LUDUS DE DECEM VIRGINIBUS
Recovery of the Sung Liturgical Core
of the Thuringian *Zehnjungfrauenspiel*

by RENATE AMSTUTZ

The musical aspects of medieval drama in Germany have been sadly neglected until recently, even in cases where the melodies for sung texts are transmitted in the manuscripts. In the case of the fourteenth-century Ten-Virgins Play from Thuringia (*Ludus de decem virginibus*), which is based on the biblical parable of the Wise and Foolish Virgins, the surviving manuscript lacks any musical notation for the chants. Moreover, the Latin texts for the sung items are normally only indicated by one or a few of the beginning words ('incipit'), while the vernacular text is always complete. As a result, the *Ludus de decem virginibus* can easily be mistaken for a spoken, predominantly vernacular drama.

This study focuses on the Latin remnants of the play and what they reveal of the nature of the Latin chants. Comprehensive research into the liturgical repertoire as known in the fourteenth century in the Province of Mainz has restored what is essentially the entire liturgico-musical dimension of the drama. Even more, once the recovered Latin chants are placed in sequence and connected through the pertinent stage directions, they emerge as a lively, coherent play in which Gregorian Chant serves as the dramatic dialogue — a Latin liturgical play that may have preceded the mixed-language drama that survived.

In the process of the inquiry, basic concepts and forms of medieval liturgy and music are discussed as needed. The study pays particular attention to the 'German dialect' of plainsong and to the special form of recitation in the Mainz Church (*Accentus Moguntinus*) — regional variations of Roman chanting that are postulated for the chants in the Thuringian play. A few facsimiles from manuscripts complement the musical transcriptions and the discussions of some palaeographical problems. Comparative studies of the peculiar *Silete* calls and their melodies as well as of the so-called travel stanzas 'B' in Easter plays extend in scope and significance to medieval drama in general. Correlated to the book is a Catalogue on microfiche which provides extensive documentation for the liturgical and dramatic sources investigated.

STUDIES AND TEXTS 140

LUDUS DE DECEM VIRGINIBUS

RECOVERY OF THE SUNG LITURGICAL CORE
OF THE THURINGIAN *ZEHNJUNGFRAUENSPIEL*

by
Renate Amstutz

PONTIFICAL INSTITUTE OF MEDIAEVAL STUDIES

ACKNOWLEDGMENT

This book has been published with the help of a grant
from the Humanities and Social Sciences Federation of Canada,
using funds provided by the Social Sciences and
Humanities Research Council of Canada.

Music, tables, Catalogue and graphics, including the map (p. 86),
were prepared by Renate Amstutz.

National Library of Canada Cataloguing in Publication Data

Amstutz, Renate, 1936-
   Ludus de decem virginibus : recovery of the sung liturgical core of the
Thuringian Zehnjungfrauenspiel

(Studies and texts, ISSN 0082-5328 ; 140)
Includes bibliographical references and index.
ISBN 0-88844-140-1

1. Eisenacher Zehnjungfrauenspiel. 2. German drama—To 1500—History
and criticism. 3. Liturgical drama—Germany—History and criticism.
4. Church music—Germany—500-1400. 5. Religious drama, German—History and criticism. 6. Gregorian chants—500-1400—History and criticism.
7. Drama, Medieval—History and criticism. 8. Theater— Germany—History—To 1500. I. Pontifical Institute of Mediaeval Studies II. Title.
III. Title: Eisenacher Zehnjungfrauenspiel. IV. Series: Studies and texts
(Pontifical Institute of Mediaeval Studies) ; 140.

PT1517.E423A47 2002   832'.209   C2001-903500-4

PT
1517
.E423
A47
2002

Printed in Canada

In memory of my husband

JAKOB AMSTUTZ

(† 1995)

Contents

Preface

The seed for this book was planted twenty years ago when I was studying a precious incunabulum, a Dominican breviary, in connection with my work on Mechthild von Magdeburg and happened upon the responsory *Sint lumbi vestri*. There it was, the complete liturgical chant, the incipit of which was cited in the edition of the Thuringian *Zehnjungfrauenspiel* as a biblical text (Luke 12: 35). Eureka! 'Just' study some more liturgical chant books — preferably, medieval ones — and it would be possible to identify the incipits in the famous Thuringian play with chants that had been in use at that time. Foolish thinking! Little did I know then of the intricacies of medieval liturgy in general and of Gregorian chant and its musical notation in particular. So the thought of 'just' studying some medieval liturgical books was naive indeed; yet the vision never really faded and carried me through intense studies of liturgy, musicology and Latin palaeography at the University of Toronto's Centre for Medieval Studies.

It is generally understood that medieval drama is — or ought to be — the interdisciplinary research field *par excellence*; in reality, however, a text-oriented, philological approach has prevailed since most medieval drama specialists are literary historians to whom the vast fields of medieval liturgy and musicology are foreign territory. Linke (1985b) outlined the multiplicity of major and subsidiary disciplines to be reckoned with in the field. Thereafter a few invaluable scholarly projects essentially of a codicological and historical nature (Bergmann [1986], Neumann [1987]) as well as some publications focusing on musicological and liturgical aspects (Mehler, Traub, Gstrein, Prüser) have considerably advanced the scholarship in the field. Research into the relevance of matters liturgical and musical for medieval religious plays, however, is still in its infancy. Scholars of medieval drama have traditionally relied on musicologists such as Lipphardt, Suppan, Traub, and Brunner (forthcoming) to provide the necessary information and material. The two pioneering musicological studies by Dreimüller (1935) and Schuler (1940), though they continue to be major reference works for dramatic research, have become partially outdated, and so the time may have come for scholars of medieval drama to venture into these 'foreign' fields at least to become familiar with the major signposts and roadways — liturgical and musical concepts, symbols, and forms. Only then will it be possible to pursue studies that take both the textual and musico-liturgical aspects of plays into concurrent consideration — as I have attempted in this book and as Mehler (1997) has done for the corpus of the *Planctus Mariae* — and to do justice to the multidimensional nature of most medieval plays. It is hoped, therefore, that the present book, in addition to recovering the sung liturgical core of the Thuringian Ten-Virgins play, may serve a second purpose: that of providing philologists with an 'interdisciplinary guide' to the fields of liturgical and musicological research.

When the first stage of this book was finally completed in the form of my Toronto dissertation (1991), the positive scholarly response to this interdisciplinary undertaking included calls for the work to be published as soon as possible and for me to prepare a new edition of the famous Thuringian drama based on my research — a project generously supported by a Canada Council grant. Owing to a number of painful losses and other circumstances beyond my control which required a new orientation in my personal life, the completion of this book has been unduly delayed. As it is about to be published now, I dedicate the book to the memory of my husband Jakob Amstutz. Without his steady encouragement I might easily have given up the complex research involved before I even reached the conclusion of the first stage back in 1991.

The research for this project, which has extended over some fifteen years, was further complicated by the fact that the major manuscript sources investigated are accessible only in European libraries and archives. Fortunately, my work has been greatly facilitated by the generous help and assistance of many institutions and individuals on both sides of the Atlantic. I am grateful to the Cornell University Library in Ithaca, NY, and particularly to the various European libraries and archives which allowed me to study the manuscripts *in situ* or as copies and provided the microfilms needed for my research and for the musical transcriptions. As a rule, most of the source material was selected on research trips to Germany and studied on microfilm copies. Only in a few cases has it been possible to verify the results and the detailed musicological analyses and transcriptions through a second consultation of the manuscripts themselves.

Colleagues at various research institutions have supported and furthered my studies in invaluable ways. In Cologne, at the Institut für deutsche Sprache und Literatur, I found doors open beyond expectation, with free access to the special library collection which includes copies of all relevant dramatic manuscripts. To the faculty and staff of this institute I am grateful for their continued assistance in my research. Hansjürgen Linke in particular generously supplied me, even by mail, with whatever material I needed, tirelessly urging me to get my work published. The late Helmut Lomnitzer (Marburg) graciously arranged to meet me on short notice (1988) and encouraged me to utilize his own research material on the *Marburg Spiel von den letzten Dingen*. In Toronto, Andrew Hughes offered valuable advice and made his private research collection available to me. Other scholars, among them Timothy McGee and Roger Reynolds of Toronto, Alan Knight and Vicky Ziegler of Penn State, Lynette Muir of Leeds, Ulrich Mehler of Cologne, and the church historian Wolfgang Petke of Göttingen, offered welcome special advice. To all of them, named or unnamed, I am deeply grateful. My gratitude extends to my family overseas and to my friends here for their understanding of my social unavailability during the process of revising and finalizing this book. To many I owe thanks for actively helping with computer problems (Catherine, Henry, Marianne), library services (Ken, Hugh), English language skills (Kari, Gloria, Barbara), or proofreading (Elisabeth).

The physical form of many parts in this book (tables, figures, chants, Catalogue) would hardly be possible without modern computer technology. Most of the music examples from the sources studied are published and transcribed here for the first time; the transcriptions were produced on an Apple Macintosh and Laserwriter, using the application 'Notewriter 2.90' created by Keith A. Hamel in Vancouver (*Opus 1 Music*), to whom I am grateful for his continued support and his availability for advice and help over the phone. The facsimiles in the appendix, also reproduced here for the first time, are developed from xerox copies (facsimiles 4 and 5) or from the microfilms provided by the libraries (facsimiles 1-3 and 6). I thank Nicole and Scott from Heer's Camera Guelph for their creativity, humor and patience in the time-consuming process of producing the photos to my minute instructions so they would fit into the given space. Due to technical and financial considerations, the Catalogue, which is an essential resource and reference for the studies in this book, particularly for those in Chapter 3, is provided on microfiches. It is hoped that this fact does not discourage the use of this resource and reference section. The date of publication did not permit the integration of articles from the second edition of the *New Grove Dictionary of Music and Musicians* (2001); readers are encouraged to consult this twenty-nine-volume work on their own, possibly even on-line, under such lemmata as *Antiphon, Divine Office, Lamentations, Liturgy and liturgical books, Notation, Plainchant* etc.

The editing and typesetting of the manuscript with a great number of graphics, tables and figures and a complicated Catalogue has been a daunting task for everyone involved. My two editors at the Pontifical Institute of Mediaeval Studies went beyond the call of duty in their efforts to give an acceptable linguistic and physical form to this book. Jean Hoff's language skills, her expertise and diligence in editing and in streamlining the argument, her acute eye in spotting incorrect citations and other blunders have amazed me. Fred Unwalla's proficiency in bibliographical referencing was a salvation for the often extensive footnoting, and his distinctive aesthetic sense helped in the overall make-up of the book with the intricate inclusion of graphics, figures, musical transcriptions and facsimiles. To both PIMS editors I express here my heartfelt thanks.

Last but not least, I am indebted to the Aid to Scholarly Publications Programme (ASPP) of the Humanities and Social Sciences Federation of Canada which made the publication of the book possible through their generous financing. My sincere thanks go to this wonderful institution for their support.

Abbreviations

[ ]	editorial additions
< >	text added within an editorial addition
AH	*Analecta Hymnica*
AMS	*Antiphonale Missarum Sextuplex*
CAO	*Corpus Antiphonalium Officii*
LOO	*Lateinische Osterfeiern und Osterspiele*
PalMus	*Paléographie musicale*
PL	*Patrologia Latina*

List of Tables

List of Figures

Liturgical and Dramatic Sources and Their Sigla

For complete information on the published works cited see the Bibliography, pp. 362-397.

KEY TO ABBREVIATIONS AND SIGLA
For most liturgical sources, letter codes in *italic* at the beginning of each siglum are used to indicate the type of liturgical book or manuscript:

A Antiphonale *AM* Antiphonale Missarum *B* Breviarium *C* Collectarium *Ev* Evangelistarium *G* Graduale *L* Lectionarium (and Homiliarium) *M* Missale *MS* Manuscript of various contents *O* Ordinarius *P* Pontificale *Pr* Processionale *Ps* Psalterium *R* Responsoriale ("Liber Responsorialis") *S* Sacramentarium

For the dramatic sources, the last part of each siglum, usually indicating the kind of play, refers to the standard Latin/English or German terminology:

Abdm	Cena domini play	"Abendmahlsspiel"
Ass	Assumption play	"Mariae Himmelfahrtspiel"
CC	Corpus Christi play	"Fronleichnamspiel"
Dir	Director's roll	"Dirigierrolle"
Emm	Emmaus play	"Emmausspiel" or "Peregrinus"
Hi	Ascension play	"Himmelfahrtspiel"
Mkl	Planctus Mariae	"Marienklage"
O	Easter play	"Osterspiel"
P	Passion play	"Passionsspiel"
Palm	Palm Sunday play	"Palmsonntagsspiel"
Par	Paradise play	"Paradiesspiel"
Sp	Play	Spiel
Vis	*Visitatio sepulchri*	*Visitatio* or "Osterfeier"
W	Christmas play	"Weihnachtspiel"
[name]	Play of a saint or other person	Dor Dorothy; Kath Katherine; Th Theophilus

Musical notation in the sources, for some or all of the chants or musical pieces, are indicated by the following symbols, placed after the siglum:

- • Non-heighted neumes in manuscript (no stave)
- <u>•</u> Neumes on a four- or five-line stave in manuscript

Abbreviations following the full name of the source indicate, where necessary, the principal forms used (not valid for the modern Vaticana or Solesmes editions listed):

MS   Manuscript
INC   Incunabulum
ED   Principal published edition(s) used (text only)
ED•   Edition with transcriptions of the music
FACS   Facsimile edition
MUS   Separate publication of music from dramatic sources
See   Selective bibliographical information

1. LITURGICAL SOURCES

*A*Ahrw.2a •
*A*Ahrw.2b •   *Antiphonal of Ahrweiler*, diocese of Cologne
MS Ahrweiler, Pfarrarchiv, Cod 2a and 2b; ca 1400.
ED [incipits only] Heckenbach (1971) 158-267.
See Heckenbach (1971) 12-18.

*A*Ambr •   *Antiphonarium Ambrosianum*
MS London, British Library, MS Add.34209; 12th c.
ED• PalMus 6 (1900).
FACS PalMus 5 (1896).
See Hiley (1993) 540-541.

*A*Erf.50a •   *Antiphonae Dominicales* in the *Liber Chori BMV*, Erfurt (not an antiphonal): fols. 147v-157v in part III; 13th c.
MS Karlsruhe, Badische Landesbibliothek, MS St. Peter perg. 50a, compilation of five different parts; 13/14th c.
See Heinzer-Stamm (1984) 119-123.

*A*Fri.117 •   *Antiphonal of St. Peter*, Fritzlar
MS Kassel, Gesamthochschul-Bibliothek, 2° MS theol. 117; 1344-1348.
See Wiedemann (1994) 151-153. CAO 5: 7, siglum 178.

*A*Fri.124 •   *Antiphonal of St. Peter*, Fritzlar
MS Kassel, Gesamthochschul-Bibliothek, 2° MS theol. 124; 1367-1378.
See Wiedemann (1994) 165-166. CAO 5: 7, siglum 181.

*A*Fri.129 •   *Antiphonal of St. Peter*, Fritzlar
MS Kassel, Gesamthochschul-Bibliothek, 2° MS theol. 129; 1344-1348.
See Wiedemann (1994) 172-174. CAO 5: 7, siglum 182.

*A*Fri.142 • Fragment of an *Antiphonal of St. Peter*, Fritzlar MS in Kassel, Gesamthochschul-Bibliothek: two loose leaves, fols. *Ir-*IIv ("membrum disjectum"), 12th c.; prefixed to 2° MS theol. 142; cf. *L*Fri.142.
See Wiedemann (1994) 195.

*A*Hartk • *Antiphonal of Hartker* (monastic)
MS St. Gall, Stiftsbibliothek, MSS 390-391; 10th/11th c.
ED one of six monastic sources in CAO vols. 2-4, siglum H.
FACS Froger (1970).
See Hesbert in CAO 2: vi-xi; Froger (1970) 15*-44*.

*A*Helm.485 • *Antiphonal from Hildesheim* (?) or *Münster* (?)
MS Wolfenbüttel, Herzog August Bibliothek, Cod. Guelf. 485 Helmst.; 14th/15th c. [Temporale: Advent-Easter; Proprium Sanctorum, no Commune Sanctorum]
See Heinemann (1884-1888) 1: 372; CAO 5: 18, siglum 592.

*AM*Med • *Antiphonale Missarum juxta Ritum Sanctae Ecclesiae Mediolanensis* (1935) Paris, Tournai, Rome: Desclée.

*A*Mon • *Antiphonale Monasticum pro diurnis horis* (1934) Paris, Tournai, Rome: Desclée.

*A*Mz.II,138 • *Antiphonal of the Weissfrauenkloster*, Mainz (?) (monastic [Cistercian])
MS Mainz, Stadtbibliothek, MS II,138; 13th/14th c.
See A. Hughes (1982) 392: A16.

*A*OP • *Antiphonarium Sacri Ordinis Praedicatorum pro diurnis horis* (1933) Rome: In Hospitio Magistri Generalis.

*A*OP(Humb) • *Antiphonal of the Dominican Order*
MS in *Codex Humberti*, Rome, Santa Sabina, Archives of the Dominican Order, MS XIV L 1, fols. 231r-322v; ca 1250.
See Bonniwell (1944) 85-86, 91-92; A. Hughes (1982) 395: B10.

*A*Pat • *Antiphonale Pataviense* (Vienna, 1519)
ED• 1519.
FACS Schlager (1985).
See Schlager (1985) iv-vii.

*A*R • *Antiphonale sacrosanctae Romanae Ecclesiae pro diurnis horis* (1949) Paris, Tournai, Rome: Desclée.

*A*Salzb • *Antiphonar von St. Peter*, Salzburg (monastic)
MS Wien, Österreichische Nationalbibliothek, MS Ser. Nova 2700; 12th c.
FACS op. cit. (1969-1973) vol. [1].
See Unterkircher in op. cit. (1974) [2]: 17-188.

*A*Sar •   *Antiphonale Sarisburiense*
MS Salisbury, Cathedral Library, MS 152, fragmentary; 13th c.
FACS Frere (1901-1924) 2-5 [The basic manuscript, complemented by other sources, mainly Cambridge, University Library, MS Mm. II 9; 13th c.]
See Frere (1901-1924) 1: 76; A. Hughes (1974) no. 505, (1982) 392: A13.

*A*Worc •   *Antiphonaire Monastique de Worcester*
MS Worcester, Cathedral Library, MS F 160; 13th c.
FACS PalMus 12 (1922).
See PalMus 12 (1922) 9-23. A. Hughes (1982) 392: A14; CAO 5: 18, siglum 894.

*B*Erf.81   *Breviary of Erfurt and Bursfelde* (monastic)
MS Vatican, Biblioteca Apostolica Vaticana, MS Rossi 81; 14th c.
See A. Hughes (1982) 396: B13.

*B*Fri.146   *Breviarium Moguntinum*, Fritzlar
MS Kassel, Gesamthochschul-Bibliothek, 2° MS theol. 146; 14th c.
See Wiedemann (1994) 205-207.

*B*Fri.161   *Breviarium Moguntinum*, diocese of Mainz
MS Kassel, Gesamthochschul-Bibliothek, 2° MS theol. 161; 14th c.
See Wiedemann (1994) 230-231. CAO 5: 7, siglum 186.

*B*Helm.145.1• *Breviarium of Kloster Marienberg*, Helmstedt
MS Wolfenbüttel, Herzog August Bibliothek, Cod. Guelf. 145.1 Helmst.; 14th c.
See Heinemann (1884-1888) 1: 140-141.

*B*OP(INC)   *Breviarium Ordinis Praedicatorum*
INC Basel, 1492. Used at the University Library of Göttingen, Germany [call number: 4° H.E.Rit.I, 8087 Inc.].

*B*OP   *Breviary of the Order of Preachers*. Part one. (1967) Dublin: St. Saviour's.

*B*R   *Breviarium Romanum* (1915), editio secunda post typicam. Regensburg, Rome: Pustet.

*B*Rh.28   *Breviary of Rheinau* (monastic)
MS Zurich, Zentralbibliothek, MS Rh. 28; 13th c., additions of 14th c. •
ED one of six monastic sources in CAO vols. 2-4: siglum R [fols. 428-642, antiphonal of the multi-section 'breviary' Rh. 28].
See Hesbert in CAO 2: ix-xi; L. Mohlberg (1951) 172. CAO 5: 18, siglum 896.

*B*Rh.61   *Breviary of Rheinau* (monastic)
MS Zurich, Zentralbibliothek, MS Rh. 61; 1484.

See L. Mohlberg (1951) 187. CAO 5: 18, siglum 897.

COP(Humb)   *Collectarium* ['The hebdomadarian's book'] *of the Dominican Order*

MS in *Codex Humberti*, Rome, Santa Sabina, Archives of the Dominican Order, MS XIV L 1, fols. 41r-57v; ca. 1250.

See Bonniwell (1944) 85-86, 89; A. Hughes (1982) 395: B10.

EvOP(Humb)   *Evangelistarium of the Dominican Order*

MS in *Codex Humberti*, Rome, Santa Sabina, Archives of the Dominican Order, MS XIV L 1, fols. 435v-454v; ca. 1250.

See Bonniwell (1944) 85-86, 93; A. Hughes (1982) 395: B10; Gastoué (1937-1939) and (1939).

GBrei.101 •   *Gradual of Breitenau* (monastic)

MS Kassel, Gesamthochschul-Bibliothek, 2° MS theol. 101; 15th c.

See Wiedemann (1994) 123-124.

GErf.16 •   *Gradual of the Neuwerkskloster*, Erfurt (Augustinian canonesses)

MS Karlsruhe, Badische Landesbibliothek, MS St. Peter perg. 16; 14th c.

See Heinzer-Stamm (1984) 38-40; Beer (1965) 44.

GErf.44 •   *Gradual of the Neuwerkskloster*, Erfurt (Augustinian canonesses)

MS Karlsruhe, Badische Landesbibliothek, MS St. Peter perg. 44; 14th c.

See Heinzer-Stamm (1984) 104-106; Beer (1965) 45.

GKath •   *Graduale von Sankt Katharinenthal* (Dominican)

MS Zurich, Schweizerisches Landesmuseum and Frauenfeld, Museum des Kantons Thurgau, MS LM 26117; ca 1312.

FACS op. cit. (1980).

See Pascal Ladner in op. cit. (1983) 298-320.

GLpz •   *Graduale der St.Thomaskirche*, Leipzig

MS in 1930 was in Leipzig, Archiv von St. Thomas, MS 371; 14th c.

FACS Wagner (1930, 1932) 2 vols.

See Wagner (1930) xi-xxi; A. Hughes (1974) no. 520.

GOP(Humb) •   *Gradual of the Dominican Order*

MS in *Codex Humberti*, Rome, Santa Sabina, Archives of the Dominican Order, MS XIV L 1, fols. 323r-369r.

See Bonniwell (1944) 85-86, 92; A. Hughes (1982) 395: B10.

GPat •   *Graduale Pataviense* (Vienna, 1511)

ED• 1511.

FACS Väterlein (1982).

See Väterlein (1982) iv-vi.

GR • *Graduale Romanum* (1974) *Graduale sacrosanctae Romanae ecclesiae de tempore et de sanctis*. Primum sancti Pii X iussu restitutum et editum, Pauli VI pontificis maximi cura nunc recognitum, ad exemplar 'Ordinis Cantus Missae' dispositum, et rhythmicis signis a Solesmibus monachis diligenter ornatum. Solesmes 1979.

GRTri • *Graduale Triplex* (1979) *seu Graduale Romanum Pauli Pp VI cura recognitum ... , neumis Laudensibus* (cod. 239) *et Sangallensibus* (codicum Sangallensis 359 et Einsidlensis 121) *nunc auctum*. Solesmes 1979. [GR (1974) augmented with the neumes of MSS Laon 239, St. Gall 359, Einsiedeln 121, and some others) *See* Foreword, pp. [i-vi] (in French, German, English).

GStrals • *Gradual of St. Nicholas*, Stralsund
MS Stralsund, Stadtbibliothek, MS without signature; 14th c.
See A. Hughes (1982) 405: G5.

GVor.22 • *Gradual of Vorau*
MS Vorau, Stiftsbibliothek, MS 22; 15th c.

GWonn • *Gradual of Wonnental* (Cistercian)
MS Karlsruhe, Badische Landesbibliothek, MS UH 1; 14th c.
See A. Hughes (1982) 405: G6.

LU • *Liber Usualis Missae et Officii pro dominicis et festis* (1962) Paris, Tournai, Rome: Desclée.

LBrsw • *Lectionarium of the Stiftskirche St. Blasii*, Braunschweig
MS Wolfenbüttel, Niedersächsisches Staatsarchiv, VII B Hs 203; 14th c.
See Lipphardt in LOO 6: 472-473. [Cf. BrswO].

LFri.142 *Lectionarium* [Homiliar] *of St. Peter*, Fritzlar
MS Kassel, Gesamthochschul-Bibliothek, 2° MS theol. 142; 1367-1389.
See Wiedemann (1994) 195-198.

LLux *Le Lectionnaire de Luxeuil*
MS Paris, Bibliothèque Nationale, MS lat. 9427; 7th/8th c.
ED Salmon (1944) vol. 1.
See Salmon (1944) xi-xlviii; Vogel (1975) 291.

LMO *Ordo Lectionum Missae* (1969) Editio typica. Vatican City.

LOP(Humb) *Lectionary of the Dominican Order*
MS in *Codex Humberti*, Rome, Santa Sabina, Archives of the Dominican Order, MS XIV L 1, fols. 142r-230v; ca 1250.
See Bonniwell (1944) 85-86, 91; A. Hughes (1982) 395: B10.

LRh.18 *Monastic Lectionary* (Matutinale), Rheinau
MS Zurich, Zentralbibliothek, MS Rh. 18; 12th c. [Pentecost-Advent].

	See L. Mohlberg (1951) 168.
*L*Rh.19	*Monastic Lectionary* (Matutinale), Rheinau
	MS Zurich, Zentralbibliothek, MS Rh. 19; 12th c. [Advent to Pentecost]
	See L. Mohlberg (1951) 168.
*L*Rh.28	*Monastic Lectionary of Rheinau*
	MS Zurich, Zentralbibliothek, MS Rh. 28, fols. 252-424; 13th c. [Lectionary for the entire year in a multi-section 'breviary']
	See L. Mohlberg (1951) 172.
*L*Weiss.76	*Gallican Lectionary*
	MS Wolfenbüttel, Herzog August Bibliothek, Cod. Weiss. 76, palimpsest from Southern France; 5th/6th c.
	ED Dold (1936) 1-68.
	See Butzmann (1964) 229-231; Vogel (1975) 290.
Manuductio •	*Manuductio Ad Cantum choralem Gregoriano-Moguntinum.*
	ED Mainz 1672.
	See Köllner (1956) 44-45.
*M*Bobbio	*Missal of Bobbio*, a Gallican Mass-Book
	MS Paris, Bibliothèque Nationale, MS lat. 13246; 8th c.
	ED Lowe et al. (1920).
	FACS Lowe et al. (1917).
	See Lowe et al. (1924) 63-106; Vogel (1975) 293.
*M*Braga •	*Missal of Braga, Portugal*
	ED• (1558) Lyon. Copy in Paris, Bibliothèque Nationale, Rés. B. 1478; Corbin (1960) 261-262 [fols. 96r-97r only, excerpts for *depositio crucis*], "Portugal 6" [text]; plates II and III, after p. 314 [music].
	ED LOO 435 [excerpts for *depositio crucis* from Corbin (1960)].
	FACS [fol. 96v] in Corbin (1960) frontispiece.
	See Corbin (1960) 66 no. 6, also 20-23, 37-39, 136-146, 220.
*M*Franc	*Missale Francorum*, a Gallican Mass-Book
	MS Vatican, Biblioteca Apostolica Vaticana, MS Vat. Reg. lat. 257; 8th c.
	ED L. Mohlberg (1957).
	See L. Mohlberg (1957) xiii-xv.
*M*Fri.100 •	*Missale plenum of St. Peter*, Fritzlar
	MS Kassel, Gesamthochschul-Bibliothek, 2° MS theol. 100; 13th c.
	See Wiedemann (1994) 119-123.
*M*Halb.888 •	*Missale celeberrimi Halberstattensis episcopatus*, Mainz
	INC (1511); used at Mainz, Bibliothek des bischöflichen Priester-seminars [call number: INC 888].

See Köllner (1950) 110-113 (INC "ohne Signatur").

*M*Helm.26 • *Missale of a monastery of canons regular*, Braunschweig
MS Wolfenbüttel, Herzog August Bibliothek, Cod. Guelf. 26
Helmst; 1456.
See Heinemann (1884-1888) 1: 20.

*M*Helm.35 • *Missale of the Leuchtenhof*, Hildesheim
MS Wolfenbüttel, Herzog August Bibliothek, Cod. Guelf. 35
Helmst; 1462.
See Heinemann (1884-1888) 1: 26-27.

*M*Helm.38 • *Missale* of unknown provenance
MS Wolfenbüttel, Herzog August Bibliothek, Cod. Guelf. 38
Helmst; 15th c.
See Heinemann (1884-1888) 1: 28.

MR • *Missale Romanum* (1933) Editio xvii juxta typicam Vaticanam.
Regensburg: Pustet.

MR.1474 • *Missale Romanum Mediolani 1474*
ED Lippe (1899, 1907).

MsHelm.628• "W$_1$", an important source for the 'Notre Dame School'
MS Wolfenbüttel, Herzog August Bibliothek, Cod. Guelf. 628
Helmst.; 13th c.
ED• [excerpts of fasc. 11 (W$_1$/11)] Stapert (1974-1976).
See Heinemann (1884-1888) 2: 87; Everist (1990); Stevens
(1986) 522, with additional bibliographical information.

MsMh.87/8 • *Vocabularius Brevilogus. Varia.*
MS Mühlhausen/Thüringen, Stadtarchiv, MS 87/8 [*olim* 60/8], fols.
387r-388r: *Oracio ieremie prophete* with musical notation; 1466.
See Fr. Stephan (1874a) 119; Lülfing (1982) 16-19.

Ordo 50 *Ordo Romanus L*, ca 950.
ED [from 21 MSS] Andrieu (1931-1961) 5: 82-407. [from 2 MSS]
PRG 2: no. XCIX (pp. 1-141); cf. editorial comment in Vogel-
Elze (1963-1972) 1: XXII.
See Vogel (1975) 169, 191, 193-194; (1986) 187, 230-237.

*O*Magd *Ordinarius of the Magdeburg Cathedral*
MS Berlin, Staatsbibliothek Preussischer Kulturbesitz, MS theol.
lat. 4° 113; 13th/15th c.
ED [excerpts] Kroos (1970) 183-186.
See Rose (1903) 758-759 no. 749.

*O*Münster *Dom-Ordinarius of Münster*
MS Münster, Domkapitel, MS 4, fols. 60-109v; 13th c.
ED [excerpts] Stapper (1917) 140-169.
See Stapper (1917) 37-39, 117-139 [tables of feasts].

OMz Ordinarius of Mainz
MS Mainz, Bibliothek des bischöflichen Priesterseminars, MS 3, fols. 193-220 (Liber fundationum et praesentiarum Ecclesiae Metropolitanae Moguntinae); 14th and 16th c.
ED [excerpts, pertaining to the feast and procession of Corpus Christi] Bruder (1901) 492-506.
See Bruder (1901) 492 n1; Klein (1962) 14.

ORh.80 Rheinauer Liber Ordinarius
MS Zurich, Zentralbibliothek, MS Rh. 80; 12th c.
ED Hänggi (1957).
See L. Mohlberg (1951) 194; Hänggi (1957) xliv-xlv.

OTrier Liber Ordinarius der Trierer Domkirche
MS London, British Library, MS Harley 2958; 14th c.
ED Kurzeja (1970) 419-556.

PAux Pontifical of Auxerre
MS Auxerre, Bibliothèque Municipale, MS 53; 14th c.
ED [fols. 24v-28r] Martène (1736) 543-546 (lib. II, cap. 6, ordo X).
See Martimort (1959) 56 no. 38, 376 no. 751; Leroquais (1937) 1: 45-49.

PAv.205 • Extract from a Roman Pontifical (Consecration of virgins, specifically, Carthusian nuns)
MS [recte, a printed book] Avignon, Bibliothèque Municipale, MS 205; 17th c.
ED [fols. 31-33] Martène (1736) 551-552 (lib. II, cap. 6, ordo XIII).
See Martimort (1959) 377 no. 754; Leroquais (1937) 1: 67-68.

PConsVirg Consecration of Virgins
ED Metz (1954) 411-455: "Le texte du Pontifical Romain actuel; origine des divers éléments." [The apparatus accounts for all the sources of the Consecration ceremony from the earliest Roman sacramentaries to the Pontifical of 1595, after which the form of the ritual was essentially unchanged.]

PDur Pontifical of William Durandus, ca 1293-1295
ED [from 14 out of 21 MSS] Andrieu (1938-1941) 3: 327-683.
See Vogel (1975) 208-210, (1986) 253-255.

PDur.Add • Pontifical of William Durandus
MS London, British Library, MS Add. 39677; 14th c.
See Andrieu (1938-1941) 3: 110-123.

PMz.XII Pontifical of Christian I, archbishop of Mainz 1167-1183 [not, as Martène states, Christian II, archbishop of Mainz 1249-1251]
MS Paris, Bibliothèque Nationale, MS lat. 946; 12th c.
ED [fols. 51r-59v] Martène (1736) 541-541 (lib. II, cap. 6, ordo IX).

See Martimort (1959) 150 no. 189, 376 no. 750; Leroquais (1937) 2: 21-26.

PMz.XIV • Pontifical of Mainz belonging to Daniel Wichterich, bishop in partibus of Modon, suffragan of Trier
MS Paris, Bibliothèque Nationale, MS lat. 948; 14th c.
See Leroquais (1937) 2: 29-31.

PR XII   Roman Pontificale of the 12th century
ED [from 5 MSS] Andrieu (1938-1941) 1: 123-303.
See Andrieu (1938-1941) 1: 3-19; Vogel (1975) 204-206, (1986) 249-251.

PR XIII   Pontifical of the Roman Curia, 13th c.
ED [from 33 MSS] Andrieu (1938-1941) 2: 327-581.
See Andrieu (1938-1941) 2: 263-315; Vogel (1975) 206-208, (1986) 252.

PRG   Pontificale Romano-Germanicum, Mainz; ca. 950-963/4.
ED [from 12 out of ca. 40 MSS] Vogel-Elze (1963-1972) 1: [nos. I-XCVIII] and 2: [nos. XCIX-CCLVIII].
See Vogel-Elze (1963-1972) 1: XI-XVII, 3: 3-6 and passim; Vogel (1975).

PR Lyon •   Pontificale Romanum of Lyon
MS Lyon, Bibliothèque Municipale, MS 5144; 15th c.
FACS [fol. 103r] Leroquais (1937) [4]: pl. CXXII.
See Leroquais (1937) 1: 196-199.

PSens   Pontificale of Sens
MS Sens, Bibliothèque Municipale, MS 11; 1671. [copy of MS London, British Library, MS Egerton 931, 14th c].
ED [fols. 129r-139r] Martène (1736) 548-551 (lib. II, cap. 6, ordo XII).
See Martimort (1959) 377 no. 753; Leroquais (1937) 2: 334-336.

PTrég   Pontifical of Pierre de Trégny, Senlis
MS Paris, Bibliothèque Sainte-Geneviève, MS 148; 14th c.
ED [fols. 79r-84r] Martène (1736) 546-548 (lib. II, cap. 6, ordo XI).
See Martimort (1959) 206 no. 302, 377 no. 752; Leroquais (1937) 2: 250-254.

PrDon.882• Processional from the Dominican nunnery Brunnenhof (near Möhringen)
MS "Donaueschingen 882," formerly Donaueschingen, Fürstlich-Fürstenbergische Hofbibliothek, MS 882; early 14th c. Present location unknown; cf. Heinzer (1995) 313, 317.
See Allworth (1970).

*Pr*Fri.87 •   *Processional of St. Peter*, Fritzlar
             MS Kassel, Gesamthochschul-Bibliothek, 4° MS theol. 87; 15th c [?].

*Pr*Mon •   *Processionale Monasticum ad usum congregationis Gallicae ordinis Sancti Benedicti* (1893) Solesmes.

*Pr*Mz.100 •   *Processional of the Mainz Cathedral*
             MS Mainz, Bibliothek des bischöflichen Priesterseminars, MS 100 [incomplete, begins with fol. 17r]; 15th/16th c.
             See Klein (1962) 16.

*Pr*Mz.105 •   *Processional of the Liebfrauenkirche* (BMV), Mainz
             MS Mainz, Bibliothek des bischöflichen Priesterseminars, MS 105; 1773.
             See Klein (1962) 17.

*Pr*Mz.110 •   *Processional of the Mainz Cathedral*
             MS Mainz, Bibliothek des bischöflichen Priesterseminars, MS 110 [pars aestivalis]; 1704.
             See Klein (1962) 16.

*Pr*Mz.118 •   *Processional of St. Peter*, Mainz
             MS Mainz, Bibliothek des bischöflichen Priesterseminars, MS 118; 14th/15th c.
             See Klein (1962) 16-17.

*Pr*Mz.II,74 •   *Processional of the Domsänger von Eltz*
             MS Mainz, Stadtbibliothek, MS II,74 [pars aestivalis]; 15th c.
             See Klein (1962) 15; Köllner (1950) 76-79.

*Pr*MzII,303 •   *Processional of the Mainz Cathedral*
             MS Mainz, Stadtbibliothek, MS II,303; 15th c.
             See Klein (1962) 15-16; Köllner (1950) 74-75.

*Pr*Mz.D652 •   *Directorium Chori of St. Stephan* (1712) Mainz
             ED• (1712) *Directorium Dominicale, Processionale, Stationale, in tres partes divisum.* Mainz: Typis Jonnis Mayeri. [Copy in Mainz, Bibliothek des bischöflichen Priesterseminars, call no. D652].
             See Klein (1962) 17-18.

*Pr*Padua •   *Processional of Padua*
             MS Padua, Biblioteca Capitolare, MS C 56; 13th c, additions of 15th c.
             ED [fols. 60r-67r] LOO 428.
             ED• [fols. 60r-67r, the 15th-century additions to the *depositio crucis* procession] Vecchi (1954) 136-143 [text], 145-160 [music].
             See Vecchi (1954) 133; Corbin (1960) 64 no. 7 [to p. 63 no. 1], also 37-39.

*Ps*Mz.D820 • *Enchiridion Psalmorum* (1607) Mainz
ED• (1607) *Enchiridion Psalmorum ferialium ad vesperas et completorium cum antiphonis et tonis.* Mainz: Typis Ionnis Albani. [Copy in Mainz, Bibliothek des bischöflichen Priesterseminars, call no. D820].
See Köllner (1950) 137-139.

*Ps*OSB •   *Psalterium cum cantis novi et veteris testamenti iuxta Regulam S.P.N. Benedicti* (1981) Solesmes.

*R*Mon •   *Liber Responsorialis pro Festis I. Classis et Communi Sanctorum juxta ritum monasticum* (1895) Solesmes.

*S*Gelas   *Sacramentarium Gelasianum*
MS Vatican, Biblioteca Apostolica Vaticana, MS Reg. lat 316; ca 750.
ED L. Mohlberg (1960).
See Vogel (1975) 48-57, (1986) 64-70; L. Mohlberg (1960) XVII-XXXV.

*S*Gell   *Sacramentarium Gellonense*
MS Paris, Bibliothèque Nationale, MS lat. 12048; end of 8th c.
ED Dumas (1981) vol. 1.
See Dumas (1981) vol. 2.

*S*Greg   *Sacramentarium Gregorianum* (8th c.)
ED [from 35 MSS] Deshusses (1971).
See Deshusses (1971) 35-45; Vogel (1975) 67-83.

*S*Pad   *Sacramentarium Paduense*
MS Padua, Biblioteca Capitolare, MS D 47, fols. 11r-100r; ca 841-855.
ED K. Mohlberg (1927). Also in Deshusses (1971-1979).
See Vogel (1975) 68-72.

*S*Ver   *Sacramentarium Veronense* [olim *Sacramentarium Leonianum*]
MS Verona, Biblioteca Capitolare, MS LXXXV [80]; early 7th c.
ED L. Mohlberg (1956).
See Vogel (1975) 31-32.
Würdtwein (Mz)
Würdtwein (Trier) in Würdtwein 1872.

2. DRAMATIC SOURCES

Manuscripts used in this study are indicated only if, for palaeographical reasons and/or for the transmission of musical items, they were directly consulted. In the more recent editions of medieval plays, the traditional line numbering of older editions is usually maintained to accommodate references in older secondary literature.

AdmP •   *Admonter Passionsspiel*
ED Polheim (1972-1980) 1: 13-104.
FACS [fols. 0r-124v] Polheim (1972-1980) 1.
See Bergmann (1986) no. 3.

AlsfDir   *Alsfelder Dirigierrolle*
ED Treutwein (1987) 280-365.
See Bergmann (1986) no. 7, supplemented (1994) 19.

AlsfP •   *Alsfelder Passionsspiel*
MS Kassel, Gesamthochschul Bibliothek, 2° MS poet. et roman.
18; 15th/16th c.
ED Froning (1891-1892) 2-3: 567-859; TRANS (English) West
(1997).
[ED• Janota (1996–) vol. 2 (forthcoming)]
MUS Dreimüller (1935) vol. 3; cf. Schuler (1940).
See Hilberg (1993) 22-23; Bergmann (1986) no. 70.

AmerP •   *Amerikaner Passion* (BozP.1495, MS B [designated MS A by
Wackernell 1897]) registered as "Tiroler Passionsspiel" at Cornell
University Library.
MS Ithaca, N.Y., Cornell University Library, MS + +4600 Bd MS
410Misc (*olim* MS F6): "Tiroler Passionsspiel"; ca 1494/95.
ED• Klammer (1986) 175-350, 435-454 apparatus; for corrections
to the melodies in this edition cf. Lipphardt-Roloff (1996) 6.2:
167-174; also below, pp. 180-183.
See De Ricci (1937) 1242; Klammer (1986) 361-369; Bergmann
(1986) no. 68, supplemented (1994) 20.

AugsO •   *Augsburger (Feldkircher) Osterspiel*
MS Feldkirch, Kapuzinerkloster, MS Liturg. 1 rtr.; 16th c.
ED Lipphardt (1975) 17-29.
FACS Lipphardt (1978b) after p. 63 (fols. 73v-92r).
See Lipphardt (1978a), (1987b) 1-11; Bergmann (1986) no. 41.

BenbEmm •   *Benediktbeurer Emmausspiel*
ED *Carmina Burana* 1.3 (1970): 184-188 (CB 26*); *Carmina
Burana* dtv (1985) 826-832 (CB 26*); LOO 820; Meyer (1901)
136-138.
FACS *Carmina Burana* (1967) ed. Bischoff, fols. VIIr-v.
See LOO 8: 267-282, 802-803; Linke (1999a) 185-190.

BenbO •   *Benediktbeurer Osterspiel*
ED *Carmina Burana* 1.3 (1970): 134-149 (CB 15*); *Carmina
Burana* dtv (1985) 742-762 (CB 15*); LOO 830.
FACS *Carmina Burana* (1967) ed. Bischoff, fols. Vr-VIv.

BenbW •   *Benediktbeurer Weihnachtsspiel*
ED *Carmina Burana* 1.3 (1970): 86-104 (CB 227); *Carmina Burana* dtv (1985) 654-684 (CB 227).
FACS *Carmina Burana* (1967) ed. Bischoff, fols. 99r-104v.
See Linke (1975b) [CB 227 and 228 as one dramatic unit].

BeRheinO •   *Berliner Rheinisches Osterspiel*
ED Rueff (1925) 136-206.
MUS Schuler (1940) nos. 336, 401 ["RHessO"].
See Bergmann (1986) no. 20.

BeThO •   *Berliner Thüringisches Osterspielfragment*
MS Berlin, Staatsbibliothek Preussischer Kulturbesitz, MS germ. 2° 757, fols. 4r-5v; 14th c.
ED Seelmann (1926) 257-267.
See Bergmann (1986) no. 19; Seelmann (1926) 257-262.

BöhmO.I •   *Böhmisches Osterspiel I*
ED Hanus (1863) 47-58, 60-66 ["Drei-Marien-Spiel" from MS NUK 17.E.1]
MUS Schuler (1940) nos. 426, 432, 435.

BozAbdm   *Bozner Abendmahlsspiel* [Debs XV]
ED Lipphardt-Roloff 1: 373-425, 515-524 [apparatus].
See Bergmann (1986) no. 137, supplemented (1994) 20.

BozHi •   *Bozner Himmelfahrtsspiel* [Debs I]
ED• Lipphardt-Roloff 1: 15-49, 465-469 [apparatus].
See Bergmann (1986) no. 137, supplemented (1994) 20.

BozO.II •   *Bozner Osterspiel ii* [Debs V]
MS Sterzing, Stadtarchiv, MS IV (Debs Codex), fols. 34v-41v; 15th c.
ED• Lipphardt-Roloff 1: 137-169, 477-482 [apparatus]; corrigenda to melodies in Lipphardt-Roloff 6.2: 140-142.
See Linke (1985a) 105-114; Bergmann (1986) no. 137, supplemented (1994) 20.

BozO.IV •   *Bozner Osterspiel IV* [Debs X]
MS Sterzing, Stadtarchiv, MS IV (Debs Codex), fols. 79r-87r; 15th c.
ED• Lipphardt-Roloff 1: 251-285, 496-501 [apparatus]; corrigenda to melodies in Lipphardt-Roloff 6.2: 147-151.
See Linke (1985a) 105-114; Bergmann (1986) no. 137, supplemented (1994) 20.

BozP.1495 •   *Bozner Passionsspiel 1495* (BozP 1495, MS A [designated MS B by Wackernell 1897])
MS Bozen, Archiv des Franziskanerklosters, MS I/51; ca 1494/95.

ED• Klammer (1986) 1-174, 405-434 [apparatus]; corrigenda to the melodies in Lipphardt-Roloff 6.2: 157-167; also below, pp. 180-183.
See Klammer (1986) 353-361; Bergmann (1986) no. 23, supplemented (1994) 19.

BozP.1514 • *Bozner Passionsspiel 1514* ("Vigil-Raber-Passion")
MS Sterzing, Stadtarchiv, MS III; 1514.
ED• Lipphardt-Roloff 3: 7-161, 405-418 [apparatus].
See Bergmann (1986) no. 136; Lipphardt-Roloff 3: 403-405.

BozPalm • *Bozner Palmsonntagsspiel*
MS Sterzing, Stadtarchiv, MS V; 1514.
ED• Lipphardt-Roloff 4: 7-87, 88-95 ['Anhang'], 345-357 [apparatus].
See Bergmann (1986) no. 138, supplemented (1994) 20; Lipphardt-Roloff 4: 341-345.

BozVerk *Bozner Verkündigungsspiel* [Debs XIII]
ED Lipphardt-Roloff 1: 335-345, 510-511 [apparatus].
See Bergmann (1986) no. 137, supplemented (1994) 20.

BrdbgO *Brandenburger Osterspielfragment*
ED Schipke-Pensel (1986) 7-61.
FACS Schipke-Pensel (1986) after p. 98.
See Bergmann (1986) no. 24, supplemented (1994) 19.

BrslO • *Breslauer Osterspielfragment*
MS Breslau, Bibliotheka Uniwersytecka, MS I Q 226a; 14th c (?).
ED Klapper (1928) 209-214.
FACS Klapper (1928) after p. 208.
See Bergmann (1986) no. 27; Klapper (1928) 180, 208.

BrswO • *Braunschweiger Osterspiel* in LBrsw (*Lectionarium St. Blasii*)
MS Wolfenbüttel, Niedersächsisches Staatsarchiv, VII B Hs 203, fols. 23r-27v; 14th c.
ED LOO 780; Sievers (1936) 25, 30, 36-38, 49, 56, 57.
MUS ['Braunschweig IV'] Sievers (1936) 27, 29, 31-34, 40, 41-43, 45, 56; also pp. 54, 60 [text and melodies complemented from other sources]. Transcriptions preferable to those in Schuler (1940).
See Sievers (1936) 3, 23-24; Lipphardt in LOO 6: 472-473; 8: 714-716.

Darmstädter Zehnjungfrauenspiel *see* Lddv(B)

DonP • *Donaueschinger Passionsspiel*
MS Karlsruhe, Badische Landesbibliothek, MS Don.137 (*olim* Donaueschingen, Fürstlich-Fürstenbergische Hofbibliothek); 15th c.

ED Mone (1846) 2: 183-350.
ED• Touber (1985) 54-258.
MUS in Schuler (1940), reproduced in Touber (1985) 251-258. For
ll. 1-2 (Touber p. 251) see improved transcription in Osthoff
(1943/44) 34.
See Touber (1985) 10-27; Bergmann (1986) no. 35 and p. 606;
Heinzer (1995) 313.
Dorotheenspiel *see* KrmsDor.
Dutch Ten Virgins Play *see* Flem.X.Virg.
Dutch Easter Play *see* EgmontO
EgerP •   *Egerer Passionsspiel* (or *Fronleichnamsspiel*)
MS Nürnberg, Germanisches Nationalmuseum, MS 7060; end 15th c.
ED Milchsack (1881).
MUS in Schuler (1940); Dreimüller (1935) 2: 134-166 [selection of
45 melodies; aphabetical index 132-133].
See Bergmann (1986) no. 122, supplemented (1994) 20.
EgmontO •   *Egmonter Osterspiel*
ED LOO 827.
ED• Smits van Waesberghe (1953) 30-37 [MS B of Egmont edited
in synopsis with MS A of Maestricht (LOO 826)].
See Smits van Waesberghe (1953) 15-21 [description of MSS A and
B of "Dutch Easter Play"]; Lipphardt in LOO 6: 254-255.
Eisenacher Zehnjungfrauenspiel *see* Lddv(A)
Erl.III •   *Erlauer Osterspiel* ["Erlau III"]
MS Eger (Hungary), Erzbischöfliche Diözesanbibliothek (Föegyház-
megyei Könyvtár), MS B.V.6, fols. 107r-116r; 15th c.
ED Kummer (1882) 35-89; superseded by
ED• Suppan (1990) 43-115.
See Bergmann (1986) no. 40, supplemented (1994) 20; Kummer
(1882) ix-xi.
Erl.IV •   *Erlauer Magdalenenspiel* ["Erlau IV"]
ED Kummer (1882) 95-119.
ED• Suppan (1990) 117-151.
FACS [fols. 13v, 15r] Osthoff (1942) 69, 73.
MUS Osthoff (1942) 76-81.
See Bergmann (1986) no. 40, supplemented (1994) 20.
Erl.V •   *Erlauer Wächterspiel* ["Erlau V"]
ED Kummer (1882) 125-146.
ED• Suppan (1990) 153-177.
See Bergmann (1986) no. 40, supplemented (1994) 20.

ErfMor   *Erfurter Moralität*
            MS Coburg, Landesbibliothek, MS Cas. 43; 1448
            ED [in preparation by H.-G. Roloff]
            See Bergmann (1986) no. 32; Linke (1995a).

Feldkircher Osterspiel *see* AugsO

Flem.X.Virg   *Flemish* (or "*Dutch*") *Ten Virgins Play*
            [MS lost; 16th c.]
            ED Hoebeke (1959) 96-153.

FriedDir   *Friedberger Dirigierrolle*
            ED [reconstruction] Zimmermann (1909) 172-203.
            See Bergmann (1986) no. 52

FrkfDir   *Frankfurter Dirigierrolle*
            ED Janota (1996–) 1: 1-33 [diplomatic], 35-52 [edition]; Froning
            (1891-1892) 2: 340-373.
            See Bergmann (1986) no. 43.

FrkfP   *Frankfurter Passionsspiel*
            ED Janota (1996–) 1: 67-421; Froning (1891-1892) 2: 379-532.
            See Bergmann (1986) no. 42.

FüssO ●   *Füssener* (or *Harburger*) *Osterspiel*
            ED Schmidtke (1983) 9-15.
            FACS [fols. 137r-141r] Schmidtke (1983) after p. 35.
            MUS Lipphardt in Schmidtke et al. (1976) 242-258.
            See Bergmann (1986) no. 11.

HeidP   *Heidelberger Passionsspiel*
            ED Milchsack (1880); [Janota (1996–) vol. 3, forthcoming].
            See Bergmann (1986) no. 62.

Hessisches Zehnjungfrauenspiel *see* Lddv(B)

HessW   *Hessisches Weihnachtspiel* ·
            ED Froning (1891-1892) 3: 904-937.
            See Hilberg (1993) 24; Bergmann (1986) no. 71.

InnsThAss   *Innsbrucker Thüringisches Spiel von Mariae Himmelfahrt*
            ED Mone (1841) 21-106.
            FACS [fols. 1r-34v] Thurnher-Neuhauser (1975).
            See Thurnher-Neuhauser (1975) 3-15; Bergmann (1986) no. 67.

InnsThO   *Innsbrucker Thüringisches Osterspiel*
            ED Mone (1841) 109-144; R. Meier (1962) 4-110.
            FACS [fols. 35v-50r] Thurnher-Neuhauser (1975).
            See Thurnher-Neuhauser (1975) 3-15; Bergmann (1986) no. 67.

KassPar   *Kasseler* (mnd.) *Paradiesspiel-Fragmente*
            ED Broszinski-Linke (1987) 42-48.
            FACS Broszinski-Linke (1987) 50-52. ·

See Bergmann (1986) no. 71a, supplemented (1994) 20.

KlstnbgO • *Klosterneuburger Osterspiel*
ED LOO 829; Young (1933) 1: 421-429.

KrmsDor *Kremsmünsterer Dorotheenspielfragment*
ED Ukena (1975) 2: 337-349.
See Bergmann (1986) no. 74.

KünzCC *Künzelsauer Fronleichnamsspiel*
ED Liebenow (1969) 1-218.
FACS [7 selected folios/details] Liebenow (1969) after p. 296.
See Bergmann (1986) no. 128.

LdbKath *Ludus de beata Katherina* ["Mühlhäuser" or "Thüringisches Kathari-
nenspiel"]
MS Mühlhausen/Thüringen, Stadtarchiv, MS 87/20, [pp.] 89b-94b;
between 1350 and 1371.
ED Beckers (1905) 128-157; Fr. Stephan (1847b) 160-173.
See Bergmann (1986) no. 114.

Lddv(A) *Ludus de decem virginibus* (MS A) ["Thüringisches Zehnjungfrauenspiel," also "Mühlhäuser" or "Eisenacher Zehnjungfrauenspiel"]
MS Mühlhausen/Thüringen, Stadtarchiv, MS 87/20 (*olim* 60/20),
[modern pagination, in 2 columns, a and b] 94b-100a; between 1350
and 1371.
ED Schneider (1964): Lddv(A) and (B) in parallel edition; Fr. Stephan
(1847b) 173-184; L. Bechstein (1855) 15-32; Beckers (1905) 96-124;
De Boor (1965) 182-202; Curschmann-Glier (1981) 274-306, 688-690
[notes]. [Citations of Lddv alone refer to Schneider's edition (1964) of
Lddv(A). Citations of other editions are always specified by the
editor's name.]
See Bergmann (1986) no. 114; Linke (1995).

Lddv(B) *Ludus de decem virginibus* (MS B) [also "Darmstädter" or "Hessisches
Zehnjungfrauenspiel," or "Thüringisches Zehnjungfrauenspiel B"]
MS Darmstadt, Hessische Landes- und Hochschulbibliothek, MS 3290,
fols. 212r-228r; 1428.
ED Schneider (1964): Lddv(A) and (B) in parallel edition; Rieger
(1865) 315-337.
See Bergmann (1986) no. 33; Linke (1995).

LOO *Lateinische Osterfeiern und Osterspiele* 1975-1981, 1990. Ed. Walther
Lipphardt. 9 vols. Vol. 1 [nos. 1-173]. Vol. 2 [nos. 174-484]. Vol.
3 [nos. 485-630]. Vol. 4 [nos. 631-769]. Vol. 5 [nos. 720-832]. Vol.
6 *Nachträge. Handschriftenverzeichnis. Bibliographie.* Vols. 7-9.
Kommentar.

LuzP   *Luzerner Passionsspiel* (or *Osterspiel*)
         ED Wyss (1967) vol. 1 [first day], vol. 2 [second day].
         See Wyss (1967) 1: 11-50. 67-68; Bergmann (1986) nos. 79, 85, 93-94, 104-108.

MaSp.532 *Marburger Spiel von den letzten Dingen* (fragments) [formerly known under the incorrect name *Marburger Weltgerichtsspiel*]
         MS Marburg, Universitäts-Bibliothek, MS 532; 15th c.
         ED unpublished; prepared by †Helmut Lomnitzer.
         See Lomnitzer (1985); Bergmann (1986) no. 110 ['MaWg'].

MedgVis • *Medinger Visitatio Sepulchri*
         MS Hildesheim, Stadtarchiv, MS Mus. 383, Orationale des Zisterziens-erinnenklosters Medingen bei Lüneburg, fols. 125b-127b; ca 1320.
         ED LOO 792.
         See Lipphardt in LOO 6: 289.

MoosbHi *Moosburger Himmelfahrtspiel*
         ED Brooks (1925) 93-96; Young (1933) 1: 484-488.
         See Brooks (1925) 91-93.

Mühlhäuser Katharinenspiel *see* LdbKath
Mühlhäuser Zehnjungfrauenspiel *see* Lddv(A)

OrignyO • *Origny Ludus Paschalis*
         ED LOO 825.
         ED• Coussemaker (1861) 256-270.
         MUS in Schuler (1940).

PfarrkP • *Pfarrkirchers Passion* [Sterzinger Passion von a. 1486]
         MS Sterzing, Stadtarchiv, MS XVI; 1486.
         ED• Lipphardt-Roloff 2: 7-205, 335-361 [apparatus, etc.); 6.2: 180-182 [addenda et corrigenda].
         See Bergmann (1986) no. 148, supplemented (1994) 20.

Prag.37 *Prag Visitatio Sepulchri* ["Prag³⁷"]
         ED LOO 806.
         See Linke (1989) 797, 799; Lipphardt in LOO 6: 468, 8: 763-764.

PragO.C • *Prager Osterspiel "C"*
         MS Prague, University Library, MS I.B.12, 135v-137v; 14th c.
         ED Máchal (1908) 98-105; also in Hanus (1863) 36-42 (*"Das zweite Drei-Marien-Spiel"*).
         FACS Máchal (1908) appendix, plates 1-5.
         MUS in Schuler (1940) as "Prager Osterspiel II."

"Raber-Passion" *see* BozP.1514

RedO   *Redentiner Osterspiel*
         ED Schottmann (1975) 22-171.
         FACS insert in Wittkowsky (1975)

See Bergmann (1986) no. 69.

RegO • *Regensburger Osterspiel*
MS Regensburg, Bischöfliche Zentralbibliothek, MS Ch 1*, fols. [22r-] 24v-29v; 17th c.
ED• Poll (1950) 37-40, 108.
See Bergmann (1986) no. 127; Poll (1950) 35-36.

Rheinisches Osterspiel *see* BeRheinO

Sponsus • *Le Sponsus* ("Mystère des Vierges sages et des Vierges folles")
ED• Thomas (1951) 174-187 [with TRANS into modern French]; Avalle-Monterosso (1965) 71-81 [text], 123-130 [text and music]; Coussemaker (1861) 1-6.
FACS Avalle-Monterosso (1965) after p. 132.

St. Dorotheenspiel *see* KrmsDor

SterzP • *Sterzinger Passionsspiel* von a. 1496 and 1503
ED• Lipphardt-Roloff 2: 207-331, 362-373 [apparatus].
See Bergmann (1986) no. 135, supplemented (1994) 20.

StGHi *St. Galler Himmelfahrtsspiel*
ED Mone (1846) 1: 254-264.
See Bergmann (1986) no. 56.

StGMrhP *St. Galler Mittelrheinisches Passionsspiel*
ED Schützeichel (1978) 99-157.
FACS [fols. 331-351] Schützeichel (1978) [modern pagination, 197-217]
See Bergmann (1986) no. 54.

Theophilusspiel *see* TrierTh

Thüringisches Zehnjungfrauenspiel *see* Lddv(A)

TirO.fr • *Tiroler Osterspiel-Fragment* ("Visitacio sepulchri")
MS Sterzing, Stadtarchiv, MS VII, fols. 13r-16v; 1520.
ED• Lipphardt-Roloff 3: 326-332, 434-435 [apparatus].
See Bergmann (1986) no. 140; Trauden (1994) 219, 226-231.

TirP • *Tiroler Passionsspiel*, fragment ("Gründonnerstagsspiel")
MS Sterzing, Stadtarchiv, MS X; 16th c.
ED• Lipphardt-Roloff 3: 249-297, 428-431.
See Bergmann (1986) no. 143; Lipphardt-Roloff 3: 427.

TirW • *Tiroler Weihnachtsspiel* ("Ludus de Nativitate Domini")
MS Sterzing, Stadtarchiv, MS XVII; 1511.
ED• Lipphardt-Roloff 3: 359-400, 441-445.
See Bergmann (1986) no. 149; Lipphardt-Roloff 3: 440.

ToursO • *Tours Ludus Paschalis*
ED LOO 824.
ED• Krieg (1956) 1*-29* [after p. 130].

MUS in Schuler (1940).

See Krieg (1956) 8-12, 106-111; Lipphardt in LOO 6: 436-437.

TrierMkl • *Trierer Marienklage*

ED• Hennig-Traub (1990) 29-51.

FACS Hennig-Traub (1990) in appendix [after p. 69] 1-19.

MUS Bohn (1877) 17-24.

See Bergmann (1986) no. 158, M 128, supplemented (1994) 21.

TrierO • *Trierer Osterspiel*

ED• Hennig-Traub (1990) 52-66; Froning (1891-1892) 1: 49-56.

FACS Hennig-Traub (1990) in appendix [after p. 69] 19-30.

See Bergmann (1986) no. 158, supplemented (1994) 21; Hennig (1988).

TrierTh • *Trierer Theophilusspiel*

ED Petsch (1908) 74-103.

MUS Bohn (1877) 24-25; [*Silete* only] Schuler (1940) no. 580.

See Bergmann (1986) no. 157, supplemented (1994) 20, 29.

VichO • *Vich Ludus Paschalis*

ED LOO 823.

ED• Anglès (1935) 276-278.

FACS [first page, fol. 58v] Donovan (1958) after p. 96.

See Lipphardt in LOO 6: 456.

WienO • *Wiener Osterspiel*

ED• Blosen (1979) 26-127.

See Bergmann (1986) no. 162.

WienP • *Wiener Passionsspielfragment*

ED Hennig (1986) 24-44; Froning (1891-1892) 1: 305-324.

FACS [fols. 1r-8v] Hennig (1986) in appendix [after p. 45].

MUS Orel (1926) appendix pp. 1-3 [melodies no. 1-17].

See Bergmann (1986) no. 167, supplemented (1994) 21.

WolfbO • *Wolfenbütteler Osterspiel*

MS Wolfenbüttel, Herzog August Bibliothek, Cod. Guelf. 965 Helmst., fols. 181r-192v; ca 1425.

ED• Schönemann (1855) 149-168.

MUS in Schuler (1940).

See Bergmann (1986) no. 172; Heinemann (1884-1888) 2: 325-327.

ZurzP • *Zurzacher Passionsspiel* (fragments)

MS Lucerne, Zentralbibliothek, MS 177 fol.; 1494.

ED Reinle (1949-1950) 79-90.

MUS Reinle (1949-1950) 77 [*Defecit gaudium*], 80 [FACS of *Contritum est*].

See Bergmann (1986) no. 97; Reinle (1981); Mundt (1919) 1-5, 81-82.

ZwiO.I • *Zwickauer Osterspiel I* [MS B]
ED LOO 789 ("Joachimsthal" Visitatio), superseded by
ED• Linke-Mehler (1990) 29-44.
FACS Linke-Mehler (1990) 140-144.
See Linke (1999d); Bergmann (1986) no. 193, supplemented (1994) 21.

ZwiO.II • *Zwickauer Osterspiel II* [MSS A and B]
ED• Linke-Mehler (1990) 47-73.
FACS Linke-Mehler (1990) 118-125 [MS A], 146-150 [MS B]
See Linke (1999d); Bergmann (1986) no. 193, supplemented (1994) 21.

ZwiO.III • *Zwickauer Osterspiel III* [MSS A and B]
ED• Linke-Mehler (1990) 74-102.
FACS Linke-Mehler (1990) 125-137 [MS A], 150-155 [MS B]
See Linke (1999d); Bergmann (1986) no. 193, supplemented (1994) 21.

Zwi.IV • *Zwickauer Maria-Salome-Rolle* [MS B]
ED• Linke-Mehler (1990) 103-108.
FACS Linke-Mehler (1990) 156 (MS B).
See Linke (1999c); Bergmann (1986) no. 193, supplemented (1994) 21.

Introduction

The fourteenth-century Thuringian Play of the Ten Virgins or *Ludus de decem virginibus* (hereafter Lddv) is one of the best known medieval German dramas and probably the most famous among numerous plays surviving from the central German area (*Mitteldeutschland*). Although this Latin-German (or 'macaronic') play has been edited a number of times since the mid-nineteenth century, it has not yet been studied as comprehensively as its poetic and dramatic qualities would warrant; important aspects of the work, essential for an adequate edition, have not been given the consideration they deserve. The present book will examine some of these basic aspects, with a focus on the play's thirty-six Latin chants, their text and music and the rich liturgical and paraliturgical heritage to which they belong; the goal is the recovery of the lost liturgico-musical dimension of the play.[1] Beyond investigating the Lddv's obvious and hidden ties to medieval liturgy, the research will extend to other medieval dramas, only a few of which deal with the biblical Parable of the Ten Virgins.

Medieval plays of the Wise and Foolish Virgins are based on the parable in Matthew 25: 1-13. They constitute one of three types of eschatological plays and represent, in a symbolic form, the individual eschatology, the salvation or damnation of the individual soul.[2] In contrast to the abundance of religious plays depicting the major events of salvation history celebrated in the course of the ecclesiastical year (Easter, Passion, and Corpus Christi plays, and to a lesser degree Christmas plays), only four texts of Ten Virgins plays have survived in Europe although, judging from performance records, they were widely known in Germany from the fourteenth to the sixteenth century.

The Thuringian *Ludus de decem virginibus* is extant in two versions which go back independently to a lost Thuringian exemplar: the Latin-German 'MS A' of Mühlhausen/Thuringia, dating from between 1350 and 1371;[3] and the purely vernacular version of 1428, 'MS B' of Darm-

---

[1]The investigations in this book are designed to lay the groundwork for a much needed new edition of the drama which I am preparing.

[2]The two other types of eschatological plays focus instead on the collective eschatology of humankind (Antichrist plays) or on the cosmic-universal eschatology of doomsday (Last Judgment plays). Cf. Linke (1987a) 223; Knight (1984) 268-269.

[3]Mühlhausen/Thüringen, Stadtarchiv, MS 87/20 (olim 60/20), [pp]. 94b-100a (hence-

stadt,[4] a Hessian revision of the lost Thuringian source which lacks the liturgical dimension of MS A and offers some changes in the vernacular dialogue and in the overall conception of the play.[5] In France the much earlier *Sponsus* play ("Jeu de l'Époux" or "Mystère des Vierges sages et des Vierges folles") from the Limoges area dates to around the turn of the twelfth century and is written in Latin and French stanzas, with the (non-liturgical) music clearly notated in the manuscript.[6] The late and very elaborate Dutch (Flemish) *Spel van de V vroede ende van de V dwaeze Maegden* (hereafter Flem.X.Virg) of the sixteenth century, surviving only in a nineteenth-century transcription, is highly allegorical; the editor Hoebeke has shown some dependency of this play on the Thuringian Lddv and its liturgical chants.[7]

In addition to these individual Ten Virgins plays there are three later, more complex German plays which have integrated the same material into a larger context. Connections to the earlier Thuringian Lddv are evident in two of them and likely, though not yet explored, in the play from Erfurt/Thuringia. The severely mutilated manuscript of the Marburg *Spiel von den letzten Dingen* (MaSp.532), written in Hesse some thirty years after the Hessian B-version of the Lddv, unfortunately remains unedited.[8] The extant parts of the manuscript contain fragments

---

forth MS A). The title *Thüringisches* (also *Mühlhäuser*) *Zehnjungfrauenspiel* has now been generally accepted in scholarly literature; cf. below, pp.12-13 with n6. References to the text of this play, if not to MS A, are to the edition by Schneider (1964), unless stated otherwise.

[4]Cf. below, p. 15 n14. Since this B-version omits all Latin texts, it is only marginally important in this study.

[5]Cf. Linke (1995), B. Neumann (1991); Beckers (1905) 19-22; synoptic edition of transmissions A and B in Schneider (1964).

[6]Editions, with music: Thomas (1951) 174-187 (with translation into modern French); Avalle-Monterosso (1965) 71-81 (text), 123-130 (text and music); Coussemaker (1861) 1-6.

[7]Cf. Hoebeke (1959) 20-33; edition ibid., pp. 96-154.

[8]This play (Marburg, Universitäts-Bibliothek, MS 532) has been discussed under the incorrect name *Marburger Weltgerichtsspiel* (e.g. Lomnitzer [1985]; Bergmann [1986] no. 110). The late H. Lomnitzer succeeded in collating the two fragmented gatherings of this manuscript and was working towards its edition under the revised name *Marburger Spiel von den letzten Dingen*. Lomnitzer (1985) 1229-1230, noted the strong dependency of large sections of the Marburg play on the Thuringian Lddv. More extensive comparisons of the two plays are found in a paper by Lomnitzer (1986), of which I received the manuscript of eleven pages. I am grateful to him for allowing me to use this and other preparatory materials for his edition. I also express my thanks to Dr. U.

of a very elaborate Ten Virgins play which is highly dependent on the A-version of the Thuringian drama, not only in the vernacular dialogue as Lomnitzer pointed out, but also in the choice of several Latin chants as will be shown below.[9] In the also unpublished *Erfurter Moralität* (ErfMor) of vast dimensions (nearly 18,000 lines), written in Thuringia in 1448,[10] the parable of the Ten Virgins is intertwined in an original and complex way with the parables of Luke 15: 11-32 (the Prodigal Son) and 16: 19-31 (the Rich Man and Lazarus); the biblical characters of the three parables are re-interpreted and figure within a new, larger plot of a highly didactic play of Virtues. This *Tugendspiel*, a "parabolische Moralität," constitutes the first part of the Erfurt morality play and leads into an "eschatologische Moralität," the concluding doomsday play; here the unforgiven characters of the parables will be judged and given eternal damnation. The somewhat later *Künzelsau Fronleichnamspiel* (1479-1522) includes around 400 lines of vernacular dialogue concerning the Ten Virgins (KünzCC 4670-5074). There is no interaction between the Wise and the Foolish Virgins; the main dialogue revolves around the Foolish Virgins, with Peter and Mary interceding on their behalf and the devils triumphantly leading them to hell after their rejection.[11]

Six reliable performance records enlarge the picture we get of Ten Virgins plays in Germany.[12] The earliest of these attested performances

Bredehorn of the University Library of Marburg for letting me use the manuscript text of this play and for providing photocopies.

[9]See Chapter 3, particularly sections [**6, 7**], and [**31, 32**] (pp. 142, 147, 280-283).

[10]Coburg, Landesbibliothek, MS Cas. 43, fols. 205r-273r; cf. Bergman (1986) no. 32. An edition of this unique German morality play is planned by Hans-Gert Roloff. As I have not seen the manuscript myself, I rely entirely on the information given by other scholars; cf. Linke (1979a), (1980), (1995a); Bergmann (1986) no. 32. See also Roloff (1993); Linke (1993b) 31.

[11]Reuschel (1906) 8-9, concluded that KünzCC drew some of this vernacular dialogue from the Lddv, probably from a lost third version, slightly different from MSS A and B.

[12]I cite these performance records from Neumann's collection (1987) by the numbers in square brackets Neumann added at the end of each entry: 1321 in Eisenach [Neumann nos. 1481-1483]; 1492 in Frankfurt/Main [nos. 1506, 1507]; fifteenth/sixteenth century in Köslin, in Germany's north-east, performance inside a church, the play of the Wise and Foolish Virgins mentioned as a particularly favorite [no. 1987]; 1545 in Pressburg (Bratislava), "ein heiligs spiel ... de quinque virginibus fatuis et prudentibus" [no. 2348]; 1551 in Eger [no. 1478]; 1552 in Munich, "lateinisch und teutsch gehalten" [no. 2323]. Neumann could find no evidence for the performances of such plays for c. 1515 in Rattenberg/Tyrol cited by Anton Dörrer; cf. Neumann (1987), note to no. [2353].

is the famous one, discussed in Chapter 1, of 1321 in Eisenach/Thuringia, given in the presence of Count Friedrich der Freidige, as recorded in a fourteenth-century chronicle.[13] While the remaining five records document the spread of these plays to other parts of Germany, they date from the late fifteenth or the sixteenth centuries. Thus, the chronological evidence of both extant manuscript transmissions and performance records of Ten Virgins plays in Germany leads to the conclusion that their cradle was in Thuringia and that they branched out from there to Hesse and other areas. The general concept we have of Thuringia's rich cultural heritage certainly supports this view.

As a geographical region, Thuringia, "in the heart of Germany," is roughly defined by the Harz mountains in the north, the *Thüringer Wald* in the south, the Werra river in the west, and the Saale river in the east, with Erfurt, Mühlhausen, Eisenach and its famous Wartburg as important centres. During the Middle Ages the major part of Thuringia always belonged to the archbishopric of Mainz, though its boundaries have otherwise not been stable through the centuries. When the counts of the Wartburg, who had been raised to the rank of landgraves (*Landgrafen*) in 1130, were at the peak of their power from 1137-1264, their territory stretched far into Hessian areas in the west, including Fritzlar and Marburg, and they held some possessions in the east as well, the palatinate (*Pfalzgrafschaft*) of Saxony.[14] Under Hermann I, *Landgraf von Thüringen* (1190-1217), who sponsored the arts and attracted renowned epic poets and *Minnesänger* to Eisenach and the Wartburg, Thuringia became an important cultural centre in Germany. Even religious plays seem to have been strongly supported by the counts of the Wartburg. As early as 1227, just prior to going on a crusade, Hermann's son and successor Ludwig IV, husband of St. Elisabeth, initiated and also covered the cost of the performance of a major Passion play by clerics in Eisenach castle.[15]

---

[13]*Cronica S. Petri Erfordensis moderna a. 1072-1335* (Neumann [no. 1481]), cited below, p. 12.

[14]Cf. Jauernig (1962) 873-874. During the politically unstable decades that followed, jurisdiction in those regions changed constantly, however.

[15]This performance is related ten years later in a *Vita* on St. Elisabeth by Caesarius von Heisterbach; the record is quoted in Schröder (1938); Neumann (1987) no. [1480]; Bergmann (1972a) 61; H. Wolf (1973) 236. See Mielke (1891) 35, and Weniger (1894) 43 n11, for earlier references to this record of the 1227 performance in Eisenach. For the literary life in medieval Thuringia in general, see H. Wolf (1973); Lemmer (1981).

Though the play itself has not survived, it is remarkable that such a major performance took place at such an early date,[16] almost a hundred years before the Eisenach performance of a *Ludus de decem virginibus* in 1321. Neither the earlier nor the later performance record of Eisenach gives us any information, however, as to whether the respective play was in Latin, in the vernacular, or in the 'macaronic' form of Latin and German.

The extant transmission of a Thuringian play of the Ten Virgins in 'MS A' of Mühlhausen is written in Latin and German and dates from thirty to fifty years after the Eisenach performance of 1321. Whether or not this A-transmission of the Lddv or its exemplar can be connected with that performance, has been a topic of much debate among scholars; the question is of minor importance, however, for the studies that follow.

The investigations of this book will focus on the play's Latin parts, in particular on the chant items and their roots in the liturgy of the church. The issue is complex since MS A indicates these chants usually by their textual incipits only, with no melodic clues.[17] The evidence of the manuscript's stage directions clearly suggests that the Latin texts referred to by the incipits are to be sung, and that most of them are liturgical chants known and used in the divine service of the Church, hence accessible in the appropriate liturgical books. The challenge is to restore the melodies as well as the texts of the Latin chants in the form in which they were most likely to have been sung in a performance of the Lddv in fourteenth-century Thuringia.

It seems obvious that medieval performers of the play, faced with a text that indicated only the incipits of the Latin chants, would have made use of local liturgical books to supply these chants. Short of miraculously recovering such local or regional sources, it will be imperative to find sources that can ensure the highest degree of authenticity for the restoration of the texts and music of the chants in the Lddv. This means tracking down, not only in the dramatic literature, but also and more importantly in the vast liturgical tradition, those sources that are proper to, or at least closely related to, the time and area of the play's performance,

---

[16]This record is among the four earliest in Germany known to date; cf. Neumann (1987) 1: 64-65.

[17]When discussing the sung items in the Lddv, I shall occasionally use the term "chant" in a generic sense for all sung Latin texts, including two stanzas and the short *Silete* calls.

i.e. sources that were known and used in fourteenth-century Thuringia and the archdiocese of Mainz, to which Thuringia belonged.

Although the chants' musical and liturgical value has been emphasized by a number of scholars, ironically, the manuscript evidence for both the stage directions and the chants has been progressively obscured in the editions of the Lddv. Friedrich Stephan, the play's discoverer and first editor (1847), misunderstood the Latin chants as mere embellishments functioning "zur Verstärkung des Eindrucks," to prepare the mood for the subsequent vernacular 'scene.'[18] Eight years later, however, Ludwig Bechstein wrote at some length, albeit in a quite unscholarly manner, about different liturgical chant forms in order to provide the background for an adequate understanding of the play which, in 1853, he had praised as "die grossartigste deutsche Opera seria alter Zeit."[19] In his major study of the play, Otto Beckers identified nine of the Latin incipits as liturgical chants and attempted to trace eighteen of them back to their biblical sources.[20] In the editions by Schneider (1958 and 1964), De Boor (1965), and Curschmann-Glier (1981), Beckers' identification of the eighteen biblical texts has become dogma; and these biblical citations, which Beckers left in the apparatus, now unfortunately appear in the main text of the play.[21]

Over the last thirty years editors of medieval plays have only hesitantly heeded the requests of leading scholars to supply the complete texts of chants indicated only by their incipits.[22] In the case of the Lddv, however, editors have been precipitate in their unquestioning acceptance of Beckers' findings.[23] As a result, even the play's more recent editors present it as a mainly vernacular text-drama in which most Latin texts conceal what are the sign-posts for the play's deep roots in medieval liturgy.

[18]Fr. Stephan (ed. 1847b) 150.

[19]L. Bechstein (ed. 1855) 1; for his description of Latin chant forms see 39-45.

[20]Beckers (ed. 1905) 43: "Unter den 29 verschiedenen lateinischen Gesängen finden wir außer den fünf dem Parabeltext entnommenen ... noch 13 andere Bibelstellen, die teils wörtlich, teils wenig verändert übernommen sind."

[21]Only those texts believed to be liturgical are printed in De Boor's edition.

[22]Such requests have been reiterated by Völker (1966/1968) 167; Linke (1970) 72, (1977) 27, (1979b) 159, (1993a) 149-150; (1999b) 158-159; Bergmann (1972a) 25-26.

[23]Cf. Schneider in the Introduction to her edition (1964) 13: "Die lateinischen Gesänge der Fassung A ... spielen ... eine so große Rolle in dieser Fassung ... , daß ich sie vollständig in den Text gesetzt habe. O. Beckers gebührt das Verdienst, die Stellen aufgesucht und ergänzt zu haben."

Because the Latin chants of the Lddv have never been seriously studied in their own right, few have recognized the need for an improved edition of their texts, much less for the restoration of their melodies. Until recently, Karl Dreimüller in his unpublished musicological dissertation on the Alsfeld Passion Play (1935) was the only one to suggest that several chants of the Lddv could be reconstructed with their Gregorian melodies from liturgical sources.[24] In my doctoral thesis (1991), I attempted to do exactly this, restore the texts and melodies of the play's Latin chants.[25] The present study is a revised version of this dissertation. Although in a sense, it seems to parallel the work done by H.M. Pflanz (1977) on the Latin liturgical chants of the St. Gall Passion Play, the objective of my study differs substantially from that of Pflanz, as a brief outline of the scope and method of the research will make clear.[26]

Since many of the play's incipits can refer to more than one chant, their correct identification requires an in-depth investigation into the liturgical background of each chant and the proper method of its performance. The scope of the research, therefore, extends beyond that with which literary historians usually feel comfortable. Yet the first-class work by musicologists and liturgical scholars in the past few decades has greatly facilitated access to important medieval sources in this field. Still, such a study poses a number of problems, and this is probably the reason it has not been attempted before. The medieval liturgy is a vast treasure trove of rites, rituals, formulas, and plainsong repertoire. Innumerable liturgical texts and tunes have been transmitted in hundreds of thousands of books, attesting to an almost unbroken chain of liturgical practice from the early to the late Middle Ages. A great number of chants, particularly for Mass, have remained virtually unchanged from the time they were composed in the sixth and seventh centuries or later.[27] Such chants can be found in practically all the appropriate liturgical Mass books.

---

[24]Dreimüller (1935) 1: 107-108: "Die Musik [in diesem Spiel] läßt sich ... zum großen Teil wenigstens ungefähr rekonstruieren: mehrere Gesänge können aus der Liturgie mit den gregorianischen Melodien ergänzt werden." See also Dörrer (1953) 1138, with reference to earlier attempts at reconstruction.

[25]Cf. Linke (1995b) 916; Körndle (1996) 1398.

[26]My main criticism of Pflanz' aims and methods has, to some extent, been articulated by Macardle (1996) 261-263 and 266-267.

[27]According to Hiley (1993) 573, "the great majority of readings on which manuscripts differ are hardly perceptible to modern ears." See also D. Hughes (1987).

This amazing uniformity and accuracy of transmission, however, goes hand in hand with innovations and accretions to the standard liturgy. For the Office and for some special Masses, for example, the tendency to preserve the inherited liturgical treasures intact was less strong, and therefore from the tenth century on, we find more and more newly composed antiphons and responsories for new or special feasts, often even whole new Offices in poetic form ("rhymed offices").[28] As new liturgical or paraliturgical categories were created, such new compositions (proses, tropes etc.) began to adorn traditional chants of Mass and Office for a growing number of new feasts in the high and late Middle Ages.[29] Many of these new liturgical creations were of only local or temporary use and consequently did not find their way into many liturgical books, even within the same diocese.[30] Thus, a great number of liturgical sources often has to be examined before a match is found for an incipit in the Lddv.

The methodology used in this study evolved from our only clues for the restoration of the Latin chants in the Lddv: the stage directions and the incipits of the chants themselves in the Mühlhausen manuscript (MS A). It involved the following steps:

(1) A palaeographical re-examination of the Latin sections in MS A and a comparison with existing editions. Particular emphasis was given to certain manuscript readings, omitted or misrepresented in the existing editions (such as *scil., seque, primarius, etc.* and *ritmus/ ritmum*). These efforts culminated in a new recension of the Latin text to provide a reliable base for subsequent studies. (Chapter 1).

(2) An analysis of the Latin stage directions in an effort to uncover their liturgical significance for the play. Liturgical terms used in the rubrics

[28]Cf. Wagner (1911-1921) 1: 300-317; Irtenkauf (1963); Hiley (1993) 273-279. Some 1500 "Late Medieval Liturgical Offices," comprising up to forty or more liturgical items each, have been catalogued by Andrew Hughes: see A. Hughes (1985, 1988, 1994, 1996).

[29]Cf. Wagner (1911-1921) 1: 277-299. As more of such innovations and additions to the old Roman repertory have been brought to light, views on and interpretations of those developments have had to be re-examined. See now Stäblein (1966); A. Hughes (1989a) 87-90; Hiley (1993) 518-520; Haug et al. (1998).

[30]This was certainly the case for chant [26] *Iniquitates nostras*; it may also be the reason I have not yet been able to find any evidence for the first chant, [1] *Testimonium domini*, as a responsory in any medieval liturgical book.

(*responsorium, invitatorium, cantare, incipere, dicere, respondere*) are discussed in a preliminary way in Chapter 2.

(3) A comprehensive examination in Chapter 3 of medieval dramatic and liturgical sources in an effort to identify the incipits found in the Lddv with chants transmitted in those sources, to compare and evaluate their textual and musical forms and to catalogue them for easy reference. The goal was to establish a sufficiently large number of sources for each chant which, by their date and place of origin, could legitimately serve as 'collateral sources' for the textual and melodic restoration of the Latin chants. Since most of such German sources exhibit a few distinctive melodic features in their transmissions of chant, it became necessary to investigate the significance of what is known as the "German dialect of plainsong" and, for items in recitation, the *Accentus Moguntinus*. (Introduction to Chapter 3). Chapter 3 is, in principle, a series of monographic studies on each chant, dealing with its dramatic and liturgical use, its melody and method of performance, and its contribution to the meaning of the play. All the data which provide the basis for the restoration of the Latin chants are collected and systematically listed in the Catalogue in the Appendix on microfiche. A list of those sources that have been retained as 'collateral' for the chants' restoration in Chapter 4 can be found at the end of Chapter 3.

(4) A musical transcription of all the chants studied and textually restored in Chapter 3 from sources selected for this purpose. In their entirety, these restored chants, together with the pertinent stage directions, constitute what I consider to be the sung liturgical core of the mixed-language Lddv. (Chapter 4). For a few of these chants facsimiles from 'collateral sources' are provided in the Appendix for comparison.

(5) Finally, a review and evaluation of the whole process of these investigations and their results. The play's restored liturgico-musical evidence will serve as the basis for a brief survey of both the interrelation between sacred and vernacular language in the macaronic dialogue as well as the alternation of various methods of performance. An attempt will also be made to outline the significance of the Latin chants for the overall design, basic thrust and sacred intent of the Lddv. It may well be that these chants contribute considerably more than was previously thought to the motivational sequence of the dramatic action and the impact it would have had on a medieval audience. (Conclusion).[31]

---

[31]Because the exclusive focus of this study is the Lddv's Latin text, not included are an examination of the twelve concluding stanzas in the vernacular, echoing the stanza

For a complete list of sources explaining the sigla by which they are cited in this study and the form in which they were used (MS, printed editions, facsimile) see pp. xv-xxxvi. Melodies from liturgical or dramatic sources cited for discussion in Chapter 3 are occasionally described by the pitch-letters of the 'Guidonian' (not the modern) system with the following meaning:[32]

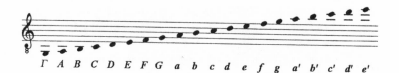

Nearly all other transcriptions from manuscript sources in Chapters 3 and 4 are done in the standard modernized notation of plainsong on a five-line stave; a 'fixed' transposing treble clef replaces the medieval 'movable' F- and C-clefs and signifies that the notes must be read an octave lower. The neumes are usually rendered by stemless round note heads ● to indicate rhythmical neutrality. The 'direct' or *custos* commonly placed at the very end of a stave, looking like a check mark (✓) and announcing the first pitch of the new stave, is omitted in the transcriptions as unnecessary in a system with a fixed clef. For more details on the transcriptions of the music see Table 1 appended to this Introduction and the Introduction to Chapter 4 (pp. 319-322).

---

form of the *Nibelungenlied* and sung by the *Fatue* in alternating solo performances, with choral refrains. The melodies for this great musical finale have already been reconstructed, and these vernacular stanzas should be recognized as an important part of the entire musical scenario of the Lddv. For the musical restoration of the concluding stanzas, see Amstutz (1994).

[32]Consisting of repeated series of the letter names *A-G, a-g*, etc. and starting with the Greek letter gamma (*Γ*), this system of 'notation' spread through the writings of Guido of Arezzo and was in general use in Europe for music teaching and theory by 1050. Cf. the description in Wagner (1911-1921) 2: 224-225; Hiley (1993) 395. For the notes of the upper octave, I changed the duplication of lower case letters (*aa, bb* etc.) to letters with a prime sign (*a', b'*, etc.).

TABLE 1 GOTHIC NOTATION AND ITS 'MODERN' TRANSCRIPTION
(CF. PARRISH [1959] 6, FIGURE 1)

	Forms of GOTHIC NEUMES	SQUARE NEUMES	Trans- cribed:
Single neumes			
Virga			
Punctum			
Two-note neumes			
Pes (Podatus)			
Clivis			
Three-note neumes			
Scandicus			
Climacus			
Torculus			
Porrectus			
Compound neumes			
Podatus subipunctis			
Torculus resupinus			
Porrectus flexus			
Strophic neumes			
Apostropha			
Distropha			
Tristropha			
Liquescent neumes			
Epiphonus			
Cephalicus			

Chapter 1

Editions of the Thuringian Lddv and
A Re-examination of Its Latin Manuscript Text

Our knowledge of a Thuringian *Ludus de decem virginibus* (Lddv) began with the discovery of the earliest medieval record for the performance of such a play, the famous performance of 1321 in Eisenach/Thuringia. According to an entry in the fourteenth-century chronicle of St. Peter's in Erfurt known as the "Sampetrinum" and later Thuringian chronicles based on it,[1] a play of the Ten Virgins was performed *a clericis et a scolaribus in orto ferarum* (a zoological garden probably belonging to the Eisenach residence of the counts of the Wartburg).[2] The performance took place on the occasion of the Dedication Feast of the Dominican Church in Eisenach, on the Monday after the Sunday *Misericordias Domini*, namely, May 4, 1321.[3] Count Friedrich der Freidige, who watched the play, is said to have been so shaken by this performance that he went home complaining in an agitated voice: *Que est fides Christiana, si peccator precibus beate Marie Dei genitricis et omnium sanctorum non debet veniam obtinere?* ("What is the Christian faith if the sinner cannot obtain forgiveness even by virtue of the prayers of Mary, blessed mother of God, and all the saints?")[4] He remained so troubled by the performance that he suffered a stroke five days later and spent the next two and a half years in bed "half alive" (*semivivus*), unable to speak or move, until his death in November 1323. Because of the count's reference to the intercessions of Mary *and all the saints* (my emphasis),

---

[1] *Cronica S. Petri Erfordensis moderna a. 1072-1335* ("Sampetrinum"), ed. Holder-Egger (1899) 351; now also in B. Neumann (1987) no. 1481; compare the records in two versions of the *Düringische Chronik* by Johannes Rothe (fifteenth century), Neumann (1987) nos. 1482 and 1483.

[2] For an explanation of the name and the locality, also the later indication "Auf der Rolle," see J. Marbach (1894) 151; and K. Koch (1909) 125.

[3] The date, mistakenly indicated in the chronicle as 1322, has been corrected by Karl Wenck (1900).

[4] All translations from the Latin are mine, unless otherwise stated.

a detail which does not seem to be reflected in the Mühlhausen MS A of the Lddv, several scholars have questioned the connection of the extant Thuringian play or its exemplar to the Eisenach performance record; the Thuringian origin of the Mühlhausen A-transmission, on the other hand, is indisputable and was confirmed by linguistic analyses of its vernacular text as early as 1866.[5] As a result of the controversy the play of MS A is now called the *Thüringisches* (or *Mühlhäuser*) rather than *Eisenacher Zehnjungfrauenspiel*.[6]

G.C. Freiesleben's discovery of the Eisenach performance record in 1760 was greeted enthusiastically by literary historians.[7] At this time, knowledge of medieval plays in Germany was limited to the Latin dramas of Roswitha and the Latin *Ludus de Antichristo*; manuscripts of the liturgical Easter and Christmas plays, with two exceptions, still remained hidden in libraries and archives.[8] Freiesleben's contemporary, Johann C. Gottsched, eager to find medieval beginnings for his collection of German plays from the fifteenth to the mid eighteenth centuries, proudly celebrated Freiesleben's 'fortunate' discovery as the first ancient trace of a religious drama in the German language.[9] Eighty-seven more years were to pass before the first manuscript of a Thuringian *Ludus de decem virginibus* came to light when Friedrich Stephan, councillor of the city of Mühlhausen/Thuringia, discovered the text of the play in 1847 while compiling a description of the manuscripts in the city archives. This manuscript was eventually called 'MS A,' after Rieger (1865) discovered a second manuscript of the Lddv ('MS B').[10]

---

[5]Cf. R. Bechstein (1866) 135-136, and in more detail, 137-163. Bechstein's results have been generally accepted in the scholarly literature; see, e.g. Beckers (1905) 2.

[6]Cf. Linke (1987a) 225, (1995); Bergmann (1986) 255 (no. 114). For the controversy regarding the play's connection with the 1321 performance record for Eisenach, see, e.g. Reuschel (1906) 7-9; Schneider (1964) 8.

[7]The reference to this performance by Joh. Manlius in 1565 went unnoticed for some three hundred years until cited by Ludwig Koch (1867) 113.

[8]The fragment of a fourteenth-century Christmas play, the *Marburger Prophetenrolle*, was published by Dieterich (1642) 122-124. And in 1716, Bernhard Pez discovered the manuscript of the Klosterneuburg Easter Play (KlstnbgO) and published two excerpts, the beginning and the end, shortly thereafter; cf. Pez (1721) p. liii. Cf. Linke (1983a), (1985c) and Bergmann (1986) no. 63.

[9]"Da also glücklicher Weise, diese erste uralte Spur eines geistlichen Trauerspiels, in deutscher Sprache glücklich entdecket worden ... ." Gottsched (1765) 42.

[10]MS A is described below, pp. 16-17; for MS B, see below, n14.

A. THE EDITIONS OF THE *LUDUS DE DECEM VIRGINIBUS*

Stephan was the first of many to publish the text of the Lddv. The most important editions, in chronological order, are the following:[11]

Friedrich Stephan, ed. "Zwei vollständige kirchliche Schauspiele." *Neue Stofflieferungen für die deutsche Geschichte, besonders auch für die der Sprache, des Rechts und der Literatur*, 2. Heft. Mühlhausen (1847) 173-184 [MS A].

Ludwig Bechstein, ed. *Das grosse thüringische Mysterium von den zehn Jungfrauen*. Wartburg-Bibliothek 1. Halle (1855) 15-33 [MS A].

Max Rieger, ed. "Das Spiel von den zehn Jungfrauen." *Germania* 10 (1865) 311-337 [MS B, with some variants from MS A].

Otto Beckers, ed. *Das Spiel von den zehn Jungfrauen und das Katharinenspiel*. Germanistische Abhandlungen 24. Breslau (1905) 96-124; repr. Hildesheim: Olms, 1977 ["critical" edition, based on MSS A and B].

Karin Schneider, ed. "Das Eisenacher Zehnjungfrauenspiel." *Lebendiges Mittelalter, Festgabe für W. Stammler*. Fribourg (1958) 163-203 [MSS A and B, synoptic edition].

Karin Schneider, ed. *Das Eisenacher Zehnjungfrauenspiel*. Texte des späten Mittelalters und der frühen Neuzeit 17. Berlin 1964 [MSS A and B, edition of 1958 revised].

Helmut De Boor, ed. "Ludus de decem virginibus." *Mittelalter: Texte und Zeugnisse* 1. In Killy, ed., *Die deutsche Literatur: Texte und Zeugnisse* I/1. München (1965) 182-202 [based on Becker's "critical" edition of 1905].

Michael Curschmann and Ingeborg Glier, eds. "Eisenacher Zehnjungfrauenspiel." *Deutsche Dichtung des Mittelalters* III, München and Wien (1981) 274-306 [based on Schneider's edition of MS A; cited as Curschmann-Glier].

Stephan's 1847 edition of this fourteenth-century play, together with that of the *Ludus de beata Katherina* (LdbKath) in the same Mühlhausen codex,[12] pays careful attention to both the Latin and the vernacular

---

[11]Not mentioned here are those editions prepared for high school students or other non-scholarly readers. In addition, several translations and modern versions of the play were created around 1921, the 600th anniversary of the famous Eisenach performance. For more details, see Linke (1995b) 915; Dörrer (1953) 1137-1138; Amstutz (1991) 13.

[12]Mühlhausen/Thüringen, Stadtarchiv, MS 87/20, [pp.] 89b-94b: LdbKath: 94b-100a: Lddv.

texts, but ignores the versification. In 1855, Ludwig Bechstein, the famous collector of German fairy tales, edited the Lddv a second time together with the performance records in Thuringian chronicles and a translation of the play into modern German.[13] Ten years later, Max Rieger discovered and published a second manuscript of the play, which he called MS B and which is based on a Thuringian exemplar close to, but not identical with, Mühlhausen MS A. This MS B from Darmstadt[14] dates to 1428 and is a Hessian revision of the play entirely in the vernacular, with the Latin chants omitted and with a few changes in the action and the portrayal of the characters. In his edition, Rieger attempted to collate the two manuscripts, indicating the variants of MS A in the apparatus or as emendations in the text. The concluding stanzas of the play, however, do not correctly reflect either A or B, since Rieger edits them to suit his own perception of their intended stanza form.[15] In his 'critical' edition of 1905, Otto Beckers tried to arrive at an original text on the basis of both manuscript transmissions, but his editorial interventions, conjectures and deletions resulted in changes to large sections of the text.

Karin Schneider decided to print the two manuscripts side by side in a synoptic edition (1958 and 1964) that makes clearly visible where the two manuscripts converge and diverge. Her plan to present the play the way it has been transmitted to us is only partially fulfilled, however,[16] since she retains several readings and misrepresentations from earlier editions and includes in her text what she considers to be the 'full wording' of the Latin chants in MS A, while in fact only adopting the biblical texts suggested by Beckers, not the true liturgical texts.[17] The more recent editions by De Boor (1965) and Curschmann-Glier (1981) cannot

---

[13]For Bechstein's comments on the general neglect of Stephan's edition, see L. Bechstein (ed. 1855) 2, 9.

[14]Darmstadt, Hessische Landes- und Hochschulbibliothek, MS 3290, fols. 212r–228r. For a description of MS B see Staub and Sänger (1991) 148; Bergmann (1986) 90; Beckers (ed. 1905) 12-14; Schneider (ed. 1964) 9.

[15]For the final stanzas of the Lddv, see Amstutz (1994), especially pp. 42-45.

[16]"Es war ... meine Absicht, das mittelalterliche Spiel einmal so darzustellen, wie es uns überliefert ist: nämlich in zwei verschiedenen Fassungen." Schneider (ed. 1964) 5.

[17]Some critics reviewed Schneider's edition very positively, e.g. Brett-Evans (1964-1965); Werner (1966). Liebenow (1969) 220, however, found it to be so full of mistakes as to be of no use.

be considered genuinely new since they rely heavily on previous editions by Beckers and Schneider.

Beside the shortcomings mentioned, the editions under review include a number of misreadings of the Latin text due to palaeographical misconceptions or negligence — readings that have been passed on from one edition to the next and that have undermined the scribe's credibility to such an extent that even liturgical directions like *responsorium* are discounted. Beckers, for example, charges the scribe with errors in the stage directions and ventures to 'correct' them.[18] Schneider too declares that she has corrected the scribe's few but serious mistakes.[19] And Curschmann-Glier go so far as to discount the liturgical information of the rubrics altogether, claiming that chants and songs in medieval plays were often simply called *responsorium* or *antiphona*.[20] A closer look at the Mühlhausen MS A will show that in most cases the manuscript text is reliable and that the 'errors' are rather to be found in the editions.

B. Palaeographical Re-Examination
of the Latin Text Sections in MS A

MS 87/20 of the Stadtarchiv Mühlhausen in Thuringia ('MS A') is a miscellaneous paper codex of 56 folios, gathered in seven quires of eight folios each, and one extra folio at both the beginning and the end.[21] A modern pagination for the 56 plus 1 folios, pages 1-114, has been added since the old folio markings (ii-xxxii) count only the pages 29-89. On the basis of the water marks examined by Beckers, the codex is dated to be-

---

[18]Beckers (ed. 1905) 44: "In den ... szenischen Angaben finden sich einige Irrtümer des Schreibers."

[19]Schneider (ed. 1964) 12: "Grobe Fehler, besonders Schreibversehen, die aber in beiden Hss. äußerst selten sind, wurden im Text verbessert."

[20]Curschmann-Glier (ed. 1981) 688: "Viele Spieltexte ... schließen sich eng an den Text der ... lateinischen Evangelien an, desgleichen an die daraus entwickelten liturgischen Gesänge (Tropen, Hymnen, Sequenzen; in den Regieanweisungen oft einfach responsorium oder antiphona genannt)."

[21]Its former call number is MS 60/20. Compare to the following the manuscript descriptions by Fr. Stephan (1847a) 126-127; Beckers (1905) 1-3; Bergmann (1986) 255-256. See also L. Bechstein (1855) 9-12 and, particularly, R. Bechstein (1866) 132-137. The description by Schneider (1964) 8, is incomplete in its indication of the contents, mentioning only three of the at least eight items in the codex.

tween 1350 and 1371. The whole manuscript is written in black ink, in a gothic minuscule by a hand of the late fourteenth century, with the text arranged in two columns to a page. The small folio volume contains various treatises and sentence collections in Latin and, on pp. 89b-100a, two Thuringian religious plays of the fourteenth century, the *Ludus de beata Kat(h)erina* and, immediately following (pp. 94b-100a), the *Ludus de decem virginibus*.[22]

In both plays, rubrics and dialogue are recorded in a continuous text wrapping within each column. The line endings of the vernacular couplets are usually marked by dots slightly above the line of writing. All Latin texts (stage directions and chant incipits) are underlined and, as a rule, preceded by a paragraph marker in the form of an ornate c. These various features of the text appearance are clear indicators (against Schneider [1964] 8) that the manuscript was intended for reading, not as a script for a performance (although the exemplar may have been a play script, since the stage directions and the dialogue necessary for a performance are all included).

The origin of MS A is in Thuringia, probably its northern part, including, possibly, Erfurt, as R. Bechstein concluded from an analysis of the dialect forms in the vernacular text.[23] Unlike the later MS B, the plays in MS A are written in a condensed, space-saving fashion with a number of abbreviations even in the vernacular texts. The Latin texts, in particular, are very highly abbreviated, and this fact probably caused many of the misreadings by the editors of the Lddv.

Serious errors and omissions in the transcription of the Latin text have been passed down in the various editions over the past 150 years. These are centered on the following readings:

- the confusion between *responsorium* and *ritmus* and of *scil.* and *Silete* in the third stage direction;
- occurrences of *ritmus/ritmum*
- other misreadings, 'emendations' or omissions (*seque, primarius, Iniquitates nostre,* the omission of *etc.* after some Latin incipits).

---

[22]Cf. facsimiles 1 and 2 in the Appendix. For a complete listing of the manuscript's contents, see Fr. Stephan (1847a) 126-127, and Bergmann (1986) 256.

[23]R. Bechstein (1866) 135-137; also L. Bechstein (1855) 11-12; cf. Bergmann (1986) 257; Linke (1995b) 915.

1. The Third Stage Direction

The third stage direction of the Lddv (ll. O, o-p),[24] the one immediately preceding the first few German couplets *Nu swigit* ... (ll. 1-6), has been a stumbling block for all the editors. Misreadings by earlier editors have been faithfully reproduced in all later editions — little wonder, then, that the play's liturgical terminology has hitherto not been taken very seriously:

ed. Stephan, 1. 4: quo finito ANGELI cantant sd (*oder* scl) R₉.

ed. L. Bechstein, 1. 4: quo finito ANGELI cantant secundum Responsorium

ed. Beckers, ll. O, f-g: quo finito ANGELI cantent scil. Responsorium *Silete.*

ed. Schneider, ll. O, o-p: quo finito ANGELI cantant scil. Responsorium

ed. De Boor, ll. 7-8: quo finito ANGELI cantent scil. Responsorium *Silete.*

ed. Curschmann-Glier, 1. O, j: quo finito ANGELI cantant scil. Responsorium

Stephan (1847) was careful not to expand what he could not read with certainty. Subsequent editors, however, decided to expand the last two words of the rubric, with strange results. Ludwig Bechstein read *secundum Responsorium*. As we shall see, palaeographically, there is no way that **R⁹** could stand for *responsorium*. Nevertheless, the reading *responsorium* has been retained by all later editors. In addition, starting with Beckers in 1905, the misreading *secundum* has been replaced with the equally wrong reading *scil*.[25] Beckers goes on to conjecture a *Silete* call after *responsorium*, and De Boor follows him in this. In the larger context, the *Silete* chorus of the Angels seems appropriate here. It was specifically composed for use in medieval plays and served as a device to mark the change of 'scenes,' like the curtain in modern theater.[26] It

---

[24]In this study, unless otherwise indicated, line numbers and quotations from the Lddv usually are from the edition by Karin Schneider (*Das Eisenacher Zehnjungfrauenspiel*, Berlin 1964).

[25]Beckers (ed. 1905) 96, note d, transcribes the manuscript reading as *cātz̄ scil. Rq*. In the manuscript, however, the second word clearly consists of three letters only. See below, pp. 21-23.

[26]This understanding of the *Silete* chorus is now generally accepted. For more details on the function of *Silete* see below, pp.44-47 and esp. 107-109.

is not a liturgical responsory, however, and nowhere in the whole dramatic tradition is the *Silete* chorus ever called a *responsorium*. Schneider and, in her footsteps, Curschmann-Glier retain Beckers' reading *scil. Responsorium*, leaving the reader of the play with the clashing juxtaposition of *Responsorium Nu swigit* ... . Thus edited, German couplets appear to be called a *responsorium*. No scribe would ever commit such an 'error,' however.[27]

Given all these confusing and misguided solutions, we must go back to the manuscript, where on page 94b we find, with a line break within the word *can/tant*:[28]

Angeli cātʒ ſdⁿ Rⁱ

The last three highly abbreviated words require closer examination.

1) R^9

An abbreviation such as the R^9-siglum, an isolated initial letter with an abbreviation mark joined to it, belongs to those abbreviations created by truncation that are difficult to interpret if taken out of context. All that the superscript ^{9} tells us is that the word with the initial letter **R** ends possibly in *-os, -is, -s*, or, more likely, in *-us*.[29] Fortunately, however, within a given context or field, in this case medieval drama, the possibilities for expanding the truncated word are limited. Given its position before a series of German couplets, the phrase *dicit ritmum* comes to mind, which is used again and again in medieval religious plays with various spellings (*ritmum, rithmum, ricmum, rikmum, rickmum, rigmum*) to refer to the whole set or sequence of vernacular couplets that follow.[30] The

---

[27]For a definition and explication of the liturgical term *responsorium* see pp. 54-60.

[28]The manuscript abbreviations rendered here and elsewhere only approximate the original, for which, compare facsimile 2, ll. 35-36.

[29]Cf. Cappelli (1973) xiv and xxv-xxvi.

[30]To my knowledge, no study has as yet been done on the use and exact meaning of *ritmus/ricmus/rigmus* in medieval German drama. See however Stevens (1986) 97-98, 510 (definition); Mohr (1977) 475; Jammers (1959) 109-110; also Bernt (1958) 842-843. "Ritmus" was used (*pars pro toto*) as the Latin technical term for medieval poems and songs in couplets. In medieval Latin poetry, this form of *ritmus* (also *versus ritmici* or *musica ritmica*) implied that the traditional quantitative *metrum* had been abandoned as an organizing principle of the Latin verses and replaced with a counting of the syllables.

siglum R^9 might conceivably be expanded to some form of *ritmus*, as Bechstein hesitantly suggested in a footnote to a later occurrence of R^9, before line 7 (MS A, p. 94b).[31]

The problem with the stage direction is compounded by grammatical considerations. In the form in which the direction has been read so far, R^9 depends grammatically on the verbal form *cantent/cantant*; hence, it would need to be in the accusative case, which excludes the nominative reading *ritmus*. The palaeographically possible expansion to *ritmos* is not satisfactory because, to my knowledge, no other example of the accusative plural form of *ritmus* to denote a series of German couplets is found in medieval manuscripts.[32]

Before continuing this discussion, it may be helpful to examine the two other abbreviated words.

2) cātz

According to palaeographical rules, this form of the verb *cantare* must be expanded to *cantent* or possibly *cantant* as most editors have done. The main problem here, however, is not the reading of the word but its meaning and grammatical function within the stage direction. It seems extremely unlikely that any fourteenth-century author or scribe would use a form of *cantare* to indicate the recitation of ordinary German coup-

---

By the eleventh century, under the influence of vernacular poetry, the word accent in the verses (alternation of stressed and unstressed syllables) became equally important in the Latin *ritmi*. The Old High German 'Ludwigslied' of the ninth century in rhymed couplets is transmitted under the title *Rithmus teutonicus de piae memoriae Hludouico* ... ; cf. Braune (ed. 1958) 128-129. The term *ritmus* in the context of medieval drama clearly refers to rhymed, vernacular couplets in the form aabbcc ... as opposed to occasional vernacular stanzas (songs).

[31]L. Bechstein (ed. 1855) 15 n3: "Fast durchgängig steht vor dem deutschen Text, wie oben R_9 [sic] oder R^m, was denn nichts anders als Rhythmus, Rhythmum oder rhythmice heissen kann." With the exception of Stephan, other editors do not even mention the occurrence of the siglum R^9 at this or any other place of the play; see Table 3, p. 26. Bechstein's spelling *Rhythmus* should be replaced, however, with the medieval spelling *ritmus* (or *ricmus*), which is found in the sources and which I shall henceforth use.

[32]Beckers' reading of *omnes rythmos* in his edition of the *Ludus de beata Katherina* (1905) is his attempt to correct a manuscript error at this place: LdbKath, 1. 610a *repetere oms R^m*. It should be emended instead to *repetere omnem rythmum*. Stephan's transcription remains more faithful to the manuscript: *debet repetere oms R^m* (sic); cf. Fr. Stephan (ed. 1847b) 171, 1. 2.

lets.[33] Something must be either missing or wrong. The uneasiness of the editors is reflected in their footnotes and strange emendations. What precisely do the *Angeli* sing?

3) ſı+

This abbreviation — which clearly consists of three letters only, with a truncation line stroking through the hast of the final letter + —, has almost unanimously been read as *scil.*, which can only be expanded as *scilicet* (cf. above, p. 18). What we would expect at this point of the play, however, after the main performers (*Dominica Persona, Maria, Angeli, Virgines*) have all proceeded to the stage is the incipit of a Latin chant, or rather, the Latin *Silete* chorus, which so often marks the opening of a medieval play. The latter would seem particularly appropriate since the first six lines of the vernacular text that immediately follows express the same request for silence in German:

> Nu swigit, liben lute!
> lazzit u bedute,
> swigit, lazt uch kunt tû ... .   (Lddv, ll. 1-3)

("Dear people, pray be still! Let it be shown to you, be quiet, let it be known to you ...")

It is probably for this reason that Beckers and De Boor conjectured a *Silete* before these first German couplets. A conjecture may not be necessary, however.

Since *Silete* calls occur at six other places later in the drama, comparisons can be made of the way in which the scribe abbreviates the word. The basis for comparison can even be enlarged to include eighteen other occurrences of *Silete* in the *Ludus de beata Katherina*, written by the same scribe and immediately preceding the Lddv in MS A.[34] The LdbKath opens with the procession of four different groups of *dramatis personae*, each singing an appropriate *responsorium*, after which the stage direction reads:

---

[33]Linke, Mehler, and other scholars have advanced the theory that even the vernacular texts of medieval drama were performed as some form of recitation in a singing voice. The rubrics always use a form of *dicere* or *legere* to refer to this method of delivery, however, *cantare* being reserved for genuinely melodic performances, usually in stanzaic form; cf. Mehler (1981) 239-242 and 257-259.

[34]Cf. above p. 17. See also facsimiles 1 and 2 in the Appendix.

Tunc ANGELI cant*ant*   *Silete*   (LdbKath, ed. Beckers, ll. h-i)

The direction of a *Silete* for the *Angeli* reappears in the same unabridged form four more times on this page (89b) and twice more on the following page (90a), with the scribe alternating between the long and the rounded forms of s- at the beginning of the word (ſ-, s-). After conscientiously writing this word out in full the first seven times in the play, the scribe seems confident that nobody will misunderstand the abbreviations he subsequently uses.

TABLE 2   OCCURRENCES OF *SILETE* IN MS MÜHLHAUSEN 87/20

MS 87/20	(1) ſilete	(2) silete	(3) ſile	(4) sile	(5) ſiꝉ	(6) siꝉ
LdbKath						
89b	2x	3x				
90a	1x	1x				
90b		1x	1x		2x	
91b				1x	1x	
92a					1x	
92b			1x			
93a	1x	1x				
94a						1x
Lddv						
94b					1x	
95b			1x	1x		
96a			1x			
96b				2x		
98a				1x		

Table 2 shows that the scribe was not very consistent about the way he abbreviated the *Silete* chant in the two plays. He obviously grew tired of spelling out the whole word in all twenty-five places where it occurs. In nine instances he abbreviates by simply writing the first two syllables (cf. Table 2, cols. 3 and 4). In six other cases, he writes only the first three letters and then uses the generic abbreviation stroke to indicate truncation of the word (Table 2, cols. 5 and 6). All the editors of both plays have unanimously read as *Silete* all the manuscript versions of this word, except the one in question on page 94b. The problem apparently arises from the position of the truncation line stroking through the third letter ꝉ: so long as the scribe started this abbreviation line above or to the right of the letter **i**, as in the first four cases noted in col. 5 of Table 2 (pp. 90b, 91b and 92a), the reading of the middle letter **i** was not affected (for pp. 90-91, see the facsimiles below). None of the editors had any problems expanding this form to *Silete,* although a dot over the **i** is not discernible in any of these cases. On pages 94a and 94b, however, this same generic line starts at the top of the undotted letter **i** in a way that makes the **i** look like a **c**.

p. 90b, 30   p. 91b, 43   p. 94a, 22   p. 94b, 36

Neither of the two editors of the LdbKath seems to have been tempted to read the first of these two abbreviations on page 94a, l. 22, as *scilicet,* since both expand it to *Silete,* which is the only reading that makes sense here, the eighteenth and final time the *Angeli* sing it in this play.[35] There is no doubt the same abbreviation on page 94b, l. 36, at the beginning of the Lddv, must be expanded to *Silete.*[36]

In this particular case, it is legitimate to elucidate the text of one play through that of another.[37] Both plays are written in the same manuscript and by the same hand. Moreover, the scribe obviously copied them in one continuous effort; in the last rubric of the LdbKath, he connects the two plays through the remark *Explicit ludus de sanctissima vir-*

---

[35]Cf. LdbKath, l. 637c, Beckers (ed. 1905); Fr. Stephan (ed. 1847b) 171, l. 19.

[36]A subsequent occurrence of *Silete* at Lddv, l. 100e is footnoted by Schneider (ed. 1964) 20 note a, with the remark that *Silete* in this play is always abbreviated as **sile**: "Hs. **sile**; und so immer." Similarly Beckers (ed. 1905) 101 note a.

[37]How important this consideration is becomes clear in an interesting comparison. In MS A of the Zwickau Easter Plays II and III (ZwiO.II and ZwiO.III), for instance, the abbreviation ſil with a truncation line through the hast of the l looks very much like the occurrences in the two Thuringian plays. In all seven instances (in ZwiO.II once each on fols 56r and 61v, twice on fol. 58v; in ZwiO.III once each on fols 66r, 76v, and 77v), however, this abbreviation does not stand for *Silete,* which does not occur in these plays, but for *simul.* This can be corroborated not only within the manuscript itself, where in similar stage directions the same word is written out in full (three times on fol. 58r, once each on fols 58v, 59r, 61v, 68v), but also through the parallel transmission of these two Easter plays in Zwickau MS B, in which *simul* is always spelled out. Cf. the pertinent folios in the facsimiles appended to the edition of these plays by Linke-Mehler (1990) 118-137 (ZwiO.II and ZwiO.III, MS A), 146-155 (ZwiO.II and ZwiO.III, MS B).

gine Katherina, sequitur de decem Virginibus ("Here ends the play of the most holy virgin Catherine, follows the one of the ten virgins").[38] Thus, the ſil abbreviation in the 'confusing' third stage direction can safely be read as *Silete*. What in almost all editions of the Lddv has been rendered as *scilicet* is, in fact, the 'curtain call' of the *Angeli*, and the first part of the rubric can be restored as:

ANGELI cantant Silete

Now that this problem has been resolved, we may return to the discussion of the siglum R^9, which is no longer seen to be governed by the verbal form *cantent/cantant* as all six editors of the play would have it. Instead, R^9 is the subject of a new one-word stage direction, hence the nominative case is appropriate. It should be expanded as ***ritmus***, the technical term for the set of vernacular couplets (ll. 1-6) that follow as the 'translation' of the *Silete* chorus. Consequently, the whole section, rubric and text, must read:

> quo finito ANGELI cantant   *Silete.*
> Ritmus   Nu swigit, liben lute!
>   lazzit v bedute,
>   swigit, lazt vch kunt tů
>   von deme liben gotis son
>   Jhesu Crist,
>   wy sůcze syn name czůe nennen ist.
>
> (ll. 0, o-6)

("Dear people, pray be still! Let it be shown to you, be quiet, let it be known to you about God's beloved son Jesus Christ. How precious is his name to call.")

---

[38]MS A 87/20, p. 94b, ll. 31-32; cf. facsimiles 1 and 2. Unfortunately, neither of the two existing editions of both plays includes this rubric *in extenso*. Fr. Stephan (ed. 1847b) 173, while maintaining the manuscript sequence of the two plays, breaks the connecting rubric into two parts by substituting *Incipit ludus* for *sequitur*, thus producing the neat, separate heading *Incipit ludus de decem virginibus*, so desirable in a modern edition. Beckers (ed. 1905), on the other hand, publishes both plays in the inverse order and gives the self-contained heading *Ludus de decem virginibus* to the manuscript's second play, which he prints first (p. 96)

As restored, the opening section of the Lddv shows the macaronic form, i.e., the *Silete* call with the subsequent vernacular lines, that was obviously echoed in the opening sections of at least three other, later plays from the fifteenth century.[39] At the beginning of the Erlau Mary Magdalene Play (Erlau IV), for instance, we read:

Deinde cantant ANGELI	*Silete etc.*
et vulgariter	Ier sweiget, lieben läite,
	und lat euch das bedäiten
	von unserm herren Jhesu Christ,
	der von dem tod erstanden ist.
	(Erlau IV, ll. 309-313)[40]

Very similar openings can be found at the beginning of the Saint Gall Ascension Play (StGHi), lines 1-8, and the Künzelsau Corpus Christi Play (KünzCC), lines 0, c-d-4.[41] This detailed examination of the third stage direction has produced two valuable results. First, the 'missing' Latin song *Silete* has been restored. Second, and even more important, the credibility of the scribe has been re-established. He did not write an almost meaningless *scilicet* here; and if the liturgical term *responsorium* incongruously appears before German couplets or a conjectured Latin *Silete* song in our editions of the play, this is the fault of the editors, not the scribe. Hence, the guiding principle in the present work will be to take the text of the manuscript seriously. When the manuscript designates a given Latin incipit as a *responsorium* or *invitatorium*, I shall regard this incipit as the beginning of a liturgical chant, the text and the music of which must be sought in liturgical books rather than in the Vulgate; and if the stage directions occasionally use some form of **R**-siglum to mark sequences of vernacular couplets as *ritmus*, this is how it shall be read.

---

[39]Compare the eight such openings listed in the Catalogue [3'C4]. The number in square brackets refers to the consecutive numbering given below, pp. 35-40, to all the chants in the Lddv and cited in this form throughout this study.

[40]Suppan (ed. 1990); line numbering in Kummer (ed. 1882) is almost identical. The Devils' Scene that precedes the *Silete* call is an interpolation.

[41]StGHi, ed. Mone (1852) 1: 254; KünzCC, ed. Liebenow (1969) 1. As Liebenow notes (p. 258): "Der gleiche Eingang—exclusive des *Silete*—liegt im Eisenacher Zehn-jungfrauenspiel in der Fassung A vor." The "exclusive des *Silete*" can now be deleted.

2. The Occurrences of 'ritmus'/'ritmum'

The use of the non-liturgical term *ritmus* as a stage direction for vernacular text would be of little interest in a study of the play's Latin components if its occurrences were always carefully reproduced in existing editions. As this is not the case, Table 3 shows where in the manuscript this term is used, which siglum is employed, and how, if at all, the editors render those sigla in their editions.

TABLE 3 OCCURRENCES OF *RITMUS* AND *RITMUM*
IN MS MÜHLHAUSEN 87/20 AND ITS EDITIONS

MS 87/20			Editions			
p.	siglum	vernacular	ST	Bechstein	Beckers	Schneider
94b	R^9	1 Nu swigit ...	R_9	Resp.	Resp.[b]	Resp.
	R^9	7 Bote ich ...	R_9	R_9[a]	_[c]	–
95a	℞	43 Eya nu ...	R	rhythmice	–	–
	R^m	63 En truwen ...	Rm	Rhythmum	–	–
95b	R^m	73 Swestere ...	Rm	Rhythmum	–	–
	R^m	89 Wy volgen ...	Rm	Rhythmum	–	–
	R^m	101 Vrowet ...	Rm	Rhythmum	–	–
96a	R^m	169 Ach wer...	Rm	Rhythmum	–	_[d]
97a	℞	237 Wer syne ...	R	Rhythmum	–	–

Notes

ST = Stephan

a. Bechstein (1855) 15 n3: "Fast durchgängig steht vor dem deutschen Text, wie oben **R_9** oder **R^m**, was denn nichts anders als *Rhythmus*, *Rhythmum* oder *rhythmice* heissen kann. Später ist diese Vorschrift in der Handschrift ... hinweggelassen."

b. 'Resp.' is short for *responsorium* in the various editions. Beckers (1905) 96, note d: **cātẑ scil. Rq. hs.**

c. Beckers (1905) 97, note d: *nuptias, dicit dominus* **R_9** Hs.

d. Schneider (1964) 24, 1. 168g, writes, without annotation, *Secunda fatua dicit* instead of the manuscript's *Quo finito dicit ritmum*.

It is evident from this table that only the first two editors, Stephan and L. Bechstein, take into account all nine instances of an **R**-siglum (**R^9**, **R^m**, or a 'stroked' **℞**)[42] while all later editors ignore them except for the **R^9**-siglum discussed above. Yet even Stephan and Bechstein seem to have difficulties with the second occurrence of the **R^9**-siglum before the vernacular text at lines 7-22; at least, neither dares to expand it,

---

[42] Stage directions before lines 1, 7, 43, 63, 73, 89, 101, 169, and 237.

although, in the apparatus, Bechstein identifies it correctly as *Rhythmus* (see note a in Table 3).[43] Such difficulties disappear, however, with the insight gained from the restoration of the 'third stage direction.' In both cases, the same siglum R^9 is used, and the same persons who previously sang the Latin chants proceed to give a translation of these chants in vernacular couplets, indicated by the term *ritmus* in its uninflected nominative case:

0h	quo finito ANGELI cantant		*Silete*
k	Ritmus	1	Nu swigit, liben lute ... (ll. 1-6)
6c	DOMINICA PERSONA cantat		*Dicite invitatis ecce prandium meum paravi. Venite ad nuptias dicit dominus.*
g	Ritmus	7	Bote ich wel dich sende ... (ll. 7-22)

It is true that the use of *ritmus* in the nominative is rare in medieval dramatic literature where forms like *dicit ritmum, rigmo finito* abound. In fact, I have found only two other instances where the nominative is used. In the Zwickau Maria-Salome-Rolle (Zwi.IV) the word is written out in the stage direction *Ultimus Rithmus* preceding the last set of seven vernacular couplets for the part of Maria-Salome.[44] And in the St. Catherine Play which precedes the Lddv in the Mühlhausen manuscript, the stage direction after the Latin incipit *Veni sponsa Christi etc.* reads ſé R^9, which can only be expanded as *Sequitur Ritmus* ("Next comes the 'ritmus'").[45] What follows is the vernacular translation of the preceding Latin chant:

DOMINICA PERSONA ... cantando   *Veni sponsa christi etc.*
Sequitur Ritmus   Kom min uzerwelte brut ...
                                     (LdbKath, ll. 669a-681)[46]

Clearly, 'ritmus' is the subject of the sentence here; therefore, it is in the nominative form.

---

[43]Beckers does note the second occurrence of the R^9-siglum, but leaves it unexpanded in the apparatus; see note c in Table 3.

[44]Zwi.IV, l. 62a; cf. the facsimile, fol. 17r, l. 14, in Linke-Mehler, eds. (1990) 156.

[45]LdbKath, l. 669; cf. facsimile 1 (MS A, p. 94b, l. 1) in the Appendix.

[46]"Come my chosen bride ...". In his edition of the LdbKath, Beckers (ed. 1905) l. 669c and note h, omits the *etc.* after the Latin incipit, changes the subsequent stage direction to *et dicit*, and relegates the manuscript's reading to his apparatus: "dafür *etc. sequitur R₉. Hs.*"

In the seven other instances in the Lddv where the term *ritmus* occurs in the stage directions, it is indicated either by R^m or by R. In all
these cases, the siglum is part of a more extensive stage direction and is
always governed by the verb *dicit*, hence the inflected accusative case
ritmum is required.[47] This is also the form used in a large number of
other medieval plays.

Palaeographically, the diagonal stroke through the leg of the R is, of
course, nothing but one of many truncation signs.[48] In liturgical books,
this R-siglum generally signifies *responsorium*. In a non-liturgical context, however, the 'stroked' R can stand for several other frequently
used words beginning in **R**. In MS A of the Lddv, R sometimes means
responsorium, sometimes the accusative form *ritmum*. Similarly, as
Table 4 shows, the scribe uses the abbreviation R^m not only for *ritmum*,
but also for *responsorium*. Since it is a commonplace in palaeography
that the same siglum or abbreviation can have different meanings, which
become clear through the context, in our play the connection of one of
the **R**-sigla with the verb *dicere* followed by German couplets is ample
evidence that it should be expanded as *ritmus/ritmum*, whereas the same
R-siglum used with the verb *cantare* and followed by a Latin text refers
to *responsorium* in its different inflected cases (R^m, R^o, etc.).

A comparison with the LdbKath will help to confirm these distinc-
tions, since the scribe is more careful there to keep the two terms
separate even in the way he abbreviates them. In the LdbKath, the term
responsorium is found in three instances only, all at the beginning of the
play and all before the Latin incipits of responsories. Each time the
scribe, in good liturgical fashion, uses the siglum R with a 'stroked' leg.
The term *ritmus/ritmum* is used a total of five times, always preceding
German couplets. In four of these cases, *ritmum*, abbreviated as R^m or
in one instance almost spelled out as Rit^m (or Ric^m), occurs with a form

---

[47]Bechstein is the only editor to recognize this; cf. Table 3. His expansion of R to
rhythmice (p. 95a) should be replaced by *ritmum*, however. To my knowledge, *rhythmice*
is never used in medieval drama.

[48] Cf. Cappelli (1973) xii-xiv.

of *dicere* (or *repetere*).[49] The last time this term is used is in the previously mentioned form of *Sequitur Ritmus* (ſê R^9).[50] Thus, in the LdbKath, which precedes the Lddv in MS A, ℞ clearly stands for *responsorium*, R^9 for the nominative form *ritmus*, and R^m (Rit^m) for the accusative form *ritmum*.[51]

TABLE 4 ABBREVIATIONS FOR *RESPONSORIUM* AND *RITMUS/RITMUM*

MS 87/20	RESPONSORIUM ABBREVIATED AS				RITMUS/RITMUM ABBREVIATED AS			
	℞	℞^m	R^m	R°	R^9	Rit^m	R^m	℞
LdbKath								
89b	3							
91b							1	
93a-b						1	1	
94a-b					1		1	
Lddv								
94b	1	1	1		2			
95a-b	1		2	1		4		1
96a-b	1					1		
97a								1

Even though the scribe is less consistent about his abbreviations in the Lddv, after five manuscript pages he might well have felt justified in thinking it should be obvious to the reader that *ritmus* is the only appropriate term to be used with *dicere* and before German couplets. Moreover, the formula *dicit ritmum* occurs so frequently in medieval plays that no scribe would have been overly concerned about the writing of a term so generally familiar to contemporary readers of his text. Beckers accused the scribe of 'errors' in the stage directions, a judgment

[49]Mühlhausen, Stadtarchiv, MS 87/20, pp. 91b, 93b, 94a (all R^m); p. 93a (Rit^m) — it is debatable whether the third letter is a t or a c. Here and in all other cases I have decided to use *ritmum* rather than *ricmum*, following Fr. Stephan (ed. 1847b) 169, l. 3, and Beckers (ed. 1905) 149, note g. Forms with a velar rather than a dental stop (e.g. *dicit ricmum, rigmum, rikmum, rickmum*) do occur in medieval drama, however.

[50]Mühlhausen, Stadtarchiv, MS 87/20, p. 94b, LdbKath, l. 669c. Cf. above, p. 27 and n45.

[51]These facts are adequately represented in the edition by Fr. Stephan (1847b), who retained all the sigla.

that has been more or less accepted by all later editors of the play, but 'inconsistency' seems to me to be a fairer assessment;[52] for while the scribe may not be consistent in the way he handles some of the abbreviations (*Silete, responsorium, ritmus*) in the stage directions, his treatment of them is correct.

3. Other Problematic Readings of the Manuscript Text

There are a few more early misreadings, 'emendations' or omissions of the manuscript's wording that have tenaciously survived into the most recent editions. Two of them concern the rubrics, others the chant incipits themselves.

(A) ll. 116c-d

The second part of the stage direction after the third *Silete* call has been rendered in the following ways by the various editors:

> *deponant se quae dormiant.* ed. Stephan (1846) 175;
> *deponant seque dormiant.* ed. L. Bechstein (1855) 19;
> *deponant se et dormiant.* ed. Beckers (1905) ll. 116b-c;[53]
> *deponant seque dormiant.* ed. Schneider (1964) ll. 116c-d;[54]
> *deponant se et dormiant.* ed. De Boor (1965) l. 153;
> *deponant seque dormiant.* ed. Curschmann-Glier (1981) l. 116c.

("Let them lie down and sleep.")

None of the editors apparently noticed that, in the manuscript, the **q** after the reflexive pronoun *se* is framed by two dots, thus making it the siglum .**q.** for *quasi*.[55] The rubric at this place of the Lddv must therefore, be restored as:

> Tunc omnes FATUE habeant convivium, deponant se quasi dormiant.[56]

---

[52]He has been shown to be just as inconsistent in the way he abbreviated the *Silete* calls, see Table 2, p. 22.

[53]Beckers' only reference is to Stephan's reading *sequae* ([ed. 1905] 102 note a).

[54]Schneider's only reference is to Beckers' reading *se et* ([ed. 1964] 21 note a).

[55]Cf. Cappelli (1973) xxxiii.

[56]MS A, p. 95b, ll. 44-45. The closest parallel to this rubric I could find is in the fourteenth-century *Visitatio sepulchri* of Vich, in which the guards at Christ's sepulcher, stricken with fear by the earthquake, fall down to the ground as though sleeping: "... *vigiles cadent in terra ... quasi dormientes.*" (Donovan [ed. 1958] 88, ll. 12-13).

("Then let all the *Foolish Virgins* have a banquet, lie down as though they were asleep.")

(B) ll. 197a-b.

Editors have clung even more persistently to the reading *Primarius* in the stage direction before *Veni electa mea*. All present this as:

QUINTA PRUDENS ducens eas
PRIMARIUS cantet (or *cantat*)   *Veni electa mea etc.*

Beckers, moreover, changes the verbal form *ducens* to *ducat*.[57]

The idea of rendering the abbreviation **p ma**[9] found on p. 96b, l. 18, of MS A as *Primarius* originates with Friedrich Stephan, the play's first editor who, with some uneasiness, explained in a lengthy footnote that the subsequent text could be spoken only by the *Dominica Persona* or *Primarius* and humorously concludes that even in those days there was already a Premier.[58] All subsequent editors repeat Stephan's 'emendation' at most adding comments such as *Id est: dominica persona*.[59]

The manuscript, however, contains no reference to a *Primarius*. Nor does any such character appear in other medieval dramas. If the abbreviation **p ma**[9] is correctly expanded to *per manus* (and, palaeographically, there is no other way),[60] the stage direction sounds very different:

QUINTA PRUDENS ducens
eas per manus cantat   *Veni electa mea etc.*

("The fifth Wise Virgin, leading them by the hand, sings, 'Come, my chosen one.'")

---

[57]Beckers (ed. 1905) 107 note a, comments only on *ducens/ducat*, thereby implicitly endorsing the traditional expansion *Primarius*: "Diese Änderung des hsl. *Quinta Prudens ducens eas Primarius cantet* ... ist wohl die richtige."

[58]"pma₉, das p ist im Schenkel durchstrichen, ich weiß es nicht anders aufzulösen, auch dem Sinne nach trotz der Construction, denn das folgende kann nur die *dominica persona* oder der *Primarius* sprechen. Also damals schon ein Premier." Fr. Stephan (1847b) 177 note **.

[59]See L. Bechstein (ed. 1855) 21 n2; Schneider (ed. 1964) 27 note b; Curschmann-Glier (ed. 1981) 287, note to ll. 196a-c.

[60]For this observation, I gratefully acknowledge the authority of the late L.E. Boyle, OP, former prefect of the Vatican Library. The abbreviation **ma**[9] for *manus* can also be found, e.g. in the St. Gall Passion Play, l. 1174b (*Jesus ... cantet: In manus tuas etc.*); cf. Schützeichel, ed. (1978) 63 and 348 (facsimile of MS St. Gall 919, p. 214, l. 7).

It is true that the subsequent Latin and German texts belong not to one of the *Virgines* but rather, as Stephan correctly argued, to the person representing Christ, i.e., the *Dominica Persona*. As transmitted in MS A, the stage direction is obviously corrupt and will be re-examined in Chapter 3, in connection with the study of the incipit [21] *Veni electa mea*.

A few chant incipits have been affected by similar kinds of editorial manipulation that were unquestioningly adopted by subsequent editors. In one instance, for example, the case ending *nostras* has been changed to *nostre*, in several other cases the *etc.* following the incipit has been omitted.

(C) l. 229

The incipit of the Foolish Virgins' chant preceding l. 229 reads in MS A:

[26] *Iniquitates nostras etc.*[61]

Stephan and L. Bechstein present the incipit in this form in their editions; Beckers, however, emends it to *Iniquitates nostrae* ... to conform to a text that he quotes in his apparatus, but for which he and all later editors fail to indicate any source.[62] In 1855 L. Bechstein had suggested that one of the biblical sources of this chant might be in Ezekiel 33:10.[63] This text now figures in all twentieth-century editions as the 'reconstructed' chant text.[64] The discussion of this incipit in Chapter 3 will show there is no need to 'emend' the text since an appropriate liturgical chant text beginning *Iniquitates nostras* has been found.

---

[61]MS A, p. 96b, l. 45.

[62]Fr. Stephan (ed. 1847b) 177; L. Bechstein (ed. 1855) 22; Beckers (ed. 1905) l. 228d. See Beckers, p. 109 note a: "*Iniquitates nostrae* (*nostras* hs., Stephan) *et peccata nostra super nos sunt, et in ipsis nos tabescimus: quomodo ergo vivere poterimus?*"

[63]Cf. L. Bechstein (ed. 1855) 43 and 41: "Folgendes sind nun im Spiele ... die Gesänge ... nach ihrem vollen Inhalte, soweit es denselben aufzufinden gelang, und *mit dem Hinweise auf ihren nur zum Theil biblischen Ursprung*, wobei es unmöglich ist, alles unzweifelhaft festzustellen." (Emphasis is mine.) Freybe in his translation of the play (1870) 22, cites the incipit as that of Ezek. 33:10, and translates the verse into modern German.

[64]Although both Beckers (ed. 1905) and Schneider (ed. 1964) ll. 228-229, indicate the manuscript reading in their apparatus, it is omitted in later editions based on their texts, i.e. by De Boor (ed. 1965) ll. 305-306, and by Curschmann-Glier (ed. 1981) ll. 228e-g. In these recent anthologies, the 'emended' chant incipit is presented as though it were the manuscript text.

(D) Omission of *etc.*

Another seemingly minor lapse in the later editions of the Lddv is the omission of the *etc.*, which in the manuscript complements thirteen of the textual incipits of the Latin chants.[65] Stephan and L. Bechstein faithfully printed all these *et cetera*'s in their editions; Beckers and Schneider do not mention them at all. In most instances, the omission does not obscure the need to supplement missing text since the incipits are clearly only the beginning words of a larger chant text (Beckers sometimes indicates those missing texts by ellipsis). For the incipit of chant no. [32] (l. 278b), however, the omission of *etc.* is critical since the incipit alone constitutes a syntactically complete invocation: *Miserere, miserere, miserere populo tuo* ("Have mercy, have mercy, have mercy on your people."). Presented in this form without the *etc.* and without ellipsis in all four of the latest editions of the play,[66] the Latin text will be understood as the complete text, although the manuscript very clearly adds an *etc.*, thus indicating that the words are only the incipit of a longer chant.[67]

A different problem, in the text for chant [27] *Qui tempus* before line 237, cannot be solved simply by reading the manuscript text in a palaeographically correct way because there is an error in transmission. This text will have to be re-examined in a broader context in Chapter 3.

Summary

A critical review of the various editions of the Lddv in the nineteenth and twentieth centuries has established the need for a palaeographical re-examination of certain manuscript readings, especially in the Latin text. As a result, a number of stage directions and a few of the Latin chant incipits must be re-edited to make them agree with MS A:

- In the third stage direction (ll. 0, o-p) immediately preceding line 1, the *scil.* after *cantant* should be replaced by the chant text *Silete*, and the liturgical term *Responsorium* changed to *Ritmus* denoting the subsequent vernacular lines.

---

[65]Chant incipits nos. [6, 8, 14-16, 19, 21, 22, 26, 30-32, 36]. (See the numbers given to the incipits in the "Preliminary Re-edition" below, pp. 34-40.)

[66]Beckers (ed. 1905) l. 278b; Schneider (ed. 1964) l. 278b; De Boor (ed. 1965) l. 375; Curschmann-Glier (ed. 1981) l. 278b.

[67]MS A, p. 97b, ll. 1-2.

- The term *ritmus/ritmum* should be restored in eight other stage directions (see p. 26 n42).
- The reading *seque* (116c-d) should be replaced by *se quasi*.
- The term *Primarius* should be omitted not only from the stage direction 197a-b, but also from the list of characters of the Lddv and returned to the realm of politics where it belongs.[68] It should be replaced by the manuscript reading *per manus*.
- The incipit of chant **[26]** (ll. 228-229) should be restored to *Iniquitates nostras etc.*
- The *etc.* found in the manuscript will have to be added to thirteen of the Latin incipits (see p. 33 n65), especially to text **[32]** (l. 278b), which, although a complete sentence in itself, functions here only as the incipit of a chant (*Miserere, miserere, miserere populo tuo etc.*)

With these restorations, the trustworthiness of the scribe of MS A is re-established. Consequently, all the information presented in the manuscript must be taken seriously, and emendations may be made only with great circumspection.

C. PRELIMINARY RE-EDITION OF THE LATIN TEXT OF MS A

The following preliminary re-edition of the Latin text sections of the Lddv found on pp. 94b-100a of Mühlhausen/Thüringen, Stadtarchiv, MS 87/20, is intended to do justice to the manuscript transmission of the Thuringian play while providing a solid basis for the investigations in the subsequent chapters.

The manuscript text, written in a continuous sequence, is arranged in three columns: the stage directions in roman to the left, the Latin chant incipits in *italics* in the centre, the cues for the German texts in a smaller font to the right. The Latin text sections are given *in extenso*; the German texts are indicated only by their beginning words followed by an ellipsis and, in parenthesis, the number of lines of each text. The (modern) page numbers of the manuscript, written in two columns [a and b], are written between slash marks in the left column (e.g. /95a/); an ellipsis before or after the page number indicates omitted vernacular text. The line numbering of the vernacular text has been retained from the

---

[68]Cf. above p. 31 and n58.

edition by Karin Schneider (1964). The Latin chants or chant incipits have been given consecutive numbers, printed in **bold**, placed in square brackets [ ] and keyed to detailed studies in Chapter 3 and to the Catalogue. A prime sign ['] is added to the numbers of the *Silete* choruses to mark their functional uniqueness as structural elements in the play. The transcription is as faithful as possible to the manuscript text. For the spelling, however, the frequent occurrences of consonantal u and v and of the elongated ∫ for s are normalized to v and s; and the superscript ° is always placed directly above the **u**, although in MS A it often appears to the right of this letter. All abbreviations have been silently expanded except for verbal forms in the stage directions: my expansions of these are indicated by *italics*. The only emendations I have made (in ll. 148b and 236b and d) are indicated by square brackets [ ] and will be discussed along with chants **[15]** and **[27]** in Chapter 3. Capitalization of the DRAMATIS PERSONAE is mine.

... **/94b/**
Explicit ludus de sanctissima virgine katherina
*se**quitur** de decem virginibus.*

0a	Primo educa*tur* DOMINICA PERSONA cum MARIA et ANGELIS cantando Responsorium	**[1]** *Testimonium domini*	
g	Deinde VIRGINES cant*ant* Responsorium	**[2]** *Regnum mundi*	
o	quo finito ANGELI cant*ant*	**[3']** *Silete*	
p	Ritmus		1 Nu swigit ... (6 lines)
6a	CORUS cant*at* Responsorium	**[4]** *Homo quidam fecit*	
d	DOMINICA PERSONA cant*at* et surgit	**[5]** *Dicite invitatis ecce prandium meum paravi. Venite ad nuptias dicit dominus.*	
g	Ritmus		7 Bote ich ... (16 lines)

/95a/ ...

22a   DUO ANGELI vad*unt*
       ad Virgines cantando   [6] *Sint lumbi vestri* etc.
j   Finito Responsorio
       UNUS dic*it* ad Virgines   23 Nû horet ...
                                                         (20 lines)
42a   ANGELI reced*unt*.
b   PRUDENTES cant*ant*
       Responsorium quod
       PRIMA incipiet [sic]   [7] *Emendemus in melius*
k   PRIMA dic*it* Ritmum   43 Eya nû ...
                                                         (20 lines)
62a   SECUNDA PRUDENS
       dic*it* Ritmum   63 En truwen ...
                                                         (10 lines)
/95b/ ...

72a   PRIMA FATUA incipit
       Responsorium   [8] *Tribularer si nescirem* etc.
h   dic*it* Ritmum   73 Swestere ...
                                                         (16 lines)
88a   SECUNDA FATUA
       dic*it* Ritmum   89 Wy volgen ...
                                                         (12 lines)
100a   Tunc FATUE corizando
       et cum magno gaudio
       vad*unt* ad alium locum.
d   ANGELI   [9'] *Silete longam horam*
f   TERTIA PRUDENS
       incipiet [sic] Resp.   [10] *Beati eritis cum vos*
                                          oderint homines
m   quo finito dic*it*
       Ritmum   101 Vrowet uch ...
                                                         (16 lines)
116a   ANGELI   [11'] *Silete*
c   Tunc OMNES FATUE
       habeant convivium,
       depona*nt* se quasi
       dormiant.
e   Tunc TERTIA incipit
       Invitatorium   [12] *Surgite vigilemus*
                                                         117 Wafen ...
                                                         (15 lines)

/96a/ ...

131a QUARTA FATUA		132 Da sul wy ...
		(9 lines)
140a ANGELI	[13'] *Silete*	
c OMNES FATUE vada*n*t		
ad Prudentes et		
QUINTA dic*it*	[14] *Date nobis de oleo*	
	vestro etc.	
		141 Wy beten ...
		(8 lines)
148a QUARTA PRUDENS		
respond*et*	[15] *Ne forte [non]*[69]	
	sufficiat nobis et vobis,	
	ite potius etc.	
		149 Liben, wy ...
		(8 lines)
156a Tunc FATUE vad*un*t		
ad emendum oleum.		
c PRIMA cant*at*	[16] *Omnipotens pater* etc.[70]	
d PRIMA dic*it*		157 O vil sûze ...
		(12 lines)
168a Et tunc SECUNDA		
FATUA cant*at*[71]	[17] *Sed eamus oleum emere*	
	preter quod nil possumus agere.	
	Qui caret hoc carebit glorie.	
e ALIE respond*ent*	*Heu quantus est noster dolor.*[72]	
g quo finito [SECUNDA]		
dic*it* Ritmum		169 Ach wer ...
		(8 lines)

---

[69]*non*] om. MS A.

[70]MS A continues here with the rubric SECUNDA FATUA, followed by the stanza *Sed eamus ... dolor* (chant [17] as printed below, ll. 168b-e, and including the rubric of l. 168e). Cf. n72 below.

[71]SECUNDA] written as a correction above an expunged QUARTA.

[72]*Sed eamus ... dolor.*] *Sed eamus* etc. MS A. The complete text for this stanza, chant [17], is provided here from the stanza that in MS A is placed, by error, immediately following the incipit for chant [16]. The rubric *Et tunc SECUNDA FATUA cantat* of ll. 168a-b should be recognized as the scribe's way of correcting his previous error; cf. n70 above, and the discussion in Chapter 3 [17], pp 189-190.

/96b/

176a	ANGELI	[18'] Silete	
c	DOMINICA PERSONA vadat ad Prudentes cum		
	ANGELIS cantando	[19] Ecce sponsus venit etc.	
g	quo finito UNUS		
	ANGELUS dicit		177 Set, hy ...
			(10 lines)
186a	PRUDENTES cantant	[20] Regnum mundi	
h	quo finito Responsorio		
	QUINTA dicit		187 Wy haben...
			(10 lines)
196a	QUINTA PRUDENS ducens eas per		
	manus cantat	[21] Veni electa mea etc.	
			197 Sint ich ...
			(12 lines)
208a	MARIA superponans		
	eis coronas cantando	[22] Transite ad me omnes etc.	
			209 Sit ...
			(6 lines)
214a	PRUDENTES cantant	[23] Sanctus sanctus sanctus	
e	et ANGELI	[24] Gloria et honor	
j	QUINTA PRUDENS		215 Gelobit ...
			(14 lines)
228a	DOMINICA PERSONA habeat magnum		
	convivium.		
c	ANGELI	[25'] Silete	
e	FATUE vadant ad		
	nuptias cantando	[26] Iniquitates nostras etc.	
j	SECUNDA FATUA		
	dicit		229 Here ...
			(8 lines)

/97a/ ...

236a	DOMINICA PERSONA	[27] *Qui tempus congrue peniten[cie][73] perdiderit, frustra cum precibus ad regni ianua[m] pervenerit.*
f	et d*icit* Ritmum	237 Wer syne ... (4 lines)
240a	TERTIA FATUA	[28] *Domine domine aperi nobis.* 241 Tû uf, here... (4 lines)
244a	DOMINICA PERSONA	[29] *Amen amen dico vobis nescio vos.* 245 Ich enweyz ... (6 lines)
250a	QUARTA FATUA	251 Sint uns nû ... (6 lines)
256a	OMNES FATUE prostrate in terram cant*ant*	[30] *Recordare virgo mater* etc.
g	QUARTA	257 Wy beten ... (8 lines)
264a	QUINTA	[31] *Exaudi* etc. 265 Maria ... (8 lines)
272a	MARIA r*espondet*	273 Hettet ir ... (6 lines)
278a	MARIA flexis **/97b/** genibus cant*at*	[32] *Miserere miserere miserere populo tuo* etc. 279 Eya libe ... (12 lines)
290a	DOMINICA PERSONA ad Mariam	[33] *Celum et terra transibunt, verbum autem meum in eternum permanet.* 291 Muter, ... (6 lines)
296a	LUCIFER ad Dominicam Personam	297 Here, dû ... (4 lines)

---

[73]*penitencie*] penitens MS A.

300a DOMINICA PERSONA

304a UNUS DYABOLUS scilicet
BELCZEBûG dici*t*

310a SECUNDUS DYABOLUS
LUCIFER

322a DOMINICA PERSONA

328a SECUNDUS LUCIFER

/98a/
334a DOMINICA PERSONA

338a OMNES DYABOLI clama*n*t

339a MARIA flexis genibus dici*t*

359a DOMINICA PERSONA ad
Mariam leniter

383a ANGELI   [34'] *Silete*
c   DYABOLI circumd*ant*
eas kathena.
d   PRIMA cant*at*   [35] *Cecidit corona*
g   Tunc OMNES FATUE
facia*n*t pendere coronas
in capite et plang*ant*.
i   PRIMA dici*t*

/98b/ ...
409a SECUNDA FATUA   [36] *Deficit gaudium* etc.

443a TERTIA

/99a/ ...
469a QUARTA FATUA

495a QUINTA FATUA

301 Recht ...
(4 lines)

305 Jhesus der ...
(6 lines)

311 Here got ...
(12 lines)

323 Nû wel ...
(6 lines)

329 Here, daz ...
(6 lines)

335 Recht ...
(4 lines)
339 Prelle ...
(1 line)
340 Eya, libez ...
(20 lines)

360 Swigit ...
(24 lines)

384 Ach der ...
(26 lines)

410 Wafen ...
(34 lines)
444 Nu horet ...
(26 lines)

470 Nû horet ...
(26 lines)
496 Owe ...
(30 lines)

/99b/ ...

525a Post hec FATUE vadant
inter populum cantando
planctos [sic].

c PRIMA cantat

526 Nû hebit sich groz schrigen ...
[NL stanza]

529a ALIE respondent ad
quemlibet versum

530 Owe und owe, sul wy ihesum
cristum nummer me gese.
(Refrain)

531a SECUNDA FATUA

532 Wy clagen uch liben ...
[NL st., var.]

535a TERTIA FATUA vertit se
ad Mariam inclinando
caput cantat

536 Maria, gotis mûter ...
[NL st., var.]

539a QUARTA FATUA

540 Nû clagit, armen alle ...
[NL st., var.]

543a QUINTA FATUA

544 Sint sich got der gûte ...
[NL st., var.]

/100a/

547a Item PRIMA FATUA

548 Got unser nicht geruchet ...
[NL st., var.]

551a SECUNDA FATUA

552 Ich clage uch liben allen ...
[NL st., var.]

555a TERTIA FATUA dicit

556 Nû habit alle rûwe ...
[NL st., var.]

559a QUARTA FATUA

560 Owe derre leyde ...
[NL st., var.]

563a QUINTA dicit

564 Owe deser swere ...
[NL st., var.]

567a QUARTA FATUA

568 Ach und we uns vil armen
[NL st., var.]

571a QUINTA

572 Vrund unde moge ...
[NL st., var.]

575a ALIE respondent

576 Des sy wy ewiclichen vorlorn.
(Refr., var.)

Explicit ludus de decem virginibus etc.

Chapter 2

The Evidence of the Stage Directions
for the Performance
of the Latin Chants

The stage directions in the Lddv do not offer a great deal of information about acting styles or stage properties, nor do they mention any specific liturgical or other collateral sources to be used for the performance of the Latin chants.[1] Yet some of the rubrics indicate the genre of a chant or the manner in which it is to be performed, thereby providing a few clues as to which kind of additional sources must be presupposed for a performance of the play. The purpose of this chapter is to identify and evaluate all such clues to ensure that the appropriate sources are searched and used to reconstruct the complete text and music of the thirty-six Latin chants.

Seven of these chants belong to the *Silete* calls that, in medieval drama, usually serve the double function of (a) structurally marking the beginning and end of 'scenes' and (b) practically permitting the procession and recession of players to and from centre stage.[2] Because of their primarily functional nature, the *Silete* chants form a category by themselves. The remaining twenty-nine Latin chants fall into three different categories according to the kind and amount of information offered by the stage directions for their performance. Thus, four groups can be distinguished for the purpose of this examination:

A   The seven *Silete* calls.
B   Twenty-one chants for which the stage directions *cantare, respondere* and/or *incipere* point to a melodic performance in a singing

---

[1] In a few other plays, such as the Zwickau Easter plays, reference is made in the rubrics to the kind of liturgical book that would contain the complete chant; see, e.g. *ut patet in antiphonario* (ZwiO.I 28a; cf. also ll. 127d-e, 134c-d), *antiphonam sequentem uel similem scilicet ex antiphonario* (ZwiO.III 48a).

[2] The function of *Silete* will be discussed in more detail in Chapter 3 [3'], pp. 107-109.

voice. In addition, nine of these specify the type of liturgical chant (*responsorium* or *invitatorium*) that is intended.

C   Two incipits for which the directions use the verbs *dicere* and *respondere*.

D   Six Latin texts which have no stage directions but only the names of the characters who are to perform them.

References to similar rubrics in other medieval plays and in liturgical books will help provide a clearer picture of the meaning of these four types of stage directions. All chant incipits or chants will be cited by the consecutive numbers in square brackets [ ] given to them in the preliminary re-edition of the excerpts from MS A in Chapter 1, pp. 35-41.

A. The *Silete* Calls

Of the seven *Silete* calls in the Lddv, only the first one contains the direction that it is to be sung:

0o ANGELI cantant   *Silete*   [3']

In the other six instances [**9'**, **11'**, **13'**, **18'**, **25'**, **34'**], the rubrics merely assign the text to the *Angeli* without any specific directions:

ANGELI   *Silete*   [**11'**, **13'**, **18'**, **25'**, **34'**]

100d-e ANGELI   *Silete longam horam.* [**9'**]

This way of handling the *Silete* calls is paralleled in at least two other fourteenth-century plays. *Silete* is found in the St. Catherine Play of the same Mühlhausen manuscript eighteen times,[3] but only the first contains the full instruction: *Tunc Angeli cantant Silete*. In the Moosburg Ascension Play (MoosbHi) as well, only the first of five *Silete* calls is prefaced by the direction *Angeli cantant,* the other four merely have *Angeli*.[4]

Two other fourteenth-century plays show a similar pattern. In the St. Gall Passion Play (StGMrhP), the verb *cantare* appears only in the initial direction *Omnibus personis decenter ornatis cantant Angeli*.[5] In nine later instances, the verb is no longer specified, though it is implied by the recurring use of *iterum:* once as *Iterum Angeli* (16a); twice as *Iterum*

---

[3]Cf. pp. 21-22 and Table 2; also the Catalogue [3'C1], p. F9.
[4]LdbKath, ll. 0i-j, ed. Beckers (1905) 128; MoosbHi, ed. Brooks (1925) ll. 4-5.
[5]StGMrhP, l. 0, ed. Schützeichel (1978) 99.

Angeli Silete (42a, 191a); five times as *Iterum Silete* (117a, 547a, 598c, 758b, 979c); and once by *Silete* alone (315a).[6] The Silesian St. Dorothy Play (KrmsDor) also uses *cantare* only for the first of seven *Silete* calls, without referring to the *Angeli* as singers.[7]

Most other plays have a form of *cantare* in their stage directions every time the *Silete* is called for, or singing is warranted by the presence of musical notation, as in some of the later plays.[8] The early fourteenth-century Frankfurt Director's Roll (FrkfDir) is, to my knowledge, the only play to use a verb other than *cantare*. At the beginning of this play, an unspecified number of boys is instructed to shout their *Silete*:

... Quo peracto surgant PUERI clamantes   *Silete, silete!*[9]

The *Silete* call was not yet in use apparently in the thirteenth century; at least, we have no record of it.[10] It appears to have developed during the fourteenth century where it is used in at least nine plays and particularly often in five of these, four of which are from the middle German area: Lddv (seven times), LdbKath (eighteen times), InnsThAss (twice), the StGMrhP (nine times), and the MoosbHi (five times). The evidence of the FrkfDir indicates that in the early fourteenth century it could still be perceived as a shouted call, an admonition to the audience

---

[6]The verb *cantare* also introduces a very special occurrence in this play of a threefold *Silete* sung by one angel only: *Hic cantet Angelus ter Silete* (StGMrhP, l. 291a).

[7]KrmsDor, ll. 71a, 97a, 125a, 135a, 171a, 223a, 249a, ed. Ukena (1975) 2: 337-349.

[8]Cf. Catalogue [3'C1-3], pp. F9-F12, the siglum • indicating musical notation. A form of *cantare* is used in the fourteenth century: four times in WienP (*Pueri cantant Silete* ll. 0b, 35a, 278a, 506a); twice in InnsThAss (*Angeli cantant Silete* ll. 1609a, 2022b); once in InnsThO (*Angeli cantant Silete* l. 361a; two additional *Silete* calls are noted in the margins without the direction *cantant*, cf. facsimile [1975] fols. 37r and 47v); once in KassPar (l. 36a *Pueri cantent Silete*). In the fifteenth century: once in FrkfP and WienO (*Nu singet ma Silete* in WienO); twice each in Erlau III, Erlau IV, Erlau V, HessW, DonP, and BozVerk; three times in KünzCC; four times in BozAbdm; five times in BeRheinO. In the sixteenth century: fourteen times in AlsfP; nine times in HeidP; four times in TirP; twice in TirW; and once each in AugsO, BozPalm, BozP.1514.

[9]FrkfDir, ll. 1b-d, ed. Janota (1996) 39. The *Silete* as a loud, shouted call is underlined in the subsequent rubric *Hoc clamore finito* (l. 1). In the fifteenth-century version of this play, the Frankfurt Passion Play (FrkfP), however, this direction is replaced by *Et primo angeli cantent Silete!* (FrkfP, ll. 0a-b, ed. Janota [1996] 69).

[10]See the chronological lists of the various *Silete* formulas in the Catalogue [3'C], pp. F9-F12. Cf. also Schuler (1951) 47. Lüdemann (1964) 56-58, is mistaken when he says that the *Silete* occurs for the first time in InnsThO (late fourteenth century).

to pay attention to the play that was about to be performed. Other four-teenth-century plays and many later religious dramas, however, over-whelmingly attest to the singing of the *Silete* call through the use of *cantare* in the stage directions. Although admittedly some of the four-teenth-century plays (Lddv, LdbKath, MoosbHi, StGMrhP, KrmsDor) use the verb *cantare* only in the first of several directions, if the *Silete* choruses were to be effective as 'curtain calls,' they must have been sung in more or less the same manner at each occurrence, at least within the same play. Hence, there would have been no need to repeat the verb *cantare* in later directions, though exactly how the *Silete* call was to be sung the directions do not tell us.

The performers, on the other hand, are clearly identified in each of the seven instances that the call occurs in the Lddv: the whole group of *Angeli* is directed to sing the *Silete*.[11] Although the size of the group is not specified, we are certainly dealing here with choral rather than solo or duet singing. In the opening procession of players, the number of the Angels is left uncertain (Lddv 0a-b: *Primo educatur Dominica Persona cum ... Angelis*), but a later stage direction orders two of them to address the *Virgines* with a responsory (l. 22a: *Duo Angeli vadunt ad Virgines cantando*). We may infer that the number of *Angeli* was meant to be as large as the staging possibilities permitted. A choir of *Angeli* serves the same function of *Silete* singing in a number of other plays of the later Middle Ages so that the formula

ANGELI cantant   *Silete*

is almost standard in the plays of the fifteenth and sixteenth centuries.[12]

---

[11]Such identification is not a matter of course. KrmsDor, for instance, does not specify who performs its seven *Silete* calls; StGHi and TrierTh open without any stage direction, just the text: *Silete silete silentium habete* (in TrierTh with two-part musical notation). BozPalm has simply *canitur Silete,* TirP *canitur Silete vel ...* . Some German stage directions are equally unspecific, e.g. WienO 195a: *Nu singet ma Silete*, TrierTh 818a: *Hyr singet men nu Silete.*

[12]KünzCC, l. 0c, and some of the Sterzing plays specify that two *Angeli* are to sing the *Silete* (PfarrkP, BozP.1495, and BrixP, ed. Wackernell [1897] 181, l. e); BozVerk 30a has *Juvenes canunt* (ed. Lipphardt-Roloff [1986] 1: 338); in AugsO only one Angel sings the *Silete* (ed. Lipphardt [1978b] fol. 74r); the seventeenth-century RegO lets three Angels "begin" the *Silete* (fol. 24v; ed. Poll [1950] 108, ll. 1-2). In BozPalm it is prob-ably not the four *Angeli* entering the dramatic action (236a-248), but a larger group who sing the *Silete* at the end of the temptation scene (*Silete canitur* 236d-e); cf. below, n19.

Three plays of the early fourteenth century have *Pueri* (boys) instead of *Angeli* sing the *Silete*. As mentioned above, the FrkfDir directs a group of boys to shout the *Silete*.[13] The recently discovered fragments of the Kassel Paradise Play (KassPar) have one occurrence of the simple formula *Pueri cantent Silete*.[14] And in four places in the Vienna Passion Play (WienP), two boys are to sing the *Silete*.[15] In the first instance, at the opening of this play (ll.0b/c-1), a kind of responsive singing seems to be called for between the *pueri* and *Lucifer*, who is still sitting in heavenly splendor below the *Dominica Persona*:[16]

Primo duo PUERI cantent   *Silete*
et *retro* quo LUCIFER sedens in claritate inf*ra*
DOMINICAM PERSONAM dicit *reclamans* (?)[17]   *Silete silentium habete*

(At the beginning two boys sing *Silete*, and Lucifer in the rear, where he is sitting in splendor beneath the *Dominica Persona*, calls out resoundingly *Silete silentium habete*.)

At the beginning of the play such a heavenly echo to the boys' *Silete* call, possibly from the opposing end of the playing area, would have been very impressive; the performance with two responding parties even suggests some kind of liturgical singing. The dialogue form for a *Silete* performance is unique to the WienP, however, and has not been adopted in any other

---

In some of the longer Passion and Corpus Christi plays, however, the *Silete* is performed only at the opening of the play, e.g. FrkfDir, FrkfP, DonP (beginning of the first and second day of the performance), KünzCC (beginning of performances at the first, second and third station), and StGHi. The statement that the *Silete* chorus is used to mark the beginning and end of 'scenes' in medieval plays (cf. above, p. 18), therefore, does not hold true for many of the later plays.

[13]FrkfDir, ll. 1c-d, ed. Janota (1996) 39 and 69.

[14]KassPar, ll. 36a-37, ed. Broszinski-Linke (1987) 43.

[15]WienP, ll. 0b/c-1, 35a, 278a, 506a, ed. Hennig (1986) or Froning (1891-1892). In Schuler's view (1951) 47, the two boys represent Angels.

[16]I offer this view, only slightly differing from Froning's edition and Liebenow's interpretation (1969) 258, for further discussion and as an alternative to other scholars' attempts to make sense of this play's opening.

[17]The last word is the reading of Menhardt (1960-1961) 3: 1279, and of Bergmann (1986) 362, which I am adopting. Froning (ed. 1891) 1: 305, omits the highly abbreviated word, Hennig (ed. 1986) ll. 0b-1, reads it as *redn* with Bischoff; cf. Hennig, pp. 7-8 and 25 notes b and c. Hennig proposes that Lucifer speaks only form line 6 on and that the stage direction after the first *Silete* is placed there by scribal error. Cf. the facsimile of the manuscript's fol. 1, ll. 1-3, in Hennig's edition, after p. 45.

play (nor is it used in the three later places in the Viennese play where an echoing of the *Silete* by the fallen *Lucifer* would not have been desirable).

If, then, most later plays have *Angeli* rather than *Pueri* sing the *Silete*,[18] the articulation of a play into 'scenes' appears to be 'arranged' by the voices of heavenly Angels rather than by the shouts of earthly Boys, and thus transforms the dramatic presentation into a heavenly message.[19] The fact that most of the fourteenth-century plays that make abundant use of the formula *Angeli cantent Silete* belong to the diocese of Mainz, or are geographically close to it, suggests that this imaginative way of calling on heavenly powers for the performance of a play may have spread from this diocese, perhaps even from Thuringia, to other areas. In the absence of a special study on this question, however, such an idea must remain a hypothesis.

The question also arises as to how the *Silete* was sung. Was it a melodious tune, or a simple two- or three-pitched call? This point will be examined in Chapter 3, where *Silete* texts and extant melodies from several other medieval dramas will provide a basis for comparison.

B. *CANTARE, RESPONDERE, INCIPERE, RESPONSORIUM, INVITATORIUM*

Unlike the seven *Silete* calls in the Lddv, the twenty-nine other Latin texts or incipits constitute a genuine part of the action and dialogue of the play. Among them is a group of twenty-one Latin chant texts for which the rubrics clearly indicate a sung performance by the use of a form of *cantare* (eighteen times), *incipere* (four times); and *respondere* (once). In nine cases,

---

[18]Of the fifteenth-century plays, apparently only the BozVerk uses *Juvenes* for the singing of *Silete*; cf. Catalogue [3'C1], pp. F9-F11.

[19]The diagram of the stage layout ("Bühnenplan") prefixed to the fifteenth-century BozPalm (MS Sterzing V, fol. 1r; ed. Lipphardt-Roloff [1990] 4: 95), for instance, shows a special location for the *Angeli cum Silete,* although only one rubric calls for a *Silete* chant. This location is at the far end of the playing area, in a central, probably elevated, position so as to overlook the entire site. From such a prominent location the *Angeli* could easily intervene with a *Silete* whenever an unforeseen situation in the performance would call for it. At two later places in this play, a *Silete* is entered by a late hand; see Catalogue [3'C1], p. F10. See also Hammerstein (1962) 80, who considers the *Angeli* in their various functions in medieval drama as representing the liturgical constant ("die liturgische Konstante").

the genre of chant is identified (*responsorium* or *invitatorium*). In the following survey, the significant terms in the stage directions of these twenty-one chants are arranged in the two centre columns (pointed brackets < > in the third column indicate that reference to the genre follows the chant incipit in a form such as *quo finito responsorio*.)

0a	Primo educatur				
	DOMINICA PERSONA				
	cum MARIA et ANGELIS	cantando	Resp.	[1]	*Testimonium domini*
0g	Deinde VIRGINES	cantant	Resp.	[2]	*Regnum mundi*
6a	CORUS (sic)	cantat	Resp.	[4]	*Homo quidam fecit*
6d	DOMINICA PERSONA	cantat et			
		surgit		[5]	*Dicite invitatis ecce prandium meum paravi. Venite ad nuptias, dicit Dominus.*
22a	Duo ANGELI vadunt				
	ad VIRGINES	cantando	<Resp.>	[6]	*Sint lumbi vestri etc.*
42b	PRUDENTES	cantant	Resp.	[7]	*Emendemus in melius*
	quod PRIMA	incipiet			
72a	PRIMA FATUA	incipit	Resp.	[8]	*Tribularer si nescirem etc.*
100f	TERTIA PRUDENS	incipiet	Resp.	[10]	*Beati eritis cum vos oderint homines*
116e	TERTIA [FATUA]	incipit	Invit.	[12]	*Surgite vigilemus*
156c	PRIMA [FATUA]	cantat		[16]	*Omnipotens pater etc.*
168a	SECUNDA FATUA	cantat		[17]	*Sed eamus oleum emere preter quod nil possumus agere Qui caret hoc carebit glorie.*
168e	ALIE [FATUE]	respondent	[Refr.]		*Heu quantus est noster dolor.*
176c	DOMINICA PERSONA				
	vadat ad PRUDENTES				
	cum ANGELIS	cantando		[19]	*Ecce sponsus venit etc.*
186a	PRUDENTES	cantant	<Resp.>	[20]	*Regnum mundi*
196a	QUINTA PRUDENS				
	ducens eas per manus	cantat		[21]	*Veni electa mea etc.*

208a	MARIA superponans		
	eis coronas	cantando	[22] *Transite ad me omnes etc.*
214a	PRUDENTES	cantant	[23] *Sanctus sanctus sanctus*
214e	et ANGELI	[cantant]	[24] *Gloria et honor*
228e	FATUE vadant		
	ad nuptias	cantando	[26] *Iniquitates nostras etc.*
256a	OMNES FATUE		
	prostrate in terram	cantant	[30] *Recordare virgo mater etc.*
278a	MARIA flexis genibus	cantat	[32] *Miserere miserere miserere populo tuo etc.*
383d	PRIMA [FATUA]	cantat	[35] *Cecidit corona*

The liturgically significant terms in the two centre columns, i.e., *cantare, respondere, incipere, responsorium,* and *invitatorium,* require preliminary definitions for an adequate understanding of the stage directions and their performance implications.

1. *Cantare*

Cantare is the most frequently used Latin verb for a musical performance with a singing voice in a liturgical as well as a secular context. Verbs like *canere* or *modulari* may occasionally be substituted for it although neither appears in the Lddv.[20] *Cantare* alone, i.e. without any complement except the subsequent Latin text or text incipit, appears in a total of twelve stage directions in the Lddv[21] — for the chants numbers [**5, 16, 17, 19, 21-24, 26, 30, 32,** and **35**]. Included in this list is the stage direction *et Angeli* for chant [**24**] because the conjunction *et* implies that the direction *cantant* of chant [**23**] extends to it as well.

The use of *cantare* in these stage directions indicates that the corresponding chants were to be sung in a musical, melodious way. Whether this would imply liturgical, semi-liturgical, or non-liturgical singing can

---

[20]For a study of these different terms see Mehler (1981) 30-38.

[21]Not counting the one for the first *Silete* call and two other occurrences of *cantat* towards the end of the play (ll. 525c and 535b), which refer to vernacular stanzas and thus are not relevant here.

be decided only by examining the Latin incipits more closely and determining their origin, chant type, and complete text. The performance of these chants, therefore, will be discussed in Chapter 3 in the larger context of the source material collected for their restoration.

2. Respondere

The verb *respondere* meaning 'to answer' is used in speech and music alike. In musical terminology, it applies to secular as well as liturgical music and usually refers to a kind of choral singing in answer to a preceding solo song or chant. Such an 'answer' is frequently a fixed formula or a refrain that is easily remembered by a congregation or other group. When used in the rubrics of a play this verb is, in itself, of little informative value for the performance. Whether the neutral *respondere* means speech, recitation, chant, or song is determined by the manner in which the text immediately preceding it is delivered: a spoken text will usually be 'answered' by speech, chant by chant, song by song.

In the Lddv we find both the spoken form (as recitation, see section C below, pp. 61-65) and the musical form. The latter sense is obviously required in three places, once referring to a Latin text, twice referring to German texts. The direction for the refrain to the sung stanza **[17]** *Sed eamus oleum emere* reads:

ALIE respondent *Heu quantus est noster dolor.*   (ll. 168e-f)

("The others respond, 'Alas, how deep is our distress.'")

The *respondent* here is the equivalent of *cantant*, reflecting the direction *cantat* (l. 168a) for the preceding stanza assigned to the *Secunda Fatua* (ll. 168b-d). This conclusion is confirmed by the *Heu*-refrain, which is sung in many Easter plays as the refrain to the "B-stanzas" of the Marys on their way to the Merchant on Easter morning.[22] In the Lddv, the refrain obviously serves a similar function. The two stanzas **[16]** and **[17]** are sung solo by the first and second *Fatue* on their way to buy oil for their lamps and the rest of the group responds (*ALIE respondent*) with a choral singing of the refrain: *Heu quantus est noster dolor.*

---

[22]For a discussion of the "B-stanzas," see below, esp. pp. 171-178, 187, 191-198.

The same function and meaning of *respondere* are evident in two stage directions which refer to vernacular refrains. As directed in the rubrics, the twelve concluding vernacular stanzas are to be sung as solos:[23]

Post hec FATUE vadant inter
populum cantando planctos.
PRIMA cantat   *Nů hebet sich ...*   (ll. 525a-c)

("After this the *Fatue* walk through the audience singing laments. The *First* [*Fatua*] sings, 'Now begins ... .'")

The direction for the sung choral refrain to eleven of these solo stanzas is:

ALIE respondent ad
quemlibet versum   *Owe und owe, ...*   (ll. 529a-b)

("The others respond to every stanza, 'Alas and alas, ...'")

For the twelfth and last refrain, with its strikingly different text, the direction again uses a form of *respondere* to indicate sung delivery:

ALIE respondent   *Des sy wy ewiclichen vorlorn.*   (l. 575a)

("The others respond, 'Thus we are eternally lost.'")

3. Incipere

Whereas *cantare* in the stage directions means singing in the broad sense, the verb *incipere* is the technical term for a special kind of liturgical singing: the intonation, i.e. solo delivery, of a chant's first few notes and syllables by the cantor before the rest of the choir joins in. At a time when few notated books were available and no instruments were used in the liturgy, such an intonation was necessary to remind the choir of the melody and, of course, to give them the right pitch. In liturgical manuscripts, especially those of the Dominican order, the end of such intonations is often marked in some way, e.g. by a single or double slash through the stave.[24]

---

[23]For a comprehensive study of the performance of these stanzas, including the refrains and a reconstruction of the melodies, see Amstutz (1994).

[24]Modern liturgical books usually have an asterisk in the text below the musical notation at the place where the choir is supposed to join in.

The author of the Lddv used the technical term *incipere* only in four of the stage directions [**7, 8, 10,** and **12**] because these four chants are part of a longer, 'macaronic' dialogue in Latin and German in which a Latin chant is immediately followed by a vernacular paraphrase:

42b	PRIMA [PRUDENS]	incipiet	Resp.	[7]	*Emendemus in melius*
42k	PRIMA	dicit	ritmum		Eya nù ... (ll. 43-62)
72a	PRIMA FATUA	incipit	Resp.	[8]	*Tribularer*
72h		dicit	ritmum		Swestere liben ... (ll. 73-88)
100f	TERTIA PRUDENS	incipiet	Resp.	[10]	*Beati eritis*
100m	quo finito	dicit	ritmum		Vrowet uch ... (ll. 101-116)
116e	TERTIA [FATUA]	incipit	Invit.	[12]	*Surgite vigilemus*
		[dicit]			Wafen, here, ...(ll. 117-131)

The author's intention is obvious. He wants to ensure that the same person performs not only the solo incipit and, in the case of a respon-sory, the solo verse of the Latin chant, but also the subsequent vernac-ular version of the chant. Such a concern does not really exist for the five other responsories: chants [**1, 2,** and **4**] are delivered in Latin only, with no vernacular paraphrase; any competent member of the group could intone the chants. Chant [**6**] is sung by only two of the Angeli, so either of them may sing the incipit and give the vernacular paraphrase. Only in the case of responsory [**20**] would we expect a singer to be designated. By analogy, we can assume that the *Quinta prudens*, who is directed to perform the vernacular paraphrase, would also have intoned the Latin chant. The author's reasons for specifying musical solo incipits only at the above-mentioned four places, therefore, have more to do with theatrical than liturgical considerations.

This arrangement is highly interesting for the performance of a 'maca-ronic' play such as the Lddv, particularly in connection with the compli-cated structure of a responsory. As we shall see, a responsory requires solo singing not only for the incipit but also for the verse, and, if applicable, for a second verse and/or the doxology. If, then, the subse-quent vernacular text is delivered by the same soloist, the alternation between solo and choir is extended even further, functioning, in a sense, to integrate the vernacular section into the performance unit of a pro-longed (or troped) 'macaronic' responsory.

4. 'RESPONSORIUM' and 'INVITATORIUM' in the Stage Directions

In nine cases, the use of the verbs *cantare* or *dicere* is paired with an indication of the genre of the liturgical chant intended by the incipit: eight times a *responsory*, once an *invitatory*. (The stage directions in what follows are condensed; pointed brackets < > indicate that the genre of chant is mentioned after the chant incipit, in the form *[quo] finito responsorio*.)

0a	DOMINICA PERSONA cum				
	MARIA et ANGELIS	cantando	Resp.	[1]	*Testimonium domini*
0g	VIRGINES	cantant	Resp.	[2]	*Regnum mundi*
6a	CORUS	cantat	Resp.	[4]	*Homo quidam fecit*
22a	Duo ANGELI vadunt	cantando	<Resp.>	[6]	*Sint lumbi vestri etc.*
42b	PRUDENTES	cantant	Resp.	[7]	*Emendemus in melius*
	quod PRIMA	incipiet			
72a	PRIMA FATUA	incipit	Resp.	[8]	*Tribularer si nescirem etc.*
100f	TERTIA PRUDENS	incipiet	Resp.	[10]	*Beati eritis cum vos oderint homines*
116e	TERTIA [FATUA]	incipit	Invit.	[12]	*Surgite vigilemus*
186a	PRUDENTES	cantant	<Resp.>	[20]	*Regnum mundi*

Despite the manuscript evidence for a liturgical origin, Beckers identified four of these chants with biblical passages (chant [1] with Psalm 18:8; [4] with Luke 14:16; [6] with Luke 12:35; [10] with Luke 6:22). Beckers had little liturgical knowledge, and the only liturgical source available in 1905 was Hartker's Antiphonary, as well as the anthologies edited by Milchsack (1886) and by Chlichtoveus (1516). Schneider and, following her the later editors, still refer to these outdated anthologies and adopt uncritically Beckers' biblical citations. Despite a growing interest in the liturgical elements of medieval plays, most liturgical chants, their form and function in the liturgy, and their implied method of performance are little understood by many scholars of medieval drama. None of the recent editors of the Lddv, for instance, ever mentions that the three responsory texts, 'restored' in 1905 by Beckers from Hartker's Antiphonal — chants [2] and [20] *Regnum mundi*; [7] *Emendemus*; and [8] *Tribularer* — are only the first section in the basically ternary structure of the liturgical chant called *responsorium*. Nor do they seem to notice that the liturgical texts are always followed in Hartker's, as well as in other antiphonals, by at least two additional elements, the verse and the *repetenda*; or if they do, they appear puzzled when they find such 'additional' elements in the liturgical sources. It is necessary, therefore, to discuss the above two genres, the responsory and the invitatory, at greater length.

a. *Responsorium*

Responsories are a complex genre of chant. Their place in the liturgy is predominantly at Matins, the Night Office. The fact that the Lddv makes use of a large number (eight) of such responsories is remarkable. For an adequate understanding of the play it seems essential that the structure and method of performance of these chants be understood.[25]

Since the sixth-century Rule of St. Benedict, the responsory has been known as a special genre of chant in the Divine Office.[26] It functions as an answer to a preceding reading, and its characteristic method of performance is alternation between a soloist and a choir rather than between two choirs as in antiphonal singing.

There are two classes of Office responsories, the short responsories (*responsoria brevia*) sung after the chapter readings of the Day Office, and the great or prolix responsories (*responsoria prolixa*) of Matins, the Night Office. The short responsories are of little interest here, their repertory being small and their music very simple, consisting of largely formulaic tunes to which the various texts are adapted.[27] By contrast, the prolix responsories of Matins with their elaborate textual and musical structure are real liturgical works of art. They are pieces of music which do not accompany any liturgical function and exist only to be listened to.[28] Hucke regards the emergence of the responsory in the Roman Rite as the actual beginning of church music.[29] All eight responsories used in the Lddv belong to this latter class of great responsories.

---

[25]This discussion is based on the following more detailed studies: Stäblein (1962) 1685-1687; Hucke (1963 and 1973); [Cutter] (1980); A. Hughes (1982) 26-30, 60-66; Hoppin (1978) 105-107; Brunner (1988); Hiley (1993) 65-66, 69-76, 85-88; also: Apel (1958) 330-351; Frere (1901-1924)1: 3-61; Wagner (1911-1921) 1: 132-140.

[26]As its earlier name *responsorium graduale* indicates, the gradual of the Mass, sung after the epistle, is also a responsory. Hucke (1973) 155-159, discusses the gradual as one of the two genres of *responsorium*.

[27]Cf. Hucke (1963) 323-324 (melody examples before col. 321, in tables III.6 and IV.7); Hiley (1993) 85-88 (with melody examples).

[28]Cf. Stäblein (1962) 1685.

[29]Hucke (1973) 159.

A prolix responsory was sung after each of the different readings of Matins (three or nine readings in the secular Office, the *cursus romanus*; four or twelve readings in the monastic Office, the *cursus monasticus*).[30] The total number of responsories contained in an antiphonal, therefore, was considerable, in the late Middle Ages often amounting to well over a thousand responsories in a single antiphonal.[31]

In performance, a choir responds to a solo recitation of one or more verses, hence the name *responsorium*.[32] The choral statement precedes the solo delivery of the verse, so the result is a basically tripartite form, which can be extended if there are additional verses. The three main sections of the responsory are:

(1) the elaborate choral part called a *respond* (R). It consists of two, three or more syntactical units (a, b, c ...);[33]

(2) the *verse* (V), sung by one or more soloists;

(3) the *repetenda* (Rep.), also called *repetendum*. It is a shortened repetition of the *respond* (*pars repetenda* = "the part that is to be repeated") sung by the choir after the *verse*.

This sequence of three parts is already highly abbreviated, compared with the old Roman form of the responsory, in which the entire respond was repeated frequently, in solo and choral performances, before and after the solo delivery of the verse.[34] In the high Middle Ages, at least

---

[30]On weekdays, Matins consisted normally of only one nocturn with, among other items, three readings and responsories (four of each in the monastic Office); on Sundays and feasts, Matins usually had three nocturns with a total of nine readings and nine responsories (twelve of each in the monastic rite). For the structure of the Divine Office see Reynolds (1984) 225-228; Hiley (1993) 25-30; Dobszay (1997) 597-599.

[31]The first two volumes of Hesbert's incipit edition of twelve early antiphonals (10th–12/13th centuries) give a concise survey of the chant repertory of the Office and its distribution on the various days and feasts of the liturgical year; see *CAO* vol. 1 for the *cursus romanus*, vol. 2 for the *cursus monasticus*.

[32]This explanation is given by Isidore of Seville (c. 555-636) in *De ecclesiasticis officiis* 1.9, quoted by Hucke (1963) 313: "Responsoria ... sunt ... vocata hoc nomine quod, uno canente, chorus consonando respondeat." See also [Cutter] (1980) 759.

[33]The liturgical terminology is sometimes confusing since the respond is also called a 'response' or even, occasionally, a *responsorium*. Andrew Hughes (1982) 27, prefers to call it a 'refrain.'

[34]For the Old Roman form as described by Amalarius in the ninth century, see Hucke (1963) 316, (1973) 160. Peter Wagner (1911-1921) 1: 134, has the highest praise for the clear structure of this form: "Diese mehrfache Wiederholung der Anfangspartie, die

from the twelfth century on, the choral respond is sung in full only once at the beginning; at other places (i.e. after the verse and the *Gloria*) it is sung in the shortened form of the *repetenda*.[35] Similarly, the solo singing is reduced to the intonation of the respond and the singing of the verse.[36] Whether or not the soloist who sings the intonation is the same as the one who delivers the verse (in a liturgical setting it usually is the cantor who does both), the whole performance of the complex responsory, even in its shortened medieval form, consists of the alternation of solo and choir parts:

solo intonation of the *respond*	(R_a intoned by soloist)
choral continuation of the *respond*	(R_{abc} continued)
solo recitation of the *verse*	(V)
choral repetition of the *repetenda*	(R_{bc} or R_c)

In the case of the third responsory (the fourth responsory in the monastic rite) of each nocturn, this sequence is usually extended through the addition of the

solo recital of a sort of second verse, the *Gloria patri* (lesser doxology)	(Dox.)
the choral repetition of the *repetenda* (often shortened)	(R_{bc} [or R_c = Rep. 2])

The basic structure can be represented as in Figure 1.[37]

---

dadurch zu einem echten Refrain wurde, und der anmutige Wechsel von Solo und Chor prägt dem Responsorialgesange des Offiziums den Charakter einer reizvollen, architektonischen Schönheit auf. Er gleicht den klaren, übersichtlichen Gebilden der Baukunst mit ihren symmetrischen Verhältnissen."

[35]In rare cases where there were several verses, the *repetenda* was sometimes progressively shortened.

[36]These changes took place between the ninth and the twelfth centuries; cf. Wagner (1911-1921) 1: 136. For more details, see Hucke (1963) 316-318, (1973) 159-162; and [Cutter] (1980) 760.

[37]Compare the variations on this basic form in Hoppin (1978b) 106. An interesting diagram, depicting the different structural elements of the responsory, has also been developed by Andrew Hughes (1982) 28, Figure 2.1.

FIGURE 1 THE COMMON MEDIEVAL STRUCTURE OF THE *RESPONSORIUM*

R_{abc}	V	$Rep_{(b/c)}$	[Dox	$Rep_{(c)}$]
solo inton./*choir* cont.	*solo*	*choir*	[*solo*	*choir*]

It is important to recognize that medieval books of chant never give all of the *repetenda* because this part was already written down as the last section of the respond. What we find in these books after the verse is the cue word only (or even only the first syllable) for the beginning of the *repetenda*. This cue is usually marked with a special majuscule initial which serves as a visual guide to the singers and directs them to the place earlier within the respond where the first word of the *repetenda* is similarly highlighted with a capitalized initial. The responsory can, consequently, be regarded as a *da signo al fine* form, the 'sign' being the highlighted initial at the beginning of the *repetenda* to which the highlighted cue word after the verse (or after the *Gloria*) corresponds.[38] In modern liturgical books, the cue is usually marked by an asterisk, but the cue word is still given after the verse, again with an asterisk. Although in my transcriptions of responsories in Chapter 4 I maintain the highlighting of the initials in the key words — beginning of the **R**esponsory/**R**espond, the **R**epetenda, the **V**erse, and the **D**oxology *Gloria patri* — in divergence from liturgical customs I will present the *repetenda* with its complete text and music after the verse; see e.g. p. 325, chant [2] *Regnum mundi*.

The alternation of choral and solo performance in responsories is paralleled by an alternation of two different musical styles — melodious, often quite ornate, singing in the respond and *repetenda*, recitation for the verse and doxology. The striking peculiarity in the performance of responsories, as Hucke points out, is that the choir has to sing the musically challenging respond, while the cantor is confined to eight responsory tones for his solo performance of the verses. Thus it is the artistic

---

[38]See, for instance, Figure 18 on p. 217, the transcription of [21] *Veni electa mea*, with the cue word *Quia* at the end to mark the beginning of the repetenda; also facsimile 3, with comment on p. 356. This custom of giving the cue after the verse, standard practice in medieval liturgical manuscripts, has obviously not been recognized by Pflanz (1977), e.g. p. 101, in his book on the Latin liturgical chants in the St. Gall Passion Play. Nor did Polheim (1980) 3: 41-42, see this connection, when he treats the *Homo quidam* chant in the Admont Passion Play as an antiphon, not recognizing the significance of the subsequent cue word *Quia* in the manuscript of the play.

skill of the choir rather than that of the cantor which is deployed in the singing of a responsory.[39] On the other hand, the eight responsory tones are much more elaborate than those for the antiphonal psalmody.[40] Indeed, the melodies of the verses were sufficiently elaborate that liturgical books of chant usually present them with full notation.[41]

The texts of the responsories are mostly, but certainly not always, taken from various books of the Bible, often in some relation to the biblical reading of the day.[42] For liturgical, musical, or other reasons, the wording of the Vulgate is frequently changed.[43] The text of the verse is not necessarily taken from the same source as that of the respond. However, composers of later responsories were usually very conscious of the need to choose verses that would lead harmoniously into the *repetenda* part of the respond.[44]

In conclusion, it is important to remember the following: The prolix responsory is a liturgical chant in which the component parts, respond and verse, are characterized by two different musical styles and two different methods of performance. Yet, through a variety of textual, melodic, and other correspondences, inner relationships are established between those two distinct parts so that they are integrated into the larger whole of the responsory as a genre, "as if combining two bodies into a single one."[45] The performance of a responsory by definition comprises alternation of solo and choral singing in this sequence: solo intonation

[39]Cf. Hucke (1973) 181 and 189. According to Hiley (1993) 73, however, the solo intonation in the Middle Ages was longer and the choir joined the singing of the responsory at a later place than in modern liturgical books.

[40]Peter Wagner (1911-1921) 3: 189, accords them the highest place in the gradation of psalmodic formulas. See also Hucke (1973) 179-181; [Cutter] (1980) 762-764.

[41]Andrew Hughes (1989a) 145, even suggests that "a stylistic distinction between complex choral phrases [in the respond] and a solo reciting formula is normally obscured by the elaborate ornamentation of the verse." For some special forms of verses in later responsories, see Hucke (1973) 179, 181, 189, and below Chapter 3 [2], pp. 99-100 with n25.

[42]See the fundamental study by C. Marbach (1907); also Hucke (1963) 314-316, (1973) 166-171; [Cutter] (1980) 760; Hiley (1993) 70; Hucke-Möller (1995) 1611-1612.

[43]Cf. C. Marbach (1907) 30-43; Becker (1971) 94-95; Hucke (1973) 167-168; Hucke-Möller (1995) 1611.

[44]In the words of Amalarius, the great ninth-century liturgical scholar: "Ideo necesse est ut hos versus quaeramus quorum sensus cum mediis responsoriorum conveniat ut fiat unus sensus ex verbis responsorii et verbis versus." (*Prologus antiphonarii*, ed. Hanssens [1948-1950] 1: 362).

[45]Amalarius, translated by Apel (1958) 513.

and choral continuation of the respond, a solo singing of the verse, and a choral *repetenda*. In some instances, this sequence may be extended by the addition of extra verses and/or the doxology. The responsory represents the unity of these three (or even more) parts.[46]

With this strong evidence of the structural complexity of the responsory, an important conclusion can be drawn regarding the restoration of the responsories used in the Lddv. In this relatively early and highly liturgical Thuringian play, those chants that are marked in the stage directions as responsories and that can be identified as such in appropriate liturgical sources should all be restored in their entirety with respond, verse, and *repetenda*. Discussion of these responsories in Chapter 3 will show that the content of the responsory verses is often echoed in the subsequent vernacular paraphrases.[47] Moreover, the cast of characters required for a performance of the Lddv can ensure the 'appropriate' alternation of solo and choral deliveries; for a group is always involved whenever a responsory is called for in the stage directions:

the ANGELI	Chants [1 and 6]
the DECEM VIRGINES	Chant [2]
the CORUS (sic)	Chant [4]

---

[46]Cf. Wagner (1911-1921) 3: 281: "Ein Responsorium ohne psalmodischen Vers wird man in der ganzen Liturgie vergeblich suchen." T.H. Klein (1962) 88: "Die Form des Responsorium prolixum besteht also in der Zusammengehörigkeit von Corpus und Versus, die erst im Miteinanderwirken ihren Sinn erhalten."

[47]The question of whether or not the verse should be included in the restoration of responsories in medieval plays has been discussed, to my knowledge, only by Polheim (1975) 195-196, in his critique of Bischoff's edition of the plays in the *Carmina Burana* Codex (*Carmina Burana* [1.3] 1970). But his main argument against a 'complete' restoration with inclusion of the verse, is not convincing, as it is based on the very late Admont Passion Play, which is far removed from liturgical customs. The music provided for the chants in the Admont play is a "reliable source of information" for this particular drama only, not for any earlier play. In fact, the opposite point could be made: this late play, in which the liturgical chants are occasionally broken up into segments, had to provide the music because it no longer used the chants in the complete form by which they were known in the liturgy. See my discussion in Chapter 3 [4] of the use of the responsory *Homo quidam* in several late plays (Admont, Eger, and Tyrol Passion plays), also the quotations from these plays in the Catalogue [4C], pp. F15-F17.

Although the verse will always be included in my restoration as an integral part of the responsory, there is less certainty with regard to whether the 'lesser doxology' *Gloria patri* should be retained as the 'second verse' in some of the responsories when the liturgical sources add it. I shall discuss this issue in Chapter 4, pp. 322-323.

and the half choruses of the Virgins:

the five PRUDENTES   Chants [7, 10, 20]
the five FATUE   Chant [8]

Unlike a religious service, however, where a single choir does all the choral singing, the play is peculiar in that the 'choirs' for ensemble singing differ depending on which of the five groups of characters the stage directions call for. The use of different solo performers, on the other hand, was already a structural element in liturgical services where solo performance of prayers, readings, and chant sections was appropriately allocated to the priest, the deacon, or the cantor.

b. *Invitatorium*
Compared with the responsory, the *invitatorium*, the genre indicated for chant [12] *Surgite vigilemus*, is a simpler genre — at least if the term is taken in its narrower meaning as 'antiphon to the invitatory,' the common liturgical name for the choral refrain which adorns the chanting of the invitatory psalm *Venite exultemus* (Psalm 94) at the beginning of Matins, the same Night Office in which the great responsories just discussed play such an important part.[48] The psalm, beginning with the joyful exclamation *Venite exultemus domino*, is performed in its entirety as a solo recitation in one of the invitatory tones. In alternation with this solo delivery, the antiphon is sung as a choral refrain at the beginning and end and, at least in part, after each of the psalm's five sections.[49] The method of performance, therefore, is responsorial.[50]

Although the invitatory psalm for Matins *Venite exultemus* remains the same throughout the year, the accompanying antiphon "varies in a way which is probably more complex than that of any other item."[51] Almost all the feasts of the Temporale and the Sanctorale, as well as many special Sundays, especially those of Advent and Lent have 'proper' invitatories, i.e. antiphons which reflect the day's specific meaning or

---

[48]The following discussion is based on Stäblein (1957); Steiner (1980b); also Frere (1901-1924) 1: 62-64; A. Hughes (1982) 30-34, 116-117; and Hiley (1993) 99-100.

[49]The text of Psalm 94 is taken from the Roman Psalter, where the psalm's five subdivisions are longer than the verses in the Vulgate. For details, see Steiner (1980b) 286; Stäblein (1957) 1391, (1962) 1684.

[50]Cf. A. Hughes (1982) 34.

[51]A. Hughes (1982) 56, with an outline of the changes over the liturgical year.

theme and which often echo some of the 'inviting' phrases of the invitatory psalm, thus establishing a close textual rapport between the two. In the liturgical sources this choral refrain is usually called *antiphona ad invitatorium* or simply *invitatorium*.[52] Musically, the invitatories form a different class from the other Office antiphons; Frere considers their melodic texture and style "more closely connected with responds."[53]

If a non-liturgical source such as the Thuringian Lddv specifies the genre of a chant as *invitatorium* and adds the chant's incipit, in this case [12] *Surgite vigilemus*, this term very likely refers to the specific invitatory antiphon rather than to the complete performance of the invitatory psalm.[54] The fact that the rubric before this incipit uses the verb *incipere* and not *cantare* (*Tunc Tertia [Fatua] incipit invitatorium Surgite vigilemus* [ll. 116e-f]) is yet another indication of the liturgical thinking of the author of the Lddv. As with other choral chants, the invitatory is intoned by a soloist who is joined by the choir for the remainder of the choral part. Thus, it must be understood that the *Tertia Fatua* does not sing the whole invitatory as a solo piece, but that the other four *Fatue* join in after the intonation.

The alternation between solo and choral performance, which marks the chanting of the complete invitatory psalm and which is built into the structure of the responsory as shown above, is a characteristic feature of liturgical chant in general. Such a lively performance style was imported, along with the chants themselves, into medieval plays such as the Lddv. This is an important point to remember.

C. DICERE AND RESPONDERE IN THE STAGE DIRECTIONS

In two of the Latin incipits in the Lddv, the stage directions use forms of the verbs *dicere* and *respondere*:

140c	OMNES FATUE vadant ad		
	PRUDENTES et QUINTA	dicit	[14] *Date nobis de oleo vestro etc.*
148a	QUARTA PRUDENS	respondet	[15] *Ne forte [non] sufficiat nobis et vobis, ite potius etc*

---

[52]Stäblein (1957) 1390, quotes Amalarius (ninth century) as clearly distinguishing between the *psalmus invitatorius* and the *invitatorium* as its antiphon.

[53]Frere (1901-1924) 1: 61; see also Hiley (1993) 99.

[54]The possibility of such a complete performance within an earlier, purely Latin play cannot be excluded, however.

("All the *Fatue* approach the *Prudentes* and the Fifth says, 'Give us from your oil' etc. The Fourth *Prudens* responds, 'Not so; lest there be not enough for us and you, but go ye rather,' etc.")

In this context, the musically neutral term *respondere* means *dicere* by extension from the previous rubric *Quinta dicit* (l. 140d).[55]

It is striking that this short dialogue between the Wise and Foolish Virgins is the only place in the Lddv where the stage directions use the verb *dicere* before a Latin incipit although it is used frequently before German texts.[56] In fact, among the first twenty-six Latin incipits of the play, incipits **[14]** and **[15]** are the only ones not to have a form of the musically unequivocal verbs *cantare* or *incipere* in their stage directions. This is certainly not an "error of the scribe" as Beckers would argue.[57] If then the *dicit* at this place is used in a purposeful way, its exact meaning for the intended form of delivery of the subsequent Latin text must be explored.

Until thirty years ago, most scholars of medieval German drama understood *dicere* in the rubrics of religious plays to mean the opposite of *cantare* and translated the term with *sprechen* or *sagen* ('to speak' or 'say'). Since most *dicere* rubrics refer to vernacular texts, the conclusion was that, as a general rule, the Latin texts in medieval plays were sung, and vernacular texts were spoken, unless they were in stanza form or were provided with musical notation.[58] As a result of these two unexamined assumptions, *dicere* in rubrics for Latin texts did not seem to make much sense. It was either declared an 'error' to be emended or an 'exception' or it was taken as proof that in the later Middle Ages, even Latin texts were often spoken.[59]

---

[55]Compare l. 168e, where *respondere* means *cantare*, as discussed above, p. 50.

[56]*Dicere* is used seventeen times with German texts, ten in the simple form *dicit*, seven as *dicit ritmum*.

[57]In his critical edition, Beckers (1905) l. 140b, emends his reading *dicat* to *cantet*, as does De Boor (1965) l. 180c. Beckers' rationale for this emendation (p. 44) is: "Selbstverständlich wurden alle lateinischen Gesetze gesungen. In den betr. szenischen Angaben finden sich einige Irrtümer des Schreibers."

[58]See e.g. Werner (1963) 49 and 60; Steinbach (1970) 142; Bergmann (1972a) 74-83.

[59]Cf. Steinbach (1970) 142 n5, 176 n13; Bergmann (1972a) 75, 81-82. Wimmer (1974) 40 and passim, discusses *cantat* and *dicit* texts in dramas with the assumption that the *dicit* texts are spoken; see e.g. p. 166.

In 1970, Hj. Linke began to challenge those theories by focusing on such rubrics as *legere* and *dicere* for German texts; *legere* (*dicere, respondere*) '*sub accentu,*' *dicere cantando*, etc. for Latin texts; or even *dicere* with subsequent musical notation. Basing his work on earlier research by the musicologists Dreimüller (1935) and Schuler (1940), sadly disregarded for decades by literary historians, Linke proposed that the verbs *dicere* and *legere* in rubrics might have functioned as technical terms to indicate a recited delivery of Latin as well as German texts. He concluded that 'normal speaking' perhaps might not have occurred in religious plays and that both Latin and German texts might have always been performed as some kind of chant, either as melodious *concentus* (*cantare*) or as a form of liturgical recitation called *accentus* (*dicere*).[60] This new theory needed to be substantiated, however, and, in some respects, revised.

In 1981, Linke's student Ulrich Mehler demonstrated in his dissertation *dicere und cantare*, how the use of these two verbs in medieval drama changed over the centuries. As a result of his studies of liturgical and dramatic rubrics from the tenth to the sixteenth century, he concluded that the meaning of *dicere* and *cantare* can be correctly assessed only when the liturgico-dramatic frame of reference is taken into consideration. The three categories of usage that he distinguishes correspond to three kinds of drama: plays in Latin only, mixed-language plays, and late medieval plays from the fifteenth and sixteenth centuries.[61]

---

[60]Cf. Linke (1970) 71, (1972b) 202, 204, (1974), 23-25, (1978a) 266-267. Independently of each other, the musicologists Dreimüller and Schuler had collected ample evidence, especially from the Alsfeld and Eger Passion plays, to conclude that, at least in these two plays, texts from the Vulgate were usually delivered as recitation, even in cases where *dicit* had no additional direction such as *sub accentu* or *dicit cantando*; cf. Dreimüller (1935) 1: 171-173; Schuler (1951) 34-36. Schuler calls this kind of recitation in medieval plays *eine neue Gattung von Gesängen* ("a new genre of chant"), which he sees as standing halfway between the genuine music items (responsories, antiphons) and the 'spoken' (vernacular) couplets. Unfortunately, the work of both musicologists remained unpublished, except for vol. 1 of Schuler's 1940 dissertation. Thanks to the initiative of Hj. Linke, the Musikwissenschaftliches Institut of Basel initiated a search for the hand- and type-written second volume of Schuler's dissertation, believed to be lost. In 1970, copies of the volume were placed in both the Musikwissenschaftliches Institut of Basel and the Institut für deutsche Sprache und Literatur in Cologne. (Information in a letter from Linke, dated Oct. 8, 1991.)

[61]Mehler (1981) 216-217, summarizes his findings for the various usages of the terms discussed in a much simplified, yet useful, table.

(1) In purely Latin (liturgical or semi-liturgical) plays, the same usage is observed as in liturgical books. Liturgical recitation is introduced by *dicere*. Simple melodic plainsong (simple antiphons, short responsories), hymns, as well as the musically elaborate great responsories are introduced by either *cantare* or *dicere* — *cantare* to indicate the musical form of delivery and *dicere* to indicate the spiritual content of a chant.[62]

(2) For the Latin sections of most of the mixed-language plays (Latin and German) of the thirteenth and fourteenth centuries, the two verbs are increasingly used for specific forms of delivery: *dicere* to indicate liturgical recitation of texts or readings from the Bible; *cantare* for musically rich, liturgical chants (responsories, antiphons, hymns, sequences, etc.) as well as non-liturgical songs usually in stanza form. Both *dicere* and *cantare* could still be used for simple kinds of melodious chanting, with a tendency to use *dicere* for very simple antiphons and *cantare* for short chants with a somewhat more melodic character.[63]

(3) In late medieval plays from the fifteenth and sixteenth centuries, a new trend can be observed. Whereas *cantare* continued to be used in stage directions for melodious items of chant, *dicere* alone no longer seemed sufficient to indicate liturgical recitation for biblical quotations. Therefore, to ensure that recitation would be used for the delivery of certain texts, new directions began to appear in these later plays such as *dicere sub accentu*, *dicere cantando* and the like (AlsfP), or a form of the verb *cantare* (Eger) or *singen* (Admont) with added musical notation for the reciting tones.[64]

---

[62]Cf. Mehler (1981) 39-132, esp. 69-70, and 214-217. This distinction between the verbs *cantare* and *dicere* would explain not only their apparent 'interchangeability' in liturgical books, but also the frequent occurrence in liturgy and drama of formulas like *dicit cum cantu*, *dicit in cantu*, *dicit cantando*, or even *dicit sine cantu*.

[63]Cf. Mehler (1981) 173-197, 214-217.

[64]Cf. Mehler (1981) 198-217. As Mehler points out, with formulas like *dicit sub accentu*, contemporary musical terminology enters into the stage directions of drama. The terms *accentus* (for all readings, prayers, and other recitation forms) and *concentus* (for pieces with more melodic expression such as antiphons, responsories, hymns, etc.) had been introduced by Ornitoparchus in his *Micrologus Musicae activae* (1517). Although such an extra-liturgical, performance-oriented distinction would have been alien to the theocentric liturgical thinking of the high Middle Ages, the difference had been felt all the time and was explained in the ninth century by Amalarius as *pronuntiatio* and

If, then, *dicere* in rubrics is used to indicate three or four different ways of delivering a Latin text, we are reminded that, in classical Latin, this verb also had a wide spectrum of meanings, from the general 'to say, speak, tell, relate' to the more specific meanings of 'to assert, affirm, pronounce, deliver,' and even 'to sing.'[65] The important point is that, thanks to the research of Linke and Mehler, German philologists have grasped the fact, long known to most musicologists and liturgical scholars, that "ceremonially heightened speech in liturgy and drama was chant";[66] and that *dicere* in stage directions often points to recitation as the simplest category of musical speech.[67]

There is little doubt that the short dialogue between the Wise and the Foolish Virgins contained in chants [14] and [15] was to be performed as liturgical recitation. At least three points can support this claim. First, according to Mehler's findings, the verb *dicere* in rubrics of mixed-language (Latin and German) plays indicates primarily liturgical recitation. Second, as most editors to date have suggested and as the discussion in Chapter 3 will confirm, the text of the dialogue seems to be quoted directly from a reading of the Parable of the Wise and Foolish Virgins in the Gospel of Matthew, and this in itself suggests liturgical recitation. In the Middle Ages, quoting a biblical text did not mean quoting from the Vulgate, but from the corresponding reading in the Mass or Office. Such lessons were read from the lectionary or the missal, with the appropriate liturgical formulas of introduction and conclusion.[68] The reading itself "was not just any kind of delivery of a text ... ; it meant a public and rhetorical kind of declamation," i.e. it was chanted to set recitation formulas and tones.[69] In Mehler's words, the text was

---

modulatio: "Lectio dicitur, quia non cantatur, ut psalmus vel hymnus, sed legitur tantum. Illic enim modulatio, hic solum pronuntiatio quaeritur." (PL 105: 1118), cited in Wagner (1911-1921) 3: 4.

[65]Cf. Lewis and Short, *A Latin Dictionary* (1879, repr. 1958) s.v. Bergmann (1972) 78 and n684a, considered the possibility that *dicere* might be used in the sense of *singen*, at least in the Wien Passion play. In translating the term *dicere*, therefore, we might be well advised to avoid limiting its meaning to either 'speak' or 'sing' and, instead, choose a more neutral verb, such as 'pronounce' or 'deliver' (in German *vortragen*).

[66]Stevens (1986) 277.

[67]For performance aspects of liturgical recitation, see Chapter 3, pp. 74-77.

[68]Cf. Jungmann (1948) 1: 498, 505-506. See also facsimile 4, fol. <229>r, ll. 7-9.

[69]Gelineau (1964) 77.

rezitativfähig ("capable of being recited"), a *conditio sine qua non* for the presence of liturgical recitation in medieval drama.[70] The third argument for a recited delivery of this dialogue has to do with the choice of performers. For the first time in the Latin sections of the Lddv, the *Prudentes* and the *Fatue* are not talking as a group but have one speaker only, the *Quinta Fatua* and the *Quarta Prudens*. In a purely liturgical setting, the recitation of a biblical text, except for the psalms, would normally require only one 'performer,' the deacon or the lector. Thus, the combined evidence of the rubrics directing through the use of *dicere* (*respondere*) a single person to deliver a biblical text that is 'capable' of being performed in a reciting tone strongly suggests that the dialogue of chants [14] and [15] should be performed in recitation. Furthermore, since the text is taken from the Gospel of Matthew, the recitation tone will be that of the *tonus evangelii*, which will be discussed at greater length in Chapter 3.

The thesis has been proposed, mainly by Linke and Mehler, that more or less everything that has been said with respect to the use and meaning of *dicere* in stage directions for Latin texts would also be valid for *dicere* preceding vernacular couplets, i.e. that even the vernacular texts were to be delivered in what Mehler calls an 'epic' as opposed to a 'liturgical' form of recitation.[71] This new view has begun to be accepted in the scholarly literature and has already considerably altered

---

[70]Mehler (1981) 183: "Nur solche Texte konnten im geistlichen Drama rezitativisch vorgetragen werden, die auch in der Liturgie im Liturgischen Rezitativ gebracht wurden. ... D.h., daß aus dem lateinischen, liturgischen Text allein auch auf seine Vortragsart geschlossen werden kann." Along with Stevens and other musicologists, I deliberately use the term 'recitation' "to avoid the anachronistic connotations of the term 'recitative'." See Stevens [1986] 509, cf. 200 n7. In German, the term '(liturgisches) Rezitativ,' adopted from Schuler (1951) 34-36, into the scholarly literature on the medieval drama, could, accordingly, be replaced by the term 'Rezitation,' which is used, e.g. by Hodes (1979) 58-61.

[71]Cf. Linke (1970) 74, (1972b) 202, (1974) 23-25, (1978b) 750, (1993b) 37. Also Mehler (1981) 239-242 and 259; (1984) 42. As early as 1855, L. Bechstein (ed. 1855) 46, had considered such a possibility with regard to the Lddv: "Wir wissen überhaupt nicht, ob nicht alle Rede in diesem Spiele recitativisch ... gesprochen wurde, ... zumal der Dichter Gewicht darauf legte, dass rhythmisch gesprochen werde, und diess eigens vorschrieb." In a similar way, Suppan (1969) 420, considers whether the phrase *dicit ritmum* might actually suggest 'accentuating' delivery in the form of recitation with a singing voice. See also other literary critics of the nineteenth and early twentieth centuries (Heinzel, Creizenach, Froning) quoted in Mehler (1981) 218-220.

our overall understanding of medieval religious drama.[72] With a few possible exceptions in the late Middle Ages, plays would have been performed in a singing voice, partly as genuinely musical chant or song, and partly as liturgical (Latin) or 'epic' (vernacular) recitation.

D. No Directions for the Performance of the Chants

For the remaining six Latin texts in the Lddv the rubrics indicate nothing but the names of the characters who are to deliver them:[73]

236a DOMINICA PERSONA	[27] *Qui tempus congrue peniten[cie] perdiderit frustra cum precibus ad regni ianua[m] pervenerit.*
240a TERTIA FATUA	[28] *Domine, domine, aperi nobis.*
244a DOMINICA PERSONA	[29] *Amen amen dico vobis nescio vos.*
264a QUINTA [FATUA]	[31] *Exaudi etc.*
290a DOMINICA PERSONA ad Mariam	[33] *Celum et terra transibunt, verbum autem meum in eternum permanet.*
409a SECUNDA FATUA	[36] *Deficit gaudium etc.*

The only information about the Latin texts that can be gleaned from these six stage directions is that every one of them is a solo performance, i.e. only the character indicated in the rubric is to deliver the text or chant. Any additional evidence for the form of delivery must come from the Latin texts or incipits themselves. The fact that the full wording is given for all but two chants [31, 36] eliminates some of the guesswork.

---

[72]Janota (1994) 109, talks about the *Kontinuum rezitativischen Vortrags* (the "continuum of recitation") in medieval drama, where melodious chants are integrated with a special function. See also Körndle (1996) 1399, (1997) 1865.

[73]When Beckers in his edition (1905) silently emended the manuscript text and added a *cantet* to the first four of these stage directions (Lddv, ed. Beckers, ll. 236a, 240a, 244a, 264a) he, once again, was acting on his idea (p. 44, cited above in n57) that all Latin texts, as a matter of course, were to be sung. De Boor (ed. 1965) ll. 330 and 357, keeps Beckers' *cantet* directions for chants [29] and [31], whereas Schneider (ed. 1958, 1964) and Curschmann-Glier (ed. 1981) re-establish the manuscript reading without *cantet* in all these directions.

For chants [28] and [29] it is easy to determine, as all editors have done, that the text is taken from the Gospel reading of the Ten Virgins parable in Matthew, as was the dialogue [14-15] with the stage directions *dicit/respondit* just examined. This would mean that the texts [28-29] are another brief dialogue using Gospel words and are also to be performed as liturgical recitation. The *dicit* was suppressed in the stage directions because the form of delivery would be obvious to a performer of the fourteenth century.

The much later Alsfeld Passion Play lends support to this conclusion. Here, in a very different context, the same verse from Matthew 25:12 (chant [29]) is preceded by a musically precise stage direction:[74]

> JHESUS dicit sub accentu ewangelii *Amen amen dico vobis nescio vos.*

If the liturgical direction *sub accentu ewangelii* introduces the Gospel words in a totally different dramatic context — the Alsfeld Passion's *Descensus ad inferos*, where Jesus addresses the damned souls who implore him for mercy — this provides external evidence that chant [29] in the Lddv is to be performed as liturgical recitation, more specifically, as recitation in the Gospel tone.[75] As the first half of the dialogue in the Lddv (and the parable of Matthew), the request of the *Fatue* in chant [28] would, of course, be recited in the same way:

TERTIA FATUA [dicit sub accentu evangelii]	[28] *Domine domine aperi nobis.*
DOMINICA PERSONA [respondet sub accentu evangelii]	[29] *Amen amen dico vobis nescio vos.*

This dialogue is another example of the "new genre of chant in medieval drama" that Schuler and Mehler noted in the later Passion plays.[76] In the Lddv, this 'new genre' in both dialogues [14-15] and [28-29] could be called Gospel recitation chants.

---

[74]AlsfP, ll. 7266a-b. Even the subsequent German lines are very close to those in the Lddv and are certainly borrowed from it; see below, Chapter 3 [28-29], p. 263 n4.

[75]To my knowledge this scene in the Alsfeld Passion is the only place in medieval drama where the Gospel tone is explicitly requested. Besides the frequent *dicit/cantat sub accentu [passionis]*, other directions in the AlsfP ask for recitation *sub accentu prophecie* (texts from Isaiah) or *sub tercio/quinto tono* (psalm texts); cf. rubrics following AlsfP, ll. 7134, 7136, 7140, 7472, 7478.

[76]Schuler (1951) 34, cited above, n60.

Chant [36], *Deficit gaudium,* the last of the six chants under discussion here and the last Latin chant of the Lddv, must be considered in connection with the preceding chant [35]:

| 383d | PRIMA [FATUA] cantat | [35] *Cecidit corona* |
| 409a | SECUNDA FATUA | [36] *Deficit gaudium etc.* |

These two Latin chants are undoubtedly meant to be performed in a parallel way. The Latin opening of the grand finale of vernacular lamentations in the Lddv, they both derive from the same ultimate source, the Lamentations of Jeremiah (Lam. 5:16 and 15). The *cantat* of the stage direction for chant [35], therefore, would carry over to chant [36]. The possible melodic form of their delivery will be discussed in Chapter 3 [35-36].

Because the origin and nature of the remaining three chants [27, 31, 33] are more difficult to determine, inquiries into the form of their delivery will have to be left until Chapter 3, when the Latin texts are studied more closely.

E. SUMMARY

The evidence the stage directions provide for the performance of the Latin chants in the Lddv can be summarized as follows:

The seven *Silete* calls [3' 9' 11' 13' 18' 25' 34'] are sung by a choir of *Angeli* and are part of the staging rather than of the dramatic action. Comparison with *Silete* chants in other plays as well as a look at liturgical customs should provide additional insight into their texts and, possibly, their music.

Singing is also clearly indicated for twenty-two Latin texts through the use of *cantare* or *incipere* in the stage directions (for the chants [24, 36] this direction is implicitly understood from the preceding chant). In nine cases, the identification of the chants' genre as *responsorium* or *invitatorium* (chants [1, 2, 4, 6-8, 10, 12, 20]) implies liturgical singing of musically rich pieces. These chants should certainly be performed in the play in exactly the same way they would be sung in the Office. To recover their complete texts and music, we must turn to medieval liturgical chant books for the Office (notated antiphonals), especially those for the Night Office, of which responsories and invitatories form such an important part.

In the thirteen other cases, chants [**5, 16-17, 19, 21-24, 26, 30, 32, 35-36**], the nature of the singing cannot be determined from the stage directions alone. Therefore, the research required to restore these chants will involve all types of liturgical books, for the Office as well as for Mass, in addition to non-liturgical sources, especially dramatic ones.

Liturgical recitation can easily be assumed for four Latin texts, the chants [**14-15**] and [**28-29**]: two short dialogue scenes, each using two consecutive verses from the parable in Matthew. The special challenge in Chapter 3 will be to find medieval sources for recitation formulas in the Mainz diocese, in particular for the Gospel tone.

For the remaining three Latin texts [**27, 32, 33**], the only evidence from the rubrics is that each is a solo. A variety of sources will have to be studied to determine the precise nature of the texts and their corresponding form of delivery.

The *dramatis personae* in this play are at the same time actors and singers and are sufficient in number to ensure an adequate performance of the chants. (Only chant [**4**] *Homo quidam* is performed by a choir). With at least one capable solo singer in each group, even a difficult responsory could be given a proper performance. And since instruments are not mentioned anywhere in the play, pure plainsong, that is, unaccompanied solo and choral performances, must be assumed for all chants.

Chapter 3

The Restoration of the Latin Chants of the Lddv
Their Significance in Medieval Liturgy and Drama

Any attempt to restore the complete texts and music of the chants and songs in the Lddv must be based on a thorough study of medieval liturgical and dramatic sources. Of particular importance for the Thuringian play are, of course, those fourteenth-century sources that have musical notation and that originate in the Thuringian region or at least in the archdiocese of Mainz, of which Thuringia was a part throughout the Middle Ages. The research carried out for this purpose resulted in such an extensive collection of data that it seemed advisable to present it in catalogue form for easy reference. This Catalogue can be found in the Appendix on microfiche with an introduction which explains its format. To a certain degree, Chapter 3 and the Catalogue in the Appendix are mutually dependent, the Catalogue presenting lists of comparative material from liturgical and dramatic sources, Chapter 3 evaluating the data in the light of the proposed restorations. The studies of individual chants as well as the Catalogue listings are correlated with the bold numbers [in square brackets] given to the chant incipits in the preliminary edition at the end of Chapter 1.

Method of Inquiry
The studies in Chapter 3 take the form of extensive 'commentaries' on each of the thirty-six Latin chants of the Lddv, with constant implicit or explicit reference to the Catalogue. The extent and focus of these 'commentaries' differ considerably from one another because of the diverse nature of the liturgical contexts in which the chants are found, some of which need to be studied in greater detail. The method followed develops naturally from the main clues for the restoration of the Latin chants — the chant incipits themselves in Mühlhausen MS A and whatever evidence is offered by the stage directions.

The research in this chapter is essentially comparative. Chants in the relevant liturgical and dramatic sources that match the incipits in the Lddv are examined for their suitability as candidates for the restoration of the chants in the Thuringian play. The search for chants matching the incipits of the Lddv was relatively easy if the genre of chant is mentioned in the rubrics, but necessarily more complex if the genre is not known since several different chants, or even different genres of chant, may share the same incipit, as is the case with incipits [21-24] and [31]. Possible matches will be evaluated from different perspectives: the text and its transmission, dramatic context including any vernacular paraphrase in the Lddv,[1] the liturgical environment of a chant incipit and its relation to action of the play, etc. If a given incipit in the Lddv cannot be satisfactorily identified with any existing chant but only with a certain section thereof, e.g. incipits [19] and [22], the possibility of an independent performance of only part of a chant will be carefully considered.

Although most of the chants in the Lddv can be traced to liturgical sources, for those that clearly stand in the dramatic tradition (chants [3' etc., 16, 17]), comparisons will be made with other plays for the textual and musical data they provide. Dramatic parallels are also discussed for those of the liturgical chants that are used in other, later medieval dramas. Such comparisons usually confirm that the chants in the Lddv are taken directly from the liturgy, not from other medieval plays.

Two observations need to be made about the music of the chants. First, in the medieval sources from Germany, plainsong and other melodies are usually found in Gothic, only occasionally in square notation, on a four- or five-line stave. As is customary in medieval music writing, the *C*- and *F*-clefs are movable, i.e. they often shift from one line to another, often even within a single chant or within a single line, to accommodate the higher and lower pitches. This practice accounts for some of the transmission errors in medieval notation of music: a scribe might change the position of the clefs to a higher or lower line, yet copy the neumes to the same line or space they occupied in the exemplar. The result is an error by a third (too low or too high), which will always be emended in the transcribed melodies. For other details regarding the musical transcriptions from the various manuscript sources, see Table 1 (p. 11) and the Introduction to Chapter 4 (pp. 319-322).

---

[1]The vernacular texts that often follow the chant incipits as a kind of free translation will be considered mainly for their general import; in two cases, chant [12] *Surgite* and [31] *Exaudi*, they can even help determine which of two versions of the liturgical chant must be presupposed for the Lddv.

A second observation concerns the melodies themselves. A careful comparison of their transmission in the various Roman and monastic sources led to the recognition that the tunes in most sources of German origin vary from most non-German and even some German monastic sources in a few characteristic features. Since the majority of the sources examined in this chapter and certainly all of the 'collateral' sources retained for the restoration of the chants originate in Germany or even central Germany, such 'German' features will be found in the chants of the Lddv as restored in Chapter 4 and must be briefly discussed here.

The 'German' Plainsong Dialect[2]

Peter Wagner in the early twentieth century was the first to recognize and study this 'German' phenomenon.[3] Although some of Wagner's views required modification or further verification, the fact remains that the majority of the 'German' liturgical sources with musical notation from the twelfth and thirteenth centuries on exhibit certain melodic peculiarities that noticeably distinguish the 'German chant dialect' from the Roman chant as transmitted in most French, Italian, and English sources.[4]

Typical in this 'German dialect' is the fondness for larger intervals at predictable places in the melodic line, frequently replacing steps in seconds or thirds (*neumae spissae*) with those in thirds or fourths (*neumae saltatrices*), especially when a semitone (*E-F* or *b-c*) is involved.[5]

---

[2]The importance of the German plainsong dialect for medieval German drama and the need to use the proper liturgical sources for any melodic restorations in these plays has also been recognized and stressed recently by Traub (1994b) 257-259, (1994c) 216, and in Lipphardt-Roloff (1996) 6.2: 11-12.

[3]Cf. Wagner (1911-1921) 2: 443-448, (1926), (1930, 1932) 2: v-lxiv. The term 'Germanic' or 'German dialect' which he applied to this form of plainchant has been questioned in more recent research, yet the geographically and ethnically more neutral term 'East Franconian dialect' (*ostfränkischer Choraldialekt*), proposed by Heisler (1985) 67, has not been generally adopted. See, with more documentation, her dissertation (1987) 138-139.

[4]See now, with some modifications to Wagner's view, Stäblein (1954a) 272-275; Brenn (1956); Tack (1960) 11; Heisler (1985, 1987); R. Stephan (1995) 1176; Hucke-Möller (1995) 1617-1618. Heisler's unpublished dissertation (1987) is the most comprehensive study of the phenomenon and includes an extensive review of the research.

[5]In his eleventh-century treatise *De Musica*, Aribo, also known as Aribo Scholasticus, mentions that his compatriots were fond of *neumae saltatrices* (larger leap intervals), while the Langobards (Italians) preferred *neumae spissae* (stepwise intervals): "Omnes saltatrices laudabiles, sed tamen nobis generosiores videntur quam Langobardis. Illi enim

Such 'leap intervals' impart a lively character to many 'German' plainsong chants without changing the musical essence of the traditional
melody.[6] Contrary to some earlier conceptions, this tendency is found
to different degrees in the various sources, as will become obvious below
in the discussion and musical comparison of some of the responsories
and antiphons used in the Lddv.[7] It appears that even the form of
recitation in German areas, at least in the Church Province of Mainz,
was noticeably affected by this 'German dialect.' Since liturgical
recitation must be assumed for several chants in the play and since the
'musical' aspects of liturgical recitation in medieval drama have rarely
been touched on by scholars in the field, this important part of medieval
liturgy will be discussed below.[8] The main emphasis will be on the
special form of recitation used throughout the Middle Ages in the
ecclesiastical province of Mainz and known as the *Accentus Moguntinus.*

Liturgical Recitation: Roman Use and the 'ACCENTUS MOGUNTINUS'
The liturgy of the Roman Church is performed in Gregorian chant,
which includes 'Textual' and 'Musical Forms.'[9] In the medieval period,

---

spissiori, nos rariori cantu delectamur." (Smits van Waesberghe, ed. [1951] 55, 78-79).
See also Wagner (1911-1921) 2: 444 n2; T.H. Klein (1962) 83.

[6]Hence Hiley (1993) 573, prefers the term 'German regional accent' to 'German
dialect,' on the grounds that "nothing of the basic vocabulary or grammar of the chants
is affected."

[7]Cf. the discussion of chants [2] *Regnum mundi,* [6] *Sint lumbi vestri,* [7] *Emendemus
in melius* (pp. 100-102, 143, 148-149), and others. Books of some religious orders, e.g.
the Cistercian antiphonal *A*Mz.II,138, are not good representatives of the German dialect, demonstrating that the customs of religious orders often override those of dialect.
Heisler (1985) 70, discusses in more detail the conflicting versions of the 'German'
plainsong dialect and the chant of the reform orders in Germany, which followed the
'Roman' version. For the reforms in Cistercian chant, see Tack (1960) 17-18; Heisler
(1987) 4, 75-76, 135; Mitterschiffthaler (1998) 2393-2396; C. Meyer (2000) 183-196.

[8]Only the recitation of the Passion narrative ("Passionston") in late medieval Passion
plays has received some attention; cf., among others, Schuler (1951) 34-35; Mehler
(1981) 210-211. Schuler (1940) presents transcriptions of such notated Passion passages
from EgerP in numbers 16, 36-37, 149, 154, 171, 188, 194, 337, 373, 384, 491, 521,
560, 568-569, 581-582, 604, 615, 619, 623, 644.

[9]Cf. A. Hughes (1982) 21-43. The older terminology, opposing 'free' and 'bound'
forms ("Freie und gebundene Formen") used by Wagner, Apel, and Hoppin, is largely
avoided in recent scholarship as misleading. The majority of musical items in liturgy use
formulaic or typical melodies that are adapted to a variety of texts; see e.g. Stevens
(1986) 286-292.

generally speaking, whatever text in Mass or Office was not sung would be chanted in liturgical recitation.[10]

For both Mass and the Daily Hours, there is an immense repertoire of genuinely musical liturgical items that are sung every day or season or that keep changing in accordance with a complex scheme of liturgical directions and rules. At the same time, there are certain liturgical texts in which the meaning of the words is of unquestionably higher value than their musical delivery: prayers, psalms, and lessons from the Old and New Testament, from the acts of the martyrs, from the homilies of the Church Fathers, etc. Such texts are delivered in recitation. As both the musical and textual categories of chant provide a wide spectrum of genres, from very simple to extremely ornate, an elaborate recitation tone of a responsory verse may sound much more 'melodic' than an unusually simple antiphon.[11] Consequently, it is sometimes not easy for an untrained ear to distinguish between them.[12] In what follows, the main focus is on the simple forms of recitation for liturgical readings, what Schuler called a "new genre of chant in medieval drama," which is often indicated in medieval plays through a form of *dicere* in the rubrics for Latin texts.[13]

Liturgical recitation, in general, is the solemn pronunciation of holy texts. Rather than spoken or sung, these texts are 'intoned' to specific recitation formulas called 'tones' (*tonus*). Because "the words must be ... understood by all, ... the musical style has to be simple, that is, basically one note to a syllable, and recited on a single pitch."[14] The music "only serves as a means of obtaining a distinct and clearly audible pronunciation of the words, so that they will resound into the farthest

---

[10]The medieval terms for these two forms were *pronuntiatio* and *modulatio* (Amalarius), or *accentus* and *concentus* (Ornitoparchus); Wagner (1911-1921) 3: 4; cf. above, pp. 64-65 n64.

[11]Cf. the discussion above, pp. 57-58.

[12]For liturgical recitation in general and for musical examples of the various intoned items, see Wagner (1911-1921) 3: 19-278; Apel (1958) 201-245; Hiley (1993) 46-48. Hiley does not subdivide chant into these two categories; he proceeds from the simplest to the more elaborate genres of recitation to a discussion of the various 'musical' genres of chant; cf. chapter 2, pp. 46-286.

[13]Cf. above, pp. 61-65, especially, p. 63 nn60-61, for a discussion of the research done by Dreimüller, Schuler, Linke, and Mehler.

[14]A. Hughes (1982) 41.

corners of the church."[15] Many reciting formulas, especially those for prayers and readings, are so simple that the medieval musicologist Johannes De Grocheo (c. 1300) excludes them from his treatise on music because they are governed by the rules of accent and grammar.[16] With due respect to De Grocheo, however, we must study them since it is precisely the knowledge of those "rules of accent and grammar" that is lacking in our modern understanding of medieval performance practices.

Three stylistic elements are basic for liturgical recitation: intonation, tenor, and cadences. These keep the musical range of the simpler recitation tones very narrow, usually within the interval of a third. The intonation (*initium*) consists of a few ascending notes leading to the tenor; in very simple forms of recitation it may even be missing. The tenor (or 'reciting note') is the pitch on which the liturgical text is recited; it permits the performer to increase the volume of his voice so that he can as it were 'trumpet' out the text.[17] The melodic cadences or punctuations correspond to the text's main syntactical caesuras: the comma, the colon, the question mark, the full stop. These are the places where inflections occur to the tone below the tenor, thus interrupting the monotonous recitation. Here, word accent is of prime importance.

In spite of the basic simplicity of liturgical recitation, in the Middle Ages the different formulas and their three elements varied according to traditions in the regional churches and monastic Orders.[18] More than just a regional variation of the Roman tones, however, can be seen in the *Accentus Moguntinus*, the special kind of liturgical recitation used in the ecclesiastical province of Mainz, which survived into the seventeenth century and in certain places even longer.[19] Since Thuringia belonged to the archdiocese of Mainz, any attempt to recover the recitation formu-

---

[15]Apel (1958) 203; compare Wagner (1911-1921) 3: 20; Handschin (1949-1951) 264, calls liturgical recitation the *Lautsprecher der alten Zeit*, "the loudspeaker of olden times." For some of liturgical recitation's other merits, see Jungmann (1948) 1: 505; Hodes (1979) 1; Stevens (1986) 200-201.

[16]"Ad musicum autem non pertinet determinare aliquid ... de lectionibus, epistulis, evangeliis et orationibus. Hae enim secundum diversos usus diversificantur et regulis accentus et grammaticalibus amplius gubernantur." (De Grocheo, *Musiktraktat*, ed. Rohloff [1972] 150.46-47, 152.1-3 [215-216]; translation into German, pp. 151, 153. English translation in Seay [1973] 31.)

[17]Cf. Wagner (1911-1921) 3: 20, 26.

[18]Cf. Wagner (1911-1921) 3: 25.

[19]Cf. Köllner (1958) 39-40; Jammers (1975b) 50-51.

las in the Lddv must take this special Mainz tradition into account. Discussion can be limited to the Gospel tone, however, as sufficient evidence suggests that only the Gospel tone would have been used for intoned Latin texts in the Lddv.[20]

The *Accentus Moguntinus* must be seen in the larger context of the 'German dialect' of Gregorian chant discussed above. There is ample evidence that the 'German dialect' was used to at least some extent in all countries under the influence of German or 'East Franconian' culture, including Germany, Belgium, the Netherlands, Poland, and Bohemia.[21] The *Accentus Moguntinus*, on the other hand, has been studied so far only in relation to the Mainz Church.[22] To my knowledge no one has as yet examined whether or not this special way of reciting lessons and prayers was known in other German areas, beyond the boundaries of the renowned Church Province of Mainz, which is outlined on the map of Figure 4 (p. 86).[23]

According to Köllner and Jammers, the most striking features of the Mainz tone are the importance of the word accents not only for the cadences but throughout the recited text, and the fact that these accents are always or almost always sung on a higher note, usually the upper third. The reciting voice continually alternates between the lower resting tone and the higher accent tone, only occasionally touching the surrounding tones. The resulting recitation formulas are extremely different from the usual Roman ones where the reciting voice rests on the tenor except for the intonation and the punctuation marks.[24]

---

[20]The chants to be restored in a form of recitation are either from the Gospel or are chanted by the *Dominica Persona*, cf. the discussion above, pp. 66-68, and below, chants [14-15, 27-29, 33], particularly pp. 260 and 296-297.

[21]Cf. Wagner (1930, 1932) 1: ix, 2: lxiv; Stäblein (1954a) 273-274; with further differentiations, Heisler (1987) 85-89, 138-139.

[22]Cf. Köllner (1950), (1956), (1958); Federl (1937) 26-27; Jammers (1975b) 49-51.

[23]See, however, the remarks in Wagner (1911-1921) 2: 446 and 3: 28.

[24]Cf. Jammers (1975b) 50. Jammers explores the significance of the *Accentus Moguntinus* for the performance of Otfried's gospel harmony, the great Old High German epic poem of the ninth century. In Jammers' view (see esp. pp. 50-54), the accents in the Otfried transmission indicate the higher accent notes of recitation in the Mainz tradition. His findings (pp. 89-90) for the performance of medieval vernacular epics in general, the 'epic recitation' of narrative works in rhymed couplets, may be of interest for the proposed 'epic recitation' in vernacular medieval drama. Cf. above, pp. 66-67 and nn71-72.

The main medieval sources evaluated so far by scholars for the *Accentus Moguntinus* are two Würzburg lectionaries of the fourteenth century in the Würzburg University Library, cited below as *L*Würz.11 and *L*Würz.169.[25] They are complemented by two non-paginated folios of fully notated lesson and Gospel readings, appended as a learning and teaching device to the *Missale Halberstattense* (*M*Halb.888) of 1511.[26] Since the examples for readings in the Mainz tone are more extensive and more completely notated in this source than in the Würzburg lectionaries, the Gospel tone presented here is the one transmitted in the Halberstadt Missal.[27]

FIGURE 2 *ACCENTUS MOGUNTINUS*: PREAMBLES FOR GOSPEL READINGS
(*M*HALB.888, FOL. <229>r)[28]

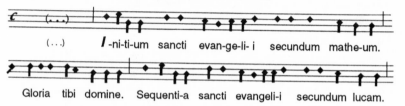

The intonations of the Gospel readings in this Mainz tone surprise with their lively sequence of intervallic leaps (e.g. [*D-C-*]*F-G-D-D-F*) which stretch to the note immediately below and above the basic third

---

[25]Würzburg, Universitätsbibliothek, MS Mp. th. f. 11 [*L*Würz.11] and MS Mp. th. f. 169 [*L*Würz.169].

[26]Mainz, Bibliothek des bischöflichen Priesterseminars, Inc. 888; cf. facsimile 4. Since this *appendix Halberstattense* can be found after fol. 227 of *M*Halb.888, I shall cite these two folios as fols. <228> and <229>. The three sources mentioned here are described in detail in Köllner (1950) 55-60 and 110-113. See also Köllner (1958) 42-45; Jammers (1975b) 50-51.

[27]The diocese of Halberstadt is part of the ecclesiastical province of Mainz and lies about fifty kilometers north of Thuringia. It is also the home of the Helmstedt sources referred to in the reconstruction of some of the chants. The Halberstadt Missal, therefore, fits well into the group of sources selected as 'appropriate' for the restoration of the Latin chants in the Lddv; cf. Figure 4 (map, p. 86) and Table 11A-B (pp. 311-312) as well as the list of 'Collateral Sources' (pp. 313-315).

[28]The transcription here is close to the original; cf. facsimile 4, fol. <229>r, ll. 7-8. Only minor sections of the *Missale Halberstattense* have been previously transcribed, in letter names only, in Köllner's typewritten dissertation (1950) 113.

for recitation. In the transcriptions in Figure 2, the original rhombic notation on four lines is maintained as closely as possible. While the preamble for the Gospel of Matthew (Figure 2, line 1) is notated in the C-clef (to accommodate the tenor a, with the upper third c), that for Luke (Figure 2, line 2) is notated in the F-clef (in the shape of a large apostrophe ') for the easier notation of the tenor D with the accentuating upper third F. The reason for the variations in notation and pitch seems to be simple: it is not the pitch as such that is important but the formula, and the formula implies that the tenor is a subtonal one (i.e. with a whole tone below), and that it has a minor third above for the accents. This is the case for the tenors a and D. The actual pitch used in recitation would more or less depend on the vocal capacities of the performer.

The tenors within a single Gospel reading in this Halberstadt source change frequently in pitch. Moreover, recitation on the same reciting note occurs more often than descriptions based on the Würzburg sources would suggest. Plain narrative reporting and less important texts are usually sung *tono recto* on the subsemitonal tenor F.[29] The special Mainz formulas with the *neumae saltatrices* seem to be used primarily for dialogue and to relate important events (see Figure 3).[30] Here, the subtonal tenor is on D, with the use of the upper third for the word accents. Occasionally, this tenor D changes to E — in the second half of a sentence or before the final close.[31]

The only complete Gospel reading given in the Halberstadt Missal is the pericope of Luke 1: 39-47, Mary's visit to Elizabeth, notated in the F-clef and reciting on D with the upper third F. Figure 3 shows, in modernized transcription, sections from the beginning and end of the dialogue between the two women (Luke 1: 41b-42, 46-47).

---

[29]See, e.g., facsimile 4, fol. <229>r, ll. 9-10. For subtonal and subsemitonal tenors in general and the preference of the latter over the former in the later Middle Ages, see Wagner (1911-1921) 3: 38-41; Apel (1958) 204.

[30]Köllner himself (1950) 113, notes this fact: "Aus den im Unterschied zu Würzburg ganz ausgeführten Beispielen [in MHalb.888] erhellt ... , dass man nicht sofort mit dieser Singweise begann. Erst im Verlauf der Rezitation geht der Sänger zu dieser Formel über, anscheinend an besonders bedeutsamen Stellen des vorzutragenden Textes."

[31]Also in questions, which, however, are not an issue in the Lddv. See Köllner (1950) 113; compare facsimile 4, fol. <229>r, ll. 3-4.

FIGURE 3 *ACCENTUS MOGUNTINUS*: GOSPEL TONE
(*M*HALB.888, FOL. <229>v)[32]

(...) Et repleta est spiri-tu sancto e-li-zabeth. et exclamavit

voce magna et dixit. Benedicta tu inter mu-li-eres. et benedictus

fructus ventris tu-i. (...) Et a-it Mari-a. Magnificat a-nima me-a

dominum. et exul-tavit spi-ritus me- us in de-o sa-lutari me-o.

The two examples from *M*Halb.888 show clearly and strikingly that the recitation in the *Accentus Moguntinus* was considerably more lively and more melodious than the plain Roman Gospel tone discussed earlier.[33] The simple Roman recitation is held in high esteem by Apel and others because it represents "an admirable solution of the difficulties involved in the loud and clear delivery of a prose text, achieving ... a remarkably high degree of liturgical propriety, artistic order, and aesthetic satisfaction."[34] Much the same could be said of the *Accentus Moguntinus*.

With such traditions for the solemn pronunciation of solo readings firmly established in the medieval Roman Church and its provinces, it appears only natural that the author of a highly liturgical medieval drama like the Lddv would make use of this form of delivery wherever he chooses to have his characters pronounce prose quotations from holy

---

[32]In the modernized transcription, the stems of the rhombic notation are indicated through short 'tenuto' lines below the notes; cf. facsimile 4, fol. <229>v, ll. 1-3, 6-8.

[33]See above, pp. 75;-76 examples for the Roman recitation can be found in the *Liber Usualis* (LU) pp. 106-108; also Hoppin (1978a) 16; Agustoni (1963) 266.

[34]Apel (1958) 208.

texts.[35] As the sections from *M*Halb.888 in Figure 3 provide authentic medieval recitation formulas for the delivery of Gospel texts that involve direct discourse in dialogue, these Mainz formulas may serve as a model for the melodic restoration of the short Gospel selections in dialogue form used in the Lddv.

The Dramatic and Liturgical Sources Used
Since many different chant genres occur in the Lddv, a large number of sources had to be studied in order to find matches for the incipits in the medieval repertoire — numerous religious plays and, particularly, various types of liturgical books. The form in which I used those sources is indicated by bold-faced abbreviations in the List of Sources at the beginning of the book, e.g. MS for manuscript, ED for published text edition.

Until ten to fifteen years ago, most of the dramatic sources were accessible only in text editions (ED), even when the manuscripts transmit the music to at least some of the chants. Since then the situation has improved greatly so that many dramatic texts can now be studied in editions with the melodies transcribed (ED•) or in facsimile (FACS) or both. For some plays, the only accessible form of the melodies is still in musicological works (MUS), e.g. by Dreimüller (1935) and Schuler (1940) for EgerP and AlsfP, by Sievers (1936) and Schuler (1940) for the Braunschweig Easter Play.[36] As some musical transcriptions in private or published works are not totally reliable, it was essential to

---

[35]Evidence of musical notation, e.g. in the Admont and Bozen ("Amerikaner") Passion plays (AdmP and AmerP), shows that even in these much less liturgically inclined late medieval plays a form of recitation was chosen for texts from the Passion story, the Passion tone. Since performers of these late plays were usually not trained in liturgical chanting, the music had to be provided in the play script, even for recitation pieces. Traub has collected a number of examples from the two plays and presented them along with the reciting tone of the 'modern' version found in the *Officium maioris hebdomadae* (Tournai 1925). See e.g. Lipphardt-Roloff (1996) 6.2: 19, 22-24 (AdmP), 28-29 (AdmP and AmerP [= "BozP.1495, Hs.B"]) and passim. A great number of notated melodies in the TirP also transmit the Passion tone; cf. Traub's transcriptions in Lipphardt-Roloff (1996) 3: 252-289, and his comments, pp. 430-431.

[36]The melodies of the Alsfeld Passion Play, transcribed by Horst Brunner, will soon be accessible in the forthcoming new edition of the play (Janota [1996-] vol. 2).

refer to the manuscripts for the melodies.[37] The as-yet unpublished *Marburger Spiel von den letzten Dingen* ("Marburg Play of the Last Things" [=MaSp.532]) was used in both its very fragmentary manuscript form and in the transcription and collation prepared by Lomnitzer for his planned edition.[38] For the two poorly edited Thuringian plays (Lddv[A and B] and LdbKath), it was also necessary to go back to their manuscripts at both Mühlhausen and Darmstadt. Manuscripts of other plays have been consulted whenever it seemed advisable, especially for the musical notation.[39]

For the liturgical sources studied, the situation is somewhat different. Antiphonals, breviaries, missals, and graduals provide most of the chants with their music, but in certain cases, lectionaries, processionals, and pontificals also had to be consulted. Thus, almost the entire gamut of liturgical books passed under review.[40] To facilitate identification of liturgical sources, the first element of the sigla in the List of Sources refers to the type of liturgical book and is printed in italics (e.g., *A* for antiphonal).[41]

Only relatively few of the thousands of extant liturgical books have been published. Such publications fall into two categories: collective editions of more than one source, and editions of single sources, often in facsimile. Among the collective editions, Hesbert's monumental works *Antiphonale Missarum Sextuplex* (AMS [1935]) and the six volumes of the *Corpus Antiphonalium Officii* (CAO [1963-1979]) offer easy access to the medieval plainsong repertoire of the Western Church. They present a total of eighteen important early sources, text only, in synopsis

---

[37]The transcribed melodies in the editions of some Tyrol plays should now be checked against Traub's *Addenda et Corrigenda* in Lipphardt-Roloff (1996) 6.2: 139-156, 180-182 for editions in Lipphardt-Roloff (1986, 1988) 1 and 2; ibid., pp. 157-174, with some caution, for Klammer's (1986) edition of the Bozen Passion 1495.

[38]For more details see above, pp. 2-3 and n8.

[39]I had the opportunity to use the excellent collection of manuscript copies of medieval plays at the Institut für deutsche Sprache und Literatur of the University of Cologne. In addition, I received much of the needed manuscript material by mail, through the generous assistance of Hj. Linke, to whom I want to express my gratitude here.

[40]For descriptions of the various liturgical books, see Hiley (1993) 287-339; A. Hughes (1982) 100-244 (chapters 6-8); and the monographs by Fiala-Irtenkauf (1963); Thiel (1967); and Huglo (1996).

[41]See "Key to Abbreviations and Sigla," p. xv. I adopted this method, with slight variations, from Andrew Hughes (1982) 390-408.

(six antiphonals for Mass, twelve for the Office). Since these two collections also provide a valuable frame of reference for many of the chants used in the Lddv, they are usually the first entry in section D of the Catalogue ("Liturgical Sources Investigated"). Other collections of sources are provided by Andrieu (1931-1961) for the *Ordines Romani*, (1938-1941) for the pontificals (*Le Pontifical Roman au Moyen Age*), and by Vogel-Elze (1963-1972) for the *Pontifical Romano-Germanique du dixième siècle* (from 12 manuscript sources).

Publications of single liturgical sources (**ED**), especially those with musical notation in facsimile (**FACS**), had more specific importance for this study. Of particular value were sources with readable notation on a stave; however, only a few such sources from the later Middle Ages have been published.[42] Of the four liturgical works published from German areas, the early printed books of the diocese of Passau (*A*Pat, *G*Pat) present the melodies in the 'German dialect' of plainsong. These two books are not only very late (1511 and 1519), however, they are also from outside the Mainz archdiocese and, therefore, of no immediate relevance for the chants in fourteenth-century Thuringia, although they have been consulted.[43] Thus, the facsimile editions of the two fourteenth-century graduals, *G*Lpz and *G*Kath, are the only published liturgical books of chant with some relevance for the restoration of the chants of the Lddv.[44]

Since the available published sources are of minor import to the specific goal of this study, they had to be supplemented by a large number of manuscript sources (**MS**). Liturgical manuscripts from Germany,

---

[42]For instance, *A*Ambr, *A*Sar, *A*Worc, *G*Lpz, *MR*.1474, *G*Kath, *A*Pat and *G*Pat.

[43]Some of the chants of the Lddv that are well documented in earlier manuscripts from the Mainz diocese and also in the antiphonals published in Hesbert's CAO are not even in the *A*Pat, e.g. the responsories [7, 8, 22] and the antiphons [23, 24] (CAO 6653, 7778, 6633, 4796, 2943). On the other hand, these two books from Passau, belonging to the ecclesiastical province of Salzburg, are helpful as regional sources for restoring chants from Mass and Office used in sixteenth-century plays from Bavaria and Austria; cf. Traub (1994b) 257-258. Traub has actually supplied facsimiles of chants from these two books as substitutes for many of the chants in the Sterzing plays indicated by incipits only (in Lipphardt-Roloff [1996] 6.2: 11-12 and passim).

[44]I.e. for the few chants from Mass, not those from the Office. The 'modern' *Vaticana* editions of Gregorian chant, initiated by the monks of Solesmes at the turn of the century, can serve only as comparative material, since they do not reliably mirror medieval usage, especially not that of central Germany.

consulted in the original or in microfilm form, provide the main basis of inquiry.[45] They were studied with a twofold purpose: a) to understand the chants of the Lddv in the liturgical context and in the textual/musical forms in which they were known in fourteenth-century Germany, particularly in Thuringia; b) to discover and locate chants that may belong to a local tradition and not found in sources outside the Mainz archdiocese.

Owing to the difficulties in gaining access to Thuringian sources, it was not possible in all cases to consult solely or mainly sources of Thuringian origin.[46] However, since Thuringia was subject to the Mainz See throughout the Middle Ages, any fourteenth-century liturgical book from this archdiocese can be considered reasonably adequate for the present purposes. In most cases, though, the sources used for the restorations are from Thuringia or close thereto and thus are more genuinely 'collateral' to MS A of the Lddv. A few Dominican sources have been included in the research not only because of their excellent transmission but also because of claims that the Lddv may have originated in Dominican circles.[47]

Selection of 'Collateral' Sources
The purpose of the comparative studies in Chapter 3 is to find for each chant incipit of the play a fully notated prototype chant that reflects as closely as possible the presumed textual/musical form of such a chant in fourteenth-century Thuringia and that, consequently, can serve as a model to recover the complete text and music of that chant in the Lddv. Liturgical and dramatic sources that contain such regional 'prototype chants' for the fourteenth century qualify as 'collateral' to MS A of the Lddv.

The criteria used for determining which of the many sources studied will serve as 'collateral' are mainly their date and their provenance, preferably fourteenth century and originating within the Mainz Church. An additional criterion would be the presence of 'German dialect' features

---

[45]I repeat here my gratitude to many European libraries for permitting me to study the various manuscripts *in situ* and for producing microfilms of certain sections thereof at my request. I am equally grateful to Andrew Hughes, Toronto, for letting me peruse microfilms in his possession.

[46]The major research for this study was done prior to 1990, in divided Germany.

[47]Representative of Dominican sources are: *A*OP(Humb), *C*OP(Humb), *Ev*OP(Humb), *G*OP(Humb), all from Humbert's Codex; *Pr*Don.882; *G*Kath; *B*OP (INC).

in the melodies of the chants — a criterion usually not met in the Cistercian antiphonal of Mainz, AMz.II,138, yet present in basically all other German sources to different degrees, apparently depending on their origin.[48] Occasionally when the preferred sources transmit only the texts of the chants or give the notation only in non-heighted neumes, the musical notation of a less preferred source is used.

The rationale behind the specific selection of 'collateral' sources for the liturgical chants is as follows. Of particular value, naturally, were sources from Thuringia, especially those of the fourteenth century.[49] However, sources from the Mainz archdiocese at large, especially those from nearby Fritzlar and Breitenau,[50] and from the Metropolis[51] itself appeared equally valuable. (All these place names are indicated on the map of Figure 4.) Sources originating elsewhere in the larger Church Province of Mainz were also acceptable, especially those in close proximity to Thuringia: sources from the Braunschweig/Helmstedt area,[52] and the 'Appendix' of a missal from Halberstadt, which provides the lesson tones for the restoration of most of the play's items in recitation.[53] Two sources from outside the Mainz Church Province, from Leipzig and Magdeburg, were included among the 'collaterals' since their transmission for specific chants is strongly supported by transmissions from within the Mainz Church.[54]

The screening process for the dramatic sources was somewhat different because of the limited number and accidental nature of their melodic transmissions (e.g. of the B-stanzas [16-17] and the Silete calls [3' etc]). Basically all the textual and musical evidence for these items in medieval German drama, even from later centuries, has been taken into

---

[48]Cf. above, p. 74.

[49]BeTh.O, AErf.50a, BErf.81, GErf.16, GErf.44 (and, possibly, MSMh.87/8).

[50]AFri.117, AFri.124, AFri.129, BFri.146, BFri.161, GBrei.101, LFri.142, MFri.100, AFri.142, and PrFri.87.

[51]AMz.II,138, PrMz.II,74, PrMz.II,303, PrMz.110, PsMz.D820.

[52]AHelm.485, BHelm.145.1, MHelm.26, MHelm.35, MHelm.38, LBrsw.

[53]MHalb.888; cf. above, pp. 78-81.

[54]GLpz for [31-32] supported by AFri.142, MHelm.35; MSMh.87/8 for [35-36] supported by LBrsw. In the case of MSMh.87/8, the slight possibility that the relevant last few pages might have been written in or for Thuringia was decisive. The codex now belongs to the same Mühlhausen collection as MS A of the Lddv. We do not know when the manuscript, written in 1466 in Magdeburg (colophon of the scribe on fol. 342r), came to Thuringia or where the text of the folios 387-388 was added.

FIGURE 4 MAP OF THE ECCLESIASTICAL PROVINCE OF MAINZ
(BASED ON WESTERMANN, *GROSSER ATLAS ZUR WELTGESCHICHTE* [1972] 89)

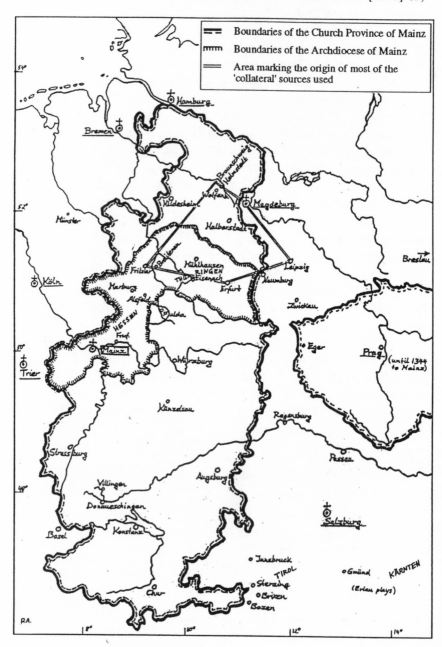

account and evaluated. 'Collateral sources' for their restoration could be selected only after comprehensive melodic comparisons (cf. pp. 183-188 and 112-119)

A list of all 'collateral sources' on which the recovery of the chants in the Lddv is based is found at the end of Chapter 3 (pp. 313-315). The map in Figure 4 shows the area within the ecclesiastical Province of Mainz in which the majority of them originate: the eastern-most part of the archdiocese of Mainz with Thuringia and some surrounding districts; the region is marked by the important centres of Erfurt, Fritzlar, Helmstedt, and Leipzig. Some 'loans' come from outside this area: i.e. Mainz for chant [21] and Breslau and Prague, Augsburg and Donaueschingen/ Villingen, for dramatic sources.

Unfortunately, all the research and scrutiny of sources was largely fruitless for the first of the chants, the responsory [1] *Testimonium domini*, although there is sufficient evidence that chants with this incipit were in liturgical use (see Catalogue [1]). Questions relating to the restoration of this responsory, its biblical source, a possible substitute etc. are studied in Chapter 3 [1].

Organization of the 'Apparatus'

In the individual studies that follow, the chants of the Lddv will be examined in their liturgical and dramatic contexts, with constant reference to the Catalogue on microfiche. For technical reasons, most melodies are discussed and described here only in words, their notation being deferred to the presentation of all the restored Latin chants in Chapter 4. Only in some special cases did it seem advisable to include the music when, for one reason or another, the melodies needed to be discussed in more detail. After a close comparison of sources, the restored text of each chant is edited at the end of each section, with an apparatus and a translation of the Latin text; the textual and melodic 'apparatus' for this edition is also included in part E of the corresponding Catalogue sections.

This apparatus notes the source selected for the textual and the melodic transcription of each chant. Textual variants found in collateral or other sources are listed in the traditional 'critical' form; melodic variants, however, having been commented on in the immediately preceding discussions, are merely indicated in the apparatus in a summary fashion.

Non-German liturgical sources are, as a rule, excluded from the comparison. They usually transmit the same basic melody for a chant, yet without the typical 'German dialect' features; they may also exhibit other significant variants. It often seemed desirable, however, to include a few ('non-collateral') German sources, *A*Ahrw, *A*Pat, *G*Pat, *G*Strals, *Pr*Fri.87, and the Dominican *A*OP(Humb), *G*OP(Humb), and *G*Kath, because the chants in these are transmitted in forms that are close in some cases to the selected Mainz version, in others to the non-German (Roman) form. Only in special cases are *A*Worc or *P*Dur.Add cited in the apparatus as an 'outside' source. The degree of similarity is indicated in a summary way through the following symbols or abbreviations:

= (or ~ =) identity (or near-identity) of the melody
~   similarity of the melody
~ *var*   similarity of the melody, with a few minor variants
var   the same basic melody, with considerable melodic variants or differences. The chants in most non-German medieval books and in the 'modern' Vaticana and Solesmes editions would fall into this category.
different (noted only, when one of the German sources studied provides a unique melody compared with the other sources).

[1] *Testimonium domini* (Lddv 0d)

The first chant in the Lddv, the responsory *Testimonium domini*, is to be sung as a processional chant by the first group of performers, the 'heavenly' players *Dominica Persona, Maria*, and the *Angeli*, as they proceed to the playing area. The same responsory, also indicated only by its incipit, is used as an opening chant in the Thuringian play of St. Catherine (LdbKath, 1. 0b) transmitted with the Lddv in Mühlhausen MS A. No other medieval play seems to make use of this chant nor has it been possible to find a responsory with this incipit in any of the liturgical sources studied. It is conceivable that such a responsory was composed and used only locally, perhaps for the feast of a local saint or for some other regional feast in Thuringia. Unfortunately, there is no vernacular paraphrase to this responsory in either the Lddv or the LdbKath, and so not much can be said about the content of the chant even by way of retranslation.

In as much as no local or regional responsory with this incipit can be found, the genre indication in the stage direction (ll. 0a-c) provides the only certainty: the opening processional chant of both the Lddv and the LdbKath was one of those festive, musically rich, prolix responsories sung during the Night Office (Matins). This means that the text of this opening chant would have been longer and more complex than the verse from Psalm 18: 8 indicated by the editors of the Lddv:

> [Lex Domini immaculata, convertens animas;]
> Testimonium Domini fidele, sapientiam praestans parvulis.
>
> ("The law of the Lord is perfect, converting the soul:
> the testimony of the Lord is sure, making wise the simple.")

This psalm verse must certainly be considered as the ultimate, but not the direct, or even the only, source for the chant in the play. And the responsory verse might have come from a totally different biblical or non-biblical source.

Interestingly, most of the textually related chants listed in Catalogue [1D] are chants from Matins: a section of a responsory verse and three different Matins antiphons (see Catalogue [1D1 and 2], pp. F1-F2). Only one Mass item, an introit, could be found (cf. Catalogue [1D3], p. F2). Both the responsory and the introit have a totally different incipit, however, and the words *Testimonium domini* occur late in the line. They would make a poor alternative for the opening chant of a play that calls for a specific responsory at this place. The three antiphons (Catalogue [1D2(a)-(c)]), on the other hand, all begin with the same two Latin words that the Lddv indicates for its opening responsory. In each case, the words seem appropriate, but not the genre.

Of the three Matins antiphons, the first

(a) *Testimonium domini fidele, sapientiam praestitit parvulae,*
    Hostis ideo saevissimus non dominatus est eius.

seems to fit into the main idea of the Ten Virgins Play, but it was composed for the feast of one virgin only, St. Margaret. The second antiphon

(b) *Testimonium domini fidele dum utriusque ...*
    Marthae activam, Mariae contemplativam.

is less appropriate because of its specific focus on the *vita activa* and the *vita passiva* of Martha and Mary. Only the antiphon for the Holy Innocents, composed for a larger number of 'weak ones,'

(c) *Testimonium domini fidele, sapientiam praestans parvulis*

appears to be textually appropriate. But the fact that this antiphon belongs to the Ambrosian Rite and is not a responsory excludes it as well.[1] Moreover, the tune to this chant is so plain that it would not qualify for the opening procession of the Thuringian play. So the search must continue.

The five liturgical chants in the Catalogue that make some use of the second half of verse 8 of Psalm 18, give a good insight into the technique of 'adaptation' in the composition of new liturgical chants, especially in new proper offices for saints. A responsory text might be used for an antiphon (in Mass or Office) or vice versa, or a part of such a text might appear as a verse for a responsory or for the *Alleluia* in Mass, usually with some kind of variation in its wording, owing mainly to the different melody associated with the other type of chant.

It seems likely, therefore, that a responsory with the incipit *Testimonium domini* did exist somewhere in Thuringia, at least in the

---

[1]The Ambrosian or Milanese Rite, named without much solid evidence after Bishop Ambrose of Milan (374-397), is an old non-Roman rite which was and still is proper to the Church of Milan. The liturgical texts and forms of this rite differ in many respects from the Roman liturgy and characteristically display a mixture of oriental and very old Latin elements. For more details see, e.g. Apel (1958) 465-483.

fourteenth century. In particular, the Matins antiphon for St. Margaret, documented in a rhymed office in some twenty-six manuscripts since the twelfth century,[2] seems to be a step towards the composition of a Matins responsory with this incipit.

Although nothing specific can be known at present about the text of the opening processional chant, it would have been delivered as a responsory in its full form with verse and *repetenda*, providing full-length singing for the solemn procession of the 'heavenly' players. The performance would have been the usual alternation of solo and choir singing: solo intonation by any one of the 'heavenly' players, probably one of the *Angeli*; choral continuation of the respond by the whole group; solo recitation of the verse by the soloist who intoned the responsory; and choral singing of the *repetenda* by the whole group. If more singing time was required for the lengthy procession, the following could be added: solo recitation of the lesser doxology *Gloria patri* (by the solo singer); choral singing of the *repetenda*; and possibly, the repetition of the respond or even of the whole responsory.

If the play were to be performed today, the lacuna could best be filled, I think, by either the first of the three antiphons with this incipit or the introit *Lex domini* [1D3]. The text of the antiphon from a rhymed office of St. Margaret [1D2(a)] could easily be adjusted to a plurality of virgins, an adjustment which is routine in liturgical texts used for different occasions. Its melody is accessible, e.g., in the antiphonal of Passau (*A*Pat), which contains the same rhymed office for St. Margaret.[3] On the other hand, the Lenten introit *Lex domini irreprehensibilis* (Catalogue [1D3]), dismissed above because of its different incipit, may yet be a better choice. The genre is not right either, but the chant would be more extended than the Matins antiphon just discussed; and the text, very close to that of Psalm 18: 8, would fit the context of the play without any changes:

Introit   *Lex domini irreprehensibilis convertens animas testimonium dei fidele sapientiam prestans parvulis.*

---

[2]See Catalogue [1D2(a)], p. F2. and AH 28: 17-19.

[3]*A*Pat, fols. 169r-171v. *Testimonium domini*, the second Matins antiphon, is on fol. 170r. The text of the whole office is almost identical to AH 28: 17-19, the main difference being that in *A*Pat the second and third nocturns are omitted for Matins.

An introit normally functions as the introductory item for Mass and accompanies the entrance procession of the clergy. To accommodate longer processions, its performance could easily be extended by adding extra psalm verses even after the singing of the doxology.[4] An introit, therefore, would appear to be an appropriate alternative for the opening procession of both the LdbKath and the Lddv. Moreover, this particular introit belongs to the old plainsong repertoire and is widely documented in medieval sources.[5] In the case of a performance of the play, the melodic version of the introit in GLpz (or even that in GPat, printed in 1511 for the diocese of Passau) could be used.[6]

In any event, the choice of this introit for chant [1] of the Lddv would only be second best, and the search for a responsory *Testimonium domini*, preferably of Thuringian origin, must continue in medieval sources from the archdiocese of Mainz.

---

[4]An introit consists of an antiphon (called *introit*), sung repeatedly in close association with a psalm which is chosen for a particular day or feast. The number of psalm verses sung was soon reduced to (usually) a single verse with the *Gloria Patri*. Not much precise information is available about the exact method of performance in the Middle Ages. It certainly was some kind of "alternation of performing bodies" (Apel [1958] 198), the two parties being either two choirs for an antiphonal performance or, more often in later times, the choir and one or two cantors for a responsorial performance. For more details, see A. Hughes (1982) 34-35; Wagner (1911-1921) 1: 66-67; Jungmann (1948) 1: 401-407; Hiley (1993) 496-497.

[5]Cf. Catalogue [1D3]. This introit was actually sung as the opening processional in a workshop performance of the Lddv (under the direction of Lynette Muir with my assistance) at the conference "The Stage as Mirror" at Pennsylvania State University in March 1993. Benedictine monks of the St. Vincent's Archabbey Schola, Latrobe, participated in the singing of the Latin chants.

[6]GLpz, fol. 28v (facsimile [1930] 57); GPat, fol. 40r. Cf. Catalogue [1D3]. See also Chapter 4, p. 324, where this introit for the Saturday of the second week of Lent is reproduced from the Solesmes edition of the Roman Gradual (GR [1974] 86).

[2] *Regnum mundi* (including [20])
(Lddv 0i and 186b)

The second group of actors, the ten *Virgines*, sing this responsory while they approach the playing area in procession. *Regnum mundi* will be sung a second time, but only by the *Prudentes*, at the climax of the play when the long awaited 'sponsus,' the *Dominica Persona*, arrives (l. 186b [20]). In each instance, the stage directions unmistakably call the chant a *responsorium*, and it has been recognized as such not only by Beckers and Schneider but also, as early as 1867, by Ludwig Ettmüller in his High German translation of the Lddv. Although Ettmüller identifies the *Consecratio virginum* as the liturgical place for this responsory,[1] Beckers and Schneider show no interest in its liturgical environment and only indicate the page number in Hartker's Antiphonal where the responsory can be found. None of the three scholars makes any reference to the verse to this responsory (*Eructavit*) or the musical notation, which, in Hartker's Antiphonal, is in neumes without lines and hence not really understandable. As pointed out earlier, however, the verse is an essential part of a responsory and must be included in the restoration of the chant.[2] And the melody can be recovered from other manuscript transmissions.

The evidence from the manuscripts examined suggests that the responsory *Regnum mundi* does not belong to the old repertoire of Gregorian chant but was created at a later time, possibly only in the twelfth century and was popular only from the thirteenth and fourteenth century on. Of the twelve antiphonals dating from the ninth to the thirteenth century in Hesbert's monumental *Corpus Antiphonalium Officii*, it is only found in the ur-texts of two late monastic sources, the Antiphonal of Rheinau and that of St. Loup of Benevent (CAO, sigla R and L; thirteenth and twelfth centuries). In the fourteenth century,

---

[1]Ettmüller (1867) 293; for this identification Ettmüller had solicited the assistance of P. Gall Morel of Einsiedeln, well known for his edition of Mechthild von Magdeburg.

[2]See above, pp. 58-59. Musicologists recognize the importance of the verse as a matter of course. See, with respect to the use of the *Regnum mundi* in the AlsfP, Schuler (1951) 303 no. 534, and Dreimüller (1935) 2: 45; for BozP.1514, Traub in Lipphardt-Roloff (1996) 6.2: 102, provides the responsory *Regnum mundi* with its verse in facsimile from *A*Pat.

however, the *Regnum mundi* chant suddenly appears in most antiphonals, often replacing older responsories.[3]

The earliest source in which I was able to find the responsory is the *Liber Ordinarius* of the Benedictine monastery of Rheinau (*O*Rh.80), written between 1114 and 1123.[4] The chant is indicated here only by the incipits of the responsory and its verse; this implies that the monastery of Rheinau must have owned chant books in the early twelfth century that contained the whole responsory *Regnum mundi* (which does not mean, of course, that the responsory was created there). The thirteenth-century Antiphonal of Rheinau (in *B*Rh.28) has the *Regnum mundi* not only *in extenso* for the Common of Virgins but also as an incipit for the proper Office of St. Agnes. At least two other sources document the spread of this chant in Europe during the twelfth century: the Antiphonal of St. Peter's in Salzburg (*A*Salzb) and the Mainz Pontifical (*P*Mz.XII) of Archbishop Christian I (1167-1183).

By the thirteenth century, the *Regnum mundi* appears more frequently in monastic sources and begins to be found in secular antiphonals.[5] The venerable Hartker Codex (*A*Hartk) did not originally have the responsory *Regnum mundi*; yet in the thirteenth century, it was added with others designated *De virginibus* to the stock of liturgical items for the Common of Virgins (*A*Hartk, p. 208). Furthermore, in the Matins formulary for All Saints Day, earlier responsories for the second nocturn were erased in order to make room for this and other new responsories.[6] The Dominican Antiphonal *A*OP(Humb), one of the fourteen basic liturgical books in the thirteenth-century Codex of Humbert, also adopted the responsory for the Common of Virgins. Since

---

[3]Judging mainly on musicological grounds, Dom Pothier (1900) 186, also does not regard it as belonging to the genuinely Gregorian repertoire. He finds it widespread only in the fourteenth century: "On ne le voit apparaître d'une façon générale que vers le XIVe siècle." Similarly, C. Marbach (1907) 104* n2: "Es war bereits allgemein bekannt im 14. Jahrhundert."

[4]This is the first book of its kind in any medieval church or monastery; in a single volume, it regulates liturgical functions and actions for the entire church year. See Catalogue [2D], p. F6, and cf. Hänggi, ed. (1957) liii.

[5]It does not appear in the thirteenth-century Cistercian Antiphonal of Mainz (*A*Mz.II,138), however.

[6]See note 4 to Catalogue [2D1(b)], p. F6, reporting on Dom Froger's research in PalMus 2.1 (1970) 36*, 40*; also CAO 2: 594-596 (no. 115b), 596 n1.

Dominican liturgical books were quickly and widely copied to ensure a uniform liturgy all over Europe for the fast growing Order of Preachers, knowledge of this new responsory would have certainly spread along with the Dominican liturgy.

The rapid diffusion of this responsory among monastic circles shows how well liked it was in the monastic and Dominican Night Office for the Common of Virgins. Its occurrence in the German antiphonals of Ahrweiler and Fritzlar and in the breviary of Helmstedt proves that, at least by the fourteenth century, it had also started to be regularly included in the secular Office for the same feasts.[7] It is interesting to note that this responsory of non-biblical origin is even included in the Carthusian breviary, despite the strict Carthusian principle to adopt liturgical chants of scriptural origin only.[8]

The dissemination of the new chant *Regnum mundi* during the thirteenth and fourteenth centuries, first in monastic and Dominican circles, later also in secular usage, is interesting in the larger context of the Lddv. The fact that the responsory is used twice (chants [2] and [20]) in this fourteenth-century play, at a time when it had only begun to be accepted in secular liturgical books, may be evidence of a relation between the Lddv's author and monasticism or the Order of Preachers. Particular attention will therefore need to be paid to the place of this responsory in secular and monastic customs. For this purpose, two very different branches of transmission must be studied, books for the Office and pontificals.

In the breviaries and antiphonals for the Office, which contain all the chants for the day and/or night hours throughout the Church year, the *Regnum mundi* is usually assigned to the Common of Virgins as the last responsory of Matins.[9] This place in the liturgy implies special treatment. The last responsory of each nocturn is always followed by the *Gloria patri* (the 'lesser doxology') as a sort of second verse, after

---

[7] Cf. the first six entries in Catalogue [2D1(a)], pp. F5-F6.

[8] Cf. Hj. Becker (1971) 233 no. 408; for the scriptural principle of selection in the Carthusian liturgy see pp. 90-97. Only eight responsories with non-biblical texts made their way into the Carthusian breviary in the sixteenth century when the Order adopted the Offices of Trinity and of Holy Women to which they belong (p. 93 n463).

[9] It is sung after the last of twelve (nine in the secular rite) readings, in some sources as the eighth responsory after the eighth reading, i.e. it is mostly found at the end of the third or, sometimes, of the second nocturn. Cf. Catalogue [2D1], pp. F5-F6.

which the *repetenda*, or a shortened form thereof, is sung again. In the Dominican liturgy, which follows the secular form of Matins and has only nine readings, there were even times when, due to the omission of the *Te deum* as the final chant of Matins during Advent and Lent, the last responsory was repeated[10] — a sure way to implant such a chant in the memory of the singers as well as the listeners. Moreover, the Common of Virgins, to which the *Regnum mundi* is assigned in most sources, is a feast which recurs frequently within the Church year, whenever a Holy Virgin is celebrated whose feast is not supplied with a proper formulary at that particular church or monastery or in that particular diocese. This fact may have contributed to the rapid dissemination of this newer responsory.

The second line of transmission for the responsory *Regnum mundi* is in the pontificals, the liturgical books reserved for special episcopal celebrations. Although the pontifical sources provide little information on the text and music of the *Regnum mundi*, which is usually indicated only by its incipit,[11] they are highly informative about the liturgical use to which the newly composed responsory was put in an episcopal ceremony — in the formulary for the *Consecratio virginum*, known from the tenth century on as one of the most 'dramatic' liturgical ceremonies of the Church. The earliest evidence I was able to find for the use of the responsory *Regnum mundi* in this context is in the twelfth-century Mainz Pontifical of Christian I (*PMz.XII*).[12] It is possible that the form of this rite as laid out in the pontifical of Christian I was known to Bishop Durandus of Mende before he composed his thorough revision of the Roman Pontifical at the end of the thirteenth century (1293-1295).[13] In

---

[10]Cf. Bonniwell (1944) 140.

[11]The existence of other liturgical books containing the complete responsory was presupposed and, in some cases, explicitly referred to; for instance in the Pontifical of Durandus (*PDur*, lib. I. ordo XXIII.28): *Et sic ... redeunt ad episcopum cantando responsorium* Regnum mundi etc. *Require in natali unius virginis*.

[12]Cf. Catalogue [2D2], p. F6. This ceremony, published by Martène (1736) 541D-543C (lib. II, cap. 6, ordo IX), must have escaped the notice of René Metz (1954) 297, 430.7, who maintains in his excellent study *La consécration des vierges dans l'église Romaine* that this responsory is found for the first time as part of the consecration rite in the late thirteenth-century Pontifical of Bishop Durandus of Mende (*PDur*).

[13]That the twelfth-century Mainz Pontifical (*PMz.XII*) was not obsolete at the time of Durandus can be seen from the fact that its formulary for the consecration of virgins is almost identical with the one in the fourteenth-century pontifical of Bishop Daniel

the consecration formulary for nuns contained in this extremely influential book,[14] Durandus has the virgins sing the *Regnum mundi* at the beginning of the consecration proper, i.e. after all the vestments and insignia have been blessed and the virgins have replaced their ordinary garments with the new vestments.[15] By the fourteenth century, the *Regnum mundi* is used in a great number of consecration formularies, even though the ceremony itself may only be partly derived from the Durandus pontifical. Although the place of this chant within the ceremony differs considerably according to local preferences,[16] what is significant is the prominence given to the new responsory in a pontifical ceremony on which the monastic life of women is founded.

One of the reasons for the popularity of the *Regnum mundi* chant in the *Consecratio virginum* is the wording of the text:[17]

R. *Regnum mundi et omnem ornatum seculi contempsi propter amorem domini mei ihesu christi Quem vidi, quem amavi, in quem credidi, quem dilexi.*

V. *Eructavit cor meum verbum bonum, dico ego opera mea regi.*[18]

Wichterich (*PMz.*XIV), fols. 4v-7r. Metz (1954) probably overlooked the Mainz Pontifical because Martène (1736) had misattributed it to the thirteenth century when another Christian was archbishop of Mainz. Leroquais (1937) 2: 24, correctly identified it with Archbishop Christian I (1167-1183), an identification accepted by Martimort (1959) no. 189. Even if Reifenberg's attribution of it ([1960] x and 64) to Archbishop Christian II of Weisenau (1249-1253) should be correct, it would still precede Durandus' pontifical by about forty years.

[14]For the importance of the Durandus pontifical see Andrieu (1938-1941) 3: v-xv, 3-20; Vogel (1975) 208-210, (1986) 253-255; De Puniet (1933) 1: 47-55; Metz (1954) 273-276. A decade or so after its compilation, Pope Clement V (1305-1314) referred to the pontifical of Durandus as an authority; cf. De Puniet (1933) 50.

[15]*P*Dur., lib. I, ordo XXIII.28 (p. 416).

[16]*PMz.*XII, *PMz.*XIV, and *P*Aux have the responsory at the end of the ceremony, *P*Sens at the very end of the consecration Mass, *P*Dur and *P*Trég have the virgins sing it at some point between the benediction of the vestments and the actual consecration ceremony; cf. Catalogue [2D2], pp. F6-F7.

[17]The first part is non-scriptural; only the verse is from the bible, Ps. 44: 2, which is considered a regal Wedding Song. The Vulgate calls it *Carmen nuptiale regis Messiae*. Cf. Wutz (1926) 215.

[18]"The kingdom of the world and all earthly trappings I have spurned for the love of my Lord Jesus Christ, * whom I have seen, whom I have loved, in whom I have believed, whom I have cherished. v. My heart overflows with noble words. To the king I must speak the song I have made." Translation from *B*OP (1967) 140.

The singers of the chant speak in the first person singular; in the consecration Mass, it is the nuns themselves who, before their investiture and consecration, sing the *Regnum mundi*. In their mouths, the words turn into a personal creed, a personal commitment to renounce all worldly interests for the sake of Christ. In short, this responsory appears to function here as a chanted confirmation of the nuns' solemn vows.

When the author of the Lddv or, rather, of its underlying Latin 'liturgical' structure, chose this responsory for the ten *Virgines* to sing at their entrance procession and again later for the five *Prudentes* at their encounter with the *Dominica Persona* (ll. 0i and 186b), was he, consciously or not, imitating this 'scene' in the consecration rite, where the novices sing the *Regnum mundi* on their way to be consecrated as God's brides by the bishop (representing Christ) and where they will receive not only veil and ring but also the crown as a symbol of their mystical marriage to Christ, as the *Prudentes* will be crowned by Mary (ll. 208a-b)? This possibility cannot be explored here, but must be kept in mind for our overall understanding of the play.[19]

In addition to the two lines of transmission for this responsory in antiphonals and pontificals, a number of processionals from the fourteenth century on call for the singing of the *Regnum mundi* on various days. According to Th. H. Klein's study of the processional chants of the Mainz Church, by the fifteenth century the *Regnum mundi* had become one of the favourite responsories for Vesper processions in commemoration of women saints on the eve of their proper feast.[20] In summary, the responsory *Regnum mundi*, initially, as it seems, used only as a Matins responsory, soon found an important place in the consecration rite for nuns. From the late fourteenth century on there is also evidence for its wider use in secular liturgies; and its melody was often adapted to other liturgical texts, as Dom Pothier noticed.[21]

Different genres of medieval plays make use of this responsory: a Ten Virgin play (Lddv), a saint's play (LdbKath), both of the fourteenth

---

[19]See also the discussion below, in section [20], esp. pp. 210-211.

[20]T.H. Klein (1962) 63, 65, 69 (twice), 70, 77, 78; see Catalogue [2D3], pp. F7-F8. Klein points out that, unlike the practice at other churches, the commemoration in Mainz occurred mainly at Vespers I. For the practice of commemorations in general, see A. Hughes (1982) 197-199.

[21]Pothier (1900) 187-188.

century, and some Passion plays of the fifteenth/sixteenth century.[22] In nearly all cases it is exceptional women who sing this responsory at an exceptional moment in the development of the dramatic action: the Wise Virgins as they meet their *Sponsus* (Lddv [20]); Saint Catherine as she is received by Christ in Heaven (LdbKath); Mary Magdalene after having lavished her love on Christ by anointing him in the house of Simon (AlsfP, AlsfDir, FriedDir), or after she has met the risen Christ and announced his resurrection to the disciples (BozP.1514). Renunciation of worldly goods, total commitment to Christ and His love is the common theme. The only instance where its appropriateness might be questioned is chant [2] in the Lddv: ten *Virgines* proceed to the performance area proclaiming their renunciation of the world for the love of Christ, yet five of them will not live up to their promise and will fail miserably.

The melody of the *Regnum mundi* is in the fifth mode which, according to Frere, is rare for the old Gregorian responsories. He counts it among those later responsories which "seem to have much claim to antiquity."[23] Dom Pothier, on the other hand, argues that two features distinguish this melody quite clearly from the classical, purely 'Gregorian' repertoire: first, the persistent use of the *B*-flat in this fifth mode, by which it approximates modern tonality, and second, the ease with which the melody runs through the whole scale (from the lower to the higher *F*) within a single phrase.[24] A third argument may be added — the striking musical form of the verse: it is not sung to one of the eight responsory tones, but has its own melody. This melody makes repeated use of melodic lines and motifs, however, that characterize the melody of the respond: the tonal movements over *Eructavit* and over *dico ego* pick up musically the beginning of the responsory (notes over *Regnum mundi*); and the melodic progressions over *cor meum* and *verbum bonum*

---

[22]Cf. Catalogue [2C], pp. F4-F5. Because the Lddv and the LdbKath are the earliest of all the plays that use the *Regnum mundi*, it seems obvious that the author took the responsory directly from the liturgy, whereas the later plays possibly adopted it from the Thuringian drama.

[23]Frere (1901-1924) 1: 40; see also T.H. Klein (1962) 116.

[24]"Ce V[e] mode, avec bémol constant, que ne motive pas la relation de triton entre si et fa, rentre déja dans les gammes modernes; et ce qui le distingue également d'un V[e] grégorien, c'est la tendance ... de parcourir toute la gamme dans une même phrase, et même parfois dans une même partie de phrase." Pothier (1900) 186. For the unique use of a b-natural in the Fritzlar sources, see below, p. 102.

correspond closely to those over *et* and *Quem* of the respond. Such correspondences and motivic repetitions function like *leitmotifs*, musically linking the three parts of the responsory (respond, verse, *repetenda*) and reinforcing its unity as a chant.[25] This is, of course, very far from the primitive Gregorian form of a responsory, which is characterized by the contrast between a melodic choral respond and a recitation tone in the solo verse.[26] These three arguments support the results of the comparison of the manuscript transmission: this responsory is relatively recent.

With the goal of restoring text and music of the *Regnum mundi* in the Lddv, I have compared the various transmissions of the responsory in medieval sources. Pontificals and processionals, listed in Catalogue [2D2 and 3], have been excluded since they usually give only the incipit. The selection, therefore, is limited to those nine sources listed in Catalogue [2D1], pp. F5-F6, that transmit the complete responsory with notation on a stave: *A*Ahrw.2b, *A*Fri.117, *A*Fri.124, *A*Fri.129, *B*Helm.145.1, *A*Pat, *A*OP(Humb), *A*Sar, *A*Worc. The following remarks may be compared with the transcription of the *Regnum mundi* from *A*Fri.117 in Chapter 4.

Three groups of variants more or less distinguish 'Roman' sources (*A*OP[Humb], *A*Sar, *A*Worc) from those of 'German' origin (*A*Ahrw.2b, *A*Fri.117, *A*Fri.124, *A*Fri.129, *B*Helm.145.1, *A*Pat), though the line of distinction is not clear cut. One variant common to all German manuscripts studied, including the early sixteenth-century printed text *A*Pat, and shared even by the 'Roman' *A*Worc, is the leap of the fifth *Fc* over *o-pera* in the verse instead of the third *ac* in the 'Roman' versions of *A*OP(Humb), *A*Sar and the modern Vaticana editions (*R*Mon and *Pr*Mon). The two other groups of variants are related to the most prominent feature of the so-called 'German' plainsong dialect, the preference for thirds over seconds in certain tonal combinations, especially when a semi-tone is involved.[27] The evidence differs in the German manu-

---

[25] Hucke (1973) 179, 181, 189, recognized such features as special to some responsories in the non-Roman Frankish tradition, particularly in some of those from the twelfth/thirteenth centuries or later.

[26] Cf. above, Chapter 2, pp. 57-58.

[27] For the characteristics of what has been called the 'Germanic,' or better, the 'German choral dialect,' see above, pp. 73-74 (with literature). Another revealing example of the 'German dialect' in plainsong is the responsory *Emendemus*; see below, Chapter 3 [7], pp. 148-149. For lack of a better, generally accepted terminology, I continue to use the qualifications 'German' and 'Roman.'

scripts studied. One such variant, the substitution of the thirds G-b^b-$G(F)$ for the seconds G-a-G occurs in the lower melodic range of the mode 5 chant (with the ambitus F-f). At this location, all five German manuscript sources have this 'typically German' variant at least three times (over *cre-didi* in respond and repetenda, and over *me-a* in the verse), while APat shares only the variant over *cre-di-di* (along with other minor 'German' variants). It is interesting that the variant over *cre-didi* appears even in the 'Roman' ASar. Variants involving the same pitches G-b^b-G abound in BHelm.145.1, with four additional instances (*secu-li, contempsi*, and, in respond and repetenda, *di-lexi*). In the following text of the responsory the syllables affected by these variants in one or all of the German sources considered are printed in bold:

R. *Regnum mundi et omnem ornatum seculi **contempsi** propter amorem domini mei ihesu christi Quem vidi, quem amavi, in quem credidi, quem **dilexi**.*

V. *Eructavit cor meum verbum bonum, dico ego opera mea regi.*

Rep. *Quem vidi, quem amavi, in quem credidi, quem **dilexi**.*

The other form of this 'typically German' variant occurs in the top range of the melody and is noticeably less common. Here, in only two of the six German sources studied, the half-tone intervals *efe* of the 'Roman' transmission are replaced with larger intervals of a third or fourth, *ege* or *egd*. By ascending to the high g, these variants affect the ambitus of the melody itself which, in all other sources considered, never moves above the f, the apex of the normal mode 5 ambitus. AAhrw.2b shows these 'apex variants' in all six instances indicated below, BHelm.145.1 in only four (over *et, **Quem**[1], cor meum*, and ***Quem**[2]*):

R. *Regnum mundi et omnem ornatum seculi contempsi propter amorem domini mei ihesu christi **Quem** vidi, quem amavi, in quem credidi, quem dilexi.*

V. *Eructavit **cor meum** verbum bonum, dico ego opera mea regi.*

Rep. ***Quem** vidi, quem ˙amavi, in quem credidi, quem dilexi.*

In the four instances common to the Ahrweiler and Helmstedt sources, the variants appear within five to seven note sequences of melismatic or neumatic style. Over the words *et, **Quem**[1]*, and *Quem*[2], for instance, the 'Roman' melisma *cdefedc* is changed from a stepwise arch to one with, at its top, the leaps *ege* (AAhrw.2b) or *egd* (BHelm.145.1, where the melisma is slightly shortened to *degdc*). Over *cor me-um*, this melismatic sequence recurs in very similar form in neumatic style with the corresponding 'German' variants. The whole melodic line and the character of the chant in both sources is, of course, noticeably affected by these 'apex variants.'

Two observations should be emphasized: first, not surprisingly, two non-German sources share at least one of the 'German' variants, *A*Sar the *G-b^b* over *credidi*, *A*Worc the *F-c* over *opera*; second, and most surprisingly, the Fritzlar Antiphonals, usually good representatives of the German plainsong dialect, do not share in the second group of 'German' variants, nor does *A*Pat of 1519. One might suspect that the position of the semi-tone *e-f* at the top end of the ambitus is partly responsible for this restraint; there may have been a certain reluctance in some German areas to adopt the 'German' preference for thirds over the semi-tone when this would imply exceeding the limits of the melody's range or, indeed, of the ambitus of its mode. Many more comparative studies are needed, however, before such a hypothesis can be asserted or disproved. In any case, for a number of other chants studied below, there is a much greater uniformity among the German sources with respect to the major 'German' variants replacing some seconds with thirds.

For the restoration of this chant in the Thuringian play, preference should, of course, be given to a melodic version from a source in the Mainz diocese, which is represented by any one of the Fritzlar Antiphonals listed in the Catalogue. In this case, the Fritzlar sources appear to be less 'German' in their melodic features when compared to *A*Ahrw.2b and *B*Helm.145.1; and yet there is a sufficient number of 'typical' and less 'typical' variants that connect all the German sources considered. A unique feature in the Fritzlar sources, however, is that they do not employ the "bémol constant" that Pothier (cf. n24 above) noticed for this chant: over the *o-* of *om-nem*, the Fritzlar transmission has a *b-natural*, not the *b-flat* of all other sources studied.

On the basis of the preceding manuscript research, I propose to restore chant [2] of the Lddv, text and music, from the responsory *Regnum mundi* as transmitted in *A*Fri.117, which is identical with the transmission in the other Fritzlar Antiphonals studied:

Responsory *Regnum mundi [et omnem ornatum seculi contempsi prop-*
ter amorem domini mei ihesu xpisti Quem uidi quem amavi[a]
In quem credidi quem dilexi.

Verse   *Eructavit cor meum verbum bonum, dico ego opera mea*
regi.

Repetenda   *Quem vidi quem amavi*[a] *in quem credidi quem dilexi.*

< Dox.   *Gloria patri et filio et spiritui sancto.*

Rep.   *Quem. >]*

Source   *A*Fri.117, fol. 339r (= *A*Fri.124, *A*Fri.129; and other
sources in Catalogue [2D], pp. F5-F8).

Variants   [a] *amavi*] *agnovi A*Sar

Melody   Mode 5. The responsory is transcribed in Chapter 4 [**2, 20**]
from *A*Fri.117, fol. 339r.

Melody ~ = *A*Fri.124, *A*Fri.129, *A*Pat; ~ *var. B*Helm.145.1,
*A*Ahrw2b, *A*OP(Humb).

Translation   "The kingdom of the world and all earthly trappings I have
spurned for the love of my Lord Jesus Christ, Whom I
have seen, whom I have loved, in whom I have believed,
whom I have cherished.
My heart overflows with noble words. To the king I must
speak the song I have made.
Whom I have …
< Glory be to the Father, and to the Son, and to the Holy
Spirit. Whom I have …" >   [cf. CAO 7524]

[3'] *Silete*, including [11' 13' 18' 25' 34']
(Lddv 0p, 116b, 140b, 176b, 228d, 383b)
[9'] *Silete longam horam* (Lddv 100e)

Chant [3'], the first of the seven *Silete* calls in the Lddv, clearly marks the end of the procession of players and the beginning of the performance. Chanted by the Angels who had entered with the first group of actors, this sung signal parallels the opening of many other medieval dramas (cf. above, pp. 43-44 with n8) and leads smoothly into the first six vernacular lines which formally announce the play's beginning.

The *Silete* chants of the Angels have been counted among the most peculiar phenomena of medieval drama.[1] Several literary historians have briefly commented on their function within the plays, but they have never been thoroughly studied. In his 1940 Basel dissertation *Die Musik der Osterfeiern, Osterspiele und Passionen des Mittelalters*, the musicologist E.A. Schuler gives a very useful survey of *Silete* occurrences in twenty of these medieval plays and devotes two pages to their discussion. The work is limited, however, by its exclusive focus on Easter and Passion plays.[2] While Catalogue [3'], pp. F9-F13, does not profess to contain a complete listing of all the *Silete* chants in medieval German drama, it adds eighteen more plays to Schuler's list.[3]

---

[1]Schuler (1951) 46: "Zu den eigenartigsten Erscheinungen des mittelalterlichen Dramas gehört der Siletegesang des Engelchores." The *Silete* chants in the Lddv as well as in most other German plays where they occur (see Catalogue [3']) are performed by *Angeli*. Four of the earlier plays — WienP, FrkfDir, KassPar, and BozVerk — mention *pueri* or *iuvenes* instead, but Schuler (1951) 47, may very well be right in believing these boys represented *Angeli*. See the listings in Catalogue [3'C1 and 3], and cf. above, the discussion of the stage directions to *Silete*, Chapter 2, pp. 45-47 and nn12-15.

[2]Schuler (1951) 316-320 no. 580, and 46-48. The research of William Boletta is similarly restrictive. Boletta (1967) 162-169, studies at some length the function of the *Silete* calls in Easter and Passion plays, especially in the Alsfeld Passion Play (AlsfP). On p. 27 n23, he gives an overview of different scholarly interpretations of the *Silete* call, and points to the difficulties of coming to general conclusions about this device. Unfortunately, some of his most valuable observations are almost lost because his summary tends to be too general (p. 205).

[3]The Easter plays of Redentin, Augsburg, Füssen, and Regensburg (RedO, AugsO, FüssO, RegO), the Ascension plays of Moosburg and St. Gall (MoosbHi, StGHi), the Saints' plays of St. Catherine and St. Dorothy (LdbKath, KrmsDor), the Innsbruck Assumption Play (InnsThAss), the Hessian and Tyrol Christmas plays (HessW, TirW), the Kassel Paradiesspiel (KassPar), three shorter plays from Bozen (BozVerk, BozAbdm,

Furthermore, since the manuscripts sometimes have the short form *Silete*, sometimes the longer form *Silete silete silentium habete*, it seems important to take into consideration which kind of *Silete* formula is used in the various plays. According to Schuler's survey, most plays use the short formula; only seven out of twenty have the extended text. Schuler seems to treat them all as the same chant text, however, regarding a simple *Silete* as an incipit and assuming that the extended formula is always intended.[4] Lipphardt obviously agrees with this view when, in reference to Schuler's list of *Silete* occurrences, he states that in most cases, only the incipit of the text is given.[5] The chronological evidence for *Silete* occurrences as collected in the Catalogue [3'C1 and 3], however, does not support this interpretation. As these chronological lists show, in the fourteenth century alone, there are over fifty short *Silete* forms in ten different plays (including the Lddv) compared to only one extended text *Silete, silete, silentium habete* at the beginning of the WienP.[6] Moreover,

---

BozPalm), two Passion plays (BozP.1514, TirP), and of course the Lddv. The RedO is not included in Schuler's survey probably because in Froning's edition the reading in l. 228a is *simul* instead of *Silete*. For the use of *Silete* in these and other plays see Catalogue [3'C1-4], pp. F9-F12.

[4]Schuler (1951) 316-320 lists all MSS occurrences of the *Silete* call under no. 580 with the heading *Silete silete silentium habete*, taken, interestingly, from the Trier Theophilus Play which is neither a Passion nor an Easter play and, consequently, should not be part of his list. Furthermore, in his index of Latin incipits (pp. 106-122) he does not enter the simple *Silete* separately (p. 119). And when he discusses the *Silete* chant in the different plays he mentions only the *stereotype Formel Silete silete silentium habete* (p. 46). Boletta does not give much thought to the two different *Silete* formulas either. Long before Schuler's publication, the musicologist Dreimüller (1935) 1: 165 and 2: 13, had also quietly extended the *Silete* chants in his dissertation on the AlsfP to the long formula and provided a misleading facsimile of this chant from the WienP. Schottmann also extends the *Silete* to the long formula in her edition (1975) of the RedO, l. 228a (see also her comment on this line), an extension rejected as *unstatthaft* by Linke (1977) 26. In the more recent popularized edition of the RedO by Andresen (1991) 54 and 58, the original simplicity of the single *Silete* is even more distorted. To the extended textual *Silete* version in l. 228b (and in l. 232a, where the manuscript does not even have a *Silete*, as Linke proved [1977] 28), the music editor Schoppmeier added the *Silete* melody of the WienP, with an additional second voice of her own making.

[5]Cf. Lipphardt in Schmidtke et al., eds. (1976) 398. On the other hand, Liebenow (ed. 1969) 258, and Linke (1977) 26, consider the extended version a rare occurrence compared with the prevailing simple *Silete*.

[6]Where, unlike the extended *Silete* chants in later plays, it appears to be used as a kind of dialogue between two boys and Lucifer before his fall. Cf. above, p. 46.

another, quite different *Silete* formula, also from the fourteenth century, is found in chant [9'] of the Lddv, *Silete longam horam*, one that has never been included in any serious discussion of the *Silete* phenomenon.[7]

In the Catalogue, the occurrences of these three different formulas in medieval drama are listed separately in three groups and arranged in a chronological sequence (see Catalogue [3'C1-3], pp. F9-F12). From these lists the following conclusions can be drawn:

1) There is no evidence for the use of the *Silete* chant in medieval plays before the fourteenth century, the earliest occurrence being that in the WienP.[8] The Lddv, then, belongs to the earlier period of this usage.

2) With the exception of the Lddv which, at one place, uses *Silete longam horam*, and the early WienP, which opens with the extended formula *Silete, silete, silentium habete*, the fourteenth-century plays contain the short *Silete* formula; with the single exception of WienP, all these earlier plays originate in the middle German areas (Middle Rhine or Thuringia/Silesia).[9] The extended formula appears more generally in plays of the fifteenth century, predominantly from southern regions, while the short *Silete* call continues to be used throughout the fifteenth and sixteenth centuries, mainly in middle German areas. Consequently, the six short *Silete* calls in the Mühlhausen manuscript of the Lddv as well as those in other plays must be considered as complete texts and not as incipits.

3) The formula [9'] *Silete longam horam* seems to be unique to the Lddv since it could not be found in any other play. It too must be regarded as a complete text.

4) Echoes of the vernacular paraphrase of the opening *Silete* call in the Lddv can be found in at least four later plays, all of the fifteenth century (see Catalogue [3'C4], p. F12).

---

[7]Cf. the Catalogue [3'C2], p. F11. De Boor (ed. 1965) 186, ll. 130-131, clearly uncomfortable with the unusual wording of this chant, which did not fit accepted notions, shortened the formula to *Silete* and rendered *longam horam* as a stage direction.

[8]See also Creizenach (1911) 220; Schuler (1951) 47. Lüdemann (1964) 56 is clearly wrong when he claims that the *Silete* chants appear only in the more developed Easter plays, and that it occurs for the first time in the Innsbruck Easter Play of 1391.

[9]Even WienP can be counted among this middle German group of plays since it has been recognized as a "Bavarian adaptation of a Rheno-Franconian model"; cf. Linke (1993b) 25; Bergmann (1972a) 41-46; Hennig (ed. 1986) 5. This observation might lead us to conclude that the use of *Silete* calls in medieval German drama originated somewhere in these middle German areas, either near the middle Rhine or perhaps in Thuringia/Silesia. Cf. above, p. 47, where a similar hypothesis was made about the stage direction *Angeli cantant Silete*.

5) Except for the seventeenth-century Regensburg Easter play, music is transmitted in various forms only for the extended call *Silete, silete, silentium
habete* (in five plays of the fifteenth, and one of the sixteenth century).[10]
Although none of these late melodic transmissions are applicable to the
Silete calls in the Lddv, the extant melodies will be taken into account and
examined in an effort to evaluate all available evidence for a possible
musical form of such simple directive calls.

Literary and musicological scholars more or less agree about the function of the *Silete* chant. In whatever form it may appear, it usually serves
as a staging device between 'scenes' to bridge the gaps in the performance
of the play while players are moving from or proceeding to the centre of the
stage; or, in larger plays, when the action moves over considerable distances
from one part of the performance area to another one and the audience
would naturally move along with it. The *Silete* call, then, brought the
attention of the onlookers back to the performance. Consequently, it often
marks the change from one 'scene' to another or, perhaps more precisely
— to include all those plays where *Silete* occurs only at the very
beginning[11] — it marks the start of a 'scene,' or of the play as such, in
much the same way as the curtain does for the modern stage.[12]

While in many plays the device is used in a random way, the Thuringian Lddv asks for it so consistently that this drama can serve as a good
example of the twofold function of *Silete* as a staging device as well as a
silentium call to the public.[13] As Table 5 clearly shows, *Silete* is always

[10]See Catalogue [3'C3], the plays marked with the siglum • (pp. F11-F12).

[11]Some of the more extended cycle plays, starting with the fourteenth-century
FrkfDir, use the *Silete* only once, at the beginning of the play or at the beginning
of each performance day.

[12]This 'scenic' function of the *Silete*-calls was recognized as early as the mid
nineteenth century by Mone (1846) 2: 157; and by R. Bechstein (1860) 97-98, (1866)
164-166, (1872) 16. Linke (1972a) 204-205, demonstrates the *szeneneinleitende Funktion*
of the *Silete* calls for the structure of the Rheinisches Osterspiel (BeRheinO).

[13]I disagree with R. Bechstein (1866) 165, who thought that, due to its mainly 'lyrical'
character, this play is not as suitable as the LdbKath for proving this thesis. The twofold
function of the *Silete* chant is perhaps best expressed by Elke Ukena (1975) 2: 354 (to
l. 71a), in her notes to the St. Dorothy Play (KrmsDor): "Seit dem Beginn der volkssprachigen Aufführungen außerhalb der Kirche nachweisbar, ... hat [der Ordnungsruf
Silete] zweifache Funktion: als Schweigeformel das Publikum zur Aufmerksamkeit zu
ermahnen und als Signalisierung einer Pause, eines Standort- oder Szenenwechsels
Inszenierungshilfe zu leisten." In many other medieval plays the use of *Silete* is less

called for whenever there is some sort of hiatus in the dialogue or in the action of the play, i.e. a) at the beginning of the performance after the procession of the players [3']; b) before, during or after a dumb show (the *Fatue* dancing and moving [9'], or dining and sleeping [11']; the *Dominica Persona* celebrating the Feast with the *Prudentes* [25']; the Devils chaining the *Fatue* [34']); c) at the beginning of a new episode that involves movement on the part of the performers (players travelling to another place [13'], or new players entering the action [18']).

In the Lddv *Silete* always denotes the beginning or end of an episode or 'scene,' although the boundaries of 'scenes' in medieval drama are never sharply delineated and often show ongoing dumb play. The only exceptions to this rule are 'scenes' 7 and 8 (cf. Table 5). The appearance of the Devils on stage at the beginning of 'scene' 7 would cause sufficient movement and disturbance for a *Silete* call to be expected here. Upon closer examination, however, 'scene' 7 appears to have been interpolated at a later stage. It is not transmitted in MS B of the Lddv (Darmstadt, MS 3290), and its dialogue, entirely in German, is very repetitive. Indeed, the rhyme and versification in this Devils' Scene are of such poor quality compared to the rest of the play that it was recognized as an interpolation as early as 1865 by Max Rieger. His findings have been corroborated by various twentieth-century scholars, including Linke in his outline of the play.[14]

---

consistent than in the Lddv (or the LdbKath), even though the action may be considerably more complex. According to Ukena, this inconsistency must be attributed less to negligence in the manuscript transmissions than to the fact that these calls served primarily as staging devices and not as a means to subdivide the text and its flow. The director of a play may well have added or dropped a *Silete* call to suit local performance conditions. On the other hand, some of the more extended cycle plays use *Silete* only once. Therefore, the function and use of the *Silete* call has to be examined individually for each play, as other scholars of medieval drama have suggested.

For the rare use of *Silete* in the medieval French plays, mainly as an instrumental call to order, see Grace Frank (1954) 177, and D. Klausner (1989) 260. It must be added that the 1486 *Passion of Angers* by Jean Michel, ed. Jodogne (1959), uses a vocal *Silete* in at least six instances, with interesting changes: a *Silete* is sung twice in paradise (ll. 2163a and 7726a), twice in limbo (ll. 7789a and 25492a); and twice Lucifer directs the Devils to "make" a *Silete* (l. 2252 *Dyables, ung petit silete*; 17230 *Dyables, faictes ung* silete). See also Jodogne, p. li.

[14]Cf. Rieger (1865) 314; Beckers (1905) 40, 113-114; Fischer (1910) 22-24; Reuschel (1906) 10; Linke (1987a) 226.

TABLE 5 THE STRUCTURE OF THE LDDV
(AS MARKED BY THE *SILETE* CHANTS)

LATIN CHANT	'SCENE'	ACTION/CONTENT [STAGE DIRECTIONS]	MOVEMENT/ DUMB PLAY
[1-2]	Overture	Entrance of main players [*Dominica Persona, Maria, Angeli, Virgines*]	Procession
[3']	*Silete*	1-6 Paraphrase of *Silete*	
[4-8]	1	7-100 Invitation to the Wedding Feast; Division of *Virgines* into two groups	Two *Angeli* approach Virgins
[9']	*S. longam horam*	[*Tunc Fatue corizando et cum magno gaudio vadunt ad alium locum*]	*Fatue* dancing move away
[10]	2	101-116 *Prudentes* respond to mockery by anticipating heavenly rewards	
[11']	*Silete*	[*Tunc omnes Fatue habeant convivium, deponant se quasi dormiant*]	*Fatue* dining and sleeping
[12]	3	117-140 *Fatue* awake, take counsel	
[13']	*Silete*	[*Omnes Fatue vadant ad Prudentes*]	*Fatue* approach *Prudentes*
[14-17]	4	141-176 *Fatue* singing search for oil	
[18']	*Silete*	Arrival of *Dominica Persona* and *Angeli*, meeting with *Prudentes*	*Fatue* searching
[19-24]	5	177-228 *Prudentes* received by heavenly host, crowned by *Mary*	
[25']	*Silete*	[*Dominica Persona habeat magnum convivium ... Fatue vadant ad nuptias*]	Wedding Feast *Fatue* return
[26-33]	6	229-296 *Fatue* beg access, are rejected; *Mary's* vain intercession	*Fatue* prostrate themselves
	7	297-339 *Devils* urge judgment over *Fatue*; dialogue with *Dominica Persona*	*Devils* enter
	8	340-383 *Mary's* second intercession; rejection and judgment of *Fatue*	*Mary* genuflects
[34']	*Silete*	[*Dyaboli circumdant eas kathena*]	*Devils* chain *Fatue*
[35-36]	9	384-525 Lamentations of *Fatue* (couplets)	*Fatue* let their crowns fall
	Postlude	526-576 Lamentations of *Fatue* (stanzas)	*Fatue* move thru audience

If then 'scene' 7 was not conceived by the playwright who inserted the *Silete* chants at the *caesuras* of the action, it becomes understandable why a *Silete* is missing at its beginning and end: the action before and after this interpolation was understood as a single scenic unit. Mary's second intercession for the *Fatue*, now 'scene' 8, would have been part of the Latin and vernacular invocations of the previous 'scene' 6. Thus it seems that, as it was originally conceived, the Lddv had an introductory *Silete* chant for each 'scene.' And in this function, the *Silete* calls provide some structure to the drama as a whole as indicated in Table 5.

It is interesting to see how thoughtfully the author placed the special formula [9'] *Silete longam horam* at the beginning of the second 'scene,' informing the audience that it will take 'a long while' for the action to unfold. The unique occurrence of *Silete longam horam*, therefore, has a threefold function, not only marking the beginning of a new scene and requesting the attention of the audience, but also providing information about the duration of the play. It is also interesting that for this longer form, the author uses one of the four main *cursus* forms of medieval Latin poetical prose, the *trispondaicus* with its alternation of stressed and unstressed syllables in the last six syllables of the phrase: *Siléte lòngam hóram*. This observation is not unimportant since the *cursus* is used in two later chants in a quite intentional way.[15]

Turning to the problem of how the *Silete* calls were performed, the question may be asked what would the medieval director of a play such as the Lddv have done when faced with the stage direction:

ANGELI cantant   *Silete.*

If he were liturgically trained, which was usually the case, some similar exhortative formulas used in the Church liturgy, *Oremus, Levate, Flectamus genua*, for example, would probably have come to his mind. Controlling liturgical actions "by addressing explanations and directions to the people," was normally the task of the deacon, who delivered such directions to a simple reciting formula.[16] The *Silete* calls, then, can well be understood as quasi-liturgical chants. Thus, liturgical books can

---

[15]Cf. the discussion of the *cursus* forms below in the sections [27] and [33].

[16]Gelineau (1964) 75-76: "The functional nature of the deacon's interventions calls for the use of a syllabic recitative in which there is no place for melismata."

be consulted for the appropriate recitation formulas. This, unfortunately, poses a problem.

It is very difficult if not impossible to get precise information about the formulas for short liturgical exhortations in local use during the Middle Ages because there was no need to notate them.[17] Nor can we draw any valid conclusions from our knowledge of recitation in general about the way in which exhortations like *Levate* or *Oremus* would have been chanted in fourteenth-century Thuringia. Nevertheless, such formulas, as well as the quasi-liturgical *Silete* calls, can be easily adapted to the most common and simple Roman reciting formulas on both the subtonal and the subsemitonal tenor. For example, we might underlay the *Silete* to one of the formulas in the 'modern' *Liber Usualis* as shown in Figure 5a.

FIGURE 5A DIRECTIVE CALLS IN THE ROMAN RITE (LU [1962] 101) TRANSCRIBED FROM THE ORIGINAL SQUARE NOTATION

In the Ambrosian Rite, calls for *silentium*, chanted before the Gospel reading, are even included (with their notation, as in Figure 5b) in the *Antiphonale Missarum*.

FIGURE 5B DIRECTIVE CALLS IN THE AMBROSIAN RITE (*AM*MED [1935] 625) TRANSCRIBED FROM THE ORIGINAL SQUARE NOTATION

On the other hand, since Thuringia belonged to the Mainz archdiocese during the Middle Ages and the province of Mainz had its own tradition for liturgical recitation known as the *Accentus Moguntinus*, we need to know how these brief exhortations were performed in medieval Mainz. Unfortunately, however, the medieval sources for the Mainz Church are no more explicit about these short directives and their

---

[17]Cf. Hiley (1993) 49.

performance than are other medieval liturgical books, so we are reduced
to conjectures based on the general characteristics of the *Accentus
Moguntinus*, i.e. a) the use of a subtonal tenor (mainly *D* or *a*); b) the
use of the upper third for the word accents; c) the close on an ascending
half step in longer recitations.[18] In the *Missale Halberstattense*, printed
in 1511, some of these features can be noted in the simple introductory
formulas for the readings of Pauline epistles as shown in Figure 6.

FIGURE 6 *ACCENTUS MOGUNTINUS*: PREAMBLES FOR EPISTLE READINGS
(*M*HALB.888, FOL. <228>r)

On the basis of these clues, it may be possible to conjecture a Mainz
formula for the even simpler recitation of short liturgical exhortations in
general and the *Silete* calls in particular. Since the Mainz sources (especially *M*Halb.888 and *L*Würz.11) give evidence for the use of both subtonal tenors *D* and *a*,[19] either would appear appropriate for a conjectu-
ral exhortation formula in the *Accentus Moguntinus*.[20]

With such criteria established from the evidence of liturgical sources
for the *Accentus Moguntinus*, it seems necessary to examine whatever
evidence is available in extant dramatic sources. At least seven notated
Silete chants have been transmitted, six for the extended formula *Silete,
silete, silentium habete* (all of the fifteenth or sixteenth centuries) and

[18]See above pp. 77-78.

[19]Cf. above, esp. pp. 78-79. Jammers (1975b) 51, gives two brief examples with the
tenor *a* from *L*Würz.11.

[20]In actual performance, however, such a tenor could have been transposed to any other
pitch. For a short directive call, the recitation formula with the tenor *D* and the upper third
F for the accent notes could possibly include a transitory note between or beyond the interval *D-F* as does the example quoted in Figure 6 from *M*Halb.888, yet its range would
basically be limited by this third *D-F* (or *a-c* respectively).

one for the shorter phrase *Silete silete* in the seventeenth-century RegO.[21] Since the melodic settings are so different from each other, it seems obvious that they are specific, independent compositions for the individual plays. Three (TrierTh, WienO, and PfarrkP) are so elaborate musically, that, except for the beginning of the *Silete* chant in PfarrkP, it is difficult to discern any melodic elements that might relate to an earlier recitation formula.[22] The remaining four versions of *Silete* (AugsO, DonP, FüssO, RegO), however, warrant closer examination. The first *Silete* phrase of PfarrkP will also be included in the comparison.

---

[21] All of these notated *Silete* chants have been published in transcription, in facsimile, or in both. Schuler (1940) 321-322 no. 580, transcribed three of them (TrierTh, WienO, DonP).

The *Silete* of Trier Theophilus (two-part version) was first transcribed by Bohn (1877) 24-25 and reproduced in Haas (1931) 64.

The *Silete* of WienO is also found in Blosen's edition (1979) 126-127, transcribed by F.E. Hansen in a non-rhythmic notation and with a more precise text setting than Schuler's; Osthoff's modal transcription of this chant (1942) 67 was reproduced by Kaff (1956) 25, and by Schottmann (1975) 181.

Schuler's transcription for the *Silete* of DonP, reproduced in Touber's edition of the play (1985) 251, has serious flaws in tune and text underlay; preferable is the transcription by Osthoff (1943-1944) 34, see, however, n23(2) below; facsimile in Bergmann (1972b) after p. 906.

The *Silete* of FüssO, with its notated vernacular paraphrase, is transcribed by Lipphardt in Schmidtke et al., eds. (1976) 242; facsimile in Schmidtke (ed. 1983) Bl. 137r.

The *Silete* of PfarrkP, with its sung vernacular paraphrase, can be found in Lipphardt-Roloff (1988) 2: 127, transcription by Traub; 2: 360, facsimile.

The *Silete* of RegO is in Poll (1950) 108, transcription, with no attempt to emend the text underlay.

The *Silete* of AugsO is transcribed here, to my knowledge, for the first time; facsimile in Lipphardt (1975) 21, and (1978b) after p. 63 (fol. 74r).

[22] This is particularly true for the TrierTh with its two-part setting for the *Silete* in a *conductus* style, both voices ascending and descending in leaps of thirds and fourths, ranging over an octave or more (*C-d*) in each of the two parts. The frequently cited *Silete* melody of the WienO (*Silete silete silete silete silencium habete*) shows an almost major tonality, with folkloristic elements and the range of an octave (*E-e*). Only the first *Silete* phrase in the *Silete* of PfarrkP, in mensural notation, is relatively simple; the rest of the melody is far removed from Gregorian chant and consists of large melodic swings spanning a whole octave (*D-d*), in both the Latin and the subsequent vernacular version. The poor text setting of this chant in the manuscript of PfarrkP has been much improved in Traub's transcription; see n21.

FIGURE 7   EXTANT *SILETE* MELODIES IN SOME LATE MEDIEVAL PLAYS[23]

[23](1) My transcription from the facsimile edition of AugsO (Feldkirch, Kapuzinerkloster, MS Liturg.1 rtr) fol. 74r; cf. facsimile in Lipphardt (ed. 1978b), after p. 63, ll. 9-10.

(2) Except for the first phrase α for *Silete* (MS: *Dilete*), my transcription from a copy of the DonP manuscript (Karlsruhe, Badische Landesbibliothek, cod. Don.137), fol. 1v, agrees with that by Osthoff (1943-1944) 34. Osthoff's omission of the beginning *G* results in a poor word underlay for the first *Silete* phrase. Schuler's transcription, adopted in Touber's edition of the play (1985) 251, misrepresents the (admittedly awkward) manuscript transmission.

(3) My transcription from the facsimile edition of FüssO (Augsburg, Universitäts-bibliothek, cod. II, 1,4°, 62), fol. 137r. Lipphardt's transcription (in Schmidtke et al. [1976] 242-243) shows a different text underlay in phrase δ (*silentium*). In phrase α', Lipphardt renders the last neume as a plain *C*. However, the manuscript clearly has an *epiphonus* at this place (a liquescent *podatus*), which means that the tune should lightly swing up a second. I present it here as such, i.e. with a gentle ("decorative") movement from the *C* to the *D*. Cf. the facsimile in Schmidtke (ed. 1983) fol. 137r.

(4) My transcription, in rough imitation of the PfarrkP manuscript's mensural notation (Sterzing, Stadtarchiv, MS XVI) fol. 63r. The complete melody in Traub's transcription and in facsimile is included in the edition of PfarrkP; cf. Lipphardt-Roloff (1988) 2: 127 and 360.

(5) My transcription from a copy of the RegO manuscript (Regensburg, Bischöfliche Zentralbibliothek, MS Ch.1*), fol. 24v. In Poll's transcription ([1950] 108), the text underlay is inaccurate and the rubric *choraliter* incorrectly accepted as part of the text.

The synoptical survey in Figure 7 shows that in each of the four medieval examples (i.e. excluding the late RegO), the repeated three-syllable word *Silete* (or *Dilete* in DonP) is given two different musical settings, the very simple melodic phrase α (α' or α'') and the slightly more ornate phrase β (or β'). For the words *silentium habete*, the last part of the tune has an expansion of phrase α to α^{ext} in AugsO, an elaboration of phrase β to β^{ext} in DonP, and new melodic material, marked δ in the example, in FüssO.[24]

Phrase α in AugsO and DonP is defined by the range of the third *D-F(G)*. In phrase α' of FüssO, the range is extended by one step down to the fourth *C-F*. Very close to this is the opening *Silete* phrase α'' of the otherwise quite elaborate *Silete* melody in PfarrkP (see Figures 7 and 8, no. 4); here, the melodic formula α' is transposed up a fifth (to *a-cbG-aa*) and preceded by an upward leap from the lower *D*, thus enlarging the range of the whole formula α'' (*[D]a-cbG-aa*) to that of the seventh *D-c*.

Phrase β in AugsO, DonP, and transposed up a second in FüssO (β'), consists of a characteristic melodic arch over the word accent of *Silete*, swinging up a fourth from *F* to *b^b* (*G-c* in FüssO) and back to the closing note *F* (*G* in FüssO). As this melodic phrase β/β' is musically quite expressive in the higher range and does not touch on any note below the finalis *F*, it appears remote from any recitation formula in the *Accentus Moguntinus*. And yet, there is some connection to the simplest way of reciting on a single pitch (*tonus rectus*): in all three examples for phrase β/β', each of the three syllables of *Si-le-te* is chanted on the pitch *F* (*G* in FüssO), with additional ornamentation only on the word accent *-lé-*.

The *Silete* tune γ of the very late (seventeenth-century) RegO (cf. Figure 7, no. 5), with an increased melodic range (*C-a*), appears to contain elements of both phrase α and β: the lower 'recitation range' (*C*)*D-F* and the upper range *F-a* alternate in the melodic waves undulating around the basic *F*. By 'closing' a step above the finalis *F*, on *G*, however, the tune has a new open ending which permits the *Silete* to be repeated almost endlessly, as the staging might require in some cases. A halt to this continuous undulating could easily be achieved by a simple cadence from the *G* to the final *F* or, rather, by substituting this *G* with an anticipation of the finalis *F*.

---

[24]In Figures 7 and 8, slurs above the notes mark compound neumes used in the manuscripts; slurs below the notes indicate note groupings for one syllable of text.

The results of this short comparison of the extant musical evidence show that of the five different *Silete* chants examined, only two, AugsO and DonP, are reasonably close to each other, with almost identical tunes for their first two phrases α and β (over the repeated *Silete* words), but with different choices for the third phrase over the words *Silentium habete* (α^{ext} in AugsO, β^{ext} in DonP). The first two *Silete* words in the *Silete* of FüssO have two melodic phrases that are similar to α and β, yet in reverse sequence (β' and α'); for *Silentium habete*, however, a tune with new melodic material is chosen (phrase δ). Most interesting is the fact that, even in the very elaborate *Silete* chant of PfarrkP, phrase α' recurs, in transposition, as the opening phrase α''.

Phrase α (α'/α'') is the simplest of the different melodic sections examined in these chants; it is the only one immediately reminiscent of recitation, the only one that is more or less defined by the limited melodic range of the interval *D-F* (*[D]a-c* in PfarrkP) so characteristic for the *Accentus Moguntinus*. It is, consequently, the only one of real interest in the search for an underlying older recitation formula for *Silete*. Moreover, in AugsO this phrase is even used, in slightly expanded form (α^{ext}), for the longer third phrase *Silentium habete*. The fact that this melodic phrase α recurs so persistently and with only minor variations in the few *Silete* melodies transmitted is remarkable. It raises the possibility that phrase α is an intact or slightly altered remnant of an earlier recitation formula for the short call *Silete* in medieval German drama. This prospect warrants an even closer comparative study.

Figure 8 shows phrase α in its different versions ($\alpha/\alpha'/\alpha''/\alpha^{ext}$) with phrase γ of RegO in comparison as found in the five different *Silete* chants discussed. The constancy of the little figure of three descending notes **FED** over the word accent *Si-lé-te* in the examples (1) to (4) is striking; it is identical in (1) AugsO, (2) DonP, and (3) FüssO, and similar in (4), the 'transposed' version (*cbG*) of PfarrkP. By contrast, a wide variety of pitches are used in these five examples for the *initium* (intonation), the unstressed first syllable of *Si-lete* — not surprisingly, perhaps, because this is the least important element in the recitation of a three syllable word.[25] Thus, the 'upbeat' leads into the central accent figure either on the same pitch as in (1) AugsO; from a step above as in

---

[25]In simple liturgical recitation, there often is no intonation at all.

(2) DonP; from a step below as in (3) FüssO; from the lower third (with a preceding leap of a fifth) as in (4) PfarrkP; or again slightly different as in (5) RegO. In face of the constancy of the rest of the formula $\alpha/\alpha'/\alpha''$, however, these differences in the initial pitch seem quite insignificant in terms of this formula's melodic form.

FIGURE 8 A 'HIDDEN *SILETE* FORMULA' IN EXTANT MELODIES?

The major difference among the various versions of formula α appears to lie in their closing on either the higher accent pitch F or on the third below, which is the unstressed reciting note D (or a in PfarrkP) in the *Accentus Moguntinus*. The result is, in the first case, a double-accent form of *Si-lé-tè* (...*F*...-*F*), in the second case, a single-accent form of *Si-lé-te* (..*F*...-*D*; or *c*...-*a*). The double-accent form of the *Silétè* formula is represented in the first two examples of Figure 8, (1) AugsO and (2) DonP and reflected in formula γ of the late example (5) RegO with the initial pitch F for both the second and third syllable of *Silete*. The examples of α' in (3) FüssO and of α'' in (4) PfarrkP, on the other hand, show the single-accent form of *Siléte* with a closing on the third below the accent pitch on the reciting note D (or a).

Both forms of terminating a recitation formula may well have been in use in the medieval Mainz Church for short directive calls, especially for the three-syllable function calls *Oremus, Levate, (Silete)*. In this context, an important, albeit late liturgical source of Mainz must be cited, the *Manuductio ad Cantum Choralem Gregoriano-Moguntinum*, printed in 1672. Federl and Köllner both concluded that even though the *Manuductio* introduces some reforms to the Mainz chorale, for the simpler recitation formulas of a syllabic nature, especially the recitation formulas for prayers and lessons, it presents faithfully old traditions of the *Accentus Moguntinus*.[26] The short calls for prayers (*Oremus*) in the *Manuductio* come, interestingly, in two forms, which Köllner distinguishes as 'solemn' and 'simple.' On Sundays and feasts, the solemn formula begins and ends on *F*, while on weekdays ("ferialiter") the simple form closes with a descending third on *D*.[27]

FIGURE 9 *ACCENTUS MOGUNTINUS*: SHORT DIRECTIVE FORMULAS
(*MANUDUCTIO AD CANTUM*, PP. 121 AND 123)
(a) SOLEMN FORM   (a') SIMPLE FORM

The two versions of *Oremus* chanting found in the *Manuductio* provide a striking parallel to the two 'hidden *Silete* formulas' just discussed: the 'solemn form' (Figure 9a) would be performed with a double accent (*O-ré-mùs*, *F-EF-F*), while the 'simple form' (Figure 9a', *O-ré-mus*, *F-F-D*) corresponds to the single-accent *Siléte* closing with a descending third. As a result, the two forms of the melodic phrase α for *Silete*, extracted above from extant melodies of *Silete* calls, may now be distinguished as a 'solemn' and a 'simple' formula (see Figure 10), although this terminology may not have been used in the fourteenth century. On the basis of the combined evidence from dramatic and liturgical sources, it ap-

---

[26]Cf. Federl (1937) 23-29; Köllner (1958) 40.
[27]Cf. *Manuductio*, pp. 120-121, 123 (*In Festis Duplicibus* ... . *In Diebus Dominicis* ... .) and p. 123 ("Modus canendi Collectas ferialiter"). Cf. Köllner (1956) 52. I would like to express here my gratitude to the librarians of both the Stadtbibliothek and the Gutenberg Museum of Mainz for their combined efforts to provide me with copies of the relevant pages of the *Manuductio*.

pears possible to conjecture a musical formula for the *Silete* calls in medieval drama.

FIGURE 10 TWO CONJECTURES FOR *SILETE* FORMULAS
IN PLAYS OF THE MAINZ CHURCH
(α) "SOLEMN" FORMULA   (α') "SIMPLE" FORMULA

Si - le - - te.

Si - le - - te.

When attempting to 'perform' the two versions of both the *Oremus* and the *Silete* calls proposed here, one effect stands out immediately: the 'solemn' formula ending in the accented higher pitch *F* has more ex- clamatory strength, more carrying power for a large audience than the 'simple' version with the closing drop of a third. In fact, the notations for the *Silete* formula α as transmitted in AugsO and DonP (cf. Figures 7 and 8) have visual symbols to underline the exclamatory character at the phrase endings: the double notes (*notae duplices*), two consecutive notes on the same pitch, for the last syllable of *Silete*. The function of these *notae duplices* is explained in the *Manuductio* as serving to empha- size words or as exclamations or expressions of admiration, pain, or joy.[28] In performance, the *Manuductio* calls specifically for two notes to be performed *distinctim*, i.e. in a clear, distinct way, that probably means to be performed as two distinguishable notes on the same pitch or, one sustained note with two stresses.[29]

In other words, if the exclamation *Silete* is recited to the formula α, as extrapolated above from extant musical transmissions, with the double note for the last syllable on the high pitch *F*, then this call would sound into the crowd like a trumpet, certainly focussing everyone's attention on whatever new action is about to happen in the performance area of a medieval play.

As a result of these admittedly speculative investigations of the *Silete* chants, I propose that the formula α as found in the AugsO be used to

---

[28]*Manuductio*, p. 10: "Hae duplices notae ... ad exprimendam Emphasim verborum sive textus, sive per modum exclamationis, sive admirationis, ... sive laetitiae ... ." See also Köllner (1956) 46-47.

[29]" ... debent uti duae notae distinctim exprimi." Cf. Köllner (1956) 46-47.

restore the *Silete* calls in the Lddv, and in other medieval plays, at least those in the area of the Mainz Church. Since the ending on the higher pitch *F* leaves the recitation in suspense, the *Silete* call may easily be repeated two or more times should the staging require a longer call.[30] The slightly extended formula α^{ext} for *Silentium habete*, transmitted in the same AugsO, can be applied as is to the longer call in the Lddv ([9'] *Silete longam horam*) because both texts consist of seven syllables and have the same accentual pattern (the *cursus* form of a *trispondaicus*, as shown above). The two different forms of *Silete* calls in the Lddv, then, will be 'musically' restored as shown in Figure 11.

FIGURE 11 CONJECTURED RECITATION FORMULAS
FOR THE *SILETE* CALLS IN THE LDDV

(1) for nos. [3' 11' 13' 18' 25' 34']   (2) for no. [9']

If the *Silete* calls were most likely delivered as recitation in the Lddv — and, presumably, in most other dramas that use the short form of *Silete* — this would appear to conflict with the direction *cantare* employed in most of the rubrics (*Angeli cantant Silete*); for, according to Mehler, *cantare* in mixed-language plays of the thirteenth and fourteenth centuries usually points to a melodious chant while *dicere* tends to indicate liturgical recitation or very simple chant forms, a distinction that also appears to hold true for the Lddv.[31] Mehler also noticed a subtle distinction in the use of the two verbs, however. While neither serves as a technical term, *dicere* refers more to the spiritual content of a given liturgical text, whereas *cantare* refers to its musical side.[32] A rubric from the LU may illustrate what Mehler means:

---

[30]In the case of RegO, the repetition of the textual-musical formula *Silete* is transmitted in the manuscript (cf. Figures 7 and 8). This phrase γ with no *finalis* to close the formula remains very much in suspense asking for repetitions; cf. above, p. 115.

[31]Cf. Mehler's results (1981) 215-217; see also the discussion above, esp. p. 64.

[32]Mehler (1981) 249: "So macht sich ein ständiger Wechsel in der rubrikalen Terminologie bemerkbar, je nachdem, ob man (mit legere, psallere und cantare) den rezitativen oder melodiösen Ausdruck durch den Choral, also seine vom heutigen Standpunkt aus 'musikalische' Seite oder aber (mit dicere) seinen ideellen Ausdruck und geistigen Gehalt meint."

Ubi pro 'Dóminus vobíscum' *dicendus* est v. 'Dómine exaúdi' sic *cantatur*[33]

("Where in place of 'The Lord be with you' the verse 'Hear, O Lord' is *said*, it is *sung* this way: …")

In this liturgical terminology, then, it would be inappropriate to use *dicere* in the rubric of a chant with as little spiritual content as the *Silete* calls. Moreover, the *Silete* calls in medieval drama are delivered by two or more characters, often a whole choir of *Angeli*, whereas recitations of prayers and lessons in the Divine Service are usually done by one person only. *Cantare* appears to be the appropriate choice of a verb to indicate the performance of a group of voices, even if the performance implies reciting or 'intoning.'

A few scholars have pondered over the origin of the *Silete* chants. Mone sees connections to the Gallican liturgy and points to the use of the formula *silentium facite* in the Mozarabic liturgy before the reading of the lessons.[34] In the old Roman custom of the *scrutinium*, the catechumens were admonished before the reading from each of the four Gospels with the words *State cum silentio, audientes intente* ("Stand in silence and listen carefully"), which of course could be one of the Gallican elements that merged into the Gelasian Sacramentary.[35] In the Ambrosian Rite — in the cathedral of Milan even today, as Jungmann points out — a deacon and two custodians alternately address the people before the reading of the Gospel with the call: *Parcite fabulis, silentium habete, habete silentium* ("Refrain from talking, be silent, keep silence").[36] As Schuler observes, however, there are no *Silete* calls in early liturgical dramas and in many later Easter plays, especially those in France and Spain.[37]

---

[33]LU, p. 101; my emphases.

[34]Mone (ed. 1846) 2: 167.

[35]*S*Gelas, lib. I.34 [nos. 302, 304, 306, 308]. For the whole subject of calling for the congregation's attention before the Gospel readings see Jungmann (1948) 1: 501-502 with n15, citing various pertinent sources from the Eastern and Western Church.

[36]Cf. *AM*Med, p. 625 (with melody); see the citation above in Figure 5b, p. 111. Cf. Jungmann (1948) 1: 501 n15.

[37]Schuler (1951) 46-47. Lüdemann (1964) 56, however, uncritically accepts Mone's view that the liturgical source for the *Silete* chants is in the Gallican liturgy: "Ihre liturgische Quelle haben sie in der gallikanischen Liturgie."

In those special cases within a liturgical service where silence is requested through specific *silentium* formulas, we are dealing with exactly the same type of exhortations which in the Roman Church were used throughout the Mass. The mere existence of *Orate, Levate, Flectamus genua* and other types of exhortations and directions within the Roman liturgy can be looked upon as a 'source' — it can account for the creation of the *Silete* chant by some inventive playwright in the fourteenth century without any direct connection to an earlier liturgical *Silentium* formula.

It is not surprising, then, that, of the seven transmitted 'dramatic' *Silete* tunes examined above, the one that appeared most likely to reflect recitation formulas for liturgical directives is found in a liturgical manuscript, the Augsburg processional in Feldkirch.[38] The Easter play AugsO in this processional is to be performed during Easter night, *in sanctissima nocte pascha*, when the procession goes to the holy sepulchre as the well-known last Matins responsory *Dum transisset sabathum* is sung.[39] Once the responsory is finished, the Angel, standing at the altar with a scepter in his hands, sings the *Silete* chant quoted above (Figure 7 [1]). The Angel continues in vernacular couplets asking for attention and informing the crowd of the meaning of the upcoming performance.

The setting is clear: the performance of AugsO occurs immediately after the Office of Matins and certainly takes place within the church. This is quite extraordinary for a sixteenth-century play written predominantly in the vernacular. In such a liturgical setting, where the Angel of the play gives directions from the altar, it makes good sense that the *Silete* would be sung to a tune reminiscent of the deacon's directive calls in a Divine Service.

---

[38]Feldkirch, Kapuzinerkloster, MS Liturg.1 rtr. According to Lipphardt (1978a), (ed. 1978b) 25-26, this sixteenth-century processional is a copy of a fifteenth-century processional and was destined, like its exemplar, for use in one of the two major churches of Augsburg. See also Bergmann (1986) 109.

[39]Cf. AugsO, ed. Lipphardt (1978b) fol. 74r. The text of fol. 74r, rubric, *Silete* chant and the first two vernacular lines, are quoted in Bergmann (1986) 109. The singing of the responsory *Dum transisset* certainly included the doxology and perhaps more than one verse, in any case more than one *repetenda* for the rubric says *finita ultima repetitione* ("repetitio" meaning "repetenda").

If in the course of this study the melodic phrase α of AugsO emerged as an almost perfect paradigm for a directive call in the *Accentus Moguntinus*, this conclusion may be corroborated by the fact that both plays which use the melodic phrase α as the opening of their extended *Silete* chants (AugsO and DonP) originate within the boundaries of the Mainz Church.[40] The resonance of this phrase in the slightly variant versions α' and α'' in two other notated *Silete* chants, of FüssO and PfarrkP respectively, provides a reasonably solid foundation for the melody proposed here for the *Silete* chants in the Lddv.[41]

The texts of the *Silete* calls in the Lddv, then, will be restored exactly as transmitted in MS A, and their 'musical' form as presented above in Figure 11, p. 120.

Texts   *Silete*   for [**3' 11' 13' 18' 25' 34'**]

            Silete longam horam   for [**9'**]

'Melody'   Liturgical recitation to formulas   'α' [**3' 11' 13' 18' 25' 34'**]
            (cf. Figure 11 above)   'α^{ext}' [**9'**]
            See Chapter 4 [**3' 9' 11' 13' 18' 25' 34'**]
            The recitation formulas 'α' and 'α^{ext}' are retrieved from AugsO, where the transmitted *Silete* melody has the structure α, β, α^{ext}. Both formulas are conjectures, based on the evidence from both liturgical sources for the *Accentus Moguntinus* (MHalb.888, *Manuductio*) and from extant melodic transmissions of *Silete* chants in late plays. Cf. the comparative Figures 7 and 8 above, and Catalogue [**3'CDE**].
            Melody for [**3' 11' 13' 18' 25' 34'**] = phrase α in AugsO (fol. 74r); ~ = phrase α in the *Silete* transmission of DonP (fol 1v); ~*var.* phrase α' in FüssO, α'' in PfarrkP; *var.* phrase γ in RegO.

---

[40]DonP probably originated in Lucerne, which also belonged to the Church of Mainz. The play was later revised, probably in Villingen, near Donaueschingen; cf. Touber (ed. 1985) 14 and 27. With the sale of the manuscripts of the Fürstlich Fürstenbergische Hofbibliothek Donaueschingen, the play's manuscript can now be found in Karlsruhe, Badische Landesbibliothek, cod.Don.137; cf. Heinzer (1995) 312-313.

[41]Füssen was also part of the Mainz Church since it belonged to the diocese of Augsburg, which, from 829-1803, had Mainz as its metropolis. Cf. Zoepfl (1955) 593, (1957).

Melody for **[9']** = phrase α^{ext} in AugsO (fol. 74r); *different* phrase β^{ext} in DonP, δ in FüssO.

Translation   "Be still" ("Keep silence")
"Keep silence for a long while."

[4] *Homo quidam fecit* (Lddv 6b)

The responsory *Homo quidam fecit* is the only chant in the Lddv sung by the *Corus*. With it the choir offers a kind of narrative introduction to the play, setting the scene for the action that is about to unfold: a man has prepared a great banquet and sent a messenger to call the invited guests. All editors of the Lddv since L. Bechstein (1855) have identified the incipit [4] with the text of Luke 14: 16. Given the stage direction of line 6a calling for a responsory and the evidence in the liturgical sources for just such a chant (Catalogue [4D]), however, there can be no doubt that the incipit *Homo quidam fecit* in the Lddv refers to the Corpus Christi responsory that begins with these words. Luke is indeed the source of this responsory, as well as of an older antiphon with the same or similar incipit since both liturgical chants use words from Luke 14: 16-17. Yet in both cases, the text is slightly different from Luke; in the responsory, it is even combined with words from the Old Testament as the following comparison shows:[1]

BIBLICAL TEXTS	LITURGICAL TEXTS
LUKE 14: 16-17	RESPONSORY
16. Homo quidam fecit coenam mag- nam et <u>vocavit multos.</u> 17. <u>Et</u> misit servum suum hora coe- nae dicere invitatis ut venirent quia <u>iam</u> parata sunt omnia.	RESPOND *Homo quidam fecit cenam magnam et misit servum suum hora cene dicere invitatis ut venirent Quia parata sunt omnia.*
PROVERBS 9: 5 Venite comedite panem meum et bi- bite vinum quod miscui vobis.	VERSE *Venite comedite panem meum et bibite vinum quod miscui vobis.* REPETENDA *Quia parata sunt omnia.*
	ANTIPHON (CAO 4536) *Quidam homo* [or *Homo quidam*] *fecit cenam magnam et vocavit mul- tos, et misit servum suum hora ce- nae dicere invitatis ut venirent, quia omnia parata sunt, alleluia.*

[1]Words in Luke omitted in the responsory are underlined. Only four of Hesbert's sources for the antiphon begin with the biblical word sequence *Homo quidam fecit* (Sigla VDFS); in the other six, the incipit is slightly changed to *Quidam homo fecit* (Sigla CBMHRL). For a translation of the responsory, see below, p. 135.

The differences between the biblical text and the liturgical versions, i.e. the omission of a few words in the responsory, and the different word order in the antiphon, often occur in chant texts. Liturgical composers were creating new textual/musical units and had to abide by other rules than strict fidelity to the scriptural text. Examining precisely this problem of scriptural conformity in Carthusian chant, Hansjakob Becker discusses the two guiding principles used in the composition of liturgical chants: *Schriftvariation* and *Schriftkomposition*. Scriptural variation refers to the omission or rearrangement of words in the underlying biblical text in response to poetical/musical needs. With scriptural composition, or *cento* technique, biblical texts of quite different origin are combined like 'patchwork' (*cento*) into a new textual unit.[2] In the responsory *Homo quidam* both principles are at work, the former in the respond, where the text of Luke is treated liberally; the latter in the selection of the verse, which is 'patched' from Proverbs 9: 5 to the Lucan text of the respond. The combination in one and the same chant of texts from the Old and the New Testament (as *prae-* and *post-figuratio*) is said to have been particularly favoured by Thomas Aquinas.[3]

No play prior to the Lddv seems to have made use of the responsory *Homo quidam*. In the fifteenth-century Bozen Ascension Play, this chant is used to introduce and accompany the scene in which the risen *Salvator* breaks bread with his disciples for the last time before he ascends to Heaven (BozHi 674 a-f):

Tunc SALVATOR cum APOSTOLIS cantat   *Homo quidam fecit …*
Cum cantant versum   *Venite comedite*
JHESUS dat cuilibet manducare
et bibere solitarie.

[2]Becker (1971) 94-95. The term 'cento technique' or 'centonization' is generally used to refer to the combination of different biblical selections into a single unit for Gospel and lesson readings in the Gallican rite; cf. Jungmann (1948) 1: 498-499; Vogel (1975) 256. Musicologists have used the term to describe the process of composing the texts and even the melodies of some liturgical chants by combining pre-existing text and musical sections; cf. Hucke (1963) 318; Stevens (1986) 287-288.

[3]C. Marbach (1907) 83*. The controversial attribution of this responsory and the entire Corpus Christi Office to Thomas will be discussed below.

The evidence for a responsory here is clear since the verse is specifically mentioned.[4] In several of the large Passion plays of the fifteenth and sixteenth centuries, such as Eger and Admont and some plays from Tyrol, the *Homo quidam* serves as an introduction to the historical scene of the Last Supper. The genre of chant is not indicated in any of these plays, but the *Homo quidam* is recognizably the responsory although until recently no editor has ever suggested as much (except Lipphardt for the BozHi).[5]

These late Passion plays[6] make very free use of the original responsory *Homo quidam* and its verse, separating respond and verse by a number of interposed vernacular or Latin lines or words, in some cases even breaking up the respond section of the responsory into two parts separated by fifty-four vernacular lines (SterzP)[7] or omitting its last part and replacing it with a new chant (EgerP).[8] The latter play appears extreme also in its treatment of the verse, which is made almost unrecognizable by interspersed Latin words and vernacular couplets. Furthermore, two of the plays, SterzP and AdmP, clearly indicate through their Latin texts that a troped form of the responsory *Homo quidam* should be sung. This hitherto overlooked fact as well as the other untraditional forms in the dramatic use of this chant are sufficiently important to deserve further investigation.[9]

A tremendous distance from liturgical customs is apparent in these late plays; the sense of respect for a liturgical work of art as a textual-musical unit has been subordinated to the new concept of a dramatic work of art: the 'appropriate' placing of the responsory's words (or other Latin texts) within the dramatic action has become more important than the unity of the liturgical chant that is being used. In the Eger play

---

[4]Lipphardt recognized it as a responsory (ed. Lipphardt-Roloff [1986] 1: 468) without, however, providing the source for the text he prints in the apparatus. See now Lipphardt-Roloff (1996) 6.2: 62, where Traub presents the entire responsory in facsimile from *A*Pat and refers to other plays that use this responsory. It should be noted, however, that the choral performance of the verse in BozHi is not proper to this liturgical genre.

[5]Traub has recently corrected this situation; see preceding note.

[6]Except TirP; in ll. 339c-e, Jesus is to sing the chant while he walks with his disciples toward the host (*hospitem*) for the Last Supper; nothing but the two-word incipit is given.

[7]Apparently, this arrangement was not liked; at least, no other Tyrol play splits the main body of the responsory into two sections.

[8]All relevant texts of the plays mentioned here are quoted in Catalogue [4C].

[9]The corresponding text passages of these two and other plays are quoted in the Catalogue [4C2], pp. F15-F17. See also below, p. 134 and n35.

and the various Tyrol plays, even the manner of performance has become non-liturgical: the whole responsory, not just the verse, is performed as a solo chant by the *Salvator*, whereas the Admont play maintains the liturgical alternation of choral singing in the main body of the responsory (Jesus and his disciples) and solo singing in the verse (Jesus alone).[10]

In the much earlier Lddv, on the other hand, the links to the liturgy are still very strong. The responsory is introduced as such in the rubrics (*Corus cantat Responsorium*), and it is sung by the choir, not by a group of characters. This in itself more or less guarantees a liturgical performance of the chant with alternation of solo and choir parts. Furthermore, the original version of the *Homo quidam* was certainly intended in the Lddv, not its later troped form for which I could find no evidence in the medieval liturgical sources except for some much later sources of Vorau and of Mainz.[11] The extended text found in these late plays, therefore, is of no relevance for the incipit in the Lddv. And since, as far as we know, no other early play uses the *Homo quidam* responsory, it can be assumed that the author of the Lddv took it directly from the Corpus Christi liturgy, which was then very new. Indeed, as we shall see, only a few years may have elapsed between the final adoption of the Corpus Christi Feast and the first known performance of a Ten-Virgins play in Eisenach.

The dissemination of the responsory *Homo quidam fecit* is closely linked to that of the Feast of Corpus Christi for which it was composed.[12] Much intensive research has been done on the institution of

---

[10]The EgerP does in fact provide for an alternation of solo and ensemble chanting by having the *Chorus* sing the added Latin chant at the place of the *repetenda*, thus interrupting the solo performance of the *Dominica Persona* through some choral responding.

[11]See Catalogue [4D2(a) and 3], pp. F18-F19: the fifteenth-century Gradual of Vorau (*GVor.22*) of the Church of Salzburg and the *Enchiridion* of Mainz, *PsMz.D820*; cf. variant (a) in the apparatus below, p. 134. Since the Council of Trent abolished all tropes, they are not normally found in liturgical books after 1568, when the breviary was thoroughly revised (Bäumer [1895] 438-466). The *PsMz.D820* of 1607 is one of the few exceptions.

[12]The church celebrated the new feast on the Thursday after Trinity because too many other liturgical customs and traditions precluded any celebration of the institution of the Eucharist on Maundy Thursday. Pope Urban IV gives this explanation in his bull of 1264: "In die namque Cene Domini, quo die ipse Christus hoc instituit sacramentum, universalis ecclesia pro penitentium reconciliatione, sacri confectione crismatis, adimple-

this feast, by such eminent scholars as Browe, Lambot, Delaissé, van Dijk, Kern, P.M. Gy, the musicologist Mathiesen, and the Dominican Zawilla in his Toronto dissertation on the topic. Two facts have somewhat obscured the history of the Corpus Christi Feast and an understanding of the liturgies connected with it. First, it took over fifty years from the time the feast received official approval in Pope Urban IV's bull *Transiturus* of 1264, until it was generally instituted in the Western Church following the publication of the *Clementines* in 1317.[13] Second, there has been much controversy regarding the date and authorship of some of the liturgies composed for the celebration of this feast in the thirteenth century and after.

The second issue is of particular interest with respect to the Lddv since the responsory *Homo quidam* has its liturgical place in the so-called Roman Office *Sacerdos in aeternum* (hereafter quoted by Zawilla's siglum *SIA*), which has been at the centre of scholarly discussion because of its controversial attribution to Thomas Aquinas.[14] Thanks to the work of Zawilla, there is now little doubt that the text of the Office *SIA*, and hence, also the responsory *Homo quidam*, was composed by Thomas, probably in 1264.[15] Moreover, Zawilla provides strong evidence that the important Paris manuscript BN lat. 1143, which contains the *SIA* with musical notation and marginal notes for the sources of the melodies, can be regarded as the official Curia prototype for the Corpus Christi liturgy, copies of which were sent to several bishops at the time of the feast's promulgation by Urban IV.

In most of the Western Church, the promulgation of the Corpus Christi Feast was halted following the early death of Urban IV in 1264,

---

tione mandati circa lotionem pedum et aliis plurimum occupata plene vacare non potest celebritati huius maximi sacramenti"; cf. Browe (ed. 1934) 31.

[13]For the most recent and comprehensive account of the origins of this feast, the legislation between 1264 and 1317 regarding its celebration, and various aspects related to its liturgies see Zawilla (1985) 1-83.

[14]The sole authority for this attribution, the Dominican historian Ptolemy of Lucca, wrote his *Historia ecclesiastica nova* fifty years after Urban's bull *Transiturus*; cf. Gy (1980) 492; Zawilla (1985) 74-76. This late witness has been contested by some scholars, mainly Delaissé (1949) and Mathiesen (1983); their major argument, however, rests mainly on their analysis of the Paris manuscript BN lat. 755, and is no longer convincing in light of the new evidence brought forward by Gy and Zawilla regarding the nature of this and other sources pertaining to the early history of the Corpus Christi Feast.

[15]Cf. Zawilla (1985) 323-337.

the very year of the bull *Transiturus*. The history of the adoption of this feast in Germany is special, however, owing to the activity of Cardinal Hugh of St. Cher, one of the first promulgators of the feast and papal legate in Germany from 1250 to 1253.[16] Indeed, he may have prepared the ground for the adoption of the Corpus Christi Feast in many German areas prior to the papal bull of 1264, so that the feast took better hold here than in other areas and countries.

Browe has collected a great deal of evidence from liturgical and ecclesiastical sources for the existence of the feast in the late thirteenth and the early fourteenth century, especially in Germany. He concludes that between 1264-1312, the Feast of Corpus Christi was introduced into more monasteries and dioceses than had hitherto been believed, especially in northern Germany.[17] Yet, even in German areas, the feast was far from being generally adopted before the Council of Vienne (1311). According to Browe, the cathedral of Mainz is one of the few churches that adopted the feast after Urban's bull was reinforced at the Council of Vienne; the rest of the archdiocese followed suit only after Pope John XXII officially published the *Clementines* in 1317.[18] This means that the Corpus Christi Feast can be assumed to have been generally adopted in Thuringia in or after 1317.[19]

A quick look at the Dominican Order's attitude to the Corpus Christi Feast might be appropriate here, since the performance of a Ten-Virgins play in Eisenach in the year 1321 took place on the annual Dedication Feast of the local Dominican Church, and since claims have been made that the author of the play was a Dominican.[20] In Germany at least, the Dominican Order was the earliest of all the Orders to support and promulgate the new feast, especially through Cardinal-Legate Hugh of St.

[16]See his decree of 1252, addressed to the entire district of his legation, in Browe (ed. 1934) 23-26; compare "Vita beatae Julianae" (pp. 16-18). Now also Zawilla (1985) 22-24. For the extent of Hugh's activity as a papal legate see Browe (1928) 141-142; Blume (1909) 339-340; Bonniwell (1944) 223-224; Stapper (1916) 323-324.

[17]Cf. Browe (1928) 141-142; Lambot-Fransen (1946) 20; Zawilla (1985) 24.

[18]Cf. Browe (1928) 143; also Gottschall (1996).

[19]To my knowledge no research has yet been done on the question of which of the various Corpus Christi liturgies was used for the sporadic celebrations of the feast in German areas before 1317.

[20]Cf. Funkhänel (1855) 11; L. Koch (1867) 116; Lienhard (1904-1905) 696; Reuschel (1906) 18; Dörrer (1953) 1132; Brett-Evans (1975) 2: 43.

Cher, a Dominican himself, who as early as 1252 had ordered the observance of the feast for all German houses of his Order.[21] A general chapter of 1304 extended his decree to the whole Order, and it became constitutional through confirmation at the two subsequent general chapters of 1305 and 1306. It was necessary, however, to repeat this legislation in a chapter of 1318 to ensure that it was followed in all houses "as stated in the Vienne Council." Regarding the question as to which office formulary was to be observed, the chapter of 1323 in Barcelona left no doubt that the choice was the office *SIA*, the *officium de corpore christi per venerabilem doctorem fratrem Thomam de Aquino editum ut asseritur* ("the Corpus Christi Office said to be composed by the venerable doctor and brother Thomas Aquinas").[22]

In conclusion, despite earlier celebrations of the Corpus Christi Feast in a few Dominican and monastic houses of the archdiocese of Mainz, it was generally accepted in the religious houses and churches of the Mainz diocese only from 1317/1318 on, after John XXII had 'published' the *Clementines* and sent them to all universities.[23] It is only after this date that the Roman office *SIA* of Corpus Christi would have been well enough known for the responsory *Homo quidam* to be included in a meaningful way in a religious play.[24] The Eisenach performance of a Ten-Virgins play in 1321, then, was immediately preceded by active attempts to promote the new feast.[25] It seems plausible that the responsory *Homo quidam* had a prominent place already in that famous perfor-

---

[21]See above, n16.

[22]For these decrees Browe see (ed. 1934) 41-42, (1928) 138; Bonniwell (1944) 224-225.

[23]This is the time when the feast started to gain a foothold in most other areas of the Western Church because many bishops and religious Orders issued decrees on its celebration. Cf. Browe (1928) 143.

[24]In the later fourteenth century, the responsory *Homo quidam* became a favourite chant for processions connected with the Corpus Christi Feast, and, in the fifteenth century, for the veneration of the Eucharist in weekly Thursday celebrations. Cf. Bruder (1901) 500-506; Browe (1933) 94-108, 149-152; T.H. Klein (1962) 34-36, 52; the Catalogue [4D3], p. F19.

[25]A revealing example of efforts to promulgate the feast in the early fourteenth century after its observance had been reaffirmed by the Vienne Council is a Mainz indulgence charter of 1313, which I found in the bishop's registry of Mainz. Forty days of indulgence are promised by the suffragan bishop Johannes Lovacensis to nuns, when they receive the body of Christ or when they celebrate the office of Corpus Christi once a week; cf. Vogt (1913) 284 no. 1598.

mance of 1321 at Eisenach, although nothing can be said with certainty since MS A of the Lddv dates from some thirty to fifty years later.

Within the *historia de corpore christi* as composed by Thomas Aquinas,[26] the responsory *Homo quidam*, sung as the prolix responsory of the first Vespers on the Eve of Corpus Christi, is part of the opening celebration of the new feast.[27] This placement of the responsory in the liturgy is strikingly paralleled in the Lddv, where the chant is placed at the very outset of the dramatic action. As the *Homo quidam* is sung in the liturgy by a liturgical choir in alternation with a solo singer, so in the play it is performed by an 'impersonal' *Corus* and a soloist, whereas all other chants in the drama are sung by characters of the play. As the singing of this responsory at the beginning of the liturgy 'sets the scene' for the Feast of Corpus Christi to come, so in the Lddv its narrative account foreshadows what the play is all about. The great Lord's Supper is ready and all the invited guests, symbolized by the Ten Virgins, are called to partake of it. The whole play could thus be understood as a play about the Holy Eucharist, a thought that should be kept in mind for an appropriate understanding of the Lddv in its earlier stages.[28] It is worth noting that the 'eucharistic' *Homo quidam* responsory rather than any of the many liturgical chants relating to the parable of the Wise and Foolish Virgins was chosen for the beginning of the dramatic action in the Lddv.

In restoring the melody for this responsory in the Lddv, it should be noted that none of the melodies used in the *SIA* of Corpus Christi is

---

[26]Thomas Aquinas (Turin 1954) 2: 275-281 [*Homo quidam* p. 275]; (Parma 1864) 15: 233-238 [*Homo quidam* p. 233]. Cf. the Catalogue [4D1], p. F17. "Historia" is the name for all the chants and readings for a given feast.

[27]The usual liturgical place for prolix responsories is at Matins. However, the first Vespers on the eve of special feasts was often adorned with the singing of a great responsory after the chapter reading — a widespread custom dating from the time of Charlemagne and Amalarius; see C. Marbach (1907) 99*-100*; Pothier (1910) 173-174; A. Hughes (1982) 68-73. In 'modern' usage, only the Dominicans and some monastic orders maintain this placement for the *Homo quidem*. Cf. Catalogue [4D2], p. F18.

[28]K.B. Ritter (1924), author of one of the twentieth-century versions of the Lddv, may have caught some of this original spirit when he called his play *Das Spiel vom grossen Abendmahl* ("The Play of the Great Supper").

original.[29] As the version found in the thirteenth-century Paris manuscript BN lat. 1143 indicates, all its chant texts are adapted to tunes from earlier chants of various Offices.[30] Thus, the mode 6 melody of the responsory *Homo quidam* is taken from the responsory *Virgo flagellatur* of the St. Catherine Office, one of the more recent Offices.[31] Owing to the late institution of the Corpus Christi Feast and its formulary and to the deferred date of its general acceptance in the Church (after 1311/1317), the liturgical chants, prayers and formulas for this feast start to appear in manuscripts only from the fourteenth century on, often as later additions to earlier manuscripts. This particular responsory cannot be found with music in any of the published medieval liturgical books except for *A*Pat (printed in 1519, repr. 1985), whereas the slightly older *Regnum mundi* responsory is an original part of such famous thirteenth-century manuscripts as *A*OP(Humb), *A*Sar, and *A*Worc.

I was able to locate the complete responsory *Homo quidam* in eleven different medieval manuscripts from the continent, all of the fourteenth or fifteenth centuries.[32] Since musical notation is either lacking or unreadable in two of these sources,[33] the number of medieval German manuscripts to be considered for the restoration of the responsory *Homo quidam* in the Lddv is reduced to nine sources of German or Austrian origin, or rather to seven from the diocese of Mainz: *A*Mz.II,138 (Cistercian, Mainz, thirteenth century);[34] three Fritzlar antiphonals (*A*Fri.117, *A*Fri.124, *A*Fri.129, all fourteenth century); and three processionals (*Pr*Fri.87, *Pr*Mz.100, *Pr*Mz.II,303, all fifteenth century). If these last three sources are disregarded as being late, the remaining four sources still provide a solid basis for the recovery of chant [4] in its

---

[29]This means that Thomas Aquinas composed the texts only of the Corpus Christi liturgy *SIA* discussed here and matched them with pre-existing melodies of the repertoire — a method that was not uncommon in the creation of newer liturgical chants.

[30]Cf. above, p. 129. The marginalia of MS BN lat. 1143 giving the sources of the melodies in *SIA* are reproduced by Lambot (1942) 95-97; and Mathiesen (1983) 24-25.

[31]See Wagner (1911-1921) 3: 351; Pothier (1910) 174-175.

[32]Cf. the Catalogue [4D2 and 3], pp. F18-F19: *A*Ahrw.2b, *A*Fri.117, *A*Fri.124, *A*Fri.129, *G*Vor.22, (*B*Erf.81), *A*Mz.II,138, (*B*Rh.28), *Pr*Fri.87, *Pr*Mz.100, *Pr*MZ.II,303.

[33]*B*Erf.81 has the text only; in *B*Rh.28, the entire responsory is added (on fol. 14r) in a fourteenth-century hand, with non-heighted neumes.

[34]This date is given in A. Hughes (1982) 392. Because of the presence of the Corpus Christi Feast in this antiphonal its dating should perhaps be revised.

fourteenth-century form for the Mainz archdiocese. This form may be compared with the untroped transmission of the responsory in other German antiphonals: that of *A*Ahrw.2b (ca. 1400, diocese of Cologne), and that of the later *A*Pat (1519, diocese of Passau), and even with the troped version of *G*Vor.22, listed with the other sources in Catalogue [4D2].

Apart from the text of the trope in *G*Vor.22, variants in these different German transmissions of the *Homo quidam* are negligible in the respond as well as in the verse, even in the later version of *A*Pat. Noteworthy in all fourteenth-century and some fifteenth-century sources is the long melisma over the penultimate syllable in the respond, the *om-* of *om-nia*.[35] Since, as with most of its chants, the Thuringian play probably drew the *Homo quidam* responsory directly from liturgical sources of the Mainz diocese, its transmission in any of the Fritzlar antiphonals will come very close to the chant the author of the Lddv had in mind. I therefore propose the restoration of chant [4] from the Corpus Christi responsory *Homo quidam* as transmitted in *A*Fri.129:

Responsory   *Homo quidam fecit* [*cenam magnam et misit servum suum hora cene dicere invitatis ut venirent. Quia parata sunt omnia.*[a]

Verse   *Venite comedite panem meum et bibite vinum*[b] *quod miscui vobis.*

Rep.   *Quia parata sunt omnia.*

< Dox.   *Gloria patri et filio et spiritui sancto.*

Rep.   *Quia.* >]

    Source   *A*Fri.129, fol. 136r (= *A*Fri.117, fol. 139r; *A*Fri.124, fol. 154v; and most other sources compared; cf. Catalogue [4D2], pp. F18-F19.)

    Variants   [a] *omnia*] *omnibus firmiter credentibus cibaria vitam* [sic] *conferencia angelica celicaque gaudia omnia.* *G*Vor.22: *Ps*Mz.D820, and AdmP [*cibaria vite*]; *omnibus* EgerP.

        [b] *vinum*] *vinum meum* Thomas Aquinas (see Catalogue [4D1], p. F17).

---

[35]The texting of this melisma resulted in the trope which is transmitted in some late sources, for instance in *G*Vor.22 and *Ps*Mz.D820, and which has been used in the two Passion plays of Sterzing and of Admont; cf. Catalogue [4CD], pp. F16-F17, F18-F19.

Melody   Mode 6. The responsory is transcribed in Chapter 4 **[4]** from *A*Fri.129, fol. 136r.

Melody = *A*Fri.117; ~ = *A*Fri.124, *A*Mz.II,138, *Pr*Mz.II,303, *Pr*Mz.100, *A*Ahrw.2b, *G*Vor.22, *A*Pat; ~ *var.* (probably a scribal error, over the words *omnibus firmiter credentibus* of the trope) AdmP; *var. Pr*Fri.87 (with a much shorter melisma over ***om***-nia). Cf. Catalogue **[4DE]**, pp. F17-F19.

Translation   "A certain man made a great supper, and he sent his servant at the hour of supper to tell the invited guests, that they should come. For all things are now ready. Come, eat my bread, and drink of the wine which I have mingled for you. For all things are now ready. < Glory be to the Father and to the Son and to the Holy Spirit. For all things are now ready. > "

[5] *Dicite invitatis ecce prandium meum paravi.*
Venite ad nuptias dicit dominus (Lddv 6e-g)

What chant **[4]** *Homo quidam* told in narrative is immediately translated into dramatic action and dialogue when the *Dominica Persona* rises to sing chant **[5]** *Dicite invitatis*, charging his messengers, the Angels, to go out and summon the invited guests since everything has been prepared for the banquet. This is the real beginning of the play's action; unlike the three preceding responsories which served as a kind of 'overture' and were all in Latin only, with no 'translation,' from here on, all Latin chants except **[23]** will be followed by a vernacular paraphrase.

Since the text is given *in extenso* in the manuscript of the Lddv, most editors have had no real problems with it. The exception is Otto Beckers who, without justifying his changes, omits the *ecce* and the last two words *dicit dominus*, the explicit of the chant, which he mentions only in the apparatus. Karin Schneider has restored the complete manuscript text for this chant, but De Boor in his edition of 1965 still adopts Beckers' truncated version. Furthermore, since all editions indicate Matt. 22: 4 as the source for this text, its liturgical nature as an antiphon has not been recognized. It is necessary, therefore, to discuss both text and music of chant **[5]**.

The text given in MS A of the Lddv is not that of Matthew 22: 4 but of the *Benedictus* antiphon for Lauds on the twentieth (or twenty-first) Sunday after Pentecost:[1]

BIBLICAL TEXT	LITURGICAL TEXT
MATTHEW 22: 4 Dicite invitatis: Ecce prandium meum paravi, <u>tauri mei et altilia occisa sunt, et omnia parata</u>: venite ad nuptias.	ANTIPHON (CAO 2202) Dicite invitatis, ecce prandium meum paravi; venite ad nuptias <u>dicit dominus</u>.

As we saw above with **[4]**, the differences between the liturgical and the biblical texts are the result of the principle of 'scriptural variation'

---

[1]The twenty-first Sunday is the twentieth Sunday after Trinity. For the different allocations in the sources see the Catalogue **[5D]**, pp. F20-F21.

(*Schriftvariation*).[2] Matt. 22: 4, then, is the ultimate, but not the immediate source of the chant in the Lddv.

The antiphon *Dicite invitatis* belongs to the old Gregorian repertoire, in the secular as well as the monastic rite, and is well documented in most sources. The only notable textual variant is found in the antiphon's explicit. All the medieval German manuscripts I have studied share the reading (i) *dicit dominus* with the Lddv. Some Roman sources (e.g. CAO 2202, the sources CDF) and the 'modern' liturgical books have (ii) *alleluia* instead.[3] According to Hesbert's studies, both explicits occur in secular and monastic sources; *dicit dominus* is found in both German and French sources, *alleluia* only in French sources, with two exceptions, Milan and Worcester.[4] Both can, of course, be sung to the same melodic clause as shown in the following examples:

*A*OP(Humb)	*A*Fri.124	*A*Mon
FE FG G G G	*E F G FG G*	*F FG G G*
di- cit do- mi- nus	di- cit do- mi- nus	al- le- lu - ia
(al- le- lu - ia)	(al-le- lu - ia)	(di- cit dominus)

To modern ears, the comment *dicit dominus* may seem inappropriate for dramatic dialogue, which is probably why Beckers deleted it.[5] At the time of the Lddv, however, such liturgical relics apparently did not present any problem. Liturgical and musical values take priority over 'theatrical illusion,' and in this sense we are still dealing with 'liturgical drama.' The *Dominica Persona* who sings the antiphon is not identical with the *dominus* of the antiphon text, the dramatic impersonation is im-

---

[2]Becker (1971) 95; cf. above, p. 126.

[3]Cf. Catalogue [5D], pp. F20-F21, last column. This antiphon occurs in 111 out of the 150 medieval manuscripts studied by Hesbert. In 66 cases the explicit is *dicit dominus*, in 43 cases *alleluia*; only two manuscripts have neither. Cf. CAO 6: 333 no. 99 *Dicite invitatis* (A. *Dicit dominus;* B. *Alleluia;* C. rien). These two alternative explicits, listed as (i) and (ii) in the Catalogue, occur frequently in liturgical chants; many chants for the Common of Saints, for instance, have an *alleluia* explicit only in the Easter season while during Lent it is replaced with *dicit dominus*.

[4]These two exceptions are the numeric codes 843 and 894 in CAO 6: 333 no. 99 B.

[5]In his attempt to provide chant texts for the St. Gall Passion Play (StGMrhP) from liturgical sources, Pflanz (1977) 121-122, 128, eliminates the *dicit dominus* wherever they occur in a chant, on the grounds that they interrupt the flow of the direct discourse.

perfect.[6] And yet, the dialogue here, both in Latin and the vernacular, is without question dramatic.

The melody of this *Benedictus* antiphon, in mode 8, is naturally much simpler than the melodies of the great responsories that precede it in the Lddv. Three melodic variants in the manuscript transmission are worth mentioning:

(1) In the Fritzlar Antiphonals, in *A*Erf.50a, and also in *A*Pat, the beginning note over *Di-cite* is an *E*, leading into the podatus *FG*, while the other medieval books (*A*OP, *A*Ahrw.2b, *A*Mz.II,138) begin on the *F*, also followed by the podatus *FG*.

(2) Over both *prand-ium* and *me-um*, the Fritzlar and Erfurt sources as well as *A*Pat have a podatus *Ga* instead of the mere *a* in other transmissions.

(3) In the clause *E-F-G-FG-G* over *dicit dominus* cited above, the three Fritzlar Antiphonals again agree with *A*Erf.50a and *A*Pat, as opposed to the slightly different clauses in the other sources, such as the one in *A*OP(Humb).

The fact that the textual and melodic transmission of the antiphon *Dicite invitatis* in the Thuringian source *A*Erf.50a is identical to that in all three Fritzlar Antiphonals can serve to corroborate the working hypothesis underlying this whole study that the medieval liturgical books of Fritzlar are valid sources for the restoration of the liturgical chants in the Thuringian play.[7] Any one of these four medieval sources could, therefore, be used for the plainsong melody of chant [5] in the Lddv. On the other hand, the discovery of a thirteenth-century set of post-Pentecost antiphons in *A*Erf.50a, the only Thuringian source among the four sources mentioned, cannot be ignored. This book, then, the Erfurt *Liber Chori*, with text and music of the chant identical to the Fritzlar transmissions, will be the immediate source for the melodic restoration of the antiphon *Dicite invitatis* in the Lddv:

---

[6]Such 'imperfect impersonation' in the use of unaltered Latin liturgical chants occurs even in late medieval Passion plays. Well known is Christ's chant *Hely, hely, lama zabathami*, in which he goes on to provide the Latin translation: ... *hoc est: deus meus, deus meus, utquid dereliquisti me?* (AlsfP, ll. 6159a-c; AdmP, l. 1073 [music on fols. 83v-84r]). A similar case is Mary Magdalene's exclamation in the *Hortulanus* Scene of the "Visitatio sepulchri": *Rhaboni quod dicitur Magister!* (e.g. BrswO 142; ZwiO.I 66, II 230, III 134; MedgVis 60); cf. also Mehler (1984) 36-37; Linke-Mehler (1989) 98-99, 105.

[7]See above, pp. 84-85, and Figure 4.

Text

Dicite invitatis ecce prandium meum paravi, venite ad nuptias, dicit dominus[a].

Source   Lddv MS A, p. 94a (= *A*Erf.50a; *A*Fri.117; *A*Fri.124; *A*Fri.129, and most other sources of Catalogue [5D], pp. F20-F21)

Variants   [a] *dicit dominus*] *alleluia A*Mon; *A*R; most Romano-French sources

Melody

Mode 8. The antiphon *Dicite invitatis* is transcribed in Chapter 4 from *A*Erf.50a, fol. 156r.

Melody = *A*Fri.117, *A*Fri.124, *A*Fri.129, *A*Pat; ~ *A*Ahrw.2b, *A*Mz.II,138, *A*OP(Humb). Cf. Catalogue [5DE], pp. F20-F21.

Translation

"Tell them who are invited: Behold, I have prepared my dinner, come to the Wedding Feast, says the Lord."

[cf. CAO 2202]

[6] *Sint lumbi vestri etc.* (Lddv 22c)

With the singing of chant [6] *Sint lumbi vestri* the *Angeli,* sent by the *Dominica Persona* to announce that the feast is ready, convey the message to the virgins. This incipit has been completed by all recent editors with the words from Luke 12: 35-36, although the subsequent stage direction specifically calls it a responsory (*Finito responsorio,* l. 22a). Schneider and Curschmann-Glier are the only ones to make a definite choice as to the extent of the biblical quotation by printing verses 35 and 36 in their entirety. A comparison with the liturgical text proves again the shortcomings of such a recourse to biblical texts:

BIBLICAL TEXT	LITURGICAL TEXT
LUKE 12: 35-36	RESPONSORY (CAO 7675)
35. Sint lumbi vestri praecincti, et lucernae ardentes in manibus vestris, 36. Et vos similes hominibus, expectantibus dominum suum quando revertatur a nuptiis: <u>ut, cum venerit et pulsaverit, confestim aperiant ei.</u>	RESPOND *Sint lumbi vestri precincti et lucerne ardentes in manibus vestris. Et vos similes hominibus expectantibus dominum suum quando revertatur a nuptiis.*
MATTHEW 24: 42	VERSE *Vigilate ergo quia nescitis qua hora dominus vester venturus sit.*
Vigilate ergo quia nescitis qua hora dominus vester venturus sit.	REPETENDA *Et vos similes hominibus expectantibus dominum suum quando revertatur a nuptiis.*

Both major principles of composing liturgical chants have been used in the creation of this responsory: the last words of Luke 12: 36 are omitted ('scriptural variation') and the text for the verse has been taken from a different biblical source ('scriptural composition' or '*cento* technique').[1]

Although the textual significance of the verse may be debatable in some of the other responsories used in the Lddv, there can be no question about the importance of this particular verse for the unfolding of the action in the play. The command *Vigilate ergo* emphasizes very strongly the theme of necessary vigilance right at the beginning of the play: all the virgins are admonished by the angelic messengers to stay awake and be prepared for the arrival of the Bridegroom. In Matthew's Parable of the Ten Virgins, on the other hand, the need for vigilance (Matt. 25: 13) is expressed only at the end as the 'moral' of the story.

---

[1]Cf. Becker (1971) 95; and above, p. 126.

Consequently, the sleep of the virgins has a different meaning and function in the parable and in the drama. In the biblical version, the sleep of all ten virgins is not considered sinful (Matt. 25: 5).[2] In the Thuringian play, however, and the much earlier Old French *Sponsus* only the Foolish Virgins fall asleep; in doing so, they clearly violate the initial command to vigilance (*Vigilate ergo* in the responsory verse of the Lddv, *Vigilate virgines* in the *Sponsus*).[3]

In his detailed analysis of the function of the sleep motif in the Matthew parable and in these two medieval plays, Ottokar Fischer concludes that the two playwrights misunderstood the biblical narrative.[4] While Fischer is correct in noting a non-biblical conception of the sleep motif, he may be overlooking an essential feature of these plays. The idea that the *Sponsus* and the Lddv are primarily dramatizations of the biblical parable is a still unexamined hypothesis which pervades the literature on medieval drama. Any judgment based on such a hypothesis seems premature. The intrinsic meaning and objective of both plays may be quite different from that of the parable in Matthew, and their authors may have purposefully used only some elements of the parable, its imagery, for instance, to convey a new message.

All we can say at this point is that, unlike the New Testament parable, at the beginning of both the *Sponsus* and the Lddv, Angels give the command to stay awake and alert; in both plays this command is expressed first in Latin, then in the vernacular, although in the Lddv, the vernacular paraphrase of the responsory is only a distant echo of the Latin verse (*Vigilate ergo*):

> daz ir alle bereyt sit
> czů siner grozen hoczit

---

[2]Their sleep has been interpreted, by Augustine and other medieval theologians, as death. Augustine in his sermon on Matt. 25: 1-13 (PL 38: 573-580): "Fatua sit virgo, prudens sit virgo, somnum mortis omnes patiuntur" (PL 38: 576). For early Christian interpretations of sleep in this parable see Fischer (1910) 13-14.

[3]The *Sponsus* (ed. Thomas [1951]) begins: *Adest sponsus qui est Christus, Vigilate virgines!* (ll. 1-2). The call for vigilance in the first Latin stanza recurs in each of the four subsequent vernacular stanzas, sung by Gabriel, as the Old French refrain: *Gaire noi dormet! aisel espos que vos hor atendet!* (*Sponsus*, ll. 24-25, 29-30, 34-35, 39-40: "Do not sleep! Here is the bridegroom who awaits you!")

[4]Fischer (1910) 11-12, 14-15, 25-26.

iz sy tag eder nacht
daz syn mit gûoten werkyn werde gedacht.   (Lddv 29-32)[5]

If this vernacular passage provides internal evidence that the Lddv used the complete responsory *Sint lumbi vestri* with its verse *Vigilate ergo*, there is also some external evidence for such a postulate. As far as I can tell, this responsory has been used in only one other medieval play, the as yet unpublished fragments of the Marburg *Spiel von den letzten Dingen* (MaSp.532) of the fifteenth century.[6] Later than the Lddv by at least one hundred years, the Marburg play also includes the incipit for the verse of the responsory *Sint lumbi*.[7] The fact that in both plays the responsory *Emendemus in melius* follows immediately after the chant *Sint lumbi vestri* further underlines the parallels of the Marburg play to the Thuringian Lddv and its dependency on it.[8]

The internal and external evidence, then, leaves no doubt that the incipit *Sint lumbi vestri* in the Lddv must be completed not from the Gospel text, but from the widely known responsory *Sint lumbi* with its verse *Vigilate ergo*. This example may even confirm the earlier conclusion that the verse should be included in all the responsories of the Lddv as a matter of course.

The liturgical place of this responsory in medieval books is usually in the Common of Confessors, as the last Matins responsory; in some cases, it also appears as a responsory of the All Saints' Feast (usually the seventh responsory of Matins). Its melody in the 'Protus' or D-tonality is unusual in so far as it does not neatly fit into the medieval system of eight modes that defines most other chants.[9] Given its range from A to b^b (to c in the verse), descending to the fourth below the finalis D, it could be considered a plagal mode; however, as the highest pitches are

---

[5]"That you are all prepared for his great feast, be it day or night, that he may be remembered with good deeds."

[6]Cf. above, pp. 2-3 and n8.

[7]MaSp.532, fol. 2v (ll. 156 and 172, my own line counting). In the Marburg play, however, the verse *Vigilate ergo* is separated from the respond by fourteen interpolated vernacular lines which provide the 'translation' to the chant, see Catalogue [6C], p. F22.

[8]For the whole text section in MaSp.532, see the quotations in the Catalogue [6C].

[9]The four 'authentic' modes 1, 3, 5 and 7 (*Protus, Deuterus, Tritus,* and *Tetrardus*) have as their *finalis* (last note) D, E, F, or G. Their *ambitus* reaches to the octave above and includes the note below the *finalis*. The 'plagal' forms of each of these modes (2, 4, 6 and 8) range a fourth lower than the 'authentic.'

beyond the octave range *A-a* of the mode 2 ambitus, the melody clearly moves in both the authentic and the plagal ambitus.[10] In such cases of "excessive ranges," the intervallic structure of a melody counted as the decisive factor in the modal assignment of a chant. Under this aspect, the responsory *Sint lumbi vestri* has traditionally been regarded as being in mode 1.[11] Its verse is sung to a melodious tune, not in a tone, an indicator of the more recent age of this chant.[12]

I compared the transmission of this responsory in seven medieval German sources (including *A*Pat) with the Dominican Codex of Humbert, the thirteenth-century Sarum Antiphonal (*A*OP[Humb], *A*Sar), and the 'modern' *Vaticana* editions, which are mainly based on medieval French manuscripts. Six of the German transmissions (*A*Ahrw.2b, *B*Helm.145.1, the three Fritzlar Antiphonals *A*Fri.117, *A*Fri.124, *A*Fri.129, and *A*Pat) are very closely related to each other, all exhibiting the features that characterize the 'German dialect' of Gregorian chant.[13] The Mainz Antiphonal *A*Mz.II,138, on the other hand, perhaps because of its Cistercian origin, has a few unique variants, shares some others with non-German transmissions, and parallels the other German sources in the melisma over *a nuptiis* at the end of the respond. An interesting common feature connects the four sources from the Mainz archbishopric: the three Fritzlar antiphonals and even the Cistercian *A*Mz.II,138 all use the same repetenda *Et vos* after the singing of both the verse and the doxology whereas the other manuscript sources studied (*A*Ahrw.2b, *A*Helm,145.1, *A*OP[Humb], *A*Sar) make use of a second repetenda, *Quando*, after the singing of the *Gloria patri*. Equally interesting is the fact that the early printed antiphonal of Passau (*A*Pat of 1519) transmits

---

[10]In the terminology of theorists of the thirteenth and fourteenth centuries such chants would be accounted for as 'mixed mode' (*tonus mixtus*); cf. C. Meyer (2000) 204-205, citing Hieronymus de Moravia and Marchettus of Padua. See also Apel (1958) 148-152.

[11]Cf. C. Meyer (2000) 205, with reference to Marchettus of Padua. In the 'modern' Solesmes editions, e.g. the *Liber Responsalis* (*R*Mon) p. 202, the responsory is also marked as a mode 1 chant. Frere (1901-1924) 1: 13, treats this responsory as a mode 2 chant. Apel (1958) 149, lists six other chants of the Protus tonality with a similar excessive range; all are proper Mass chants, four of them in mode 1, two in mode 2.

[12]C. Marbach (1907) 95* mentions specifically the two responsories *Sint lumbi vestri* and *Regnum mundi* (see above [2]) as not following the regular melodic formula for the verse.

[13]The 'German dialect' in Gregorian chant was discussed above, pp. 73-74. Cf. additional observations on pp. 100-102 and 148-149.

this chant in a melodic form which, although transposed up a fifth, is quite close to the Fritzlar transmission, not only in most of the 'German' variants, but also in the choice of the repetenda *Et vos*.

The versions of the antiphonals from Fritzlar, which, like Thuringia, belonged to the archdiocese of Mainz, again appear to be the most appropriate sources for the restoration of the *Sint lumbi vestri* chant in the Lddv. Except for two inconsequential melodic differences, all three Fritzlar versions are more or less identical. I therefore propose the restoration of the responsory *Sint lumbi vestri* as transmitted in *A*Fri.124:

Responsory   *Sint lumbi vestri [precincti et lucerne ardentes in manibus vestris. Et vos similes hominibus expectantibus dominum suum quando revertatur a nuptiis.*

Verse   *Vigilate ergo quia nescitis qua hora dominus vester venturus sit.*

Rep.1   *Et vos similes hominibus expectantibus dominum suum quando revertatur a nuptiis.*

<Dox.   *Gloria patri et filio et spiritui sancto.*

Rep.2   *Et vos*[a].*>]*

      Source   *A*Fri.124, fol. 364r-v (= *A*Fri.117, fol. 335v; *A*Fri.129, fol. 269v; and most other liturgical sources consulted)

      Variants   [a] *Et vos] Quando* (as Rep. 2) *A*Ahrw.2b; *B*Helm.145.1; *A*OP(Humb); *A*Sar.

Melody   Mode 1 (with 'excessive range'). The responsory is transcribed in Chapter 4 **[6]** from *A*Fri.124, fol. 364r-v.

      Melody = *A*Fri.117, *A*Fri.129; ~ *B*Helm.145.1, *A*Ahrw.2b, *A*OP (Humb), *A*Pat (transposed up a fifth); ~ *var.* *A*Mz.II,138. Cf. Catalogue **[6DE]**, pp. F22-F24.

Translation   "Let your loins be girded about and your lamps lit in your hands, **And you yourselves** like those who wait for their Lord when he will return from the wedding.

      Keep awake, then; for you do not know what hour your Lord will come.

      And you yourselves ..."   [cf. CAO 7675]

[7] *Emendemus in melius* (Lddv 42d)

The singing of the penitential responsory *Emendemus in melius* is the *Prudentes'* response to the Angels' command in chant [6]. The *Prudentes* have not been mentioned before in the play; they are singled out from the previously uniform group of the *Virgines* by this response, which is continued in the vernacular paraphrase (ll. 43-72). The remaining Virgins will establish themselves as the *Fatue* when they sing their own response, chant [8] *Tribularer*.

The incipit [7] *Emendemus in melius* was first recognized as the beginning of a responsory *in quadragesima* by Reinhold Bechstein (1866), who quoted the text from the *Elucidatorium ecclesiasticum* by Chlichtoveus (Paris, 1516) in the following form:[1]

> *Emendemus in melius quae ignoranter peccavimus, ne subito praeoccupati die mortis quaeramus spatium poenitentiae et invenire non possimus. Attende, domine, et miserere: quia peccavimus tibi.* (Lddv 42d-j)

This text, adopted in all subsequent editions, requires some improvements. First, none of the editions refers to either the verse or the chant's melody, both of which should be provided from medieval sources. Second, the source cited by Beckers and succeeding editors is Chlichtoveus' outdated liturgical anthology; it must be replaced by more authentic sources. Third, the liturgical and musical implications of this responsory have been neglected, although Ettmüller in his translation of the Lddv and Reuschel in his study on doomsday plays also referred to it as a responsory of Quadragesima.[2]

The liturgical place for this responsory, which clearly belongs to the old Gregorian repertoire, is the first Sunday in Lent ("Quadragesima") where it is sung, very consistently, as the third responsory of Matins.[3]

---

[1]R. Bechstein (1866) 164. For the final complete text of the responsory with its verse, including an apparatus, see below. p. 149; also Catalogue [7E], p. F27.

[2]Ettmüller (1867) 295; Reuschel (1906) 11.

[3]See also the list of responsories for the first Sunday in Quadragesima in CAO 6: 250-251, where the responsory *Tribularer* discussed in Chapter 3 [8] is listed with a similar consistency. It might be noted in passing that, while the value of the data collected by Hesbert in CAO vols. 5 and 6 is undeniable, his proposed reconstruction of an 'archetype' of the Roman antiphonal has met with considerable criticism; see Möller (1984) and esp. (1987) 2, 11 n14.

In addition, this chant was in widespread use as a processional responsory mainly on Ash Wednesday, but also on the first Sunday of Lent, as
it still is today according to the *Processionale Monasticum* (see Catalogue [7D], pp. F25-F27).[4]

A wide variety of liturgical sources is available for the textual and
musical recovery of this chant, which, of course, must include the verse.
The fact that these sources provide four different verses for this chant
(verses A-D, see the last column of Catalogue [7D]) does not really
present a problem. The overwhelming majority of the sources studied,
in fact all the medieval German sources, have verse A (*Peccavimus cum
patribus nostris*); verses B and C (*Converte nos* and *Angelis suis*) are
extremely rare, and verse D (*Adiuva nos*) is limited to *A*Worc and to the
'modern' liturgical books.[5] In Thuringia and in other German areas,
then, the responsory *Emendemus in melius* would have verse A:

V. *Peccavimus cum patribus nostris, injuste egimus, iniquitatem fecimus.*

And since, according to the stage directions, the *Prima Prudens* is to
begin the responsory with her sisters joining in after the intonation, this
same First Wise Virgin would probably also be expected to sing the solo
verse in the Lddv (cf. above, pp. 50-51).

Unlike verses B, C and D, verse A does not convey any really new
idea, but is merely an extension of the penitential text of the respond
section (Lddv 42d-j); it is difficult, therefore, to determine whether the
subsequent vernacular 'translation' (ll. 43-72) includes the verse. Some
reflections of the Latin verse may be recognized, however, in the vernacular lines that follow:

> ... wy sin geladen alle gemeyne,
> beyde groz unde cleyne,
> daczů dy iungen und dy alden,
> czů den vroůden manicvalden.
> wy sullen in unser kyntheit

---

[4]It is surprising that this widely known responsory is not included in the *A*Pat of 1519.

[5]Had more French and Mediterranean sources been included in this study there would
certainly be more evidence for the medieval use of verse D. Cf. the findings of Hesbert
in CAO 6: 268-269, for the use of the verses A and D in *Emendemus*. The official editions of the 'modern' liturgical books, by the monks of Solesmes, draw almost exclusively on manuscripts of the Romance areas, which, according to Hesbert, present the
'romano-franciscan' or 'Latin' tradition of chant (Hesbert, CAO 6: 245 and 265-269).

werbyn umme eyne sicherheit;
wert iz an daz alder gespart,
we magen vorsûmen dy wirtschaft.   (Lddv 51-58)[6]

While the Latin verse refers to the confession of past sins, including those of the fathers, the vernacular couplets emphasize that although both young and old are invited to the feast, a prudent lifestyle from early childhood is more likely to ensure admission than conversion in old age. Thus, the sins of youth and old age are a concern of both the Latin verse and the German paraphrase.

The only other medieval play that includes this responsory, also after the responsory *Sint lumbi vestri*, is the fifteenth-century Marburg *Spiel von den letzten Dingen*, another argument for this play's dependency on the Thuringian drama.[7] In this fragmentary Hessian play, however, the *Emendemus* responsory is immediately preceded by the verse *Vigilate*, which belongs to *Sint lumbi vestri* but is separated from it by fourteen vernacular lines, a very strange arrangement from a liturgical point of view. It is also open to question whether the responsory *Emendemus* in the Marburg play was to be sung with its verse. Since the stage direction does not indicate the genre and calls for only one of the Wise Virgins to sing the *Emendemus* (see Catalogue [7C], p. F25), the interplay of choir and solo singing, so essential in a responsory and still intact in the Lddv, is lost in the later Marburg play.

Within the Lddv, the choice of a popular Lenten responsory of penitential character at this point seems very appropriate for the development of the dramatic action. All ten *Virgines* have sung their ascetic *Regnum mundi* at the beginning. The five wise ones among them, the *Prudentes*, now sing another responsory as evidence of their readiness to repent and confess in response to the preceding angelic admonition. There is a suggestion that the hitherto unified group of virgins may split into two opposing camps, a division which becomes more evident with the responsory that follows ([8] *Tribularer*).

Musically, the responsory *Emendemus* is in the second mode, i.e. in the plagal mode of the Protus tonality. The typical responsories of this

---

[6]"We are all invited, both strong and weak, also young and old, to the manifold delights. We should strive for a covenant in our childhood; if we leave it for old age we might miss the heavenly feast."

[7]MaSp.532, fol. 2v (1. 174).

mode have been studied and analyzed by Frere for their use and different combinations of 'typical' or 'original' musical phrases or formulas.[8] For the purpose of comparison, Frere has lettered the component members (phrases, formulas) of a given plainsong melody usually after their closes. He distinguishes them further by numerals, so that different phrases with closes in D, for example, are marked as D^1, D^2, D^3 etc. For the second mode he observes that many of the responsories, all belonging to the early Roman collection of responsories, are combinations of various common, "well-defined formulas" and their melodic structure follows an "unusually homogeneous scheme."[9] The *Emendemus* responsory diverges slightly from this scheme with two phrases (marked by a line —) not included in the common formulas. Frere summarizes its melodic structure as:[10]

$$O \ D^1 - - D^1 \ \Gamma \ D^{3\hat{u}}$$

My studies of the melodic transmission of this responsory were limited to the nine medieval manuscripts with readable musical notation listed in the Catalogue [7D1(a) and (b), siglum •], eight of them secular, one monastic. 'Modern' liturgical books were consulted for additional comparisons. The striking result of this comparison is that all six German sources abound in those melodic features that are typical for the 'German' chant dialect with its avoidance of semitones and its preference for thirds and other melodic leaps over tunes in tonal steps.[11] These 'German' variants (e.g. *aca* instead of *aba*)[12] occur mostly in the middle of a phrase, or at its end as the cadence *ca*, or sometimes within a melisma. Even the verse, which is a recitation tone, shows this feature

---

[8]Frere (1901-1924) 1: 5-16 (mode 2 responsories). To Frere's method may be compared the slightly different and more recent approach by Hucke (1973). The *Emendemus* responsory would belong musically to the 'typical' responsory tune of mode 2, for which Hucke (pp. 182-185) transcribes three examples, all transposed up a fifth. See also Apel (1958) 332-337.

[9]Frere (1901-1924) 1: 5. Frere (p. 7) lists a total of thirty-nine responsories that strictly conform to this type.

[10]Frere (1901-1924) 1: 7. *O* stands for 'Opening phrase,' the Greek Γ for a phrase that descends to the 'Gamma' below the bottom *A*. Compare the formula in Apel (1958) 332.

[11]Cf. the discussions above on pp. 73-74, also 100-102 (regarding *Regnum mundi*).

[12]Many of the German sources studied have the notation of this chant transposed up a fifth, so the *finalis* appears as an *a* instead of the *D*. In the regular mode 2 notation, the corresponding melodic variants would be *DFD* instead of *DED*.

in a total of five places. In the following text, the syllables affected by these variants are highlighted:

R. Emendemus in me**lius** quod igno**ran**ter peccavi**mus** ne subito preoccupati die mortis queramus spatium peni**ten**tie et invenire non pos**simus**. Attende domine et mise**rere** quia peccavimus **tibi**.

V. Peccavimus cum patribus **nostris** iniuste **egimus** iniqui**ta**tem fe**cimus**.

Rep. Attende domine et mise**rere** quia peccavimus **tibi**.

Of the twelve occurrences of the variants in the respond section (R), ten can be found in all six of the selected German sources (*A*Ahrw.2a, *A*Fri 117, 124, 129, *A*Helm.485, *B*Helm.145.1); only the seventh and eleventh occurrence (over *invenire* and *peccavimus*) are unique for the Fritzlar or Helmstedt sources respectively. Of the five occurrences in the versus (V), the second and the last are general for all six, the three others can be found only in one or several of the German sources considered.[13]

The obvious source, then, for a valid restoration of chant [7] *Emendemus in melius* in the Lddv is again a liturgical book of German origin, preferably from the Mainz diocese, hence one of the Fritzlar antiphonals which also present the German dialect of the Gregorian melody. I propose as a model the Lenten responsory *Emendemus* as transmitted in *A*Fri.124:

Responsory *Emendemus in melius [quod^a ignoranter peccavimus ne subito preoccupati die mortis queramus spatium penitentie et invenire non possimus^b. Attende domine et miserere quia peccavimus tibi.*

Verse *Peccavimus^c cum patribus nostris iniuste egimus iniquitatem fecimus.*

Rep. *Attende domine et miserere quia peccavimus tibi.]*

---

[13]For a sense of the peculiarities of this 'German' version of the responsory *Emendemus*, its transcription from one of the Fritzlar Antiphonals in Chapter 4 [7] may be compared with the published 'Roman' versions in *A*Sar, *A*Worc, or in one of the 'modern' liturgical books (*G*R, LU, or *Pr*Mon; see the Catalogue [7D1], p. F26), which represent the Romano-French tradition. The observations concerning the melodic form of this responsory may also be compared to Klein's analysis of the second mode responsory *Laetentur caeli* as transmitted in five Rhenish manuscripts; see T.H. Klein (1962) 94-96.

Source   *A*Fri.124, fol. 75r (= *A*Fri.117, fol. 63r; *A*Fri.129, fol.
          71v; *A*Helm.485, fol. 83v; *B*Helm.145.1, fol. 192r),
          collated with other sources listed in Catalogue [7D1], p.
          F26.

Variants [a] *quod*] *que* *A*Ahrw.2a; *A*Sar.; *A*OP(Humb); *B*OP(incun.);
          *B*R; LU; A Worc; *Pr*Mon; Lddv ed. Schneider
          [b] *possimus*] *possumus* *A*Fri.124;
          [c] *Peccavimus*] a different verse (B, C, or D) is used by a
          few other sources; see Catalogue [7D], last column.

Melody   Mode 2. The responsory is transcribed in Chapter 4[7]
                  from *A*Fri.124, fols. 75r-v, where the tune is transposed up
                  a fifth to *a*.

                  Melody = *A*Fri.117 (untransposed, in *D*), *A*Fri.129 (in *a*); ~ =
                  *A*Ahrw.2a (in *a*); ~ *var.* *A*Helm.485 (in *a*), *B*Helm.145.1 (in *D*);
                  var. *A*OP(Humb) (in *D*). Cf. Catalogue [7DE].

Translation   "Let us atone where we have unknowingly sinned, lest
                  we are preoccupied on the day of our death and, all of
                  a sudden, have to seek an opportunity for penitence and
                  cannot gain access. Listen, o Lord, and have mercy, for
                  we have sinned against you.
                  We have sinned with our fathers, we have acted
                  unjustly, we have done evil.
                  Listen, o Lord, ..."   [cf. CAO 6653]

[8] *Tribularer si nescirem* etc. (Lddv 72b)

Chant [8] *Tribularer*, another penitential responsory of Lent, is the response of the second group of *Virgines* to the Angels' call in chant [6]. At the end of this 'scene,' when the Angels sing their next *Silete* call ([9']), it will be apparent to everyone in the audience, even those who did not follow the words closely, that the group of ten *Virgines* has split into two groups, since the *Fatue* literally dance away from their sisters and move to a different place: *Tunc* Fatue *corizando et cum magno gaudio vadunt ad alium locum* (ll. 100a-c).

Ever since Otto Beckers identified this incipit [8] as that of the responsory *Tribularer si nescirem* in Hartker's Antiphonary, the different editions of the Lddv have provided the 'complete' text of the chant essentially as follows:

> *Tribularer si nescirem* [*misericordias tuas domine; tu dixisti nolo mortem peccatoris* **sed convertatur** *et vivat, qui chananeam et* **publicanam** [sic] *vocasti ad poenitentiam*]

This text, of course, lacks the verse, which is essential to any re-sponsory as shown above; furthermore, it contains some variants (high-lighted above) that do not agree with the German sources studied.[1] Of the two verses listed in Catalogue [8D], only verse A (*Et Petrum lacri-mantem suscepisti misericors domine,* "And you accepted the weeping Peter, merciful Lord") can be claimed for the Thuringian play since it is the only one in the medieval German tradition, as is clear not only from my own limited research but also from Hesbert's extensive scrutiny of sources.[2] Verse B (*Secundum multitudinem*), found in the 'modern' *Breviary* and the *Liber Responsalis*, probably belongs to what Hesbert calls the 'Latin' tradition of liturgical chant.[3]

The stage direction for this chant, *Prima Fatua incipit responsorium*, implies that this same *Prima Fatua* is also to deliver both the solo verse to the responsory and the set of sixteen vernacular lines following it, before the *Secunda Fatua* continues with her own paraphrase of the Latin chant. Although none of these twenty-eight vernacular lines explicitly

---

[1] For the final text, with apparatus, see below, p. 154; also the Catalogue [8E], p. F29.
[2] See Catalogue [8D], pp. F28-F29, last column; Hesbert in CAO 6: 267-269.
[3] Cf. Hesbert, CAO 6: 269; compare above, p. 146 n5.

refers to the responsory's verse, except for the allusion to St. Peter (see n5 below), the idea behind the entire text of respond and verse is reflected in the vernacular text, albeit in a distorted and presumptuous way. Paraphrasing the words of the respond about God's great mercy ("God in His mercy does not want the death of the sinner, but rather that he live and be converted"), the first *Fatua* ignores the Angels' counsel for vigilance, suggesting to her sisters that they play games instead and indulge in other amusements inappropriate to times of penitence (ll. 76-88). A sacred text with its promise of God's mercy is misused as an excuse for self-indulgence. Furthermore, when the *Secunda Fatua* in her vernacular speech (ll. 90-100) ridicules the prayers and fasting of the *Prudentes* and calls them names (*dy alten tempeltreten*, "the old temple trodders," l. 92), she not only disparages her wise sisters but also betrays the *Fatue*'s own promise of self-abnegation in the opening chant *Regnum mundi*.[4] Her calculated proposal of thirty years of worldly pleasures before repenting and turning to a monastery somehow parallels the betrayal of Peter referred to in the verse of the responsory: *Et Petrum lacrimantem suscepisti misericors domine*. Peter's repentance, however, was genuine whereas the virgins' 'deferred' penitence is self-contradictory.[5]

The liturgical place of *Tribularer* is close to that of the preceding chant [7] *Emendemus*, both of which are documented in the oldest liturgical sources and belong to the traditional Gregorian repertoire for Lent, more specifically to the Matins chants for the first Sunday of Quadragesima. The *Tribularer* is usually sung as one of the responsories in the third nocturn, in both the secular and the monastic rite.[6] As used in the Lddv, this chant of penance loses its original significance; the *Fatue*, in their light-hearted overconfidence bordering on presumption, twist the meaning of the words, turning a genuine penitential responsory into one of defiance.

---

[4]"The kingdom of the world and all earthly trappings I have spurned for the love of my Lord Jesus Christ ... ." Translation from *BOP* (1967) p. [140].

[5]Betrayal as the common denominator between Peter and the *Fatue* is not made explicit in the vernacular words, since the *Secunda Fatua* cites Peter's name in a different context — Peter as the doorkeeper of Heaven: *hat uns got syn riche beschert, ich weiz wol, daz iz uns nummir sente peter gewert* (ll. 99-100: "I know that if God has given His kingdom to us Saint Peter will never banish us").

[6]See Catalogue [8D1], pp. F28-F29, and Hesbert in CAO 6: 267-269, 281. It is surprising that this responsory, like the *Emendemus* that precedes it, is not part of *A*Pat.

We are witnessing here an extreme in the use of liturgical chants for dramaturgical purposes. The transfer of liturgical chants or texts from one liturgical place to another, typologically similar place was practised throughout the Middle Ages and thereafter, a practice that facilitated the use of liturgical items in religious plays. The responsory *Tribularer*, however, has been transferred from its original place within the Lenten penance to a typologically dissimilar place in the Lddv, a place that is non-liturgical, even anti-religious. The chant here has a purely dramaturgical function in singling out its singers as rebels. It perverts the religious intention of a given liturgical chant while maintaining its textual and musical integrity. Thus the author of the play succeeds in expressing the very opposite of genuine worship by liturgical means. The outcome of the play will balance the scales and set the account straight.

The melody of the responsory *Tribularer* is in the eighth mode, different in its structure from most other chants of this mode but using melodic formulas common to all of them.[7] Variants in the chant's musical transmission are of the kind observed in the earlier chants, the German manuscripts again presenting a more uniform version compared with the 'Roman' or Dominican sources. It is surprising that the monastic *A*Worc agrees with several of the 'typically German' variants.

For the recovery of the full text and music of this chant [8] in the Lddv, the Fritzlar antiphonals, along with the Erfurt Breviary, should again be consulted. I propose to use the following Lenten responsory from *A*Fri.124 as a model:

Responsory	*Tribularer si nescirem* [*misericordias tuas domine; tu dixisti nolo mortem peccatoris sed ut*[a] *convertatur et vivat. Qui chananeam et publicanum*[b] *vocasti ad penitentiam.*
Verse	*Et petrum*[c] *lacrimantem suscepisti misericors domine.*
Rep.	*Qui chananeam et publicanum vocasti ad penitentiam.*[d]]
	Source *A*Fri.124, fol. 76r (= *A*Fri.117, *A*Fri.129, *B*Erf.81)
	Variants [a] *ut*] om. *A*OP(Humb), *B*OP(incun.) *A*Sar, *A*Worc; previous editions of the Lddv since Beckers (1905); *ut magis* *R*Mon

---

[7]Cf. Frere (1901-1924) 1: 56. The opening and closing formulas of the *Tribularer* can be related, e.g. to the corresponding sections in the 'typical' melody for mode 8 responsories as presented by Hucke (1973) 185-187.

^b *publicanum*] *publicanam* editions of the Lddv since Beckers (1905)
^c *Et petrum*] 'modern' sources have a different verse, v. B (*Secun-dum multitudinem* ...); om. editions of the Lddv since Beckers (1905). Cf. Catalogue [8D], pp. F28-F29, last column.
^d *Qui chananeam* ...] *Tu dixisti* ... (as repetenda) *A*Ahrw.2a; *B*Helm.145.1.

Melody

Mode 8. The responsory is transcribed in Chapter 4 [8] from *A*Fri.124, fol. 76r-v.

Melody = *A*Fri.117, *A*Fri.129; ~ *A*Helm485, *B*Helm.145.1, *A*Ahrw.2a; ~ *var*. *A*OP(Humb).

Translation

"I would be distressed did I not know your mercy, Lord. You have said, 'I do not want the death of the sinner, but rather that he convert and live.' You who have called to penitence the Canaanite woman and the publican.
And you accepted the weeping Peter, merciful Lord. You who have ..."   [cf. CAO 7778]

[10] *Beati eritis cum vos oderint homines*
(Lddv 100h)

Before chant [10] is sung, the Angels' signal [9'] *Silete longam horam* has given a clear message to the audience: "Be quiet and attentive for a long while! The preceding little 'scene' is only the beginning. There is more to come."[1] While the worldly amusements of the *Fatue* would most likely continue in the background,[2] the focus changes to the *Prudentes*, who respond to their sisters' sneering and mockery with chant [10] *Beati eritis cum vos oderint homines* ("Blessed are you when people hate you ... ").

A major problem here is the chant's liturgical genre. Luke 6: 22, which in the various editions has been given as the source of the chant ever since L. Bechstein first suggested it in 1855, can be regarded only as the ultimate source. The Lddv clearly calls the chant a *responsorium*; yet an examination of medieval liturgical manuscripts has shown that the full wording of its incipit can so far only be identified as an antiphon (cf. Catalogue [10D1 and 2], pp. F30-F31):

> *Beati eritis cum vos oderint homines, et cum separaverint vos, et exprobraverint, et ejecerint nomen vestrum tamquam malum propter filium hominis; gaudete et exsultate, ecce enim merces vestra multa est in coeli.*[3]

A responsory beginning *Beati eritis* is found in a few liturgical sources, yet only its first three words match the play's chant incipit. The phrase *cum vos oderint homines*, however, begins verse A of this responsory in four out of six sources documented by Hesbert (cf. Catalogue [10D1]:

---

[1] Cf. the discussion above in Chapter 3 [3'], especially pp. 106 and 110. For the musical delivery of chant [9'], discussed in the context of the other *Silete* calls, see particularly pp. 114-120, with Figure 11 offering the proposed recitation formula for both *Silete* and *Silete longam horam*.

[2] Cf. ll. 100a-c: *Tunc Fatue corizando et cum magno gaudio vadunt ad alium locum.* See also below, p. 161. The *Simultanbühne* ("simultaneous stage"), customary on the continent, made it easy to stage ongoing pantomime action in the background; the localities or *loca* required for a performance were always 'simultaneously' in sight, and "the actors remained in their respective *loca* throughout the entire play," entering the action from those basic stations. Cf. Linke (1993b) 34-35.

[3] CAO 1580 (MSS CEMV HRDFSL). For a translation, see below, p. 160.

Resp. *Beati eritis cum maledixerint vobis homines et persecuti vos fuerint,*
       et dixerint omne malum adversum vos, mentientes, propter me.
       Gaudete et exultate, quoniam merces vestra copiosa est in coelis.
V.   *Cum vos oderint homines et cum separaverint vos, et exprobra-*
       verint et ejecerint nomen vestrum tamquam malum propter filium
       hominis.
Rep.   *Gaudete ... .*[4]

With such findings the decision for the 'right' chant is difficult. The choices are:

1) the responsory *Beati eritis cum maledixerint* because the rubric iden-
    tifies the chant as a *responsorium*; in this case, the incipit would have
    to be considered faulty.
2) the antiphon *Beati eritis cum vos oderint homines* because its incipit
    is identical to that in the Lddv; this would imply that *responsorium* in
    the stage direction is faulty.
3) to declare that a responsory with the given six word incipit has not yet
    been found.

Before deciding on any of these three options, some other factors need to be taken into account. There is very little difference in content between the texts of the chants as quoted above; both are based on the biblical Beatitudes, the antiphon using the words of Luke 6: 22-23, the responsory using the parallel version from Matthew 5: 11-12 as well as Luke 6: 22 for the verse. No secure indication as to which of the two chants is meant can be found in the subsequent vernacular couplets, which are in any event only a paraphrase, not a real translation of the Latin chant. The paraphrase appears appropriate for both (I translate from Lddv, ll. 101-116):

Rejoice, dear sisters, God endured hardship and pain so that we would have comfort. Whatever did or could happen to us, our reward will be hundredfold. If we are hated by others, excluded from society, what harm could it mean to us? God himself will love us. And if people despise us,

---

[4]CAO 6174 (MSS HFSL). "Blessed are you if people speak ill of you and persecute you and are lying when they speak all manner of evil against you because of me. Rejoice and exult, for your reward in heaven is great. [V] If people hate you, if they exclude you and insult you and reject your name as evil because of the Son of Man. [Rep.] Rejoice and exult, for your reward in heaven is great."

how kindly will God receive us! Thus be merry and cheerful! The good God is so gentle, he will certainly give us the heavenly kingdom.

After a closer look at the manuscript transmission of the two chants, it may be possible to draw a few conclusions. First, given the fact that a responsory and an antiphon with very similar incipits *Beati eritis cum* did exist in the Middle Ages, it is in my opinion unlikely, although not impossible, that a third chant would have used the same three words as an opening; much less likely even, that a responsory would share all six opening words with the antiphon. The search for a third chant that would perfectly match the data in the Lddv could prove endless and should therefore be given up. Second, the antiphon is contained in a great number of sources, but it is hard to find any manuscript, at least in German areas, that transmits the responsory *Beati eritis cum maledixerint.* Hartker's Antiphonal from the turn of the eleventh century is the only German evidence I could find for this responsory.[5] The fact that it reappears in the monastic *Liber Responsalis* (RMon), which is based on Romano-French sources and was published by the monks of Solesmes at the end of the nineteenth century with the incipit slightly changed to *Beati estis cum*, supports the suspicion that this responsory may belong to what Hesbert calls the 'Latin' tradition of Gregorian chant and that it may have been totally unknown in fourteenth-century Thuringia.[6]

The antiphon, on the other hand, was well established throughout the Mainz diocese and beyond as a Vespers antiphon for the feasts of apostles, in secular as well as monastic usage (see Catalogue [10D2], p. F31). Furthermore, unlike the responsory, the antiphon shows exactly the six-word-incipit spelled out in the Lddv for chant [10] *Beati eritis cum vos oderint homines.* As transmitted in the medieval sources, this antiphon is a long, substantial chant with an elaborate melody in mode 1. Nevertheless, it is an antiphon, and should this chant have been intended in the Lddv, the designation *responsorium* in the stage direction would certainly be incorrect. Such an error could, of course, be explained as negligence on the part of the scribe who, after having written a whole set of incipits of responsories ([1] [2] [4] [6] [7] and [8]) with

---

[5]I could not locate it in any medieval source other than the six collated by Hesbert in CAO 6174 (see Catalogue [10D1], p. F30). Five of these manuscripts (sigla CE FSL) are of French, Spanish or Italian (Beneventan) origin, hence not relevant in our context.

[6]Cf. Hesbert in CAO 6: 269; compare above, p. 146 n5.

correct stage directions such as *cantat/incipiet responsorium*, added one more direction of this kind for chant **[10]**.

Considering all the facts, there seems to be an error here, either in the Latin incipit of chant **[10]** or in the preceding stage direction. In my view, it is much more likely that the scribe would err in the rubrics, i.e. that he would continue, after a series of similar rubrics, to write *incipiet responsorium* (instead of *incipiet antiphonam*), than that he would have changed the actual incipit of the chant. I therefore propose to emend the stage direction to

TERTIA FATUA incipiet [antiphonam] …

Consequently, the six-word incipit for chant **[10]** can remain unchanged, in the form transmitted in MS A of the Lddv.

The antiphon *Beati eritis cum vos oderint homines* appears to be extremely appropriate in the context of the Lddv.[7] Its liturgical place is usually the second Vespers of apostle feasts in both the secular and monastic Office, mostly for the canticle *Magnificat*. As such, it belongs to that class of musically rich, solemn Office antiphons among which Bruno Stäblein finds real gems.[8] In its neumatic setting and with its lively melody spanning an octave, this antiphon would fit very well into the careful selection of outstanding liturgical chants in the Thuringian play.

In the manuscript transmissions, the German sources show the typically German variants. By comparison with the Dominican version of Humbert's Codex, the German versions, particularly the settings in the

---

[7]Even if the reasoning for the emendment of the stage direction is mistaken, the choice of the antiphon would still have good medieval precedents. Often in medieval performances, a chant required in a play but not known locally would have been replaced by a similar one from the available liturgical books; see, for instance, ZwiO.III 48a: *Tunc chorus canit antiphonam sequentem vel similem ex antiphonario*.

[8]"Unter diesen Melodien sind die Juwelen antiphonischer Kunst zu suchen." Stäblein (1949-1951a) 528. Some literary scholars have expressed uncertainty about the musical quality of antiphons for which the melody is not transmitted in the plays (see e.g. Janota [1994] 109-110), but by identifying the liturgical place of an antiphon within the Office, it is often possible to ascertain whether we are dealing with very simple, syllabic settings (most of the psalter antiphons of the week) or with more elaborate, melodious tunes in neumatic or even melismatic settings (usually the antiphons of Matins, Lauds, and Vespers, especially those to the Gospel canticles *Benedictus* and *Magnificat*; also Marian antiphons.) Cf. Stäblein (1949-1951a) 528; Nowacki (1994) 651-659; Huglo (1980a) 476 and 478-479.

three Fritzlar antiphonals, which are more or less identical with each other, are, in general, somehow brighter, more dramatic, with more use of exciting intervals. Interestingly, the Cistercian Mainz antiphonal *A*Mz.II,138 stands somewhat in the middle as it does for other chants, going along largely with the Dominican version but also sharing some variants with the other German sources.[9]

The existing editions of the Lddv, in which the chant incipit is completed from Luke 6: 22 only (ll. 100h-l; see Catalogue **[10B]**, p. F30), overlook not only the beautiful melody but also the joyful textual ending of the antiphon (*gaudete et exultate, ecce enim merces vestra multa est in celis*) — joy over the heavenly reward and recompense expected for all the slander and hatred presently endured; such joy is very clearly echoed in the vernacular words of the third *Prudens*, especially in the last four lines of her speech:

nû sit vro und wol gemût!
der milde got, der ist so gût,
he gebet uns sicherliche
daz schone hemelriche.   (Lddv 113-116)[10]

The antiphonals from Fritzlar with typically 'German' variants will serve as reliable sources for the recovery of the chant *Beati eritis* in the Lddv. With the emendation of the preceding stage direction *incipiet responsorium* to *incipiet [antiphonam]*, I propose the following antiphon from *A*Fri.129 for the restoration of chant **[10]** in the Lddv:

Antiphon   *Beati eritis cum vos oderint homines [et cum separaverint et exprobraverint et eiecerint nomen vestrum tamquam malum propter filium hominis; gaudete et exultate, ecce enim merces vestra multa est in celis.*[a]*]*

Source   *A*Fri.117, fol. 325r (= *A*Fri.129, fol. 262r; *A*Fri.124, fol. 352v; and most other sources listed in Catalogue **[10D]**, p. F31)

Variants   [a] *celis*] *celo* *A*OP(Humb), *B*OP(INC)

[9]Such occasional ambivalence in the chant transmission of the reform orders is noted also by Heisler (1985) 70.
[10]For a translation see above, pp. 156-157.

Melody

Mode 1. The antiphon *Beati eritis* is transcribed in Chapter 4 from *A*Fri.129, fol. 262r.

Melody = *A*Fri.117, *A*Fri.124; ~ *A*Ahrw.2b; ~*var.* *A*Mz.II,138, *A*OP(Humb.). Cf. Catalogue [**10DE**], pp. F30-F31.

Translation

"Blessed are you if people hate you and if they exclude you and insult you and reject your name as evil because of the Son of Man. Rejoice and exult, for behold, your reward in heaven is great."   [cf. CAO 1580 (6174)]

[12] *Surgite vigilemus* (Lddv 116f)

It must be assumed that a great deal of dumb play has been going on during and after chant [10] *Beati eritis* of the *Prudentes* and before the *Tertia Fatua* starts to sing chant [12] *Surgite*. The dancing, playing of games etc. of the *Fatue* (cf. the rubric ll. 100a-c, cited above, p. 155 n2) would have continued in the background while the *Prudentes* attempted to deflect the belittling comments of their 'foolish' sisters (chant [10] and the vernacular ll. 101-116). With the *Silete* call [11'] of the *Angeli* the background action of the *Fatue* is brought back into focus, and the show continues in pantomime since the rubric directs the *Fatue* to have a banquet and, eventually, lie down 'as if they were asleep' (ll. 116c-d).

Suddenly, one of them, the third *Fatua*, begins (*incipit*) the wake-up call [12] *Surgite vigilemus* ("Get up, let's stay awake") to rouse her sisters, and the four other *Fatue* join the chanting.[1] This chant is called an "invitatory" in the stage direction, the kind of chant which is always sung at the beginning of Matins. In his edition of the play (1905) Beckers was able to identify two chants with this incipit in Hartker's Antiphonal.[2] Though their texts differ in length and in content, both seem appropriate for the Advent season to which they belong. Similar to most other invitatories, they are reveilles, so to speak, admonishing those present to get up and stay awake and alert. The shorter invitatory (i) maintains that the king is coming whereas the longer chant (ii) says that the hour of the Lord's arrival is not known. The difference in content is one of urgency:

Inv. (i) *Surgite vigilemus quia veniet rex.*　　　　　(= CAO 1164)
Inv. (ii) *Surgite vigilemus, venite adoremus quia nescimus horam quando veniet Dominus.*　　　　　(= CAO 1165)

Beckers gives no preference to either of these two chants in his edition, though he seems to opt for the shorter form (i). He fails to see the close relationship between invitatory (ii) and the subsequent vernacular paraphrase, particularly lines 125-127, which give an almost exact translation of the chant text:

---

[1]Cf. the discussion above, pp. 60-61.
[2]Beckers' note b to l. 116e is cited in Catalogue [12B], p. F32. Cf. n5 below.

truwen, wy solden wache
und uns bereyte mache!
wy wizzen nicht, wanne der brutegum komit; ... [3]

Instead Beckers states with some surprise that a large textual gap exists
between the invitatory of line 116e and what he assumes to be its vernacular rendering in lines 177-186.[4] Over fifty years later, Karin Schneider
too clearly gives preference to the shorter invitatory (i) by printing it
in her text while burying the longer form (ii) in the apparatus, without
giving any reason for this choice. As a consequence, we now find the
shorter invitatory (i) in all recent editions, since neither De Boor nor
Curschmann-Glier rescued the second invitatory (ii) from its hiding
places in the apparatus of Beckers' and Schneider's editions.[5]

Although medieval antiphonals often do not indicate an invitatory in
their Matins formularies,[6] the longer invitatory (ii) was found in six of
the medieval liturgical sources studied, in three of them with musical
notation on a stave (cf. Catalogue [12D], pp. F32-F33). The only important textual variant, *nescitis* instead of *nescimus* (CAO 1165), is common
to all German sources consulted except *A*Salzb, and it is supported by
*A*OP(Humb). For this reason, the form *nescitis* is preferable in the restoration of chant [12], even though the vernacular text in the Lddv uses
the first person plural (*wy wizzen nicht*, l. 127).

For the musical setting of this invitatory antiphon I have only three
sources for comparison, the Dominican *A*OP of Humbert's Codex and
two books from the Helmstedt collection in Wolfenbüttel (*A*Helm.485
and *B*Helm.145.1) since the antiphonals from Fritzlar do not contain this

---

[3]Lddv, ll. 125-127; "Surely, we should stay awake and make ourselves ready! We do
not know when the Bridegroom will come."

[4]I.e. *Set, hy komit der ware brutegum* ... , which actually paraphrases the immediately
preceding chant [19] *Ecce sponsus venit* of l. 176d. Beckers (ed. 1905) 41: "(Es) ist zu
beachten, daß [der Autor] dort ein Invitatorium gibt, die Worte der Textstelle aber erst
später (v. 177-186) benutzt."

[5]It is probably insufficient familiarity with liturgical terminology and customs that led
Beckers and Schneider (ed. 1964) to these strange choices. Beckers (ed. 1905) 102, note
b to l. 116e, cites the shorter invitatory (i) as *Inv.* "Surgite etc." (*A*Hartk p. 34), the
longer one (ii) as *Antiph.* "Surgite etc." (*A*Hartk p. 149); see Catalogue [12B], p. F32.
However, the rubric in *A*Hartk p. 149, clearly reads *Ant. ad Invit.*, which is what the
term *Invitatorium* means: the antiphon sung to the invitatory psalm (Ps. 94) at the beginning of Matins, the Night Office. Cf. the discussion in Chapter 2, pp. 60-61, with n52.

[6]See A. Hughes (1982) 56.

chant. The Erfurt breviary *B*Erf.81 provides textual evidence, however, that this Advent invitatory was known in fourteenth-century Thuringia.[7] Compared with the thirteenth-century Dominican version from Humbert's Codex, the two Helmstedt sources, which are almost identical, show the typically 'German' leaps of a third over *Surgite, vigilemus, nescitis*, and *horam*. In addition, there are major musical variants over the last phrase of the antiphon, *quando veniet dominus*, as shown in the following melodic comparison:[8]

Humb.Codex	*FE*	*DC*		*DGGF*	*E*	*D*	*EFD*	*C*	*D*
	quan-	do		ve-		ni- et	do -	mi-	nus.

Helmst. MSS	*C*	*E*	*FGF*	*DCDEDE*	*FD*	*DF*	*GF*	*ED*	*EFD*	*CD D*
	quando	ve-	ni - -		et	do- -	-	-		mi- nus.

While the melodic range of a fifth for this final phrase, from *C* to *G*, is the same in both versions, the Helmstedt books provide a much more elaborate, melismatic tune than Humbert's Codex with its simpler neumatic setting. This musically richer version of the invitatory *Surgite vigilemus* will, of course, more likely be the form in which chant [12] of the Lddv was sung, since both Helmstedt manuscripts, dating from the thirteenth and fourteenth centuries, originate in the Church of Mainz, in an area close to Thuringia. And as the text of this antiphon in the Helmstedt sources is identical to that in the non-notated Thuringian breviary *B*Erf.81, both sources can be regarded as authentic for the recovery of text and music of the *Surgite vigilemus*-invitatory in the Thuringian play.

On the basis of the preceding investigations, I propose the restoration of chant [12] in the Lddv from the Advent invitatory as transmitted in *A*Helm.485:

Invitatory *Surgite vigilemus, [venite adoremus quia nescitis[a] horam quando veniet dominus.]*

  Source   *B*Erf.81, fol. 163v (= *A*Helm.485, fol. 20r; *B*Helm.145.1, fol. 49r; *A*Hartk, p. 34)

  Variants   [a] *nescitis*] *nescimus A*Salzb; 6 of the 10 CAO sources (BEMVFL)

---

[7]Cf. Catalogue [12D] Single sources (b), p. F33.
[8]Cf. *A*OP(Humb), fol. 232v; *A*Helm.485, fol. 20r and *B*Helm.145.1, fol. 49r.

Melody   Mode 2. The invitatory is transcribed in Chapter 4 **[12]**
                  from *A*Helm.485, fol. 20r.
                  Melody = *B*Helm.145.1; *var. A*OP(Humb.). *Text* = *B*Erf.81 (no
                  musical notation).

Translation   "Get up, let us be awake, come let us adore, for you do not
                  know the hour when the Lord comes."
                  [cf. CAO 1165 (1164)]

[14] *Date nobis de oleo vestro etc.* (Lddv 140e)
[15] *Ne forte [non] sufficiat nobis et vobis, ite potius etc.*
(Lddv 148b-c)

After another *Silete* call [13'], which ends the *Fatue*'s belated deliberations about how to prepare for the Bridegroom's arrival, the focus widens again to include both the *Fatue* and the *Prudentes*. Implementing their plan to make amends for their foolish behaviour, the *Fatue* approach their sisters to ask for oil (rubric 140c-d), and a short dialogue ensues with the chants [14] and [15], which may be discussed as a unit.

Since the words of these chants figure as direct discourse in the parable of the Wise and Foolish Virgins in Matthew 25: 8-9, this Gospel text is generally considered to be the direct source for the two entries in the play (ll. 140d-e and 148a-c).[1]

QUINTA [FATUA] dicit   [14] *Date nobis de oleo vestro [quia lampades nostre extinguuntur].*

QUARTA PRUDENS respondet   [15] *Ne forte [non] sufficiat nobis et vobis, ite potius [ad vendentes, et emite vobis].*[2]

Although some of the phrases in the parable of the Ten Virgins are used in a variety of medieval chant texts, there is hardly any evidence for the liturgical use of the dialogue words under discussion. Only for incipit [14] could I find a corresponding chant, and that only in the thirteenth-century monastic Antiphonal of Worcester Cathedral (*A*Worc) as the fourth in a set of eight Matins antiphons for the Common of Vir-

---

[1] L. Bechstein (ed. 1855) 42; Beckers (ed. 1905) 103 notes b and c; Schneider (ed. 1964) 22 notes a and b; De Boor (ed. 1965) 187-188; Curschmann-Glier (ed. 1981) 690.

[2] [15] "Not so; lest there be not enough for us and you: but go ye rather to them that sell, and buy for yourselves." (Matt. 25: 9; King James version) In MS A, the beginning of the incipit [15] is *Ne forte sufficiat*, and that is what Fr. Stephan (ed. 1874b) as well as Beckers (ed. 1905) and De Boor (ed. 1965) present in their editions. L. Bechstein (ed. 1855) 19, supplied the <non> after *forte*, on the basis of Matt. 25: 9; Schneider (ed. 1964) ll. 148b-d, and Curschmann-Glier (ed. 1981) l. 148b, also insert the *non*, without, however, marking it as an emendation. Only the biblical wording with *non*, of course, makes sense here as the *Prudentes* reject the request of the *Fatue* for oil.

gins.[3] All six antiphons of the first nocturn and the first two antiphons of the second present a condensed, continuous narrative interspersed with direct discourse of the parable of the Ten Virgins from Matthew 25: 1-13. The text of the fourth and fifth antiphon reads:

> A4 *Date nobis de oleo vestro, dixerunt fatue virgines, quia lampades nostre extinguuntur.*
>
> A5 *Responderunt prudentes virgines dicentes, ne forte non sufficiat nobis et vobis, ite potius ad vendentes et emite vobis.* (*A*Worc, p. 431)

It is highly unlikely that even A4 despite its matching incipit was used in the Lddv. The subsequent antiphon, A5, which contains the reply of the *Prudentes*, would be even less suitable (and in fact does not occur) in the Lddv, since its incipit, taken from Matt. 25: 9, is very different from that in the Thuringian play. What is needed in the dialogue of a play is direct discourse only.[4]

As was discussed earlier, antiphons and responsories in the Lddv are usually introduced by a stage direction with the verb *cantare* or *incipere*. Since the rubrics for the two incipits [14] and [15] use *dicere* and *respondere* instead, the intended chants are very likely not musical chants but rather some kind of liturgical recitation.[5] This conclusion is strongly supported by the fact that in the Divine Service the recitation of holy texts is usually done by one person only. In the Lddv, as well, a single *Fatua* delivers the text of chant [14], and a single *Prudens* gives the reply [15], whereas all previous Latin texts were sung by the whole group of *Prudentes* or *Fatue* or even by all ten *Virgines*.[6] Apart from the missing *non*, an error of transmission, no changes to the biblical text, so frequent in liturgical chants, can be detected in incipits [14] and

---

[3]*A*Worc, pp. 430-431; cf. Catalogue [14D1], p. F35. The whole set of eight antiphons from Matthew 25 at this place in the Worcester Antiphonal appears to be proper to the Worcester Rite since I was unable to find them in any other source.

[4]It is true, however, that medieval plays occasionally make use of chants with narrative texts; cf. the discussion above for chant [5], pp. 137-138 and n6.

[5]See Chapter 2, pp. 61-66.

[6]In the only dramatic parallel to this short dialogue in the unedited Marburg *Spiel von den letzten Dingen* (MaSp.532, fol. 8v, ll. 757, 776; cf. the quotations in Catalogue [14C] and [15C], pp. F34 and F37), both Latin lines are introduced by *dicere* and performed by one speaker only, thus also indicating liturgical recitation for the dialogue.

[15].[7] Hence, these chants belong to a text that is usually intoned as a liturgical reading in the Church service, a *conditio sine qua non*, according to Mehler, for the use of liturgical recitation in medieval drama.[8]

Proof that the Gospel text of Matthew 25: 1-13 was read on different occasions throughout the liturgical year comes from the earliest capitularies as well as from later lectionaries. At least from the seventh century on, this pericope was required reading at feasts of holy virgins, later also in the Common of Virgins.[9] At the end of the thirteenth century, Durandus introduced it into the Roman rite for the consecration of nuns,[10] where it had always had a place in the old Gallican rite.[11] Thus, a number of times each year, the verbal exchange between the Wise and Foolish Virgins was chanted to the Gospel tone within the context of the pericope from Matt. 25: 1-13. Surely, liturgically trained singers would have had no problems performing these short phrases outside the usual lesson context in the form they were chanted at Mass. In a dramatic context, such 'intoned' items constitute what Schuler called a new genre of chant in the drama.[12]

From the stage directions in the Alsfeld Passion Play we know that the different biblical texts used in that play were chanted in a reciting formula indicative of their specific biblical origin, i.e., texts from the Prophets were delivered *sub accentu prophecie*, those from the psalms *sub tercio* (*quinto* etc.) *tono*, and those from the Gospel *sub accentu evangelii*, except for texts from the Passion for which *sub accentu* (i. e., *sub accentu passionis*) was sufficient.[13] Simply by listening to the respective reciting formulas, the attentive audience would thus have known what kind of sacred text they were hearing, even though the exact meaning of the Latin words may have escaped them. It can be safely concluded, therefore, that the dialogue in the Lddv which uses the text from Matthew 25: 8 and 9 was chanted to the Gospel tone, the *tonus*

---

[7]Whether the *non* was written in the MaSp.532 is not known because the beginning of this quotation has been trimmed off along with the whole margin of fol. 8v.

[8]Cf. Mehler (1981) 183 and 216; see also above, pp. 65-66 and n70.

[9]See Catalogue [14DII1 and 2], pp. F34-F35.

[10]See Catalogue [14DII3], p. F35.

[11]Cf. Catalogue [14DII1(c)], p. F34.

[12]" ... eine neue Gattung von Gesängen." Cf. above, Chapter 2, p. 63 and n60.

[13]See above, p. 68 n75; cf. Dreimüller (1935) 1: 172-174; Schuler (1951) 34-36; Mehler (1981) 205.

rectors of plays, at least in the fourteenth century, that there was no need to spell out what kind of recitation was required for a given Gospel text. For a reasonably authentic restoration of this dialogue in the play, then, it is essential to find or approximate the recitation formula for the Gospel tone that would have been used in fourteenth-century Thuringia or, rather, within the limits of the Mainz Church. As was discussed earlier, the conclusion was to focus on the *Accentus Moguntinus* and to use the Mainz recitation formulas, as recovered from the Halberstadt Missal *M*Halb.888, for the melodic restoration of all the short Gospel selections in the Lddv, i.e. for the chants **[14-15]**, **[28-29]**, and **[33]**.[14]

An additional factor in determining the Gospel recitation used within the Lddv may deserve some consideration, the fact that some of these chants **[14, 15, 28]** are performed by either a *Fatua* or a *Prudens*, others **[29, 33]** by the *Dominica Persona*. In the *Accentus Moguntinus*, where the tenor for the Gospel recitation was usually on a pitch with a whole tone below ("subtonal tenor"), the sources offer *D* or *a*, always with the upper third for the accent notes.[15] The implication seems to be that the choice of the lower or higher pitch was left open, dependent on the vocal abilities of the person who was responsible for performing it. It may be suggested, then, that the lower-pitched tenor *D* (with the upper third *F*) should be reserved for the *Dominica Persona*, whereas the higher-pitched tenor *a* (with *c* as the upper third) seems more appropriate for the female characters of the Wise and Foolish Virgins.

With this consideration in mind, I propose that the dialogue between the *Fatue* and the *Prudentes*, chants **[14]** and **[15]** in the Lddv, be restored as Gospel recitation in the *Accentus Moguntinus* in the form presented in Figure 12.[16]

[14]Cf. above, especially pp. 78-81, and the example from *M*Halb.888 in Figure 3.
[15]See above, p. 78.
[16]The example given from *M*Halb.888, fol. <229>v in Figure 3 (above, p. 80; cf. facsimile 4) served as the model to which the Gospel words of Matthew 25: 8-9 have been adapted. The tenor *D* of the model, however, is changed here to the tenor *a* (with the accentuating upper third *c*) for female characters.

FIGURE 12 THE DIALOGUE OF MATTHEW 25: 8-9,
ADAPTED TO THE GOSPEL TONE
OF THE *ACCENTUS MOGUNTINUS*

The vivacity of the musical form of this recitation is striking, and the lively intervallic leaps in the opening formulas are rare melodic features in Roman recitation. Admittedly, there is much less firm ground for an authentic restoration of such 'recitation chants' than for responsories and antiphons, the texts and melodies of which are transmitted in their entirety in liturgical books. And yet, if the purpose is to achieve a closer understanding of a medieval performance such as the Lddv, conjectures are sometimes necessary. In any case, the attempt has been made here to make circumspect use of the available evidence for Gospel recitation in the Mainz Church. The resulting proposal may approximate the medieval reality to a reasonable degree.

Text [14] *Date nobis de oleo vestro [quia lampades nostre extinguuntur.]*

[15] *Ne forte [non]*[a] *sufficiat nobis et vobis; ite potius [ad vendentes et emite vobis.]*

Sources   Lddv, ll. 140e, 148b-c (MS A, p. 96a); cf. Matthew 25: 8-9; *EvOP* (Humb), fol. 454r (with *positurae* markings);[17] *LFri*.142, fols. 224v-225r (text incomplete).

Variants   [a] *non*] Matt. 25: 9; *om.* Lddv MS A.

---

[17]Liturgical books containing the texts for the Gospel and lesson readings usually provided the so-called *positurae* (or *pausationes*) over certain words to help the lector recite the text with the appropriate voice inflections at the various points of punctuation.

'Melody'   Set in liturgical recitation to the Gospel tone, according to the *Accentus Moguntinus* as transmitted in *M*Halb.888 (cf. pp. 78-81, with Figure 3), with the subtonal tenor *a* and the upper third *c* for both [14] and [15]. See Figure 12 above, and Chapter 4 [14]-[15].

Translation   [14] "Give us from your oil; for our lamps have gone out."

[15] "Not so; lest there be not enough for us and you: but go ye rather to them that sell, and buy for yourselves."   (King James Version)

[16] *Omnipotens pater etc.* (Lddv 156d)

This is the first of two chants sung by the *Fatue* at the start of their journey to buy oil for their lamps, as the *Prudentes* had advised them to do in chant [15].[1] Whereas chant [16] is indicated only by its incipit *Omnipotens pater etc.*, the full wording is given for the second chant [17]: *Sed eamus oleum emere preter quod nil possumus agere. Qui caret hoc carebit glorie. Heu quantus est noster dolor.* The beginning words of these two chants as well as the stanza form of chant [17] *Sed eamus* with its refrain *Heu, quantus est noster dolor* immediately remind the scholar of medieval drama of the decasyllabic stanzas 'B1' and 'B3' in many Easter plays from France and Germany, where such stanzas (*Wegstrophen*, 'travel stanzas') are sung by the three Marys on their way to the merchant to purchase ointments for the body of Christ.

The two chants or songs [16] and [17] in the Lddv, sung as solos by the *Prima* and *Secunda Fatua* respectively, are the only Latin musical items in stanza form in the Lddv.[2] The Latin B-stanzas to which they allude are not part of the Church liturgy, nor were they originally part of the *Visitatio sepulchri*, but were composed for the so-called 'Merchant Scene' in Easter plays, the first evidence for which we find in the twelfth-century Catalan Easter play of Vich.[3] In Germany, these stanzas begin to appear in Easter plays of the fourteenth century. The chants [16] and [17] of the Lddv, therefore, are best discussed in the context of the Easter play tradition in Germany.[4]

The following is the text of the three travel stanzas B1-3 in their most common German form:

---

[1]Cf. also the vernacular paraphrase of ll. 149-156.

[2]They will be more than balanced by the twelve vernacular stanzas sung at the end of the play by the *Fatue* as the conclusion of their extensive lamentations. Cf. Lddv, ll. 526-576. For a brief comparison of the Latin stanzas [16-17] and the concluding vernacular stanzas and their function in the play see Amstutz (1994) 41-42.

[3]Cf. Donovan (1958) 78-81.

[4]Most of the Latin and macaronic Easter and Passion plays that contain these B stanzas are listed in Catalogue [16C], pp. F39-F42; their musical notation is usually transmitted in the sources. The Latin plays from Catalonia and France, which include earlier stages of this scene, have been added to the list in the Catalogue for comparison. Also added are two liturgical dramas or rather, 'dramatic ceremonies' called *Osterfeiern* in German. For the elusive distinction between *Feier* and *Spiel* in German scholarship, and John Stevens' (1986) carefully chosen term '(dramatic) ceremony' see below n18.

B1   Omnipotens pater altissime,
       angelorum rector mitissime,
       quid faciemus nos miserrime?
       Heu quantus est noster Dolor!

B2   Amisimus enim solatium,
       Ihesum Christum, Marie filium.
       ipse erat nostra redemptio.
       Heu quantus est noster Dolor!

B3   Sed eamus unguentum emere,
       cum quo bene possumus ungere
       corpus Domini sacratum.

In the German tradition of Easter and Passion plays, the three deca-syllabic travel stanzas of the Marys, with subsequent vernacular para-phrases, are usually followed by three decasyllabic purchase stanzas (*Kaufstrophen*). Together they form the much-discussed Ointment Pur-chase or Merchant Scene (*Salbenkauf* or *Krämerszene*), which was prob-ably created in Spain, possibly as early as the eleventh century, from where it spread to France (e.g. Tours) and most other European coun-tries. A convenient way of referring to these two stanza groups of the Merchant Scene is by the sigla that W. Meyer attached to them: B1-3 for the travel stanzas *Omnipotens pater* etc., C1-3 for the purchase stanzas.[5]

In the first travel stanza (B1), *Omnipotens pater altissime*, the invocation of God Almighty and the lamentations are so general that, even though the stanza was originally composed for the three Marys in Easter plays, the words could be transferred into the new context of the Lddv without changes. Certainly the two-word incipit [16] in the Lddv refers to the B1 stanza: the incipits are identical; the subsequent chant [17] *Sed eamus* with the same incipit as B3, its decasyllabic verse

[5]See W. Meyer (1901) 59, esp. pp. 106-110. A welcome overview of all the Latin stanza groups A-F examined by Meyer is the fold-out "Textschlüssel" in Wimmer (1974), after p. 308. The survey in Smoldon (1980) 308-311, can be confusing because it differs considerably from standard surveys of these stanzas and their numbering. In the Lddv, the author naturally had no use for stanza B2, in which the three Marys give the reason for their lamentations on Easter morning. Stanza B3, however, in which they declare their intention to buy ointments, clearly served as a model for the second stanza of the *Fatue* chant [17]; the text had to be adapted to a similar, but different situation — purchase of oil for their lamps. The C stanzas are of no interest in this study because no merchant appears in the Lddv.

structure, and its *Heu*-refrain clearly alludes to the stanzas of the three Marys in the Easter plays. Even the dramatic function of the two stanzas is exactly the same: lamenting women sing the stanzas on their way to purchase a precious oil for a worthy cause.

This typological sameness permits what Stemmler calls *typologische Übertragung* ('typological transfer'), a technique by which textual and other details are transferred from one scene to a typologically similar one in a different context, e.g. *Visitatio sepulchri — Visitatio praesepis.*[6] There is nothing new in principle about this technique since typological thinking was the driving force in the interpretation of the Holy Scripture and penetrated nearly all areas of religious life throughout the Middle Ages.[7] It also affected the choice and composition of liturgical texts and chants, their 'transfer' and adaptation from one feast to another, similar one. In medieval drama, such typological transfers occurred again and again, as Stemmler has shown for the English cycle plays.[8] Yet, while several chants and details from the *Visitatio* scenes have been used in Christmas plays of various countries, the Lddv is the only play outside the Easter cycle that has adapted to a new context some of the stanzas from the Merchant Scene in the Easter plays.

Most editors of the Lddv see this connection quite clearly, yet they are strangely hesitant to include the complete text of travel stanza B1 *Omnipotens pater* in their editions or even their footnotes.[9] Cursch-

[6]Cf. Stemmler (1970) 123-150 and passim.
[7]See, e.g. Ohly (1977) 312-337, 361-400, passim.
[8]Cf. Stemmler (1970) 165-299.
[9]Beckers' (ed. 1905) 104 note a, only comment is: "Nur so viel in der Hs. Wahrscheinlich der bekannte Hymnus der Marien." Schneider (ed. 1964) 23, surprisingly, does not comment on this incipit. De Boor (ed. 1965) 188 note to ll. 204ff., footnotes both stanzas with an explanation of their source in the Easter plays but does not quote the full text of the first stanza.
Beckers is not alone in using the term 'hymn' for this stanza from the Merchant Scene. Kummer, for instance, persistently calls it a hymn, as do Sievers and Dürre; even De Boor and Flemming employ the term occasionally for the travel stanzas. Cf. Kummer, ed. (1882) xxxiv, 35 note b, 36 note b, 37 note b. Sievers (1936) 29. Dürre (1915) 18: "Der geistliche Dichter hat den Marien einen in sich geschlossenen Hymnus geschaffen." De Boor (1967) 353. Flemming (1971) 14: "Gelegentlich wird noch die Hymne *Omnipotens pater altissime* verwendet." This usage is inappropriate since, as a poetical genre, *hymnus* is restricted to liturgical use and usually ends with a doxology stanza, whereas these travel stanzas are obviously composed for the performance of a play and lead into a secular dialogue. Moreover, they are laments, not songs of praise, and their

mann-Glier are the only editors to refer the reader to the corresponding text of the travel stanzas of the Marys in the Erlau Easter Play (Erl.III), which is included in their anthology.[10]

The text of stanza B1 *Omnipotens pater altissime* is the same in both French and German sources, except for line 3.[11] Of the twenty-nine German plays and ceremonies listed in Catalogue [16], pp. F39-F43 (including the Dutch play of Egmont = EgmontO), twenty-five transmit the full text for stanza B1. Since in these German plays the stanza usually appears in the form quoted above (p. 172), this should also be the suggested text for the Lddv. The stanza displays the general stanza form of the Merchant Scene: three decasyllabic lines and an octosyllabic fourth line, which also serves as a refrain in most other B and some C stanzas. In the German play tradition, the refrain *Heu quantus est noster dolor* is sometimes missing in B2, and usually in B3; with only two exceptions, however, it is always present in B1.[12] It should, therefore, be included in the restoration of stanza [16].

What seems surprising is the relatively early date of the adaptation of stanzas from the Easter plays in the Lddv. A performance of a Ten-Virgins play similar to the Lddv is recorded for the year 1321 in Eisenach/Thüringen, while the earliest Easter or Passion plays with the B-

---

decasyllabic verse structure is one of secular vernacular poetry, to my knowledge never used in Latin hymns; see e.g. the survey of the metrical structure of hymns in Schulte (1916) 10-14. Lipphardt (1948) 33, objects to the term 'hymn' for these stanzas from a purely musical point of view in an analysis of their melody. The more neutral terms 'stanza' or 'song' (*Strophe, Gesang, Lied*), which are preferred by most scholars, are certainly appropriate. The dramatic sources, including the Lddv, usually omit any indication of genre. I found *versus* twice (Narbonne Visitatio [LOO 116], ToursO), *antiphona* in four plays (BozO.IV, TrierO, ZwiO.I and III), and *cantus, canticum* once each (BeThO, AlsfP). Of these, only *antiphona* has a specific liturgical meaning which, in medieval drama, however, is occasionally extended to any kind of sung text.

[10]Curschmann-Glier (ed. 1981) 690, ll. 13-17: reference to no. 29 of their anthology (p. 337).

[11]The different readings of l. 3 are: *Quid facient iste miserrime?* (Vich). *Quid faciunt iste miserrime?* (Tours) as opposed to the German form *Quid faciemus nos miserrime?* For variants within the German stanza transmission see the apparatus below, p. 188.

[12]Cf. the Catalogue [16C1-2], pp. F39-F41, the first column (siglum R). In the Brandenburg (stanzas B1-3) and the Wolfenbüttel (stanzas B1-2) Easter Plays, the refrain is missing in the travel stanzas, yet used as a separate chant of the Marys in the dialogue with the merchant.

stanzas in Germany just barely precede that date.[13] The early adaptation of the stanzas in the Lddv appears surprising, however, only if the dissemination of the Easter plays in Germany is seen as a movement from the West to the East. This view, based on Rueff's thesis (1925) of a hypothetical German *Urspiel* in the Rheinhessen area, went unchallenged for fifty years and was supported by De Boor's additional hypothesis of a lost original Latin Easter play in the Middle or Lower Rhine districts.[14]

The discovery and publication of additional fourteenth-century Easter plays from east-central Germany and U. Hennig's convincing refutation (1975) of Rueff's thesis has completely reversed the picture.[15] The east-central areas, including Silesia and Bohemia, are now seen as the cradle of the German Easter plays; from there the tradition radiated westward to Thuringia and Wolfenbüttel and southward to Erlau and Tyrol.[16] Thuringia, consequently, emerges as an area where the Easter plays, with or without a Merchant Scene, would have been firmly established in the fourteenth century; they survive in such important dramatic documents as the Innsbruck Thuringian Easter Play (InnsThO) and the earlier Berlin Thuringian Easter play fragments (BeThO).[17] Moreover, there is evidence in this east-central area (and even in northern Germany) that prior to the full-blown German Easter plays, the B-stanzas were adopted in Latin liturgical ceremonies of the type III *visitatio*.[18] Consequently,

---

[13]Although the manuscript of the Lddv can be dated to some thirty to fifty years later, it is conceivable that the 1321 performance already included all the Latin texts and, possibly, most of the texts transmitted in both manuscripts A and B. For the controversy over whether or not the Mühlhausen MS A reflects the 1321 Eisenach performance, cf. above, p. 13 and n6, also the discussion below, pp. 248-250 and 290-291.

[14]Cf. Rueff (1925) 81-82; De Boor (1967) 329-345.

[15]Cf. Hennig (1975) 108-138, esp. 112-118, 137-138. Her results have been generally accepted in the literature; see e.g. Linke (1987a) 165-166 and Thoran (1994) 187-190.

[16]The Rhenish plays of Trier (c. 1400) and Rheinhessen (1460) are later revisions of the eastern forms.

[17]Cf. Linke (1987a) 166. The fragments of the BeThO were published in 1926, those of Breslau (BrslO) in 1928, those of Brandenburg (BrdbgO) only in 1986. It was only in 1975 that the origin of InnsThO was ascribed to Thuringia; cf. Thoran (1994) 188.

[18]B1 in MedgVis of ca. 1320, B1-3 in Prag.37. As U. Hennig has shown (1977) 98-100, the fourteenth-century ceremony of Prag.37 can be regarded as the immediate basis for the Prague Easter Play PragO.C. Among the three types of Easter ceremonies (*Oster-feiern*), the type III *visitatio* (or ceremony) includes not only the visitation to the sepulcher by the Marys (type I) and the 'race' of the disciples (type II), but also the *Hortu-lanus* 'scene' (the encounter of Mary Magdalene with the risen Christ whom she mis-

the B-stanzas were known in this region in the early fourteenth century. The fact that only the incipit *Omnipotens pater* is given for chant [16] in the Lddv provides additional proof that, by the time MS A was written in the later fourteenth century (between 1350 and 1370), the travel stanzas B1-3 were not unknown in Thuringia. Had the stanza B1 [16] been unfamiliar in the area, the scribe of MS A would have written in the complete text.[19]

The manner of performance for the two chants [16] and [17] is clearly indicated in the stage directions. Solo performance in a singing voice is required in both cases:

PRIMA FATUA cantat   *Omnipotens pater etc.* (ll. 156c-d)

Tunc SECUNDA. FATUA cantat   *Sed eamus ...* (ll. 168a-b)

This corresponds perfectly with the Easter play tradition in which in about twenty-one of the thirty-two plays listed in the Catalogue the three

---

takes for a gardener). In the two works cited, at least one of the three travel stanzas, *Omnipotens pater etc.* (MedgVis), or all three (Prag.37), are sung by the three Marys on their way to Christ's tomb (i.e. not to the merchant). It is generally accepted among researchers that this placement of the travel stanzas at the beginning of the type III Easter ceremonies is not original and must be regarded as an import from the Merchant Scene; see, e.g. De Boor (1967) 289 and 292, where the Easter plays of Zwickau and Braunschweig are still discussed as ceremonies, 'Osterfeiern'; they have since been redefined as Easter plays (together with seventeen more texts edited in LOO); cf. Linke (1983b), 34, (1994) 130-131.

For the most recent definition of 'Osterfeiern' and the distinction between *Feier* and *Spiel*, superseding that made by De Boor and Lipphardt on the basis of the type of manuscripts transmitting the texts, see Linke (1994); Linke-Mehler (1989) particularly 99-100. John Stevens' term '(dramatic) ceremonies' is probably a better equivalent to the German term *liturgische Feier* than 'liturgical drama' because it denotes the semi-liturgical character of these texts, associated with the liturgy and yet separable; cf. Stevens (1986) 311, 313, and compare pp. 324-347. While anglophone scholars of medieval drama still cling to the term 'liturgical drama,' other musicologists besides Stevens also prefer the term 'ceremony;' see Rankin (1981); Hiley (1993) 252, also 253-267. Strangely, however, both Stevens (pp. 324-336) and Hiley (pp. 250-273) still maintain the term 'Liturgical Drama' in the section headings of their books.

[19]It is generally surmised that, although hundreds of *visitatio* texts survive in liturgical books from the tenth to the sixteenth century, only relatively few vernacular Easter plays are known to us since they were no longer tied to the liturgy and, hence, were not transmitted in liturgical books, but in separate or miscellaneous manuscripts which were more likely to be lost or destroyed. Cf. Donovan (1958) 73.

Marys (*Maria Magdalena*, *Maria Iacobi*, and *Maria Salome*, often called *Prima*, *Secunda*, *Tercia Maria* or *Persona*) take turns singing one of the three B-stanzas.[20] Indeed, the solo performance of these B-stanzas can be looked upon as a common trait of the plays in east-central and southern Germany, including Prague and Tyrol.[21] In this respect, then, the Lddv stands firmly in the east-central tradition.

While the textual form and the significance of the B-stanzas in the various Easter plays have received much attention in the field of medieval drama, little work has been done on their musical form. In fact, the transcriptions of the melodies included in some editions of Easter plays, or published elsewhere, are not always reliable. Hence, primary comparative research of the manuscript transmission of those melodies is required to provide a solid basis for the melodic restoration of the two stanzas [16] and [17]. Fortunately, the melody of the B-stanzas is extremely well documented. All but three of the plays listed in Catalogue [16C], not counting the incipit versions of Prag.37 and FrkfDir, have musical notation for them.[22] In most cases, this music is accessible (in transcription and/or facsimile) in older or more recent editions of the plays.[23] For at least some travel stanzas, the melody can also be con-

---

[20]Cf. Catalogue [16C], pp. F39-F42, where the performance of the stanzas is indicated in the third column with the sigla S (for Solo) or E (for Ensemble). In only nine cases do all three Marys sing the stanzas together: in OrignyO, BrswO (only stanza B1), WolfO (B1-2), BeRheinO, ZwiO.II (B2+1), AlsfP, AugsO (B1), RegO (B1-2), and in TrierO (only stanza B3). For two other sources, specific directions are missing.

[21]Prag.37, PragO.C, InsThO, BeThO, BrdbgO, BöhmO.I, FrkfDir, ZwiO.I and III, EgerP, Erl.III, BozO.II and IV, PfarrkP, BozP.1495, AmerP, BozP.1514, TirO.fr.

[22]The manuscripts of the BrdbgO and the InnsThO are both without music; that of the BeRheinO was meant to have musical notation, yet all the staves, except for two chants (ll. 1005a-d *Nunc vadamus* and l. 1073b *Raboni*), are empty.

[23]The published melodies for all or some of the B stanzas can be found in the following editions or monographs (cf. also Catalogue [16C1-2]): ZwiO.I ed. Linke-Mehler (1990) 31-32 (transcription), 141 (facsimile). ZwiO.III, ibid., 76-78 (transcription), 126-127, 150-151 (facs.). BrslO ed. Klapper (1928) after p. 208 (facs., Bl. 2v). PragO.C in Schuler (1940) nos. 426, 432, 435 (as "PragO.II"), Lipphardt (1948) 32 (as "Prag.I"), facs. in Máchal (1908), appendix, plate 1, and in Svejkovsky (1966) after p. 80. Erl.III, ed. Suppan (1990) 51-53. EgerP in Schuler (1940) nos. 426, 432, 435. AlsfP in Schuler loc. cit., Dreimüller (1935) 3: 78-80 (transcription, handwritten), 86 (facs.). BozO.II in Lipphardt-Roloff (1986) 1: 139-140. BozO.IV, ibid., 260-261. PfarrkP in Lipphardt-Roloff (1988) 2: 154. BozP.1495, ed. Klammer (1986) 141; AmerP ibid., 317. BrswO, in Sievers (1936) 29, Schuler (1940) 426, Lipphardt (1948) 32. WolfO, ed.

sulted, with due caution, in the synoptic musicological publications by Schuler, Lipphardt, and Smoldon.[24]

Basically, the melody of the travel stanzas is the same for the whole broad Easter play tradition. A comparative survey of the various melodic versions shows that most of the few variants follow the pattern of the geographical distribution of the sources. I compared the B-melody of sixteen German plays (ZwiO.I and III, BethO, BrslO, PragO.C,[25] Erl.III, EgerP, AlsfP, BozO.II and IV, PfarrkP, BozP.1495 [A and B], BozP.1514, TirO.fr, BrswO, WolfO, AugsO, RegO) with each other and with that of the four Easter plays of the West (Vich, Tours, Origny, and Egmont). For all of the German plays was it possible to work from the manuscript versions of the melody, at least in the form of microfilm, xerox copies or facsimiles.[26]

The melodic structure of the four-line stanza — $\alpha\alpha\beta\gamma$ — is the same in the Spanish, French, and German versions: phrase α in line 1 is repeated in line 2; line 3 has its own tune in phrase β; and the refrain in line 4 is sung to a third tune γ.[27] With regard to the range of the melody, the various plays agree for phrase α (range of a fourth, F-b^b) as well as phrase β (range of a sixth, F-d). Only the range for phrase γ, the

---

Schönemann (1855) 151-153, also in Schuler (1940) nos. 426, 432, Smoldon (1980) 314. AugsO, ed. (facs.) Lipphardt (1978b), fols. lxxvr-v. BozP. 1514 in Lipphardt-Roloff (1996) 3: 133-134. TirO.fr, ibid., 326-327. RegO, ed. Poll (1950) 108.

[24]See Schuler (1940) nos 426, 432, 435; Lipphardt (1948) 32 (BrswO, WolfO, PragO.C, OrignyO, ToursO); Smoldon (1980) 174-175, 308-309, 314 (VichO, WolfO, Origny, Dutch plays).

[25]Prague, University Library, MS 1.B.12, fols. 135^v-137^v. The play was edited by Máchal (1908) 18-19, 98-105, as "Marienspiel C"; cf. Hennig (1977) 90; Schuler (1940-1951) calls the play "PragO.II," obviously in reference to its edition by Hanus (1863), who edited it as the second of three "Drei-Marien-Spiele." Lipphardt (1948) 32 refers to the play as "Prag.I." Of the four different transmissions of the B stanzas in Latin-Czech plays transcribed in Schuler (1940), nos. 426, 432, 435, I selected PragO.C as the oldest among them (fourteenth century); cf. Hennig (1977) 89-92.

[26]I am grateful to Hj. Linke, who has kindly sent me manuscript images for most of the relevant melodies (e.g. of the plays from Tyrol, from Eger, Erlau, Braunschweig, Wolfenbüttel, and Prague), mainly from the facsimile collection at the Institut für deutsche Sprache und Literatur in Cologne. My thanks go also to various libraries for sending me copies of other sources for the B stanzas: the Stadtarchiv und Stadtbibliothek of Hildesheim (for MedgVis), the Staatsbibliothek Preussischer Kulturbesitz in Berlin (for BethO), and the Gesamthochschulbibliothek in Kassel (for AlsfP).

[27]See Table 6, p. 187, for the transcription of the melody in German plays.

refrain, varies considerably among the sources: a third in most German versions (*F-a*); a fourth in a few other German (*F-b^b*) and in the 'Norman' versions of Origny and Egmont (*G-c*);[28] a fifth in Tours (*E-b^b*): and almost an octave in the Vich play (*C-b^b*).[29]

The stanza melody clearly belongs to the *F*-tonality (finalis *F*);[30] yet, whether it is in the authentic or the plagal mode (mode 5 or mode 6) is not so clear in the German versions because of the limited melodic range: in the three decasyllabic lines, the range does not extend beyond a sixth above the finalis *F*, and this sixth *d* is reached only once in phrase β; the range of the refrain is even more limited. As Apel points out, however, medieval theorists usually considered small-range melodies as plagal,[31] thus the melody of the B-stanza even in German sources can be assigned to mode 6. The older Vich play supports this, as its melody of the B-stanza is clearly of mode 6, evident not only in the abundant use of *a* as the reciting note,[32] but also in the extension of the melodic range in the refrain to the lower fourth *C-F* of the mode 6-ambitus.

In general, the stanza melody consists of gentle arches in each of its phrases, always rising from the finalis *F* (*G* in the 'Normanic' plays, *C* in the transposed version of the late AugsO) and returning to it in simple

---

[28]According to De Boor (1967) 360-361, the French play of Origny and the Dutch play of Egmont present what he calls the 'Norman' tradition of the Merchant Scene. In these two plays, the melody of the travel stanzas is transposed up a second, i.e., the tune, which normally is in the *F*-mode, starts and ends on *G*. Since this does not influence the shape of the small-range melody in any way, I will not always cite the specific note names for these two sources.

[29]For the melodies in these last four plays see the respective editions: EgmontO ed. Smits van Waesberghe (1953) 31; OrignyO ed. Coussemaker (1861) 21; ToursO ed. Krieg (1956) 3*; VichO ed. Anglès (1935) 276.

[30]In 'Rabers Passion' of 1514 (BozP.1514) the B1 stanza is one pitch higher, beginning and ending on *G*, with no change in the shape of the small-range tune. Since this rather unusual notation is 'corrected' in the subsequent stanzas B2 and B3, both notated in *F*, I disregard it as erroneous. Cf. Traub (Lipphardt-Roloff [1996] 6.2: 14), who explains such notational errors in some Sterzing manuscripts as manifesting the scribe's "unsicheres Modusbewußtsein."

[31]Apel (1958) 144-148. Medieval theories concerning chants with limited melodic range are also discussed by C. Meyer (2000) 210-211.

[32]In mode 5 the reciting tone would be *c*.

cadences at the end of each line. Only in some of the plays (Vich, Tours, Egmont, BrswO and WolfO) does a phrase (β in 1. 3) begin on the third *a* instead of on the *F*. The entire melody is basically a syllabic tune, with short melismas only over the last syllable of line 3 and the first syllable of the plaintive *Heu* in line 4, the refrain.[33] In spite of the basic uniformity in the transmission of this melody, there are sufficient variants, even among the German sources retained for this study, that a more detailed musical comparison is warranted. The goal is, in any case, to find a suitable paradigm for the melodic restoration of the B1 stanza in the Lddv.

As a primary paradigm for a comparative study of the German transmissions of the stanza, the melodic version from the Zwickau Easter plays appears to be suitable for at least two reasons: Zwickau is geographically close to Thuringia, slightly east of it and to the south of Leipzig in Saxony (see the map, Figure 4, p. 86); and its excellent transmission of the B-stanzas, supported by three parallel manuscripts from around 1500 (one for ZwiO.I, two for ZwiO.III), is very reliable and accessible in the model edition by Linke-Mehler.[34] Of the seven Tyrol plays that transmit one or all three of the B-stanzas, only those of the fifteenth century are accounted for in Table 6 and may suffice to represent the Tyrol tradition of this stanza.[35] The form in which the B-stanzas have been transcribed in the editions of the Tyrol plays requires some discussion, however, regarding the text underlay.[36]

---

[33]In a syllabic musical style, "every syllable of text was set to a single pitch." A. Hughes (1989a) 95. The different setting in the editions of some of the later Tyrol plays is discussed below, pp. 181-182

[34]The RegO, on the other hand, shows a larger number of variants and some serious scribal errors in the transmission of the stanza; for the textual variants see the critical edition of the stanza below, p. 188. Since it is a late source (seventeenth-century), it is not included in the comparative survey of Table 6. Nor does the stanza version of the MedgVis figure in the survey because its fourteenth-century notation in neumes without lines is too difficult to interpret. The melody seems to be closer to the Braunschweig/Wolfenbüttel transmission.

[35]In any case, the evidence of the two sixteenth-century plays, BozP.1514 and TirO.fr, is too late, their notation of the various B-stanzas too negligent and open to interpretation (see below), to be of much value for this comparison.

[36]For the following discussion see the editions of these stanzas in Lipphardt-Roloff (1986) 1: 139-140 (BozO II), 260-261 (BozO IV); 2: 154 (PfarrkP); 3: 133 (BozP.1514), 326 (TirO.fr); Klammer (1986) 141 (BozP.1495), 317 (AmerP). The principles govern-

For BozO.II, BozO.IV, and PfarrkP, the text setting in the editions corresponds to the syllabic setting in the other German plays, with short melismas only over the last syllable of line 3 and over *Heu* of the refrain (Table 6). For BozP.1495, AmerP, BozP1514, and TirO.fr, however, the editors interpret and present line 3 as having a 3-note neume ('ligature') over syllable 7, or some other ligatures over other syllables. This totally alters the traditional text underlay for the last four or more syllables of the line in those stanzas. As a result, the strictly syllabic style of the tune is lost in these transcriptions, along with the final melisma of phrase β, both so characteristic for the decasyllabic stanzas of the Merchant Scene (as is clear in Table 6).[37]

Genuine ligatures, i.e. compound neumes, are accurate forms of assigning more than one pitch to a given syllable (see Table 1). The deci-

---

ing those transcriptions were established and outlined by Lipphardt; cf. Lipphardt-Roloff (1986) 1: 10-13.

[37]For BozP.1495, the strange text setting of l. 3, syllables 7-10, in Lipphardt's transcription of B1 (ed. Klammer [1986] 141) has been corrected by Traub in Lipphardt-Roloff (1996) 6.2: 164 (although no effort has been made to emend the manuscript's erroneous pitches over syllables 6-10). Unfortunately, in correcting the third of five pitches over *Heu* from *b* to *a* in l. 4, a new error slipped in; the last two pitches had been correct in Klammer's edition. Traub's version (p. 164) *FG aFG* over *Heu* must be corrected to the traditional *FG aGa*. See below, Table 6, no. 12 with n5.

For AmerP as well (MS B of BozP.1495), the improper text underlay for B1 l. 3 in Lipphardt's transcription (ed. Klammer [1986] 317) has been corrected by Traub in Lipphardt-Roloff (1996) 6.2: 171. The letter names Traub gives for this line are incorrect, however. He cites the neumes over *nos mi-ser-ri-me* (syllables 6-10 of l. 3) not as the traditional *b♭-b♭-G-b♭-aGF*, but as the pitches *G-G-E-G-FED* — a tonal sequence absolutely foreign to the *F*-tonality of the stanza tune — because of an alleged *C*-clef on l. 4 of the stave (*auf der zweitobersten Linie*), which is mistaken. The Ithaca manuscript of the play does not have a clef for either of the two stanzas, *Hew nobis* and *Omnipotens pater*, notated on fol. 52r. (This fact was verified by Patrick Stevens, curator of the manuscript collection at Cornell University, to whom I am grateful for supplying me other relevant information and a copy of the manuscript page.) Should a *C*-clef be conjectured in the notation of this stanza, it would have to be on l. 3 of the 5-line stave (as Lipphardt has done in the edition of BozP.1495, ll. 3140-3143), because the *finalis* on l. 1 is certainly meant to be an *F*. The whole stanza melody of B1 in AmerP can, consequently, be understood as being in the traditional mode 6. Cf. Table 6, no. 12 with n4.

For Tir.O.fr, the manuscript's inaccurate text setting for B1 l. 3 as well as Traub's transcription of it in Lipphardt-Roloff (1996) 3: 326, can be corrected through the traditional syllabic text setting of B2 l. 3 in the manuscript, fol. 13v (which is also misrepresented in the edition).

sion, however, to place a three-note 'ligature' over syllable 7 depends entirely on the interpretation of the editors/transcribers and is to be questioned.[38] In fact, the manuscripts can quite readily be interpreted to support the traditional syllabic setting of this line in all cases discussed here: none of the plays (except AugsO) included in this comparison of the B-stanzas gives real evidence for the use of ligatures in the notation of the main body of line 3, phrase β.[39] Apart from a five-note ligature in EgerP over *Heu* of the refrain, the only unequivocal compound neume for the B-stanzas in all plays listed in Table 6 is the *clivis*, and it is used primarily over the second syllable of lines 1 and 2 (phrase α). The *clivis* is occasionally employed in the octosyllabic phrase γ of the refrain, but, except for AugsO and EgerP, never in phrase β for the decasyllabic line 3.[40] In my view, the notation of line 3 in the Tyrol B-stanzas must be understood as one using single, one-note neumes, *virga* and *punctum* (in the form of gothic 'rhombs' with or without a 'tail' or 'cauda') to indicate a syllabic style of melody which allows a melisma to occur over the last syllable as well as the occasional use of a *clivis*.[41]

[38]The various Tyrol plays use a kind of rhombic notation. The editors interpret the "kaudierte Rhombe" (actually a *virga*, a rhomb with a 'tail' [thick vertical stroke or stem] below) as usually 'attracting' two or three of the preceding notes to form a ligature (Lipphardt in Lipphardt-Roloff [1986] 1: 11). This principle may hold true in some cases (see e.g. J. Wolf [1913] 160, Munich, MS mus 1573); yet in others, the *virga* in a sequence of rhombic notes serves a different function (see n41 below, cf. also Suppan [ed. 1990] 11). Gstrein (1994) 92-93, demonstrates that the principle underlying the transcriptions in the Tyrol plays often produces confusion rather than clarity and results in editions that are inadequate for musicological comparisons.

[39]Only in AugsO is a clear indicator given, through the use of the *clivis* over syllables 7 and 9 of l. 3, that these two syllables will each receive two pitches of the (slightly extended) melodic line; yet the final melisma is still intact here; see Table 6, no. 15.

[40]In EgerP, a *podatus ab*[b] indicates the beginning of the end-melisma of phrase β.

[41]J. Wolf (1913) 162, noticed a side-by-side usage of *virga* and *punctum* for single notes in rhombic notation in a number of German manuscripts of the fifteenth/sixteenth century, mainly from the South. Contrary to the transcription in Lipphardt-Roloff (1996) 3: 133, the manuscript of BozP.1514 ('Rabers Passion') provides clear evidence for such a syllabic setting: the notation of the B stanzas in this play (Sterzing, MS III, fol. 60r) shows rhombic neumes only as *punctum* or *clivis*, not as a rhombic *virga* ('kaudierte Rhombe'; cf. n38), which, for the music editors of the Tyrol plays, is the designated criterion in the determination of ligatures.

The comparison that follows, therefore, is based on my own transcriptions from the manuscripts in a 'syllabic' style for the main body of
line 3.[42] Understood in this 'syllabic' style, the B-stanzas of all four
late Tyrol plays (BozP.1495, AmerP, BozP.1514, TirO.fr) basically
agree with the general textual-musical form in the other German plays
recorded in the comparative Table 6, even though their transcriptions in
the editions present a different picture. The B-melodies of BozP.1514
and TirO.fr, not included in Table 6, are, consequently, close to those
of PfarrkP and AmerP (Table 6, nos. 11 and 12), although there is some
inconsistency in the notation of phrase β in the B-stanzas of the former
two plays.[43]

Fifteen plays, then, remain for a comparison of the various extant
melodies of B1. They are listed in the synoptical Table 6 more or less
according to the degree to which their stanza melodies diverge from the
Zwickau transmission. All melodies for the B1 stanza included in the
table have been studied in their manuscript versions (original or
facsimile).[44] Only those melodic sections of the sources are indicated

---

[42]This is also the form in which Lipphardt transcribed the B stanzas in BozO.II and
BozO.IV, where the 'problem' of the 'kaudierte Rhomben' does not really exist (ed.
Lipphardt-Roloff (1986) 1: 139-140, 260-261). Traub too seems to abandon the
'principle of the *kaudierte Rhomben*' in some instances: for B1 and B2 in PfarrkP (ed.
Lipphardt-Roloff [1996] 2: 154), he chooses a strictly syllabic setting of syllables 8 and
9 of phrase β despite the 'kaudierte Rhomben' in the manuscript (MS XVI, fols. 74v-75r)
and despite the manuscript's setting, which he recognizes as a scribal error and as a
"melodisch sinnwidriger Zeilenwechsel" (p. 358). When he corrects Lipphardt's
transcriptions and text underlay of B1 in BozP.1495 and AmerP, he also ignores the
'kaudierten Rhomben' in favour of a strictly syllabic setting; see above, n37.

[43]The inexact and inconsistent fashion in which most of the B stanzas are transmitted
in some of the Tyrol manuscripts may be interpreted as a rough but, at the time,
sufficient form of pointing to stanzas well known in the tradition of Easter and Passion
plays. In this sense, Traub appropriately assesses these notations as having a
"Gebrauchscharakter" (cf. Lipphardt-Roloff [1996] 6.2: 7).

[44]The notes to Table 6 concern mainly scribal errors in the sources or incorrect transcriptions in the various publications. An additional comment on the error in PragO.C
is necessary (cf. n2 to play no. 5). PragO.C has a double scribal error in B1, at the
beginning of phrase β, over *faciemus* (pitch is off by a third for the first two neumes of
the new stave; also, after the first two wrongly pitched neumes a third neume is missing
for the third syllable of *fa-ci-e-mus*). These two scribal errors can easily be emended
through the corresponding phrase β of the subsequent stanza B2 on the same manuscript
page (fol. 135v; facsimile in Máchal [1908] plate 1). Schuler's unemended transcription
has a most bizarre text underlay for l. 3 (phrase β) of B1 (Schuler [1940] 233 no. 426,

in the table that differ from the chosen paradigm of Zwickau. A quick glance at this synopsis shows that the last three plays of the survey, BrswO, WolfO, and particularly AugsO (nos. 13-15), stand somewhat outside the rest of the German tradition. With two characteristic variants — the opening *a-c-c* (instead of *F-c-bb*) for the first three syllables in phrase β, and the richer, seven- instead of five-note melisma at the beginning of phrase γ over *Heu* — BrswO and WolfO appear to be more closely related to the four 'western' plays, especially those of Egmont, Origny, and Tours. AugsO (no. 15) is the only play in which the mode 6 tune for the B1 stanza is not notated in *F* but in *C* (transposed up a fifth or down a fourth). In addition, this tune shows several melodic variants, mainly in phrase β, which distinguish it slightly from the majority of the German transmissions.

The other twelve sources in Table 6 (including BeThO) are very similar to each other in their transmission of the basic stanza melody.[45] In fact, there is only one substantial variant that affects the shape of the melody, and that is in line 3 of the stanza. While the two Zwickau plays and the plays of Breslau, Prague, and Erlau are characterized in phrase β by a stepwise melodic descent from *d* to *G* (on the syllables 4 to 8), the next six plays of Table 6, nos. 7-12, share the variant of a repeated *b^b* on syllable 7. This results in a subsequent leap of a third (to *G* on syllable 8), and thus the gradually descending melodic line of phrase β is disrupted here.[46] These six plays (EgerO, AlsfP, BozO.II, BozO.IV,

---

"PragO.II"). He did not recognize that the scribe, ignoring his error over *faciemus* (or is there no error but perhaps a hole in the manuscript page where the missing third neume *d* had been written), clearly relates, through thin separating strokes, the first three neumes of the stave to *faciemus*, and the subsequent *b^b* to *nos*, as the general transmission of this l. 3 would have it.

[45]Unfortunately, the manuscript of the BeThO (no. 3), the only Thuringian notation for the stanza, cannot be properly transcribed because the neumes are not heighted. Nevertheless, this source can provide some valuable information for comparison. Its stanza version is clearly not very different from the Zwickau transmission.

[46]The WolfO (no. 14) also shares this variant, yet its stanza melody for B1 was recognized above (along with nos. 13 and 15) as being somewhat removed from the prevailing German transmission. BozP.1495 (no. 12) has the repetition and the subsequent leap mistakenly notated one syllable too early and, hence, one pitch too high (*ccaca*); an emendation is proposed below, Table 6, n5. The evidence of the two sixteenth-century Tyrol plays BozP.1514 and TirO.fr is mixed: the leap of a third at this place only in B1 of the former; a stepwise descent in B2 of BozP.1514 and in B1 and 2 of TirO.fr.

PfarrkP, AmerP) are of the fifteenth and sixteenth centuries, and pre-dominantly from the south.[47]

In searching for a model for chant **[16]** *Omnipotens pater* in the Thuringian Lddv, I limit the choice to the melodic versions presented in nos. 1-6 of Table 6 — the "east-central group" of plays, especially since two of them are dated to the fourteenth century (BrslO and PragO.C). The few variants among these sources are so negligible that any of them except BeThO could serve as a model for the B1 stanza in the Lddv.[48] The version from Zwickau will be excluded, however, because BeThO, the only Thuringian play with notation, albeit vague, for this stanza, does not support their three-note neume over the last syllable of phrase β, only the five-note melisma of the other three plays.

Considering all the facts discussed, it seems likely that the melodic form in which the B1 stanza became known in Thuringia in the four-teenth century was very close to the version transmitted in these three plays, BrslO, PragO.C, and Erl.III. The fact that they differ from the well-documented B-melody in the plays of nearby Zwickau (of around 1500) in only one variant, a melisma of five instead of three notes at the end of line 3 (phrase β), places a restoration of chant **[16]** by any of these transmissions on a secure basis. The Thuringian version of this stanza in BeThO in non-heighted neumes appears to support this deci-sion. Minor differences in the three versions exist only in the use of notational symbols in phrase γ, the refrain. As the quilisma-like figure over the penultimate *do-lor* is unique in PragO.C, I consider it a local (folkloristic?) variant and exclude this version, although PragO.C is from

[47]Regarding this geographical grouping, it is interesting to note that the first five plays with the stepwise descent in phrase β (ZwickO.I and III, BrslO, PragO.C, Erl.III) all belong to what Hennig (1978), (1975) 116-120, 137-138, has recognized as the east-central tradition of German Easter plays, which had radiated west, and south to Erlau. Most interesting is the fact that Hennig's discovery of the existence of this east-central tradition (cf. above, p. 175) seems to be corroborated by this musicological comparison of the B stanzas of the Easter plays. It seems noteworthy that of the last three plays in Table 6, the only one to maintain the stepwise descent in phrase β is BrswO (no. 13); since this play belongs to the fourteenth century, it probably stayed closer to the east-central transmission of the stanza.

[48]Erl.III, for instance, is the only one of these five plays with a single *punctum G*, not the *clivis GF*, for the penultimate syllable *do-lor* of the refrain (phrase γ). This is offset by the fact that B2 and B3 of Erl.III show the *clivis GF* at the corresponding places.

Notes to Table 6

1) For the plays nos. 3-15, only the melodic variants to the paradigm transmission of the two Zwickau plays are indicated in this synopsis. Where letter names are cited, *b'* stands for *b^b*. Not included in the table are the sixteenth-century Tyrol plays TirO.fr and BozP.1514 ('Raber's Passion'). For the transmission of the B1 stanza in these plays and their editions, see the discussion above, pp. 180-183. For the stanza's transmission in the French plays of Tours and Origny, see Lipphardt (1948) 32, and above, p. 179 n29.

2) The error of notation in PragO.C for stanza B1 (line 3, syllables 2-5) can be emended through the correct notation in B2 (*Amisimus enim*) on the same folio 135v of this manuscript; cf. above n44.

3) In stanza B1 of BozO.IV, the error of notation (line 3, syllables 5-7, notation too low by one pitch), can be emended through the correct notation of this manuscript's stanza B2, which is identical with that of BozO.II. In stanza B3 of BozO.IV, a similar error of notation (one pitch too low in line 3, over syllables 7 and 9-10, and in the entire refrain) can equally be emended through stanza B2. Cf. fols. 80v-81r of the MS of BozO.IV and Lipphardt's unemended transcriptions in Lipphardt-Roloff (1986) 1: 260-261. For stanza B3, lines 3-4, see now Traub's correction in Lipphardt-Roloff (1996) 6.2: 147-148.

4) In AmerP, the B1 stanza must be understood as being in the traditional *F*-tonality, although its notation in the manuscript, fol. 52r, is without a clef; see above n37.

5) In BozP.1495, an error of notation occurred over syllables 6-10 of line 3 (MS fol. 47v): the scribe started to write repeat pitches one syllable too early, repeating *c*'s over syllables 5 and 6 instead of *b^b*'s over syllables 6 and 7. As a result, the rest of the melodic phrase is thrown off pitch and the three-note group over *-me* (syllable 10) increased to four notes. This erroneous notation over syllables 5-10 *c-c-a-c-a-b^b aGF* must be emended to the traditional *c-b^b-b^b-G-b^b-aGF* of AmerP in both Klammer's edition (1986) 141, and Traub's correction of it; cf. above n37. The neumes over *Heu* of the refrain, on the other hand, are clearly notated in the manuscript as the traditional *FGaGa*-melisma; both Klammer's edition and Traub's 'correction' of it (see n37) should be corrected accordingly.

6) In WolfO, the two pitches *ab^b* between the syllables 9 and 10 of line 3 are not clearly set (MS fol. 182r). They appear to form a three-note group with the preceding *b^b* over syllable 9 *-ri-*. This untraditional setting is changed in stanza B2 of this play through omission of those two pitches *ab^b*.

7) The refrain in WolfO is not part of the B-stanzas; it is used only at a later place, in response to a vernacular stanza; cf. above, p. 174 and n12.

8) In AugsO, the reading [*rector*] in line 2 is an emendation of the manuscript's flawed *pater* (fol. 75r) which repeats the *pater* of line 1.

TABLE 6 THE MELODIC TRANSMISSION OF THE B1-STANZA
OMNIPOTENS PATER IN GERMAN PLAYS[1]

the ecclesiastical province of Mainz.[49] Since of the remaining two versions of the stanza melody BrslO is probably of the fourteenth century rather than the fifteenth, I give preference to it as the direct source for the restoration of chant [16] in the Lddv.

Stanza 'B1'   *Omnipotens   pater [altissime[a],*
angelorum   rector[b] mitissime,
quid faciemus[c] nos[d] miserrime?
Heu quantus est noster dolor[e]!]

Source   BrslO, fol. 2v (text = PragO.C, fol. 135v; BeThO, fol. 4v; Erl.III and most other German Easter plays listed in Catalogue [16C2)

Variants   [a] *altissime] mitissime* RegO, fol. 25r
[b] *rector] pater* AugsO, fol. 75r
[c] *faciemus] faciamus* AlsfP, fol. 80av; PfarrkP, fol. 74v; AmerP, fol. 52r; AugsO, fol. 75v; BozP.1514 fol. 60r; TirO.fr., fol. 13v; *facimus* RegO, fol. 25r.
[d] *quid faciemus nos] quid facimus* RegO, fol. 25r; *quid facient iste* VichO; *quid faciunt iste* ToursO.
[e] *noster dolor] dolor noster* RegO, fol. 25r.

Melody   Mode 6. Transcribed in Chapter 4 from B1-stanza *Omnipotens pater* in BrslO (MS Breslau [Wroclaw], UB, MS I Q.226a, fol. 2v). Cf. the comparative Table 6, p. 187.

Translation   "Almighty Father in the highest heaven,
Most gentle ruler of the angels,
What shall we do in our deep misery?
Alas, how vast is our woe and pain!"

---

[49]The diocese of Prague belonged to the ecclesiastical province of Mainz until 1344; cf. Brück (1960) 613; Weizsäcker (1961) 499. See also the map on p. 86 (Figure 4).

[17] *Sed eamus oleum emere*
preter quod nil possumus agere.
Qui caret hoc carebit glorie.
Heu quantus est noster dolor!
(Lddv 168b-f)

This decasyllabic stanza, sung by the second *Fatua*, is a sequel to the lament of the first *Fatua* (chant [16]) in the Foolish Virgins' desperate attempt to find oil for their lamps. The text of chant [17] is transmitted in its entirety in the Lddv, and for this reason it should not require much discussion. Yet, the state of the manuscript for this whole passage and its presentation in the different editions require some clarification. Furthermore, the four-line form of this stanza differs considerably from the standard B3 stanza in the German tradition of Easter plays after which it is modelled. A study of the metrical and musical transmission of the B3 stanza in the various plays, therefore, is needed before we can draw any valid conclusions about the melodic restoration of chant [17] in the Lddv.

The way in which the *Sed eamus* stanza is presented in MS A has given rise to some confusion. The *Prima Fatua* is called upon to sing chant [16] *Omnipotens pater*, which is indicated by its incipit (l. 156d). This is followed immediately in the manuscript (p. 96a) by the stage direction *Secunda Fatua* and the complete stanza of *Sed eamus oleum emere*, which in turn is followed by the vernacular paraphrase (ll. 157-168) to *Omnipotens pater*. Next comes another stage direction: *Et tunc Secunda Fatua cantat Sed eamus etc.* (ll. 168a-b). Beckers and Schneider saw an error of the scribe after the incipit *Omnipotens pater* and emended it in their editions by correctly placing the complete stanza *Sed eamus* (Schneider) or its incipit (Beckers) after line 168a.[1]

My impression is that the scribe himself was very much aware of his error and rushed to correct it through his second stage direction. Something like the following probably happened: the scribe saw, in the exemplar before him, the complete stanza B1 *Omnipotens pater* and, noticing that it was the familiar stanza from the Easter plays, reduced it to its

---

[1]Dreimüller (1935) 1: 109 (after the citation on p. 108 of the complete stanza) interprets it as an instruction to repeat the previously quoted *Sed eamus* stanza: "Später wird diese Strophe ... noch einmal wiederholt."

incipit. Then, curious as to whether there was any other stanza that he knew from the Merchant Scene of the Easter plays, he spotted the *Sed eamus* stanza and, recognizing it as a remarkable variation of the B3 stanza, immediately copied the whole text. When he realized he had skipped all the vernacular lines after the first stanza, he wrote them down and added the new stage direction (l. 168a) to inform the user of the manuscript that the *Secunda Fatua* should now sing the *Sed eamus* stanza:[2]

Et tunc SECUNDA FATUA cantat   *Sed eamus etc.* (l. 168a)

The *Et tunc* in this stage direction should be understood in the sense of "And only after this," thereby cancelling the earlier stage direction for the *Secunda Fatua* after the incipit *Omnipotens pater*. The scribe himself 'emended' his initial error, and the intended sequence of the manuscript is clear.

The form of chant **[17]** must be considered identical to that of chant **[16]** *Omnipotens pater* with its three decasyllabic verses and the final octosyllabic line *Heu quantus* as refrain:[3]

Sed eamus oleum emere
preter quod nil possumus agere.
Qui caret hoc carebit glorie.
Heu quantus est noster dolor!

The music for this chant should not present any problem. Dreimüller recognized this in 1935, when he demonstrated that the *Sed eamus* stanza of the Lddv can be set and sung to the stanza melody of B3 in the Alsfeld Passion Play.[4] De Boor, on the other hand, in stressing the textual

---

[2]The error seems to be one of remembering ("Behalten des Textes"), stage 2 of the four stages of copying texts; cf. Touber (1992) 124-125.

[3]Beckers (ed. 1905) 104, and De Boor (ed. 1965) 188, banish the full text of the *Sed eamus* stanza to the apparatus of their editions. In Schneider's edition (1964) 23 and in that of Curschmann-Glier (1981) 284-285, the whole passage from *Omnipotens* to the second *Sed eamus* is now in the order that the scribe obviously intended. Unfortunately, however, the lines are not printed as a stanza; this is done only in the apparatus of De Boor's edition. Fr. Stephan (ed. 1847b) 176 and L. Bechstein (ed. 1855) 20, gave diplomatic editions of this passage.

[4]Dreimüller (1935) 1: 107-109. Since the Alsfeld B3 stanza has an error of notation in l. 1 over syllable 3, which Dreimüller did not emend, the more accurate B1 stanza of AlsfP would have been a better choice.

parallel of the stanzas [16-17] with the travel stanzas B1 and B3 in the Easter plays,[5] indirectly refers to the standard three-line form of B3 in German plays with only two decasyllabic lines and one octosyllabic line, but no refrain:[6]

Sed eamus unguentum emere,
cum quo bene possumus ungere
corpus Domini sacratum.

Scholarly discussions of this special German B3 stanza have focussed on the change in the stanza's rhyme and verse structure and particularly the content[7] and paid little if any attention to its musical form, probably because the music was not readily accessible.[8] A study of the melody for this reduced B3 stanza reveals that it is also musically impoverished. Lines 1 and 2 are each sung, as usual, to the melodic phrase α.[9] The new line 3 of the German stanza with the octosyllabic verse *corpus Domini sacratum* adopts tune γ of the octosyllabic refrain *Heu quantus est noster dolor*.[10] The remaining melody α-α-γ is, consequently, much

[5]Cf. De Boor (ed. 1965) note to ll. 204ff.

[6]Cf. De Boor (1967) 354. See the text of stanzas B1-3 on p. 172.

[7]Namely, a more reverential attitude towards the sacred body of Christ in the German B3 stanza in contrast to the realistic views of the older versions of Vich and Tours that had pondered the perishable body of Christ, which the ointments were to prevent from decomposing. Cf. De Boor (1967) 354; Thoran (1976) 239-240.

[8]Until quite recently, Schuler's handwritten second volume of his dissertation (1940) *Die Musik der Osterfeiern, Osterspiele und Passionen des Mittelalters* was the only 'published' source of information for many of the melodies in medieval German dramas, including that for the special German B3 stanza in different plays. Within the last fifteen years, however, a number of new editions of medieval plays have been published, which include the transmitted music in transcriptions and/or facsimiles; see above, Chapter 3 [16] n23, and Catalogue [16C], pp. F39-F42.

[9]Cf. the melodic analysis of the B1 stanza in Chapter 3 [16], pp. 178-180, especially the comparative Table 6 on p. 187

[10]This may well be the reason why the standard B3 stanza in German plays lacks the *Heu*-refrain. The final cadence of tune γ in the shortened l. 3 is musically so strong that it more or less precludes a repetition for the words of the refrain. Nevertheless, such a repetition of phrase γ has been experimented with in the Zwickau tradition where, in ZwiO.I and III, the refrain is maintained for the standard German B3 stanza (not, however, for the vernacular version of this stanza in ZwiO.III); cf. Linke-Mehler (eds. 1990) 72, 78, 79; compare the discussion below, p. 195 and n18.

poorer than that of the regular B-stanzas.[11] It has the metric/musical formula: 10α | 10α | 8γ, which lacks both the third decasyllabic text line and the corresponding, musically dynamic phrase β. Thus, the somewhat "organgrinding character" that Lipphardt noticed in its first two lines is maintained throughout the stanza.[12] This melodic formula would certainly not fit the *Sed eamus* chant in the Lddv with its four-line stanza form.

While it is interesting to see that, in imitating the third travel stanza *Sed eamus* of the Easter plays, the Lddv departs from their special three-line form, it is not the only play to do so. A few attempts have also been made in German Easter and Passion plays to restore the normal four-line form of the B-stanzas. These plays, however, are all much later than the Lddv, and, except for the two Zwickau plays, the changes have been made in each case independently of any other play, as the evidence of their diverse textual/musical solutions shows.[13] In three cases, the *Heu*-refrain has simply been tacked on to the standard three-line B3 stanza, so the stanzas read:

[11]The special B3 stanza is deprived of the only line, phrase β, that brought the melodic range up to the fifth and sixth in the *F*-mode. The two different melodic patterns of the two stanza forms are listed in the chronological survey of Table 7 below, p. 198. In Suppan's index of the melodic incipits in the six Erlau plays ([1990] 227-241), only the rhyme pattern, not the metrical form of the stanza text, is accounted for (p. 234) because the main focus is on the melodies. The textual/melodic form of the 'reduced' B3 stanza (M III/3) is indicated here as having three lines, 'rhyming' A A B, with the melodic range of a fourth (1-4, i.e. *F-b*^{b}) as opposed to the melodic range of a sixth (1-6, i.e. *F-d*) in stanzas B1 and B2 (M III/1 and III/2); for two forms of phrase γ in the Erlau stanzas, see p. 248 (M III/3, M III/2) in the 'Register der Klauseln' (pp. 241-252).

[12]Lipphardt (1948) 33. For easily accessible examples of the 'reduced' B3 stanza, with transcription of the music, see TrierO ed. Hennig-Traub (1990) 54, Erl.III ed. Suppan (1990) 53, BozO.II ed. Lipphardt-Roloff (1986) 1: 140. Cf. also Schuler (1940) nos. 435-437, where only the samples from Alsfeld and Origny show the 'complete' melodic sequence α-α-β-γ.

[13]The Trier Easter Play in Hartl's 1937 edition appears to have restored the decasyllabic third line for the B3 stanza: *corpus domini sacratissimum* (2: 49-50, l. 43). However, Hartl's editions are known to be unreliable; see, e.g. Polheim (1975) 202-203. Hartl himself in his preface (1: 17-18) admits to making a number of conjectures in his editions. The Trier manuscript of the play clearly presents the B3 stanza as the normal German reduced stanza form B3 (10α-10α-8γ); see TrierO, ed. Hennig-Traub (1990) 53, with facsimile in the appendix, fol. 20. Cf. Froning's 1891-1892 edition, ll. 40c-e, and Schuler's musical transcription (1940) no. 435-437.

(1) ZwiO.I, ll. 23-26, and

(2) ZwiO.III, ll. 39-42   *Sed eamus unguentum emere*
de quo bene possumus unguere
corpus domini sacratum.
Hew quantus [est noster dolor!][14]

(3) TirO.fr, ll. 16b-c   *Sed eamus unguentum emere*
cum quo bene possumus ungere
corpus domini sacratum.
Heu quantus est noster dolor!

In three other plays, the obvious effort to recreate the normal deca-syllabic B-stanza form for B3 had strikingly different results:[15]

(4) BeRheinO, ll. 936 c-f: *Sed eamus ferventes opere*
caritatis unguentum emere,
quo dominum possimus ungere.
Heu quantus est noster dolor.

(5) BozO.IV, ll. 191-194:   *Sed eamus nunc Jhesum querere,*
Festinemus unguentum emere
Cum quo bene possumus ungere
Corpus domini sacratum.

(6) AlsfP, ll. 7535 b-e: *Sed eamus unguentum emere,*
cum quo bene possumus ungere
corpus domini sanctissimi.
Heu quantus est noster dolor.

---

[14]It is worth noting that ZwiO.II does not have a B3 stanza. Thus reduced to two travel stanzas, B1 and B2 are sung in reversed order as ensemble performances by the three Marys, while in ZwiO.I and III with three travel stanzas, each of the three Marys sings one of the stanzas as a solo. It appears that, at least in the Zwickau tradition, the number of available stanzas was a factor in deciding on a solo or choral performance.

[15]The fifteenth-century Dutch Easter play of Egmont, EgmontO, ed. Smits van Waes-berghe (1953) 31 (LOO 5: no. 827, ll. 13-17), with its equally independent version of stanza B3 and the formula 10α-10α-10β-R8γ could be added as another attempt in the same direction:

Sed eamus unguentum emere,
quo Dominum possimus ungere.
ipse erat nostra redemptio.
    Heu quantus est noster dolor.

This play has been classified by Smits van Waesberghe and De Boor as belonging to the Norman text tradition, although De Boor (1967) 342-345, recognized typically German stanza choices and textual variants in it. In my view, the play is best understood within the German tradition.

The stanza revision in BozO.IV is the only one of these six versions not to restore the refrain for line 4 but to move the octosyllabic line 3 of the usual B3 stanza (*corpus domini sacratum*) to this place instead. This stanza is interesting also from a chronological point of view, at least if Gstrein's tentative dating ([1994] 92) of the four Easter plays in the 'Debs' Codex, on the basis of the water marks, is correct: in the earlier play of BozO.IV ("nach 1428") the stanza was revised to a four-line form, while for the later BozO.II ("nach 1492") the reduced three-line form (ll. 25-27) seemed to be satisfying.

Important for the melody of this B3 stanza in its 'new' four-line form is the fact that the original decasyllabic form 10-10-10-R8 has been (almost) achieved in the last three plays of the survey (nos. 4-6, p. 193), with BozO.IV sacrificing the refrain by moving the usual octosyllabic third line into its place, and Alsfeld producing just nine syllables for a non-rhyming line 3.[16] The two Zwickau plays, ZwiO.I and III, on the other hand, and TirO.fr retain the octosyllabic line three. The metrical/syllabic structures of these 'new' four-line stanzas, then, are as follows (R stands for refrain):

ZwiO.I and III	10 - 10 - 8 - R8
TirO.fr	10 - 10 - 8 - R8
BeRheinO	10 - 10 - 10 - R8
BozO.IV	10 - 10 - 10 - 8
AlsfP	10 - 10 - 9 - R8

Given its four-line stanza form and its metrical structure (10-10-10-R8), chant **[17]** *Sed eamus* of the Lddv is closer to each of the above stanzas than to any of the standard B3 stanzas of three lines in German plays. The really interesting question for the melodic recovery of chant **[17]**, therefore, is whether in those six Easter plays the complete melody α-α-β-γ of the travel stanzas B has been restored for B3 along with the metrical restoration (or quasi restoration) of its decasyllabic stanza form of four lines.

Fortunately, the manuscripts for all but one of the 'new' four-line versions of the B3 stanza in German plays transmit the melodies; only

---

[16]The new texts in the stanzas of BeRheinO and BozO.IV have been briefly discussed by Thoran (1976) 239-240, and Rueff (1925) 58-59. The additional musical evidence, examined below (pp. 195-198), will shed new light on the various three- and four-line versions of stanza B3.

BeRheinO has the text under empty staves.[17] These musical transmissions in German sources show that the metrical/musical challenge of the B3 stanza was met in various fashions that are highly interesting. The first three plays, nos. 1-3 of the survey, appear to offer almost identical solutions by adding the refrain as a fourth line to the normal 'reduced' German B3 stanza. The musical evidence, however, reveals two very different approaches: in ZwiO.I and III (nos. 1 and 2), the B3 stanza is, basically, still the impoverished version of the standard three-line stanza since the dynamic melodic phrase β, created for a decasyllabic line 3, is missing; the traditional, octosyllabic line 3 is sung to phrase γ, as is the refrain. However, through a seemingly minor, yet remarkable musical variant of this phrase γ in line 3, over its first syllable *cor-pus*, the melodic line is modified to γ^{var}, thus preventing an exact repetition of it in the conventional phrase γ of the refrain.[18] The metrical/musical formula for this Zwickau stanza is 10α- 10α- $8\gamma^{var}$- 8γR. In TirO.fr (no. 3), on the other hand, the standard German line 3 *Corpus domini sacratum* is sung, in spite of its octosyllabic structure, to the musically richer phrase β, which is slightly varied to fit eight syllables (β'); hence the melodic form of the normal B-stanzas is recovered here, although the metrical form of line 3 is not. The stanza's metrical/musical form is 10α- 10α- $8\beta'$- 8γR.

It comes as no surprise, then, that in two of the remaining three plays, where the re-creation of a decasyllabic line 3 was genuinely attempted, this metrical change is matched with the re-appearance of the melodic phrase β for line 3: in BozO.IV and even in AlsfP with its not-

---

[17]Transcriptions and/or facsimiles of the melodies for these B3 stanzas can be found in some of the editions or in the secondary literature: for ZwiO.I and III ed. Linke-Mehler (1990) 32 and 78 (facsimiles pp. 141, 127, and 151); BozO.IV ed. Lipphardt-Roloff (1986) 1: 261; TirO.fr ed. Lipphardt-Roloff (1996) 3: 327; for AlsfP, see Drei-müller (1935) 3: 80 (Beilage 64) and p. 86 (facsimile), Schuler (1940) nos. 435-437, and especially Brunner's transcription in the forthcoming edition by Janota (1996-).

[18]The opening 'melisma' over the first word *cor-pus* in l. 3 is enlarged to a total of seven notes (*FGab^baG-a*) thus extending the melodic range of this phrase γ^{var} to that of a fourth, while in the refrain of l. 4, phrase γ appears in the usual German form with a five-note melisma over *Heu* (*FGaGa*) and the more limited melodic range of a third (*F-a*). The longer 'melisma' chosen for the beginning of l. 3 [phrase γ^{var}] is, interestingly, the one which distinguishes the *Heu*-refrain γ in BrswO, WolfO, and AugsO from the rest of the German transmission (see Table 6) and is more closely related to Origny and Egmont.

quite-perfect stanza of only nine syllables in line 3. Such a musical structure α-α-β-γ can, consequently, also be assumed for the 'perfectly' decasyllabic B3 stanza of BeRheinO (without musical notation) so that the metrical/musical form for these B3 stanzas (nos. 4-6) may be noted as 10α- 10α- 10[9]β- 8γR.

The version of the AlsfP is indeed particularly interesting because the re-instalment of phrase β for line 3 has been achieved here by two extremely simple means: first, in the text of line 3 of the standard German B3 stanza, one word of three syllables (*sacratum*) was merely replaced by a four-syllable word (*sanctissimi*), thus increasing the number of syllables to nine; second, the melodic phrase β was reduced by one neume to fit the new nine-syllable text. This 'reduction' was effected not through the loss of a pitch in the melodic line but through the merging of two repeated pitches b^b (notes 6 and 7 of phrase β in the Alsfeld transmission)[19] into a single pitch b^b for the sixth syllable *sanc-tissimi*. Such a statement calls for some modification, however. It seems that, in a performance of the new line 3, the sixth syllable with its nasal consonant cluster -*nct*- (of *sanctissimi*) would be sung with a sustained tone so as to take up the performance space of two syllables;[20] this means that the line with nine syllables would, in the reality of a performance, have the effect and duration of a sung decasyllabic line. In other words, this line 3 of nine syllables exists within the metrical/musical frame of a decasyllabic verse for which phrase β was originally created.

---

[19]Cf. Table 6, no. 8 (p. 187).

[20]In the pronunciation of consonant clusters involving nasals or liquids (*sanctus, corpus*, etc.) "the voice performs a kind of glottal stop" (A. Hughes [1989] 57), which is often reflected in a special kind of notation (*plicas* or *liquescents*), special neumes that imply, in addition to the main pitch, an ornamental second note of indeterminate pitch; cf. Table 1. The 'liquescent' performance seems to "facilitate clear enunciation of the text" in these special cases (Hoppin [1978b] 62). The added time required for such 'liquescent' performance does not seem to be a major issue in plainsong and, therefore, is mentioned only in passing by musicologists; see, e.g. Apel (1958) 105-106. If in the manuscript of AlsfP the neume over *sanc-tissimi* is not a plica or liquescent of some kind but a simple *virga*, this may just be one of the many cases where the special performance is not reflected in a corresponding notational symbol. In any case, the consonant cluster in the syllable *sanct*- of AlsfP is sufficient reason for an extended "clear enunciation" on a sustained tone, which then may well take up the 'duration' of two syllables in a decasyllabic verse.

With regard to its performance, therefore, the new line 3 of the Alsfeld stanza qualifies as a decasyllabic line: 10α- 10α- $10[9]\beta$- $R8\gamma$.

To conclude this comparative study of the B3 stanza in the various Easter or Passion play traditions, the chronological survey in Table 7 shows the metrical/melodic structure of the stanza in all the plays that transmit its complete text and are listed in the Catalogue [**16C**], pp. F39-F42. In the left column (1) are the four-line stanzas which show the regular metrical/ melodic structure of the decasyllabic B-stanzas; included are the earlier Catalan and French stanzas as well as the slightly irregular stanza forms of BozO.IV, AlsfP, TirO.fr, and the 'regular' stanza form of BeRheinO for which the 'regular' melodic structure α-α-β-γ can only be conjectured. The right column (2) lists the 'reduced' stanzas considered typical for the German plays and having an octosyllabic line 3, thereby lacking (except TirO.fr) the musically dynamic phrase β of the traditional B-stanza. Included in this column (2) are the metrically reduced B3 stanzas of InnsThO and BrdbO for which the impoverished melody α-α-γ, not transmitted in the manuscripts, can be reasonably assumed. Included as well is the four-line stanza of the two Zwickau plays I and III which, in spite of the added refrain, still represent the metrically and musically reduced 'German' B3 stanza.[21]

The survey in Table 7 and the preceding comparative discussion lead to the conclusion that chant [**17**] of the Lddv, with its decasyllabic stanza form of four lines including the refrain, would have been sung to the melody α-α-β-γ of the regular decasyllabic travel stanzas B. The author of the fourteenth-century Lddv certainly knew the regular four-line B-stanzas of the Merchant Scene and used stanza B1 for chant [**16**] *Omnipotens pater*. Of the B3 stanza *Sed eamus* he most likely knew only its reduced German version, 10α-10α-8γ, since the surviving four-line recreations of this stanza in German plays are of a later date and the two Thuringian Easter plays (BeThO and InnsThO) as well as the closely re-

---

[21]On the basis of all metrical and musical evidence for the various B3 stanzas in German Easter and Passion plays, Thoran's statement (1976) 234, that all three German B stanzas have four lines and end with the *Heu*-refrain, needs revision; it does not hold true even against her own documentation (pp. 234-238), where she cites four plays (Tr, Inns, Erl, Eg) as having B3 stanzas with three lines only and no *Heu*-refrain. See Table 7, col. 2, listing ten plays with a 3-line stanza B3.

lated PragO.C (all of the fourteenth-century like the Lddv) have the
reduced three-line form.[22]

TABLE 7 THE METRICAL/MELODIC STRUCTURE OF THE B3-STANZA
SED EAMUS IN THE EASTER PLAYS[23]

DATE	(1) REGULAR B3 STANZA $(10\alpha\text{-}10\alpha\text{-}10\beta\text{-}8\gamma)$		(2) 'REDUCED' B3 STANZA $(10\alpha\text{-}10\alpha\text{-}8\gamma)$	
12c	VichO	$10\alpha\text{-}10\alpha\text{-}10\beta\text{-}8\gamma$		
13c	ToursO	$10\alpha\text{-}10\alpha\text{-}10\beta\text{-}8\gamma$	(a) *3-line stanza form*	
14c			BeThürO	$10\alpha\text{-}10\alpha\text{-}8\gamma$
			PragO.C	$10\alpha\text{-}10\alpha\text{-}8\gamma$
			TrierO	$10\alpha\text{-}10\alpha\text{-}8\gamma$
			[InnsThO	10 - 10 - 8]
			[BrdbO	10 - 10 - 8]
15c	EgmontO	$10\alpha\text{-}10\alpha\text{-}10\beta\text{-}8\gamma$	Erl.III	$10\alpha\text{-}10\alpha\text{-}8\gamma$
	[BeRheinO	$10\alpha\text{-}10\alpha\text{-}10\beta\text{-}8\gamma$]	EgerP	$10\alpha\text{-}10\alpha\text{-}8\gamma$
	BozO.IV	$10\alpha\text{-}10\alpha\text{-}10\beta\text{-}8\gamma$	BozO.II	$10\alpha\text{-}10\alpha\text{-}8\gamma$
			BöhmO.I	$10\alpha\text{-}10\alpha\text{-}8\gamma$
			(b) *4-line stanza form*	
			ZwiO.I+III	$10\alpha\text{-}10\alpha\text{-}8\gamma^{\text{var}}\text{-}R8\gamma$
16c	AlsfP	$10\alpha\text{-}10\alpha\text{-}10(9)\gamma\text{-}R8\gamma$	(a) *3-line stanza form*	
	TirO.fr	$10\alpha\text{-}10\alpha\text{-}8\beta'\text{-}R8\gamma$	BozP.1514	$10\alpha\text{-}10\alpha\text{-}8\gamma$

When the author of the Lddv decided to use stanzas from the Easter
play for the oil-searching scene in his Ten Virgins play he was, of
course, less dependent on his model than a compiler of an Easter play.
He, therefore, adopted the B1 stanza entirely, but took only a few words
of the B3 stanza, mainly from the beginning. Obviously, he wanted this
second stanza, sung by the *Secunda Fatua*, to have the same complete
melody that the *Prima Fatua* had sung in the preceding chant [16] *Omnipotens pater*. Thus he composed a new *Sed eamus* stanza in the regular

[22]It seems to me that the lack of the distinctive melodic phrase β in the three-line B3
stanza in German plays would have been the main reason for the changes observed in
the form of the B3 stanza. All four-line versions of this stanza, in the Lddv and in the
six later Easter/Passion plays examined above, must be understood as independent
recreations, motivated by the desire to restore the regular metrical and melodic structure
of the decasyllabic B stanzas.

[23]Square brackets [ ] indicate the absence of musical notation in the manuscripts.

B-structure of four-lines, 10-10-10-R8. The melodic sequence was doubt-less α-α-β-γ (words identical with B3 are printed in bold):

> **Sed eamus** oleum **emere,**
> preter quod nil **possumus** agere.
> Qui caret hoc carebit glorie.
> Alie respondent   Heu quantus est noster dolor!

As far as I can tell, this is the earliest, independent rewriting of the German three-line stanza *Sed eamus unguentum emere* as a perfect deca-syllabic stanza, in a totally different context, yet with a similar dramatic function. This little composition proves the author of the play to be a poet who was metrically and musically acutely aware.[24]

In fact, the author wrote in chant [17] a genuine *contrafactum* to the B3 stanza (with restitution of its underlying B-stanza structure). The widespread practice of *contrafactum* compositions has been defined as substituting "one text for another while retaining the same, or nearly the same, music."[25] In instances where the melody of the new composition is not transmitted, non-musical criteria are considered indicative of an author's intention to create a *contrafactum* (maintaining an unusual stanza form with its rhythmical-metrical structure, imitating the rhyme scheme, the syntax, and/or the content, and particularly, adopting some key words or the first line of the model).[26] Such criteria certainly hold true for chant [17] as a *contrafactum* of the B3 stanza.[27]

With all this evidence, it will be safe to restore the melody of chant [17] *Sed eamus oleum emere* with the same stanza melody that was

---

[24]The discussion below of chants [27] and [33] will confirm this observation.

[25]A. Hughes (1989a) 82; cf. Stevens (1986) 506, explaining a *contrafactum* as "a song ... to which a new set of words has been fitted — normally ... with precise syllabic equivalence." See also Kippenberg (1962) 158, cited in Amstutz (1994) 9-10; Stevens (1986) 441, with further literature.

[26]Cf. Reichert (1958) 883; Kippenberg (1962) 158; Falck (1980) 701.

[27]In contrast, the twelve concluding vernacular stanzas of the Lddv (ll. 526-576), which were probably sung to the (reconstructed) melody of the *Nibelungenlied* whose stanza form they imitate, cannot be regarded as *contrafacta* but rather as adaptations of new texts to a pre-existing melody. The *planctus* stanza *Nu hebyd sych groeß weynen unde schryen ummerme* in TrierMkl and AlsfP, however, which use the beginning line of the first of those concluding stanzas in the Lddv, have been shown to be *contrafacta* to this first stanza *Nù hebit sich groz schrigen und weynen ummerme* (ll. 526-529). For the whole complex issue, see Amstutz (1994).

adopted for chant **[16]** *Omnipotens pater*, i.e., with the B1-melody from the Breslau Easter Play (BrslO). The Lddv is special, however, in that the manner of delivery of the stanza *Sed eamus oleum emere* is in 'dialogue' form. The three first lines are sung solo by one of the *Fatue*, and the refrain is an ensemble response by the other four *Fatue*. Such a 'dialogue' form sometimes occurs in the purchase stanzas (C) of the Merchant Scene (in ToursO, InnsThO, BrdbO, Erl.III) when the three Marys sing their refrain *Heu quantus est noster dolor* in response to the Merchant's words,[28] but it is rare in any of the B-stanzas. In fact, the only case to my knowledge where the performance changes within a B-stanza is again a Thuringian source, the fourteenth-century Thuringian Easter Play fragments of BeThO: stanza B2 in this play, *Amisimus enim solatium,* is sung solo by the *Secunda Maria* (ll. 1-3), followed by the stage direction for all three Marys to sing the refrain together: *Omnes tres heu quantus.*[29]

Thus, there are two Thuringian Easter plays (InnsThO and BeThO) and the closely related BrdbgO,[30] all of the fourteenth century, which, independently of the much earlier Easter play of Tours, use the refrain as a group response in one or more stanzas (of the B- or C-group). It comes as no surprise, then, that in the more or less contemporaneous Lddv, the performance changes in a similar way from solo for the first three lines of chant **[17]** to choral singing for the fourth line, the refrain. This common feature in the manner of delivery is additional proof that the Lddv stands firmly within the rich and lively play tradition of Thuringia.

We do not know whether the author intended an ensemble singing of the refrain in chant **[16]** *Omnipotens pater*, which is indicated in the

[28]InnsThO (C1 and C3); BrdbgO (C1 and C3; only *Tercia Maria* in dialogue with Merchant); Erl.III (C3); and three times in ToursO (ed. Krieg, ll. 36-39, 44-47, 48-51; LOO 824, ll. 49-53, 60-64, 65-70).

[29]Seelmann in his edition (1926) 265, reads *heu quater* BeThO, l. 75a; the nasal stroke above the *a* and the final siglum-*us* are clearly recognizable, however, even in the microfilm copy of the manuscript. Of the C stanzas in this play fragment, only C1 is extant, with no change of performers; thus nothing can be said about the performance of the other C stanzas in this play. In the Erlau Easter Play, the *Heu*-refrain, sung solo in B1 and B2, is used quite effectively as a group response after the third Mary has delivered both stanza B3 (three lines) and the subsequent sixteen lines of vernacular paraphrase (Erl.III 36a-52b).

[30]The editors of the newly discovered BrdbgO see a close relationship between this play and the InnsThO; cf. Schipke-Pensel (1986) 62.

manuscript only by its incipit. However, frequent alternation of solo and choral singing is evident in most of the liturgical chants of the Lddv. Moreover, the twelve vernacular stanzas at the end of the play, sung solo by the various *Fatue*, are always rounded off by a choral refrain of the rest of the group (cf. Lddv, A529a *Alie respondent ad quemlibet versum* and A575a *Alie respondent*). By analogy, we may assume that the author had a similar method of performance in mind also for both Latin stanzas [16] and [17], not just for the latter.

These two stanzas, then, will be presented in Chapter 4 in the form of the regular travel stanza B, with three perfect decasyllabic lines in solo performance (phrases α-α-β) and the final octosyllabic line *Heu quantus* sung as a choral refrain (phrase γ) by the rest of the group. As the text for the chant [17] is complete in the transmission of MS A, only its melody needs to be restored; this will be done with the mode 6 melody of B1 in the BrslO used for the melodic restoration of chant [16] *Omnipotens pater*.

Stanza	*Sed eamus oleum emere*
	preter quod nil possumus agere.
	Qui caret hoc carebit glorie.
	Heu quantus est noster dolor!
	Source Lddv 168b-f (a *contrafactum* to the B3 stanza of the Easter plays).
Melody	Mode 6. Transcribed in Chapter 4 [17], like chant [16], from the B1 stanza *Omnipotens pater* in BrslO (MS Breslau [Wroclaw], UB, MS I Q.226a) fol. 2v).
	Melody Cf. the comparative Tables 6 and 7 (pp. 187 and 198).
Translation	"But let us go and buy oil
	Without which we cannot do anything.
	He who lacks this will lack also glory.
	Alas, how vast is our woe and pain!"

[19] *Ecce sponsus venit etc.* (Lddv 176e)

The triumphant announcement **[19]** *Ecce sponsus venit etc.* is sung by the Angels as they accompany the *Dominica Persona*, when he finally arrives to meet the *Prudentes*:

DOMINICA PERSONA vadat ad
PRUDENTES cum ANGELIS cantando   *Ecce sponsus venit etc.* (ll. 176c-d)[1]

With the preceding *Silete* call **[18′]**, the laments of the *Fatue* in the Latin stanzas **[16-17]** (and the corresponding vernacular ll. 157-176) are suddenly suspended. Although their futile search for an oil merchant probably continues in the background, the focus is now on the new action about to unfold. This new action is the climax of the play: the long awaited encounter of the Bridegroom with those of the *Virgines* that have heeded the call of the *Angeli* and are prepared for the Wedding Feast.

There does not seem to be any liturgical chant with the incipit *Ecce sponsus venit*, nor could I find it used as a chant in any other medieval play.[2] All editors of the Lddv have suggested that this text was taken directly from the parable in Matthew 25: 6. In that case it would have to be recited in the *tonus evangelii* like the short dialogue **[14-15]** *Date nobis etc.* studied above. The verb in the stage direction clearly contradicts such a choice, however; as we have seen, *cantare* implies a melodious Gregorian chant.

A closer study of the liturgical sources shows that the joyful exclamation *Ecce sponsus venit etc.* occurs at the end of several different chants. The three antiphons (i)-(iii) cited in Catalogue **[19D]** are transmitted in a great number of medieval antiphonals, usually in the Office for the common feasts of virgins.[3] The first two can be found as regular

---

[1]The stage direction is not precise in designating which character(s) should deliver the chant. The gerund *cantando* can refer to either the *Dominica Persona* or the *Angeli*, or both of them. But as one of the *Angeli* delivers the subsequent vernacular lines, 177-186, and the chant is about the arrival of the Bridegroom, its performance by the *Angeli* alone would make sense. See also Ettmüller's translation (1867) 300. Curschmann-Glier (1981) 285 (translation of ll. 176a-f) have the *Dominica Persona* sing this chant, however.

[2]See, however, below p. 206 and n8.

[3]In addition to the three antiphons listed in Catalogue **[19D]**, p. F46, at least two other chants, both responsories, end with the words of this 'incipit.' The texts of the responsories are listed in CAO 7444 and 7496. The responsory no. 7444 *Prudentes virgines aptate ... obviam ei* is complete only in the Antiphonal of Ivrea (siglum E) for the

psalm antiphons (mostly for Matins or Lauds), while the longer and
more elaborate antiphon (iii) of Figure 15 is usually reserved for the
Gospel canticle in Lauds (*Benedictus*) or Vespers (*Magnificat*).

The first two antiphons are particularly interesting for different reasons:

  i *Prudentes virgines aptate lampades vestras, ecce sponsus venit, exite
    obviam ei.*
  ii *Media autem nocte clamor factus est, ecce sponsus venit, exite obviam ei.*

Both are concise in terms of both text and music, consisting of four
clauses (melodic phrases) each and ending with the exclamation *Ecce
sponsus venit etc.*, which furnishes the second half of the chant. Their
melodies are basically the same, although the different words in the first
part cause a few minor melodic variants. The two examples from *A*Fri.117
(Figure 13) can be found in very similar forms in other German and in
Dominican sources.

FIGURE 13 ... *ECCE SPONSUS VENIT* IN TWO ANTIPHONS OF *A*FRI.117

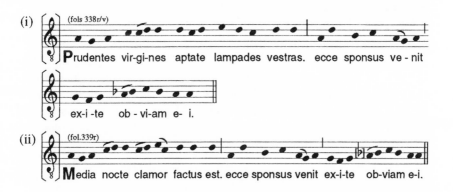

Within the same manuscript, the text and tune of the *Ecce sponsus venit*
are usually identical in both antiphons. In its syllabic style the melody

---

Common of Virgins; as an incipit it appears in Hartker's Antiphonal (siglum H) for All
Saints' Day. The responsory no. 7496 *Quinque prudentes virgines acceperunt ... obviam
Christo Domino* is only complete in the monastic antiphonals of Hartker (H) and that
from St. Maur-les-Fossés (F) for the Common of Virgins; it is indicated by incipits in
the antiphonals of Compiégne and St. Denis (sigla C and D in CAO). As sufficient evidence suggests that one or two of the antiphons to be discussed here provided the model
for chant [19], the responsories are excluded from this study.

of this final section has a very distinct character, almost like a bugle call, that is easily remembered, and this means that it is also easily separable from the antiphons, e.g. for use in a play like the Lddv:[4]

FIGURE 14 THE "BUGLE CALL" *ECCE SPONSUS VENIT*
(AFRI.117, FOLS. 338v AND 339r)

... Ec-ce spon-sus ve- nit   ex- i- te   ob -vi-am   e- i.

The melodic similarity between antiphons (i) and (ii) is not surprising when we learn that this tune is "one of the commonest prototypes" for antiphons and was adapted to a large number of texts comprising four clauses.[5] Since around ninety different texts have this melody, the tune was certainly well known generally, and the separate performance of its final section should not have presented any problem.

By comparison, the long, multiphrase antiphon (iii) beginning *Quinque prudentes virgines* also listed in Catalogue [19D], pp. F46-F47, seems less known. Its final *Ecce sponsus venit* section (Figure 15) with a number of two-note neumes in the undulating pattern over *exite obviam xristo domino* has a more gentle character than the melody of (i) and (ii). The tune does not stand out musically and, hence, appears less easily separable from the chant than the *Ecce sponsus* exclamation of the two antiphons (i) and (ii) just discussed.

---

[4]It is interesting to see that this melody's bugle-like character gets lost in a chant with a less syllabic style. In two of the sources studied, an antiphon with the same melody and incipit as (i) continues with a different text (*Prudentes virgines acceperunt oleum in vasis suis cum lampadibus*); the result for the final section of the antiphon is as follows (example from *B*Helm.145.1, fol. 370v; similar in *A*Ahrw.2b, fol. 215r):

... in vasis su - is   cum lam-pa- di - bus.

[5]Huglo (1980a) 471-480, esp. 473-474, shows how this mode 4 prototype melody (see his example 3) was adapted to various texts through contraction of occasional notes or expansion of the formulas with extra notes.

FIGURE 15 *ECCE SPONSUS VENIT* **IN THE ANTIPHON** *QUINQUE PRUDENTES*
(*A*FRI.117, FOL. 339v)

As a result of the study of the three antiphons that contain the phrase *Ecce sponsus venit etc.* in their last section, I consider the antiphons (i) *Prudentes virgines* and (ii) *Media nocte* most likely to have provided the model for chant **[19]** of the Lddv. The cheerful leaps in their proclamation *Ecce sponsus venit* (Figure 14) articulate musically the change in action that results from the sudden arrival of the *Dominica Persona* announced in this chant. And since most antiphonals contain both antiphons in their formulary for the common feasts of holy virgins, this *Ecce sponsus* call could be heard a number of times throughout the year whenever a holy virgin who did not have a proper Office was celebrated. Thus, even though it is only the final part of an antiphon, it must have been quite familiar. Because of its simple tune, it is relatively easy to deliver even in the totally different context of a religious play.

Last, but not least, antiphon (i), in which the *Prudentes virgines* are directly addressed and told to take up their lamps and go out to meet the Bridegroom, had a special function in a pontifical celebration. By the late thirteenth century Bishop Durandus of Mende chose this antiphon for the beginning of the Consecration of Virgins. With the singing of this antiphon, the archpresbyter invites the virgins to come forward to the bishop to be consecrated as nuns.[6] The Lddv provides a striking parallel to this opening of the consecration ceremony when the *Angeli* sing the antiphon's last section *Ecce sponsus*, thus inviting the *Prudentes* to come forward to meet the Bridegroom. This connection would suggest that the antiphon (i) *Prudentes virgines* rather than (ii) *Media nocte* was the source for chant **[19]** in the play. Such parallels between the Lddv and the consecration rite for nuns must be kept in mind along with other similar associations with the same ceremony mentioned earlier.[7] In this context, the fifteenth-century Roman pontifical in the municipal library

---

[6]Cf. *P*Dur lib. I, ordo XXIII.4, ed. Andrieu (1938-1941) 412.
[7]Cf. the discussion above of chant **[2]** *Regnum mundi*, pp. 96-98.

of Lyon (MS 5144) is of interest. A full-page illustration for the formulary of the Consecration of Virgins, fol. 103r (cf. copy in Leroquais [1937] Pl. CXXII), uses the antiphon *Prudentes virgines* as its caption. The complete text is given, but only the 'bugle call' is set to music.

FIGURE 16   *ECCE SPONSUS VENIT* AS CAPTION FOR A MINIATURE
(LYON, BIBL.MUN. MS 5144, FOL. 103 [DETAIL])

Photo: Didier Nicole, cliché Bibliothèque municipale de Lyon.
Detail, used by permission.

An as yet unedited later Thuringian play, the Erfurt Morality of 1448 (ErfMor), may lend some unsuspected support to the preference for antiphon (i) *Prudentes virgines* over (ii) *Media nocte* as the more immediate source for chant [19]. On fol. 262ra of the Coburg manuscript, as described by Linke, the rubric calls for a chant with the incipit *Prudentes virgines* in a dramatic context comparable to that of chant [19] in the Lddv. Since the incipit remains without notation, under an empty stave, and the genre of the chant is not indicated in the rubrics, however, either the antiphon (CAO 4404) or the responsory (CAO 7444) could be intended here.[8]

---

[8]Cf. Linke (1995a) n20. As Linke has shown, the subsequent vernacular text in the Erfurt play is a paraphrase of both the antiphon (i) discussed above (CAO 4404) and the responsory (CAO 7444), which uses the same words, at least for the respond section. Linke concludes that it is impossible to decide between the two. It may be noted, however, that the responsory's verse (*Tunc surrexerunt omnes virgines illae, et ornaverunt lampades suas*) does not really fit the play's context; moreover, a liturgical source from Erfurt, BErf.81, fol. 298r, has additional narrative text for the responsory's respond section (*Prudentes virgines, ... exite obviam ei. Et que parate erant intraverunt cum eo ad nuptias. V. Tunc surrexerunt* etc.) Thus, the antiphon *Prudentes virgines* with its text entirely in direct discourse would seem more appropriate at this place in ErfMor.

There is an unusual diversity in the way the mode 4 melody of the antiphons (i) and (ii) is transmitted in the various sources listed in the Catalogue. Only the Pontifical of Durandus (consulted in its London manuscript Add. 36677) and the Passau Antiphonal *A*Pat present it in the expected mode 4 range with the finalis *E*; the other sources, except two, have it transposed to the upper fourth (finalis *a*).[9] The substantially different transmissions in *A*Ahrw.2b and particularly *A*Mz.II,138 can be explained through the 'ambiguous' modality of this particular prototype melody, an ambiguity which led to various medieval modifications of the tune and which is discussed at some length by Huglo.[10]

Except for *A*Mz.II,138, the melody of the two antiphons is basically the same in all sources studied. The main true variants of transmission for the final section are the different ways in which the melodic line is shaped over the two words *Ecce sponsus*. The opening leap of a rising minor third over *Ecce* occurs only in three of the sources studied; all other versions except that in the Durandus Pontifical have an ascending fourth at this place. By extending the comparison to the next word *sponsus*, we find:

(1) two different melodic zigzag lines over *Ecce sponsus*, beginning

(a) with a minor third	**bdbc**	in	*A*OP(Humb); *A*Mz.II,138; PR.Lyon 5144
(b) with a fourth	**adbc**	in	*A*Fri.117; 124; 129; BHelm.145.1; LU; *A*R
	DGEF	in	*A*Ahrw.2b

---

[9]Such transpositions are not uncommon in the plainsong tradition. See Apel (1958) 157-165.

[10]Cf. Huglo (1980a) 474. In *A*Ahrw.2b the greater part of the tune, except the last four notes, is notated one pitch too low, probably by mistake, causing melodic problems. The Cistercian antiphonal *A*Mz.II,138 provides a quite different melody in mode 7 (*finalis G*) for both antiphons. This may be the completely reshaped version of the prototype that the Cistercians created following proposals of twelfth-century theorists (cf. Huglo, loc. cit.). Nevertheless, the musical phrase **b-d-b-c-aG-a** over the words *Ecce sponsus venit*, is retained in this Cistercian source in almost exactly the form and pitch known from other 'transposed' versions of the melody.

(2) three moderate, smoother versions, beginning
    (a) with a major third   **FaGF**   in   *P*Dur.Add.39677
    (b) with an ascending fourth   **adcb**   in   *A*Worc
    (c) "   "   "   "   **EaGG**   in   *A*Pat

The first group of variants with the melodic zigzag line over *Ecce sponsus*, especially when it opens with an ascending fourth over the reveille word *Ecce* (version 1.b), gives a joyful, bugle-like character to the call. This cheerful way of singing the *Ecce sponsus* section in both antiphons (i) and (ii) was certainly well known in the Mainz diocese as evidenced in the three Fritzlar Antiphonals and supported for other German areas by *B*Helm.145.1 and *A*Ahrw.2b. Chant **[19]** in the Lddv will, therefore, be restored in this form from the final section of the Matins antiphon *Prudentes virgines* as transmitted in *A*Fri.117:

Text   (second part of the antiphon *Prudentes virgines aptate lampades vestras*):

                      Ecce sponsus venit, [exite oviam ei.]

                      Source   *A*Fri.117, fol. 338r/v (= *A*Fri.124, *A*Fri.129, *B*Fri.146, *B*Erf.81, *B*Helm.145.1, *A*Ahrw.2b, *A*Mz.II,138, and others); cf. Catalogue **[19D]**, pp. F46-F47.

Melody   Mode 4, in most sources transposed up a fourth. See Figures 13 and 14 above. Transcribed in Chapter 4 from *A*Fri.117, fols. 338r-v.

                      Melody = *A*Fri.124, *A*Fri.129, *B*Helm.145.1; ~ = *A*OP(Humb); ~ (untransposed) *A*Pat, *P*Dur.Add; *var.* *A*Ahrw (errors in notation?); *different* *A*Mz.II,138 (a mode 7 tune).

Translation "Look, the Bridegroom is coming! Go out to meet him!"

                                                    [cf. CAO 4404]

[20] *Regnum mundi* (Lddv 186b)

At the beginning of the Lddv, the responsory *Regnum mundi* was sung by all Ten *Virgines* (chant [2]) as they proceeded to the playing area. At the climax of the play when the Bridegroom arrives and the *Angeli* summon all to come and meet him ([19] *Ecce sponsus* with the vernacular ll. 177-186), it is only the *Prudentes* who are ready for this encounter.

The fact that this intrinsically monastic responsory, professing denial of worldly goods and honors for the sake of Christ, is sung twice in the Lddv is remarkable and, in my view, quite significant for a deeper understanding of the play. During the opening procession all Ten Virgins were apparently able to identify with the ascetic attitude and content of chant [2] *Regnum mundi*, and in this way the responsory helped characterize its singers. Their promise and commitment, however, were manifest only on the Latin-liturgical level since the chant was not followed by any vernacular paraphrase. Sung a second time at the climax of the play by the *Prudentes* alone, chant [20] is followed by a vernacular text in which the *Quinta prudens* provides an almost literal rendering of the Latin liturgical text except that the first person singular has been changed to the first person plural:

Wy haben der werlde ere
vorsmet dorch dy gotis lere,
hochvart und kundickeit
habe wy vorkorn dorch dy ewickeit,
und alliz, daz in der werlde ist,
daz habe wy gelazen dorch unsen heren jhesum crist,
an den wy gelouben
und han ge[se] mit unsen ougen
und den wy von herczen minnen
mit alle unsen synnen.   (ll. 187-196)[1]

Only now, through this translation, is it clear on the vernacular level that with the singing of chants [2] and [20] *Regnum mundi*, the *Virgines*

---

[1] "We have despised the world's glory and splendour for the sake of God's direction. We have renounced honor and prudence for the sake of eternity. And we have abandoned everything in the world for the sake of our Lord Jesus Christ, in whom we believe, and whom we have seen with our eyes, and whom we love with all our heart and with all our understanding."

have made a very deep religious commitment. And it becomes obvious in retrospect that the *Fatue* by indulging in all kinds of worldly pleasures did not live up to such a promise.

Most aspects of the responsory *Regnum mundi* have been discussed in Chapter 3 [2], but because I consider it to be a key chant for the Lddv and its roots in the ritual of the Church, a few observations may be added here regarding its place and function in the play and in the religious life of the time.[2] In a Mainz pontifical of the twelfth century, *PMz.XII*, one of the earliest occurrences of this responsory, the *Regnum mundi* had a prominent place in the consecration ceremony: after the nuns are consecrated and veiled and, as brides of Christ, have received the symbolic insignia of ring and crown, they all sing the responsory *Regnum mundi* "cum versu et Gloria patri" in confirmation of their vows and their commitment to their *sponsus* Christ.[3] It comes as no surprise, then, that, as early as the first half of the thirteenth century, 'brides of Christ' were identified with this responsory, at least, in monastic and Dominican circles.[4]

The later form of the *Consecratio virginum* as designed by William Durandus at the end of the thirteenth century seems to be even more closely reflected in the Lddv and the action surrounding the singing of this responsory. If chant [19] *Ecce sponsus venit* recalls the opening antiphon of this ceremony, *Prudentes virgines*, inviting the virgins to come forward to be consecrated as nuns (see above, pp. 205-206), chant [20] *Regnum mundi*, sung by the *Prudentes* when they meet the *Dominica Persona* brings to mind the point in Durandus' consecration ceremony when the virgins, having put on the blessed vestments, sing this responsory while they return to the bishop to be consecrated as nuns and brides of Christ (*PDur lib. I, ordo XXIII.28*). And when the *Dominica Persona*,

---

[2]Compare to the following the discussion above, pp. 94-97.

[3]Cf. *PMz.XII* ed. Martène (1736) 542D-543A.

[4]See e.g. Jordan of Saxony, second general of the Dominican Order (1222-1237), in a letter to Diane, sister in the women's convent of St. Agnes/Bologna, after her solemn vows in June 1223: "Regnum mundi et omnem ornatum saeculi ... propter amorem Iesu Christi dilecti sponsi tui (contempsisti) ... ." (ed. Walz [1951] 20, letter xvii). And the mystic Henri Suso (Heinrich Seuse, early fourteenth century) regards the responsory *Regnum mundi* as the joyous chant that accompanies the departure of God's elected bride from this treacherous world into a heavenly life on the day of her consecration (ed. Bihlmeyer [1907] 410).

with chant [21] *Veni electa mea* (ll. 196b-c), invites the *Prudentes* to come towards him and be rewarded and crowned by his mother Mary, there is another parallel with this particular consecration ceremony, where, after the consecration proper, the bishop, representing Christ, uses that responsory (*PDur* lib. I, ordo XXIII.33, cited below, p. 222 n20) to call the new nuns to receive the veil and the ring and crown, as symbols of their mystical marriage to Christ.[5]

The evidence for these and other parallels and reminiscences between *ludus* and rite exists more on the play's Latin-liturgical level than it does in the vernacular text.[6] For a liturgically educated medieval audience, however, such connections were certainly just as relevant as, for instance, the connection of chants [16-17] *Omnipotens* and *Sed eamus* to the Easter plays, of chant [4] *Homo quidam* to the new feast of Corpus Christi, or of chants [7] *Emendemus* and [8] *Tribularer* to the season of Lent. If the entire liturgical dimension inherent in these chants is not immediately evident in the 'theatrical' reality of the play, this is just one of the ways in which the hybrid character of many mixed-language plays, on the threshold between liturgy and drama, manifests itself.[7] To some degree, however, the intrinsically liturgical connotations of the *Regnum mundi* and the other chants are carried over into the macaronic Lddv, at least into its Latin parts. An awareness of these underlying liturgical connections can only help deepen the understanding of the extant play.

---

[5]Cf. *PDur* lib. I, ordo XXIII.3-5, 28-51. For more details on this consecration ceremony and its relevance for the Thuringian Lddv, see Amstutz forthcoming.

[6]The statement that my 1991 Toronto dissertation suggested "that the Thuringian A text was written ... for the Celebration of the Profession of a Nun" (Muir [1995] 261 n21) is an unfortunate misunderstanding. What I did propose is that, first, the consecration rite for nuns must be regarded as one of the main liturgical sources for a hypothetical original conception of the play in Latin; the Thuringian MS A with its various interpolations does not transmit an 'original' version of the Lddv. And, second, that, given the historical context — lack of discipline in women's convents, the Dominicans' *cura monialium*, etc., — the original intent of the author of an earlier, possibly Latin-only version, may have been an admonition addressed to a monastic audience, especially nuns who had pronounced, or were about to pronounce, solemn vows in the rite of their consecration. See Amstutz (1991) 386-396, 411-420, 451-454; also p. 98 above.

[7]Linke ([1987a] 183) talks about the "Zwitternatur" of such plays.

For the complete text of the responsory *Regnum mundi*, see its 'critical' edition, with apparatus and melodic indicators in [2], p. 103, and with the melody in Chapter 4 [2] and [20].

[21] *Veni electa mea etc.* (Lddv 196c)

The place of this chant **[21]** in its dramatic context cannot yet be determined since the rubric in MS A is obviously flawed:

QUINTA PRUDENS ducens
eas per manus cantat   *Veni electa mea etc.* (ll. 197a-b)[1]

Both the chant incipit and the stage direction need to be examined first.

Two other German plays, both of Thuringian origin, the LdbKath and the Innsbruck Thuringian Assumption Play (InnsThAss), each employ this incipit twice, yet the genre of the chant is not indicated in any of these places.[2] Both an antiphon and a responsory with this incipit are well documented in medieval liturgical books, and the choice between them is not easy.[3]

Whereas in the other plays, the rubrics clearly direct the *Dominica Persona* to deliver this chant,[4] the stage direction in the Lddv has the *Quinta Prudens* sing or begin it. Yet even examples from mystical wri-

---

[1]"While the fifth *Prudens* leads them by the hand she sings: *Come, my chosen one etc.*" Fr. Stephan's reading of this stage direction (1847b) 177, *Quinta Prudens ducens eas Primarius cantet*, repeated in all subsequent editions, attempted to emend the questionable rubric by having the *Primarius* ("i.e. *Dominica Persona*") sing the chant. For the rejection of this reading and the related palaeographical discussion see above, Chapter 1, pp. 31-32.

[2]See the quotations in Catalogue **[21C]**, p. F50. Only once is a more extensive text given, with a stage direction that suggests liturgical recitation: DOMINICA PERSONA dicit *Veni electa mea, veni coronaberis* (InnsThAss, l. 1520a). For good reasons it has never been suggested that this could be the complete text in the Lddv or the other three instances, where the use of the verb *cantare* in the preceding stage directions points rather to a musical chant.

[3]See Catalogue **[21DI and II]**, pp. F51-F53. In their editions of the Thuringian play, Beckers and Schneider show little concern for the genre of the chant, although the responsory would have additional text and more elaborate music than the antiphon. Beckers (ed. 1905) 107, note b, cites the complete text of the antiphon, referring to two places in Hartker's Antiphonal (pp. 298 and 384); yet only on p. 82 does he explain that the first reference (p. 298) is not to the antiphon, but to the responsory. Nowhere does he give a reason for his preference for the antiphon. Schneider (ed. 1964) ll. 196c-f and note c, simply inserts the text of the antiphon in the play text while maintaining Beckers' two references. In the editions of De Boor (1965) 190, ll. 258-259, and Curschmann-Glier (1981) 287, ll. 196b-c, only Schneider's text version is given with no references.

[4]LdbKath, ll. 529a and 647a; InnsThAss, l. 1492a: *dominica persona cantet Veni electa mea.* Cf. InnsThAss, l. 1520a: *dominica persona dicit Veni electa mea, veni coronaberis.*

tings and from a medieval painting assign these or similar words to Christ.[5] Every reader of the play will surely agree that the Latin words as well as the subsequent twelve vernacular lines belong in the mouth of the *Dominica Persona*. MS B of the Lddv, which omits all the Latin texts and rubrics, has the German stage direction (B 272a) *Jhesus sprichet zu den wisen*, which introduces the vernacular couplets B 273-278 as spoken by the *Dominica Persona*.[6]

While the singing of a Latin liturgical chant by a character who does not quite fit the expected role seems acceptable in some cases, the German text after the Latin chant in the Lddv should so obviously be spoken by the person of Jesus that the stage direction must be considered corrupt. The speaker of the vernacular text addresses the *Prudentes* in eight lines, praising them for their vigilance and promising them eternal life and reward. He then turns to his mother Mary and, in four lines, commends the five *Prudentes* to her company for joy and recompense:

> Sint ich uch habe vůnden
> bereyt czů allen stunden,
> darumme wel ich uch geben
> ewic lon und ewic leben
> und wel uch selben brenge
> uz deseme enelende
> czů der ewigen selickeyt,
> dy uch myn vatir hat bereyt.
> Maria, libe muter myn,
> ich bevele dy dese iuncvrowelyn:
> dů salt sů bi dich selben seczen
> und alle ers ungemachs ergetzen.   (ll. 197-208)[7]

---

[5]Cf. Mechthild von Magdeburg, *Das fließende Licht der Gottheit*, I.46, 51-52, ed. H. Neumann (1990, 1993) 1: 35: "So sprichet únser herre zů siner userwelten brut: *Veni, dilecta mea, veni, coronaberis!*". A painting by a middle German master (c. 1350) shows Christ crowning Mary with a banderol belonging to Christ saying: *Veni electa mea.* (Frankfurt/Main, Städel Museum, no. SG 443).

[6]See also the Ten-Virgins Scene in KünzCC, ll. 4669a-5074f, in which the *Dominica Persona* speaks the corresponding words "Komt her, mein auss er welten ewiglich, In meiness vatter reich" (ll. 4750a-4754). Since the stage directions in Lddv(B) and KünzCC refer to the vernacular text only, their evidence is not very strong.

[7]"Since I have found you prepared at all times, I shall give you eternal reward and eternal life. And I will myself bring you from this life of exile to eternal bliss, which my father has prepared for you. Mary, dear mother mine, I commend these maidens to Thy care: Thou shalt seat them by Thy side and compensate them for their distress."

Mary then welcomes the *Prudentes* and crowns them while singing chant [22] *Transite ad me* and adding vernacular verses.

This whole 'scene' is the climax of the play, and the twelve vernacular lines quoted above, if assigned to the *Dominica Persona*, would be his only speech. As we have seen, the basic structure of the Lddv is that a vernacular speech is preceded by a Latin chant sung by the same character as gives the speech, in this case, the *Dominica Persona* himself. The simplest way of solving the problem here, therefore, seems to be to emend the stage direction and attribute the chant to the *Dominica Persona* in keeping with the existing editions:

> QUINTA PRUDENS ducens eas per manus
> [DOMINICA PERSONA] cantat   *Veni electa mea etc.*

This conjecture, although unsatisfactory because of its awkward Latin syntax, would have the *Dominica Persona* perform both the Latin chant and the vernacular couplets. On the other hand, it may be premature to emend the rubric for a chant of which neither the genre nor the melody nor the complete text is known. The restoration of chant [21] should, therefore, be attempted first, at least tentatively.

As mentioned before, the incipit *Veni electa mea* can be found in an antiphon as well as in a responsory. The antiphon exists in two forms (i) and (ii) (see Catalogue [21DI], p. F51). Most medieval books have the slightly longer form (ii) *Veni ... speciem tuam* (CAO 5323), with a quite simple melody in mode 6, as transcribed in Figure 17.[8]

FIGURE 17 THE ANTIPHON *VENI ELECTA MEA*
IN A FRITZLAR ANTIPHONAL (*A*FRI.124, FOL. 365r)

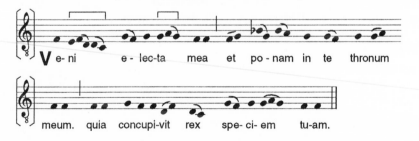

[8]In *A*Pat, fols. 192r and 267r, antiphon (ii) has a very different tune in mode 3. The very short form (i) *Veni ... thronum meum* (CAO 5322), rare in the Middle Ages, is the one retained in the 'modern' liturgical books LU (pp. 1211 and 1233) and *A*Mon (p. 67) and has a very simple, syllabic tune in mode 1.

For the responsory *Veni electa mea*, most German sources studied have the verse **A** *Specie tua*, while verse **B** *Audi filia* seems rare and verse **C** *Surge virgo regia* almost absent from the German transmission.[9] Surprisingly, in two liturgical books from the Mainz diocese, the monastic breviary *B*Erf.81 and the monastic antiphonal *A*Mz.II,138, the responsory has a verse, which I shall call verse **D** (*Surge propera*), that does not appear in any of the twelve antiphonals edited in Hesbert's CAO. The potential importance of this verse **D** for the Lddv surfaces in juxtaposition to the verses **A** and **B**, which belong to this responsory in other German transmissions studied:[10]

<table>
<tr><td align="center">Most German sources</td><td align="center">BErf.81 and AMz.II,138</td></tr>
<tr><td>R *Veni electa mea et ponam in te thronum meum Quia concupivit rex speciem tuam.*
V **A** *Specie tua et pulchritudine tua, intende prospere procede et regna.*
B *Audi filia et vide et inclina aurem tuam.*</td><td>R *Veni electa mea ... Quia concupivit rex speciem tuam.*
V **D** *Surge propera amica mea, veni de libano et coronaberis.*</td></tr>
</table>

If, out of a random list of over twenty manuscripts for this responsory listed in the Catalogue, the only two such responsories with verse **D** *Surge propera* are in monastic sources from the Mainz diocese, one even from Thuringia (*B*Erf.81), the evidence is quite strong that the responsory *Veni electa mea* was known in Thuringia in this form, at least in monastic circles. Verse **D**, then, would be just as valid a choice as verse **A** for this responsory in the Thuringian Lddv if indeed the genre of incipit **[21]** is a responsory rather than an antiphon.

The interesting element in this discovery is the wording of verse **D**, especially the announcement *coronaberis* ("you will be crowned"), which introduces a totally new idea into the responsory not conveyed

---

[9]See Catalogue [21DII1 and 2], pp. F52-F53, where the last column indicates the choice of verse in the various sources.

[10]Translation of the four verses: (**A**) "In your splendor and beauty, strive, proceed and prevail in triumph." (**B**) "Listen, o daughter, look, and lend an ear." (**C**) "Rise up, royal Virgin, worthy of eternal beauty, ascend to the glorious palace of the eternal King." (**D**) "Rise up, my beloved, be quick, come with me from Lebanon and you will be crowned."

through the other extant verses **A**, **B**, or **C**. The coronation of the *Pru-dentes* in the Lddv by Mary (ll. 208a-b), foreign to the parable in Matthew, is the visual culmination in this important 'scene' of the Bridegroom's Wedding Banquet. Yet the act of crowning seems to be an unmotivated action on the part of Mary.[11]

FIGURE 18 THE RESPONSORY *VENI ELECTA MEA*
IN A MAINZ ANTIPHONAL *(AMZ.II,138,*
FOL. 218r [WITH VERSE D *SURGE, PROPERA*])[12]

[11]In the Dutch Play of the Ten Virgins (Flem.X.Virg, ed. Hoebeke [1959] ll. 450, 499 and 502g-k), it is the Bridegroom himself who crowns the Wise Virgins in heaven after having announced his intention to do so twice before. In the KünzCC, ll. 4765-4766, the act of crowning, although not shown, is announced by the *Dominica Persona* himself.

[12]The transcription is from the Mainz Antiphonal, since the Thuringian source with this verse **D** (*B*Erf.81) does not have musical notation.

If verse **D** is claimed for this 'scene' in the Lddv as part of the responsory *Veni electa mea*, the whole situation appears in a new light (cf. Figure 18). It seems natural that the *Dominica Persona* would be the singer of the verse, which is always the solo section in a responsory. By singing this text **D** with its promise of crowning (*coronaberis*), he would so to speak delegate the power for this action to his mother Mary while remaining himself the dominant figure. In this sense, the text of the responsory *Veni electa mea* with verse **D** contributes to the unfolding of the action here.

Besides the special significance of verse **D** for the action of the play, the responsory *Veni electa mea* is musically much richer than the extremely simple antiphon of the same incipit presented in Figure 17 (p. 215). Its prolix performance appears to complement the long-awaited encounter of the *Dominica Persona* and the *Prudentes*. So this responsory may well be the chant meant in the Lddv with incipit **[21]** *Veni electa mea*. With its verse **D** *Surge propera*, it effectively sets the scene not only for the action to follow (crowning of the *Prudentes*), but also for the subsequent words by Mary (*Ich wil uch selben lonen mit den ewigen cronen*).[13] Indeed, verse **D** seems to be the missing link in the manuscript transmission for the extraordinary 'scene' where the Bridegroom meets the Virgins and leads them to the celestial banquet. Such a motivational link appears particularly important since neither the act of crowning nor the person of Mary have any basis in the biblical parable. Chant **[21]** in the Lddv, then, will be restored through this responsory with verse **D**, *Surge propera amica mea*.

The problem of the questionable rubric to chant **[21]** must finally be dealt with. As transmitted in MS A it reads:

QUINTA PRUDENS ducens
eas per manus cantat   *Veni electa mea etc.* (ll. 196a-c)

In my Toronto dissertation (1991) I tried to defend this stage direction, arguing that the *Prudentes* must be understood here as being not completely impersonated, i.e., as fulfilling the liturgical function of singing a chant in which the voice of someone else is speaking. The perceived inadequacy of the words for the *Prudentes*, then, would be due

---

[13]Lddv, l. 211f: "I will reward you myself with crowns of eternal life" (transl. Gloria Dent).

to some kind of a liturgical relic in the play. I have since distanced myself from this position and am offering here a new emendation which I consider well founded.

In view of the fact that the Lddv assigns liturgical chants to the various players in a highly appropriate way, the text of the responsory, or at least its first two phrases (*Veni electa mea ... thronum meum*) must be sung by the *Dominica Persona*. Since the problem in this stage direction is no longer with the words *per manus*, the error may well reside in the name of the person to which both the action and the words are assigned in the rubric. If *Dominica Persona* is placed at the beginning of the complex sentence, instead of *Quinta Prudens*, the syntactical awkwardness of the previous proposal (p. 215) would disappear; the *Dominica Persona* would be the one and only grammatical subject in a satisfying sentence structure:

[DOMINICA PERSONA] ducens
eas per manus cantat   *Veni electa mea* etc.

In this form, the emended stage direction appears in a new light by directing the *Dominica Persona* not only to perform chant [21] including the subsequent vernacular lines but also to take the Wise Virgins by their hands and lead them. It will be necessary to examine whether such an emendation is supported by the larger context.

Immediately preceding chant [21], the *Prudentes* have sung the responsory [20] *Regnum mundi*, with the *Quinta Prudens* adding ten vernacular lines. Beyond the appropriateness of the chant text, it makes dramaturgic sense that the performer would change at this point, i.e. that the *Dominica Persona*, not the *Quinta Prudens*, would be directed to sing the next chant. With the subsequent vernacular lines assigned to him as well (197-208), the basic 'macaronic' principle of the Lddv of Latin chant succeeded by vernacular paraphrase would also be restored for this important 'scene.' Moreover, if it is the *Dominica Persona*, and not the *Quinta Prudens*, who leads the *Prudentes* by the hand, the Latin form *ducens eas* ("leading them") is appropriate here; whereas, if the *Quinta Prudens* were the grammatical subject of the phrase, the form *ducens alias* ("leading the others") would have been more logical.[14] Furthermore, with the singing of the 'bugle call' [19] *Ecce sponsus venit* by the

---

[14]Compare the rubric in ll. 168e-f: ALIE respondent *Heu quantus est noster dolor!*

Angeli, the *Dominica Persona* had advanced, together with the Angels, towards the *Prudentes*:

DOMINICA PERSONA vadat ad
PRUDENTES cum ANGELIS cantando   *Ecce sponsus venit etc.*   (ll. 176c-e)

So, at the time chant **[21]** is sung, he actually is in a position to take the virgins by the hands and guide them to his heavenly kingdom. Not only that, in the vernacular paraphrase he announces very clearly: "I myself want to bring you out of this 'exile' into eternal bliss, which my father has prepared for you":

> und wel uch selben brenge
> uz deseme enelende
> czů der ewigen selickeyt
> dy uch myn vatir hat bireyt.   (ll. 201-204)

On his arrival, the *Dominica Persona* had been greeted by the *Prudentes* with their responsory **[20]** *Regnum mundi*. Chant **[21]** *Veni electa*, then, would be the sung reply of the Bridegroom inviting the Wise Virgins to come with him. The performance of chant and paraphrase implies processional movement, this time to the Heavenly Feast where the *Prudentes* will be crowned by Mary. The responsory *Veni electa* with its more involved performance structure and longer duration is certainly more appropriate than the simple antiphon (Figure 17) to accompany this solemn procession towards that place in the playing area where the heavenly realm is represented and where the great banquet will take place.

With all this evidence, I consider the emended stage direction, [*Dominica Persona*] *ducens eas per manus cantat* not only preferable to earlier emendations, but the only one that makes sense in the context.[15] In copying the text, the scribe, mentally preoccupied with the *Quinta Prudens* as the performer of the preceding vernacular lines 187-196, may have inadvertently transferred this direction into the next rubric, line 196a.

Another problem remains to be solved. If the rubric is emended in this way and chant **[21]** *Veni electa* restored as a responsory, only the *Dominica Persona* can deliver the chant. Yet for the proper performance

[15]KünzCC, ll. 4750a-4766, provides an interesting parallel with the stage direction *Dominica Persona capit virgines* ("the *Dominica Persona* takes the virgins") preceding a vernacular version of the *Veni electa mea*: "Komt her, mein auß er welten ewiglich, ..." which culminates in the promise of an eternal crown as reward (ll. 4765-4766).

of a responsory additional singers are required to sing the choral sections.[16] Any liturgically conscious medieval director of the Lddv would most likely have employed the *Angeli* for an adequate performance of the responsory; in their company the Bridegroom had arrived at the beginning of this 'scene,' and while proceeding they had been singing chant [19] *Ecce sponsus venit*. They would be the obvious choral group to alternate with the *Dominica Persona* as the soloist in the delivery of chant [21] *Veni electa*. Thus, with the emendation of the stage direction proposed here, the responsory *Veni electa mea* in the Lddv can be performed in the proper, liturgical way, i.e., the same person who sings the solo intonation is also the solo singer of the verse; and the accompanying *Angeli* would respond with the choral chanting of respond and *repetenda*. This method of performance seems to have been observed in all the other responsories used in the Lddv.[17]

It is rare in medieval drama that the precise form in which a liturgical chant should be performed is spelled out in every detail, although it does occur.[18] In the Lddv, the direction of who within a group of characters should begin (*incipere*) a chant is given only in four instances, for the chants [7, 8, 10 and 12]:

PRUDENTES cantant Responsorium quod PRIMA incipiet	*Emendemus*	(ll. 42b-d)
PRIMA FATUA incipit Responsorium	*Tribularer*	(ll. 72a-b)
TERTIA PRUDENS incipiet Responsorium	*Beati eritis*	(ll. 100f-h)
TERTIA [FATUA] incipit Invitatorium	*Surgite*	(ll. 116d-f)

In the other instances of choral chanting in this play, the direction *cantare* leaves that decision to the director of the play.[19] In none of these

---

[16]If the *Quinta Prudens* had performed the responsory as the rubric in MS A originally indicated, she could easily have been joined by her four sisters in the choral sections.

[17]See, for instance, the discussion of the term *incipere* in Chapter 2, pp. 51-52; compare pp. 55-60.

[18]In the AlsfP, for instance, the rubric for the responsory *Regnum mundi* directs *Maria* [*Magdalena*] to begin and the *Chorus* to continue the chant: "Maria recedit et incipit canere *Regnum mundi etc.* et chorus continuabit. Post hoc dicit" [16 vernacular lines] (AlsfP, ll. 2875a-c).

[19]For the chants [1, 2, 4, 6, 19-21, 23, 24, 26, 30].

cases is it ever mentioned who else is to join in; it is more or less understood that the rest of the group will continue the chant.

For the performance of chant **[21]** *Veni electa mea*, then, it may be
concluded that the *cantat* of the rubric should be understood to mean
incipit. Moreover, the *Dominica Persona* and the *Angeli*, having entered
the action as a group at the beginning of this 'scene' (after the *Silete* call
[18′]), are certainly perceived as a 'group,' i.e. the group of heavenly
players, which had entered at the opening of the play, singing the first
responsory **[1]** *Testimonium domini*. Thus, the *Angeli* would naturally
join in the performance of the responsory for the choral parts. In this
particular case, the solo intonation would probably be slightly extended
to the point in the respond where the voice shifts from the first to the
third person singular:

[DOMINICA PERSONA] ducens eas per
manus cantat [i.e. incipit responsorium]   *Veni electa mea [et ponam in*
                     te thronum meum.

[ANGELIS prosequentibus]   *Quia concupivit rex speciem*
                     tuam.

[DOMINICA PERSONA] versus   *Surge propera amica mea,*
                     veni de libano et coronaberis.

[ANGELI]   *Quia concupivit rex speciem*
                     tuam.]

If this conjecture seems complicated, it only appears that way.[20]
The liturgically trained director of a performance of the Lddv in the
fourteenth century may well have chosen a similar method of performance, even on the basis of a much simpler emendation:

[DOMINICA PERSONA] ducens
eas per manus cantat [responsorium] *Veni electa mea etc.*

---

[20]There is some external evidence to support this method of performance in the
parallel 'scene' (cf. above, pp. 210-211) of the Consecration of Nuns in the thirteenth-
century Pontifical of Durandus, where the rubrics are more explicit (*P*Dur lib. I, ordo
XXIII.33): "Prefatione finita *pontifex* vocat illam vel illas si plures sint inchoando et
schola prosequente responsorium *Veni electa mea.*" ("After the Preface the bishop calls
this or those [virgin(s)], if there are several, by beginning to sing the responsory *Veni
electa mea* which the *schola* is to continue.") Cf. Catalogue **[21DII2]**, p. F50.

A performance structure comparable to the one proposed here is specified for another responsory in the fourteenth-century Moosburg Ascension Play (MoosbHi), which consists almost exclusively of Latin liturgical chants and has more detailed stage directions.

SALVATOR incipit responsorium	*Ite in orbem [universum et predicate dicentes]*
APOSTOLI prosecuntur cantantes,	*[alleluia. Qui crediderit et baptizatus fuerit, salvus erit, alleluia, alleluia, alleluia.]*
circu[m]eundo domunculam. Deinde	
... SALVATOR cantat versum	*In nomine patris [et filii et spiritus sancti]*
APOSTLI repeticionem	*[Qui crediderit ...]*

The intention here is to have the *Salvator* sing the first section of the responsory and to have the *Apostoli*, probably after *dicentes*, continue with the rest of the respond. The *Salvator*, then, sings the solo verse, and the *Apostoli* conclude the responsory with the singing of the *repetenda* ("repeticio") *Qui crediderit.*[21] Thus, the solo and choral parts of this responsory are distributed among the *Salvator* and the *Apostoli* in exactly the way suggested above for the *Dominica Persona* and the *Angeli* in chant [21] of the Lddv.

Since the *Angeli* are not mentioned in the faulty rubric of the Lddv, however, it is possible that this chant [21] was meant to be sung by the *Dominica Persona* alone, or that the antiphon, not the responsory, was intended. Consequently, without even considering verses **A** and **B**, there are three possible ways of restoring the chant with the incipit [21] *Veni electa mea:*

(1) as the responsory (with verse **D**), sung in alternation by the *Dominica Persona* for the solo sections and the *Angeli* for the choral parts;

---

[21]MoosbHi, ed. Brooks (1925) 95, ll. 26-33. Brooks places the first rubric for the *Apostoli* after the last *alleluia*, as does Karl Young. In his edition of the Moosburg play, Young (1933) 1: 484-488, does not seem to recognize that the *Qui crediderit* (of Hartker's Antiphonal, p. 264) is not part of the verse but rather the beginning of the *repetenda* (or *repeticio*), to be sung by the *Apostoli* (p. 487, ll. 19-20). Polheim and Pflanz had similar difficulties recognizing the cue for the beginning of a *repetenda* section; see above, p. 57 with n38.

(2) as the responsory (with verse **D**), sung by the *Dominica Persona* only;

(3) as the simple antiphon, sung by the *Dominica Persona*.

Scholars of medieval drama may come to different conclusions as to whether the responsory or the simple antiphon should be given preference here; views may differ also as to which method of performance would be preferable for the responsory at this place: (1) the liturgically proper form of alternating solo and choral chanting; or (2) the non-liturgical solo performance. I certainly regard the first of these options as the most appropriate choice for the Lddv.[22]

Whether the responsory or the antiphon is meant in the two other Thuringian plays that use the incipit *Veni electa mea* can be discussed here only briefly in a tentative way.[23] In both plays the context is very different. In the LdbKath (ll. 529a-b), the *Dominica Persona* welcomes the soul of the martyred queen with the *Veni electa mea* chant, promising her in the subsequent vernacular couplets (ll. 530-537) the crown and other heavenly joys as reward that may well 'translate' the text of the 'Thuringian' responsory with verse **D**. When the incipit appears a second time as an answer to Catherine's prayer just before her martyr's death, the short, two-line 'translation' of the chant may suggest that here the antiphon is meant.[24] In the Innsbruck Thuringian Assumption (InnsThAss), Jesus appears at the home of his mother Mary just before her death, greeting her with the chant *Veni electa mea* (l. 1492a). The subsequent eight lines of vernacular text may possibly reflect the text of the antiphon.[25] It may not be necessary to come to a definite decision here. Both chants were certainly available and accessible at the time of these plays, no matter where they were performed; and the responsory would have been sung with whatever verse was in use in that particular area or

---

[22]Unfortunately the Marburg *Spiel von den letzten Dingen* (MaSp.532), which has so much in common with the Lddv, cannot be compared to this scene. In its fragmentary manuscript, the stage directions at the bottom of fol. 9v indicate the entrance of the *Prudentes* into heaven, but the two pages that should follow are missing. Reconstruction of the two fragmented gatherings by H. Lomnitzer; cf. above, p. 2 n8.

[23]The relevant passages of these plays are quoted in Catalogue [**21C**], p. F50.

[24]LdbKath, ll. 647a-649.

[25]When, shortly later (in l. 1520a), he greets her with the words *Veni electa mea, veni coronaberis*, we may not be dealing with a chant at all since the stage direction uses a form of *dicere* which probably implies liturgical recitation.

church. If the texts of the plays were not sufficiently clear about which of the two chants was to be chosen, the director would use his own judgment and make a decision based on the availability of singers and liturgical books.[26]

The only clear evidence for the use of the responsory *Veni electa* in an analogous semi-dramatic context is in liturgical sources, specifically in the thirteenth-century Pontifical of Durandus mentioned above.[27] Here, in the formulary for the *Consecratio Virginum*, the bishop as the representative of Christ sings the *Veni electa mea* to invite the newly consecrated nuns to come forward and be invested with veil, ring and crown. Notwithstanding the elaborate rituals and additional chants surrounding these liturgical actions, the correspondences between the liturgical ritual and the central 'scene' of the Lddv are remarkable and might even suggest that the 'coronation scene' of the Thuringian play was modelled after this highly dramatic investiture 'scene' in the pontifical rite. The fact that the responsory *Veni electa* was sung at the beginning of this 'scene' by a person representing Christ (the bishop) may provide addi-

---

[26]Such an open choice due to the vagueness of the manuscript directions is, in fact, inherent in medieval performance practice. An interesting case in point is the York Cycle of English mystery plays where, in one of the two manuscripts, a chant *Veni electa mea* (text of the antiphon only) is set to proper, two-part music in two different versions, without any indication as to which version should be given preference. Cf. Catalogue [21C], p. F50 and n52, under York Plays: Music versions (i) and (ii). The only version of MS Ashb.137 is transcribed in L.T. Smith, ed. (1885) 521; facsimile, frontispiece. Both versions are published next to each other in Dutka (1980) 48-50. "Perhaps the capabilities of the singers determined the choice, or perhaps the requirements of a particular year's performance decided which setting was to be used," says Dutka (p. 66). Dutka's statement may be applied to the Lddv and other German plays with the understanding, however, that when a complete chant is not found in the play's manuscripts, the choice depended on the availability of liturgical books and a profound knowledge of the chants therein.

Considerations of this kind may explain why, in the MoosbHi, a choice of two different chants is offered at two places, with no preference indicated: in response to the apostle Philip, the *Salvator* is directed to sing the antiphon *Philippe, qui videt* or the much longer communion *Tanto tempore*; and, at the end of the play, the *Angeli* are to sing either the antiphon or the offertory *Viri Galylei*. Cf. MoosbHi, ed. Brooks (1925) 94, ll. 31-33 and 96, ll. 3-6 (ed. Young [1933] 1: 486, ll. 15-18, and 487, ll. 22-26). In both instances, the shorter antiphon and the longer alternative chant have more or less the same verbal message but, of course, different music.

[27]Cf. pp. 210-211, 222 n20; see also pp. 96-98.

tional support for the choice of the responsory over the antiphon *Veni electa* for chant [21] in the Lddv.

A few remarks are necessary regarding the manuscript transmission of the chants discussed here. The antiphon *Veni electa mea* in its more common medieval form was quoted earlier with its melody from the Fritzlar Antiphonal *A*Fri.124 (Figure 17). As this antiphonal, along with the other closely related liturgical antiphonals from Fritzlar (*A*Fri.117 and *A*Fri.129), has been shown to be a reliable source for liturgical chants from the Mainz diocese, any one of the Fritzlar transmissions could serve to restore chant [21] in the Lddv if the antiphon should be chosen.

The responsory *Veni electa mea* with its mode 2 melody has been presented above from the Cistercian antiphonal *A*Mz.II,138 (Figure 18), the only manuscript studied that transmits the melody for the responsory with verse D. Regardless of the verse, the melody of this chant in other manuscripts is basically the same in all sources consulted.[28] The German books show only minor melodic variants from each other and display again their fondness for the minor third so characteristic of the German plainsong 'dialect.' Owing to its Cistercian origin, the Mainz antiphonal only partially shares these special dialect features.[29]

For the restoration in Chapter 4 of chant [21], I have broken editorial rules and traditions by conflating manuscripts. The respond is presented from a Fritzlar antiphonal for its characteristic German dialect forms in the melody; the verse, however, is taken from the Cistercian antiphonal of Mainz (*A*Mz.II,138) because, so far, it is the only source

---

[28]A surprising exception to this near-uniformity in the musical transmission is the version in the above-mentioned Pontifical of Durandus, at least in BL Addit. 39677, which is fully notated. In particular, the verse (B *Audi filia*) as sung in the *Consecratio Virginum* (fol. 56r) is so highly ornamented, that it looks as if this solo tune had been specifically chosen, if not created, to adorn this special moment in the ceremony. I am grateful to the British Library London for sending me a copy of the consecration formulary of MS Addit. 39677, fols 48r-61r, with the musical notation.

[29]*A*Mz.II,138 has the interval of a third instead of the second at two places only (over *Veni* and *speciem*), while the other German sources use the third up to seven times, over *Veni, concupivit, speciem tuam;* and in the verse over *tua, prospere,* and *regna.* (The corresponding words in the Mainz text of the verse are *mea, libano,* and *coronaberis.*) See, for instance, facsimile 3 from *B*Helm.145.1; also *A*Ahrw.2b, fol. 212v. Cf. the edition of this chant in Chapter 4 [21], where, in the transcription of the verse from *A*Mz.II,138, the typically 'German' variants to be expected in a non-Cistercian source are proposed at the corresponding places in letter names above the stave.

accessible to me that transmits this verse **D** with music. Letter names above the stave of the verse will indicate where certain 'German' intervals would have to be substituted in the Mainz melody.[30] Such a conflation of manuscripts can, of course, be disputed, yet it is backed up by the text transmission in the Erfurt Breviary (*B*Erf.81), which also has the verse **D** for this responsory, unfortunately without musical notation.[31]

This much said by way of apology, I propose for the restoration of Chant **[21]** in the Lddv the prolix responsory *Veni electa mea* of the Common of Virgins, with the text restored from *B*Erf.81 (= *A*Mz.II,138), the music, however, from both a Fritzlar source and *A*Mz.II,138:

Responsory   *Veni electa mea [et ponam in te*[a] *thronum meum Quia concupivit rex speciem tuam.*

Verse   *Surge*[b] *propera amica mea, veni de Libano et coronaberis.*

Rep.   *Quia concupivit rex speciem tuam.*]

Source   *B*Erf.81, fol. 366r (= *A*Mz.II,138, fol. 218r)

Variants   [a] *in te*] *te in A*Ahrw.2b.

[b] *Surge propera ... coronaberis*] *B*Erf.81, *A*Mz.II,138; different verses in most other sources: (verse **A**) *Specie tua ...* [*A*Fri.117, 124, 129: incipit only], *B*Fri.145.1, *A*OP(Humb), *B*OP, *B*R, *R*Mon; (verse **B**) *Audi filia ... A*Sar, *A*Salzb, *P*Dur; (verse **C**) *Surge virgo ...* See Catalogue [21DII1 and 2], pp. F52-F53.

Melody*   Mode 2. Transcribed in Chapter 4 from *A*Fri.124, fol. 367r (respond) and *A*Mz.II,138, fol. 218r (verse **D** *Surge ... coronaberis*).

Melody of respond = *A*Fri.117, *A*Fri.129; ~ *B*Helm.145.1; ~ var. *A*Mz.II,138, *A*Ahrw.2b, *A*Pat;

Melody of verse = *A*OP(Humb); ~ var. ("German dialect" variants) *B*Helm.145.1, *A*Ahrw.2b, *A*Pat; *incipits only A*Fri.117, *A*Fri.124, *A*Fri.129; *no notation B*Erf.81. Cf. facsimile 3 (*B*Helm.145.1)

Note In the transcription of the verse, the typically 'German' features, lacking in *A*Mz.II,138 and *A*OP(Humb), but present in *B*Helm.145.1, *A*Ahrw, *A*Pat at three locations, are proposed by letter names in brackets *[...]* placed above the corresponding notes of *A*Mz.II,138; cf. p. 335, ll. 2-3.

---

[30]Cf. above n29. For the reforms in Cistercian chant and its avoidance of the typically 'German' interval features, see e.g. above, p. 74 n7.

[31]I firmly believe that some day another Mainz/Thuringian source will be found that transmits the responsory *Veni electa mea* with the verse **D** along with its melody.

The complete responsory as transmitted in *A*Mz.II,138 is transcribed in Figure 18 above, p. 217, the antiphon *Veni electa mea* in Figure 17, from *A*Fri.124, p. 215.

Translation "Come, my chosen one, and I will set my throne in you: For the king has desired your beauty. **R**ise up, my beloved, be quick, come with me from Lebanon and you will be crowned."   [cf. CAO 7826 (and 5323, as antiphon)]

[22] *Transite ad me omnes etc.* (Lddv 208c)

The rubric of lines 208a-b, "*Maria* superponans eis coronas cantando," directs Mary to sing chant [22] *Transite ad me omnes* while she rewards the *Prudentes* with heavenly crowns, an act which Mary herself mentions in the short vernacular paraphrase to her Latin chant (ll. 209-214): "ich wil uch selben lonen mit den ewigen cronen" (ll. 211-212). Editions of the Lddv since Beckers propose restoring the chant with the biblical text of Ecclesiastes 24: 26, which begins with the same words; yet it has not been easy to match the incipit *Transite ad me* with a liturgical chant known in Thuringia in the early fourteenth century. After some diligent searching, however, various genres of chant using these words can be found in medieval liturgical books listed in Catalogue [22D], pp. F51-F53.

From early times, the whole of Ecclesiastes 24, the *Praeconium sapientiae* ("Praise of Wisdom"), has been used for readings at Marian feasts. It is therefore not surprising to find at least three different chants with the given incipit. Two of them, an introit for the Visitation of St. Mary and an antiphon from a Carthusian rite for the Consecration of Virgins, use the text of Eccles. 24: 26. A third chant, a Matins responsory for the Immaculate Conception of Mary, takes only the first half of the biblical verse and continues with a different text for the respond and the verse. In addition, the incipit can also be found in a section of the responsory *Ego sicut vitis* from Eccles. 24: 23, where the words *Transite ad me* are used for the last part of the respond (cf. Catalogue [22D2], p. F53). Of these four choices, only the first three have the incipit indicated in the Lddv for chant [22]. It seems paradoxical, but, on closer examination, likely that those three choices (Catalogue [22D1(i)-(iii)]) will have to be eliminated because their sources are all very late.

From a liturgical viewpoint, the introit *Transite* for the Visitation Mass of BMV would be a good choice for the Lddv, line 208c: a Mass introit, followed by the singing of a *Sanctus* and a *Gloria* chant (chants [23-24]), all leading to the great Wedding Banquet of the *Dominica Persona* (ll. 228a-b). This would be a meaningful sequence in a play that abounds in allusions to the eucharist. The only evidence I have found for this introit, however, is in an addition to the Worcester Antiphonal in which Office and Mass for the *Visitatio BMV* are noted by a late hand on fol. 131r.[1] The feast was prescribed for the whole Church by Urban VI only in 1389.[2] The earliest extant manuscript of the Lddv, MS A of Mühlhausen, therefore, antedates the general adoption of this feast by at least fifteen years. Thus, from a purely chronological viewpoint, the introit cannot be the chant with the incipit *Transite ad me omnes* meant in the Lddv.

For the responsory *Transite*, sung at Matins of the Immaculate Conception, the situation is confusing in a different way. The feast, first celebrated only in the East, was introduced to the West via southern Italy, from whence it spread first to Norman and then to English monasteries (twelfth century). It was not adopted by the Roman Church until the late fifteenth century under Sixtus IV.[3] Although the feast was celebrated in Germany before this date,[4] a special liturgical formulary for it had probably not yet been created. The fourteenth-century Erfurt Breviary is a case in point, as it gives for the celebration of the Immaculate Conception the formulary for the *Nativitas BMV* with the appropriate textual changes.[5] The proper Mass and Office were promulgated together at the time of the feast's approval under Sixtus IV between 1476 and 1480. The responsory *Transite* from this proper Office, therefore, cannot be used for the restoration of chant [22] in the much earlier Lddv.[6]

The antiphon *Transite* as found in MS 205 of the Avignon Bibliothéque Municipale marks the beginning of the Carthusian addition to the

---

[1]The facsimile publication of the Worcester Antiphonal in PalMus 12 does not include the fourteenth-century additions, of which only a text version is given on pp. 120-125. I am grateful to the University Library of Birmingham for sending me a copy of fol. 131r-v of the Ms Worcester Cathedral F 160 with the introit *Transite*.

[2]For more details see *The Oxford Dictionary of the Christian Church* (1974) 1446; *The New Catholic Encyclopedia* (1967) 14: 721; Holweck (1892) 126-129.

[3]The exact date of its adoption is indicated as 1477 (Thalhofer-Eisenhofer [1912] 1: 702-703); 1476 (*Oxford Dictionary of the Christian Church* [1974] 692-693); 1477 and 1480 (*The New Catholic Encyclopedia* [1967] 7: 381). Only under Clement XI, in 1708, was the observance of the feast officially prescribed and extended to the Universal Church.

[4]The Franciscans celebrated the Immaculate Conception as early as 1263; and the feast was known in Mainz by 1318 and in Trier between 1338 and 1343; cf. Thalhofer-Eisenhofer (1912) 1: 702-703.

[5]BErf.81, fol. 396r: *Conceptionis Mariae: Omnia ut in die nativitatis eiusdem mutato nomine nativitatis in conceptionis etc.*

[6]I could not find any evidence for this responsory in medieval sources, only its version in the 'modern' *Liber Responsalis* (RMon); cf. Catalogue [22D], p. F52.

Roman ceremony of the Consecration of Virgins. With the singing of this antiphon the bishop invites the virgins to come forward for the final specifically Carthusian ritual act, in which they will genuflect in front of him to receive the Carthusian insignia of maniple, stole, and cross:[7]

> Finitâ oratione *Da quaesumus* Pontifex cum mitra stans incipit scholâ prosequente hanc Antiphonam: *Transite ad me omnes qui concupiscitis me, & à generatiónibus meis implémini.*

> Inceptâ Antiphonâ sedet Pontifex cum mitra & eâ finitâ praesentantur ei à paranymphis duae primae virgines ... coram eo genuflexae.

There is an interesting affinity between this scene in the Consecration of Virgins and the one in the Lddv, but the source is from the late seventeenth century, and from France. This antiphon therefore has no relevance for the Lddv, even though the late source from Avignon may reflect older customs of the Carthusian order.

Because these three *Transite* chants have had to be rejected due to their very rare and late appearance in liturgical sources, the responsory *Ego sicut vitis* with its repetenda *Transite ad me omnes* needs to be examined more closely. A well-known, widely documented responsory for the Sunday after the Octave of Easter, this chant is usually sung as the second responsory in the first nocturn of Matins. Of the sources studied, all the German books, except *A*Ahrw.2a, have the verse **A** *Ego diligentes me*.[8] In this case, the verse itself is of less interest, however, since only the *repetenda*, i.e. the part of the respond that is repeated after the verse, would be used here as a chant.

Resp.	*Ego sicut vitis fructificavi suavitatem odoris, alleluia. Transite ad me omnes qui concupiscitis me et a generationibus meis adimplemini, alleluia, alleluia.*
V.	*Ego diligentes me diligo, et qui mane vigilaverint ad me invenient me.*
Rep.	*Transite ...*

---

[7]*P*Av.205, pp. 31-32. See also the edition in Martène (1736) 551D (lib. II, cap. 6, ordo XIII). The Carthusian addition is introduced with the words (slightly different in Martène's edition): *Quae sequuntur non habentur in Pontificali Romano, adhibentur autem è Pontifice in consecratione virginum Cartusianarum ex antiquissimo usu, & consuetudine Ordinis.*

[8]Cf. Catalogue [22D2 (last column)]. *A*Pat does not include this responsory.

The two phrases of the respond in this responsory are punctuated by the paschal exclamations *alleluia* (after *odoris* and after *adimplemini*). They are thus clearly marked as two different sections, the second section being the *repetenda*, which is quite easily separable from the rest of the responsory, and so it may well have been used as an 'independent' chant in the Lddv. Two of the Fritzlar Antiphonals (*A*Fri.124 and *A*Fri.129) even mark the beginning of the *repetenda* with, in addition to the traditionally larger initial, a distinct vertical slash through the stave as can be seen in the transcription of this responsory in Figure 19.[9]

It may seem surprising that only a part of a responsory should be used in a religious play, but this is often the case in other medieval dramas.[10] In this instance, at least two more arguments can be brought forward to support its usage here. First, the monologue style of section one of the responsory (*Ego sicut vitis*) turns into dialogue in its second section, where a group of adherents is addressed directly: *Transite ad me*. Second, this section stands out musically, having an especially expressive melody over the words *Transite ad me*, to which the first section appears as a mere introduction. Moreover, this melodic line is a common opening formula for mode 3 responsories.[11] As a result, the *repetenda* section of this responsory forms an almost independent little unit, suitable for use as a separate chant.

The only other medieval play in which this chant incipit is used is, interestingly, again the Innsbruck Thuringian Assumption of Mary of 1391 (InnsThAss), where Mary sings the *Transite ad me omnes* after her Assumption (see Catalogue [22C], p. F54). A Thuringian origin has been suggested for this 'Innsbruck' play mainly on linguistic grounds.[12] These findings may now be corroborated by the fact that the InnsThAss makes use of two Latin chants ([21] *Veni electa mea* and [22]) *Transite ad me*), which had been given a 'dramatic' function in one or two other Thuringian plays, the Lddv and the LdbKath. It may further be concluded that in the InnsThAss, the incipit *Transite* can probably also be completed through the repetenda *Transite* from the responsory *Ego sicut vitis*.

---

[9]Cf. the observation below, pp. 321-322.

[10]Indeed, as discussed above, the second part of an antiphon was probably the source for chant [19] *Ecce sponsus venit*.

[11]See the examples in Frere (1901-1924) 1: 31; T.H. Klein (1962) 96.

[12]See Thurnher-Neuhauser (1975) 4; Bergmann (1986) 160-161.

FIGURE 19 THE RESPONSORY *EGO SICUT VITIS*
WITH THE REPETENDA *TRANSITE AD ME*
(AFRI.124, FOL. 127v)

A comparison of the melodic transmissions of this responsory in mode 3 shows, at certain places in the German manuscripts, the typically German preference for the minor third over the second; the Mainz antiphonal *A*Mz.II,138 seems again to maintain a moderate position between German and non-German sources. Two additional features of some German sources become evident in the *repetenda*. There is, firstly, an obvious delight in reaching the reciting tone *c*, or descending from it, by the leap of a fourth (*Gc* or *cG*), which occurs a total of six times in the short section *Transite ... omnes qui* (three times each ascending and descending, cf. Figure 19) while, for instance, the Dominican *A*OP(Humb) shows this leap only twice, in the opening phrase *Transite*. The second 'German' feature is related — a clear tendency, mainly in the Fritzlar antiphonals, to emphasize the sixth *c* in the Deuterus tonality rather than the fifth *b*, especially at the end of phrases. This is particularly striking in the closes over *omnes* and *me*, where all other sources studied close with the clivis *cb*. Both these features give the Fritzlar versions of this third mode chant a very bright colour, which is abandoned only for the *alleluias*, in the middle and at the end of the respond, with the cadence of a fourth into the finalis *E*.

As reliable sources and examples for the plainsong tradition in the Mainz diocese, these Fritzlar transmissions should, of course, be retained for chant [22] of the Lddv. I therefore propose the restoration of this chant through the repetenda of the Matins responsory *Ego sicut vitis* as transmitted in *A*Fri.124:

Text (*Repetenda* of the responsory *Ego sicut vitis*, with verse *Ego diligentes me*):

Transite ad me omnes [*qui concupiscitis me et a generationibus meis adimplemini, alleluia, alleluia.*]

Source   *A*Fri.124, fol. 127v (= *A*Fri.117, *A*Fri.129, and most other sources studied); cf. Catalogue [22D2], p. F55.

Melody Mode 3. Transcribed in Chapter 4 from *A*Fri.124, fol. 127v.

Melody ~ = *A*Fri.117, *A*Fri.129; ~*A*Ahrw.2a; *var.* *A*Mz.II,138, *A*OP(Humb).

The entire responsory is transcribed above in Figure 19, from *A*Fri.124.

Translation "Come to me, all who desire me and eat your fill of my fruit."   [cf. CAO 6633]

[23] *Sanctus sanctus sanctus* (Lddv 214b)

Having been received into the heavenly kingdom and crowned by Mary, the *Prudentes* sing a song of adoration [23] which starts with a threefold *Sanctus*. Another song of praise, [24] *Gloria et honor*, immediately follows, sung by the *Angeli* (l. 214f). Only after chant [24] does the *Quinta Prudens* deliver the vernacular paraphrase (l. 215-228) before the whole 'scene' at the climax of the play concludes in the Great Banquet of the *Dominica Persona*.

As the quotations in Catalogue [23C1-3], pp. F57-F58, show, chants with a triple *Sanctus* incipit were used in a number of medieval German plays. In three cases the complete texts are supplied in the manuscripts; in six other instances only the incipits are given.[1] The function and dramatic context of such triple *Sanctus* chants vary considerably in the plays. The three different categories or types of context distinguished in the Catalogue [23C] are:

I   the angelic adoration of the Lord in heaven before or after the Fall of Lucifer;

II   the heavenly revelation in connection with Christ's life on earth (Annunciation and Temptation);

III   praise to the deity at the entry of redeemed humans into heaven (praise by the Redeemed Souls after Christ's *Descensus*; by the Wise Virgins in heaven; or by another group [Angels or choir]).

Given these three categories, it is not surprising that in those scenes belonging to categories I or II the singers of the chant are Angels whereas for category III scenes it is often the Redeemed Souls or the Wise Virgins themselves who sing the *Sanctus* chant.[2]

In the liturgy, there are at least five *Sanctus* chants: the *Sanctus* following the Preface in the ordinary of Mass, two antiphons (CAO 4796 and 4797), and two hymn stanzas (the third stanza of the *Te deum*, and the eighth stanza of the hymn *Christe celi Domine*.[3] In dramas that pro-

---

[1]Complete text in WienP, KünzCC, EgerP; the incipit once each in the Lddv and HessW, twice each in StGMrhP and the Dutch play of the Ten Virgins (Flem.X.Virg); cf. the quotations in Catalogue [23C1-3]. No claim is made that the list is complete.

[2]Only in the Dutch play of the 'Maegden' (Flem.X.Virg) are the stage directions at both places too vague (*men zingt Sanctus*) to identify the singers (see Catalogue [23C3]).

[3]Cf. Schuler (1951) no. 559; his references are not always accurate, however.

vide the complete wording, the triple *Sanctus* chant can be identified as either the Trinity antiphon of CAO 4796 (WienP) or the third stanza of the *Te deum* (KünzCC and EgerP).[4] In all three instances, the chant is part of the angelic adoration in heaven. Since in the four other plays (Lddv, HessW, StGMrhP, and Flem.X.Virg) the chant is indicated only by its incipit, we must examine which one of the liturgical chants mentioned might have been used here.

The *Sanctus* of the *Ordinarium missae* is so familiar and well known that it comes to mind immediately on reading the incipit in a play.[5] On the other hand, this chant preceding the Canon of Mass is a very sacred part of the eucharistic liturgy.[6] In the Lddv, the quasi-eucharistic import of the play might provide an almost congruent context since the Wise Virgins sing their triple *Sanctus* immediately before the *Dominica Persona* holds the great Wedding Banquet. But there are other chants with that incipit, which must also be examined.

The hymn *Christe celi Domine* with its triple *Sanctus* stanza, listed in Schuler (1959) no. 559, is not sufficiently known to be seriously considered here. The third stanza of the *Te deum*, used in KünzCC and EgerP, is a very specific praise of the Deity by all the angelic choirs, introduced as such in the second stanza, *Tibi omnes Angeli ... proclamant: 'Sanctus, sanctus, sanctus'*;[7] it would be inappropriate to have the *Prudentes* sing this chant in the Lddv. The second of the two antiphons with a threefold

---

[4]Cf. Catalogue [23C1 and 2], p. F58 ("Context I").

[5]*Sanctus, sanctus, sanctus Dominus Deus Sabaoth. Pleni sunt caeli et terra gloria tua. (Benedictus qui venit ...).* For the function and performance of the *Sanctus* during Mass and the history of its development see e.g. Jungmann (1948) 2: 156-168. Musical aspects are discussed by A. Hughes (1982) 89 and Hiley (1993) 161-165 with further literature and a few examples from the hundreds of different melodies transmitted.

[6]For this reason I cannot accept Mone's suggestion (1846) 1: 56-57, that the *Sanctus* of Mass should be the chant which the Angels in the St. Gall Passion Play (StGMrhP) sing at the end of the Temptation Scene, where it functions just like a *Silete* chant between scenes, with the scene of the worldly life of Mary Magdalene following immediately thereafter. Schützeichel in his 1978 edition of the StGMrhP does not complete the incipit at this place (l. 161b) nor later, in l. 1289b. Bergmann (1972a) 210 n1696 and (1978) 222 n11, refers only to Schuler's listings, no. 559. Pflanz (1977) does not comment at all on the two *Sanctus* incipits in this play.

[7]Cf. Schulte (1916) 30; three different melodic versions in *GR* (1974) and, with identical pagination, *GRTri* (1979): pp. 838, l. 3-6 (tonus sollemnis); 841, l. 4-6 (tonus simplex); 844, l. 6-845, l. 1 (alio modo).

Sanctus listed in the Catalogue [23D(i) and(ii)], p. F59, is documented only in the Beneventan antiphonal of St. Lupus (Siglum L in CAO 4797), hence of little value in our context.

The first of these two antiphons, on the other hand, CAO 4796, used in the WienP and well known in medieval liturgical books, appears to be a most suitable chant for the Lddv at this place (cf. Catalogue, p. F59):

Sanctus, sanctus, sanctus dominus deus omnipotens,
qui erat et qui est et qui venturus est.

The subsequent chant [24] *Gloria et honor* belongs to the same liturgical formulary for the feast of the Holy Trinity; both antiphons are used almost side by side in either Matins (or Lauds) or the second Vespers of this feast.[8] This proximity seems to be reflected in the immediate succession of the two chants in the play. It can be inferred, then, that it is this Trinity antiphon *Sanctus* which was meant by incipit [23].[9]

The feast of the Holy Trinity was first celebrated in the ninth/tenth century in the Frankish areas only and was not adopted in Rome until the twelfth century. Prescribed for the whole Church by John XXII only in 1334, it is not found in many older sources although it is sometimes inserted at odd places in manuscripts of the eleventh/twelfth centuries.[10] By the thirteenth and fourteenth centuries, it is generally found in its usual place on the Sunday after Pentecost,[11] although in some of the German manuscripts (*A*Ahrw.2a, *A*Helm.485, *B*Helm.145.1), the two

---

[8]For a synoptic view of the places of these antiphons within the Trinity Office in the different manuscripts studied, see Table 8 below, in Chapter 3 [24], p. 242.

[9]When Beckers (ed. 1905) proposed this antiphon, he omitted the *et* in the last phrase (*et qui venturus est*), an omission repeated by subsequent editors. See Catalogue [23B, n57]. The melody of the chant, however, has a sequence of four to five notes over this conjunction; cf Chapter 4 [23], line 2.

[10]For the gradual introduction of the Trinity Feast see Thalhofer-Eisenhofer (1912) 1: 665-666; Eisenhofer (1950) 143; Apel (1958) 8; Braun (1938) 44. In Hartker's Antiphonal, the *Ystoria de sancta Trinitate* appears somewhere between Epiphany and Septuagesima (pp. 101-105); in *A*Salzb it is presented at the end of the *Commune sanctorum* after the *Dedicatio ecclesie* (pp. 793-798), demonstrating the wavering attitude of the twelfth century toward the liturgical location of this feast; cf. Unterkircher-Demus (1974) [2]: 120.

[11]For more details on the history and development of the Trinity feast see Wagner (1911-1921) 1: 305-307; (1908) 13-19; Klaus (1938); Browe (1950) 65-81.

antiphons in question, *Sanctus* and *Gloria*, are to be found not in the formulary for Trinity, but in that for the first Sunday after Epiphany.[12]

Regardless of where in the liturgical books this *Sanctus* antiphon appears, its melody is always the same bright, 'modern' tune in the fifth mode: very jubilant, with triads in *F* moving up and down several times, then easily ascending to high *f*, in the German sources reaching it a second time over *erat*, before descending down to the lower *F* within one short phrase and concluding with another brisk up and down movement. The impression is that of an F-major tonality, particularly in the Ahrweiler antiphonal which, for the last two phrases, makes consistent use of the *b*-flat. The whole spirit of this chant surpasses in brightness that of the *Regnum mundi* discussed earlier. It almost seems as if this fifth mode was meant to characterize the Wise Virgins.[13]

The musical transmission of this antiphon in the German sources is quite homogeneous and even close to that of the Worcester Antiphonal.[14] Only the last six words (*qui est et qui venturus est*) are given some kind of individual treatment in each source, with no major, yet distinctive minor variants. The version of the Fritzlar antiphonals should again be preferred for the Thuringian play.

The *Sanctus* chant in the Lddv is not followed by a vernacular 'translation,' but by the next Latin chant, **[24]** *Gloria et honor*, sung by the

---

[12]Cf. Catalogue [23D], p. F59.

[13]This exultant and well-known Trinity antiphon *Sanctus*, sung by the Angels in the WienP and, as inferred, by the Wise Virgins in the Lddv, would appear to be very fitting in the other plays where the chant is indicated by its incipit only; cf. the quotations in Catalogue [23C3], "Context II and III": in HessW, Angels sing it during the Annunciation to the shepherds; in StGMrhP, it is sung a first time (l. 161a-b) by the Angels (as a kind of angelic *jubilus* after the 'Temptation scene'), a second time (l. 1289a-b) by the Redeemed Souls in heaven. In the Flem.X.Virg, where no singers are specified for the two occurrences of *Sanctus* (l. 434d and 502m), the same antiphon would appear appropriate, as Hoebeke also suggests ([1959] 30 and n2, 130, 135 note to l. 502m). On the other hand, the particularly sacred context at the second occurrence of *Sanctus* in this Dutch play (cf. l. 502a-n) may permit a different choice. Hoebeke (p. 135, note to l. 502m) considers the *Sanctus* of the Mass Preface as an alternative; my proposal is rather for the third stanza of the *Te deum* at this place, since this hymn is mentioned twice in the context, l. 502l-m and p. For the *Te deum* and its *Sanctus* stanza, see n7 above.

[14]The Mainz Antiphonal *A*Mz.II,138, probably again due to its Cistercian origin, has major variants, especially in the opening of the chant, while maintaining the same general spirit of brightness for the chant.

Angeli. As both antiphons have their usual liturgical place in the same Trinity Office, this close relationship will have to be kept in mind in the discussion of chant **[24]**. On the basis of this evidence and all the preceding investigations I propose for the restoration of chant **[23]** in the Lddv the Trinity antiphon *Sanctus sanctus sanctus* as transmitted in *A*Fri.124:

Antiphon   *Sanctus sanctus sanctus [dominus deus omnipotens qui erat et qui*[a] *est et*[b] *qui venturus est.*[c]]

Source   *A*Fri.124, fol. 153v (= *A* Fri.129, fol. 58r, and most other liturgical sources consulted. Incipits only in *A* Fri.117, fol. 138v; *A* Fri.129, fol. 135r); cf. Catalogue **[23D]**, p. F59.

Variants   [a] *et qui*] om. WienP 33b-c
[b] *et*] om. Lddv ed. Beckers, Schneider, De Boor, Curschmann-Glier
[c] *qui erat ... venturus est*] *qui eras et qui es et qui venturus es.* CAO 4796 (sigla D, L).

Melody   Mode 5. Transcribed in Chapter 4 from *A* Fri.124, fol. 153v.
Melody ~*A* Fri.129, *A*Helm.485, *B*Helm.145.1; ~ *var. A*Ahrw.2a, *A*Worc; *var. A*Mz.II,138.

Translation   "Holy, holy, holy is the Lord God Almighty, who was, and who is now, and who will come."
[cf. CAO 4796 (and 4797)]

[24] *Gloria et honor* (Lddv 214f)

This chant is sung by the Angels immediately after the *Sanctus* chant [23] of the *Prudentes*, with no intervening vernacular paraphrase. The joint adoration of the Deity by the *Prudentes* and the *Angeli* in these two chants suggests symbolically that the virgins have been raised to the angelic life. And the whole 'scene' will culminate in the Great Banquet of the *Dominica Persona* (1. 228a-b).

Within the tradition of medieval drama, the incipit *Gloria et honor* seems to be unique to the Lddv since other plays use different *Gloria* chants as songs of praise (see Catalogue [24C], p. F61). In the liturgical repertoire, two antiphons from the Trinity Feast and the final doxology stanza from a hymn for Good Friday begin with these words (see Catalogue [24D], pp. F62-F63). The two Trinity antiphons *Gloria et honor* are closely related in the liturgy of the Holy Trinity with the antiphon *Sanctus sanctus sanctus* just discussed. All three are Office antiphons for this feast. And in the Lddv, the incipits of chants [23] and [24] are implicitly connected by the stage direction.

PRUDENTES cantant   *Sanctus sanctus sanctus*
et ANGELI   *Gloria et honor*   (1. 214 a-f)

This seems to reflect the common link the two chants have to the same liturgical office. It is, therefore, unlikely that the author of the play would have used the hymn stanza *Gloria* sung mainly on Good Friday. The two Trinity antiphons, then, need to be examined for their suitability to the context of the Lddv.

(i) *Gloria et honor Deo in Unitate Trinitatis, Patri et Filio cum
     Sancto Spiritu, in sempiterna saecula ...*   (CAO 2943)

(ii) *Gloria et honor et benedictio sedenti super thronum, viventi
     in saecula saeculorum.*   (CAO 2944)

In deciding between the two, all the information on the incipit in the context of the play must be taken into consideration, including the subsequent 'translation' of the chant:

MS A, ll. 215-223[1]

Gelobit sist dů, milder crist!
dů hast uns in korczer vrist
wol gelonit alle unser erbeyt
mit der ewigen selickeyt.
ere und lob si dy, mildir crist,
wan dů eyn recht richter bist.
gelobit sist dů, heylger geyst,
wan dyn hulfe aller meyst
uns czů desen vrouden hat bracht.

MS B, ll. 283-291

Gelobet sistu, milder got!
du hast uns bracht uß großer not
unde uns wol gelonet unser erbeit
mit der ewigen selekeit.
ere unde lob sy dir, milder crist
want du ein rechter richter bist.
gelobet sistu, heiliger geist,
want din hulffe allermeist
uns zu diesen freuden hat bracht.

These vernacular lines delivered by the *Quinta Prudens*, clearly contain a Trinitarian praise which is intact only in MS B of Darmstadt.[2] Since only antiphon (i) contains such praise, the evidence is very strong that it was meant in the Lddv and paraphrased in the quoted vernacular couplets. Moreover, there are a few liturgical sources, all of monastic origin, which provide only form (i) of the antiphon: the Thuringian *B*Erf.81 as well as *A*Salzb, *A*Worc and *A*Mz.II,138 (cf. Table 8, last four columns). If the author of the play used primarily monastic books, he could be confident that the three-word incipit *Gloria et honor* would suffice to identify clearly the Trinity antiphon meant. The combined internal and external evidence, then, can confirm the antiphon *Gloria et honor deo*, suggested in 1905 by Beckers and adopted in all later editions of the play, as the one that was probably intended.

In a comparison of the transmission of this chant it is noteworthy that of the six secular sources listed in Catalogue [24D], p. F62, only the three Fritzlar antiphonals transmit this antiphon (i), while it is present in all the five monastic antiphonals or breviaries in that list (see Table 8, last five columns). The only textual variant *in unitate trina* (instead of *trinitatis* in most CAO sources and *A*Worc) is common to all German sources (Hartker, Rheinau, Fritzlar, Erfurt), except the Mainz

---

[1]"Praise be to you, gentle [God]. You have speedily compensated us with eternal bliss for all our pains. Praise and glory to you, gentle Christ, for you are a fair judge. Praise be to you, Holy Spirit, since it was first of all through your help that we have been brought to these delights."

[2]Lines A215-217 need to be emended from MS B, as Beckers has done in his critical edition of the Lddv, so that the vernacular paraphrase begins with the praise of the first person of the Trinity ("Gelobit sist du, milder Got! du hast und bracht uz grozer not"). In Schneider's edition (1964), these three lines are printed as found in MS A.

antiphonal, and should be retained for the Lddv. Five of the sources studied transmit the melody of the antiphon in readable notation with neumes on a stave; of these, the three Fritzlar antiphonals stand out again as representing the German 'dialect' version. The use of the thirds *aca*, for instance, at the two places over *honor deo* (where *A*Worc has the half steps *ab^{b}a*) gives a much brighter, less subdued character to the whole opening phrase of the antiphon than the Worcester version with the *b^b* in the sequences *Dab^{b}a* and *aGab^{b}aG*.[3] This means that, in the Lddv, the Fritzlar version of this *Gloria* antiphon (i) in mode 1 would go particularly well with the preceding *Sanctus* chant and its quasi-major tonality; it avoids the *b^b* altogether and twice reaches high *c*, which is the important pitch in the Virgins' chant [23] of the *Sanctus sanctus sanctus*.

TABLE 8 THE TRINITY ANTIPHONS *SANCTUS SANCTUS SANCTUS* AND
GLORIA ET HONOR IN SELECTED SOURCES

SUNDAY 1 AFTER EPIPHANY LAUDS	TRINITY VESPERS 2		TRINITY MATINS, NOCTURN 2, ETC.			
*A*Ahrw.2a *A*Helm485 *B*Helm.145.1	*A*Fri.117 *A*Fri.124 *A*Fri.129	*A*Hartk.	*A*Salzb.	*A*Worc.	*A*Mz.II,138	*B*Erf.81
Indutus est *Gloria* ii *Deus misere.* *Benedictio* *Sanctus*	*Gloria* i *In patre* *Sanctus* *Gloria* ii *Benedic.*	*Benedic.* *Gloria* i *In patre* *Sanctus* *Gloria* ii *Benedic.*	*Karitas* *Verax* *Una* *Gloria* i *Gratias* *In patre* ad l: *Sanctus*	*Karitas* *Verax* *Una* *In patre* *Ex quo* *Sanctus* ad Cant: *Gloria* i	*Karitas* *Benedic.* *Gloria* i *In patre* *Sanctus* *Tibi laus*	*Karitas* *Benedic.* *Tibi laus* *Gloria* i *Sanctus* *In patre*

As a result of textual, liturgical, and musical considerations, the Fritzlar antiphonals are again regarded as transmitting the desired chant in the form which was likely to be known in fourteenth-century Thuringia. I, therefore, propose to use the Trinity antiphon (i) *Gloria et honor deo* as transmitted in *A*Fri.124 for the restoration of chant [24]:

---

[3]*A*Mz.II,138, where this chant is notated a fifth higher starting on *c*, again maintains a middle position with the third over the first place *honor* and the half step over *deo*.

Antiphon   *Gloria et honor [deo in unitate trina,*[a] *patri et filio cum sancto spiritu in sempiterna secula.]*

                Source   *A* Fri.124, fol. 153v (= *A* Fri.117, *A* Fri.129, *B*Erf.81, *A*Hartk, *A*Salzb).

                Variants   [a] *trina] trinitatis A*Mz.II,138; *A*Worc; CAO 2943 (sigla D, F, S, L). Cf. Catalogue [**24**D1], p. F62.

Melody   Mode 1. Transcribed in Chapter 4 from *A*Fri.124, fol. 153v

                Melody ~ = *A*Fri.117, *A*Fri.129; ~ *var. A*Mz.II,138; *var. A*Worc.

Translation "Glory and honor to God, three in one, to the Father and to the Son with the Holy Spirit, world without end."

                                        [cf. CAO 2943 (and 2944)]

[26] *Iniquitates nostras etc.* (Lddv 228f)

Prior to this chant [26], the Angels had sung another *Silete* call [25'], punctuating the preceding 'scene,' which had culminated in the Great Banquet of the *Dominica Persona* (1. 228a-b). It must be assumed that the heavenly feast is ongoing, and will continue in the background or remain as a 'living picture,' while, after the *Silete* call, the *Fatue* are brought into the 'limelight.' As they return from their vain search for oil, they realize that they have missed the arrival of the Bridegroom and the beginning of the Wedding Feast, to which they too had been invited. Recognizing and admitting their 'iniquities,' they approach the site of the Wedding Banquet singing chant [26] *Iniquitates nostras*, which will be paraphrased by the *Second Fatua* in eight vernacular lines (1. 229-236).

As shown in Chapter 1, the editors' handling of the chant incipit *Iniquitates nostras etc.* progressively deteriorated through the various editions of the Lddv.[1] The biblical text proposed for incipit [26] since Freybe and Beckers (*Iniquitates nostrae* [*et peccata nostra super nos sunt, et in ipsis nos tabescimus: quomodo ergo vivere poterimus?*])[2] suggests wailing lamentations and resignation. Such an attitude does not fit well into the play context, where the distressed *Fatue* would be expected to pray for access to the Wedding Feast, as they do in the subsequent vernacular couplets:

> Here vater, homelische got,
> wy beten dich dorch dynen bittirn tot,
> den dû ledes an deme cruce vrone:
> nû hab unser armen vrowen schone!
> Uns hat vorsumit unse tumpheyt,
> nû laz uns genize dynir großen barmeherczicheyt
> und Marian, der liben muter dyn,
> und laz uns armen czû dyner wertschaft in.   (1. 229-236)[3]

---

[1] See above, p. 32 with nn62-64, and the quotations in Catalogue [26B], p. F64.

[2] Cf. Schneider (ed. 1964) 1. 228f-i. "Our transgressions and our sins weigh upon us, and we waste away because of them; how then can we live?" Translation from *The Holy Bible NRSV* (1989) 550.

[3] "Lord father, heavenly God, we implore you on account of your bitter death that you suffered on the holy cross, be mindful of us poor women! Our foolishness made us neglectful. Now let us enjoy your great mercy and that of Mary, your dear mother, and let us, poor ones, gain entrance to your feast."

The *Dominica Persona* in his Latin response **[27]** also refers to their chant as 'prayers': *Qui tempus congrue peniten[cie] perdiderit frustra cum precibus ad regni ianua[m] pervenerit.* (l. 236 b-d) An *oratio* with the required incipit *Iniquitates nostras* exists and is well documented in sacramentaries from the eighth century on.[4] The stage direction, however, calls for a chant (*cantando*), and so the search must continue.

The incipit *Iniquitates nostre* conjectured by all editors since Beckers can indeed be found as the beginning of a widely known Rogation antiphon, the text of which is even in the form of a prayer.[5]

> *Iniquitates nostrae, domine, multiplicatae sunt super capita nostra; delicta nostra creverunt usque ad caelos; parce, domine, et inclina super nos misericordiam tuam. Alleluia.*

This antiphon is well documented in sources that transmit the Litany processions for St. Mark's Day (April 25) and for the three Rogation days before Ascension.[6] All these features, however, cannot eliminate the fact that its incipit does not match the accusative form *Iniquitates nostras* of chant **[26]**.

Intensive research into a number of regional sources, mainly processionals, led to the discovery of a processional antiphon *Iniquitates nostras*, which apparently remained tied to liturgical/processional customs within the archbishopric of Mainz and did not enter into books of the Church Province at large. Its wording fits the context of the Lddv to an astounding degree:

> *Iniquitates nostras aufer a nobis pater omnipotens, ut hoc templum tuo nomini dedicatum puris mereamur meritibus introire, sancta Maria cum istis omnibusque sanctis intercedente celestes portas nobis dignare Aperire.*[7]

---

[4]Cf. Catalogue **[26D1]**, p. F64. An *oratio* would probably have been introduced by a form of *dicere* and would most likely have been assigned to one speaker only.

[5]Quoted here in the spelling of Andrieu's edition (1931-1961) Ordo 50, XXXVI.13; see also PRG XCIX.423; CAO 3346; and Hesbert's *Antiphonale Missarum Sextuplex* (1935) nos. 94a and 201b.

[6]Terence Bailey (1971) 125 (Table 1), in his study of over one hundred Rogation antiphons, found it in seventeen out of twenty manuscripts from the eighth to the twelfth century. See Bailey's transcription of this antiphon from the eleventh-century Gradual of Saint-Yrieix (Paris, BN, lat. MS 903) in (1971) 144-145.

[7]*PrMz.*II,303, fols. 26r-27r. I am grateful to the Stadtbibliothek of Mainz for sending me microfilm copies of these pages in MS II,303.

("Take away from us, almighty Father, our iniquities that we may be worthy to enter with pure minds this temple dedicated to Thy name. As Saint Mary with these and all the saints is interceding, deign to open to us the heavenly doors." Translation based on *Aufer a nobis* in *The Roman Missal* [1917] 4.)

Klein, who researched the Mainz processions from the fourteenth to the eighteenth centuries, gives the two principal liturgical occasions on which this antiphon was used as the Ash Wednesday procession after the imposition of the ashes and the *Jejunium bannitum* procession, limited to the Mainz archdiocese.[8] The only (indirect) source for the use of this chant on Ash Wednesday seems to be Würdtwein's *Commentatio ... de Stationibus Ecclesiae Moguntinae* in which the medieval processional rites of the Mainz Church are presented for the whole liturgical year, with texts and rubrics "from old sources."[9]

For the second occasion, the *Jejunium bannitum*, most processionals of the Mainz Cathedral contain the formularies with the complete chants, text and music.[10] The *Jejunium bannitum* ("Bannfasten") is an extremely important penitential tradition proper to the archdiocese of Mainz.[11] Little is known about its origin, but from at least the fourteenth century on, it was regularly observed twice a year on three days of the week with a general fast, penitential processions, stational services, and litany

[8]Cf. T.H. Klein (1962) 57 and 38-39.

[9]The chants sung during the procession from the Cathedral to St. Jakob's were Resp. *Paradisi portas*, Resp. *Emendemus*, Ant. *Iniquitates nostras*. Cf. Würdtwein (1782) 106-113, and Catalogue [26D2b]; T.H. Klein (1962) 57 (incipits). Unfortunately, Würdtwein refers to his "old sources" only in a very perfunctory way at the end of his book (p. 278), and I have not been able to identify his formulary for Ash Wednesday in any of the Mainz sources I studied.

[10]See Catalogue [26D2], p. F65. T.H. Klein (1962) 38, quotes only the incipits of the chants and in a very general way refers readers to the Mainz processionals for their texts: "Die Gesänge sind nur in den Prozessionalien des Domes und im Direktorium Chori von St. Stephan enthalten" (n95).

[11]*Jejunium bannitum* means "jejunium ... publice statutum et indictum" (Würdtwein [1782] 200 note ss), i.e. a fast which was proclaimed and established by public decree. The name was obviously developed from the phrase "ieiunium banno seu edicto publico indictum" (*Capitularius Caroli Magni*, lib. 5, cap. 87, cited in Würdtwein, p. 199).

singing.[12] The two dates of these fasts were the week after the Sunday *Misericordia Domini* (Monday, Wednesday, Friday following the second Sunday after Easter); and the week after the Sunday *Salus populi* (Monday, Wednesday, Friday following the twentieth Sunday after Pentecost).[13] This institution is so characteristic of the Mainz archdiocese that its mention in a liturgical book is a sure indicator of the book's origin in this diocese.[14]

All Mainz processional sources consulted agree on the liturgical place of the antiphon *Iniquitates nostras* in these very special processions.[15] It is sung during the Fall procession of the *Bannfasten* on the Wednesday (*Feria IV*) after the Sunday *Salus populi*, on the way to the *Liebfrauenkirche* ('Church of Our Lady'); and it is followed, in the choir of this church, by the singing of another long antiphon, *Sancta Maria, succurre miseris, ... tuum nomen*. The pervasive spirit of penitence in both attitude and practice in these processions provides a significant background for and parallel to the use of the antiphon in the Lddv. Moreover, the singing of the antiphon before the procession enters the church parallels the situation of the *Fatue*, who sing it in hope of being granted mercy and access to the heavenly kingdom.

The first part of the antiphon as quoted above is closely related to *Aufer a nobis*, one of the priest's preparation prayers for Mass (MR, p. 266). Its second part, with the indirect invocation of Mary and all the

---

[12]There are different theories about the origin of these fasts. Serarius, a historiographer of Mainz in the early seventeenth century, explains that "Jejunium banni in tota diocesi Moguntina institutum est contra plagam aboriendi, quae olim in diocesi Moguntina graviter in hominibus et bestiis saeviebat, curataque est et remota a Domino misericorditer per hanc observantiam" (quotation in Würdtwein [1782] 201, note; see also Bruder [1900-1901] 555). Bruder (pp. 552-555) reports on several similar, temporary institutions of 'Bannfasten' in the Mainz diocese, 'ordered' by Mainz bishops and archbishops as early as the eighth and tenth centuries for different reasons (flooding rains, drought, etc.); and he concludes that by the fourteenth century, such various "ordered" fasts developed into the permanent institution of the *Bannfasten*, documented from the fourteenth century on. T.H. Klein (1962) 38-39, tries to combine the two above-mentioned theories.

[13]Bruder (1900-1901) 554-555; T.H. Klein (1962) 38; Reifenberg (1971-1972) 1: 670. In modern use, the Mass introit *Salus populi* is sung on the nineteenth Sunday after Pentecost; cf. LU, p. 1059.

[14]I received this hint from Konrad Wiedemann, author of the Catalogue of the theological folio manuscripts in the Kassel library; see now Wiedemann (1994) p. xxv.

[15]See Catalogue [26D2(b)], p. F65; cf. T.H. Klein (1962) 38.

saints and the repeated plea that heaven's door be opened to them, appears particularly fitting in the context of the Lddv when the *Fatue*, full of repentance, arrive at the closed door asking for admittance to the Wedding Feast (l. 228e): *Fatue vadant ad nuptias cantando Iniquitates nostras etc.* The whole antiphon is the kind of penitential prayer-entreaty that would be expected here, and the subsequent vernacular paraphrase (ll. 229-236, see above, p. 244) reflects this prayer as closely as does any other vernacular paraphrase of a preceding Latin chant.

Beyond the immediate action-related function of the text, this processional antiphon is also important in the larger context of the play. Hoping to win access to the Wedding Feast, the *Fatue* start what can be considered a penitential procession within the drama; it extends from chant **[26]** *Iniquitates nostras* to chant **[32]** *Miserere* in an intensifying series of five appeals including one to the Virgin Mary herself **[32]**:

[26] *Iniquitates nostras*
[28] *Domine domine aperi nobis*
[30] *Recordare virgo mater*
[31] *Exaudi*
[32] *Miserere miserere miserere populo tuo etc.*

This dramatic 'rogation procession' is interrupted twice by the *Dominica Persona*, who rejects the *Fatue* with his two chants **[27]** *Qui tempus*, and **[29]** *Amen amen dico vobis*; and it comes to an abrupt end with the final rejection of the *Fatue* in chant **[33]** *Celum et terra.*[16] As we shall see, the last two chants before this final rejection, **[31]** *Exaudi* and **[32]** *Miserere*, belong to another important penitential procession, that of the Rogation Days, where they are sung at the beginning of the *Aufer a nobis* litany.[17] The penitential spirit of this whole dramatic sequence in the Lddv is overwhelming: the chants would have evoked memories of the singing of litanies, of penitential processions, and of relics of saints carried during those processions. This penitential spirit is amplified by other penitential observances integrated into the action of the play: the *Fatue* prostrating themselves (l. 256a) when they invoke the Virgin Mary

---

[16]See also below, the commentary to chant **[31]** *Exaudi*, p. 278.

[17]The textual relations of the processional antiphon *Iniquitates nostras aufer a nobis* to both the Rogation litany *Aufer a nobis, domine* and the prayer of access *Aufer a nobis quaesumus* at the beginning of Mass (*MR*, p. 266) can, of course, not be overlooked.

with the *Recordare* chant [30], and Mary's genuflexion (l. 278a) when she intercedes on their behalf with the *Miserere* chant [32].

Even more striking, the last phrase of the first chant [26] in this 'rogation' sequence of the Lddv includes this noteworthy petition

sancta maria **cum istis omnibusque sanctis** *intercedente*

Since the carrying of relics happened in many processions, e.g. on the three days of Rogation,[18] this suggests that the presence of saints was probably made manifest during the performance: if not through characters on 'stage,' then perhaps in symbolic form through images, statues, or relics set out in the playing area.[19]

If a 'real' presence of the saints, as perceived by a medieval audience, can be inferred for the performance of the Lddv, then the restoration of this chant [26] may have an impact on our understanding of the play as a whole. It also opens up a new perspective on the controversy over the question of whether or not the Mühlhausen manuscript basically transmits the famous performance of 1321 in Eisenach, in the presence of Count Friedrich der Freidige, whose angry words about the useless

---

[18]Cf. Beissel (1892) II, 2-3. In the ritual of these important processions as outlined in the tenth-century Ordo 50 XXXVI the texts of the antiphons "to be sung for the carrying of the relics" are given *in extenso* ("Antiphonae vero ad reliquias deducendas ... hic subscriptae videntur." Ordo 50 XXXVI.4). That a real presence was perceived in those relics becomes evident in the wording of the chants: the saints are directly addressed, e.g. in the first two antiphons when the relics are lifted and carried outside: *Surgite, sancti, de mansionibus vestris, loca sanctificate, plebem benedicite et nos homines peccatores in pace custodite. Alleluia.* And: *De Hierusalem exeunt reliquiae et salvatio de Monte Syon, propterea protectio erit huic civitati et salvabitur propter David famulum eius. Alleluia* (XXXVI.8). See also the rubrics in the twelfth-century *Liber Ordinarius* of Rheinau (*O*Rh.80), cited below in Chapter 3 [32], p. 290 n7, with details as to how the relics of the saints are to be elevated and carried.

[19]Beissel (1892) II, 1-18, cites a number of instances in which relics of saints were considered to represent the saints themselves. Their relics were exhibited inside and outside of churches for veneration and were carried not only in special liturgical processions but also to battlefields or to places of important political negotiations to ensure a successful outcome. Moreover, in some Corpus Christi plays, particularly the Künzelsau Play, the monstrance showing the host was set up on stage and repeatedly referred to throughout the play to demonstrate that the Lord was present *realiter*. Cf. KünzCC, l. 4a-26; references by the performers such as *der da gegenwertig ist* ("who is present here") recur like a *leitmotif;* cf. l. 1563, 1684, 4173; similarly, l. 3870: the heavenly bread *das da gegenwertick ist*.

"prayers of St. Mary *and all the saints*" (my emphasis) did not appear to reflect the extant play, where only Mary intercedes for the *Fatue*.[20] With the restoration of the complete text for chant [26] *Iniquitates nostras*, the picture has changed: the *Fatue* in their appeal for God's mercy express total trust that "Mary and these and all the saints" will intercede for them; they may even gesture to Mary and to the relics of the saints exhibited in the playing area. When a procession reminiscent of a Rogation procession is subsequently enacted complete with prostrations and genuflexions and the singing of chants from an All Saints litany, then the evidence of 'all the saints' being part of the whole intercessory endeavour is extremely strong. The Mühlhausen manuscript of the Lddv may, therefore, essentially transmit the Eisenach performance.

The processional antiphon *Iniquitates nostras* discussed here meets the main requirements for the restoration of chant [26]: matching incipit, sung performance, penitential prayer content, and textual relevance for the action of the play. All the Mainz processionals that transmit this antiphon, however, are more recent than the Lddv, i.e. from the fifteenth century or later.[21]

Fortunately, the antiphon *Iniquitates nostras* is transmitted in sources other than the Mainz processionals,[22] chief of which are two fourteenth-

----

[20]For this controversy see, for instance, Reuschel (1906) 8-9; Schneider (ed. 1964) 8; Bergmann (1986) 256-257; Linke (1987a) 225. For the words of the Count as reported in the *Cronica S. Petri* ("Sampetrinum") of Erfurt, see above, pp. 12-13.

[21]Cf. Catalogue [26D2(b)], p. F65. The oldest among them, *PrMz.*II,74 (early fifteenth century), does not have the complete antiphon in its original formulary. Only the incipit appears on fol. 33v, with a reference in the margin to the sixteenth-century addition of the complete chant on fol. 76v (=LXXXIIII of the old pagination). On fol. 33v of this processional, which is a *Pars aestivalis*, reference is made to an earlier notation ("*ut supra*") of the complete antiphon (possibly for Ash Wednesday), which would probably have been included in the *Pars hiemalis* that no longer exists. As the complete antiphon was added in the sixteenth century, on fol. 76v, with specific reference to fol. 33v, this proves that the *Jejuniumn bannitum* continued to be observed in the sixteenth century, a thesis maintained also by Bruder (1900-1901) 556, and by T.H. Klein (1962) 39.

*PrMz.*II,303 is from the late fifteenth century, and *PrMz.*110 only from the year 1704. However, the *Jejunium bannitum* formulary in this late manuscript is an almost exact copy of those in the fifteenth-century processionals.

[22]The date of its use in Trier, according to Würdtwein (1782) 244, on the last day of the Rogation processions, can, unfortunately, not be determined; cf. Catalogue [26D2(b)]. The text of the antiphon in Trier has the variant "*sancto Petro ... intercedente*"; cf. Catalogue [26E], p. F65 and below, p. 253.

century graduals of the Badische Landesbibliothek in Karlsruhe.[23] As both manuscripts, GErf.44 and GErf.16, originate in Erfurt and were written for the Neuwerkskloster of Augustinian canonesses, the conditions are close to perfect for the restoration of chant [26] *Iniquitates nostras* from these contemporaneous Thuringian sources. There is no indication of the liturgical context for this antiphon in either source,[24] yet the transmission of text and music is good. In the older of these two Erfurt graduals, GErf.44, dating from the first quarter of the fourteenth century, the text is complete, but only the first two lines are notated; GErf.16 of the mid-fourteenth century transmits the antiphon with its complete text and melody.

With the fortunate discovery of the Erfurt graduals, the music of this long processional antiphon *Iniquitates nostras* is now accessible in four manuscript sources, three from Mainz and one from Erfurt, partly paralleled by a second Erfurt source. A detailed comparison of these various transmissions of the antiphon and its context leads to some remarkable conclusions regarding the faithfulness of the Mainz tradition:

(1) The late Mainz processional *Pr*Mz.110 (of 1704) presents the whole long formulary for the *Jejunium bannitum* procession, fols. 33v-43v, in more or less the same form this procession has in the fifteenth-century source *Pr*Mz.II,74, fols. 76v-77r: the rubrics are approximately, the chants exactly, the same in both sources.[25]

(2) In *Pr*Mz.II,74, the processional antiphon *Iniquitates* has been added, with its complete text and music, by a sixteenth-century hand on fols. 76v-77r. Its textual-musical form here is absolutely the same as that in the fifteenth-century processional *Pr*Mz.II,303. The only difference between these two transmissions and the early eighteenth-century processional *Pr*Mz.110 is that notation in the latter is on a five-line stave, whereas the two earlier processionals use a four-line stave.

(3) In the earlier versions of the antiphon in GErf.44 (early fourteenth century) and GErf.16 (mid-fourteenth century), the text is absolutely iden-

---

[23]MS St. Peter perg. 44, fols. 133v-135v and MS St. Peter perg. 16, fols. 208r-211r; cf. Catalogue [26D2(a)], p. F65.

[24]In both graduals, the antiphon is surrounded by various other liturgical items. Heinzer-Stamm (1984) 40, 160, classify it under *Varia*.

[25]On fol. 33v of *Pr*Mz.II,74, the antiphon *Iniquitates* is given only with its incipit with reference to a part of the book that is now missing; see above, n21.

tical to that in the later Mainz sources. The tune is basically the same in all these sources except for a few variants of minor importance.[26]

The amazing faithfulness in the tradition and transmission of the whole *Jejunium bannitum* procession and, in particular, the antiphon *Iniquitates nostras* in the different liturgical books of Mainz and its diocese tends to corroborate the conservatism and longevity of the old tradition that musicologists have ascribed as special characteristics and attributes of the Mainz choral on the whole, including the liturgical Recitation.[27] A faithful tradition for the chants in the processionals in particular, Klein contends, can be guaranteed from the fourteenth to the late seventeenth century, new processionals having been produced only from the early eighteenth century on.[28]

As a processional antiphon, the *Iniquitates* chant belongs to a special category of antiphons that are independent of the Office, no longer necessarily connected with the singing of a psalm, and often of considerable length, although, of course, 'regular' antiphons were also used in processions.[29] The melody of this *Iniquitates* antiphon is in mode 2 (finalis *D*) and extends over a range of a tenth, from *A* to *c*. More neumatic than syllabic in style, as is typical for processional antiphons, it includes several beautiful melismas of up to nine notes, especially in the first part and towards the end. While the melody progresses largely in steps, again in accordance with the genre, the tune is enlivened by an amazing number of larger intervals, certainly evidence of the basic German dialect: numerous thirds, fourths (five times), fifths (four times, one of them a fifth-plus-third). Successive thirds, however, occur only once in a descending form. Several cadences are made from the tone below

---

[26]In addition to a slightly differently shaped melisma over *pater*, the variants are mainly one-, two-, and three-note neumes which, compared to *G*Erf.16, in the Mainz sources often have a note missing or sometimes added, usually only in the interval of a second, without really affecting the shape of the melody. The transmission in *G*Erf.44, basically supporting that of *G*Erf.16, stops after the first two lines.

[27]Cf. T.H. Klein (1962) 141-145, with references to the studies by Federl and Köllner. According to Federl (1937) 79, some of the regional peculiarities of the Mainz recitation tones, for instance, persisted even into the late nineteenth century.

[28]Cf. T.H. Klein (1962) 141-142.

[29]For the characteristics of processional antiphons see Wagner (1911-1921) 3: 319-320; Apel (1958) 403-404; Bailey (1971) 133-142 (Rogation antiphons); Hiley (1993) 100-104; Nowacki (1994) 657-658.

the finalis (**C-D-D**), a non-Gregorian form which is explained as being of Gallican origin.[30]

As a result of the related investigations, chant [26] of the Lddv will be restored from the antiphon *Iniquitates nostras* as transmitted in the Thuringian gradual *G*Erf.16, the only fourteenth-century source with complete musical notation for this chant.

Antiphon   *Iniquitates nostras [aufer a nobis pater omnipotens, ut hoc templum tuo nomine dedicatum puris mereamur mentibus introire, sancta maria*[a] *cum istis omnibusque sanctis intercedente celestes portas nobis dignare aperire.]*

Source   *G*Erf.16, fol. 210r-v (= *G*Erf.44; *Pr*Mz.II,74; *Pr*Mz.II,303; *Pr*Mz.110; Würdtwein, p. 112 [Mainz]; ~ Würdtwein, p. 244 [Trier]); cf. Catalogue [26D2], p. F65.

Variants   [a] *sancta maria] sancto petro* Würdtwein (Trier)

Melody   Mode 2. Transcribed in Chapter 4 from *G*Erf.16, fol. 210r-v.
Melody ~ *Pr*Mz.II,74, *Pr*Mz.II.303, *Pr*Mz.110. ~ = *G*Erf.44, fol. 135v (notated only up to *puris*).

Translation   "Take away from us, almighty Father, our iniquities that we may be worthy to enter with pure minds this temple dedicated to Thy name. As Saint Mary with these and all the saints is interceding, deign to open to us the heavenly doors."

---

[30]Cf. Hiley (1993) 104.

[27] *Qui tempus congrue peniten[cie] perdiderit,*
frustra cum precibus ad regni ianua[m] pervenerit.

(Lddv 236b-e)

The stern words **[27]** "He who wasted the time of proper penitence comes in vain to the door of the kingdom with prayers," pronounced by the *Dominica Persona* in response to the fervent entreaties of the *Fatue* in their chant **[26]** *Iniquitates*, are the first of three rejections (**[27, 29, 33]**) that the *Fatue* will experience during their continued efforts to gain access to the heavenly Wedding Feast. The text is complete in MS A of the Lddv although it does require some emendation:[1]

> *Qui tempus congrue penitens perdiderit*
> *frustra cum precibus ad regni ianua pervenerit.*

The first editor of the Lddv, Friedrich Stephan, suggested the emendation with an added [*non*]: *Qui tempus* [*non*] *congrue penitens perdiderit*, a conjecture which was to be perpetuated in the editions to the present day (see Catalogue **[27B]**, p. F66). Beckers' additional manipulation of the two text lines and the preceding stage direction was presumably based on the idea that some kind of versification would be expected when a non-biblical Latin text is used in a dramatic work.[2] The text of chant **[27]** is clearly not biblical. It may have been part of a liturgical reading, however, and if so, the appropriate form of performance, in the liturgy as well as in drama, would be that of liturgical recitation. This possibility must be pursued here since the text of chant **[27]** can be identified as a sentence from a homily by Pope Gregory the Great on the

---

[1]The manuscript seems to provide complete texts whenever the chants are either very short (**[28, 29]**), little known or not readily accessible (**[5, 27, 33]**), or especially composed for this play (**[9', 17]**, and possibly **[33]**).

[2]Cf. Lddv ed. Beckers (1905) ll. 236b-c and note b. Beckers adds an unwarranted *cantet* to the direction, and omits the important *regni* of the manuscript in order to adapt the two phrases to what he thinks are intended to be two fourteen-syllable verses. De Boor (ed. 1965) ll. 315b-c, unfortunately presents Beckers' edited form of the text (not the rubric) in his anthology with no editorial brackets or notes. While verses of eight, ten, twelve, and fifteen syllables are popular in romance poetry, fourteen-syllable verses, to my knowledge, are virtually unheard of. Thus the restoration of the manuscript version of this text, *ad regni ianua[m]*, resulting in two phrases of unequal length, is mandatory. This has been done in Schneider's edition (of 1958 and 1964).

Parable of the Ten Virgins. I quote the sentence from the edition in the *Patrologia Latina*, in the spelling found there:

Qui tempus congruae poenitentiae perdidit,
frustra ante regni ianuam cum precibus venit. (PL 76: 1121C)

Several medieval lectionaries and breviaries provide evidence that this homily, originally given on the Feast of St. Agnes, was used for many feasts, particularly those of the *Commune Virginum*, when Matthew 25: 1-13 was the required Gospel reading (Catalogue [27D2a and b], p. F67). In general, sections from homilies were read at Matins as the three lessons (or four in the monastic Office) in single nocturn services and in the last nocturn on Sundays and feasts with three nocturns.[3] These homily lessons as *Expositio evangelii* were taken from sermons and other writings of the Fathers, often collected in a homiliary.[4]

All Matins readings were originally very long and not specified in the lectionaries. Instead, it was the responsibility of the celebrant to subdivide the *lectio continua* to fit into the available time by intoning the *Tu autem, domine, miserere nobis*.[5] From the eleventh century on, the lesson books tend to present only the specified reading sections for each *lectio*. These sections became progressively shorter, particularly during the thirteenth century when the Franciscans helped spread the very concise Breviary of the Roman Curia.[6] Such a gradual shortening of the reading material for the above-mentioned homily of Gregory is reflected in the liturgical sources listed in the Catalogue under [27D2], p. F67. Nevertheless, lectionaries for the Office and homiliaries that presented the original readings in their entirety or as a *continua* series did exist into the fourteenth century.[7] *L*Fri.142, a fourteenth-century homiliary from Fritzlar, is just such a lectionary; it contains the entire homily of St. Gregory in the second formulary for the Common of Virgins.[8]

---

[3]Cf. A. Hughes (1982) 61-62.
[4]See, e.g. Reynolds (1984) 224.
[5]Thalhofer-Eisenhofer (1912) 2: 559-560.
[6]Bäumer (1895) 338-339; cf. Thalhofer-Eisenhofer (1912) 2: 556-557.
[7]Cf. Bäumer (1895) 339; Thalhofer-Eisenhofer (1912) 2: 557.
[8]Kassel, MS 2° theol. 142, fols. 224v-229r; see Catalogue [27D2a]. Wiedemann (1994) 195-198, classifies this book correctly as a homiliary, a term that is not included in the "Versuch einer liturgischen Nomenklatur" by Fiala-Irtenkauf (1963). My use of the letter *L* for lectionary in the siglum for *L*Fri.142 is meant in a generic sense. Cf. Fiala-Irtenkauf (1963) 118 (*Lectionarium officii*) and Thiel (1967) 2387 (*Homiliarium*).

Matins readings were, of course, intoned to specific formulas. Gregory's sentence in chant **[27]** of the Lddv, can, therefore, be assumed to have been performed in recitation, just as prose texts from the Prophets, the Passions, or other biblical passages were, when used in plays.[9] Versification of such a text then, as Beckers had it in mind, was not necessary although it was the rule for freely created texts that had no basis in the Vulgate or the liturgy. Nevertheless, the author of the Lddv revised the text that he adopted from Gregory. I quote from the critical edition (CCL 141: 86) and MS A, p. 97a, with my emphases:

Gregory   Qui tempus congruae paeniten**tiae** perdi**dit**
             frustra **ante** regni ianuam cum precibus **uenit**.

Lddv   *Qui tempus congrue penitens perdiderit*
             *frustra cum precibus **ad** regni ianua[m] pervenerit.*

As mentioned earlier, the text of this chant in the Lddv is faulty and needs to be emended. In the light of the quotation from Gregory's homily, the emendation *Qui tempus [non] congrue penitens perdiderit* appears questionable; the form *congrue* has been understood here as an adverb modifying *penitens*, whereas in Gregory's sentence it is clearly an adjective modifying the noun *paenitentia*. If the error of transmission lies in the form of the word *penitens*, changing it to the genitive form *penitencie* (*paenitentiae* in classical spelling) as in Gregory's text gives genitive status also to *congrue* (*congruae*) as the modifying adjective. The result is an elegant, less clumsy version of this whole passage in the Lddv:

Qui tempus congrue peniten[cie] perdiderit
frustra cum precibus ad regni ianua[m] pervenerit.

This emendation appears preferable to the addition of [*non*] not only because of its simplicity and its closeness to the Gregorian text but also because the phrase *tempus penitencie* (like *tempus venie*) is a technical term in liturgical language and very likely to have been used by Pope Gregory, *tempus congrue penitencie* being those times in the year that are prescribed by the Church for fast and penance, particularly the Lenten period. Last, but not least, the reading *tempus penitencie* is supported by the vernacular 'translation' of the chant, which also uses a genitive

[9]Cf. Schuler (1951) 33-36; Mehler (1981) 183, and the discussion above. in Chapter 2, pp. 65-67, and Chapter 3, p. 75.

construction, MS B reflecting the original Latin phrase even more literally than MS A:

Wer syne **czit der jogent** vorsumit hat ... (A, 1. 237)

Wer die **zyt der ruwe** versumet hat ... (B, 1. 365)[10]

Even in its emended form the Latin text of the Lddv still presents some noteworthy variants in comparison with the 'original' sentence of Gregory's homily. The most obvious change is in the two verbal forms at the end of the two clauses: *perdidit : venit* to *perdiderit : pervenerit.* This is hardly accidental since the changed forms strike the ear with their accentual accord. If the comparison includes the words immediately preceding these two verbal forms, the sequence of accents is even more striking; in the following example, the figures 7 and 3 mark the last two word accents when the syllables are counted from the end:

peniténcie perdíderit : iánuam pervénerit

' __ _' __ : ' _ _ _' _ _

7   3   :   7   3

Such an 'accentual echo' in the endings of the two lines seems to be the touch of 'poeticizing' that the author may have desired when he extracted a single sentence from a liturgical reading for use in his drama.[11] A similar technique is evident in chant [33], the final speech of the *Dominica Persona:*

Celum et térra transíbunt   ' _ _ ' _   5 - - 2 -

Verbum autem meum in etérnum permánet.   ' _ _ ' _   5 - - 2 -

The 'accentual accord' of the line endings in the two chants [27] and [33] of the *Dominica Persona* is, in fact, a special form of what is known as medieval *cursus* or 'poetical prose,' often referred to as 'rhythmical prose'.

---

[10]"He who wasted his *time of youth* ..." (A 237); "He who wasted *the time of penitence* ..." (B 365), with my emphases.

[11]Strangely enough, this pattern holds true even for the unemended manuscript versions *pénitens perdíderit : iánua[m] pervénerit* with the accentual pattern 7---3-- in each case.

In medieval Latin prose, *cursus* is the practice of ending sentences and clauses in certain cadences or accent patterns.[12] What was important in the *cursus* was not the 'accentual accord' in consecutive phrase endings as in the two chants [27] and [33]; all that mattered was to make the end of a sentence or clause pleasing to the ear through the use of one of the preferred accentual patterns for the last two words.[13]

Chant [27] in the Lddv and its source in Gregory's homily can now be 'notated' and compared with respect to the *cursus* used:

Gregory	*Qui tempus congruae paeniténtiae pérdidit*	6--3--	(pp 3pp)
	frustra ante regni ianuam cum précibus vénit.	5--2-	(pp 2)
Lddv [27]	*Qui tempus congrue peiténcie perdíderit*	7---3--	(pp 4pp)
	frustra cum precibus ad regni iánuam pervénerit.	7---3--	(pp 4pp)

And the notation for the last reply of the *Dominica Persona* in chant [33] would be:

| Lddv [33] | *Celum et térra transíbunt* | 5--2- | (p 3p) |
| | *Verbum autem meum in etérnum permánet.* | 5--2- | (p 3p) |

---

[12]Used by Marcellinus and Leo the Great as early as the fourth and fifth centuries and in a great number of prayers in the early Latin liturgy, this form of Latin prose became widespread among medieval authors from the tenth and eleventh centuries on and was in wide use in the papal and other chanceries. For more information on the *cursus* see W. Meyer (1905); Janson (1975); a brief survey in Smedick (1984). For the use of the *cursus* in Bible and liturgy, see Stummer (1954).

[13]Different procedures have been developed for the analysis and description of the *cursus*. In W. Meyer's method, used here, the number of syllables in the last two words are counted from the end of the sentence or clause and the last two accents are marked. Tore Janson has developed a system in which the accentual structure of each of the last two words is considered, rather than the total number of syllables. For an explanation of his system of 'notation,' see Janson (1975) 13-15. Meyer's system has been almost universally accepted, as even Janson (p. 11) admits.

The four most favoured cadences can be described as follows (Janson's method of 'notation' is added in parentheses):

Planus	*íllum dedúxit*	' - - ' -	5--2-	(p 3p)
Tardus	*resilére tentáverit*	(- -) ' - - ' - -	6--3--	(p 4pp)
Velox	*hóminem recepístis*	' - - - - ' -	7----2-	(pp 4p)
Trispondaicus	*ágnos àdmittátis*	' - ' - ' -	6-4-2-	(p 4p)

Besides these four main cadences, there were numerous other patterns more or less desired. Some authors developed a personal style of *cursus*, or they used a regional one that was taught at certain school centres.

While the *cursus planus* 5--2- (p 3p) used in chant **[33]** occurs frequently in medieval Latin prose, the cadence 7---3-- (pp 4pp) of chant **[27]** is more rare. In both chants the same *cursus* cadence is repeated. This is certainly not an accident, but was fully intended by the author of the play for these two speeches of the *Dominica Persona*. It is interesting to note that, according to Friedrich Stummer's studies, many Mass prayers show a similar 'accentual accord' of two consecutive clauses, especially at the end of prayers.[14]

Gregory also used the *cursus* in each of the two clauses of his sentence; the cadences are different in nature, but they represent the most common types: the *tardus* 6--3-- (pp 3pp) in the first and the *planus* 5--2- (pp 2) in the second clause. The author of the Lddv achieved a repetition of the same *cursus* for chant **[27]** by simply replacing Gregory's verbal forms, i.e. changing the perfect tense (*perdidit* and *venit*) to the future perfect (*perdiderit* and *pervenerit*). In addition, the author changed the word order within the second clause, probably to avoid the hiatus of *frustra ante* found in Gregory's homily — a change that did not affect the accentual structure at the end of the phrase. The result of these two minute changes to the original Gregorian sentence is a harmonious, elegant wording for text **[27]** with the *cursus* cadence 7---3-- (pp 4pp) in both its clauses, a perfect accentual accord. Since the cadence 7---3-- (pp 4pp) is one of the less frequently used *cursus* forms in the Middle Ages, the fact, that it is employed in repetition within a single sentence seems even more purposeful.[15]

In Gregory's homily, the phrase was embedded in a larger unit of poetical prose, where the use of two different *cursus* patterns in two consecutive clauses is completely in line with the rules of medieval *cursus*. By isolating this one sentence and transplanting it into the totally different medium of a religious play, the author of the Lddv obviously wanted to give some poetical form to this prose text which is recited by the *Dominica Persona* at a very important juncture in the drama.

[14]Cf. Stummer (1954), esp. pp. 271-272, with a large number of examples. Stummer finds that a parallelism in content and thought in two phrases is often underlined through an audible parallelism of their *cursus* clauses.

[15]For the frequency of the 7---3-- (pp 4pp) cadence check the tables in Janson (1975) 107-115; compare his discussion (pp. 53-54) on the more frequent use of pp 4pp cadence with Adalbert of Magdeburg in the tenth century.

Since the liturgical source of chant [27] is a homily reading of Matins, mainly in the Common of Virgins, the method of performance — in the Office as well as in the drama — would be liturgical recitation. The question as to which particular recitation formula should be used for chant [27] in the Lddv cannot be answered with absolute certainty. Having its liturgical place in the Office of Matins, this text would 'normally' be intoned to the lesson tone for Matins. Since the phrase is not from a Gospel, indeed not biblical at all, it might appear inappropriate to use the Gospel tone as in the earlier 'recitation chants' [14] and [15].[16] However, since it is the *Dominica Persona* himself who is pronouncing these words, which constitute the first of three harsh rejections of the Foolish Virgins, and since he addresses them with his full authority using words from the Gospel in both later replies, [29] *Amen amen, dico vobis* and [33] *Celum et terra transibunt*, the use of the Gospel tone, i.e. the form in which the word of God had been pronounced for centuries in the liturgical context of Mass, would seem appropriate and meaningful for the reciting of all three 'speeches' of the *Dominica Persona*.

I shall, therefore, set this chant [27] to the Gospel tone of the *Accentus Moguntinus* as transmitted in *M*Halb.888, that is, to the same recitation formula that was proposed above for the performance of the short dialogue between the two groups of the Virgins, chants [14] and [15], with words from Matthew.[17] However, while the higher pitched tenor *a* (with the upper third *c*) was suggested for the female characters of the Virgins, the lower-pitched tenor *D* (with the upper third *F*) as found in the 'model' of *M*Halb.888 would appear more suitable for the *Dominica*

---

[16]It is worth noting that even in this short dialogue between the Wise and the Foolish Virgins using the Vulgate text, the cadences of the four clauses show the use of *cursus*:

[14] *Date nobis de óleo véstro*	5--2-	(Planus)
quia lampades nóstre extinguúntur.	6---2-	(Trispondaicus)
[15] *Ne forte [non] sufficiat nóbis et vóbis;*	5--2-	(Planus)
ite potius ad vendentes et émite vóbis.	5--2-	(Planus)

Here, the very common *cursus* form of the *planus* appears three times, the less common *trispondaicus* only once. With the repetition of the *planus*, chant [15] shows the kind of 'accentual accord' or echo that was noticed in chant [27]. It may not be unjustified to suggest that this echo form of *cursus* in the verse from Matthew could have inspired the author to strive for a similar accord of cadences in chants [27] and [33]. For use of *cursus* in Latin Bible translations see Stummer (1954) 237-269.

[17] See Chapter 3 [14-15], pp. 168-169, with Figure 12 showing the musical setting.

Persona.[18] And in its text, chant **[27]** will be emended through the Gregorian homily as shown above.

Text   *Qui tempus congrue peniten[cie]*[a] *perdiderit*[b]
        frustra cum precibus ad regni ianua[m][c] *pervenerit.*[d]

Source   Lddv(A), ll. 236b-d (MS A, p. 97a), collated with a phrase from Gregorius Magnus, Homily on Matt. 25: 1-13 (*L*Fri.142, fol. 227v; CCL 141: 86; PL 76: 1121c).

Variants   [a] *penitencie*] *L*Fri.142; *penitens* Lddv A; *paenitentiae* (*poenitentiae*) Gregorius (CCL 141; PL 76); [*non*] ... *penitens* all previous editions.
        [b] *perdiderit*] Lddv A; *perdidit* Gregorius (*L*Fri.142; CCL 141; PL 76).
        [c] *cum precibus ad regni ianua*m] *cum precibus ad regni ianua* Lddv A; *ante regni ianuam cum precibus* Gregorius (*L*Fri.142; CCL 141; PL 76).
        [d] *pervenerit*] Lddv A; *venit* Gregorius (*L*Fri.142; CCL 141; PL 76). Cf. Catalogue [27D1 and 2a], p. F67.

Melody   Set in liturgical recitation to the Gospel tone, according to the *Accentus Moguntinus* as transmitted in *M*Halb.888 (cf. above, Figure 3, p. 80), with the subtonal tenor *D* and the upper third *F*; compare facsimile 4. See Chapter 4 **[27]**.

Translation "He who wasted the time of proper penitence comes in vain to the door of the Kingdom with prayers."

---

[18] Cf. the discussion above, p. 168, and below, p. 264.

[28] *Domine domine aperi nobis* (Lddv 240b)
[29] *Amen amen dico vobis nescio vos* (Lddv 244b)

Despite the *Dominica Persona*'s stern rejection in chant [27], the *Fatue* try a second time to gain entry to the Heavenly Banquet when they sing chant [28], entreating the *Dominica Persona* to open the door for them, only to receive a second harsh reply. The words of the *Fatue*, [28] *Domine, domine aperi nobis*, and those of the *Dominica Persona*, [29] *Amen, amen, dico vobis, nescio vos*, like the earlier short dialogue of chants [14] and [15], can easily be identified as the words of direct discourse in the Parable of the Wise and Foolish Virgins where they form the brief dialogue of Matthew 25: 11 and 12. The only textual change in the direct discourse is the emphatic repetition of the beginning word *Amen* in speech [29] of the *Dominica Persona*. The author of the play may have deliberately chosen this repetition in analogy to the repeated *Domine* in the preceding speech [28] of the *Fatue*. Both texts are given in their full wording in MS A of the Lddv; they are discussed here together as they continue the macaronic 'dialogue' between the two parties that had started with chant [26].

While the other plays of the Ten Virgins include this dramatic rejection scene, they do not all use the Latin words from the parable. Only the Marburg *Spiel von den letzten Dingen* (MaSp.532) has the fragment of a parallel text to chant [29]:[1]

[SALVAT]OR respondit   ... *nescio vos, nescio vos.* (MaSp.532, fol. 10v)[2]

---

[1]Cf. Catalogue [29C], p. F70. The Old French *Sponsus* ed. Thomas (1951) makes use of a slightly different wording (*Amen dico, vos ignosco*) at the beginning of the final Latin stanza, sung by *Christus* before he concludes the play with three vernacular lines consigning the Foolish Virgins to hell; cf. ll. 99-105. In the Dutch *Spel van de Maegden* (Flem.X.Virg), ed. Hoebeke (1959), the scene is entirely in the vernacular and stretches over twenty-five lines in five individual verbal exchanges between the Foolish Virgins and the Bridegroom (ll. 543-567); the vernacular equivalent of the Latin *nescio vos* is in l. 556 and, more specifically, l. 564. In KünzCC, ll. 4779-4786, the vernacular version of the dialogue from Matt. 25: 11-12 occurs at the outset of the scene with the *Fatue*, which is also quite extended and in the vernacular only.

[2]Since in this fragmentary manuscript the beginnings of all lines on fol. 10v are trimmed off, it can only be conjectured that the same Latin speech from Matt. 25: 12 was used here. The repetition of *nescio vos*, not found in the biblical model, may be explained as an added emphasis by the author, comparable to the *Amen amen* in the Lddv. Chant [28] does not seem to occur in any other play.

Although the scanty stage directions in the Thuringian play give no indication of how this dialogue should be performed, its origin in the Gospel reading of Matthew is a sufficient indicator that it was meant to be intoned in the Gospel tone. For chant [29] *Amen amen dico vobis,* the external evidence from the corresponding stage direction in the Alsfeld Passion Play (AlsfP) not only supports this assumption, but even indicates the exact reciting formula in which it should be delivered;[3] here, in the scene of the *Harrowing of Hell,* Jesus pronounces the same words of Matthew 25: 12 to the damned souls:

Jhesus dicit sub accentu ewangelii   *Amen amen dico vobis nescio vos.*
                                                              (AlsfP, ll. 7266 a-b)

This invaluable information shows the respect shown to the words of the Gospel even in a very short text and in a scene as far removed from its original place in the Matthew parable as hell is from the gates of heaven. Whether this short condemnatory speech of Jesus is addressed to the Foolish Virgins in front of heaven's portal or to the damned souls in hell, it is a quotation from holy Scripture, and implies the whole authority of the Gospel. Therefore it is delivered in the only appropriate form — *sub accentu evangelii,* in the Gospel tone.[4]

What is operating here is the typological manner of medieval thought. The scenes in the Harrowing of Hell and in the Ten Virgins play may be remote from each other in an objective sense; yet, typologically, they are closely related. Both exemplify the Lord's exclusion of unworthy human beings from heavenly bliss. This typological identity makes it possible for the parable words to be transferred to the 'historical' scene of the *Descensus* (or 'Harrowing of Hell'), a process discussed above as *typologische Übertragung.*[5]

---

[3]See Catalogue [29C], p. F70; also above, Chapter 2, especially p. 64 n64.

[4]It is worth noting that the subsequent vernacular lines in the Alsfeld play are also very close to those in the Lddv; they must be regarded as one of the many borrowings from the Thuringian drama: "Vorware, ich enweiss nicht, wer er sijt, / want ir nach nye zu keyner zyt / mich selber erkant hot / noch gedienet frue adder spade!" (AlsfP, ll. 7267-7270). Compare Lddv, ll. 245-248: "Ich enweyz nicht, wy ir sit, / wan ir czů icheyner czyt / mich selben erkant hat / noch den andirn armen ny eyn gut getat." ("I do not know who you are, for at no time have you known me, nor have you done anything good for other poor creatures.")

[5]Cf. Stemmler (1970) 123-163 and 247-299; see above, p. 173.

The strong evidence that chant **[29]** *Amen amen dico vobis* is to be intoned as a Gospel recitation must also apply, by analogy, to the preceding plea of the *Fatue*, chant **[28]** *Domine domine aperi nobis*. This form of delivery within a play for any kind of Gospel text, even very short ones, was so much a matter of course, at least at the time of the Lddv, that there was no need to give the special directions for performance that are included in the much later Alsfeld play. The performance of this dialogue is certainly similar to the earlier one between the *Fatue* and the *Prudentes*, chants **[14-15]**, which also contained direct discourse from the Matthew parable. The significant difference is that the *Fatue* are in dialogue not with other *virgines* but with the *Dominica Persona*. This may translate into the use of two different tenors in the recitation as suggested above.[6] If the *Dominica Persona* recited his first rejection **[27]** of the *Fatue* with the tenor *D*, the *Fatue* would intone their second plea for entrance **[28]** *Domine domine aperi nobis* on the higher-pitched tenor *a* (with the upper third *c*) in imitation of female voices. The *Dominica Persona* would resume the lower-pitched tenor *D* (with the upper third *F*) in his dismissive reply **[29]** *Amen amen dico vobis nescio vos*. Such musical aspects of the chants **[28]** and **[29]** are the main concern here since the texts of both are complete in MS A of the Lddv.

Texts   **[28]** *Domine domine aperi nobis.*

[29] *Amen amen dico vobis nescio vos.*

Sources   Lddv, ll. 240b, 244b (MS A, p. 97a); cf. Matthew 25: 11-12; EvOP(Humb), fol. 454r (with *positurae* markings); LFri.142, fol. 224v-225r (text incomplete).

Variants   [a] *Amen amen*] Lddv; AlsfP 7266b; *Amen* Matthew 25: 12.

Melody   Set in liturgical recitation to the Gospel tone, according to the *Accentus Moguntinus* as transmitted in MHalb.888 (cf. pp. 79-81, with Figure 3); compare facsimile 4. See Chapter 4 **[28-29]**:

for **[28]** *Domine*, with the subtonal tenor *a* and the upper third *c*;

for **[29]** *Amen amen*, with the subtonal tenor *D* and the upper third *F*.

Translation   **[28]** "Lord, Lord, open to us!"

[29] "Verily, verily, I say unto you, I know you not!"

---

[6]Cf. pp. 168 and 260-261.

[30] *Recordare virgo mater etc.* (Lddv 256c)

In deep despair over their second rejection by the *Dominica Persona*, the *Fatue* turn to his mother Mary and implore her in chant **[30]** to be their advocate. As a display of their helplessness, their contrition, and the urgency of their appeal, they throw themselves on the ground in prostration, as the rubric for this chant directs: *Omnes Fatue prostrate in terram cantant* (ll. 256a-b).[1] The rubric does not, however, indicate any genre for this chant **[30]**, which is given by its incipit only. The liturgical text *Recordare virgo mater*, proposed by Beckers in his critical edition of the Lddv (1905, p. 111) and adopted in all subsequent editions, was mistakenly perceived as introducing the 'sequence' *Ob hac familia*;[2] it must be recognized as an offertory for Masses in honor of the Virgin Mary, however, although the offertory's last two words *a nobis* are lacking in what is presented as the 'complete' text of this chant in the editions of the Lddv.[3] This offertory, the only chant with such an incipit, was obviously much liked in the Middle Ages and gave rise to a number of tropes after the twelfth century, the trope (not 'sequence') *Ab hac familia* being the most famous among them. In the edition by Clemens Blume

---

[1]For the significance of prostration in liturgy and ritual, see Suntrup (1978) 166-169; also Braun (1937) 170.

[2]Sequences are additions to the *Alleluia* of Mass, texting in a very structured form the alleluia *jubilus*, the long final melisma on *-a*. Beckers' only source ([1905] 44) for this chant was a liturgical anthology by Gustav Milchsack (1886), *Hymni et Sequentiae*, where the *Recordare* is inadequately edited (p. 219) and figures as no. 248 under "Carmina vagorum." As Blume mentions (AH 49: 322), the *Recordare virgo* was presented as a 'sequence' in an earlier anthology by Misset-Weale, from a single missal, printed in Paris in 1547. Did Milchsack use this source for his edition of the *Recordare*? For the affinity of this particular (troped) version of the offertory to sequences see below, p. 270 n20.

[3]An offertory, originally the antiphon to the psalm chanted during the offertory procession, is sung by the choir and is one of the proper chants of Mass. For its liturgical function and general musical characteristics see Wagner (1901-1921) 3: 418-434; Apel (1958) 363-375; Scharnagl (1961); Baroffio-Steiner (1980). This particular offertory *Recordare virgo mater* (without the trope) was generated from the first verse to another offertory (*Recordare mei*); see Ott (1935) 125-126; Björkvall-Steiner (1982) 28-30. When offertory verses fell into disuse in the eleventh century, this verse, with a few textual and musical changes, eventually became an independent offertory. Cf. Björkvall-Steiner (1982) 30, 35 n35, with more literature; Johner (1940) 101 n2; Stäblein (1966) 810; Haug et al. (1998) 906-907.

of the Tropes of the Mass, which appeared one year after Beckers' edition of the Lddv, the type setting clarifies the chant's structure, the original offertory in *italics*, the trope in Roman type:[4]

A.　*Recordare, virgo mater, dum consteteris in conspectu Dei, ut loquaris pro nobis bonum et ut avertas indignationem suam [a nobis]*,

1a. Ab hac familia　tu propitia,　　　1b. Mater eximia,　pelle vitia;
2a. Fer remedia　reis in via,　　　　2b. Dans in patria　vitae gaudia,
3a. Pro quibus dulcia　tu praeconia　3b. Laudis cum gratia　suscipe, pia
　　　　　　　　4　Virgo Maria, *a nobis*.[5]

Tropes are textual and/or musical accretions to existing chants for Office and Mass. They can take different forms. The famous *Quem queritis* dialogue, for example, is often understood as an 'introductory trope' to the Easter introit *Resurrexi*; other tropes are appended to or inserted into chants.[6] In the trope *Ab hac familia*, the new poetic text or 'prosula' with three paired verses and a concluding seventh line makes use of the long melisma over the *a* of *a nobis* in such a way that each syllable of the newly created text is matched with a note of the pre-existing, yet, in

---

[4]AH 49: 321-322 (no. 634). The text of the offertory proper is based on Jeremiah 18: 20. When Beckers quoted the chant from Milchsack's anthology he omitted, together with the trope (which he perceived as a sequence) also the last two words *a nobis* which belong to the original offertory. In liturgical and musical terms such a truncated version is inconceivable since, as we shall see, those last two words, carrying the long melisma over the preposition *a*, are highly important for the offertory's musical message.

[5]It should be noted that the text of the basic offertory given here (in *italics*) is not identical with that established for the Lddv from other sources at the end of section [30], notably *consteteris/steteris* and *bonum/bona*. Translation of the troped offertory, by Johansson (1985) 83 and 85: "Remember, Virgin Mother, while you stand in the presence of God, to plead on our behalf and to turn his wrath away [from us] — from this family, you favourable, exceptional mother, expel the vices, bring remedy to the sinners on their way, bringing joy of life in the native land. For this, receive sweet proclamations of praise with pious grace, Virgin Mary — from us."

[6]Earlier theories on tropes, e.g. by Wagner and Apel, have been partly superseded by recent research on the topic; see now particularly Haug et al. (1998); Hiley (1993) 196-238 (prosulas for offertories: 201-204); Stäblein (1966); Crocker (1966b); Steiner (1980c); Planchart (1988); for further references see A. Hughes (1974) 103-110. For the newest editions of tropes see the monumental series in progress, *Corpus troporum* (in *Studia Latina Stockholmiensia*). My citations here and in the Catalogue are from the easily accessible editions of tropes in *Analecta Hymnica* (AH).

this case, expanded, melisma.[7] Thus the melisma is dissolved, giving way to a texted version, a strictly syllabic melody.[8] The vowel *a* recurs frequently in internal and end-rhymes and serves as a bridge reaching over and beyond the textual interpolation to connect with the final *a nobis* of the offertory.[9]

The trope *Ab hac familia* was evidently very popular from the thirteenth century on. It is transmitted in a large number of manuscripts from all over Europe and was the model for at least eight *contrafacta*, i.e. texts of a similar poetical structure to the same melisma.[10] Moreover, there are so many polyphonic settings surviving for the main trope and its contrafact versions that the musicologist M.L. Göllner counts it "among the longest lived and most popular tropes of all, encountered in various settings of from two to four voices from the thirteenth through the sixteenth centuries."[11]

Since previous scholarship has been preoccupied with the interesting textual and musical settings of the trope, discovering the text and music of the original plain untroped offertory and its place in the liturgy requires some diligent searching. In 'modern' liturgical books of the Vaticana edition, the simple form of the offertory exists as one of five options for an offertory in the formulary *Commune BMV*, which is chanted at various occasions throughout the year (see catalogue [30D1]);[12] in medieval books, the plain offertory *Recordare* belongs to some formularies for the Saturday Votive Mass of the Virgin Mary. This weekly ob-

---

[7]In order to accommodate musically the second member of those three paired verses, each of the melisma's first three melodic phrases was duplicated; see below, pp. 270-271 and Figures 20 and 21.

[8]It is the same technique, basically, that had produced the trope (or *prosa* in medieval terminology) for the responsory *Homo quidam* mentioned above in Chapter 3 [4]; cf. pp. 127 and 134 with n35.

[9]Other prosulas to this offertory have different ways of integrating the last two words into the new, longer textual unit. See tropes nos. 635-642 in AH 49: 322-325.

[10]Blume lists twenty-six manuscripts and early printed books for no. 634, and this list is far from complete. For the contrafact trope texts see AH 49, nos. 635-642.

[11]Göllner (1985) 91. Göllner publishes and discusses seven of the polyphonic settings of this trope; see Catalogue [30D2], p. F74 n77.

[12]Cf. p. F73. The offertory is also used in some very late feasts that were not generally introduced and accepted until the eighteenth and nineteenth centuries. For instance, the Feast of the *Seven sorrows of BMV* on September 15, since 1814; the Feast of *Our Lady of Mt. Carmel* on July 16, since 1726. Cf. Catalogue [30D1], last four entries.

servance of the *Officium BMV* on Saturdays was introduced in 1096 at the Council of Clermont when Urban II prescribed it in place of the ferial office.[13] Once this liturgical place is known, the different formularies for this important year-round celebration can be found in medieval liturgical chant books for Mass.

TABLE 9 THE SATURDAY VOTIVE MASS OF THE VIRGIN
IN SOME MEDIEVAL MSS

SOURCE	TITLE	LITURGICAL SEASONS				
		I	II	III	IV	V
GOP(Humb)	Commemoratio BMV	*Rorate*	*Gaude*	*Salve*	*sancta*	*parens*
*M*Helm.26	De BMV	—	—	*Salve*	—	*Salve*
*M*Helm.35	De domina nostra generaliter	*Vultum* or *Rorate*	*Salve*	*<Salve>*	*Salve sancta parens* or *Vultum tuum*	
*M*Helm.38	Officium generale de domina nostra	*Vultum* or *Rorate*	*Salve* or *Vultum*	—	*Salve sancta parens* or *Vultum tuum*	
*G*Brei	Missa votiva BMV	*Rorate*	*Salve*	*Salve*	*sancta*	*parens*

I = Advent   II = Christmas to Purification   III Purification to Septuagesima
IV = Passion to Pentecost   V Trinity to Advent

The formulary for the Saturday Mass of Our Lady, which comes under different titles,[14] usually varies from season to season with a total of three or four different Masses supplied in the sources over the course of the year. As a norm, the rubrics assign each of them clearly to a certain period of the liturgical year, sometimes giving a choice between two formularies.[15] The Mass with the introit *Salve sancta parens* is the one of interest here, because in medieval sources it usually contains the *Recordare virgo mater* as its offertory.[16] Table 9 and catalogue [30D1] show that, for the sources studied, the Mass formulary *Salve sancta parens* is

---

[13]Cf. Holweck (1892) xiv; also Beissel (1909) 307-310.

[14]Cf. Table 9, second column ("Title"); see also Catalogue [30D1], p. F73.

[15]See the survey in Table 9 and in Catalogue [30D]; also A. Hughes (1982) 157. Mass formularies are usually named after the incipit of their introit.

[16]Six out of eleven sources provide the alternate offertory *Felix namque es*; cf. Catalogue [30D1], where the choice of the offertory is marked with an asterisk (*) (*R* for *Recordare* or *F* for *Felix*). The 'modern' formularies for the Saturday Mass *BMV* have other offertories; see LU, pp. 1269-1272; *G*RTri (1979) 662-663.

by far the most favoured in most seasons except Advent, and thus it would have been sung in many regions almost every Saturday from Purification to Advent (i.e., from the beginning of February to the end of November). Moreover, in the thirteenth century, the celebration of the Saturday Mass of Our Lady grew so popular that it gradually became a daily observance.[17] Each of its chants must have been extremely well known by the early fourteenth century.

Among the sources studied, the Mass *Salve sancta parens* with its complete, untroped offertory *Recordare* is found in eleven manuscripts of the thirteenth to the fifteenth century, as well as in the early sixteenth-century printed book *G*Pat. Almost all are Mass books of German origin, with music provided in all except *M*Helm.35.[18] Of the two Mass books from the Mainz diocese, the thirteenth-century *M*Fri.100 has the chant notated only in non-heighted neumes; thus the version in the fifteenth-century monastic Gradual of Breitenau (just east of Fritzlar), *G*Brei.101, with its notation on a five-line stave will be preferred for the melodic restoration of chant [30]. This transmission is identical to that in *M*Helm.38, and very close to that of *G*Lpz.[19]

For an appropriate restoration of chant [30] *Recordare* in the Lddv it is necessary to take a close comparative look at the textual and melodic transmission of this offertory, especially its final melisma. In its simplest, possibly original, form, the long *a*-melisma (over *a nobis*), which

[17]Cf. Baltzer (1989) 671.

[18]See Catalogue [30D1], p. F73.

[19]Considering the attention the different tropes for this offertory have received in musicological research, it is interesting to note that a trope could be found in only five of the twelve German sources studied, in three of them only as additions by a later hand: in *G*Lpz and *G*Strals, the respective tropes (AH 49, no. 634 in *G*Lpz; AH 49, no. 641 in *G*Strals) are squeezed under the *a*-melisma of the plain version; and in *Pr*Don.882, the trope *Ab hac familia*, together with other Latin and German additions, is found on fol. 325r-v, separated from the offertory *Recordare* (fol. 240v), with no marginal reference mark. It would be rash, however, to conclude that this trope was little known in Germany. As non-essential parts of the liturgy, the tropes were often noted in tropers or other books accessible to the few singers who had to sing them. Cf. A. Hughes (1989b); Hiley (1993) 314-317; Huglo (1996) 1416.

*M*SHelm.628, which contains the trope *Ob hac familia* in a two-voice setting of the whole Mass (cf. Catalogue [30D2]), is not a German source. It is a manuscript of the Notre Dame School and is known to the musical world as MS W$_1$, written probably in Scotland (cf. Stapert [1976] 18: 10; Göllner [1985] 92). Recently, Everist (1990) redated the manuscript and reinstated it as the earliest of the four main 'Notre Dame' sources.

starts and ends on the finalis **D**, is characterized by an upward progression of three short melodic phrases (α, β, α^1), separated by thirds, followed by a downward swing (phrase γ) from the *c* to the final **DEFD-D** over *nobis* (see Figure 20). This form of the melisma is preserved, with some minor variants, in four of the medieval sources listed in the catalogue (*G*OP[Humb], *G*Kath, *G*Wonn, *Pr*Don.882) and in the 'modern' liturgical books *G*R, *G*RTri, LU. Since the third of the four phrases is an exact echo of the first one, just a fifth higher, the structure of the whole melisma in this version may be indicated by the letters α-β-α^1-γ as in Figure 20.

FIGURE 20 THE OFFERTORY *RECORDARE VIRGO:*
a-MELISMA IN SIMPLE FORM
(*G*WONN, FOL. 192v)

In the other sources with readable notation for the untroped offertory (*G*Lpz, *G*Strals, *M*Helm.26, *M*Helm.38, *G*Brei.101, *G*Pat), each of the first three phrases is duplicated, resulting in the melodic sequence $\alpha\alpha$-$\beta\beta$-$\alpha^1\alpha^1$-γ (see Figure 21). This is also the musical form of the final melisma in the different tropes. Here the first three musical phrases of the melisma, α, β, α^1, all of equal length, were simply repeated in order to accommodate the new poetical text of three paired verses, with the final concluding line sung to the last phrase γ. Hence there is no newly created 'trope' melody, only an expansion of the existing melisma through repetition of its sections.[20]

---

[20]Such reduplication of melismas or sections thereof is not rare in tropes; see, for instance, Kelly's observations, (1985) 165-167. It is this musical and metrical repeat structure that is reminiscent of the poetical-musical form of sequences. In Stäblein's view (1966) 810, the *a*-melisma in the *Recordare* offertory is texted "in Sequenzen-Art." Cf. the definition of 'sequence' given under this lemma by Stevens (1986) 510.

If some of the medieval sources have this expanded melodic structure without the text of the trope, or with the trope text added by a later hand as in *G*Lpz and *G*Strals, this suggests that the trope was very likely known in these places. The trope had obviously influenced the performance of the plain offertory in a way that even here, without the new text, the final melisma was sung with the repetition duplicating each of its first three phrases.[21]

FIGURE 21   THE OFFERTORY *RECORDARE VIRGO*:
a-MELISMA IN DUPLICATION FORM
(*M*HELM.26 FOLS. 192v-193r)

The final long melisma of the offertory in its untroped form, consequently, exists in two versions:

1) the 'simple' melisma α- β- α^1- γ
2) the 'duplication' melisma $\alpha\alpha$-$\beta\beta$-$\alpha^1\alpha^1$-γ

---

[21]The form in which the offertory is transmitted in *G*Pat may prove exactly that: on fol. 172r, the plain offertory shows the long melisma over *a* with a duplication of all its first three melodic phrases ($\alpha\alpha$, $\beta\beta$, $\alpha^1\alpha^1$), in a version almost identical with that of the Munich MS 11763, transcribed by Wagner (1901-1921) 3: 507-508. And the words for the trope in *A*Pat are provided separately, below the chant, as *Prosa*.

This observation may, in turn, shed some light on the performance of such a trope, which is generally considered to be a solo chant for the simple reason that the new trope text was only available to one or a few singers. Cf. Wagner (1901-1921) 3: 502. A. Hughes (1989b) 208 points to the very small size of most tropers as a clear indicator that performance of tropes was by a soloist. The duplication of the melodic phrases α, β, and α^1 in so many untroped versions of the offertory seems to support the view that the choir continued chanting the melisma while one or more soloists were singing the words of the trope. The choir had to repeat each of those three musical phrases in order to keep in step with the solo singers of the trope. For the various theories about the method of performance for texted melismas, cf. Haug et al. (1998) 901. See also Kelly (1985), who examines various possibilities for the performance of responsory tropes.

The troped form of the offertory, on the other hand, always has the tune in a 'syllabic' style, with the duplication structure $\alpha\alpha$-$\beta\beta$-$\alpha^1\alpha^1$-γ, a structure that remains the same whether the trope continues as plainsong or in a polyphonic setting, whether it is the main trope *Ab hac familia* or any of the contrafact tropes.[22]

Given the dramatic context of the Lddv, it is not difficult to decide whether the troped version or the plain untroped form of the offertory *Recordare* should be retained for chant [30]. The despair of the *Fatue* and the urgency of their situation leave no room for sophisticated poetical language and flowery praise of the Virgin in the manner of a trope. The original plain offertory text with its concise supplication and the long melisma at the end fits perfectly: *Remember, Virgin Mother, while you stand in the presence of God, to plead on our behalf and to turn his wrath away from us.*[23] This simple supplication is expressed in the vernacular paraphrase that follows, spoken by the *Quarta Fatua*:

Wy beten dich, Maria, muter und mayt,
wan dů dyne barmeherczickeyt nimane vorsayst,
daz dů betes den milden got

...

daz he synen czorn und synen unmůt von uns kere
dorch sich selben und dorch aller iuncvowen ere.[24]

If the decision, then, is for the untroped offertory, which remained in wide use in all churches, it seems almost idle to ask whether the simple

---

[22]For a musical discussion of the troped offertory and seven of the polyphonic settings in the thirteenth and fourteenth centuries, with publication of most of these settings, see Göllner (1985). The text of the offertory and trope is discussed by Johansson (1985).

[23]How powerfully the appeal to the Virgin Mary is intensified through the purely vocal, wordless chanting of the *a*-melisma by the *Fatue* at the end of their chant [30] has been demonstrated in a workshop performance of the Lddv, under the direction of Lynette Muir (with my assistance), on the occasion of a conference on medieval drama ("The Stage as Mirror") at Pennsylvania State University in March 1993. I want to acknowledge here with thanks the participation (for the chants) of members of the Benedictine St. Vincent's Archabbey Schola of Latrobe, Pennsylvania, in this workshop performance.

[24]Lddv, ll. 257-264: "Mary, mother, maiden, we beg thee because you deny not your mercy to anyone: pray, ask the God benign ... that his wrath and displeasure he might turn away to honour himself and all virgins today." (Translation with the assistance of Gloria Dent.)

or the 'duplication' structure should be chosen for that final melisma.[25] Either would do, and the local tradition would certainly be followed wherever the play was performed. For the Lddv, the choice will depend on the source chosen for the restoration of the chant, in this case one of the Helmstedt sources or, better still, *G*Brei.101, close to Fritzlar and within the Mainz diocese, which all have the extended structure $\alpha\alpha$-$\beta\beta$-$\alpha^1\alpha^1$-γ.

In the manuscript transmission of this popular offertory there are a few textual variants of minor importance, though of sufficient interest to be noted in the 'critical' edition of the offertory below. Variant c (*avertas/avertat*) is the only really noteworthy one. Of the twelve medieval sources (including *G*Pat) consulted for the untroped offertory, seven have the verbal form for the second person singular (*ut avertas*), five for the third person (*ut avertat*). Although the latter form is supported by the subsequent vernacular paraphrase in the Lddv ... *daz he synen czorn und synen unmût von uns kere* (l. 263), I shall retain the reading *ut avertas* for the restoration of the chant since it is backed by the two sources from the Fritzlar area (*G*Brei.101 and *M*Fri.100), which are both close to Thuringia and part of the Mainz diocese.

The musical transmission of this offertory in the manuscripts listed in Catalogue [30D1 and 2], pp. F73-F74, shows a remarkable homogeneity although at a closer look, regardless of the final melisma's structure, two groups can be distinguished. One is close to the Dominican version in *G*OP from Humbert's codex (the Dominican *G*Kath is almost identical to it): the German Graduals *Pr*Don.882 (also Dominican), *G*Wonn (Cistercian), and the 'modern' version in LU share most of the melodic turns and melismas, except for the final cadence; of the troped versions, MS Helm.628 (W$_1$), the Notre Dame manuscript written in Scotland, would also belong to this group. A second group centers around *G*Brei.101 and *M*Helm.38 with an identical transmission of the tune; *G*Lpz and *G*Strals are close (except for the melodic phrase over *indignationem suam*). All four sources share the long final descent ('phrase γ') over *a nobis* and also two variants with leaps of a third and a fourth (over **de-i** and **loqua-**

---

[25]Even churches that had enthusiastically embraced the use of tropes for Mass and Office continued to perform the simpler, untroped forms on ordinary weekdays, the more festive troped forms being reserved for feast days; cf. Wagner (1901-1921) 3: 502; Haug et al. (1998) 900.

ris) which are typical for the German dialect. Also related are *M*Helm.26, and less closely, *G*Pat, and MS München 11763 (transcribed in Wagner [1901-1921] 3: 507). The two different renderings of the final *a*-melisma as quoted in Figure 20 from *G*Wonn. (α-β-α^1-γ) and in Figure 21 from *M*Helm.26 ($\alpha\alpha$-$\beta\beta$-$\alpha^1\alpha^1$-γ) may be compared to its form in *G*Brei.101 ($\alpha\alpha$-$\beta\beta$-$\alpha^1\alpha^1$-γ), transcribed in chapter 4 **[30]**.

The offertory as a whole and its exceptional dorian melody can be understood as consisting of three sections, (1) *Recordare ... dei*; (2) *ut loquaris ... suam*; (3) *a nobis*. The tune has an amazing melodic structure with musical correspondences and 'rhymes' within and between those three sections, and with a clear melodic upward progression from section to section. It has been said that the final melisma section (3) over the words *a nobis* "constitutes a summary in musical terms of that which preceded it in the offertory proper."[26] And the whole chant is rounded off by the concluding phrase γ, descending from the high *c* and leading into the final cadence over *nobis* (**DEFDD** in Dominican and related sources, **FGFEDCD** in some German sources). The German transmission of the cadence **FGFEDCD** in six manuscripts is of special interest because, unlike all other sources, their closing cadence picks up the 'musical end rhyme' of earlier phrases (over *-cordare*, *steteris*, *bona* and *-vertas*): in an identical form in *G*Brei.101 and *M*Helm.38 (**FGFEDCD**); in two slightly varied forms in *G*Strals (**FGFDCD**) and *G*Lpz, *G*Pat, and the above-mentioned Munich manuscript 11763 (**DEFEDCD**).

As a basis for the textual and musical restoration of chant **[30]** in the Lddv, the German versions of this offertory, particularly the two from the Fritzlar area, should, of course, have priority over the other sources. Therefore, I propose to restore this chant **[30]** from the offertory *Recordare* as transmitted in *G*Brei.101 and, textually, in *M*Fri.100.[27]

Offertory *Recordare virgo mater [dum steteris*[a] *in conspectu Dei ut loquaris pro nobis bona*[b] *et ut avertas*[c] *indignationem suam a nobis.*[d]]

Source   *G*Brei.101, fol. 68r-v (= *M*Fri.100; *M*Helm.26; *G*Wonn; *Pr*Don.882; *G*OP[Humb]; collated with other sources from Catalogue **[30D1]**, p. F73).

---

[26]Göllner (1985) 90.

[27]The final *alleluia* in *G*Brei.101, missing in *M*Fri.100, will be omitted because it is an addition for the Easter season only.

Variants   [a] *dum steteris*] om. MSHelm.628; LU; Milchsack (ed. 1886) 219; Lddv, ed. Schneider; *dum consteteris* AH 49, nos. 634, 636, 642.

[b] *bona*] *bonum* MSHelm.628; Milchsack (ed. 1886) 219; Lddv, ed. Schneider.

[c] *avertas*] *avertat* GLpz; GStrals; MHelm.35; MHelm.38; GPat; MS Munich 11763 (ed. Wagner 3: 507); GR; LU.

[d] *a nobis*] om. Lddv, ed. Beckers; ed. Schneider; ed. De Boor; ed. Curschmann-Glier; *alleluia* added (for time after Easter) in some sources: GBrei.101, GOP(Humb), GKath, MHelm.38, PrDon.882, MSHelm.628.

Cf. Catalogue [30D1 and 2], pp. F73-74.

Melody   Mode 1. Transcribed in Chapter 4 from GBrei.101, fol. 68r-v (the final *alleluia* is omitted in the transcription).

Melody = MHelm.38; ~ = MHelm.26, GLpz; ~ GStrals, GPat; ~ *var.* GOP(Humb), GKath, PrDon.882, GWonn, MSHelm.628.

Translation   "Remember, virgin mother, in the sight of God, that you speak well of us, so that you turn away His wrath ... from us."   (Stapert [1974-1976] 18: 11).

[31] *Exaudi etc.* (Lddv 264b)

Exaudi is the only word given as incipit for chant [31] with which the *Quinta Fatua* continues the supplications of the whole group. Judging from the subsequent vernacular paraphrase (ll. 265-272, cf. p. 279), the words are again addressed to the Virgin Mary asking her to intercede on their behalf. As all five *Fatue* together had appealed to her in chant [30] *Recordare* with, essentially, the same request, this appeal by one of them serves to intensify the efforts of the whole group to gain entry to the Feast, if not directly, then through the intercession of Mary.

The manuscript of the Lddv does not supply much information either on the genre of chant [31] nor its method of performance nor which sources to consult for its identification. The stage direction (l. 264a-b) simply indicates:[1]

QUINTA [FATUA]   *Exaudi etc.*

With no clue beyond the word *Exaudi*, a precise identification of the text is difficult. Beckers' suggestion that the incipit be completed with Psalm 16: 6 (*Exaudi verba mea*), although adopted by all subsequent editors, must be rejected. Not only is this text extremely weak at this point in the drama, it is also highly unlikely since the words occur at the end of the suggested psalm verse (*Ego clamavi, quoniam exaudisti me Deus; Inclina aurem tuam mihi, et exaudi verba mea.*) If a psalm verse were meant at this place in the Lddv, there are at least five with the required incipit to choose from.[2] Yet, surely, if any of these psalm verses were intended, the author or scribe would have extended the incipit to permit correct identification of the selected text.

---

[1]Beckers (ed. 1905) and subsequently De Boor (ed. 1965) took the same liberties Beckers had taken for chants [27], [28], and [29], adding a *cantet* that the manuscript does not have; this has fortunately been corrected in Schneider's 1964 edition.

[2]Psalm 16: 1 *Exaudi, Domine, iustitiam meam*; Psalm 26: 7 *Exaudi, Domine, vocem meam, qua clamavi ad te; miserere mei, et exaudi me*; Psalm 54: 2-3 *Exaudi, Deus, orationem meam, Et ne despexeris deprecationem meam Intende mihi et exaudi me. Contristatus sum in exercitatione mea*; Psalm 60: 2 *Exaudi, Deus, deprecationem meam, Intende orationi meae*; Psalm 63: 2 *Exaudi, Deus, orationem meam cum deprecor; A timore inimici eripe animam meam.*

The list of liturgical pieces which start with the word *Exaudi* is almost endless. Besides the above-mentioned psalms, numerous prayers start with this Invocation,[3] as do a great number of chants for Mass and Office. The sixteen *Exaudi* incipits listed in Catalogue [31D1, nos. 1-16], pp. F77-F78, include at least five different genres: three introits, two offertories, eight antiphons, two responsories, and one litany verse. Nor is this list intended to be complete. It seems futile to weigh all these chants and prayers against one another to find out which might have been the one intended in the Lddv. Again, one would expect the author or scribe to have added a few more words to the incipit to permit proper identification of the chant, unless he was sure there were sufficient other cues.

And indeed there are, at least for a medieval mind intimately familiar with the liturgy and traditions of the Church. Chant no. 16 of the Catalogue listing, the one with the triple *Exaudi* incipit, stands out as particularly suitable not only because of its text, but also, and perhaps mainly, because of its liturgical context, which matches the corresponding dramatic context to a remarkable degree.

The triple *Exaudi* chant forms part of the *Aufer a nobis* litany, sung during the litany processions that took place on St. Mark's Day (*Letania Maior*, on April 25, a Roman institution) and on the three Rogation Days before Ascension (*Letania Minor* or *Letaniae minores*, a Gallican institution).[4] Occasionally the *Aufer a nobis* litany was used as well during other litany processions of more local importance. The Rogation Days were considered so important that no one, including servants and maids, was allowed to work, and all were required to join the procession bare-footed and in sackcloth and ashes.[5]

---

[3]For the prayers see Deshusses-Darragon (1982-1983) 1: nos. 1447-1512, where over sixty prayers with the incipit *Exaudi* are listed for the early sacramentaries.

[4]For these important processions see e.g. Reifenberg (1971) 679-682; Reynolds (1986); Bailey (1965) 95-98. Ordo 50 XXXV.1-4 (*Letania Maior*), XXXVI.1-3 (*Letania Minor* = Rogation). The liturgical formularies for these two occasions in the tenth century transmit over sixty processional antiphons, some prayers and several litanies to be sung during these processions; cf. Ordo 50 XXXV-XXXVI(Andrieu, ed. [1931-1961] 5: 314-340), or PRG XCIX.419-434 (Vogel-Elze [1963-1972] 2: 119-131). Later processional sources contain fewer items, but usually more extensive rubrics.

[5]Cf. Ordo 50 XXXVI.1-3; PRG XCIX.420. See also Beissel (1892) II, 2-3.

After a long series of processional antiphons and other items, sung during the procession, the sources present a set of three 'litany verses' introducing the All Saints' Litany *Pater de caelis*:[6]

> *Aufer a nobis, domine, iniquitates nostras ut mereamur puris mentibus introire ad sancta sanctorum.*
>
> *Exaudi, exaudi, exaudi preces nostras, sanctorum omnibus* (or *omnium*) *suffragantibus meritis.*
>
> *Miserere, miserere, miserere populo tuo quem redemisti, Christe, sanguine tuo ne in aeternum irascaris nobis.*

("Take away from us, Lord, our iniquities that we may be worthy to enter with pure minds the holy of holies." — "Hear, hear, hear our prayers, and let the merits of all the saints speak on our behalf." — "Have mercy, have mercy, have mercy on your people who you, Christ, have redeemed with your blood, lest your wrath be upon us in eternity.")[7]

The verses *Exaudi* and *Miserere miserere miserere* are sung at this place of the *Letania* procession in exactly the same sequence as in the Lddv (chants [31] and [32]). The first of the three chants, *Aufer a nobis, domine, iniquitates nostras,* calls to mind chant [26] *Iniquitates nostras aufer a nobis*, with which the *Fatue* began their supplications after the arrival of the *Dominica Persona*. Moreover, as was pointed out in the discussion of that chant, the whole sequence of appeals by which the *Fatue* try to gain access to the heavenly Wedding Feast, with supplications reiterated in ensemble and solo chanting and with Mary as intercessor, are like a small-scale Rogation procession within the drama itself. The scribe of the Mühlhausen manuscript of the Lddv obviously felt that there were sufficient indicators in the play pointing to the Litany processions as the liturgical home of chant [31]. Even the very short incipit *Exaudi etc.,* followed by the more extensive incipit [32] *Miserere miserere miserere*

---

[6]Occasionally the second day of Rogation is indicated for this litany. For the Gallican origin of these introductory chants or 'verses,' which Gastoué calls a "sorte d'antienne triple," see, with the music from early French sources, Gastoué (1937-1939) 41: 174-176; repr. (1939) 17-19.

[7]Ordo 50 XXXVI.78; or PRG XCIX.428/29. The relation between the PRG (*Pontificale Romano-Germanicum*) and Ordo 50, their date and origin are discussed by Andrieu (1931-1961) 1: 494-505; Vogel (1975) 193-197, (1986) 187, 230-237; Vogel-Elze (1963-1972) 1: xvi. Ordo 50, the *Ordo Romanus L* (in Andrieu's counting), was previously known as *Ordo Romanus Antiquus* through Melchior Hittorp's edition of 1568; for bibliographical details of this edition see Vogel (1975) 191 n205.

populo tuo etc., would leave no doubt in the mind of a singer with some liturgical awareness which chants were meant.

The vernacular text following the *Exaudi* chant in the Lddv, however, does not exactly correspond to the prayer content of the chant as cited above from Ordo 50:

> Maria, mûter unde mayt,
> ia ist uns dicke von dy gesayt,
> daz dů sist allir gnaden vol;
> nů bedorve wy gnade also wol
> und beten dich vel sere
> dorch allir iuncfrowen ere,
> daz dů betis dynen son noch vor uns armen,
> daz he sich obir uns erbarmen. (ll. 265-272)[8]

Here it is clearly the Virgin Mary, who is being entreated to intercede for the *Fatue*, whereas the words in the triple *Exaudi* chant cited above are directed to the Lord and ask for the support of all the saints only in an indirect way (*sanctorum omnibus suffragantibus meritis*). It is interesting, therefore, to find that in the manuscript transmission of this *Exaudi* chant two different textual forms coexist:

> *Exaudi exaudi exaudi*
> (i) *preces nostras **sanctorum omnibus** (or omnium) **suffragantibus meritis.***[9]
> (ii) ***domine, preces nostras. Sancta Maria ora pro nobis.***[10]

While (i) is found only in Ordo 50 and in the PRG,[11] I was able to locate form (ii) of this chant in several other German sources of the twelfth to the fourteenth centuries, three of which have musical nota-

---

[8]"Mary, mother and maiden, you are said to be so full of grace. We now are so much in want of grace and beseech thee for the sake of all the holy Virgins and their glory to pray for us to thy son so that he may have mercy upon us."

[9]Ordo 50 and PRG; see above and Catalogue [31D2], p. F78.

[10]CAO 2, no. 148b; *A*Fri.142, fol. *Iv; *G*Lpz, fol. 71v; *G*Strals, fol. 59r; *G*Pat. fol. 2v; Würdtwein (1782) 219; French sources, ed. Gastoué (1937-1939) 41: 175, (1939) 19. Cf. Catalogue [31D2], p. F78.

[11]The tenth-century Roman-Germanic Pontifical spread quickly throughout the Western Church. Over fifty manuscripts of the PRG attest to its wide influence and rapid dissemination; see, e.g. Vogel-Elze, ed. (1963-1972) 3: 44-57; Vogel (1975) 187-203.

tion.[12] The second phrase of form (ii), *Sancta Maria ora pro nobis*, offers precisely the kind of direct invocation of Mary that seems to be reflected in the vernacular paraphrase quoted above. Thus, the author of the Lddv probably knew form (ii) of the triple *Exaudi* chant.

Whatever the textual form may be, however, the triple *Exaudi* chant is always found together with the two other chants, the *Aufer a nobis* and the triple *Miserere* chant, usually in conjunction with the Rogation procession. The sequence of the three verses within the set of three may vary, and one or more of them may be repeated (cf. Catalogue, p. F78):

Aufer—Exaudi—Miserere	Ordo 50; PRG; CAO (F = St. Maur);
Aufer—Miserere—Exaudi	*A*Fri.142; *M*Helm.35; *G*Lpz; *G*Strals; *G*Pat;
	and sources collated by Würdtwein (1782) 219;
Miserere—Aufer—Exaudi	French sources, ed. Gastoué (1939) 19.

There is even some external evidence that points to the litany processions (Rogations) as the direct source for the two chants [31-32]. In the parallel section of the *Marburger Spiel von den letzten Dingen* (MaSp.532), for which a strong dependency on the Lddv has already been pointed out by Lomnitzer, the connection to the Rogation procession is even closer since all three litany verses are used. I present here the corresponding scene in a condensed version from its Marburg manuscript:[13]

(10r)	FATUE VIRGINES omnes cantant fl[exis genibus]		
	Aufer a nobis, domine, cunctas iniq[uitates nostras]		
	MARIA cantant flexis g[enibus]		
	Exaudi exaudi exaudi domin[e preces nostras]		
	FATUE VIRGINES omnes can[tant]		
	Sancta Maria ora pro nob[is]		
	MARIA dicit ad Salva[torem]	(1ST INTERCESSION)	(12 lines)
	SALVATOR dicit ad Mar[iam]		(16 lines)
	ROSENKRANCZE diabo[lus dicit]		(8 lines)
	TERCIA FATUA dicit		(4 + lines)

---

[12]Cf. Catalogue [31D2]. Even the later printed books, *G*Pat of 1511, and *Ps*Mz.D820 of 1607 (cf. facsimile 5), transmit the chant in a very similar form. Form (ii) might be regarded as a later development, yet Gastoué (1937-1939) 41: 174-175, (1939) 17-19) found it in French sources from the ninth century on, which he used for his edition.

[13]MaSp.532: Marburg, UB, cod. 532, fols. 10r-11v. Prior to fol. 10r, two leaves are missing in the manuscript. For more details on this manuscript and Lomnitzer's preparations for the edition, see p. 2 n8.

(10v)	[MARIA dicit ad Salvatorem]　　(2ND INTERCESSION)	([..] + 6 lines)
	[SALVATO]R dicit Marie	(10 lines)
	[SPIGELDR]UT diabolus dicit Marie	(10 lines)
	[FATUE VIRGI]NES omnes cantant	
	[... miser]ere nobis	
	FATUA dicit	(8 lines)
	[SALVAT]OR respondit	
	... nescio vos, nescio vos	
	[SALVAT]OR dicit immediate	(8 lines)
	[FATUE VIRGINE]S omnes cantant	
(11r)	**Aufer a nobis, domine, cunctas iniquitates nostras**	
	MARIA cantat	
	Exaudi exaudi exaudi domine preces nostras	
	FATUE omnes cantant	
	Sancta Maria ora pro nobis	
	Et MARIA flexis genibus dicit　　(3RD INTERCESSION)	26 lines
	SALVATOR dicit	(14 lines)
	SPIGELDRUT diabolus dicit	(4+ lines)
(11v)	[SALVATOR dicit]	([..] + 2 lines)
	SPIGELDRUT diabolus dicit	(4 lines)
	FATUE omnes cantant flexis genibus	
	Ave regina celorum mater regis angelorum	
	MARIA dicit:　　(4TH INTERCESSION)	(12 lines)
	SALVATOR dicit Marie	(8 lines)
	MARIA cantat	
	Miserere miserere miserere populo tuo	
	Et MARIA dicit　　(5TH INTERCESSION)	(4 lines)
	SALVATOR dicit	(10 lines)
	PRIMA FATUA dicit　　(LAMENTATIONS)	(3+ lines)

In this play, the *'Letania* procession' of the *Fatue* is considerably more extended and elaborate than in the Lddv, spanning 192 lines, not counting its first part which is missing, but can be assumed to have contained the *Fatue* begging the *Salvator* for admission to the Feast.[14] What is preserved in the Marburg fragments is a sequence of supplications by the *Fatue*, leading to five intercessions by St. Mary, partly in Latin, mostly in

---

[14]Lacuna of two folios before fol. 10v based on Lomnitzer's reconstruction of the gatherings of the Marburg MS 532; cf. above p. 2 n8.

vernacular lines.[15] Although somewhat obscured by the expansion and dra-
matization of the dialogue,[16] the *Aufer a nobis* litany and other more
general litany-like features are used so extensively that a close relation
to the *Rogationes* processions is very evident. All three opening verses
of this litany are used in the same sequence as in the Rogation formulary
of Ordo 50 and of the PRG,[17] except that Latin and vernacular texts are
delivered between *Exaudi* and *Miserere* (line count is mine):

Aufer a nobis	MaSp.532 fols. 10r and 11r [ll. 886, 988]
Exaudi exaudi exaudi	ibid. [ll. 888-890, 990-992]
Miserere miserere miserere	MaSp.532 fol. 11v [l.1072]

The first two of these verses on fol. 10r [ll. 886-890] are repeated on
fol. 11r [ll. 988-992], and in both places they are kept together with no
intervening vernacular lines. Comparison with liturgical sources indicates
that this repetition reflects liturgical usage. At least three different medieval sources, two of them of middle German origin, call for some kind
of repetition of the verses:[18]

CAO 2, no. 148b	*Aufer—Exaudi—Miserere—Exaudi—Miserere*
AFri.142, fol. *Iv	*Aufer—Aufer—Miserere—Miserere—Exaudi*
GLpz, fol. 71v	*Aufer—Aufer—Miserere—Miserere—Exaudi—Aufer*

Even the distribution of the verses to different groups of singers, in one
case the division of the *Exaudi* verse into two sections for different performers (as in MaSp.532, fols 10r and 11r), can be found in rubrics for

---

[15]The increase in the number of intercessions to five suggests a numeric correlation
with the five Foolish Virgins. In the Dutch Play of the Ten Virgins, each of the five
Foolish Virgins approaches the Bridegroom individually, and he pronounces his rejection
a total of five times; see Flem.X.Virg ed. Hoebeke, ll. 543-567. Cf. KünzCC, ll. 4779-
5028, where the five *Fatue* also make their appeals individually; the third request is
directed to Peter, the fifth and an additional sixth to Mary. Yet there are only three
intercessions, one by Peter, two by Mary.

[16]In long verbal exchanges with Mary, with the Devils, and once also with the *Fatue*,
Salvator dooms the Foolish Virgins to hell seven times. The Devils *Rosenkrancz* and
Spigeldrut repeatedly intervene to counteract the Blessed Virgin's intercessions and to
hasten the *Salvator*'s harsh judgment over the *Fatue*.

[17]Cf. above, p. 280, and Catalogue [31D2], p. F78.

[18]Cf. Catalogue [31D2] last column under 'Sequence.' Repetition is maintained even
in 'modern' usage for the Major and Minor Litanies: in the litany *Pater de caelis* all the
verses are marked for duplication (Rubric: *Duo Cantores ante altare maius genuflexi
Litanias incipiunt, et **omnes versus duplicantur**)*; cf. LU, p. 835 (my emphasis).

the litany processions.[19] Other features indicative of litanies or processions in general confirm the impression that this scene in the Marburg play MaSp.532 represents a litany procession:[20] four instances of genuflexions (the *Fatue* twice, fols. 10r, 11v; the Virgin Mary also twice, fols.10r, 11r), the repeated invocation *Sancta Maria ora pro nobis* (ll. 890 and 992) as part of the *Exaudi* chant, and the litany formula *miserere nobis* used by the *Fatue* (fol. 10v).

With the Rogation connection thus firmly established for both the Lddv and the later MaSp.532, it is safe to complete the incipits [31] *Exaudi* and [32] *Miserere* from this background; the *Exaudi* chant will, of course, be in form (ii) with the invocation to St. Mary. This connection also warrants a musical performance of both chants, although the direction *cantat* is used only for [32] *Miserere*.

The genre of these Rogation chants, on the other hand, is difficult to grasp since the sources call them by different names.[21] The only reliable sources indicating their function as introductory verses to a longer litany are OR 50, the PRG, and the late *Ps*Mz.D820, all of which provide the complete litanies.[22] Since any genre label for the chants of the

---

[19]See, for instance, CAO 2, no. 148b (MS F): "Finita missa ante altare cantent cantores duo: *Aufer a nobis* ... Respondet scola: *Exaudi exaudi exaudi* ... [Cantores]: *Sancta Maria ora pro nobis. Et scola: Miserere miserere miserere* ... Cantores: *Exaudi ut supra.*" *O*Trier, fol. 42v (ed. Kurzeja [1970] 503): "In Platea pontis incipiatur letania *Aufer a nobis.* Domini nostri cantent primum versum, domini de s. Paulino secundum et domini de s. Symeone tertium." Here, the litany is sung on the occasion of the *Statio luporum*, a local litany procession. In the later *Ps*Mz.D820, fols. 289r-290r, the performance alternates between the *pueri* and the *chorus*, in the sequence *Exaudi—Aufer—Exaudi—Miserere—Exaudi*; cf. facsimile 5.

[20]On the whole, the interweaving of processional, penitential ritual with dramatic dialogue in this elaborate section of MaSp.532 effectively reflects the interaction of the antagonistic forces represented here.

[21]Cf. the column 'Genre' in Catalogue [31D2] and [32D], pp. F78 and F81.

[22]In other medieval German and French sources, usually music books, which give the musical items only, not the litany formulas, such a connection is at most hinted at, and the chants are qualified in the rubrics as *letania, versus, antiphona*, if at all:

*O*Trier	In Platea pontis incipiatur letania *Aufer a nobis.* (Subsequently, only directions are given for the different performers of the three chants called **versus**).
*G*Strals	Letania *Aufer a nobis*—**Ant**. *Miserere*—**Ant**. *Exaudi.*
*M*Helm.35	Cantatur a duobus **versus** *Aufer a nobis etc.* ut sequitur ...
*A*Fri.142	(All three chants described as **antiphona** during procession)

Aufer a nobis triad should indicate their connection with a litany, particularly for the Rogation days, I tend to call them "'verses' or 'chants'
of the litany antiphon *Aufer a nobis*."

The fact that later liturgical sources rarely indicate a connection
between the three chants and the litany does not mean that such a connection no longer existed. Long tradition and rubrics in ritual books or
processionals would have ensured that the correct sequence of chant, prayers, litanies, and action was followed, as the late Mainz source *Ps*Mz.D820
proves.[23] The rubrics for the Rogation litany in this *Enchiridion Psalmorum* direct the *Pueri* and the *Chorus* to sing alternately the verses *Exaudi — Aufer — Exaudi — Miserere — Exaudi*, which are all fully notated (fols. 289r-290r, see facsimile 5); subsequently, the complete text of
the All Saints Litany is printed without notation (fols. 290r-292v).

The music to these chants can be provided from a few medieval
sources although it is generally not easy to locate processional items in
liturgical books. I found the set in four German noted manuscripts of the
twelfth to the fifteenth centuries.[24] Only two of them, the graduals from
Leipzig and Stralsund (*G*Lpz and *G*Strals), provide readable notation for
all three verses.[25] The previously cited later sources, *G*Pat of 1511 and

---

*G*Lpz	Rubric Feria III. Letania. (The three chants are noted but no genre given)
*G*Pat	**Antiphona** for the sequence *Aufer—Miserere—Kyrie—Exaudi—Aufer*
CAO 2, 148b	Finita missa ante altare cantent cantores duo: *Aufer a nobis* (All three verses are given with directions for the various performers but no genre. The subsequent invocation *Sancta Dei Genitrix hora pro nobis* is obviously the beginning of a litany).
Gastoué	Gastoué [1939] 17-18, calls the chants "preces" or "série de supplica-tions," "la triple prière *Miserere* ... , *Aufer a nobis* ... , *Exaudi* ... , encadrant des invocations litaniques," and "sorte d'antienne triple."

[23]This *Enchiridion Psalmorum* was printed in 1607 for the instruction of congregation
and students: "In gratiam parochialium Ecclesiarum et usum iuuentutis Scholasticae,"
as its title page indicates. What was usually kept in separate books is combined here for
the purpose of instruction. The existence of this formulary in the *Enchiridion* is evidence
that the tradition of the *Aufer a nobis* litany for the Rogation processions was kept alive
in Mainz at least into the early seventeenth century.

[24]Cf. Catalogue [31D2] and [32D], pp. F78 and F81, sigla ● (notation on a stave),
● (non-heighted neumes), and = (empty stave).

[25]The missal from Hildesheim, *M*Helm.35, which contains the melody for both other
verses, unfortunately breaks off right after the incipit *Exaudi* under an empty stave. In
*A*Fri.142, a two-page remnant of a ritual or processional, probably of the twelfth cen-

*Ps*Mz.D820 of 1607, provide the melodies for each of the three verses in a form so close to the medieval German transmissions that they can be used for comparison despite their late date and their brief additions.[26]

The melody for all three texts, *Aufer, Miserere,* and *Exaudi,* is basically the same, especially for the two latter 'verses,' with major adjustments made for differences in phrasing and in the number of words and syllables. In this sense, the designation *versus* appears justified, and this melodic bond may well explain why the three chants always remained together as "a sort of triple antiphon," a designation preferred by Gastoué. To show this musical relatedness I have arranged the musical notation for the three chants, from *G*Lpz, in a vertical synopsis (see Figure 22 below). A comparison of this transcription with that by Gastoué from early French sources[27] will reveal the degree to which the transmission in the German sources is characterized by the special features of the 'German plainsong dialect.' Unlike the mainly stepwise melodic progression in the French transmission of the tune, the German sources show an abundance of ascending and descending thirds, with an occasional larger leap, thus providing more life and colour to the melody and placing this transmission firmly in the German tradition of plainsong.

In all three verses, the mode 3 melody is essentially syllabic and moves in beautiful lines mainly between *E* and *c* (*d*). In the second phrase, it descends to the lower *C,* thus stretching over more than an octave.[28] At the beginning of the *Aufer a nobis* verse, there is some recitation on the high *c.* Such recitation turns into more melodic up and down movements in the *Miserere* and *Exaudi,* where the threefold repetitions of the beginning words need to be musically balanced.

The *Exaudi* verse here has one long melodic arch over *Exaudi ... Maria.* It rises from the opening *G* (*-ac-c*) and descends gradually from the high *c* (*d*) to the low *D-C,* over *sancta Maria,* before it closes with a second short arch, in the middle range, for the invocation *ora pro no-*

---

tury, bound at the beginning of the Fritzlar Lectionary *L*Fri.142, the chants are notated in non-heighted neumes only, so they cannot be read properly.

[26]In *G*Pat, a *Kyrie* section is inserted between the verses *Miserere* and *Exaudi*; in *Ps*Mz.D820, each of the verses closes with an *alleluia*; cf. facsimile 5.

[27]Cf. Gastoué (1937-1939) 41: 175; (1939) 19.

[28]The frequent use of the lower *C* has been recognized by Gastoué as a characteristic feature of this and other Gallican chants; cf. Gastoué (1937-1939) 41: 174, also 131, 169-170.

FIGURE 22 THE THREE LITANY VERSES *AUFER A NOBIS*:
COMPARATIVE TRANSCRIPTION FROM *GL*PZ, FOL. 71v[29]

bis. The two German graduals *GL*pz and *GS*trals are almost identical in their transmission of this melody, and show the 'typically German' leap of a minor third at four places (over the words *Exaudi, domine, preces, sancta Maria*).[30] For the restoration of chant **[31]** in the Lddv, these

[29]Cf. facsimile in Wagner (ed. 1930) 1: 143. My transcription is designed to show the three verses in a melodic synopsis.

[30]The later books, *GP*at and *Ps*Mz.D820, basically agree on the 'German dialect' features and on two non-essential variants for this melody (two-note neumes, instead of a *virga*, over the second *ex-au-di* and over *no-stras*); *GP*at has a third minor variant over *sancta Maria* (*E-E-G-E-D* instead of *E-G-E-E-D*).

graduals from Leipzig and Stralsund, though not from the Mainz Church province, should be given preference over later sources.

Given the similarity in the melodic transmission of this *Exaudi* verse in the four German sources examined, it can be concluded that the fourteenth-century Leipzig Gradual *G*Lpz transmits it in a version that was known in a very similar form in nearby Thuringia.[31] As this famous book is almost contemporaneous with the Lddv, I propose the restoration of chant **[31]** in the Thuringian play from the *Exaudi* verse as transmitted in the litany antiphon (or 'triple antiphon') *Aufer a nobis* of *G*Lpz:

Text *Exaudi*[a] *[exaudi exaudi domine*[b] *preces nostras, sancta Maria ora pro nobis.*[c]]

Source *G*Lpz, fol. 71v (= *A*Fri.142, *G*Strals, *G*Pat, Würdtwein [Trier], p. 219; Gastoué [1939] 19), collated with other sources listed in Catalogue **[31D2]**, pp. F78-F79.

Variants [a] *Exaudi ... nobis*] *Exaudi* (incipit only) in *M*Helm.35, fol. 102r.
[b] *domine*] om. Ordo 50; PRG
[c] *sancta Maria ... nobis*] *alleluia* added *Ps*Mz.D820; *sanctorum omnibus suffragantibus meritis* Ordo 50, PRG; *sanctorum omnium suffragantibus meritis* MS S of Ordo 50; om. MS G of Ordo 50.

Melody Mode 3. Transcribed in Chapter 4 from *G*Lpz, fol. 71v; see Figure 22 above and compare facsimile 5 (from *Ps*Mz.D820).
Melody = *G*Strals; ~ = *G*Pat; ~ *Ps*Mz.D820 [added *alleluia*]; *var.* Gastoué (1939) 19.

Translation "Hear, hear, hear our prayers, o Lord! Holy Mary, pray for us!" [cf. CAO 2: 787]

---

[31]Leipzig is less than fifty kilometres from the eastern border of the Mainz Church Province; cf. the map in Figure 4, p. 86. It belonged to the Merseburg diocese as part of the Church province of Magdeburg.

[32] *Miserere miserere miserere populo tuo etc.* (Lddv 278b)

In the context of the Lddv it is highly appropriate that Mary should sing the *Miserere* chant, which, in the litany triad *Aufer a nobis* just discussed, is closely linked to the verse *Exaudi*. Sung by the *Quinta Fatua*, this chant [31] had ended in a direct invocation of Mary for intercession and was preceded by the offertory chant [30] *Recordare* through which all the *Fatue* had begged Mary for help. In response to these supplications, each subsequently paraphrased in the vernacular (ll. 257-264, 265-272), Mary first speaks a few vernacular lines to the *Fatue* (ll. 273-278), gently reproving their conduct, yet promising to try to obtain mercy for them from her son. She then genuflects when she sings this litany verse [32] (*Maria flexis genibus cantat 'Miserere ...'* [l. 278a]). The evidence, presented above in section [31], is conclusive that both chants [31] and [32] belong to the *Aufer a nobis* litany of the Major and Minor Litanies.

In the editions of the Lddv since Beckers, the *etc.* after the incipit of chant [32] *Miserere miserere miserere populo tuo* has been omitted, leaving readers with the impression that these five words form the entire chant, when in fact a major part of it has been suppressed.[1] I cite here only the second verse of the litany triad from the Leipzig Gradual (*GLpz*, fol. 71v):[2]

> *Miserere, miserere, miserere populo tuo quem redemisti christe sanguine tuo ne in eternum irascaris nobis. Miserere ...*

Of the three other plays that make use of a *Miserere* chant, the fifteenth-century Marburg *Spiel von den letzten Dingen* (MaSp.532) is of special interest.[3] Here, as was shown above, the whole triad is sung, the

---

[1]See the discussion in Chapter 1, p. 33.

[2]For a translation, see below, p. 293. All three litany verses are transcribed above in Figure 22, p. 286, with text and music.

[3]The two other later plays that use a *Miserere* chant, the Künzelsau Corpus Christi and the Alsfeld Passion plays (KünzCC and AlsfP), do not offer many new insights into a discussion of the chant. Although in both plays this chant begins with only a twofold *Miserere* (see Catalogue [32C2], p. F80) and the context does not indicate any connection with the Rogation processions, some relation to the *Miserere* chant discussed above can be assumed. In KünzCC, the chant is also delivered by Mary, in the scene of the Last Judgment, and the incipit has been extended to the second phrase. The third phrase might have been purposefully

verses *Aufer* and *Exaudi* in immediate succession in two places (fols. 10r and 11r), *Miserere* at a later place (fol. 11v), as Mary's fifth intercession.[4] The integration of all three chants in this play, during the *Fatue*'s long supplication sequence is clear evidence for its link to the liturgy of the Rogation procession; it provides also external evidence for the relation of the Lddv to this important penitential celebration. In both plays the *cantat* of the stage directions leaves no doubt that this *Miserere* chant is performed with a singing voice, as is the chant in AlsfP:

MARIA flexis genibus cantat *Miserere miserere miserere populo tuo etc.*

(Lddv 278a-b)

MARIA cantat *Miserere miserere miserere populo tuo*

(MaSp.532, fol. 11v)

ANIMAE INFERNALES cantant *Miserere miserere populo tuo*

(AlsfP 7262a)

---

left out as being not quite fitting for Mary. Since the stage direction uses the verb *dicere*, not *cantare*, it may be assumed that the text was delivered in recitation:

MARIA flectat genus et dicat *Misserere misserere populo tuo quem redemisti, criste, sangwine tuo.*   (KünzCC, ll. 5738a-c)

In the equally late AlsfP, the Damned Souls sing the *Miserere* chant, during the Harrowing of Hell, and Jesus rejects them with the words from the Ten Virgins Parable:

Tunc ANIME INFERNALES cantant *Miserere, miserere populo tuo!*

JHESUS dicit sub accentu ewangelii *Amen, amen dico vobis: nescio vos!*

(AlsfP, ll. 7262a-b and 7266b)

The sequence of these two Latin chants not traditionally connected with the *Descensus* scene looks like a borrowing from the Lddv (chants [**32**] *Miserere* and [**29**] *Amen amen*). This can be confirmed through close parallels in the vernacular text immediately preceding and following the two Latin chants; indeed, a total of eleven of these eighteen lines in AlsfP appear to have been copied almost literally from the Thuringian play. See also above, p. 263 n4. These similarities and other obvious influences of the Lddv on the Alsfeld play have been discussed by Beckers (ed. 1905) 69-95, esp. 85-87. It is not possible to tell, however, whether the melody to the *Miserere* chant in this play was borrowed from the Lddv along with the other sections, or taken directly from the liturgy or some other source. Dreimüller (1935) 2: 93 no. 306, in his musicological dissertation on the AlsfP does not give any information about the music or the liturgical background of this chant. Very likely he did not find it in any source since he consulted mainly 'modern' liturgical books of the *Vaticana* editions. In any case, the liturgical connection for this chant is much weaker in the two late plays of Alsfeld and Künzelsau than in the Lddv and the MaSp.532. Nevertheless, the ultimate source for the *Miserere* in these two late plays remains the *Aufer a nobis* litany discussed above. Schuler's suggestion (1951) 244 no. 368, of the responsory *Miserere domine populo tuo quia volunt nos* as a liturgical source for the *Miserere* chant in the AlsfP is consequently no longer tenable.

[4]See pp. 280-281, with excerpts from MaSp.532.

The fact that only Mary appears to intercede for the *Fatue* has been much discussed by literary historians in trying to define the relationship between the extant manuscript texts of the Lddv and the only performance record we have of such a play in Eisenach (Thuringia) on May 4, 1321, with the famous comment by Count Friedrich der Freidige about "the prayers of the blessed Mary, Mother of God, and of all the saints" in this play.[5] Since the extant manuscripts of the Lddv do not contain any intercessory prayers of all the saints, so the argument goes, they cannot reflect the performance of Eisenach.[6]

Given the close connection of chants [31] and [32], *Exaudi* and *Miserere,* to the All Saints litany of the Rogation processions, this argument loses some of its force. For an attentive medieval audience, the idea of the involvement of all the saints, expressed already in chant [26] *Iniquitates nostras*, would certainly have been reinforced through such borrowings from the Rogation litanies. On the three consecutive days before Ascension Day, the relics of the saints were carried along in procession;[7] and not only Mary, but all the saints were invoked in various litanies, prayers and chants. Since the whole supplication sequence in the Lddv can be perceived as a small-scale re-enactment of the Rogation processions, the reaction of Count Friedrich der Freidige over the ineffectiveness of the prayers of "Mary and all the saints" is conceivable, even though only St. Mary actually appears in the play. Moreover, the newly-discovered text of chant [26] *Iniquitates nostras* with its phrase *cum istis omnibusque sanctis* allows for the suggestion that, at least in an earlier stage of the extant play, relics of the saints in reliquaries and precious boxes, images, and perhaps even small statues might have been present in the playing area; and since such relics implied the 'real pres-

---

[5]See Chapter 1, pp. 12-13, for more details on the early Eisenach performance and its effect on Count Friedrich; also above, section [26], pp. 249-250 and n20.

[6]Cf. Linke (1987a) 225; Bergmann (1986) 255 (no. 114), also above, p. 13 n6.

[7]See for instance the pertinent rubrics for the three Rogation days in *ORh.*80 (pp. 150.24–154.10): "pulsantur omnia signa et interim a custodibus ecclesie sanctorum relique, quotquot sunt, cruciculis, capsulis vel nuxis incluse, per fratres dividuntur, ut ab eis collo suspense portentur" (p. 151, ll. 19-22) ("All the bells are tolled, and meanwhile the custodians of the church distribute the relics of the saints, however many, among the brethren — relics that are held in small crosses, boxes or other reliquaries — so that they can be carried by them on their shoulders."). Here too through the singing of the antiphon *Surgite sancti,* the saints are directly invoked to join the procession for the blessing and protection of the people. See also the quotations above, p. 249 nn18-19.

ence' of the saints,[8] the *Fatue* could have referred to them with gestures while appealing to Mary and the *Dominica Persona*.[9] The performance of 1321 in Eisenach may quite well have been based on a play script that, in essence, is extant in the transmission of MS A of Mühlhausen, written some thirty to fifty-five years later.

The few textual variants for the *Miserere* chant among the sources studied are of minor importance and are noted in the 'critical' edition of the text below and in Catalogue [32E]. The dual *Miserere* (variant **a**) is found only in some manuscripts of the PRG and in the two later plays AlsfP and KünzCC; the inserted *domine* (variant **b**) appears only in the French transmissions. Variant **c** (*irasceris*) occurs in *M*Helm.35 and *G*Pat; and variant **d** (the final *alleluia*) seems to be a late addition, only in *Ps*Mz.D820. Thus, the text is more or less identical in all medieval liturgical sources from Germany mentioned.

The melodic form of this chant in the liturgy has been briefly discussed in the previous section [31] on *Exaudi*, along with a transcription from the Leipzig Gradual of all three introductory 'verses' of the litany.[10] Compared with the two other verses, the verse *Miserere* stands out with its musical rendering of the first phrase: since the cadence with its descending line from d to a is texted with the words *po-pu-lo tu-o*, the twelve syllables of the threefold *Miserere* had to be musically accommodated on the few pitches of the ascending line in the initial melodic phrase (cf. Figure 22, line 2). While the equally long text of verse 1 permitted extended recitation on c, the repetition of *Miserere* in verse 2 requires a different solution, resulting in a very lively sequence of two almost identical melodic arches between the pitches G and d. Such a musical repetition intensifies the urgency of the appeal and underlines

---

[8]See Beissel (1892) II, 1-18, summarized above, Chapter 3 [26] p. 249 n19.

[9]See above, Chapter 3 [26], p. 250. The *Dominica Persona* himself, in his reply to Mary, might have pointed to such representations of the saints, thus including them as (indirect) actors, when he pronounces his harsh vernacular words:

... hemel und erde solde er czů ge,
er myne wort in bruchen solden ste;
dar noch alliz hemelische her
mochte eynen sunder nicht erner. (ll. 293-296)

"Heaven and earth shall pass away ere my words shall be destroyed. The whole heavenly host, therefore, could not rescue a sinner."

[10]Cf. Chapter 3 [31], pp. 285-287, and Figure 22, p. 286.

effectively the insistent verbal repetition of *Miserere* — certainly an impressive beginning for the Virgin's intercession on the *Fatue*'s behalf.

In the musical transmission, the Helmstedt source *M*Helm.35, which has only the incipit for the *Exaudi* chant, joins the other German manuscripts in providing a melody for the *Miserere* verse. As has been shown, the main differences in the musical transmission of the whole triad of the *Aufer a nobis* antiphon are between the Roman and the German sources rather than within either of these groups. Therefore, any of the medieval German versions, all quite close to each other, would be suitable for the restoration of chants [31] and [32] in the Lddv. For the *Miserere* verse [32], however, there are a few more variants among the German sources, possibly due to the larger number of syllables to be set to the basic melody. These variants concern primarily the implementation of the 'German dialect features,' i.e. how frequently and where exactly in the verse those special *neumae saltatrices* occur in the melody. Of the five German sources compared, *G*Lpz and *M*Helm.35 are very closely related, sharing five such melodic leaps and showing three additional ones at almost identical places. (For *G*Lpz, see Figure 22, p. 286). The remaining three sources, *G*Strals, *G*Pat, *Ps*Mz.D820, vary slightly in the way they apply those special intervals or replace them with tonal sequences in steps, yet they differ jointly from the former group in two variants for the final verse section: a stepwise ascending movement over *e-ter-num* and a sudden cadence from *Ga* (*GaG* in *Ps*Mz.D820) into the final *E-E* over *nobis*; cf. facsimile 5 from *Ps*Mz.D820.

Because the *Exaudi* and the *Miserere* chants of the Lddv have their origin in the same liturgical function and are verses of a larger liturgical unit, one and the same source should be used for the reconstruction of both chants. I will, therefore, restore chant [32] using the litany verse *Miserere* for Rogations as transmitted in *G*Lpz, the fourteenth-century gradual of Leipzig:

Text   *Miserere*[a] *miserere miserere*[b] [*populo tuo quem redemisti Christe sanguine tuo ne in eternum irascaris*[c] *nobis.*[d]]

       Source   *G*Lpz, fol. 71v (= *A*Fri.142; *G*Strals; Würdtwein (Trier), p. 219; Ordo 50; collated with the other sources listed in Catalogue [32D], p. F81.

      Variants   [a] Triple *Miserere*] Dual *Miserere* PRG;

                [b] *miserere*] add. *domine* CAO MS F; Gastoué (1939) 19;

                [c] *irascaris*] *irasceris* *M*Helm.35; *G*Pat;

                [d] *nobis*] add. *alleluia* *Ps*Mz.D820.

Melody   Mode 3. Transcribed in Chapter 4 from *G*Lpz, fol. 71v; see also Figure 22, p. 286, and compare facsimile 5 (from *Ps*Mz.D820).

  Melody ~ = *M*Helm.35; ~ *G*Strals, *G*Pat; ~*var. Ps*Mz.D820; *var.* Gastoué (1939) 19.

Translation "Have mercy, have mercy, have mercy upon your people whom you have redeemed, Christ, with your blood, lest your wrath be upon us in eternity."   [cf. CAO 2: 787]

[33] *Celum et terra transibunt, verbum autem meum in eternum permanet.* (Lddv 290b-d)

With chant **[33]** and the subsequent six lines of vernacular paraphrase (ll. 291-296), the *Dominica Persona* sternly rejects his mother Mary's intercession for the Foolish Virgins, as, in lines 360-383, he will reject her second and last intercession for them in the vernacular only. The scanty stage direction *Dominica Persona ad Mariam* (l. 278a) fails to give any indication as to how this reply is to be performed. However, the relatively long text for chant **[33]** *Celum et terra* is given in its full wording, as were the *Dominica Persona*'s two previous rejections **[27]** and **[29]**; this may indicate that there was no readily available chant with such a text to which the author or scribe could refer. Tracing the Latin text back to its source will help determine the type of chant and what the form of its delivery should be.

In each of the three synoptic Gospels there is a biblical verse whose first half is identical with the text in the Lddv; the second half differs slightly in wording, but not in content:

> *Caelum et terra transibunt, verba autem mea non praeteribunt.*
>
> (Matthew 24: 35)
>
> *Caelum et terra transibunt, verba autem mea non transibunt.*
>
> (Mark 13: 31 and Luke 21: 33)

Beckers and Schneider indicate the passages from Matthew and Mark as sources for text **[33]**; De Boor and Curschmann-Glier refer only to the verse from Matthew. Yet strictly speaking the source should be Luke 21: 33, for it is Luke's account of the *Parousia* of the Son of Man (Luke 21: 25-33) that has had an established place in the lectionary of the Church from early times on. Part of Jesus' eschatological speech, this pericope was the required Gospel reading in Advent, usually in the third week before Christmas, in the Roman capitularies of the seventh and eighth centuries.[1] It was, of course, always delivered in an intoned form.

The author of the Lddv obviously felt that, if he extracted for use in his play a biblical verse from a pericope other than the Ten Virgins Parable, he had to give it some poetical form, just as he had done with the sentence from the Gregorian homily for chant **[27]** *Qui tempus*. In any

---

[1] Cf. Catalogue **[33D1(a)]**, pp. F83-F84.

case, the verse from Luke 21: 33 is used here in a slightly edited form with a *cursus planus* in both of its phrases:[2]

Celum et térra transíbunt,	5--2-	(p 3p)
verbum autem meum in etérnum permánet.	5--2-	(p 3p)

The two final accents of each phrase are on the fifth and the second syllable counting from the end and have the kind of 'accentual accord' of the phrase endings observed in the earlier chants **[15]** *Ne forte* and **[27]** *Qui tempus*. The author achieved this effect through two minor changes to the Gospel verse: instead of the plural *verba autem mea* he used the singular *verbum autem meum*, and he turned the negative statement *non transibunt* into the positive declaration *in eternum permanet*, thus avoiding the awkward repetition of the verbal form *transibunt*. With these changes, the second phrase of chant **[33]** sounds much more poetic than the plain prose version of the Gospel.

Since this second phrase does not seem to exist as such anywhere in the Bible or in the liturgy, the author most likely composed it himself from textual elements which he had in front of him or which he reconstructed from memory. Among such textual elements, contributing directly or indirectly to the composition of chant **[33]**, are the "Related biblical texts" quoted in Catalogue **[33D]**, p. F83. The last of these, Lamentations 5: 19, is the biblical source for the Rogation antiphon *Tu autem domine*, which displays some interesting textual connections to the play context in the Lddv: *Tu autem, domine,* **in eternum permanes;** *solium tuum a generatione in generationem; ... sed proiciens repulisti nos, iratus es contra nos vehementer.*[3] This very long processional antiphon belongs to the formulary of the Rogation procession, which was the liturgical place for chants **[31]** and **[32]**. Furthermore, the text of this antiphon is taken from the last four verses of the *Oratio Jeremiae* (Lam. 5: 19-22), which is the biblical source for the last two Latin chants, **[35]** and **[36]** *Cecidit corona* and *Deficit gaudium.*

Whether or not the author made conscious use of these and other related biblical or liturgical texts listed in Catalogue **[33D]** is, of course, impossible to say. His intimate familiarity with Scripture and other holy texts as well as his sense for poetic language are sufficient to explain the

---

[2]The technique of the cursus in medieval Latin was discussed above, pp. 257-259.
[3]Ordo 50 XXXVI.70; and PRG XCIX.425; cf. Catalogue **[33D2]**, p. F84.

specific changes to pre-existing texts in the chants [33] and [27]. There is nothing really unusual about this method of textual composition since the large majority of Gregorian chant texts were created using this same principle of 'scriptural variation' or 'scriptural composition.'[4] What is different is that the author did not, as far as we know, add a melody to either of these chants, and that both were apparently composed specifically for the Lddv rather than for a Church Office.

The fact that the *cursus* form is applied to chants [27] *Qui tempus* and [33] *Celum et terra*, both pronounced by the *Dominica Persona*, may reveal yet another aspect of the concern the author had for his chants. Changed in their original wording and isolated from their original homily or Gospel context, these texts acquire an authenticity and dignity that the use of the *cursus* also bestowed on sermons of Leo the Great, on many of the oldest Latin prayers, and on papal and other chancery documents of the Middle Ages.[5] The vernacular paraphrase following chant [33] is proof that the Latin was conceived as authentic, scriptural text:

> Muter, gedenke an *dy wort,*
> *dy sů vunden beschreben dort:*
> hemel und erde solde er czů ge,
> er myne wort in bruchen solden ste (ll. 291-294)[6]

Chant [33], therefore, in spite of some textual changes, is designed to be recognizably from the Gospel; intoning it in the Gospel tone would be appropriate in a performance. The same kind of recitation, then, would be posited that was proposed for the two earlier chants of the *Dominica Persona*, [27] *Qui tempus* and [29] *Amen amen dico vobis*. Thus, the three 'speeches' of the *Dominica Persona* in which he rejects the *Fatue* either directly (chants [27] and [29]) or indirectly by refusing to accede to his mother Mary's intercession (chant [33]), would all be intoned to the Mainz recitation formula for Gospel readings with the

---

[4]Cf. above, p. 126 (Chapter 3[4]). An excellent survey of the ways and means used to compose liturgical chant texts for older and newer offices is given by C. Marbach (1907) esp. 30*-56*.

[5]For the importance of the Leonine *cursus* as a criterion of authenticity see e.g. Klauser-Meyer (1962) 59; Boyle (1976) 86.

[6]"Mother, remember *the words which they find written there* [i.e. in the Bible]: 'Heaven and earth shall pass away ere my words shall be destroyed'" (my emphases).

tenor **D** (and the upper third **F** for the accent syllables).[7] This form of delivery would convey the same authority that emanates from the words themselves:

[27]   *Qui tempus congrue penitén[cie] perdíderit,*
       frustra cum precibus ad regni iánua[m] pervénerit.

[29]   *Amen amen dico vobis nescio vos.*

[33]   *Celum et térra transíbunt,*
       verbum autem meum in etérnum permánet.

The chant is proposed here and restored in Chapter 4 [33] as liturgical Gospel recitation according to the *Accentus Moguntinus*, with the tenor **D** (**F**):

Text   *Celum et terra transibunt,*
       verbum autem meum in eternum permanet.[a]
       Source Lddv, ll. 290b-d (MS A, p. 97b); cf. Luke 21: 33.
       Variants   [a] *verbum ... permanet]* verba autem mea non transibunt
             Luke 21: 33; Mark 13: 31; *verba autem mea non*
             praeteribunt Matthew 24: 35.

Melody   Set in liturgical recitation to the Gospel tone, according to the *Accentus Moguntinus* as transmitted in *M*Halb.888 (cf. pp. 79-81, and Figure 3), with the subtonal tenor **D** and the upper third **F**. Compare facsimile 4 and Chapter 4 [33].

Translation "Heaven and earth shall pass away; my word, however, remains in eternity."

[7]Cf. the discussion of this recitation formula above, pp. 78-81, and in Chapter 3 [14/15], [27], and [28/29]; see esp. pp. 168, 260-261, and 264, also Figure 3, p. 80, and facsimile 4.

[35] *Cecidit corona* (Lddv 383e)
[36] *Deficit gaudium etc.* (Lddv 409b)

With the chants *Cecidit corona* and *Deficit gaudium*, the *Fatue* begin the series of lamentations that conclude the play. After the *Dominica Persona* has rejected not only the first of his mother Mary's intercessions (chants [32-33] with vernacular paraphrases), but also her repeated plea (in the vernacular only, cf. ll. 339a-383), the long 'Rogation procession' of the *Fatue* has come to an indisputable end. The *Silete*-call [34'] by the *Angeli*, the last one in the Lddv (ll. 383a-b),[1] marks this ending, at the same time signaling that a new action is about to begin. This new action presumably contained a great deal of dumb play as the Devils, with no dialogue assigned to them, rush in to encircle the *Fatue* with a chain (l. 383c, *Dyaboli circumdant eas kathena*).[2]

Thus captured in the Devils' chain — an image reminiscent of some pictorial representations of the Last Judgment — the *Fatue* begin their desperate lamentations, bemoaning their fate first in a sequence of five monologues in vernacular couplets (ll. 444-525), then in the concluding vernacular stanzas (ll. 526-576) which they sing while leaving the 'stage' and withdrawing through the audience. The only Latin chants sung in this prolonged final section of the macaronic Lddv are the two to be discussed here, [35] *Cecidit corona* at the outset of the laments (l. 383e), and [36] *Deficit gaudium* (l. 409b).

While the *Prima Fatua* sings chant [35], all of the *Fatue* enact the chant's words, letting the crowns on their heads drop as directed by the rubric (ll. 383g-h, *Tunc omnes* FATUE *faciant pendere coronas in capite et plangant*) — a scene that seems to be captured in a few works of art of the time and area.[3] This silent gesture paraphrases the Latin chant more accurately than the singer's subsequent vernacular lines 384-409 with their general wailing. The *Secunda Fatua*'s chant [36] *Deficit gaudium* also seems to function mainly as a starting point for the subsequent

---

[1]Cf. above, Chapter 3 [3'] and Table 5, p. 109.

[2]In MS B of the Lddv, this pantomime is the only appearance of the Devils, while MS A has an added Devils' Scene (ll. 295a-339) placed between the two intercessions of Mary. For this interpolation, see above, pp. 108-110.

[3]Cf. the images nos. 3-10, appended to my dissertation (1991) 552-558, of sculptures in Erfurt and stained glass windows in Mühlhausen and Naumburg.

lamentations of all the *Fatue*. These two chants [35-36] are so closely related in their liturgical origin and their dramaturgical function that they
are discussed here jointly. As all editions of the Lddv since Beckers have
indicated, their ultimate biblical source is verses 15 and 16, *Deficit gaudium* and *Cecidit corona*, of the *Oratio Ieremiae* (Lam. 5: 1-22).[4]

The Lamentations of Jeremiah reflect the desolation of the prophet
and his people over Judah's sins and the destruction of Jerusalem in the
year 586 BC. They were re-interpreted by the Christian Church and used
as a lament over Christ's Passion and death in two liturgical contexts in
the pre-Easter period: as nocturnal readings on the three last days of
Holy Week and — generally less known because limited to the monastic
rite — as one of the Matins canticles during the Lenten period.[5]

---

[4]L. Bechstein (ed. 1855) 44-45, referred to Lam. 5: 16 as the source for the chant *Cecidit corona*, not noticing that the next Latin incipit, [36] *Deficit gaudium*, can be identified with Lam. 5: 15. The use of the present tense *Deficit* in chant [36] does not quite
agree with the biblical form in the perfect tense (*Defecit*), but it is difficult to tell
whether this change was intended or the result of a scribal error.

The only other medieval play to my knowledge that makes use of these two verses,
or parts thereof, is the Zurzach Passion or Easter Play (ZurzP) of 1494, where (fol. 18r-
v) Mary Magdalene laments the death of Christ with the words *Defecit gaudium cordis
nostri, cecidit corona capitis nostri*, followed by fourteen vernacular lines (ll. 32a-48).
The verses maintain their biblical sequence, whereas in the Lddv the order is reversed.
Only the first halves of the two verses are used in the ZurzP, however, and combined
they form a new textual-musical unit. This unit is reinforced by a sort of circular melody
repeating the initial fifteen-note melisma over *Defecit* in the same way at the end, over
capitis nostri. Fol. 18r-v of this Lucerne manuscript had been separately published by
Mone (1846) 1: 202-203, and became known as the fragment of a *Lucerne Planctus
Mariae* ("Luzerner Marienklage"). Owing largely to Erika Mundt's research (1919), this
fol. 18 is now recognized as belonging, together with various other folios, to the larger
unit of the severely fragmented Zurzach Passion (or Easter) Play. A. Reinle (1949-1950)
provided the definitive edition; for an account of the complicated manuscript transmission of this play, see Reinle, pp. 15-16 and (1981). Cf. also Mundt (1919) 3-5; Bergmann (1986) no. 97; B. Neumann (1987) 1: no. 3570-3572; Eggers (1985).

The music is transmitted in Lucerne, 2° MS 177, fol. 18v. I am grateful to the Zentralbibliothek Lucerne for providing me with a copy of fol. 18r-v with the musical notation of this Latin chant. Modern transcription by H. Sidler in Reinle, ed. (1949-1950)
77. The chant was probably composed especially for the ZurzP, although it may also
have been part of the local Good Friday liturgy in the Constance diocese to which Zurzach belonged. It would be inappropriate to 'borrow' this melody for the chants [35] and
[36] in the much older Ten Virgins Play of far-away Thuringia; in spite of the same
biblical source, the text and particularly the play context is very different.

[5]See Catalogue [35-36D1 and 2], p. F86.

Canticles are psalm-like chants of biblical texts other than the psalms, slightly more solemn and festive in their musical delivery.[6] Usually chants of praise they have been in special use in the Church from the fourth and fifth centuries on. The Rule of St. Benedict required that on Sundays and feastdays three canticles be chanted at the beginning of the third nocturn instead of the usual psalms.[7] Therefore, a large number of canticles, including Lamentations 5: 1-22 (*Recordare domine*), were integrated into the monastic Office of Matins. Over the centuries, a schedule was developed assigning groups of three canticles to certain liturgical occasions or seasons of the year.[8] The canticle based on Lamentations 5 always belongs to the group of canticles for Lent and always comes with the same selection of verses: Lam. 5: 1-7, 15-17, and 19-21;[9] the verses 15 and 16, used in the Lddv, therefore, are always included.[10]

Better known than the monastic canticles and far more widely discussed in scholarly research are the Lamentations chanted as the three lesson readings of Matins on the *triduum sanctum*, the so-called 'dark Matins' (or *tenebrae*) of the three days before Easter. In these Offices, the mourning over Christ's death is manifest not only in the chants and readings but also in the liturgical color black and, particularly, in the gradual extinction of a certain number of candles (seven, fifteen, or twenty-four, according to different local customs) in the course of Matins and Lauds.[11] Originally, major parts of the Lamentations were to be

---

[6]An excellent study on the subject, focusing primarily on the English transmission of the monastic canticles, is that by Korhammer (1976). For further literature see pp. 6-7; also Steiner (1980a). The canticles that remain in use into modern times are the *Benedictus* of Lauds, the *Magnificat* of Vespers, and the *Nunc dimittis* of Compline.

[7]Cf. Benedict (ed. Walzer 1929) 34-35 [Chapter 11].

[8]For more details, see Korhammer (1976) 10-11 (for England), 26-31 (France and Germany). Especially valuable is the survey on pp. 14-15.

[9]One exception mentioned by Korhammer (1976) 42, 32, 58-63, is a Spanish manuscript where, following mozarabic traditions, the *Recordare* canticle includes the whole of the *Oratio Ieremiae*, Lam. 5: 1-22.

[10]The selection of verses is the same in the modern edition of the Benedictine Psalter (*Ps*OSB, pp. 60-61), where the *Recordare* has its place as the third canticle in the group *Cantica in Quadragesima*. Cf. Catalogue [**35/36**D2], p. F86.

[11]Cf. Ordo Romanus XXVII.5 in Andrieu (1931-1961) 3: 348. Very detailed descriptions of this ritual can also be found in later ritual books, e.g. in the Cathedral Ordinarius of Magdeburg, Berlin, Staatsbibliothek, MS theol. lat. 4° 113, fol. 75v.

read at Matins on each of these three days. From the eleventh century on, however, these lessons were gradually shortened by papal legislation of Gregory VII.[12] In the mid-thirteenth century Dominican Codex of Humbert, for instance, the three readings for Holy Saturday, which consisted of 89 verses before the time of Gregory VII, have been reduced to Lam. 4: 1-12. The text of Lam. 5: 15-16, therefore, was often no longer included in these readings.[13] The fourteenth-century lectionary of the Stiftskirche St. Blasius in Braunschweig (*L*Brsw.), on the other hand, provides for the entire *Oratio Ieremiae* of Lam. 5, except for the last verse, to be chanted on Holy Saturday.[14]

If, then, two different, well-established liturgical usages for the texts of Lam. 5 coexisted in the medieval church, the question arises as to which of the two traditions should serve as the basis for restoring the chants [35] and [36] in the Lddv. There is no doubt that, while the canticle was restricted to monastic use on Lenten Sundays, the lesson chanting of the *Oratio Ieremiae* on Holy Saturday was in general use and, indeed, more relevant because the *tenebrae* offices were so very prominent in the pre-Easter liturgy throughout the Western church. This prominence rested not only on the special liturgical season and the gradual extinction of the candles during the Office, but also on the very special and melodious reciting formulas to which the Lamentation lessons were chanted.[15] The following discussion will, therefore, disregard the monastic canticle and focus instead on the chanting of the Lamentations.[16]

---

[12]Cf. Bäumer (1895) 333; Stäblein (1960a) esp. col. 134, where local differences in shortening the lessons are explained.

[13]Cf. Catalogue [35/36D1], pp. F86. Compare the gradual shortening of Gregory's homily discussed above in Chapter 3 [27], p. 255, and Catalogue [27D1-2], p. F67.

[14]Cf. Catalogue [35/36D1]. For the three first lessons on Maundy Thursday, *L*Brsw has Lam. 1: 1-9; on Good Friday, Lam. 3: 1-33. On Holy Saturday, Lam. 4: 1-11 for the first two lessons, and Lam. 5: 1-21 for the third lesson; cf. Catalogue, p. F86.

[15]Various musical settings for the Lamentations are discussed by Wagner (1911-1921) 3: 235-243; Massenkeil (1980) 410; and especially Stäblein (1960a) 133-140.

[16]The fact that the *Oratio Ieremiae* was also used in monastic circles as a canticle may, however, have contributed to the author's choice of text for the two last chants of the Lddv. A third occasion where texts from Lam. 5 were put to liturgical use should at least be mentioned, although this occurrence is late and limited to a few distant local traditions. According to Corbin (1960) esp. pp. 13-39 and 113-143, the liturgical celebration of the *Depositio crucis* on Good Friday, known since the tenth century in countries north of the Alps, yet always ignored in Rome, was introduced into some churches

Trying to find the 'right' Lamentation tone, or, more specifically, the recitation tone for the *Oratio Ieremiae* that might have been in use in fourteenth-century Thuringian liturgy, could prove difficult, however, since according to Stäblein's estimate, as many as two hundred different Lamentation tones are transmitted in medieval sources.[17] Often of only local importance, especially in the later Middle Ages, they have not yet been systematically collected and studied, but are known to range from simple recitation formulas to extensive melodies in which the character of recitation is almost lost. Yet whatever the Lamentation tone, all the verses are usually sung to the same formula, with melodic adjustments for verses of different length. Most manuscripts, however, provide the notation for the whole text in order to ensure the correct melodic inflections and cadences for the various points of punctuation within the verses.

---

in Italy and other southern countries from the thirteenth century on. It was only in the fifteenth century that this purely liturgical event was transformed into a large scale procession for which the formulary is transmitted in a processional from Padua (*Pr*Padua). Cf. Biblioteca Capitolare di Padova, MS C 56, fols. 60r-67r, published in Vecchi (1954) 136-143 (texts), 145-160 (music); the description in Corbin (1960) 23 and 117. For the texts see also LOO 428, and LOO 9: 881-882. Cf. Catalogue [35/36D3], p. F86. Before the procession moved outside the church, a series of lamentations was sung, in two-part compositions, among them a few selected verses from the Lamentations of Jeremiah: Lam. 5: 3; 5: 16; 4: 20; 5: 15 (in that order). By the middle of the sixteenth century, those four texts from Lamentations recur, in the same sequence as in Padua, in a much shorter ceremony in Portugal, transmitted in the Missal of Braga (*M*Braga) of 1558; cf. Catalogue, p. F86. Here, the Lamentation verses are chanted to a simple recitation formula, not too different from the Roman formula, which extends over a fourth (*F-b^b*), with *a* as the main reciting note. Cf. Corbin (1960) 261-262 (text); frontispiece (facsimile of fol. 96); plate (II), after p. 314 (transcription of fol. 96: 'Planctus de la Déposition'; the date in the heading should be corrected to 1558). Corbin includes most of the later versions of this ceremony, surviving in Portugal into the twentieth century, all more or less dependent on the version from Padua. Text only of Braga 1558 also in LOO 435, printed from Corbin's edition.

    The interesting point is that the same verses as in the Lddv are chanted here (Lam. 5: 15 and 16), also in a non-biblical sequence. Of course, neither of these two deposition ceremonies are of any relevance for the restoration of the chants [35] and [36] in the Lddv, which is much earlier and geographically distant. These ceremonies can, however, serve as evidence that the verses of Lamentations were liturgically available for insertion into other ceremonies, especially on the days before Easter.

[17]Cf. Stäblein (1960a) 136. A number of such local formulas have been published in Wagner (1911-1921) 3: 238-243, and by Stäblein (1960a) 135-140.

By the end of the Middle Ages, the 'Roman' recitation tone for the Lamentations which was used in the Roman Curia, had superseded most other Lamentation tones.[18] Set to this Roman recitation tone, the two laŝt chants of the Lddv could have been delivered in the form presented in Figure 23.

FIGURE 23 LAM. 5: 16 AND 15 SET TO A ROMAN LAMENTATION TONE
IN A 13TH-CENTURY ANTIPHONAL OF THE PAPAL CURIA

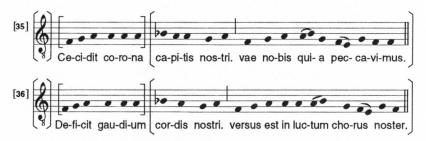

On the other hand, Stäblein has pointed out very clearly that the *Oratio Ieremiae* is usually treated differently from the Lamentation readings. Most often it has its own melodic formula, one and the same for all twenty-two verses except the first, or sometimes even two different formulas chanted in alternation. And there is a large diversity of locally different tunes, persisting into the baroque time.[19]

An extremely fortunate discovery in a fifteenth-century Mühlhausen manuscript, codex 87/8, turned out to be a completely notated version of the entire *Oratio Ieremiae* (Lam. 5: 1-22).[20] I found it thanks to Friedrich Stephan's mention of a 'sacred music piece without indication

[18]Cf. Wagner (1911-1921) 3: 236-237. Wagner published this Lamentation tone from the Antiphonarium secundum consuetudinem curiae romanae in a Munich manuscript, which is also from the thirteenth century. The manuscript belongs to the Franciscan Library in Munich. Stäblein (1960a) 135 presents a slightly different Roman formula from a Naples source of the eleventh century. For the 'modern' Roman formula, see LU, pp. 758-759. It had also been adopted in the Dominican liturgical model book of Humbert's Codex.

[19]Cf. Stäblein (1960a) 136, 139-140.

[20]MsMh.87/8 = Mühlhausen, Stadtarchiv, MS 87/8 (olim 60/8), fols. 387r-388r; cf. Catalogue [35/36D1], p. F83. I had an opportunity to study this manuscript in Mühlhausen in 1984 and again in 1994, and I am grateful to the Stadtarchiv Mühlhausen for providing microfilm copies of this precious 'music piece.'

author or scribe' in his 1847 description of the codex.[21] This codex has 390 folios, most of which (fols. 3r-348v) are devoted to a Latin *vocabularius*, written in 1466 in Magdeburg.[22] The last entry in a series of short, miscellaneous additions is the *Oracio ieremie prophete* (fols. 387r-388r).[23] The incipit *Oracio ieremie prophete* and explicit *Jerusalem ierusalem convertere ad dominum deum tuum*, the proper 'refrain' for all Lamentations lessons, provide clear evidence that this piece is a version of the liturgical reading of the *Oracio ieremie*.[24]

The recitation formula for the *Oracio ieremie* in this manuscript has a gentle melodic line with a range of almost an octave (from D to c).[25] With its opening E-G-a and the recitation on a, it is very close to the older E-type of Lamentation formulas quoted by Stäblein.[26] That the tune reaches high c and closes on a is also common in most older formulas. A special feature in the Mühlhausen version seems to be the richer melismas concluding the two phrases of the formula. The final cadence *GabcbaG-aa* (over *peccavi-mus* in [35] and *nos-ter* in [36]) echoes a part of the melodic progression of the first phrase (over *ca-pi-tis no-stri* in [35] and *cor-dis no-stri* in [36]). Yet even these melismas are traditional melodic material used in those E-type Lamentation tones for the singing of the Hebrew letters *Aleph* etc.[27] Two melodic turns seem to be special, however: the last melisma of phrase one, *baGFG* over *no-stri* (the implied 'tritone' is discussed below), and the strong melodic movement in the second phrase, descending from the high c to the lower D and rising again to the high c before the final cadence which closes on

---

[21]Fr. Stephan (1847a) 119: "Der übrig bleibende ... Theil des Codex enthält verschiedene Collectaneen aus den Gebieten der Scholastik, auch ein geistliches Musikstück, ohne Vermerke über Verfasser und Schreiber." In a more recent, typewritten description of the manuscripts of the "Kreisarchiv" (now "Stadtarchiv") Mühlhausen by D. Lülfing (1982) 19, the 'music piece' in MS 60/8 (now 87/8) is correctly identified as "*Oratio Ieremiae propheta* [sic] (Lam. 5: 1-22) mit gotischen Neumen im 4-Linien-System."

[22]Colophon of the scribe, Joachim Gronbergk, on fol. 348v.

[23]I hereafter adopt the spelling of the Mühlhausen manuscript, *Oracio ieremie*.

[24]In this Mühlhausen version, only verse 13 of Lam. 5 is missing, probably accidentally.

[25]See the transcription of Lam. 5: 16 and 15 (chants [35] and [36]) in Chapter 4 [35] and [36].

[26]Cf. Stäblein (1960a) 137-138, examples 2 and 4-7.

[27]Cf. Stäblein (1960a) 137, examples 2, 3, and 4.

a. In its overall character, then, the Mühlhausen formula for the *Oracio ieremie* appears to belong to a general, older tradition of Lamentations chanting. Some typically German uses of thirds and fourths, with the characteristic leaps of the third *a-c-a* (over *Recordare* and *Intuere*) at the beginning, are evidence that this version stands within the German tradition of plainsong.[28]

The manuscript was written in Magdeburg, north-east of and not far from Thuringia; it is not known when the codex came to Thuringia. The version transmitted here for the *Oracio ieremie*, however, may be the closest we can presently get to a local medieval reciting formula for the two verses from Lam. 5 in the Lddv. Although dating from the fifteenth century, this Mühlhausen source should be seriously considered for the restoration of the two last chants of the play.

Another fourteenth-century notation of the entire *Oratio Ieremiae*, also from central Germany, is almost identical to that of the Mühlhausen source. The manuscript, of Wolfenbüttel, is the lectionary *L*Brsw of the Stiftskirche St. Blasius in Braunschweig, well known for its transmission of the fourteenth-century Latin Easter play BrswO. The ten folios immediately preceding this play transmit a completely notated version of the Lamentation lessons for the *tenebrae* offices on the three days before Easter.[29] As the whole chapter of Lam. 5 (except v. 22) is noted here for the third lesson of Holy Saturday, the verses 15 and 16 at issue in this study are included.

The two versions of the *Oratio Ieremiae* in the Mühlhausen and the Wolfenbüttel manuscripts differ mainly in their text underlay, especially in the first half of the verses.[30] They also differ, to some degree, in the form of their cadences. While the 'final cadences' at the end of each verse are very similar in both sources — the final *a* is reached in an ascending motion from one degree below, i.e. from *G* as the last pitch of the short melisma *GabcbaG* — the 'inner cadences' concluding the first halves of the verses on a *G* betray the only real melodic difference

---

[28]Cf. MsMh.87/8, fol. 387r.

[29]*L*Brsw (Wolfenbüttel, Niedersächsisches Staatsarchiv, VII B Hs 203), fols. 14r-23r; fol. 22v is reproduced in facsimile 6. Cf. Catalogue [35/36D1], p. F86.

[30]In MsMh.87/8, the main melodic movement in the first half of the verses occurs as melismatic turns over the last two syllables *nos-tri*, whereas in *L*Brsw the same notes are distributed more evenly over the last four/five syllables.

between the two versions of the recitation formula, interestingly, however, not in all twenty-two verses. In *LBrsw* (cf. facsimile 6), the cadence over the last few syllables before the caesura is consistently a descending motion, leading stepwise into the last pitch *G* (*abaG-G-[G]*). MSMh.87/8, on the other hand, has a similar cadential motion (*aba-G-[G]*) at the corresponding places only in ten of the verses (Lam. 5: 1-2, 4, 6-7, 10-11, 17, 19, 21); in the remaining eleven verses (v. 13 is missing here, see n. 24) and in the refrain *Jerusalem, Jerusalem* …, this cadence is varied in an extraordinary manner: the melismatic turn before the final *G* descends to the *F* as the penultimate pitch of the inner cadence, resulting in a sequence of three whole tones (*baGFG*), the 'infamous' tritone which is generally avoided in medieval music as the *diabolus in musica*.[31] Such a selective use of this 'awkward' interval in MSMh.87/8 gives the appearance of being fully intended, since it is employed in a progressively increasing way as the despair of the singers intensifies: the tritone in the cadence of the first phrase occurs only four times in Lam. 5: 1-11, compared to eight times in verses 12-22, including the refrain. Both verses 15 and 16 of the *Oratio Ieremiae* in the Mühlhausen manuscript are, consequently, affected by this 'awkward' *tritonus*.

With the twofold evidence of a late medieval recitation formula for the *Oratio Ieremiae* in central-German areas, a solid basis is provided for the restoration of chants [35] and [36] in the Lddv. The variants between the two transmissions appear minor in nature, especially considering the multitude of Lamentation tunes transmitted from the Middle Ages. Thus, either source could serve as a model for these two chants, MSMh.87/8 being of the fifteenth century and possibly from Thuringia in the archdiocese of Mainz, *LBrsw* of the fourteenth century and clearly from within the Church province of Mainz. In this particular case, an external circumstance may be decisive for selecting the fifteenth-century source over the earlier one: MSMh.87/8 is located in the same Mühlhausen archives as MS A, the leading manuscript of the Lddv. The two last chants of this play, therefore, will be presented in Chapter 4 with the melodic version as found in MSMh.87/8 of the Stadtarchiv Mühlhausen; for comparison, the version from *LBrsw* is provided as facsimile 6. As

---

[31]A. Hughes (1989a) 504. For more details on the tritone and the attempts of medieval musicians to avoid it (often by employing a *b*♭), see Seay (1975) 34.

a result of this choice, the restored chants [35] and [36] will include in the middle of the recitation formula the awkward, 'diabolic' interval of a tritone — a feature that may appear even congruent with the desperate dramatic situation of the *Fatue* who are already in the hands of the devils:

Texts

[35] *Cecidit corona [capitis nostri, we^a nobis quia peccavimus].*

[36] *Deficit^b gaudium [cordis nostri, versus est in luctum chorus noster].*

Sources Lddv, ll. 383d and 409b (MS A, pp. 98a and b); MSMh.87/8, fol. 387v; cf. LBrsw, fol. 22v; Lam. 5: 16 and 15.

Variants ^{a} we] ve LBrsw; vae Lam. 5: 16.
^{b} Deficit] Defecit MSMh.87/8; LBrsw; Lam. 5: 15.

Melody*

Liturgical recitation in the Lamentation tone for the *Oratio Ieremiae*. Transcribed in Chapter 4 [35] and [36] from MS Mühlhausen 87/8, fol. 387v.

Melody ~ = LBrsw, fol. 22v (slightly different text underlay, with less *tono recto* recitation; no tritone over *no-stri*); *different* LU, pp. 758-759. Cf. facsimile 6 (from LBrsw).

* *Note* to [35]: *peccavimus*] The four-neume notation **FEDE** over the second syllable of *pec-ca-vimus* in MSMh.87/8 has been emended to the three-neume form **FED** which prevails in this manuscript at this place of the recitation formula in a ratio of 21 : 1.

Translation

[35] "The crown is fallen from our head: woe unto us, that we have sinned!"

[36] "The joy of our heart ceases; our dance is turned into mourning."   (cf. King James Version)

Summary

The goal of Chapter 3 has been to lay the groundwork for the recovery of the complete text and music for the Latin chants and songs in the Lddv in the most authentic form now possible. With this focus, the indebtedness of the play's Latin texts to both the medieval dramatic and liturgical traditions has been examined in detail.

The author of the comparatively early Lddv has been shown to be thoroughly familiar with the liturgical repertoire and customs. It is legitimate, therefore, in Chapter 4 to restore essentially from liturgical sources the twenty-six 'liturgical chants' that have been transmitted in MS A in a radically truncated form and without music. As Table 10 shows,

TABLE 10 THE CHANTS OF THE LDDV BY GENRE

I CHANTS FROM THE LITURGICAL TRADITION	
a) *Entire Chants*	
7 prolix responsories	[2] [4] [6-8] [20-21]
4 Office antiphons	[5] [10] [23-24]
1 processional antiphon	[26]
1 invitatory	[12]
1 offertory	[30]
b) *Sections of a Chant:*	
1 second half of an antiphon	[19]
1 repetenda of a responsory	[22]
2 verses from a "triple litany antiphon"	[31-32]
c) *Lesson Chants* (Intonations)	
6 chants in the Gospel tone	[14-15] [27-29] [33]
2 chants in the Lamentation tone	[35-36]
II CHANTS FROM THE DRAMATIC TRADITION	
2 decasyllabic stanzas (Easter plays)	[16-17]
7 directive calls	
6x *Silete*	[3'] [11'] [13'] [18'] [25'] [34']
1x *Silete longam horam*	[9']

many different genres exist among these restored chants; various kinds of antiphons, surprisingly many responsories and some other chants from Office or Mass have been taken directly from liturgical sources, not conveyed through other dramatic works. In addition, however, there are two decasyllabic 'travel stanzas' **[16]** *Omnipotens pater* and **[17]** *Sed eamus* and the seven directive calls of *Silete* which must be seen primarily in the context of medieval drama.

In the course of studying the large number of manuscripts containing the various chants, there was clear evidence of, on the one hand, a basic uniformity in the general transmission of these chants[1] and, on the other hand, undeniable deviations from it in most German sources through a few distinctive melodic features that characterize the 'German dialect of plainsong.' More particularly, the features of the 'German' phenomenon have been implemented in the melodies of German sources to different degrees, according to regional and other preferences (especially in religious orders).[2] Thus, sources originating within the boundaries of a certain ecclesiastical area, such as the archdiocese or the whole Church Province of Mainz, often differ slightly not only from 'Roman' but also from many other German, non-Mainz sources where these features may appear less frequently. Since Thuringia belonged to the archdiocese of Mainz, such considerations became decisive in selecting the 'collateral' sources to be used for a reasonably authentic restoration of the liturgical chants. As a result, essentially all of the twenty-six liturgical items in the Lddv could be restored through regional sources originating within the limited area delineated on the map of Figure 4, an area which comprises Thuringia, in the east of the Mainz diocese, with some surrounding sites.[3]

For the restoration of the chant items from the dramatic tradition, the geographical reach for 'collateral sources' had to be extended beyond the defined area, because the transmission of medieval plays is so much thinner than that of the liturgical chant repertoire. In order to attain a solid basis for the restoration of the two stanzas **[16]** and **[17]**, basically, all the musical evidence for the travel stanzas B1 and B3 in the various Easter and Passion plays has been studied comprehensively (cf. Tables 6 and 7). Three manuscripts, representing the east-central form of Easter plays, were retained as 'collateral' sources for chant **[16]**: BrslO, PragO.C, and Erl.III, all transmitting text and melody of the B1 stanza

---

[1]For the accuracy in the transmission of Gregorian chant in general see, among others, D. Hughes (1987), esp. pp. 398-401. Cf. above, pp. 7-8 with n27.

[2]Cf. above, pp. 73-74 with n7; also pp. 100-102 and 148-149.

[3]See the map on p. 86 and the list of the Collateral Sources below, pp. 313-315. The criteria of their selection have been discussed in more detail in Chapter 3, pp. 84-87.

in an almost identical form, one that seems to be supported also by the only Thuringian source for this stanza, the BeThO of the fourteenth century.[4] The recovery of chant [16] also provided the melody for chant [17].

In the special case of the directive calls (*Silete* and *Silete longam horam*), the kinship with drama is not quite as clear cut, however, since they show links to liturgical as well as dramatic traditions. In their function as structuring the sequence of dramatic events and dialogue in the play, they are parallel to and are comparable with similar directive calls in Mass and Office (for praying, kneeling down, standing up, etc.), which were always chanted in recitation. On the other hand, it seemed important to include and evaluate the musical evidence of the seven more complex notated *Silete* calls transmitted in later medieval plays. The analytical studies of these twofold connections resulted in a conjecture for the melody of the *Silete* calls which appears congruent with both directive calls in the Mainz Church and some of the extant *Silete* melodies in medieval drama (cf. Chapter 3 [3']).

Table 11 lists the selected regional sources in a 'geographical' survey and indicates the chants restored in Chapter 4 for which they provided the paradigm. The degree of authenticity that can be asserted for these restorations differs for the various categories of chants (musical chants, intoned items or directive calls).

All twenty-two genuinely musical chants, including the 'dramatic' stanzas [16-17] and even the two intoned items from the *Oratio Ieremiae* [35-36],[5] have been recovered in a highly authentic form since they could be transcribed from chant paradigms of carefully selected 'collateral sources,' most of which were in use in the fourteenth century in the larger Thuringian region, or at least in the Mainz Church Province. For the six items in the simple form of Gospel recitation (chants [14-15, 27-29, 33], the restorations are less 'secure.' Unlike the lesson texts from the Lamentations, no liturgical book transmits those specific texts with notation. The recitation formula chosen, i.e., the Gospel tone of the

---

[4]The BeThO has notation without lines which permits only a rough comparison.

[5] Because of their special and melodic recitation formula these two chants could almost be classified as 'musical items.'

TABLE 11A ORIGIN OF SOURCES USED FOR THE RESTORATION OF THE CHANTS
(■ PRINCIPLE SOURCES, □ SUPPORTING SOURCES; {} ITEMS RESTORED USING □)

SOURCES FOR THE RESTORATION	DATE	RESTORED MUSICAL ITEMS	
		TEXT ONLY	TEXT & MUSIC
MAINZ ARCHDIOCESE			
a) Thuringia			
■*A*Erf.50a	13+14c		[5]
□*B*Erf.81	14c	{12} [21]	
■*G*Erf.16	14c		[26]
□BeThO	14c	{16}	
b) Archdiocese at large			
■*A*Fri.117, ■124, ■129	14c		[2, 4, 6-8, 10, 19-24]
□*M*Fri.100	13c	{30}	
□*A*Fri.142	12c	{31-32}	
■*G*Brei.101 + □*M*Fri.100	15c		[30]
■*A*Mz.II,138	13/14c		[21]
+ □*A*Fri.124 + □*B*Erf.81			
□*Ps*Mz.D820	1607		{31-32}
MAINZ CHURCH PROVINCE			
■*A*Helm.485, □*B*Helm.145.1	14c		[12]
+ □*B*Erf.81			
□BeThO + □PragO.C	14c		{16} {17 music only}
□*M*Helm.35	14c	{31 ‖ }	{32}
OUTSIDE MAINZ CHURCH			
■BrslO + □PragO.C, □BeThO,	14c (14c)		[16] [17 music only]
+ □Erl.III	(15c)		
■*G*Lpz + □*A*Fri.142, □*M*Helm.35	14c		[31-32]

Accentus Moguntinus from *M*Halb.888 (cf. Figure 3, p. 80), appears authentic; the way in which the given texts of the Lddv have been set to this formula may contain some arbitrary elements, however.[6] Yet the

---

[6]The recitation of a text to any pre-existing melodic formula may differ according to local traditions or the interpretation of the person who delivers it. Even in the case of the Lamentations or the *Oratio Ieremiae*, which are always transmitted with notation, a consistent form of delivery was not guaranteed, as shown above for chants [35] and [36]: the recitation formula in MsMh.87/8 and LBrsw is practically the same, the performance reality (text setting) as transmitted in the two manuscripts, however, shows differences in style. See also Traub's collection of chants in Lipphardt-Roloff (1996) 6.2, where

form proposed here seems more authentic than any alternative. It is also more melodious and, consequently, less different from the musical items than Roman recitations would be. Since an intonation formula for the

TABLE 11B ORIGIN OF SOURCES USED FOR THE RESTORATION OF THE CHANTS
(■ PRINCIPLE SOURCES, □ SUPPORTING SOURCES; {} ITEMS RESTORED USING □)

SOURCES FOR THE RESTORATION	DATE	RESTORED INTONED ITEMS	
		TEXT	RECITATION FORMULA
MAINZ DIOCESE/PROVINCE			
■LFri.142 + □NT	14c	[14-15, 27-29, 33]	
■MHalb.888	1511		[14-15, 27-29, 33]
□LBrsw	14c	{35-36}	{35-36}
OUTSIDE MAINZ CHURCH?			
■MsMh.87/8 + □LBrsw	15c (14c)	[35-36]	[35-36]
		RESTORED DIRECTIVE ITEMS (*SILETE* AND *SILETE LONGAM HORAM*)	
MAINZ CHURCH PROVINCE			
■AugsO + □DonP	16c (15c)	[3', 9', 11', 13', 18', 25', 34']	
+ □MHalb.888	(1511)		
+ □*Manuductio*	(1672)		

simple *Silete* calls in medieval drama is nowhere transmitted, the one proposed here for the seven *Silete* calls, in a short and an extended version, is definitely a conjecture. While not 'authentic' in itself, it is based on the combined evidence of various authentic sources from the Mainz Church Province: MHalb.888 and *Manuductio* as liturgical, and AugsO and DonP with their extant *Silete* melodies as dramatic sources (cf. Chapter 3 [3'], Figures 7-11).

In the following list of 'collateral sources,' those actually used for the restoration of one or several chants in the edition in Chapter 4, are preceded by ■; those preceded by □ in most cases support the selected transcriptions

---

some notated recitation texts in different late medieval plays exhibit very different melodic forms: for instance the juxtaposed versions of BozP 1495 (MS B) and AdmP (pp. 79, 95), while the *Ecce homo* (p. 48) is notated in an identical form in both plays.

(cf. Table 11). A more precise identification of the sources used for and/or compared with the chosen transmission of each chant is given in the apparatus that concludes and summarizes the discussion of that chant in the respective section of Chapter 3.

Collateral Sources for the Edition of the Latin Chants
(a) Liturgical Sources

■AErf.50a •   *Antiphonae Dominicales* in the *Liber Chori BMV*, Erfurt, part III; 13th c.
               Karlsruhe, Badische Landesbibliothek, MS St. Peter perg. 50a, fols. 147v-157v.

■AFri.117 •   *Antiphonal of St. Peter*, Fritzlar (begins 3rd Sunday in Advent).
               Kassel, Gesamthochschul-Bibliothek, 2o MS theol. 117; 1344-1348.

■AFri.124 •   *Antiphonal of St. Peter*, Fritzlar
               Kassel, Gesamthochschul-Bibliothek, 2o MS theol. 124; 1367-1378.

■AFri.129 •   *Antiphonal of St. Peter*, Fritzlar
               Kassel, Gesamthochschul-Bibliothek, 2o MS theol. 129; 1344-1348.

□AFri.142 •   Fragment of an *Antiphonal of St. Peter*, Fritzlar (12th c.)
               Kassel, Gesamthochschul-Bibliothek, 2o MS theol. 142, fols. *Ir-*IIv.

■AHelm.485 •   *Antiphonal from Hildesheim* (?) or *Münster* (?)
               Wolfenbüttel, Herzog August Bibliothek, Cod. Guelf. 485 Helmst.; 13/14c.

■AMz.II,138 •   *Antiphonal of the Weissfrauenkloster*, Mainz (?), monastic [Cistercian]
               Mainz, Stadtbibliothek, MS II,138; 13/14th c.

□BErf.81   *Breviary of Erfurt and Bursfelde*, monastic
               Vatican, Biblioteca Apostolica Vaticana, MS Rossi 81; 14th c.

□BHelm.145.1 • *Breviarium of Kloster Marienberg*, Helmstedt
               Wolfenbüttel, Herzog August Bibliothek, Cod. Guelf. 145.1 Helmst.; 14th c.

■GBrei.101 •   *Gradual of Breitenau* (Melsungen, East of Fritzlar), monastic
               Kassel, Gesamthochschul-Bibliothek, 2o MS theol. 101; 15th c.

■GErf.16 •   *Gradual of the Neuwerkskloster,* Erfurt (Augustinian canon-
                esses)
                Karlsruhe, Badische Landesbibliothek, MS St. Peter perg.
                16; 14th c.
□GErf.44 • ‖   *Gradual of the Neuwerkskloster,* Erfurt (Augustinian canon-
                esses)
                Karlsruhe, Badische Landesbibliothek, MS St. Peter perg.
                44; 14th c.
■GLpz •   *Graduale der St. Thomaskirche,* Leipzig
                MS in 1930 in Leipzig, Archiv von St. Thomas, cod. 371;
                14th c. FACS Wagner (1930-1932)
□LBrsw •   *Lectionarium of the Stiftskirche St. Blasii,* Braunschweig
                Wolfenbüttel, Niedersächsisches Staatsarchiv, VII B Hs
                203; 14th c.
■LFri.142   *Lectionarium* [Homiliar] *of St. Peter,* Fritzlar
                Kassel, Gesamthochschul-Bibliothek, 2○ MS theol. 142;
                1367-1389.
□*Manuductio* • *Manuductio Ad Cantum choralem Gregoriano-Moguntinum.*
                Mainz 1672
□*M*Fri.100 •   *Missale plenum of St. Peter,* Fritzlar
                Kassel, Gesamthochschul-Bibliothek, 2○ MS theol. 100;
                13th c.
■*M*Halb.888 • *Missale celeberrimi Halberstattensis episcopatus.* Mainz,
                1511. Incunabulum.
□*M*Helm.26•   *Missal of a Braunschweig monastery*
                Wolfenbüttel, Herzog August Bibliothek, Cod. Guelf. 26
                Helmst.; 1456.
□*M*Helm.35 •   *Missal of the Leuchtenhof,* Hildesheim
                Wolfenbüttel, Herzog August Bibliothek, Cod. Guelf. 35
                Helmst.; 1462.
□*M*Helm.38•   *Missal of unknown provenance*
                Wolfenbüttel, Herzog August Bibliothek, Cod. Guelf. 38
                Helmst.; 15th c.
■MSMh.87/8 •   *Vocabularius* etc. (fols. 387r-388r: *Oracio ieremie prophete*).
                Mühlhausen, Thüringen, Stadtarchiv, MS 87/8 [*olim* 60/8];
                1466.
□*Pr*Mz.110 •   *Processional of the Mainz Cathedral* (Pars aestivalis)
                Mainz, Bibliothek des bischöflichen Priesterseminars, MS
                110; 1704.

□*Pr*Mz.II.74 •   *Processional of the Domsänger von Eltz* (Pars aestivalis)
                 Mainz, Stadtbibliothek, MS II,74; 15th c.
□*Pr*Mz.II.303 • *Processional of the Mainz Cathedral*
                 Mainz, Stadtbibliothek, MS II,303 15th c.
□*Ps*Mz.D820 •   *Enchiridion Psalmorum,* printed Mainz 1607.

(b) Dramatic Sources

■AugsO •   *Augsburger Osterspiel* ("Feldkircher O")
                 Feldkirch, Kapuzinerkloster, MS Liturg. 1 rtr.; 16th c.
□BeThO •   *Berliner Thüringisches Osterspielfragment*
                 Berlin, Staatsbibliothek Preussischer Kulturbesitz, MS germ.
                 2° 757, fols. 4r-5v; 14c.
■BrslO •   *Breslauer Osterspielfragment*
                 Breslau, Bibliotheka Uniwersytecka, MS I Q 226a; 14th c.
                 (?)
□DonP •   *Donaueschinger Passionsspiel*
                 Karlsruhe, Badische Landesbibliothek, MS Don.137; 15th c.
□Erl.III •   *Erlauer Osterspiel* ["Erlau III"]
                 Eger (Hungary), Erzbischöfliche Diözesanbibliothek
                 (Föegyházmegyei Könyvtár), MS B.V.6; fols. 107r-116r;
                 15th c.
□PragO.C •   *Prager Osterspiel "C"*
                 Prague, University Library, MS I.B.12, fols. 135v-137v;
                 14th c.

The liturgical and dramatic sources listed here and used in Chapter 4 to restore the musical and intoned items of the play qualify as 'collateral sources' to the MS A of the Lddv; most of them originate in the geographical area delineated in Figure 4, p. 86. Being reliable in their transmission of chant, they can essentially ensure that the Latin texts and restored chants in Chapter 4 will closely approximate what must be postulated as the hitherto much undervalued Latin foundation and liturgical core of the extant Thuringian Lddv. This restored core should, at the same time, remain open for textual or musical adjustments should new identifications and manuscript evidence emerge.

Chapter 4

The Sung Liturgical Core of the
Ludus de Decem Virginibus
with Text and Music Restored
from 'Collateral' Medieval Sources

The Latin chants of the Lddv, transmitted in MS A with no musical notation and usually with their incipits only, are presented here with their
complete texts and their melodies. The purpose is to reclaim for the
macaronic Thuringian play the liturgico-musical dimension which is al-
luded to again and again in the stage directions. Such an enterprise
implies necessarily the 'edition' of large parts of the play that are not
transmitted in its only extant manuscript. The edition of the Latin chants,
therefore, has to transcend the frame of their dramatic source, and this
is, *per definitionem*, an experiment.[1]

The way in which MS A of the Lddv has been 'transcended' here
corresponds, in principle, to the way in which, in the Middle Ages, the
rubrics of a ritual book or, for that matter, the script of a play referring
to chants by incipits would have been complemented through other liturgical books that provided the entire text and music of the chants. The
difference is that such collateral books would have been readily available
at a medieval church in Thuringia, whereas now, some six hundred years
later, painstaking research is required to select among the many surviv-

---

[1]Andreas Traub (1994b) 255, has clearly pointed out the need to do this for all
medieval plays that indicate the Latin chants only by incipits: "Hier wird die Edition den
Rahmen der Quelle überschreiten müssen." For reasons beyond his control, Traub was
unable to carry out this resolution in the edition of the Sterzing plays. However, in the
complementary volume Lipphardt-Roloff (1996) 6.2, he provided an approximate form
of the complete text and music for most of the 'incipit chants' of these plays (ed.
Lipphardt-Roloff [1980-1996] 1-5) from other, mostly liturgical sources as a kind of
'Liederbuch' ('chant book') to the plays (Lipphardt-Roloff 6.2: 5 note *). See also Traub
(1994c) 211, 216, and in Lipphardt-Roloff 6.2: 5, 11; Janota (1994) 118; Dreimüller
(1935) 1: 82, 99, 108, (1950) 27-29.

ing liturgical books those that may qualify, if only by approximation, as collateral sources for the particular chants in the Thuringian play.

If, in addition to restoring the texts and melodies of the Latin chants as a kind of 'Liederbuch' for the play, I presume to present these chants in their entirety together with the pertinent rubrics as "the sung liturgical core" of the Lddv, this may strike some as an audacious proposition. Yet the studies in Chapter 3 of the thirty-six chants in their contextual sequence have shown an astounding dramatic coherence within the play's 'Latin-liturgical level'; the vernacular passages up to and including chant [33] offer little more than paraphrases to the Latin paradigm.[2] The experiment, therefore, to present the restored Latin chants in their Latin-only context, seems warranted.

A. NOTES ON THE EDITION OF THE CHANTS

The Sources Used for the Edition

The leading source for the edition is, of course, the only extant manuscript of the macaronic play, Mühlhausen/Thuringia, Stadtarchiv, MS 87/20 (formerly MS 60/20); it is always cited by its siglum MS A. The collateral and supporting sources that serve to 'transcend' this basic dramatic frame by providing the complete chants for the play are listed in alphabetical order of their sigla on pp. 313-315.[3] They have been selected in the study sections of Chapter 3 and are always cited by their sigla.[4] Table 11A-B and the map of Figure 4 (p. 86) help locate the places of origin of these sources within Thuringia or the Church Province of Mainz.

The Presentation of the Text

The edition below is of the play's Latin foundation only: all vernacular texts of MS A and all Latin rubrics relating to them are omitted. The extent of these omissions is indicated in each case by the number of vernacular lines, set in pointed brackets < >.

---

[2]Cf. the account given below, pp. 345-347. On the 'vernacular level,' text and action are greatly expanded only from l. 297 to the end (l. 576), i.e. before and after the last two Latin chants [35] and [36]; cf. Tables 5 and 12.

[3]For more detailed information on these sources, see the List of all the Liturgical and Dramatic Sources, pp. xv-xxxvi.

[4]For the principles of selection, see pp. 84-87.

The text of MS A and of all the restored chants is printed as faithfully as possible: no attempt has been made to normalize the spelling in any of the manuscripts used, except for the letters s and u, which in MS A are sometimes written as the long-shafted ∫ or as v respectively. Abbreviations have been silently expanded,[5] except for the verbal forms in the stage directions; since it is often open to interpretation whether the indicative or the subjunctive forms are meant my expansions of the verb endings are marked by *italics*.[6] Emendations, in square brackets [ ], are kept to a minimum. The names of the DRAMATIS PERSONAE are highlighted through small capitals. The line numbering of Schneider's edition of the Lddv is indicated in the margins of the Latin stage directions to mark their place within the entire macaronic play. Arabic page numbers between slash marks approximate the modern pagination of MS A, which is written in two columns (a and b) on pages 94b-100a.[7] The Latin chants have been numbered in sequence, as throughout this study, with the numbers in bold set in square brackets.

For the presentation of the chant texts, I chose to mark the first word in the manner of medieval liturgical books with special, though considerably less ornate initials: larger initials for musical items, simpler ones for items in liturgical recitation. In the responsories, I tried to imitate the use in manuscripts of different size letters to mark the beginnings of the *respond*, the *repetenda* and the *verse*, which serve as visual guides for the chant's structural elements and as clues to their performance.[8] In addition, the verse of a responsory is always indicated through a special *V*-abbreviation imitating manuscript customs. Although, in the perfor-

---

[5]For those abbreviations that are rendered differently in the existing editions of the Lddv, see the studies in Chapter 1, with a summary on pp. 33-34.

[6]The siglum ₃, which customarily stands for a final *-et, -us, -m,* or the enclitic *-que* (cf. Capelli [1973] xxxi-xxxiii, [1982] 20-22), seems to be employed in MS A indiscriminately for the verbal endings *-et, -at, -it* and, with a nasal stroke above, *-ent, -ant* and, possibly, *-unt* (ll. 42a, 383h). In my expansions I have generally opted for the indicative forms, limiting the subjunctive forms to those eight occurrences where they are clearly written as such, with two additional forms for ll. 42a and 383h.

[7]Schneider in her edition of the Lddv (1964) refers to the manuscript pages as folios 47v-50v. The concordance between the two ways of page/folio counting is as follows: MS A, p. 94b = Schneider, fol. 47vb; pp. 95-96 = fol. 48r-v; pp. 97-98 = fol. 49r-v; pp. 99-100 = fol. 50r-v.

[8]For the importance of initials of different sizes in medieval liturgical books see, e.g. A. Hughes (1982) 117-118, 161-164, 198.

mance of the chants, especially of the responsories, delivery alternates frequently between solo and choral singing, no attempt has been made here to facilitate such a distribution of sections of the chants to solo singers or ensemble groups among the performers, i.e. no additional stage directions beyond the rubrics in MS A have been proposed for this purpose, except for some additions to the rubric for chant [21].[9] On the other hand, the *repetenda* section of responsories and, in some cases, the doxology, which in liturgical manuscripts are usually indicated only with their beginning word(s), are always presented here with the full text and melody. Those chants of the Lddv which have been identified in Chapter 3 as a section only of a liturgical chant ([19, 22]) or as a fragment of a liturgical reading ([14-15, 27-29, 33, 35-36]) are presented here as independent chants.

The Transcriptions of the Chants from the Collateral Sources
The notation in almost all sources used for restoring the chants of the Thuringian play is some form of 'Gothic' or *hufnagel* on a four- or five-line stave, the notation customary in most German and eastern European sources of the later Middle Ages;[10] only a few of the selected sources have square notation. As a rule, the liturgical books are notated with great care; even though the neumes may often appear crowded and compacted as a space-saving practice in manuscript writing, the text setting is usually clearly discernable.

For my transcriptions I used the standard modernized notation of plainsong on a five-line stave in which the medieval *F*- and *C*-clefs are replaced by a 'transposing' treble clef, signifying that the notes should be read one octave lower.[11] It must be understood, however, that the

---

[9]A 'dramatic' presentation of the chants is deferred to the planned new edition of the Lddv.
[10]See facsimiles 3-6 in the Appendix. Cf. Hiley (1993) 438-441 (plates 17-18).
[11]The decision to use modernized transcriptions of the medieval melodies was dictated by the desire to render the musical material accessible and understandable to readers and users without musicological training. This decision is made in full awareness of the "vast gulf" that exists between medieval and modern notation and its interpretation. The differences between the two systems have perhaps best been described by A. Hughes (1989) xxvii-xxviii. The solution proposed by Traub to use a 'regulated' kind of Gothic notation carries over the medieval barriers to an immediate understanding of the music into modern publications (cf. Traub [1994b] 256-257 and in Lipphardt-Roloff [1996] 6.2: 8-9, partly based on Lipphardt in Lipphardt-Roloff [1986] 1: 10-12). It seemed more advisable here, where multiple sources are involved, to offer modernized transcriptions and

medieval notation unlike the modern system does not imply absolute pitches. The clef is, therefore, enclosed in brackets. Moreover, the melodic possibilities, basically limitless in a modern notational system, in plainsong are restricted usually to an octave, according to the definition of each of the eight modes.[12] As an attempt to bridge this gap between the two systems, the transcriptions of the chants are prefixed with a brief diagram of the mode of the chant, indicating the tonal range or 'ambitus' of the mode and marking in it the *finalis* (o) and the *subfinalis* (•), which is one degree below the octave range and serves as an important extra note in many chants.[13]

The neumes of the manuscripts are rendered in the transcriptions by stemless round note heads (•) to indicate rhythmical neutrality. Table 1 on Gothic Notation (p. 11) gives a survey of the various Gothic neumes and their equivalents in a modern transcription. A 'regular' (pitch by pitch) transcription of longer groupings of notes with extended melismas would take up considerable space, with the result that prolonged melodic phrases and melismas could not easily be grasped in their totality. The notes belonging to one syllable or word of text, therefore, have been crowded together, leaving some space between the notated words for easier readability of both text and music. Also in the service of readability, horizontal brackets (⌐⌐) are placed above the note groupings that pertain to one syllable of text or to one melodic unit within a melisma.[14] Instead of trying to indicate faithfully all the ligatures

---

provide some facsimiles (in the appendix) for comparison. Cf. the arguments by Hiley (1993) 400, supporting modern transcriptions.

[12]The eight modes are briefly described above, p. 142 n9.

[13]Cf. Apel (1958) 135. Visual presentation of the modes are offered also by Seay (1975) 33 and Johner-Pfaff (1956) 58. Occasionally, other criteria such as the intervallic structure of the melody can be more decisive than the ambitus for the modal assignment of a chant. This is the case, e.g. in chant [6] *Sint lumbi vestri* with an 'excessive' melodic range. Although it descends to the plagal fourth below the *finalis*, the chant is traditionally classified as a mode 1 responsory; cf. above, Chapter 3 [6], pp. 142-143. For the modal assignment of chants with an excessive tonal range or even a limited range (e.g. chant [16]), see Apel (1958) 148-152 and C. Meyer (2000) 204-206.

[14]These note groupings may comprise several sequences of ligatures, single and compound neumes. Ligatures are notational symbols 'binding' together two or more notes that are to be sung over a syllable of text. These and other note-groupings are an ex-

or compound neumes used in the manuscripts, such syllable markers have been preferred for two reasons. First, different manuscripts consulted often use different neumatic symbols to notate the same melodic movement; second, and more importantly, the manuscripts in many cases show clusters of ligatures and other neumes over one syllable of text in a very compressed way, often leaving it open to interpretation where one 'ligature' ends and another begins. A slur is used, therefore, to mark only those of the ligatures that literally 'bind together' two or more notes to form a single graphic symbol.[15] The horizontal bracket seemed a reasonable alternative, serving as a graphic sign to assemble all the note heads intended to indicate the melodic movement over one syllable of text.

On the other hand, two types of notational symbols, the strophic (repercussive) and the liquescent neumes (cf. Table 1), are rendered in close imitation of the medieval manuscript forms, because they imply not only pitch, but apparently also a special kind of performance. Strophic (or repercussive) neumes are represented by rhombic signs resembling an apostrophe (*♪♪*); they indicate repetition of the same pitch over a syllable. Liquescent neumes, occurring primarily over liquid and nasal sounds (l, r, m, n), occasionally over diphthongs or consonant clusters, are drawn as large, round apostrophe-like symbols (*,* or *,* or *♪*); they probably indicate a pitch direction between two pitches, some kind of a gliding performance, which seems to be closely linked to the pronunciation of the 'liquid' word sound.[16]

The b^b, which serves special functions in medieval music, primarily to temper the *tritonus*, is usually placed before the group of notes in which it occurs and it is not repeated within the same stave; this practice is basically maintained in the transcriptions.

Additional signs, used only sparingly in the sources, are employed to punctuate the structure of some chants, particularly the responsories. Distinct vertical strokes (≣) through the stave mark the beginning

---

tremely compact way of relating a long sequence of notes to a single syllable that are unique to medieval notation and provide a very condensed visual image for a quick grasp of long melismatic lines. 'Modern' Solesmes/Vatican books use square notation for this purpose.

[15]This excludes ligatures such as *scandicus, climacus, pes subbipunctis, virga cum punctis*.

[16]Cf. Stevens (1986) 507; A. Hughes (1989a) 57.

of *repetenda*, verse and doxology. In the offertory **[30]** *Recordare,* such strokes are retained from *G*Brei.101, where they indicate sections of the melodic line. The end of the solo intonation of a chant is rarely specified in the sources; the short double strokes (≝) on the stave after the first or the first few words are my proposal as to where the other singers might join the soloist. Single short strokes (≝) in the top part of the stave indicate proposed breathing places in the performance of the chants.

Since all of the melodies and most of the chant texts are missing in MS A of Mühlhausen, a variety of brackets are used to enclose the additions and reflect the rudimentary transmission of the play's Latin-liturgical dimension:

[ ]   large square brackets on the stave mark the addition of music only;

( )   somewhat larger angled brackets enclose the addition of both text and music as well as the modern treble clef;

⟨ ⟩   large pointed brackets are used within the bracketed sections of some responsories to enclose the doxology, if this is transmitted in the liturgical sources; it may have no relevance for the play's performance.

The Apparatus

The 'textual apparatus' at the bottom of the pages of this edition pertains only to the stage directions. For technical and other reasons, the apparatus for each of the restored chants is provided at the end of each study section of Chapter 3 as a summary of the pertinent comparative discussions; it can also be found at the end of section E in the corresponding entry in the Catalogue. For more details see Chapter 3, pp. 87-88.

Some Special Remarks

The restored Latin 'core' of the Lddv as presented below may be debatable in some details; yet every effort has been made to restore it with as much authenticity as presently attainable. In at least one respect I made an arbitrary decision already, which can easily be altered. In four of the seven responsories transcribed here, i.e., in chants **[2]**, **[4]**, **[6]**, and **[20]**, I retained the lesser doxology, found as the 'second verse' in most of the sources. Since the lesser doxology *Gloria patri etc.* was sung only in the last responsory of each nocturn of Matins, it is doubtful whether it was meant to be sung in the Lddv. On the other hand, maintaining the doxology in these four responsories would make tremendous liturgical sense in this very liturgically oriented play, particularly in an earlier, possibly Latin-only version. The first three of these responsories are sung in turn by the main performers and the choir at the beginning of the play — chant [2] by the ten *Virgines*, chant [4] by the *Corus*, and chant [6] by the *Angeli*. With the additional singing of the *Gloria patri* at the end of the responsories, each of these groups of players would honor the Trinity at the very outset of the performance. Thus the whole presentation would be understood as a service.[17] And at the end of chant [20], the repeated *Regnum mundi*, the chanting of the doxology by the *Prudentes* only at their encounter with the heavenly Bridegroom would be equally significant; indeed, it is later echoed by another trinitarian praise, the antiphon [24] *Gloria et honor* sung by the *Angeli*. Such liturgical extensions of the responsories, however, would have been more likely, if at all, in an earlier, purely Latin liturgical drama, not in the Latin-German form of the play that survives today.

Since it has not yet been possible to match the incipit *Testimonium domini* of the introductory responsory [1] of the Lddv with an appropriate chant in the liturgical repertoire, the following Lenten introit *Lex domini* may serve as a substitute should it be desired to have an opening chant, e.g. in the case of a performance of the play.[18] The text of this introit for the Saturday of the second week in Quadragesima is certainly similar to the text meant with the given incipit in the Lddv; the melody of the responsory and its verse, however, would be different. The search for a medieval responsory *Testimonium domini* will have to continue; it may have belonged to a very localized liturgy in Thuringia.

---

[17]In a similar way, Traub (1994c) 211, claims liturgical propriety for the chants used in the much later Sterzing plays: "Das Geistliche Spiel ist als representatio heilsgeschichtlicher Ereignisse eine Form des Gottesdienstes ... . So ist dem Gesang in den Spielen grundsätzlich derselbe Rang zuzugestehen wie in der Liturgie, und die Ausführenden werden sich nach diesem Vorbild gerichtet haben."

[18]Cf. the discussion in Chapter 3 [1], also Catalogue [1D3], p. F2. Other textually related chants are listed in Catalogue [1D1-2], pp. F1-F2.

THE INTROIT *LEX DOMINI* FOR THE SECOND SATURDAY IN LENT[19]

SABBATO

[19]The introit here is taken from the *Graduale Romanum, GR* (1974) 86, for the first week in Lent. In medieval books, this introit consistently begins the Saturday Mass of the second week in Lent (see Catalogue [1D3], p. F2). Compare the versions of this introit in *G*Lpz, fol. 28v (ed. Wagner [1930] 1: 57), or in *G*Pat, fol. 40r, where the melodies show the special features of the German dialect of plainsong.

B. THE SUNG LATIN CORE OF THE LDDV

/94b/ Se*quitur* [ludus] de decem virginibus.

0a Primo educa*tur* DOMINICA PERSONA cum MARIA et ANGELIS
cantando Responsorium
[1]
Testimonium domini ...

0g Deinde VIRGINES cant*ant* Responsorium

0o quo finito ANGELI cant*ant*

[3']

S i - le - te.

<6 vernacular lines, 1-6>

6a CORUS cant*at* Responsorium

6d DOMINICA PERSONA cant*at* et surgit

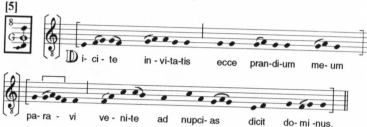

i- ci - te in - vi-ta-tis ecce pran-di-um me- um
pa- ra - vi ve - ni-te ad nupci- as dicit do- mi -nus.

/95a/ < 16 vernacular lines, 7-22 >

22a DUO ANGELI vad*unt* ad Virgines cantando

int lumbi vestri pre - - - - - - cincti et lu-
cer - ne ardentes in ma- ni- bus ves - tris. Et vos simi-
les ho-mi-ni - - bus ex-pec-tan -ti - - bus do - - -
- - - minum su - um quando rever-ta - - - tur a
nup-ci - - is. Vi-gi-la - te ergo qui-a
ne- sci -tis qua ho-ra do-minus ves - ter ventu-rus sit. Et vos
simi-les ho -mi-ni - - bus ex-pec-tan -ti - - bus do -

- - - - - - minum su - - um quan-do re-ver- ta - - - tur
a nup-ci - - is. ℣ Glo- ri - a
pa-tri et fi - li - o et spi-ri - - tu - i sanc - to. Et vos simi-
les ho-mi-ni - - bus ex-pec-tan - ti - - bus do - - -
- - - minum su - um quando rever- ta - - - tur a
nup-ci - - is.

<Finito Responsorio: 20 vernacular lines, 23-42>

42a ANGELI reced*unt*

42b PRUDENTES cant*ant* Responsorium quod PRIMA incipiet [*sic*]

[7]

2
a
D
E -mende - mus in me - li - us quod igno-ran - - ter
pec - - ca-vi - - - mus ne sub-i -to preoc-cu-pa - - ti di -e mortis
quera -mus spa-ci - um pe-ni-ten-ci-e et inve-ni-re non pos-

-si - - mus. **A**tten-de do- mi - ne et mise-re - re quia

pecca - vi - mus ti - - bi. ℣ **P** ec-ca - -vimus cum pa-tri -bus

no - stris in-iu-ste e- gimus i-niqui-ta - - tem fe - - ci - - mus.

A tten-de do -mi - ne et mise-re - re quia pecca - vi -

mus ti - - bi.

/95b/   < 30 vernacular lines, 43-72 >

72a   PRIMA FATUA incipit Responsorium

[8]

T ribu-la - rer si ne-sci- rem mise-ri- cor - -

-dias tu - as do-mi - - ne tu di- xi - sti nolo mor-tem

pec-ca - to - - ris sed ut con -ver-tatur et vi - - vat. **Q**ui

chana - neam et publi-ca - - num vo-ca - sti ad

pe - ni - - - - ten-ti - - am. ℣ **E**t pe- trum la - cri-

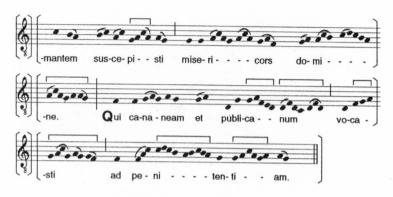

<28 vernacular lines, 73-100>

100a Tunc FATUE corizando et cum magno gaudio vad*unt* ad alium locum.

100d ANGELI

[9']

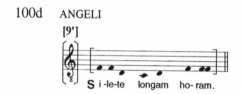

100f TERTIA PRUDENS incipiet [Antiphonam][1]

[10]

---

[1]Antiphonam] *Responsorium* MS A; cf. the discusson in Chapter 3 [10], esp. pp. 157-158. The *incipiet* of MS A, here and in l. 42b, could be emended to either the indicative form *incipit* or the subjunctive *incipiat*.

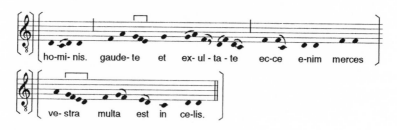

<16 vernacular lines, 101-116>

116a   ANGELI

[11']

116c   Tunc OMNES FATUE habeant convivium, depona*n*t se quasi dormiant.

116e   Tunc TERTIA incipit Invitatorium

[12]

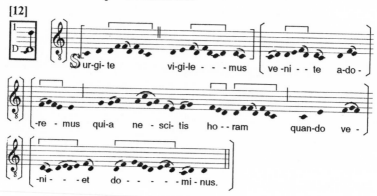

/96a/   <center><24 vernacular lines, 117-140></center>

140a   ANGELI

[13']

140c   OMNES FATUE vada*nt* ad PRUDENTES et QUINTA dic*it*

<8 vernacular lines, 141-148>

148a   QUARTA PRUDENS r*espondet*

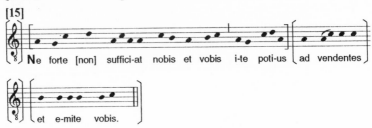

<8 vernacular lines, 149-156>

156a   Tunc FATUE vad*unt* ad emendum oleum. PRIMA cant*at*[2]

<12 vernacular lines, 157-168>

168a   Et tunc SECUNDA FATUA cantat

[2]The refrain *Heu quantus est noster dolor* would probably be sung by the rest of the *Fatue* as in chant [17] ('Alie respondent'). For the arrangement of stanzas [16-17] and their paraphrases in MS A, see the apparatus on p. 37 nn 70-72, also p. 189.

qui caret hoc carebit glori- e.

168e   ALIE respond*ent*

[Refr.] Heu quantus est noster do- lor.

<8 vernacular lines, 169-176>

/96b/
176a   ANGELI

[18']

S i - le - te.

176c   DOMINICA PERSONA vadat ad Prudentes cum ANGELIS cantando

[19]

Ec-ce sponsus ve -nit exi-te ob -vi-am e-i.

<10 vernacular lines, 177-186>

186a   PRUDENTES cant*ant*

[20]

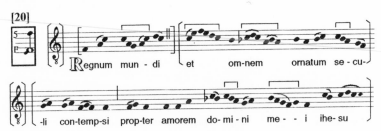

Regnum mun - di et om-nem ornatum se - cu-

-li con-temp-si prop-ter amorem do- mi - ni me - - i ihe- su

< quo finito Responsorio: 10 vernacular lines, 187-196 >

196a   [DOMINICA PERSONA][3] ducens eas per manus[4] cant*at*
    [ANGELIS prosequentibus][5]

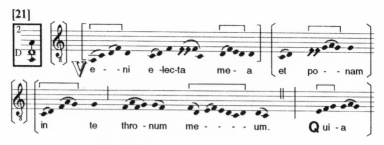

---

[3]Dominica Persona] *Quinta Prudens* MS A; all editions of the Lddv. Cf. Chapter 3 [21].
[4]per manus] MS A. *Primarius* All editions of the Lddv. Cf. Chapter 1, p. 31.
[5]Angelis prosequentibus] proposed here as an aid to the performance of the responsory. *Note to p. 335, line 3: letter names above the notation of the verse indicate typically 'German' intervals found in other German transmissions.

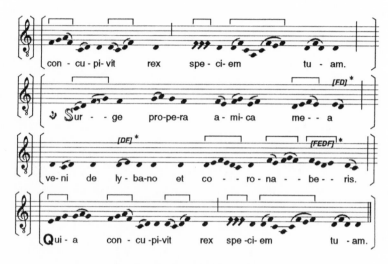

con - cu - pi- vit   rex   spe - ci- em   tu - am.

ᵕ **S**ur - - ge   pro-pe-ra   a - mi- ca   me - - a   [FD]*

ve- ni   de   ly - ba-no   et   co - - ro - na - - be - - ris.   [DE]* [FEDF]*

Qui - a   con - cu -pi-vit   rex   spe -ci- em   tu - am.

<12 vernacular lines, 197-208>

208a   MARIA superponans eis coronas cantando

[22]

Trans- i - - te   ad   me   om - - - - -nes   qui

concu-pis-ci-tis   me   et   a   ge-ne- ra- ti - o - ni-bus

me - is   ad-im-ple - mi - - ni.   **A**l - le - -lu -ia.

al - - le -lu - - ia.

<6 vernacular lines, 209-214>

214a   PRUDENTES cant*ant*

[23]

Sanc - tus   sanc - -tus   sanc- tus   dominus   de - us   om-ni-

-po-tens qui e-rat et qui est et qui ven-tu-rus est.

214e   *et* ANGELI

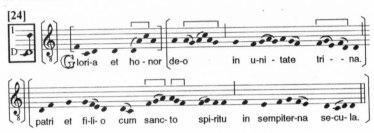

Glori-a et ho-nor deo in u-ni-tate tri - - na.

patri et fi-li-o cum sanc-to spi-ritu in sempiter-na se-cu-la.

< 14 vernacular lines, 215-228 >

228a   DOMINICA PERSONA habeat magnum convivium.

228c   ANGELI

S i-le - te.

228e   FATUE vada*n*t ad nuptias cantando

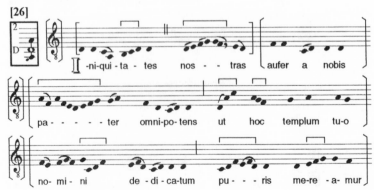

-ni-qui-ta-tes nos - - tras aufer a nobis

pa - - - - - ter omni-po-tens ut hoc templum tu-o

no-mi-ni de-di-ca-tum pu - - ris me-re-a-mur

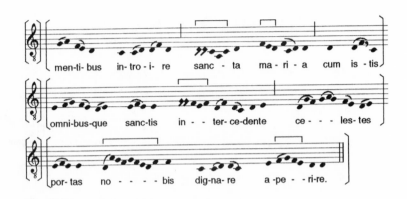

men-ti- bus in- tro - i- re sanc - ta ma - ri - a cum is - tis

omni-bus-que sanc-tis in - - ter- ce-dente ce - - - les- tes

por- tas no - - - - - bis dig-na- re a -pe - - ri-re.

/97a/   <8 vernacular lines, 229-236>

236a   DOMINICA PERSONA

[27]

Qui tempus congru-e peni-ten-[ci-e] perdi-derit frustra

cum pre-ci-bus ad reg-ni ia - nu-a[m] pervene-rit.

<4 vernacular lines, 237-240>

240a   TERTIA FATUA

[28]

Domi-ne domi-ne a-pe-ri no-bis.

<4 vernacular lines, 241-244>

244a   DOMINICA PERSONA

[29]

A -men a-men dico vo-bis nesci-o vos.

<6 vernacular lines, 245-250, by DOMINICA PERSONA
+ 6 vernacular lines, 251-256, by QUARTA FATUA>

256a   OMNES FATUE prostrate in terram cant*ant*

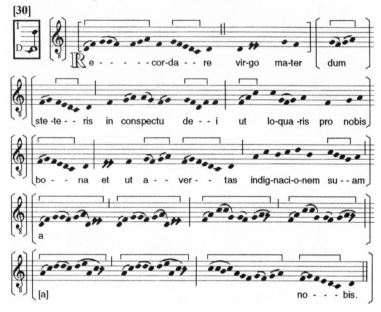

<8 vernacular lines, 257-264>

264a   QUINTA

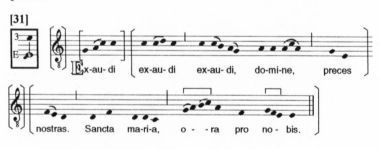

<8 vernacular lines, 265-272, by QUINTA FATUA,
+ 6 vernacular lines, 273-278, by MARIA>

278a   MARIA flexis /**97b**/ genibus cant*at*

[32]

Mi-se-re- re   mi-se-re- re   mi-se-re - re   populo   tu - o

quem   re-de-misti,   chri-ste,   sanguine   tu- o.   ne   in   e- ter-num

i-ras-ca-ris   no - bis.

< 12 vernacular lines, 279-290 >

290a   DOMINICA PERSONA ad Mariam

[33]

Celum et   terra   transibunt   verbum autem me - um   in   eternum permanet.

< 6 vernacular lines, 291-296, by DOMINICA PERSONA
/**98a**/   + 87 vernacular lines, 296a-339 (Devils' scene);
         339a-383 (Mary's 2nd intercession) >

383a   ANGELI

[34']

S i - le - te.

383c   DYABOLI circumd*ant* eas kathena.

383d PRIMA cant*at*

[35]

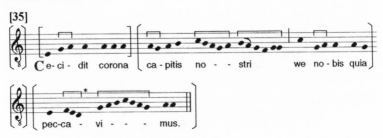

e- ci - dit corona ca - pitis no - - stri we no - bis quia

pec-ca - vi - - - mus.

383g/h Tunc OMNES FATUE facia*nt* pendere coronas in capite et plang*ant.*

/98b/ < 26 vernacular lines, 384-409 >

409a SECUNDA FATUA

[36]

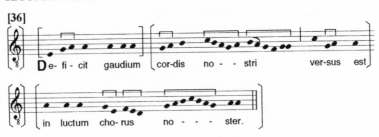

De- fi - cit gaudium cor-dis no - - stri ver-sus est

in luctum cho- rus no - - - ster.

/99a/b/ < 116 vernacular lines, 410-525 (lamentations in couplets) >

525a Post hec FATUE vada*nt* inter populum cantando planctos [*sic*].

/99b/100a/ < 60 vernacular lines, 525a-576
(lamentations in 12 stanzas with refrain) >

Explicit Ludus de Decem virginibus etc. [*sic*].

Conclusion

The research of this study, designed to restore the Latin foundation of the Lddv, was guided by one basic principle: that the Latin rubrics and the chant incipits in MS Mühlhausen 87/20 (pp. 94b-100a) must be taken seriously, and that their transcription, interpretation and restoration must be handled with extreme care. Consequently, every effort was made to ensure that abbreviations and scribal peculiarities were clearly understood and accurately reflected in the transcription.[1] The result was a new edition of the Latin excerpts from MS A in Chapter 1, pp. 34-41.

Those Latin remnants, notably the stage directions, were thoroughly analyzed in Chapter 2 with a view to interpreting correctly the nature of the chants, the general design of the play, and the structure of its performance. The play was shown to abound in liturgical singing and recitation of various kinds. This did not come as a surprise since general statements praising the play's oratorio-like character have often been made;[2] the re-evaluation of the evidence of the stage directions has made it possible to substantiate such claims, however, and has motivated an exploratory journey into the concealed liturgico-musical scenario of the extant Lddv.

What is fundamentally new in this study, therefore, is that the Latin incipits have been taken seriously with respect to what they do not transmit.[3] This implies full acknowledgement of the fact that the transmission of the play in MS A is deficient: the complete texts of most Latin chants as well as all melodies are missing.[4] The reasons for these omissions are

---

[1]Although such practices are a matter of course in editing, they have not always been heeded in the existing editions of the Lddv.

[2]See, among others, L. Bechstein (ed. 1855) 1 (quoted above, p. 6); Reuschel (1906) 10-11; Dörrer (1953) 1138; Dreimüller (1935) 1: 107-108; more recently Schneider (ed. 1964) 13. Cf. n13 below.

[3]As Traub (1994c) 216, has pointed out, it is necessary to make adequate provision for the material that is not transmitted in the manuscripts, but only indicated in the rubrics by the chant incipits: "Darüberhinaus muss das Nichtaufgezeichnete in angemessener Weise greifbar gemacht werden." See also above, p. 316 and n1.

[4]The melody of the twelve concluding stanzas in the vernacular is also missing; see above pp. 9-10 n31.

obvious: copying the complete text and music of the chants was unnecessary because most of them belonged to the traditional liturgy and were
therefore accessible in local liturgical books. Moreover, the use of
incipits alone to indicate chants and other items had long been standard
practice in ordinal and ritual books; the complete texts of prayers and
readings, and the music of chants with their texts were available in other
liturgical books suited to the needs and functions of the various agents
of the liturgy: the celebrant, the sacred ministers, the deacon, the cantor,
and the choir.[5] In this sense, the Latin rubrics and incipits in MS A may
be compared to an ordinal for a liturgical service, describing in rubrics
the sequence of word and action in the liturgy. As Linke notes, the
textual forms in which medieval plays are transmitted have been shaped
by two different traditions of manuscript writing, the long-standing
practice of liturgical transmissions and the new way of play writing.[6] In
MS A of the Lddv these two forms — that of a liturgical ordinal for the
Latin components and the 'new' form of play writing for the vernacular
dialogue — are amalgamated. This combination of two heterogeneous
forms of manuscript writing in the transmission of a single play resulted
in the hybrid form in which the text of the macaronic Lddv has been
recorded in the Mühlhausen manuscript. As a consequence, the extant
script provides only "half the evidence" of the entire play.[7] If the other

---

[5]For works on the content and format of liturgical books (sacramentaries, lectionaries,
missals, breviaries for the texts; graduals, antiphonals, noted missals and noted breviaries
for both text and chant; ordinals for the order of service, etc.) see above, p. 82 n40.

[6]Linke (1993a) 139. For the direction of the more complex, mainly vernacular Passion
plays, the special form of a *Dirigierrolle*, 'director's roll,' was eventually created, providing complete stage directions, but only the beginnings of the (Latin or vernacular)
text. Such a director's copy for religious plays can in turn be compared to an ordinal for
a religious service; in this sense, the Latin components of the Lddv function for the Latin
liturgical level of the play like a *Dirigierrolle*. The five extant examples of a *Dirigierrolle* for medieval plays, among them FrkfDir and AlsfDir, are described in Linke
(1988) 530-531.

[7]Cf. A. Hughes (1991) 52: "Any study of the drama that sets the music aside is scholarship that ignores half the evidence." Hj. Linke (1988) 527-28, takes this argument
even further. Because the reality of a medieval play was in its live performance and,
thus, was much larger than the combined total of texts and melodies, he considers all
transmitted records thereof as necessarily fragmentary, even when all the texts and melodies are written down. The modern interpreter, therefore, is required to describe and elucidate the dramatic work of art as comprehensively as possible.

half of the evidence is accessible in the manuscript only indirectly through the rubrics and incipits, it is nonetheless just as important.[8]

Recovering "the other half of the evidence" for the Thuringian Lddv, therefore, was the task here. It meant recognizing that it is possible to restore the complete text and music of most of the chants in an almost authentic form because the fourteenth-century sources for them are, essentially, still available among the thousands of surviving liturgical manuscripts — not, of course, the exact same books that the author of the play or the scribe of the extant manuscript would have referred to, but numerous similar sources survive that are almost identical in content and closely related in time and place of origin.[9] The search for such sources, with a necessary degree of circumspection and with constant consideration of other plays that use the same chant incipits, became the major undertaking of Chapter 3. This resulted in the recovery of almost the entire Latin core of the Lddv in Chapter 4.

In Table 12 an attempt is made to show at a glance how these Latin components are integrated into the extant macaronic play, i.e. how the two "halves of the evidence," once both are complete, relate to each other with regard to their language and the dialogue they provide. Two facts are clearly reflected in this survey: first, that up to the end of 'scene' 6, basically every Latin chant (with the exception of the first three 'processional' responsories and most of the *Silete* calls) is followed by one or sometimes two short entries in the vernacular, supplying paraphrases of the preceding Latin; second, that the remainder of the play consists of long stretches of vernacular text, with hardly any Latin chant, providing new vernacular material: 87 lines in the purely vernacular 'scenes' 7 and 8 (ll. 297-383); and 202 vernacular lines of lamentations (in couplets and stanzas) in 'scene' 9 and the 'Postlude' (ll. 384-576).[10]

---

[8]Traub (1994c) 211, expresses a similar view with regard to the transmission of the Sterzing Passion plays: "Zwischen Aufgezeichnetem ... und Nichtaufgezeichnetem — den nur mit Rubriken angegebenen Gesängen, darunter Responsorien und Antiphonen von hohem musikalischem Anspruch — fällt es nicht leicht, den Rang der Musik ... einzuschätzen. ... Die Quellenhandschriften sind ... , anders als etwa ein Plenarmissale, vordringlich der Überlieferung der gesprochenen Texte verpflichtet."

[9]This is, basically, what Janota (1994) 118, has in mind when he calls for more research of relevant local liturgical sources ("*Quellen der jeweiligen Ortsliturgie*") for a more comprehensive understanding of medieval plays. See also Traub (1994c) 216.

[10]The ten lines of refrains for stanzas 2-11 in the last text section (ll. 526-576) are not repeated in the manuscript, hence not included in the line count of Schneider's (1964) edition.

TABLE 12 RELATION OF THE VERNACULAR TO THE LATIN TEXTS
(< = 'TAKEN FROM' OR 'ADAPTED FROM')

'SCENE'		LATIN CHANTS	GENRE	VERNACULAR TEXTS		
Overture	[1]	Testimonium	Responsory	—		
	[2]	Regnum mundi	Responsory	—		
	[3']	Silete		1 entry:	6 ll.	1-6
1	[4]	Homo quidam	Responsory	—		
	[5]	Dicite invitatis	Antiphon	1 entry:	16 ll.	7-22
	[6]	Sint lumbi	Responsory	1 entry:	20 ll.	23-42
	[7]	Emendemus	Responsory	2 entries:	20+10 ll.	43-72
	[8]	Tribularer	Responsory	2 entries:	16+12 ll.	73-100
	[9']	Silete longam horam				
2	[10]	Beati eritis	Antiphon	1 entry:	16 ll.	101-116
	[11']	Silete				
3	[12]	Surgite	<Invitatory	2 entries:	15+9 ll.	117-140
	[13']	Silete				
4	[14]	Date nobis	<Gospel	1 entry:	8 ll.	141-148
	[15]	Ne forte	<Gospel	1 entry:	8 ll.	149-156
	[16]	Omnipotens	Stanza	1 entry:	12 ll.	157-168
	[17]	Sed eamus	Stanza	1 entry:	8 ll.	169-176
	[18']	Silete				
5	[19]	Ecce sponsus	<Antiphon	1 entry:	10 ll.	177-186
	[20]	Regnum mundi	Responsory	1 entry:	10 ll.	187-196
	[21]	Veni electa	Responsory	1 entry:	12 ll.	197-208
	[22]	Transite	<Responsory	1 entry:	6 ll.	209-214
	[23]	Sanctus sanctus	Antiphon	—		
	[24]	Gloria et honor	Antiphon	1 entry:	14 ll.	215-228
	[25']	Silete				
6	[26]	Iniquitates	Antiphon	1 entry:	8 ll.	229-236
	[27]	Qui tempus	<Homily	1 entry:	4 ll.	237-240
	[28]	Domine domine	<Gospel	1 entry:	4 ll.	241-244
	[29]	Amen amen	<Gospel	1 entry:	6 ll.	245-250
		— ⌣:		1 entry:	6 ll.	251-256
	[30]	Recordare	Offertory	1 entry:	8 ll.	257-264
	[31]	Exaudi	<Litany	1 entry:	8 ll.	265-272
		—		1 entry:	6 ll.	273-278
	[32]	Miserere	<Litany	1 entry:	12 ll.	279-290
	[33]	Celum et terra	<Gospel	1 entry	6 ll.	291-296
7		—		8 entries:	43 ll.	297-339
8		—		2 entries:	44 ll.	340-383
	[34']	Silete				
9	[35]	Cecidit corona	<Lam.Ier.	1 entry:	26 ll.	384-409
	[36]	Deficit gaudium	<Lam.Ier.	4 entries:	116 ll.	410-525
Postlude		—		12 entries:	60 ll.	526-576
				(12 long-line stanzas + refrain)		

Since these last vernacular 'scenes' all follow in succession, interrupted only by a *Silete* call [34'] and the two short Latin chants [35] and [36] at the beginning of the lamentations, the final third of the play (ll. 297-576) is essentially a vernacular performance. These 289 verses comprise roughly fifty per cent of the entire vernacular text. Thus, in spite of the almost perfect equilibrium of the Latin and vernacular texts in the play's first and major part (ll. 1-296), there is a considerable linguistic imbalance in the macaronic play as a whole, as transmitted in MS A. Such an imbalance towards the end of the play could be due to interpolations in the vernacular.[11] An earlier macaronic version of the play may well have comprised no more of the extant vernacular text than the immediate paraphrases of the Latin chants.[12]

In the complete Thuringian *Play of the Wise and Foolish Virgins* of MS A, the two linguistic layers surveyed here correspond to two layers or levels of word and action, the Latin, liturgical level making use of traditional liturgical material as the sung Latin dialogue, and the vernacular (secular) level, using vernacular dramatic dialogue created for this purpose. Since the latter is greatly enriched by the former and since both dimensions are so closely intertwined in the reality of the extant Lddv, an obvious question arises: did the restored Latin layer, the recovered 'core' of the Lddv, serve only as the Latin basis for the mixed-language ('macaronic') play, or did it exist as a separate, purely Latin earlier stage of the drama, as Karl Reuschel and other twentieth-century schol-

---

[11]The "Devils' Scene" 7 (ll. 297-339), which is not transmitted in MS B, has long been recognized as an interpolation; cf. Rieger (1865) 314; Reuschel (1906) 10; Fischer (1910) 22-24, against Beckers (1905) 30-32, who wanted to rescue part of the scene as belonging to an older tradition. More recently, Linke (1987a) 226, stresses that only the Devils' pantomime, in ll. A383c and B476a, can be considered original. On closer examination, even 'scene' 8, Mary's second, purely vernacular intercession (ll. 340-383), and 'scene' 9, the long lamentations of the *Fatue* in vernacular couplets (ll. 384-525), may be considered early interpolations because of the very different nature of their dialogue and performance structure. See the preliminary discussion in my dissertation (1991), esp. pp. 420-428.

[12]Because of their lyrical expressiveness, I consider the twelve concluding stanzas (ll. 526-576) a closer paraphrase of the Latin lamentations in chants [35] and [36] than the quite didactic vernacular lamentations in couplets (ll. 384-525) that immediately follow the Latin chants. See also Amstutz (1994) 45-46.

ars have suggested?[13] There is, of course, no definite answer to this question. The fact is that the restored liturgico-musical components of the Lddv constitute a coherent Latin play, complete in itself.[14] This is a magnificent ensemble of Latin dialogue through chant, chants from a variety of liturgical backgrounds that appear to be chosen for their dramatic potential and their abundant use of direct discourse. Connected as they are through brief yet effective stage directions that occasionally call for pantomime, they provide for a continuous dramatic action.

Chant [4] *Homo quidam fecit* is the only chant performed by the liturgical *Chorus*. It functions as a brief introduction to the play, somewhat in the way a *Precursor* or *Rector ludi* would present introductory remarks at the outset of a performance in many later plays.[15] The opening responsory [1] *Testimonium domini*, sung in procession by one group of players (*Dominica Persona cum Maria et Angelis*), might also fall into the category of introductory proclamation, as far as we can judge from the few clues for a textual restoration of this chant. The second responsory, [2] *Regnum mundi*, kept in the first person singular, is a proclamation of a more personal nature, thus serving to characterize the ten *Virgines* who sing it while proceeding to the playing area.[16]

Given the title of the play, *Ludus de decem virginibus*, it may seem somewhat odd that none of these introductory chants is directly related to the Parable of the Wise and Foolish Virgins, although numerous litur-

---

[13]"Zieht man nun die kirchensprachlichen Bibelstellen, Responsorien und Hymnen in Betracht, so ergibt sich ein völlig in sich abgeschlossenes oratorienartiges Werk." Reuschel (1906) 11, 17. Cf. Beckers (ed. 1905) 45; Creizenach (1911) 120; Dörrer (1953) 1131, 1132, 1134.

[14]Cf. also Linke (1995b) 916.

[15]Most of the more complex later plays have a 'stage director' in their cast who, as a rule, explains to the audience the significance of the upcoming performance, often reappearing at the beginning of a new action sequence or a new day's performance, and sometimes concluding the play with a final comment. He is referred to by various names, *Rector ludi* or *processionis* (KünzCC), *Precursor* (WienO and many of the Tyrol plays), *Proclamator* (AlsfP), etc. In StGMrhP, FrkfDir, FrkfP, this role is given to Augustine. Cf. Liebenow (ed. 1969) 258-259; Bergmann (1972a) 246-247, (1978) 258-259. It is interesting to note that in MS B of the Lddv, which excludes the Latin chants and does not give a title to the play, a prefatory note introduces the dramatic text as if it pertained to Augustine's exposition of the parable of the Ten Virgins; cf. Lddv(B), ed. Schneider (1964), ll. 0a-f.

[16]Cf. above, Chapter 3 [2], pp. 97-98 and 209.

gical chants based on Matthew 25: 1-13 exist. Might this imply that an earlier, purely Latin, liturgical version of the Lddv, contemplated above, actually existed? and that its author, perhaps not primarily interested in dramatizing the parable, made use of its imagery for a different purpose, more closely related to the message of the chants he selected for the opening of the play, notably [2] *Regnum mundi* and [4] *Homo quidam*?[17]

In any case, by assigning all the remaining chants to the various *dramatis personae*, who deliver their sung dialogue in alternation of solo and group performance, the author has produced a lively play in chant, with a minimum of text borrowed from Matthew, effectively enlarging the story of the biblical Parable of the Ten Virgins through additional characters (Mary, the Angels, and the Devils[18]) and supplementary action — dancing, playing, and dining of the *Fatue*, crowning of the *Prudentes* by Mary, Mary's intercession for the *Fatue*, the latter's seizure by the Devils, and their concluding lamentations.[19] This basically is also the scenario of the macaronic play as we know it. Thus, the textually and musically restored Latin layer of the Lddv emerges as the intrinsic liturgical core of the Latin-German *Zehnjungfrauenspiel*. It constitutes a dramatic conception of such poetic beauty and so powerful a message that I personally believe that it was conceived and probably performed as a play in itself, possibly with a few vernacular paraphrases.

Looking at the liturgical roots of those recovered Latin chants and recitation items (excluding the seven *Silete* calls), a quite remarkable observation can be made, particularly in comparison with many other small-scale religious plays that center around a single feast or event of the salvation history. Table 13 shows that these chants belong to a highly di-

---

[17]Cf. the reflections above, particularly pp. 97-98, 132, 209-211 with n6.

[18]The Devils, however, have no speaking part in the Latin layer of the play nor do they have any dialogue in the vernacular transmission of MS B; cf. above, n11.

[19]The *Fatue*, dancing and separating themselves from the *Prudentes* (ll. 100a-c, before [9′] *Silete*), then dining and falling asleep (ll. 116c-d, before chant [12]); the celebration of the great Wedding Banquet (ll. 228a-b, before chant [25′]); the Devils encircling the *Fatue* with a chain (l. 383c, before chant [35]); cf. the survey in Table 5.

Although it could be argued that the seven *Silete* calls in the Lddv might not have been part of a purely Latin play since such calls served a primarily structural function in more complex plays, there is no reason to make such an assumption. The Moosburg Ascension Play, for instance, is composed almost entirely of Latin liturgical chants, yet its manuscript includes five *Silete* calls; cf. MoosbHi, ed. Brooks (1925) 94-95, and Catalogue [3′C1], where the *Silete* occurrences in MoosbHi are indicated.

verse range of seasons, feasts, processions, and other occasions of the
Church year from Advent to beyond the twentieth Sunday after Pentecost.
Although some chants relate to more than one liturgical occasion (chants
[2], [14], [15], [19], [20], [21], [28] and [29]), each derives its own specific significance from the liturgical environment in which it has its usual
place. When transferred from ritual to drama, each chant becomes integrated into the completely new stream of action in the Thuringian play,
yet maintains to a certain degree its original intrinsic meaning.

In a medieval performance of this play, therefore, the singing of the
various chants would have evoked strong liturgical associations in its
fourteenth-century audience even as they watched the new dramatic action unfold before their eyes[20] — evocations of their own experiences
of litany processions, penitential rites and prayers, invocations of Mary
and the saints (chants [7-8, 12, 26, 30-32, 35-36]), as well as recollec-
tions of joyful events of veneration and celebration: the feasts of Corpus
Christi [4], of Easter [16-17], of the Holy Trinity [23-24], feasts of various saints, particularly the Common of Virgins (cf. Table 13) and, last but
not least, the spectacular ceremony of the Consecration of Nuns [2, 19-21].
The modern reader may never be able to appreciate fully the extent to
which a medieval audience would have been affected by those associations, or the degree of identification they would have felt with the players when what they heard and saw enacted in the Lddv reminded them
of liturgical rituals and customs familiar to them from their own religious
experience.[21]

What made it possible, however, for all those chants to serve as the
continuous 'dialogue' in a play, even in the presumed Latin-only stage
of it, is the form of their texts or, rather, the special kind of discourse
found in most of them. It has often been pointed out that a large number
of Gregorian chants in general, and the responsories of Matins in parti-

---

[20]Cf. Traub's observation (1994c) 214, about the interpenetration of two different layers of time in the far less 'liturgical' Sterzing plays and the way liturgical time, represented by the antiphons and responsories, enters into the performance of the play as if from
outside, tying the dramatic development into the liturgical year: "Die liturgische Zeit,
die durch die Antiphonen und Responsorien angezeigt wird und wie von aussen in die
Spiele hineinragt, deren Entfaltung in das liturgische Jahr zurückbindend ... ."

[21]Cf. Linke's (1987a) 227, comment on the Erfurt chronicle's report of the Eisenach
performance of 1321 with its impact on the audience of the time, particularly on Count
Friedrich der Freidige.

TABLE 13 LITURGICAL SEASONS AS REFLECTED IN THE LDDV CHANTS

PLACE IN CHURCH YEAR	CHANT	THEME
PROPER OF TIME		
Christmas Season — Advent	[12] [33]	Vigilance God's Eternity
Lent — Quadragesima Triduum Sanctum	[7, 8] [35-36]	Penitence Lamentations
Easter Season — Easter 2nd Sunday after East. Rogation Days	[16, (17)] [22] [31, 32]	Visitatio Sepulchri Mary's grace Supplication
Post-Pentecost — Trinity Corpus Christi 20th Sunday Wedn. after 20th Sun. (*jejunium bannitum*)	[23, 24] [4] [5] [26]	Trinitarian praise Eucharist Eucharist Penitence (prayer)
PROPER OF SAINTS		
Marian Feasts — Assumption *BMV* Votive Mass *BMV*	[21] [30]	Heavenly bliss Mary's grace (prayer)
COMMON OF SAINTS — of Virgins of Confessors of Apostles	[2, 20] [19] [21] [14-15] [27] [28-29] [6] [10]	Dedication to Christ Vigilance Heavenly bliss Gospel reading Homily reading Gospel reading Vigilance Vigilance
PONTIFICAL CELEBRATIONS — Consecration of Virgins	[2, 20] [19] [21] [14-15] [28-29]	Dedication to Christ Vigilance Heavenly bliss Gospel reading Gospel reading

cular, display an inherent dialogue quality and, hence, dramatic potential, inasmuch as they are often in direct discourse and use various forms of address, questions, or exclamations, expressing grief or joy, contrition or encouragement, lamentation or celebration, occasionally in the form of prayer or praise.[22] The responsories acquired such textual forms because their function and purpose in Matins was to provide appropriate emotional, reflective, or other responses to each of the successive nocturnal lessons. Thus, in performing the responsories, the *precentor* (cantor) and the choir often assume the voice and 'role' of one or more of the figures in the lesson's narrative, including the voice of God or Christ. This results in a remarkable "voice structure" which closely approximates genuine dialogue within the "composite unit" of recited *lectio* and musical response, as a single lector, a cantor and the choir alternate in solo and choral performances.[23] The texts of antiphons and invitatories, sung usually with a psalm or canticle, often have similar forms of direct discourse; the interchange in antiphonal singing being between two semi-choirs, however, the sense of 'dialogue' in this liturgical setting is much less pronounced.

As Table 14 shows, the author of the Lddv, or of a preceding Latin stage of it, drew most of the chants for his play from Matins. Using to advantage the chants' intrinsic voice patterns and the particular forms of their discourse, he allotted the 'speeches' to appropriate characters in order to create a sung dialogue among them fitting the new dramatic context. What had functioned as quasi-dialogue in their various liturgical contexts, and had been performed by 'liturgical' singers able to assume a multiplicity of roles, was thus transferred into a context of genuine, dramatic dialogue distributed among a whole cast of players impersonating those roles. And if at Matins a responsory was 'responding' to the preceding narrative of a *lectio*, in the play the chants are responses to preceding chants as part of a new mimetic representation. As a consequence, a sequence of chants such as the three responsories **[6-8]** is no longer 'liturgical,' since these responsories are stripped of their liturgical function — responding to a preceding *lectio* — and sung in succession by the *Angeli* **[6]** *Sint lumbi*, the *Prudentes* **[7]** *Emendemus*, and the *Fatue*

---

[22]Cf. Marbach (1907) 86*-91*, Schuler (1951) 37-39, Gstrein (1994) 96; also Dunn (1972) esp. 47-51, on earlier French research, particularly by Sepet and Battifol.
[23]Cf. Dunn (1972) 49-50.

TABLE 14 THE CHANTS OF THE LDDV AND THEIR LITURGICAL PROVENANCE
(< = 'TAKEN' OR 'ADAPTED FROM')

CHANTS		LITURGICAL PLACE	OFFICE	TYPE OF CHANT
[1]	Testimonium	?	?	(Responsory)
[2]	Regnum mundi	Comm. Virg.	Matins	Responsory 9
		Consecr. Virg.	Mass	Responsory
[4]	Homo quidam	Corpus Christi	Vesp.1	Responsory
[5]	Dicite invitatis	Dom. 20 p.P.	Lauds	Antiphon ad Benedictus
[6]	Sint lumbi	Comm. Conf.	Matins	Responsory 9
[7]	Emendemus	Dom. 1 in XL	Matins	Responsory 3
[8]	Tribularer	Dom. 1 in XL	Matins	Respsonsory 7
[10]	Beati eritis	Comm. Apost.	Vesp. 1	Antiphon ad Magnificat
	(Responsory?)		Vesp. 2	Antiphon 3 or 4
[12]	Surgite	Hebd. IV Adv.	Matins	Invitatory
[14]	Date nobis	Comm. Virg.	Matins	< Gospel recit. (Matt. 25:8)
		Consecr. Virg.	Mass	
[15]	Ne forte	Comm. Virg.	Matins	
		Consecr. Virg.	Mass	< Gospel recit. (Matt. 25:9)
[16]	Omnipotens	Easter	Play	Travel stanza "B1"
[17]	Sed eamus	[Easter]	[Play]	< Travel stanza "B3"
[19]	Ecce sponsus	Comm. Virg.	Mat./Laud.	< Antiphon
		Consecr. Virg.	Mass	< Antiphon
[20]	Regnum mundi	Comm. Virg.	Matins	Responsory 9
		Consecr. Virg.	Mass	Responsory
[21]	Veni electa	Comm. Virg.	Mat./Vsp. 1	Resp.7/Ant. ad Magnificat
		Consecr. Virg.	Mass	Responsory
[22]	Transite	Dom. 1 p. Pas.	Matins	< Responsory 2
[23]	Sanctus s. s.	de Trinitate	Vesp. 2	Antiphon 3
		Dom. 1 p. Ep.	(Lauds)	(Antiphon 5)
[24]	Gloria et h.	de Trinitate	Vesp. 2	Antiphon 4
		Dom. 1 p. Ep.	(Lauds)	(Antiphon 4)
[26]	Iniquitates	Feria 4 p. Dom.	Jejunium	Processional Antiphon
		20 p. Pent.	bannitum	
[27]	Qui tempus	Comm. Virg.	Matins	< Homily recitation
[28]	Domine domine	Comm. Virg.	Matins	< Gospel recit. (Matt. 25:11)
		Consecr. Virg.	Mass	
[29]	Amen amen	Comm. Virg.	Matins	< Gospel recit. (Matt. 25:12)
		Consecr. Virg.	Mass	
[30]	Recordare	Mass BMV	Mass	Offertory
[31]	Exaudi	Rogation-	Litany	Litany Antiphon
[32]	Miserere	Procession	Litany	Litany Antiphon
[33]	Celum et terra	Hbd. 3 ante Nat.	Mass	< Gospel recit. (Luke 21:33)
[35]	Cecidit	Sab. sancto	Matins	< Lamentations (5:16)
[36]	Deficit	Sab. sancto	Matins	< Lamentations (5:15)

[8] *Tribularer*; but the chants themselves maintain their liturgical character along with their unchanged text, melody and method of performance.

Of the twenty-eight restored chants in the Lddv (excluding the *Silete* calls), only one, [4] *Homo quidam*, is narrative in nature, serving as the kind of introductory proclamation mentioned above; yet even here, the responsory's verse is in direct discourse (*Venite, comedite* ...), thus anticipating and connecting with the subsequent invitation of chant [5] *Dicite invitatis*. Four other chants employ an impersonal form of discourse. Two of them, [23-24] *Sanctus* and *Gloria et honor*, are sung at the climax of the play as praise of the Deity by the *Prudentes* and the *Angeli* in Heaven — a realm that seems beyond ordinary dialogue anyway. The two other 'impersonal' chants, [27] *Qui tempus* and [33] *Celum et terra*, pronounced by the *Dominica Persona* in rejection of the *Fatue* at the play's anti-climax, proclaim the eternal authority of God perhaps in a stronger form than ordinary discourse would.

All other chants of this Thuringian play are in some form of personal discourse, i.e. in the first or second person singular or plural; a form of address prevails in many of them [5, 6, 10, 12, 14-15, 19, 21, 22, 28, 30-32]. While this chant-as-dialogue form of interchange between characters or groups of characters may be very different from the more individualized vernacular dialogue in the macaronic Lddv, it nevertheless approaches dramatic dialogue to a high degree, especially if an entire chant is sung by a single character (chants [5, 14-15, 22, 27-29, 31-36] and, with a group response, [16-17]). Yet even the 'choral chants,' sung by the *Prudentes*, the *Fatue*, or the *Angeli*, usually imply different voice patterns in their discourse, i.e. some kind of dialogue or group discussion, since there are always solo parts, at least in the solo intonation of a chant and particularly in the delivery of a responsory verse to which the group or an individual responds.[24]

Connected through stage directions that provide for continuity of dialogue and action, including some pantomime, the chants selected for this play show an astounding textual coherence and dramatic congruency, as noted throughout Chapter 3. The author has provided Latin chants for

---

[24]Some kind of group discussion or group meditation certainly occurs in chants [2, 7, 8, 20], and to some degree even in the antiphons [10] and [12, 26, 31] with their solo intonations. Various forms of address seeking a response are found, for instance, in chants [6-7, 10, 12, 21, 22, 30].

almost every turn in the action. In most cases these chants were readily available from the liturgy (responsories, antiphons, an offertory, lamentations), or from other religious plays (the B1-stanza from the Easter plays, cf. chant [16]). In a few other cases, he either selected an easily separable section of an existing liturgical chant (as for chants [19] *Ecce* and [23] *Transite*), or used the dialogue sections from the liturgical reading of the Matthew parable (cf. chants [14], [15], [28], and [29]). In three additional cases, where the complete text is transmitted in the manuscript, the author created a chant himself by slightly adapting traditional material to suit his purposes in the play. This creativity is apparent in chant [17] *Sed eamus oleum emere*, a decasyllabic stanza modelled after the B3-stanza of the Easter plays to fit the new dramatic context of the Lddv.[25] It also manifests itself in two chants sung by the *Dominica Persona*, [27] *Qui tempus congrue penitencie* and [33] *Celum et terra*, which are both taken from liturgical readings (a homily and a gospel *lectio*), hence performed in recitation. By slightly revising the wording of these texts the author achieved a special kind of *cursus*, i.e. a more poetic form, thereby adding to the authority of their message.[26] The special concern and attention given to the continuity and dramatic propriety of the Latin texts in the play may serve to corroborate the hypothesis that such a purely Latin liturgical form of the Lddv possibly preceded the macaronic version transmitted in MS A.

Apart from the three chants [17, 27, 33], which have been creatively 'edited' by the author, all chants in the Thuringian play, including the B1-stanza [16] *Omnipotens pater*, were probably performed in the same textual and melodic form in which they were known in the local liturgy and the Easter plays. In this sense, the restored Latin core of the Lddv may be compared to two other plays that are also more or less exclusively composed of Latin liturgical chants: the thirteenth-century Benediktbeuren Emmaus play CB26* (BenbEmm) and the fourteenth-century Moosburg Ascension Play (MoosbHi). While the chants in the latter play are only indicated by their incipits,[27] the BenbEmm chants are transmitted

---

[25]Cf. the discussion in Chapter 3 [17], passim, esp. pp. 198-199.

[26]Cf. the discussion in Chapter 3 [27] and [33], esp. pp. 256-258, 296-297.

[27]Most of these incipits have been completed from contemporary liturgical books by the first editor of the play, N. Brooks (1925). It would be possible and desirable to restore these chants with their melodies from local medieval sources.

with their complete texts and melodies in the codex of the *Carmina Burana*.[28] The Benediktbeuren Emmaus play can thus serve, along with the MoosbHi, as a convincing example of how an entire play and a vivid Latin dialogue could be composed simply through the coordination of dramaturgical directions and carefully selected liturgical chants assigned to the different characters of the play.[29] Recognizing this and the rich dramatic life inherent in the liturgy of the Church already by the year 1000 (date of *A*Hartk), Meyer exclaimed in awe:

> What an amazing dramatic life this liturgy must have carried in itself! Compared with this abundance of dramatic antiphons and responsories, the emergence of that seedling of the Easter play and its gradual development appears as an almost insignificant matter.[30]

The recovered Latin core of the Thuringian Lddv must certainly be regarded as another impressive testimony to the ingrained dramatic possibilities of chant. Even the reduction of the complete liturgical evidence to rubrics and chant incipits in the skeletal transmission of the play in Mühlhausen MS A cannot diminish this fact. Though some of the Latin chants proposed in Chapter 4 of this study may require adjustments in text and music if or when other, more authentic sources surface, I am confident that they provide the intrinsic core of the Lddv, the liturgical scenario and musical score that have been lost in the transmission of the play. As with any other play, though, the fact is that a mixed-language

---

[28]Notation without lines. As early as 1901, W. Meyer noted that the text and melody for most of the chants in the BenbEmm are identical with their counterparts in Hartker's Antiphonal (*A*Hartk); cf. his comparative studies of BenbEmm with the two French plays from Beauvais and Orléans, in *Fragmenta Burana* (1901) 134-138. In the new edition of the *Carmina Burana* [1.3] (1970) 187-188, Bischoff identified the antiphons in the BenbEmm with the liturgical repertoire of Hesbert's CAO.

The confusion surrounding the two plays, CB26* and CB26a*, arising from their transmission in the Codex Buranus and their contradictory modern editions and interpretations, has been convincingly resolved recently by Linke (1999a) 186-190: despite their edition under the same heading, CB26* and CB26a* are two separate Latin plays. CB26* is a 'complete' Emmaus (or *Peregrinus*) play; CB26a*, a fragment of a play on the Assumption of the Virgin Mary.

[29]See also Schüttpelz (1930) 80-81.

[30]W. Meyer (1901) 134: "Welch ein dramatisches Leben muss diese Liturgie in sich geborgen haben! Verglichen mit dieser Fülle dramatischer Antiphonen und Responsorien erscheint die Entstehung jenes Keimes des Osterspiels und dessen langsame Ausbildung fast eine unbedeutende Sache."

play such as the Lddv comes to real life only in performance; and this presupposes that "both halves of the evidence," the vernacular texts and the Latin liturgical chants with the stage directions are taken fully into account. This is now possible. Deo gratias.

Appendix 1

Facsimiles

Most reproductions are considerably reduced; line numberings are added.

1. MS A: Mühlhausen/Thüringen, Stadtarchiv, MS 87/20, p. 94a-b:
   End of *Ludus de beata Katherina* (LdbKath), beginning of *Ludus de decem virginibus* (Lddv).
   Photo: Dieter Gerlach, Stadtarchiv Mühlhausen/Thüringen. Reproduced by permission of the Stadtarchiv Mühlhausen/Thüringen.

2. MS A: Mühlhausen/Thüringen, Stadtarchiv, MS 87/20, p. 94b, lines 31-44:
   Beginning of Lddv with chants [1] to [3] indicated in ll. 34-36, chant [4] in ll. 39-40, chant [5] in ll. 40-42.
   Reproduced by permission of the Stadtarchiv Mühlhausen/Thüringen.

3. *B*Helm.145.1: Wolfenbüttel, Herzog August Bibliothek, Cod. Guelf. 145.1 Helmst. fol. 367vb, lines 1-7:
   Responsory *Veni electa mea* with verse *Specie tua*, showing melodic features of the 'German plainsong dialect' not present in the version from *A*Mz.II,138, which served as a model for chant [21]. Contrary to common practice (cf. the discussion above, p. 57) the *quia* in l. 3, beginning of the *repetenda*, is not highlighted; yet in l. 7, after the verse, it is marked with a capital *Q* (*Quia*) and provided with an extensive melodic cue for the *repetenda* which helps find the corresponding place in l. 3.
   Reproduced by permission of the Herzog August Bibliothek Wolfenbüttel.

4. *M*Halb.888: *Missale celeberrimi Halberstattensis episcopatus.* Incunabulum. Mainz 1511, fols. <229> recto and verso:
   Examples for the gospel tone in the *Accentus Moguntinus*: Introductory formulas (fol. <229>r, ll. 7-8); recitation of Luke 1: 39-47 (fol. <229>r, ll. 8 to fol. <229>v, end). Cf. the discussion on pp. 78-81, with transcriptions in Figures 2 and 3. On fol. <229>r, ll. 1-6, the final section of the tone for Revelations (Rev. 7: 14-17).

5. *Ps*Mz.D.820: *Enchiridion Psalmorum ferialium ad vesperas et completorium cum antiphonis et tonis.* Mainz 1607: fol. 287v (beginning of Rogation procession), fols. 289r-290r ('Triple antiphon' for Rogation litany). The *Aufer a nobis* triad or 'triple antiphon' for the Rogation litany here in the sequence *Exaudi — Aufer — Exaudi — Miserere — Exaudi*; the *alleluia* at the end of each verse seems to be a later addition. To be compared with the transcription of the chants from GLpz in Figure 22, p. 286. Cf. the discussion on pp. 277-287, particularly p. 284 n23.

6. *L*Brsw: Wolfenbüttel, Niedersächsisches Staatsarchiv, VII B Hs 203, fol. 22v:
   A section from the *Oratio Ieremiae* (Lam. 5) which begins on fol. 21rb and ends on fol. 23rb, immediately followed by the Braunschweig Easter Play (BrswO). Lam. 5: 15 and 16, which correspond to chants [36] and [35] of the Lddv are on fol. 22va, ll. 3-6 and 6-8.
   Reproduced by permission of the Niedersächsisches Staatsarchiv Wolfenbüttel.

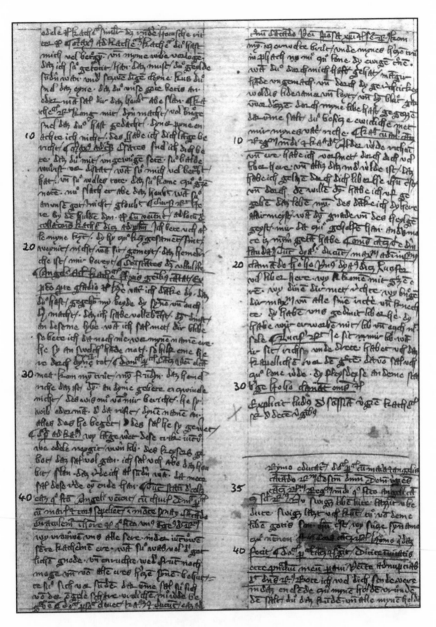

1. MS A: Mühlhausen/Thüringen, Stadtarchiv, MS 87/20, p. 94a-b.
Photo: Dieter Gerlach

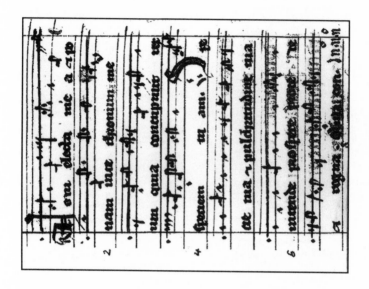

3. *B*Helm 145.1: Wolfenbüttel, Herzog August Bibliothek, Cod. Guelf. 145.1 Helmst.: fol. 367vb, ll. 1-7.

2. MS A: Mühlhausen/Thüringen, Stadtarchiv, MS 87/20: p. 94b, ll. 31-44.

4. *MHalb. 888: Missale Halberstatense*, Mainz 1511: fols. <229>r–<229>v.

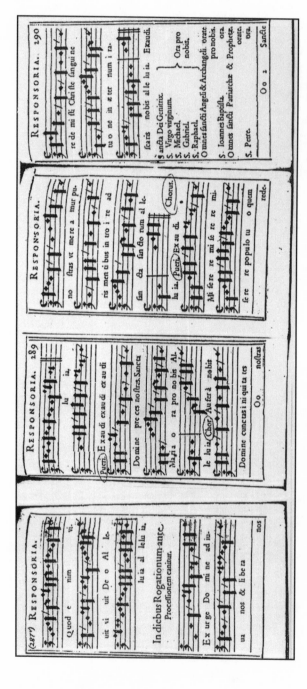

5. *PsMz.D.820: Enchiridion Psalmorum ferialium ad vesperas et completorium cum antiphonis et tonis.*
Mainz 1607: fols. 287v (beginning of Rogation procession), 289r–290r ('Triple antiphon' for Rogation litany).

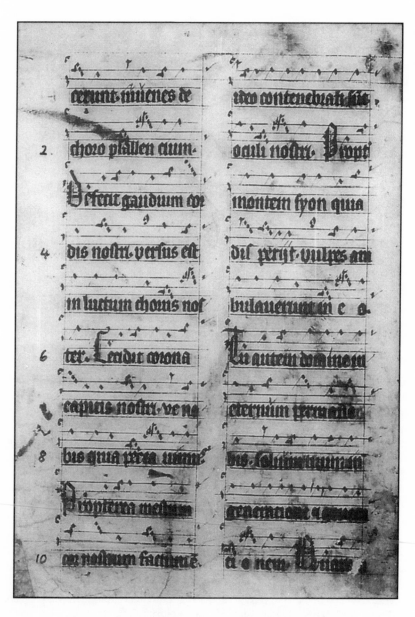

6. LBrsw: Wolfenbüttel, Niedersächsisches Staadsarchiv,
VII B Hs 203, fol. 22v.

Bibliography

AfdA   *Anzeiger für deutsches Altertum und deutsche Literatur* (in *ZfdA*)
Beiträge   *Beiträge zur Geschichte der deutschen Sprache und Literatur* [conventionally cited as *PBB*, Paul und Braunes Beiträge.]
DMA   *Dictionary of the Middle Ages*
JAMS   *Journal of the American Musical Society*
KmJb   *Kirchenmusikalisches Jahrbuch*
MGG   *Die Musik in Geschichte und Gegenwart.* 1949-1986. 1st ed.
²MGG   *Die Musik in Geschichte und Gegenwart.* 1994-1999. 2nd ed. *Sachteil.*
New Grove   *The New Grove Dictionary of Music and Musicians*
PalMus   *Paléographie musicale*
RL   *Reallexikon der deutschen Literaturgeschichte.* 1958-1984. 2nd ed.
VL   *Die deutsche Literatur des Mittelalters. Verfasserlexikon.* 1st ed.
²VL   *Die deutsche Literatur des Mittelalters. Verfasserlexikon.* 1978-. 2nd revised and enlarged ed.
ZfdA   *Zeitschrift für deutsches Altertum und Literatur*
ZfdPh   *Zeitschrift für deutsche Philologie*

Agustoni, Luigi. 1963. *Gregorianischer Choral. Elemente und Vortragslehre mit besonderer Berücksichtigung der Neumenkunde.* Freiburg i. Br., Basel, Vienna: Herder.

AH 28 (1898), AH 47 (1905), AH 49 (1906). See *Analecta Hymnica Medii Aevi*.

Allworth, Christopher. 1970. "The Medieval Processional: Donaueschingen MS 882." *Ephemerides Liturgicae* 84: 169-186.

Amalarius, of Metz, Archbishop of Lyon. See Hanssens, ed. 1948-1950.

Amstutz, Renate. 1991. "The Latin Subsratum of the Thuringian 'Ludus de decem virginibus.' Its Liturgical Roots and its Dramatic Relevance for the Mixed-Language Music Drama." PhD dissertation. University of Toronto.

———. 1994. "Zum musikalischen Vortrag der Schlußstrophen des Thüringischen Zehnjungfrauenspiels." In Mehler-Touber, eds., 1-47.

———. Forthcoming. "Die liturgisch-dramatische Feier der *Consecratio virginum* nach dem Pontifikale des Bischofs Durandus. Eine Studie zur Rezeption der Zehn-jungfrauen-Parabel in Liturgie, Ritus und Drama der mittelalterlichen Kirche." In *Ritual und Inszenierung.* Proceedings of the conference "Ritual und Inszenierung" in Cologne, March 1999. Tübingen: Niemeyer.

Analecta Hymnica Medii Aevi [AH]. 1886-1922. Ed. Guido Maria Dreves, Clemens Blume, and Henry M. Bannister. 55 vols. Leipzig: O.R. Reisland. Repr. 1961. New York: Johnson Reprint.

AH 28 (1898): *Historiae rhythmicae. Liturgische Reimofficien des Mittelalters VII.* Ed. Dreves.

AH 47 (1905): *Tropi graduales. Tropen des Missale im Mittelalter I. Tropen zum Ordinarium Missae.* Ed. Blume and Bannister.

AH 49 (1906): *Tropi graduales. Tropen des Missale im Mittelalter II. Tropen zum Proprium Missarum.* Ed. Blume.

Anderson, Gordon A. 1971. "A Troped Offertorium-Conductus of the 13th Century." *JAMS* 24: 96-100.

Andresen, Dieter, and H. Schoppmeier, eds. 1991. *Dat Osterspeel vun Redentin,* Heide: Westholsteinische Verlagsanstalt.

Andrieu, Michel, ed. 1931-1961. *Les Ordines Romani du haut moyen âge.* 5 vols. Spicilegium Sacrum Lovaniense 11, 23-24, 28-29. Louvain. Repr. 1960-1965.

———, ed. 1938-1941. *Le Pontifical Romain au moyen âge.* 4 vols. Studi e Testi 86-88, 99. Vatican City: Biblioteca Apostolica Vaticana.

[86] (1938): *Le Pontifical romain du xiie siècle.*

[87] (1940): *Le Pontifical de la Curie romaine au xiiie siècle.*

[88] (1940): *Le Pontifical de Guillaume Durand.*

[99] (1941): *Tables alphabétiques.*

Anglès, Higini. 1935. *La Música a Catalunya fins al segle XIII.* Publicacions del Departament de Música 10. Barcelona: Biblioteca de Catalunya.

Antiphonaire monastique de Worcester. See PalMus 12 (1922).

Antiphonale Missarum juxta Ritum Sanctae Ecclesiae Mediolanensis [*AMMed*]. 1935. Paris, Tournai, Rome: Desclée.

Antiphonale Missarum Sextuplex [AMS]. 1935. *Édité ... d'apres le graduel de Monza et les antiphonaires de Rheinau, du Mont-Blandin, de Compiegne, de Corbie et de Senlis.* Ed. René-Jean Hesbert. Brussels: Vromant et Co.

Antiphonale Monasticum pro diurnis horis [*AMon*]. 1934. Paris, Tournai, Rome: Desclée.

Antiphonale Pataviense. See Schlager, ed. 1985.

Antiphonale sacrosanctae Romanae Ecclesiae pro diurnis horis [AR]. 1949. Paris, Tournai, Rome: Desclée.

Antiphonale Sarisburiense. See Frere, ed. 1901-1924.

Das Antiphonar von St. Peter [ASalzb]. 1969-1974. 2 vols. Codices Selecti, phototypice impressi 21 (*Facsimileband*), 21* (*Kommentarband* [Franz Unterkircher and Otto Demus]). Graz: Akademische Druck- und Verlagsanstalt.

Antiphonarium Ambrosianum du Musée Britannique. See PalMus 5 (1896), 6 (1900).

Antiphonarium Sacri Ordinis Praedicatorum pro diurnis horis [AOP]. 1933. Rome: In Hospitio Magistri Generalis.

Apel, Willi. 1958. *Gregorian Chant.* Bloomington: Indiana University Press.

Aribo, Bishop of Freising. *See* Smits van Waesberghe, ed. 1951.

Avalle, D'Arco Silvio, and Raffaello Monterosso, eds. 1965. *Sponsus. Dramma delle vergini prudenti e delle vergini stolte.* Documenti di Filologia 9. Milan, Naples: Riccardo Ricciardi.

Axton, Richard. 1974. *European Drama of the Early Middle Ages*. London: Hutch-inson.

Badstübner, Ernst, and Wolfgang Hanke. 1984. *Die Blasiuskirche zu Mühlhausen. Das Christliche Denkmal 56*. 3rd edition. Berlin: Union Verlag.

Bailey, Terence W., ed. 1965. *The Fleury Play of Herod*. Toronto: Pontifical Insti-tute of Mediaeval Studies.

——. 1971. *The Processions of Sarum and the Western Church*. Studies and Texts 21. Toronto: Pontifical Institute of Mediaeval Studies.

——. 1988. "Processions (Liturgical)." In *DMA* 10: 130-133.

Baltzer, Rebecca. 1989. "Wolfenbüttel, Helmstedt MS 628 (St. Andrews MS)." In *DMA* 12: 670-672.

Baroffio, Giacomo B., and Ruth Steiner. 1980. "Offertory." In *New Grove* 13: 513-517.

Baumann, Winfried. 1978. *Die Literatur des Mittelalters in Böhmen*. Veröffent-lichungen des Collegium Carolinum 37. Munich, Vienna: Oldenbourg.

Bäumer, Suitbert. 1895. *Geschichte des Breviers. Versuch einer quellenmäßigen Darstellung der Entwicklung des altkirchlichen und des römischen Officiums bis auf unsere Tage*. Freiburg i. Br.: Herder.

Bechstein, Ludwig, ed. 1855. *Das grosse thüringische Mysterium von den zehn Jungfrauen*. Wartburg-Bibliothek 1. Halle: C.E.M. Pfeffer.

Bechstein, Reinhold. 1860. "Einiges über Silete." *Germania* 5: 97-99.

——. 1866. "Zum Spiele von den zehn Jungfrauen." *Germania* 11: 129-166. (Repr. of *Zum Spiele von den zehn Jungfrauen*. Diss. Jena 1866).

——. 1872. *Das Spiel von den zehn Jungfrauen, ein deutsches Drama des Mittelal-ters*. Rostock.

Becker, Hansjakob. 1971. *Die Responsorien des Kartäuserbreviers. Untersuchungen zu Urform und Herkunft des Antiphonars der Kartause*. Münchener Theologi-sche Studien, 2 Systematische Abteilung 39. Munich: Max Hueber.

Beckers, Otto, ed. 1905. *Das Spiel von den zehn Jungfrauen und das Katharinen-spiel*. Germanistische Abhandlungen 24. Breslau: M & H Marcus. Repr. 1977. Hildesheim: Olms.

Beer, Ellen J. 1965. *Initial und Miniatur. Buchmalerei aus neun Jahrhunderten in Handschriften der Badischen Landesbibliothek*. Basel: Feuermann.

Beissel, Stephan. 1892. "Die Verehrung der Heiligen und ihrer Reliquien in Deutschland während der zweiten Hälfte des Mittelalters." *Stimmen aus Maria Laach. Erg.-Heft 54*. Repr. as "Zweiter Teil" (pp. 1-143) in Beissel, Stephan, *Die Verehrung der Heiligen und ihrer Reliquien in Deutschland im Mittelalter*. Darmstadt: Wissenschaftl. Buchgesellschaft, 1976. [Part 1: pp. 1-148; followed by part 2: pp. 1-143, cited as (1892) II, (page number)]

——. 1909. *Geschichte der Verehrung Marias in Deutschland während des Mittelalters*. Freiburg i. Br.: Herder. Repr. 1972. Darmstadt: Wissenschaftl. Buchgesellschaft.

Benedict, Saint. 1980. *Die Benediktus-Regel: Lateinisch-deutsch.* Ed. Basilius Steidle OSB. 4th ed. Beuron: Beuroner Kunstverlag.

——. 1929. *Regula Sancti P. Benedicti. Cum approbatis a sede AP. congregationis S. Martini de Beuron constitutionibus.* 3rd edition by Raphael Walzer. Beuron.

Berger, Blandine-Dominique. 1976. *Le drame liturgique de Pâques du xe au xiiie siècle: liturgie et théâtre.* Théologie Historique 37. Paris: Éditions Beauchesne.

Bergmann, Rolf. 1972a. *Studien zu Entstehung und Geschichte der deutschen Passionsspiele des 13. und 14. Jahrhunderts.* Münstersche Mittelalter-Schriften 14. Munich: Wilhelm Fink Verlag.

——. 1972b. "Zur Überlieferung der mittelalterlichen geistlichen Spiele. Mit 6 Abbildungen." In *Festschrift Matthias Zender, Studien zu Volkskultur, Sprache und Landesgeschichte,* ed. Edith Ennen and Günter Wiegelmann, 2: 900-909. Bonn: L. Böhrscheid.

——. 1978. "Interpretation." In Schützeichel, ed., 217-260.

——. 1979. "Spiele, Mittelalterliche geistliche." In *RL* 4: 64-100.

——. 1985. "Aufführungstext und Lesetext. Zur Funktion der Überlieferung des mittelalterlichen geistlichen deutschen Dramas." In *The Theatre in the Middle Ages,* ed. Herman Braet et al. Mediaevalia Lovaniensia ser. 1, studia 13, pp. 314-351. Leuven: Leuven University Press.

——. 1986. *Katalog der deutschsprachigen geistlichen Spiele und Marienklagen des Mittelalters.* Munich: C.H. Beck.

——. 1994. "Geistliche Spiele des Mittelalters—Katalogerfassung und Neufunde." In Siller, ed., 13-32.

——, and Kurt Gärtner, eds. 1993. *Methoden und Probleme der Edition mittelalterlicher deutscher Texte.* Bamberger Fachtagung 26.–29. Juni 1991. Beihefte zu editio 4. Tübingen: Niemeyer.

——, and Stefanie Stricker. 1994. "Zur Terminologie und Wortgeschichte des Geistlichen Spiels." In Mehler–Touber, eds., 49-77.

Bernt, Günter. 1958. "Nachwort." In *Carmina Burana.* dtv, 837-862.

——. 1978. "Carmina Burana." In ²*VL* 1: 1179-1186.

Bertamini, Tullio. 1968. "La bolla 'Transiturus' di papa Urbano IV e l'ufficio del 'Corpus Domini' secondo il codice di S. Lorenzo di Bognanco." *Aevum* 42: 29-58.

Bihlmeyer, Karl, ed. 1907. *Heinrich Seuse, Deutsche Schriften. Im Auftrag der Würtembergischen Kommission für Landesgeschichte herausgegeben.* [pp. 360-393 *Briefbüchlein,* pp. 403-554 *Das grosse Briefbuch*]. Stuttgart: Kohlhammer.

Bischoff, Bernhard. 1979. *Paläographie des römischen Altertums und des abendländischen Mittelalters.* Grundlagen der Germanistik 24. Berlin: Erich Schmidt.

Björkvall, Gunilla, and Ruth Steiner. 1982. "Some prosulas for offertory antiphons." *Journal of the Plainsong and Mediaeval Music Society* 5: 13-35.

Block, K.S., ed. 1922. *Ludus Coventriae or The Plaie called Corpus Christi, Cotton Ms. Vespasian D.viii.* Early English Text Society, e.s. 120. Repr. 1960.

Blosen, Hans, ed. 1979. *Das Wiener Osterspiel. Abdruck der Handschrift und Lese-ausgabe.* Texte des späten Mittelalters und der frühen Neuzeit 33. Berlin: Erich Schmidt.

Blume, Clemens. 1909. "Das Fronleichnams-Fest. Seine ersten Urkunden und Offizien." *Theologie und Glaube* 1: 337-349.

Bohn, P[eter]. 1877. "'Marienklage.' 'Theophilus' [Trier]." *Monatshefte für Musik-Geschichte* 9: 1-4, 17-25.

Boletta, William L. 1967. "The Role of Music in Medieval German Drama: Easter Plays and Passion Plays." PhD dissertation. Vanderbilt University.

Bonniwell, William R. 1945. *A History of the Dominican Liturgy.* 2nd ed. New York: Joseph F. Wagner.

Bourgeault, Cynthia. 1985. "Liturgical Dramaturgy." *Comparative Drama* 17: 124-140. Repr. in Campbell–Davidson, eds., 144-160.

Boyle. Leonard E. 1992. "Diplomatics." In *Medieval Studies. An Introduction,* 2nd ed. James M. Powell, pp. 82-113. Syracuse: Syracuse University Press.

Braun, Joseph. 1937. *Liturgia Romana. Eine Darstellung des römischen Ritus in lexikalischer Gestalt.* Hannover: Joseph Giesel.

Braune, Wilhelm, ed. 1958. *Althochdeutsches Lesebuch.* 13th edition by Karl Helm. Tübingen: Niemeyer.

Brenn, Franz. 1956. "Zur Frage gregorianischer Lesarten." *Die Musikforschung* 9: 442-443.

Brett-Evans, David. 1975. *Von Hrotsvit bis Folz und Gengenbach. Eine Geschichte des mittelalterlichen deutschen Dramas.* 2 vols. Grundlagen der Germanistik 15, 18. Berlin: Erich Schmidt.

——. 1964-1965. Review of Karin Schneider, ed. *Das Eisenacher Zehnjungfrauen-spiel* (1964). *German Life and Letters* 18: 226-227.

Breviary of the Order of Preachers [BOP]. 1967. Dublin: St. Saviour's.

Breviarium Romanum [BR]. 1915. Regensburg, Rome: Pustet.

Brooks, Neil C., ed. 1925. "Eine liturgisch-dramatische Himmelfahrtsfeier." *ZfdA* 62 (NF 50): 91-96.

Broszinski, Hartmut, and Hansjürgen Linke, eds. 1987. "Kasseler (mnd.) Paradies-spiel-Fragmente." *ZfdA* 116: 36-52.

Browe, Peter. 1928. "Die Ausbreitung des Fronleichnamsfestes." *Jahrbuch für Liturgiewissenschaft* 8: 107-143.

——. 1933. *Die Verehrung der Eucharistie im Mittelalter.* Munich: Max Hueber. Repr. 1967. Rome: Heider.

——, ed. 1934. *Textus antiqui de Festo Corporis Christi.* Opuscula et textus 4, series liturgica. Münster: Aschendorff.

——. 1950. "Zur Geschichte des Dreifaltigkeitsfestes." *Archiv für Liturgiewissen-schaft* 1: 65-81.

Brück, Anton Philipp. 1960. "Mainz. I. Bistum und Erzbistum." In *Religion in Ge-schichte und Gegenwart* 4: 613-615.

Bruder, P. 1901. "Die Fronleichnamsfeier zu Mainz um das Jahr 1400." *Der Katholik* 81: 489-507.

——. 1900-1901. "Das Bannfasten oder 'Ieiunium bannitum'." *Pastor bonus* 13: 550-556.

Brunner, Lance W. 1988. "Responsory." In *DMA* 10: 336-337.

Bugge, John. 1975. *Virginitas. An Essay in the History of a Medieval Ideal.* Archives Internationales d'Histoire des Idées, series minor 17. The Hague: Martinus Nijhoff.

Butzmann, Hans. 1964. *Die Weissenburger Handschriften.* Kataloge der Herzog August Bibliothek Wolfenbüttel. Die neue Reihe 10. Frankfurt/Main: Klostermann.

Bužga, Jaroslav. 1997. "Prag, tschech. Praha." In ²*MGG* 7: 1776-1792.

——, and Adrienne Simpson. 1980. "Prague." In *New Grove* 15: 192-201.

Cabrol, Fernand. 1906. *Die Liturgie der Kirche.* Transl. by Georg Pletl. Kempten and Munich: Kösel.

Campbell, Thomas P. 1981. "Liturgy and Drama: Recent Approaches to Medieval Theatre." *Theatre Journal* 33: 289-301.

——, and Clifford Davidson, eds. 1985. *The Fleury Playbook. Essays and Studies.* Early Drama, Art, and Music Monograph Series 7. Kalamazoo: Medieval Institute.

Cappelli, Adriano. 1973. *Dizionario di Abbreviature latine ed italiane ... Lexicon abbreviaturarum.* 6th ed. Milan: Ulrico Hoepli.

——. 1982. *The Elements of Abbreviation in Medieval Latin Paleography.* Transl. by David Heimann and Richard Kay. University of Kansas Publications. Library Series 47. Lawrence: University of Kansas Printing Service. Repr. 1984.

Cargill, Oscar. 1930. *Drama and Liturgy.* New York: Columbia University Press.

Carmina Burana. [Facsimile] 1967. Faksimile-Ausgabe der Handschrift Clm 4660–Clm 4660a. Ed. Bernhard Bischoff. Veröffentlichungen mittelalterlicher Musikhandschriften 9. Munich: Prestel.

——. [1.3.] 1970. Mit Benutzung der Vorarbeiten Wilhelm Meyers kritisch herausgegeben von Alfons Hilka und Otto Schumann. Vol. 1.3. *Die Trink- und Spielerlieder–Die geistlichen Dramen.* Nachträge. Ed. †Otto Schumann and Bernhard Bischoff. Heidelberg: Carl Winter.

——. [dtv] 1985. Die Lieder der Benediktbeurer Handschrift. Zweisprachige Ausgabe. dtv Klassik 2063. 3rd ed. Munich: Deutscher Taschenbuch Verlag. [Vollständige Ausgabe des Originaltextes nach der von B. Bischoff abgeschlossenen kritischen Ausgabe von A. Hilka und O. Schumann (1930-1970). Übersetzung der lateinischen Texte von Carl Fischer, der mittelhochdeutschen von Hugo Kuhn. Anmerkungen und Nachwort von Günter Bernt.]

Chronici Saxonici Continuatio (Thuringica). See Holder-Egger, ed. 1899.

Concilia Germaniae. See Hartzheim, ed. 1761.

Corbin, Solange. 1960. *La Déposition Liturgique du Christ au Vendredi Saint. Sa place dans l'histoire des rites et du théâtre religieux. (Analyse de documents portugais).* Collection Portugaise. Paris: "Les Belles Lettres." Lisbon: Bertrand.

———. 1977. *Die Neumen*. Palaeographie der Musik 1, fasc. 3. Cologne: Arno Volk.

Corpus Antiphonalium Officii [CAO]. 1963-1979. Ed. René-Jean Hesbert. 6 vols. Rerum Ecclesiasticarum Documenta, series maior, fontes 7-12. Rome: Herder.

1 [7] (1963): *Manuscripti 'Cursus Romanus'* [6 manuscripts: C Compiègne, G 'Gallicanus,' B Bamberg, E Ivrea, M Monza, V Verona].

2 [8] (1965): *Manuscripti 'Cursus Monasticus'* [6 manuscripts: H Hartker, R Rheinau, D St. Denis, F Saint-Maur-les-Fossées, S Silos, L St.-Loup de Benevent].

3 [9] (1968): *Invitatoria et Antiphonae*.

4 [10] (1970): *Responsoria, Versus, Hymni et Varia*.

5 [11] (1975): *Fontes earumque prima ordinatio*.

6 [12] (1979): *Secunda et tertia ordinationes*.

[vols. 3-4 are cited by chant number]

Corpus troporum 1 (1975), 3 (1982). *Tropes du propre de la messe*. Studia Latina Stockholmiensia 21, 25. Stockholm: Almquist & Wiksell.

CT 1 (1975): *Cycle de Noël*. Ed. Ritva Jonsson.

CT 3 (1982): *Cycle de Pâques*. Ed. Gunilla Björkvall, Gunilla Iversen, and Ritva Jonsson.

Coussemaker, Edmond de, ed. 1860. *Drames liturgiques du Moyen Âge. Texte et musique*. Rennes: Vater. Repr. 1964. New York: Broude Bros.

Creizenach, Wilhelm. 1911. *Geschichte des neueren Dramas* 1: *Mittelalter und Frührenaissance*. 2nd ed. Halle: Max Niemeyer.

Crocker, Richard L. 1966a. *A History of Musical Style*. McGraw-Hill Series in Music. New York: McGraw-Hill.

———. 1966b. "The Troping Hypothesis." *Musical Quarterly* 52: 183-203.

Cronica S. Petri Erfordensis moderna a. 1072-1335 (vulgo "Sampetrinum"). See Holder-Egger, ed. 1899.

Curschmann, Michael, and Ingeborg Glier, eds. 1981. *Deutsche Dichtung des Mittelalters* 3: *Spätmittelalter*. Munich and Vienna: Hanser Verlag.

[Cutter, Paul F.] 1980. "Responsory." In *New Grove* 15: 759-765.

Dauven-van Knippenberg, Carla. 1994. "Ein Anfang ohne Ende: Einführendes zur Frage nach dem Verhältnis zwischen Predigt und geistlichem Schauspiel des Mittelalters." In Mehler–Touber, eds., 143-160.

Davidson, Clifford. 1974. "Medieval Drama: Diversity and Theatricality." *Comparative Drama* 8: 5-12.

———. 1979-1980. "On the Uses of Iconographic Studies: The Example of the 'Sponsus' from St. Martial of Limoges." *Comparative Drama* 13: 300-319.

———, et al., eds. 1974. *Studies in Medieval Drama in Honor of William L. Smoldon on His 82nd Birthday*. *Comparative Drama* 8. Kalamazoo: Western Michigan University.

———, and John H. Stroupe, eds. 1993. *Medieval Drama on the Continent of Europe*. *Comparative Drama* 27. Kalamazoo: Western Michigan University.

De Boor, Helmut, ed. 1965. *Mittelalter* 1: *Die deutsche Literatur: Texte und Zeugnisse 1, 1.* Munich: C.H. Beck.

——. 1967. *Die Textgeschichte der lateinischen Osterfeiern.* Hermaea. Germanistische Forschungen, NF 22. Tübingen: Niemeyer.

Decker, Otmar. 1935. *Die Stellung des Predigerordens zu den Dominikanerinnen (1207-1267).* Quellen und Forschungen zur Geschichte des Dominikanerordens in Deutschland 31.

De Grocheo. *See* Rohloff, ed. 1972, and Seay, transl. 1973.

Delaissé, L.M.J. 1949. "Les remaniements d'un légendier témoins de l'évolution de la liturgie romaine au XIIIe siècle." *Scriptorium* 3: 26-44.

——. 1950. "À la recherche des origines de l'Office du Corpus Christi dans les manuscrits liturgiques." *Scriptorium* 4: 220-239.

De Puniet, Pierre. 1933. *Das Römische Pontificale. Geschichte und Kommentar.* 2 vols. Stift Klosterneuburg.

De Ricci, Seymour. 1937. *Census of Medieval and Renaissance Manuscripts in the United States and Canada.* Vol. 2. New York: Wilson Company.

Deshusses, Jean, ed. 1971, 1979, 1982. *Le Sacramentaire Grégorien [SGreg]. Ses principales formes d'après les plus anciens manuscrits.* Édition comparative. 3 vols. Spicilegium Friburgense 16, 24, 28. Fribourg/Switzerland: Éditions Universitaires.

——, and Benoit Darragon. 1982-1983. *Concordances et tableaux pour l'étude des grands sacramentaires.* 3 vols. Spicilegii Friburgensis Subsidia 9-14. Fribourg: Éditions Universitaires.

1 [9] (1982): *Concordances des pièces.*

2 [10] (1982): *Tableaux synoptiques.*

3 [part 1] [11] (1982): *Concordance verbale;* [parts 2-4] [12-14] (1983).

Die deutsche Literatur des Mittelalters. Verfasserlexikon [VL]. 1933-1955. 1st ed. Ed. Wolfgang Stammler and Karl Langosch. 5 vols. Berlin.

Die deutsche Literatur des Mittelalters. Verfasserlexikon [²VL]. 1978- . 2nd rev. ed. Ed. Kurt Ruh et al. Berlin, New York: de Gruyter. Vols. 1-10 (1978-1999). Vol. 11 ('Nachtragsband') forthcoming.

Dictionary of the Middle Ages [DMA]. 1982-1989. Ed. Joseph R. Strayer. 13 vols. New York: Scribner.

Dieterich, Johann Conrad, ed. 1642. *Specimen Antiquitatum Biblicarum, quo libris tribus varia instituta, mores et ritus ... e Sacris literis exhibentur.* Marburg. [pp. 122-124: "Marburger Prophetenspielfragment": *De Nativitate Christi.*]

Dobszay, László. 1997. "Offizium." In ²*MGG* 7: 593-609.

Dold, Alban, ed. 1936. *Das älteste Liturgiebuch der lateinischen Kirche: Ein altgallikanisches Lektionar des 5./6. Jahrhunderts aus dem Wolfenbütteler Palimpsest-Codex Weissenburgensis 76.* Texte und Arbeiten 26-28. Beuron i. Hohenzollern: Kunstverlag Beuron. Beiträge zur Ergründung des älteren lateinischen christlichen Schriftums und Gottesdienstes.

Donovan, Richard B. 1958. *The Liturgical Drama in Medieval Spain*. Studies and Texts 4. Toronto: Pontifical Institute of Mediaeval Studies.

Dörrer, Anton. 1953. "Zehnjungfrauenspiele." In *VL* 4: 1130-1139.

———. 1965. "Schicksale des Sterzinger Spielarchivs." *ZfdA* 94: 138-141.

Dreimüller, Karl. 1935. "Die Musik des Alsfelder Passionsspiels: Ein Beitrag zur Geschichte der Musik in den geistlichen Spielen des deutschen Mittelalters. Mit erstmaliger Veröffentlichung der Melodien aus der Kasseler Handschrift des Alsfelder Spiels (Landes-Bibliothek Kassel 2° fol. Mss. poet. 18)." 3 vols. Dissertation. University of Vienna.

1: "Abhandlungen."

2: "Das musikalische Szenarium des Alsfelder Passionsspiels. Mit Ergänzung und Bestimmung der liturgischen Texte und einem Anhang von 45 Melodien zu lateinischen Textparallelen im Egerer Fronleichnamsspiel, aus der Handschrift 'Ludus de creacione mundi no 7060' des Germanischen Nationalmuseums in Nürnberg."

3: "Die Melodien des Alsfelder Passionsspiels. Übertragungen der Melodien aus der Kasseler Handschrift des Alsfelder Spiels."

———. 1950. "Die Musik im geistlichen Spiel des späten deutschen Mittelalters, dargestellt am Alsfelder Passionsspiel." *KmJb* 34: 27-34.

Dumas, A., ed. 1981. *Liber Sacramentorum Gellonensis* [*SGell*]. 2 vols. Corpus Christianorum, Series Latina 159 (*Textus*), 159A (*Introductio*). Turnhout: Brepols.

Dunn, E. Catherine. 1972. "Voice Structure in the Liturgical Drama." In Taylor–Nelson, eds., 28-43.

Düringische Chronik. See Rothe.

Durandus, Gulielmus. 1995. *Guillelmi Duranti Rationale divinorum officiorum I-IV*. Ed. A. Davril and T.M. Thibodeau. Corpus Christianorum, Continuatio Mediaevalis 140. Turnhout: Brepols.

Dürre, Konrad. 1915. *Die Mercatorszene im lateinisch-liturgischen, altdeutschen und altfranzösischen religiösen Drama*. Halle (Saale): Heinrich John.

Dutka, JoAnna. 1980. *Music in the English Mystery Plays*. Early Drama, Art, and Music Reference Series 2. Kalamazoo: Medieval Institute.

Eggers, Hans. 1985. "Sog. 'Luzerner Marienklage.'" In ^{2}*VL* 5: 1093.

Eisenhofer, Ludwig. 1950. *Grundriss der Liturgik des römischen Ritus*. 5th ed. rev. by Joseph Lechner. Freiburg i. Br.: Herder.

Engel, Hans. 1966. *Musik in Thüringen*. Mitteldeutsche Forschungen 39. Cologne: Böhlau.

Ettmüller, Ludwig. 1867. *Herbstabende und Winternächte: Gespräche über deutsche Dichtungen und Dichter* 3: *Die höfischen Minnesänger und Meister des 13. Jahrhunderts, das Volkslied und das Schauspiel des 14.-16. Jahrhunderts*. Stuttgart: J.G. Cotta.

Everist, Mark. 1990. "From Paris to St. Andrews: The Origins of W$_1$." *JAMS* 43: 1-42.

Falck, Robert. 1980. "Contrafactum." In *New Grove* 4: 700-701.

Federl, Ekkehard. 1937. *Spätmittelalterliche Choralpflege in Würzburg und in mainfränkischen Klöstern.* St. Ottilien, Oberbayern: Missionsdruckerei.

Feldkamm, Jacob. 1900. *Geschichtliche Nachrichten über die Erfurter Weihbischöfe.* Mitteilungen des Vereins für Geschichte und Altertumskunde von Erfurt 21.

Fellerer, Karl Gustav. 1956. "Kirchenmusikalische Vorschriften im Mittelalter." *KmJb* 40: 1-11.

Fiala, Virgil, and Wolfgang Irtenkauf. 1963. "Versuch einer liturgischen Nomenklatur." *Zeitschrift für Bibliothekswesen und Bibliographie* (Sonderheft), pp. 105-137. Frankfurt am Main: Klostermann.

Fischer, Ottokar. 1910. "Die mittelalterlichen Zehnjungfrauenspiele." *Archiv für das Studium der neueren Sprachen und Literaturen* 125. N.S. 25: 9-26.

Flanigan, C. Clifford. 1973-1974. "The Roman Rite and the Origins of the Liturgical Drama." *University of Toronto Quarterly* 43: 263-284.

——. 1974. "The Liturgical Context of the *Quem Queritis* Trope." *Comparative Drama* 8: 45-62.

——. 1985. "The Fleury *Playbook* and the Traditions of Medieval Latin Drama." *Comparative Drama* 18: 348-372. Repr. in Campbell-Davidson, eds., 1-25.

Flemming, Willi. 1971. *Die Gestaltung der liturgischen Osterfeier in Deutschland.* Wiesbaden: Verlag der Akademie der Wissenschaften und der Literatur, Mainz.

Fluck, Hans, ed. 1932. *Das Spiel von den zehn Jungfrauen.* Ferdinand Schöninghs Dombücherei 108. Paderborn: Schöningh.

Frank, Grace. 1954. *The Medieval French Drama.* Oxford: Clarendon Press. Repr. 1967.

Fransen, J. *See* Lambot-Fransen.

Freiesleben, Gottfried Christian. 1765. *Kleine Nachlese zu des berühmten Hrn. Prof. Gottscheds nöthigem Vorrathe zur Geschichte der deutschen dramatischen Dichtkunst.* In Gottsched, Appendix.

Frere, Walter Howard, ed. 1901-1924. *Antiphonale Sarisburiense* [*ASar*]. *A Reproduction in Facsimile of a Manuscript of the Thirteenth Century with a Dissertation and Analytical Index.* 6 vols. London: Plainsong and Mediaeval Music Society. Vol. 1: *Introduction*; Vols. 2-6: *Facsimile.* Repr. 1966. Farnborough.

Freybe, Albert. 1870. *Das Spiel von den zehn Jungfrauen, eine Opera seria, gegeben zu Eisenach am 24. April 1322.* Leipzig: Justus Naumann.

——. 1907. "Das Spiel von den zehn Jungfrauen." *Allgemeine ev.-lutherische Kirchenzeitung* 40, no. 46: 1087-1091, no. 47: 1109-1113. Leipzig.

Froger, Jacques, ed. 1970. *Antiphonaire de Hartker, manuscrits Saint-Gall, 390-391* [*AHartk*] PalMus 2.1. Bern: Lang [Repr. of 1900 Solesmes ed.].

Froning, Richard, ed. 1891-1892. *Das Drama des Mittelalters.* 3 vols. Deutsche Nationalliteratur 14, 1-3. Stuttgart. Repr. 1964. Darmstadt: Wissenschaftliche Buchgesellschaft.

Funkhänel, Carl Hermann. 1855. *Ueber das geistliche Spiel von den zehn Jung-frauen*. Vortrag am 23. Juni 1855 im Carl Friedrichs-Gymnasium Eisenach. Weimar: H.Böhlau.

Gärtner, Kurt. *See* Bergmann–Gärtner.

Gastoué, Amédée. 1937-1939. "Le chant gallican." *Revue du Chant Grégorien* 41 (1937) 101-106, 131-133, 167-176; 42 (1938) 5-12, 57-62, 76-80, 107-112, 146-151, 171-176; 43 (1939) 7-12, 44-46. Repr. *see* next entry.

———. 1939. *Le chant gallican*. Grenoble: Librairie Saint-Grégoire.

Gelineau, Joseph. 1964. *Voices and Instruments in Christian Worship. Principles, Laws, Applications*. Transl. by Clifford Howell. London: Burns and Oates.

Göllner, Marie Louise. 1985. "Musical Settings of the Trope *Ab hac familia*." In Silagi, ed., 89-109.

Gottschall, Dagmar. 1996. "Papst Urban IV." In ^2VL 10: 121-123.

Gottsched, Johann Christoph. 1765. *Des nöthigen Vorraths zur Geschichte der deut-schen dramatischen Dichtkunst, Zweyter Theil, oder Nachlese aller deutschen Trauer-, Lust- und Singspiele, die vom 1450sten bis zum 1760sten Jahre im Drucke erschienen*. Leipzig: Teubner.

Das Graduale von Sankt Katharinenthal. Eine wissenschaftlich bearbeitete Faksimile-Ausgabe. 1980, 1983. Ed. Editionskommission of the Schweizerisches Landes-museum, the Gottfried Keller Stiftung and the Kanton of Thurgau. 2 vols. Lucerne: Faksimile Verlag.

1 (1980): *Faksimile*, gen. ed. Johannes Duft et al.

2 (1983): *Kommentar*, gen. ed. Lucas Wüthrich et al.

Graduale Romanum [GR]. 1974. *Graduale sacrosanctae Romanae ecclesiae de tem-pore et de sanctis*. Solesmes.

Graduale Triplex [GRTri]. 1979. *seu Graduale Romanum Pauli Pp VI cura recogni-tum ... , neumis Laudensibus* (cod. 239) *et Sangallensibus* (codicum Sangallen-sis 359 et Einsidlensis 121) *nunc auctum*. Solesmes.

Gregorius I. 1999. *Homiliae in Evangelia*. Ed. Raymond Étaix. Corpus Christiano-rum, Series Latina 141. Turnhout: Brepols.

———. *XL Homiliarum in Evangelia libri duo*. PL 76: 1075-1312.

Gstrein, Rainer. 1994. "Anmerkungen zu den Gesängen der Osterspiele des Ster-zinger 'Debs'-Codex." In Siller, ed., 91-98.

Gümbel-Seiling, Max. 1925. *Das Spiel von den zehn Jungfrauen [Eisenach 1322]*. Deutsche Volksspiele des Mittelalters 8. Leipzig: Breitkopf & Härtel, 1919, 5th ed. 1925.

Gy, Pierre-Marie. 1980. "L'office du Corpus Christi et S. Thomas d'Aquin." *Re-vue des sciences philosophiques et théologiques* 64: 491-507.

Haas, Robert. 1931. *Aufführungspraxis der Musik*. Handbuch der Musikwissen-schaft. Potsdam: Akademische Verlagsgesellschaft Athenaion.

Habermann, Paul, and Wolfgang Mohr. 1958. "Deutsche Versmaße und Strophen-formen." In *RL* 1: 231-244.

Hammerstein, Reinhold. 1962. *Die Musik der Engel. Untersuchungen zur Musikanschauung des Mittelalters*. Bern and Munich: Francke.

Handschin, Jacques. 1949-1951. "Akzent." In *MGG* 1: 260-266.

Hänggi, Anton, ed. 1957. *Der Rheinauer Liber Ordinarius* [ORh.80]. Spicilegium Friburgense 1. Fribourg/Switzerland: Universitätsverlag.

Hanssens, Johannes M., ed. 1948-1950. *Amalarii Episcopi Opera Liturgica Omnia*. 3 vols. Studi e Testi 138-140. Vatican City: Biblioteca Apostolica Vaticana.

Hanus, Dr. Ignac Jan, ed. 1863. *Die lateinisch-böhmischen Oster-Spiele des 14.-15. Jahrhunderts. Handschriftlich aufbewahrt in der k. k. Universitäts-Bibliothek zu Prag*. Prague: Carl Bellmann.

Hardison, Osborne B. 1965. *Christian Rite and Christian Drama in the Middle Ages*. Essays in the Origin and Early History of Modern Drama. Baltimore: John Hopkins Press.

Hartl, Eduard, ed. 1937. *Das Drama des Mittelalters* 1: *Osterfeiern*; 2: *Osterspiele*. Deutsche Literatur. Sammlung literarischer Kunst- und Kulturdenkmäler in Entwicklungsreihen. Reihe Drama des Mittelalters. Leipzig: Reclam. Repr. 1964-1966. Darmstadt: Wissenschaftliche Buchgesellschaft.

Hartzheim, Josephus. 1761. *Concilia Germaniae* 4 (1290-1400). Cologne. Repr. 1970-1996. Aalen: Scientia Verlag.

Haug, Andreas. 1997. "Melisma." In *²MGG* 6: 19-29.

——, SL (Bruno Stäblein), and David Hiley. 1998. "Tropus." In *²MGG* 9: 897-921.

Heckenbach, Willibrord Alfons. 1971. *Das Antiphonar von Ahrweiler* [AAhrw]. *Studien am Codex 2a/b des Pfarrarchivs Ahrweiler (um 1400)*. Beiträge zur rheinischen Musikgeschichte 94. Cologne: Arno Volk-Verlag.

Heinemann, Otto von. 1884-1888. *Die Helmstedter Handschriften*. 3 vols. Kataloge der Herzog August Bibliothek Wolfenbüttel. Die alte Reihe 1.1-3. Wolfenbüttel. Repr. 1963-1965. Frankfurt am Main: Klostermann.

Heinzer, Felix. 1995. "Die neuen Standorte der ehemals Donaueschinger Handschriftensammlung." *Scriptorium* 49: 312-319.

——, and Gerhard Stamm. 1984. *Die Handschriften von St. Peter im Schwarzwald* 2: *Die Pergamenthandschriften*. Die Handschriften der Badischen Landesbibliothek in Karlsruhe 10. Wiesbaden: Harrassowitz.

Heisler, Maria-Elisabeth. 1985. "Die Problematik des 'germanischen' oder 'deutschen' Choraldialekts." *Studia Musicologica Academiae Scientiarum Hungaricae* 27: 67-82.

——. 1987. "Studien zum ostfränkischen Choraldialekt." Dissertation. Frankfurt am Main.

Helwig, Paul. *See* Höfer–Helwig.

Hennig, Ursula. 1975. "Die Klage der Maria Magdalena in den deutschen Osterspielen." *ZfdPh* 94 (Sonderheft *Mittelalterliches deutsches Drama*): 108-138.

——. 1977. "Die lateinisch-liturgische Grundlage der tschechischen Marienspiele." *ZfdPh* 96: 89-102.

——, ed. 1986. *Das Wiener Passionsspiel. Cod. 12887 (Suppl. 561) der Österreichischen Nationalbibliothek zu Wien* [WienP]. *Mit Einleitung und Texabdruck in Abbildung*. Litterae 92. Göppingen: Kümmerle.

——. 1988. "Trierer Marienklage und Osterspiel." *Beiträge* 110: 63-77.

——. 1994. "Die Osterereignisse in den deutschen Passionsspielen." In Siller, ed., 99-108.

——, and Andreas Traub, eds. 1990. *Trierer Marienklage und Osterspiel. Codex 1973/63 der Stadtbibliothek Trier* [TrierO]. Litterae 91. Göppingen: Kümmerle.

Hesbert, René-Jean, ed. 1935. See *Antiphonale Missarum Sextuplex*.

——, ed. 1963-1979. See *Corpus Antiphonalium Officii*.

Heyne, Hildegard. 1922. *Das Gleichnis von den klugen und törichten Jungfrauen: Eine literarisch-ikonographische Studie zur altchristlichen Zeit*. Leipzig: Haessel Verlag.

Hilberg, Birgitt. 1993. *Manuscripta poetica et romanensia. Manuscripta theatralia*. Die Handschriften der Gesamthochschul-Bibliothek Kassel, Landesbibliothek und Murhardsche Bibliothek der Stadt Kassel 4,2. Wiesbaden: Harrassowitz.

Hiley, David. 1993. *Western Plainchant. A Handbook*. Oxford: Clarendon Press.

Hilka, †Alfons, O. Schumann, and B. Bischoff, eds. See *Carmina Burana* [1.3] 1970.

Hintzenstern, Herbert von. 1955. "Vom Eisenacher Zehnjungfrauenspiel." *Thüringer Tageblatt* (22 Nov. 1955) 12.

Hodes, Karlheinrich. 1979. *Der Gregorianische Choral. Eine Einführung*. 2nd rev. ed. Darmstadt: Wissenschaftliche Buchgesellschaft.

Hoebeke, Marcel, ed. 1959. *Het Spel van de V vroede ende van de V dwaeze Maegden*. Zwolse Drukken en herdrukken voor de Maatschappij der Nederlandse Letterkunde te Leiden 37. Zwolle: Tjeenk Willink.

Höfer, Conrad, and Paul Helwig. 1921. *Das Eisenacher Spiel von den zehn Jungfrauen 1321*. Beiträge zur Geschichte Eisenachs 27. Eisenach: H. Kahle.

Holder-Egger, Oswald, ed. 1899. *Monumenta Erphesfurtensia saec. XII, XIII, XIV.* MGH, SS, ed. separatim [42] [pp. 150-369 *Cronica S. Petri Erfordensis moderna* or "Sampetrinum"; pp. 447-485 *Chronici Saxonici Continuatio* (*Thuringica*) *Erfordensis a. 1227-1353*]. Hannover, Leipzig: Hahn.

Holweck, Frederick George. 1892. *Fasti Mariani, sive Calendarium festorum sanctae Mariae Virginis Deiparae*. Freiburg i. Br.: Herder.

Hoppin, Richard. 1978a. *Anthology of Medieval Music*. The Norton Introduction to Music History. New York: Norton and Co.

——. 1978b. *Medieval Music*. The Norton Introduction to Music History. New York: Norton and Co.

Hucke, Helmut. 1963. "Responsorium I-III and V-VII." In *MGG* 11: 313-318, 320-325.

——. 1973. "Das Responsorium." In *Gattungen der Musik in Einzeldarstellungen. Gedenkschrift Leo Schrade*, ed. W. Arlt, E. Lichtenhahn, and M. Haas, pp. 144-191. Bern: Francke Verlag.

——, and Hartmut Möller. 1995. "Gregorianischer Gesang." In ²*MGG* 3: 1609-1621.

Hughes, Andrew. 1974. *Medieval Music: The Sixth Liberal Art*. Toronto Medieval Bibliographies 4. Toronto: University of Toronto Press. Rev. ed. 1980.

——. 1982. *Medieval Manuscripts for Mass and Office. A Guide to Their Organization and Terminology*. Toronto: University of Toronto Press.

——. 1985. "Late Medieval Rhymed Offices. Research Report." *Journal of the Plainsong and Medieval Music Society* 8: 33-49.

——. 1988. "Rhymed Offices. " In *DMA* 10: 366-377.

——. 1989a. *Style and Symbol. Medieval Music: 800-1453*. Musicological Studies 51. Ottawa: The Institute of Mediaeval Music.

——. 1989b. "Troper." In *DMA* 12: 208.

——. 1991. "Liturgical Drama: Falling between the Disciplines." In Simon, ed., 42-62.

——. 1994, 1996. *Late Medieval Liturgical Offices (LMLO). Resources for Electronic Research* 1: *Texts*; 2: *Sources and Chants*. Subsidia Mediaevali 23, 24. Toronto: Pontifical Institute of Mediaeval Studies.

Hughes, David G. 1987. "Evidence for the Traditional View of the Transmission of Gregorian Chant." *JAMS* 40: 377-404.

Huglo, Michel. 1980a. "Antiphon." In *New Grove* 1: 471-481.

——. 1980b. "Gospel." In *New Grove* 7: 544-549.

——. 1996. "Liturgische Gesangbücher." In ²*MGG* 5: 1412-1437.

——, et al. 2000. *Die Lehre vom einstimmigen liturgischen Gesang*. Geschichte der Musiktheorie, ed. Thomas Ertelt and Frieder Zaminer, vol. 4. Darmstadt: Wissenschaftliche Buchgesellschaft.

Irtenkauf, Wolfgang. 1963. "Reimoffizium." In *MGG* 11: 172-176.

Jammers, Ewald. 1959. "Der musikalische Vortrag des altdeutschen Epos." *Der Deutschunterricht* 11: 98-116.

——. 1965. *Tafeln zur Neumenschrift*. Tutzing: Hans Schneider.

——. 1975a. *Aufzeichnungsweisen der einstimmigen ausserliturgischen Musik des Mittelalters*. Palaeographie der Musik 1, fasc. 4. Cologne: Arno Volk.

——. 1975b. "Das mittelalterliche deutsche Epos und die Musik." *Heidelberger Jahrbücher* 1: 31-90.

Janota, Johannes. 1994. "Zur Funktion der Gesänge in der hessischen Passionsspielgruppe." In Siller, ed., 109-120.

——. ed. 1996 [recte 1997]. *Die Hessische Passionsspielgruppe: Edition in Paralleldruck* 1: *Frankfurter Dirigierrolle. Frankfurter Passionsspiel. Mit den Paralleltexten der 'Frankfurter Dirigierrolle,' des 'Alsfelder Passionsspiels,' des 'Heidelberger Passionsspiels,' des 'Frankfurter Osterspielfragments' und des 'Fritzlarer Passionsspielfragments.'* Tübingen: Niemeyer Verlag.

Janson, Tore. 1975. *Prose Rhythm in Medieval Latin from the 9th to the 13th Century*. Acta Universitatis Stockholmiensis. Studia Latina Stockholmiensia 20. Stockholm: Almquist & Wiksell.

Jauernig, R. 1962. "Thüringen." In *Die Religion in Geschichte und Gegenwart* 6: 873-880.

Jodogne, Omer, ed. 1959. *Jean Michel: Le mystère de la Passion (Angers 1486)*. Gembloux: Éditions J. Duculot.

Johansson, Ann-Katrin. 1985. "Observations on the Text of the Offertory Trope *Ab hac familia.*" In Silagi, ed. 83-87.

Johner, Dominicus. 1940. *Wort und Ton im Choral. Ein Beitrag zur Aesthetik des gregorianischen Chorals*. Leipzig: Breitkopf und Härtel.

——, and Maurus Pfaff. 1956. *Choralschule*. 8th ed. Regensburg: Pustet.

Johnston, Alexandra F. 1976. "The Guild of Corpus Christi and the Procession of Corpus Christi in York." *Medieval Studies* 38: 372-384.

Jordanus de Saxonia. *See* Walz, ed. 1951.

Jungmann, Josef Andreas. 1948. *Missarum sollemnia. Eine genetische Erklärung der römischen Messe*. 2 vols. Vienna: Herder.

Kaff, Ludwig. 1956. *Mittelalterliche Oster- und Passionsspiele aus Oberösterreich im Spiegel musikwissenschaftlicher Betrachtung*. Schriftenreihe des Institutes für Landeskunde von Oberösterreich 9. Linz: Oberösterreichischer Landesverlag.

Kelly, Thomas Forest. 1985. "Melisma and Prosula: The Performance of Responsory Tropes." In Silagi, ed., 163-180.

Kern, Anton. 1954. "Das Offizium *De Corpore Christi* in österreichischen Bibiotheken." *Revue bénédictine* 64: 46-67.

Kindermann, Heinz. 1980. *Das Theaterpublikum des Mittelalters*. Salzburg: Otto Müller.

Kippenberg, Burkhard. 1962. *Der Rhythmus im Minnesang*. Münchener Texte und Untersuchungen zur deutschen Literatur des Mittelalters 3. Munich: Beck.

Klammer, Bruno, ed. 1986. *Bozner Passion 1495. Die Spielhandschriften A und B*. Mittlere deutsche Literatur in Neu- und Nachdrucken 20. Bern, Frankfurt am Main, New York: Peter Lang.

Klapper, Joseph. 1928. "Das mittelalterliche Volksschauspiel in Schlesien." *Mitteilungen der schlesischen Gesellschaft für Volkskunde* 29: 168-216.

Klaus, A. 1938. *Ursprung und Verbreitung der Dreifaltigkeitsmesse*. Werl.

Klauser, Renate, and Otto Meyer. 1962. *Clavis Medievalis. Kleines Wörterbuch der Mittelalterforschung*. Wiesbaden: Harrassowitz. Repr. 1966.

Klauser, Theodor. 1935. *Das römische Capitulare evangeliorum. Texte und Untersuchungen zu seiner ältesten Geschichte*. Liturgiegeschichtliche Quellen und Forschungen 28. Münster: Aschendorff.

Klausner, David N. 1989. "Music." In *A Companion for the Medieval Theatre*, ed. Ronald W. Vince, pp. 257-264. New York, London: Greenwood Press.

Klein, H.A., ed. 1926. *Das Spiel von den zehn Jungfrauen*. Diesterwegs deutschkundliche Schülerhefte, Reihe 2, 33. Frankfurt am Main: Diesterweg.

Klein, Theodor Heinrich. 1962. *Die Prozessionsgesänge der Mainzer Kirche aus dem 14. bis 18. Jahrhundert*. Quellen und Abhandlungen zur mittelrheinischen Kirchengeschichte 7. Speyer: Jaegersche Buchdruckerei.

Knight, Alan. 1984. "Drama, French." In *DMA* 4: 263-266.

Koch, K. 1909. "Das Eisenacher Spiel von den zehn Jungfrauen und seine Wirkung." *Thüringer Monatsblätter* 16, no. 10: 125-128.

Koch, Ludwig. 1867. "Das geistliche Spiel von den zehn Jungfrauen zu Eisenach. Nach Sinn und Tendenz beleuchtet." *Zeitschrift des Vereins für thüringische Geschichte und Altertumskunde* 7: 111-132.

Köllner, Georg Paul. 1950. "Der Accentus Moguntinus. Ein Beitrag zur Frage des 'Mainzer Chorals.'" Diss. Mainz. [Available at the Bibliothek des bischöflichen Priesterseminars Mainz.]

——. 1956. "Der Accentus Moguntinus nach den 'Schönborn-Drucken'." *KmJb* 40: 44-62.

——. 1958. "Zur Tradition des Accentus Moguntinus." *KmJb* 42: 39-46.

Korhammer, Michael. 1976. *Die monastischen Cantica im Mittelalter und ihre altenglischen Interlinearversionen*. Studien und Textausgabe. Münchener Universitäts-Schriften: Philosophische Fakultät 6. Munich: Wilhelm Fink.

Körndle, Franz. 1996. "Liturgische Dramen, Geistliche Spiele." In ²*MGG* 5: 1388-1412.

——. 1997. "Vortragsformen." In *Lexikon des Mittelalters* 8: 1861-1868.

Kretzmann, Paul Edward. 1916. *The Liturgical Element in the Earliest Forms of the Medieval Drama. With Special Reference to the English and German Plays*. Minneapolis: Bulletin of the University of Minnesota, December 1916.

Krieg, Eduard, ed. 1956. *Das lateinische Osterspiel von Tours*. Literarhistorisch-Musikwissenschaftliche Abhandlungen 13. Würzburg: Konrad Triltsch.

Krollmann, Christian. 1933. "Geistige Beziehungen zwischen Preußen und Thüringen im 13. und Anfang des 14. Jahrhunderts." *Thüringisch-Sächsische Zeitschrift für Geschichte und Kunst* 22: 78-91.

Kroos, Renate. 1970. *Niedersächsische Bildstickereien des Mittelalters*. Berlin: Deutscher Verlag für Kunstwissenschaft.

Kummer, Karl Ferdinand, ed. 1882. *Erlauer Spiele. Sechs altdeutsche Mysterien. Nach einer Handschrift des XV. Jahrhunderts*. Vienna: Alfred Hölder. Repr. 1977. Hildesheim, New York: G. Olms.

Kunze, Konrad, and Hansjürgen Linke. 1999. "Theophilus." In ²*VL* 9: 775-782.

Kurzeja, Adalbert, ed. 1970. *Der älteste Liber Ordinarius der Trierer Domkirche* [*OTrier*]. London, Brit. Mus., Harley 2958, Anfang 14. Jh. Liturgiewissenschaftliche Quellen und Forschungen 52. Münster: Aschendorff.

Lambot, Cyrille. 1942. "L'office de la Fête-Dieu: Aperçus nouveaux sur ses origines." *Revue bénédictine* 54: 61-123.

——, and J. Fransen. 1946. *L'Office de la Fête-Dieu primitive. Textes et Mélodies retrouvés*. Maredsous: Éditions de Maredsous.

Lateinische Osterfeiern und Osterspiele [LOO]. 1975-1981, 1990. Ed. Walther Lipphardt. 9 vols. Ausgaben deutscher Literatur des 15. bis 18. Jahrhunderts, 61-65, 96, 136-138. Reihe Drama 5. Berlin, New York: De Gruyter. 1 (1975): [nos. 1-173].

2 (1976): [nos. 174-484].
3 (1976): [nos. 485-630].
4 (1976): [nos. 631-769].
5 (1976): [nos. 770-832].
6 (1981): *Nachträge. Handschriftenverzeichnis. Bibliographie.*
7-9 (1990): *Kommentar. Aus dem Nachlass herausgegeben von Hans-Gert Ro-loff, redaktionell bearbeitet von Lothar Mundt.* Vol. 7 [commentary to LOO 1-630]. Vol. 8 [commentary to LOO 631-832]. Vol. 9 [Repertorium der gesungenen und gesprochenen Texte].

Lawrence, C[lifford] H[ugh]. 1984. *Medieval Monasticism. Forms of Religious Life in Western Europe in the Middle Ages.* London, New York: Longman.

Lehnen, Brigitte. 1988. *Das Egerer Passionsspiel.* Europäische Hochschulschriften. Reihe I. Deutsche Sprache und Literatur 1034. Frankfurt am Main, Bern, New York, Paris: Peter Lang.

Lemmer, Manfred. 1981. *'Der Dürnge bluome schînet dur den snê.' Thüringen und die deutsche Literatur des Mittelalters.* Eisenach: Wartburg Stiftung.

Leroquais, Victor. 1937. *Les Pontificaux manuscrits des bibliothèques publiques de France.* 3 vols. [descriptions] and 'Planches.' Paris [Mâcon: Protat Frères.]

Lexikon des Mittelalters. 1980-1999. 9 vols. and *Registerband* ('vol. 10'). Munich and Zurich: Artemis and Winkler (vols. 1-7); Munich: Lexma (vols. 8-9); Stuttgart and Weimar; Metzler ('vol. 10').

Liber Responsorialis pro Festis I: *Classis et Communi Sanctorum juxta ritum monasticum* [RMon]. 1895. Solesmes.

Liber Usualis Missae et Officii pro dominicis et festis [LU]. 1962. Paris, Tournai, Rome: Desclée.

Liebenow, Peter K., ed. 1969. *Das Künzelsauer Fronleichnamspiel.* Ausgaben deutscher Literatur des 15. bis 18. Jahrhunderts. Reihe Drama 2. Berlin: De Gruyter.

Lienhard, Fritz. 1904-1905. "Ein Festspiel im alten Eisenach." *Der Türmer* 7: 695-705.

Liliencron, R[ochus] von, ed. 1859. *Johannes Rothe. Düringische Chronik.* Thüringische Geschichtsquellen 3. Jena: Frommann.

Linke, Hansjürgen. 1970. Review of Peter Liebenow, ed., *Das Künzelsauer Fronleichnamspiel* (1969). *AfdA* 81: 69-75.

——. 1971. "Zwischen Jammertal und Schlaraffenland." *ZfdA* 100: 350-370.

——. 1972a. "Bauformen geistlicher Dramen des späten Mittelalters." In *Zeiten und Formen in Sprache und Dichtung. Festschrift für Fritz Tschirch zum 70. Geburtstag,* ed. Karl-Heinz Schirmer and Bernhard Sowinski, pp. 203-225. Cologne, Vienna: Böhlau.

——. 1972b. Review of Rolf Steinbach, *Die deutschen Oster- und Passionsspiele des Mittelalters* (1970). *AfdA* 83: 199-207.

——. 1974. Review of Rolf Bergmann, *Studien zu Entstehung und Geschichte der deutschen Passionsspiele des 13. und 14. Jahrhunderts* (1972). *AfdA* 85: 19-26.

——. 1975a. Review of Karl K. Polheim, ed., *Das Admonter Passionsspiel* 1 (1972). *AfdA* 86: 28-33.

——. 1975b. "Der Schluss des mittellateinischen Weihnachtsspiels aus Benediktbeuren." *ZfdPh* 94 (Sonderheft *Mittelalterliches deutsches Drama*): 1-22.

——. 1977. "Zu Text und Textkritik der Auferstehungsszene im Redentiner Osterspiel." *ZfdA* 106: 24-31.

——. 1978a. "Alsfelder Passionsspiel." *²VL* 1: 263-267.

——. 1978b. "Das volkssprachige Drama und Theater im deutschen und niederländischen Sprachbereich." In *Europäisches Spätmittelalter*, ed. Willi Erzgräber. Neues Handbuch der Literaturwissenschaft 8, pp. 733-763. Wiesbaden: Athenaion.

——. 1979a. "Die Komposition der Erfurter Moralität." In *Medium Aevum deutsch. Beiträge zur deutschen Literatur des hohen und späten Mittelalters. Festschrift für Kurt Ruh zum 65. Geburtstag*, ed. Dietrich Huschenbett et al., pp. 215-236. Tübingen: Max Niemeyer.

——. 1979b. Review of Rudolf Schützeichel, ed., *Das Mittelrheinische Passionsspiel der St. Galler Handschrift 919* (1978). *AfdA* 90: 154-160.

——. 1980. "Erfurter Moralität." *²VL* 2: 576-582.

——. 1983a. "Klosterneuburger Osterspiel." In *²VL* 4: 1259-1263.

——. 1983b. Review of Walter Lipphardt, ed., *Lateinische Osterfeiern und Osterspiele* 1-6 (1975-1981). *AfdA* 94: 33-38.

——. 1984. "Das missverstandene *Heu.*" *ZfdA* 113: 294-310.

——. 1985a. "Die Osterspiele des Debs-Codex." *ZfdPh* 104: 104-129.

——. 1985b. "Drama und Theater des Mittelalters als Feld interdisziplinärer Forschung." *Euphorion* 79: 43-65.

——. 1985c. "Marburger Prophetenspiel." In *²VL* 5: 1227-1228.

——. 1987a. "Drama und Theater." In *Die deutsche Literatur im späten Mittelalter, 1250-1370*, part 2, ed. Ingeborg Glier. Geschichte der deutschen Literatur von den Anfängen bis zur Gegenwart 3,2, pp. 153-233, 471-485. Munich: C.H. Beck.

——. 1987b. "Moosburger Himmelfahrtspiel (lat.)." In *²VL* 6: 684-685.

——. 1988. "Versuch über deutsche Handschriften mittelalterlicher Spiele." In *Deutsche Handschriften 1100-1400*, Oxforder Kolloquium 1985, ed. Volker Honemann and Nigel F. Palmer, pp. 527-589. Tübingen: Max Niemeyer.

——. 1989a. "Prager Osterspiele." In *²VL* 7: 797-803.

——. 1989a. "Regensburger (alemannisches) Osterspiel." In *²VL* 7: 1092-1093.

——. 1991. "Germany and German-speaking Central Europe." In Simon, ed., 207-224, 278-284.

——. 1993a. "Die Gratwanderung des Spieleditors." In Bergmann and Gärtner, eds., 137-155.

——. 1993b. "A Survey of Medieval Drama and Theater in Germany." *Comparative Drama* 27: 17-53.

——. 1994. "Osterfeier und Osterspiel. Vorschläge zur sachlich-terminologischen Klärung einiger Abgrenzungsprobleme." In Siller, ed., 121-133.

——. 1995a. "Figurengestaltung in der 'Erfurter Moralität.' Geistliche Dramatik als Lebensorientierung." *ZfdA* 124: 129-142.

——. 1995b. "Thüringische Zehnjungfrauenspiele." In *²VL* 9: 915-918.

——. 1998a. "Wiener Passionsspiel I." In *²VL* 10: 1031-1034.

——. 1998b. "Wiener (schlesisches) Osterspiel." In *²VL* 10: 1036-1039.

——. 1999a. "Beobachtungen zu den geistlichen Spielen im Codex Buranus." *ZfdA* 128: 185-193.

——. 1999b. Review of Janota, ed. (1996-). *Beiträge* 121: 156-162.

——. 1999c. "Zwickauer Maria-Salome-Rolle." In *²VL* 10: 1625-26.

——. 1999d. "Zwickauer Osterspiele." In *²VL* 10: 1626-1629.

——. Forthcoming. "Benediktbeurer Spiele." In *²VL* 11 (1. Lieferung): 229-236.

——. Forthcoming. "Braunschweiger Osterspiel." In *²VL* 11 (1. Lieferung): 281-282.

——, and Ulrich Mehler. 1989. "Osterfeiern." In *²VL* 7: 92-108.

——, and Ulrich Mehler, eds. 1990. *Die österlichen Spiele aus der Ratsschulbibliothek Zwickau* [ZwiO.I, II, III]. *Kritischer Text und Faksimilie der Handschriften*. Altdeutsche Textbibliothek 103. Tübingen: Max Niemeyer.

——, and Ulrich Mehler, eds. 1993. "Die Steinacher Salvator-Rolle." *Der Schlern* 7: 489-506.

Lippe, Robert, ed. 1899, 1907. *Missale Romanum Mediolani, 1474.* [MR.1474]. 2 vols. Henry Bradshaw Society 17, 33. London.

    [1] (HBS 17): *Text* (1899).

    [2] (HBS 33): *A Collation with Other Editions Printed before 1570* (1907).

Lipphardt, Walther. 1933. "Altdeutsche Marienklagen." *Die Singgemeinde* 9: 65-79.

——. 1948. *Die Weisen der lateinischen Osterspiele des 12. und 13. Jahrhunderts.* Musikwissenschaftliche Arbeiten 2. Kassel: Bärenreiter.

——. 1960. "Liturgische Dramen des Mittelalters." In *MGG* 8: 1012-1051.

——, ed. 1975. "Ein lateinisch-deutsches Osterspiel aus Augsburg (16. Jhdt.) in der Bibliothek des Kapuzinerklosters Feldkirch." *Jahrbuch des Vorarlberger Landesmuseums-Vereins*, pp. 14-29. Bregenz.

——, ed. 1975-1981, 1990. See *Lateinische Osterfeiern und Osterspiele* [LOO].

——. 1978a. "Augsburger Osterspiel." *²VL* 1: 524-525.

——, ed. 1978b. *Das lateinisch-deutsche Augsburger Osterspiel und das deutsche Passionslied des Mönchs von Salzburg. In Abbildung aus dem Ms Liturg. 1 rtr. des Kapuzinerklosters Feldkirch.* Litterae 55. Göppingen: Kümmerle.

——. 1980. "Füssener Osterspiel." In *²VL* 2: 1032-1034.

†——, and Hans-Gert Roloff, eds. 1980- . *Die geistlichen Spiele des Sterzinger Spielarchivs.* 6 vols. Mittlere deutsche Literatur in Neu- und Nachdrucken 14-19 [MDL]. Bern: Peter Lang.

1 (MDL 14) (1986): ed. †W. Lipphardt; 2nd rev. ed. [15 plays from the 'Debs Codex,' including BozHi, BozO.II, Boz.OIV, Boz Verk, BozAbdm.]
2 (MDL 15) (1988): ed. H.-G. Roloff [text] and Andreas Traub [melodies] [Two transmissions of the Sterzing Passion play, PfarrkP 1486 and SterzP 1496/1503.]
3 (MDL 16) (1996): ed. H.G. Roloff [text] and Andreas Traub [melodies] [Seven plays, including BozP.1514, TirP, TirO*, TirW].
4 (MDL 17) (1990): ed. H.-G. Roloff [text] and Andreas Traub [melodies] [Five plays, including BozPalm].
5 (MDL 18) (1980): ed. H.-G. Roloff [Texts of 5 plays].
6.2 (MDL 19.2) (1996): *Kommentar zur Edition der Melodien.* By Andreas Traub with assistance from Sabine Prüser.
Literatur Lexikon. 1988-1993. Ed. Walther Killy. 15 vols. Gütersloh and Munich: Bertelsmann.
Lomnitzer, Helmut. 1985. "Marburger Weltgerichtsspiel." In *²VL* 5: 1229-1230.
———. 1986. "Das Marburger Weltgerichtsspiel. Vortrag" [Typescript].
†——, [ed.] "Marburger Weltgerichtsspiel" [recte "Marburger Spiel von den letzten Dingen." Typescript in preparation for an edition]
Lowe, Elias A. et al., eds. 1917-1924. *The Bobbio Missal. A Gallican Mass-Book (MS. Paris. Lat. B246). Critical edition.* 3 vols. Henry Bradshaw Society
[1] (HSB 53) (1917): *Facsimile.*
[2] (HSB 58) (1920): *Text.*
[3] (HSB 61) (1924): *Notes and Studies* [André Wilmart, H.A. Wilson, Lowe].
Lüdemann, Lutz. 1964. "Wesensformen des Chores im mittelalterlichen Drama." Dissertation. University of Vienna.
Lülfing, D. 1982. "Die Handschriften des Stadtarchivs Mühlhausen" [Available at the Stadtarchiv Mühlhausen].
Macardle, Peter. 1996. "Die Gesänge des 'St. Galler Mittelrheinischen Passions-spiels.' Ein Beitrag zu Rekonstruktion und Lokalisierung." In *Die Vermittlung geistlicher Inhalte im deutschen Mittelalter. Internationales Symposium, Roscrea 1994,* ed. Timothy R. Jackson, Nigel F. Palmer, and Almut Suerbaum, pp. 255-270. Tübingen: Niemeyer.
Máchal, Jan, ed. 1908. *Staroceské skladby dramatické puvodu liturgického* ["Old-Czech Dramatic Works of Liturgical Origin"]. Rozpravy Ceské Akademie Císare Frantiska Josefa pro vedy, slovesnost a umeni 3.23. Prague: Nákadem Ceské Akademie císare Frantiska Josefa.
Marbach, Carolus. 1907. *Carmina scripturarum. Scilicet antiphonas et responsoria ex sacro scripturae fonte in libros liturgicos sanctae ecclesiae Romanae deriva-ta.* Strassburg. Repr. 1963. Hildesheim: Olms.
Marbach, Joh. 1894. "Die Aufführung des geistlichen Spiels 'von den zehn Jung-frauen' zu Eisenach am 24. April 1322." Vortrag. *Korrespondenzblatt des Gesamtvereine der deutschen Geschichts- und Altertumsvereine* 42: 150-155.

Marshall, Mary H. 1972. "Aesthetic Values of the Liturgical Drama." In *English Institute Essays*. New York: Columbia University Press. Repr. in Taylor-Nelson, eds., 44-63.

Martène, Edmond, ed. 1736. *De Antiquis Ecclesiae Ritibus libri tres*. Vol. 2. 2nd ed. Antwerp. Repr. 1967. Hildesheim: Olms.

Martimort, Aimé-Georges. 1978. *La documentation liturgique de Dom Edmond Martène. Étude codicologique*. Studi e Testi 279. Vatican City: Biblioteca Apostolica Vaticana.

Massenkeil, Günther. 1980. "Lamentations." In *New Grove* 10: 410-412.

Mathiesen, Thomas J. 1983. "'The Office of the New Feast of Corpus Christi' in the *Regimen Animarum* at Brigham Young University." *The Journal of Musicology* 2: 13-44.

McGee, Timothy J. 1976. "The Liturgical Placement of the 'Quem queritis' Dialogue." *JAMS* 29: 1-29.

——. 1984. "Drama, Liturgical." In *DMA* 4: 272-277.

McKinnon, James W. 1980. "Performing practice 2. Medieval monophony." In *New Grove* 14: 371-375.

Mechthild von Magdeburg. *See* Neumann, H., ed. 1990, 1993.

Mehler, Ulrich. 1981. *Dicere und cantare: Zur musikalischen Terminologie und Aufführungspraxis des mittelalterlichen geistlichen Dramas in Deutschland*. Kölner Beiträge zur Musikforschung 120. Regensburg: Gustav Bosse Verlag.

——. 1984. "Musik im geistlichen Drama des Mittelalters." *Concerto* 2: 35-42.

——. 1997. *Marienklagen im spätmittelalterlichen und frühneuzeitlichen Deutschland. Textversikel und Melodietypen*. 2 vols. Amsterdamer Publikationen zur Sprache und Literatur 128-129. Amsterdam, Atlanta: Radopi.

——, and Anton H. Touber, eds. 1994. *Mittelalterliches Schauspiel. Festschrift für Hansjürgen Linke zum 65. Geburtstag*. Amsterdamer Beiträge zur älteren Germanistik 38-39. Amsterdam, Atlanta: Rodopi.

See also Linke–Mehler.

Meier, Rudolf, ed. 1962. *Das Innsbrucker Osterspiel. Das Osterspiel von Muri. Mittelhochdeutsch und neuhochdeutsch*. Universal-Bibliothek 8660/61. Stuttgart: Philipp Reclam jun.

Meier, Theo. 1959. *Die Gestalt Marias im geistlichen Schauspiel des deutschen Mittelalters*. Philologische Studien und Quellen 4. Berlin: Erich Schmidt.

Menhardt, Hermann. 1960-1961. *Verzeichnis der altdeutschen literarischen Handschriften der Österreichischen Nationalbibliothek*. 3 vols. Deutsche Akademie der Wissenschaften zu Berlin. Veröffentlichungen des Instituts für deutsche Sprache und Literatur 13. Berlin.

Meredith, Peter, and John E. Tailby. 1983. *The Staging of Religious Drama in Europe in the Later Middle Ages: Texts and Documents in English Translation*. Early Drama, Art, and Music 4. Kalamazoo: Medieval Institute.

Metz, René. 1954. *La consécration des vierges dans l'église romaine. Étude d'histoire de la liturgie.* Bibliothèque de l'Institut de Droit Canonique de l'Université de Strasbourg 4. Paris: Presses Universitaires de France.

Meyer, Christian. 2000. "Die Tonartenlehre im Mittelalter." In Huglo et al., pp. 135-215.

Meyer, Otto. *See* Klauser–Meyer.

Meyer, Wilhelm. 1901. *Fragmenta Burana.* Berlin: Weidmannsche Buchhandlung.

——. 1905. *Die rhythmische lateinische Prosa. Abhandlungen zur mittellateinischen Rhythmik.* Berlin.

Michel, Jean. *See* Jodogne, ed. 1959.

Michael, Wolfgang F. 1971. *Das deutsche Drama des Mittelalters.* Grundriss der germanischen Philologie 20. Berlin, New York: De Gruyter.

Mielke, Hellmuth. 1891. "Die heilige Elisabeth, Landgräfin von Thüringen." *Sammlung gemeinverständlicher wissenschaftlicher Vorträge,* Neue Folge 6, 125.

Migne, J.P., ed. 1844-1864. *Patrologiae cursus completus: series Latina* [PL]. 221 vols. Paris.

Milchsack, Gustav, ed. 1880. *Heidelberger Passionsspiel.* Bibliothek des Litterarischen Vereins in Stuttgart 150. Tübingen: L. Fr. Fues.

——, ed. 1881. *Egerer Fronleichnamsspiel.* Bibliothek des Litterarischen Vereins in Stuttgart 156. Tübingen: L. Fr. Fues.

——, ed. 1886. *Hymni et Sequentiae cum compluribus aliis et latinis et gallicis necnon theodiscis carminibus medio aevo compositis.* Part I. Halle: Niemeyer.

Missale Romanum [MR]. 1933. 17th ed. Regensburg: Pustet.

Mitterschiffthaler, Karl. 1998. "Zisterzienser." In ^{2}MGG 9: 2390-2401.

Mohlberg, [Leo] Cunibert, ed. 1927. *Die älteste erreichbare Gestalt des Liber Sacramentorum anni circuli der römischen Kirche* [SPad] *(Cod. pad. D 47, fol. 111r-100r).* Liturgiegeschichtliche Quellen und Forschungen 11/12. Münster: Aschendorff.

——. 1951. *Mittelalterliche Handschriften.* Katalog der Handschriften der Zentralbibliothek Zürich 1. Zurich.

——, ed. 1956. *Sacramentarium Veronense* [SVer]. *(Cod. Bibl. Capit. Veron. LXXXV [80]).* Rerum Ecclesiasticarum Documenta, series maior, Fontes 1. Rome: Herder.

——, ed. 1957. *Missale Francorum* [MFranc]. *(Cod. Vat. Reg. lat. 257).* Rerum Ecclesiasticarum Documenta, series maior, Fontes 2. Rome: Herder.

——, ed. 1960. *Liber Sacramentorum Romanae Aeclesiae ordinis anni circuli (Sacramentarium Gelasianum)* [SGelas]. *(Cod. Vat. Reg. lat. 316/Paris Bibl. Nat. 7193, 41/56).* Rerum Ecclesiasticarum Documenta, series maior, Fontes 4. Rome: Herder. 3rd ed. rev. by Leo Eizenhöfer, 1981.

Mohr, Wolfgang. 1977. "Rhythmus." In *RL* 3: 456-475.

Möller, Hartmut. 1984. "Auf dem Wege zur Rekonstruktion des Antiphonale S. Gregorii? Kritisches zu den Klassifizierungen des 'Corpus Antiphonalium Officii'." *Die Musikforschung* 37: 219-228.

——. 1987. "Research on the Antiphonar—Problems and Perspectives." *Journal of the Plainsong and Medieval Music Society* 10: 1-14.

Mone, Franz Joseph, ed. 1841. *Altteutsche Schauspiele.* Bibliothek der gesammten deutschen National-Literatur 21. Quedlinburg, Leipzig: Basse.

——, ed. 1846. *Schauspiele des Mittelalters.* 2 vols. Karlsruhe: Macklot. Repr. 1852. Mannheim: Bensheimer; 1970. Aalen: Scientia Verlag.

——, ed. 1853-1855. *Lateinische Hymnen des Mittelalters.* 3 vols. Freiburg i. Br.: Herder. Repr. 1964. Aalen: Scientia Verlag.

Monumenta Erphesfurtensia saec. XII, XIII, XIV. See Holder-Egger, ed. 1899.

Morin, D.G. 1910. "L'office cistercien pour la Fête-Dieu comparé avec celui de saint Thomas d'Aquin." *Revue bénédictine* 27: 236-246.

Muir, Lynette R. 1995. *The Biblical Drama of Medieval Europe.* Cambridge, New York: Cambridge University Press.

Mundt, Erika. 1919. "Das Luzerner Spiel von Christi Tod und Grablegung." Dissertation. Marburg.

Die Musik in Geschichte und Gegenwart [MGG]. 1949-1986. *Allgemeine Enzyklopädie der Musik.* 1st ed., Friedrich Blume. 17 vols. Kassel: Bärenreiter.

Die Musik in Geschichte und Gegenwart [²MGG]. 1994- . *Allgemeine Enzyklopädie der Musik, begründet von Friedrich Blume.* 2nd ed., Ludwig Finscher. *Sachteil* in 9 vols. (1994-1998); *Register zum Sachteil* (1999). Kassel: Bärenreiter; and Stuttgart: Metzler.

Neumann, Bernd. 1975. "Geistliches Schauspiel im spätmittelalterlichen Friedberg." *Wetterauer Geschichtsblätter* 24: 113-131.

——. 1983a. "Innsbrucker (thüringisches) Osterspiel." In *²VL* 7: 400-403.

——. 1983b. "Innsbrucker (thüringisches) Spiel von Mariae Himmelfahrt." In *²VL* 7: 403-406.

——. 1987. *Geistliches Schauspiel im Zeugnis der Zeit. Zur Aufführung mittelalterlicher religiöser Dramen im deutschen Sprachgebiet.* 2 vols. Münchener Texte und Untersuchungen zur deutschen Literatur des Mittelalters 84, 85. Munich, Zurich: Artemis.

——. 1991. "Thüringisches Zehnjungfrauenspiel." In *Literatur Lexikon* 11: 353-354.

Neumann, Hans, ed. 1990, 1993. *Mechthild von Magdeburg. Das fließende Licht der Gottheit.* 2 vols. Münchener Texte und Untersuchungen zur deutschen Literatur des Mittelalters 100 (*Text*), 101 (*Untersuchungen*). Munich: Artemis.

The New Grove Dictionary of Music and Musicians [New Grove]. 1980. Ed. Stanley Sadie. 20 vols. London: Macmillan.

Nowacki, Edward. 1994. "Antiphon." In *²MGG* 1: 636-660.

Ogden, Dunbar H. 1974. "The Use of Architectural Space in Medieval Music-Drama." *Comparative Drama* 8: 63-76.

Ohly, Friedrich. 1977. *Schriften zur mittelalterlichen Bedeutungsforschung*. Darmstadt: Wissenschaftliche Buchgesellschaft.

Ordo Lectionum Missae [LMO]. 1969. Vatican City.

Orel, Alfred. 1926. "Die Weisen im 'Wiener Passionsspiel' aus dem 13. Jahrhundert." *Mitteilungen des Vereines für Geschichte der Stadt Wien* 6: 72-95.

Osthoff, Helmuth. 1942. "Deutsche Liedweisen und Wechselgesänge im mittelalterlichen Drama." *Archiv für Musikforschung* 7: 65-81.

——. 1943-1944. "Die Musik im Drama des deutschen Mittelalters. Quellen und Forschungsziele." *Deutsche Musikkultur* 8: 29-40.

Ott, Carolus. 1935. *Offertoriale sive Versus Offertoriorum Cantus Gregoriani*. Paris, Tournai, Rome: Desclée.

The Oxford Dictionary of the Christian Church. 1974. 2nd ed., F.L. Cross and E.A. Livingstone. London, New York: Oxford University Press.

Paléographie musicale [PalMus]. 1889-1974. *Les principaux manuscrits de chant grégorien, ambrosien, mozarabe, gallican. Publiés en facsimilés phototypiques* (Première série; deuxième série [Monumentale]). 21 vols. Solesmes, Tournai, Bern etc. [various imprints].

PalMus 5 (1896), 6 (1900): *Antiphonarium Ambrosianum du Musée Britannique* [AAmbr]. 2 vols. 5 [facs.], 6 [transcription]. Repr. 1972. Bern: Herbert Lang.

PalMus 12 (1922): *Antiphonaire monastique, xiiiᵉ siècle, codex F.160 de la Bibliothèque de la cathédrale de Worcester* [AWorc]. Tournai: Desclée.

PalMus 2.1 (1970): *See* Froger, ed. 1970.

Parrish, Carl. 1959. *The Notation of Medieval Music*. New York: Norton. Repr. 1978. New York: Pendragon Press.

Patrologia Latina. See Migne, ed. 1844-1864.

Patze, Hans, and Walter Schlesinger. 1973. *Geschichte Thüringens 2, 2: Hohes und spätes Mittelalter*. Mitteldeutsche Forschungen 48, 2.2. Cologne, Vienna: Böhlau.

Petsch, Robert, ed. 1908. *Theophilus. Mittelniederdeutsches Drama in drei Fassungen*. Germanistische Bibliothek. Untersuchungen und Texte 2. Heidelberg: Carl Winter.

Pez, Bernhard, ed. 1721. "Klosterneuburger Osterspiel." In *Thesaurus anecdotorum novissimus* 2: liii. Augsburg. [First edition, only beginning and end of the play.]

Pflanz, Hermann Manfred. 1977. *Die lateinischen Textgrundlagen des St. Galler Passionsspieles in der mittelalterlichen Liturgie*. Europäische Hochschulschriften, ser. 1: Deutsche Literatur und Germanistik 205. Frankfurt am Main, Bern, Las Vegas: Peter Lang.

Planchart, Alejandro Enrique. 1988. "On the Nature of Transmission and Change in Trope Repertories." *JAMS* 41: 215-249.

Polheim, Karl Konrad, ed. 1972-1980. *Das Admonter Passionsspiel*. 3 vols. Munich, Paderborn, Vienna: Ferdinand Schöningh.

1 (1972): *Textausgabe. Faksimileausgabe.*

2 (1980): *Untersuchungen zur Überlieferung, Sprache und Osterhandlung.*

3 (1980): *Untersuchungen zur Passionshandlung, Aufführung und Eigenart. Nebst Studien zu Hans Sachs und einer kritischen Ausgabe seines Passionsspieles.*

——. 1975. "Weitere Forschungen zu den Oster- und Passionsspielen des deutschen Mittelalters." *ZfdPh* 94 (Sonderheft *Mittelalterliches deutsches Drama*): 194-212.

Poll, Joseph, ed. 1950. "Ein Osterspiel enthalten in einem Prozessionale der Alten Kapelle in Regensburg." *KmJb* 34: 35-40, 108.

Pothier, Joseph. 1900. "Répons *Regnum mundi.*" *Revue du Chant Grégorien* 8: 185-189.

——. 1910. "Répons *Discubuit Jesus.*" *Revue du Chant Grégorien* 18: 169-178.

Processionale Monasticum ad usum congregationis Gallicae ordinis Sancti Benedicti [*PrMon*]. 1893. Solesmes.

Psalterium cum cantis novi et veteris testamenti iuxta Regulam S.P.N. Benedicti [*PsOSB*]. 1981. Solesmes.

Rankin, Susan K. 1981. "The Mary Magdalene Scene in the 'Visitatio Sepulchri' Ceremonies." *Early Music History* 1: 227-255.

Reallexikon der deutschen Literaturgeschichte [*RL*]. 1958-1988. 2nd ed. 5 vols. Vols. 1-3: ed. Werner Kohlschmidt and Wolfgang Mohr. Vol. 4: ed. Klaus Kanzog and Achim Masser. Redaktion: Dorothea Kanzog. Vol. 5: Sachregister, ed. Klaus Kanzog and Johann S. Koch. Berlin and New York: De Gruyter.

Regesten der Erzbischöfe von Mainz. See Vogt, ed. 1913.

Regula Sancti P. Benedicti. See Benedict, Saint.

Reichert, Georg. 1958. "Kontrafaktur." In *RL* 1: 882-883.

Reifenberg, Hermann. 1960. *Messe und Missalien im Bistum Mainz seit dem Zeitalter der Gotik.* Liturgiewissenschaftliche Quellen und Forschungen 37. Münster: Aschendorff.

——. 1964. *Stundengebet und Breviere im Bistum Mainz seit der romanischen Epoche.* Liturgiewissenschaftliche Quellen und Forschungen 40. Münster: Aschendorff.

——. 1971. *Sakramente, Sakramentalien und Ritualien im Bistum Mainz seit dem Spätmittelalter.* 2 vols. Liturgiewissenschaftliche Quellen und Forschungen 53-54. Münster: Aschendorff.

Reinle, Adolf, ed. 1949-1950. "Mathias Gundelfingers Zurzacher Osterspiel von 1494. 'Luzerner Grablegung'." *Innerschweizerisches Jahrbuch für Heimatkunde* 13/14: 65-96.

——. 1981. "Gundelfinger, Mathias." In ²*VL* 3: 310-312.

Die Religion in Geschichte und Gegenwart. 1957-1965. *Handwörterbuch für Theologie und Religionswissenschaft.* 3rd ed., ed. Kurt Galling et al. 7 vols. Tübingen: J.C.B. Mohr.

Reuschel, Karl. 1906. *Die deutschen Weltgerichtsspiele des Mittelalters und der Reformationszeit.* Teutonia: Arbeiten zur germanischen Philologie 4. Leipzig: Avenarius.

Reynolds, Roger E. 1984. "Divine Office." In *DMA* 4: 221-231.
——. 1986. "Litanies, Greater and Lesser." In *DMA* 7: 587-588.
——. 1987. "Rites of Separation and Reconciliation." In *Segni e Riti nella chiesa altomedievale occidentale. 11-17 Aprile, 1985. Settimane di Studio del Centro Italiano di Studi sull'alto Medioevo 33*, 1: 405-433. Spoleto: La Sede del Centro.
Rieger, Max, ed. 1865. "Das Spiel von den zehen Jungfrauen." *Germania* 10: 311-337.
Ritter, Karl Bernhard, ed. 1924. *Das Spiel vom großen Abendmahl. Das thüringische Mysterium von den zehn Jungfrauen in neuer Gestalt mit Musik für zwei Frauenchöre, Solostimmen, Streichinstrumente, Flöten und Orgel von Spes Stahlberg*. Frankfurt am Main: Verlag des Bühnenvolksbundes.
Roeder, Anke. 1974. *Die Gebärde im Drama des Mittelalters: Osterfeiern, Osterspiele*. Münchener Texte und Untersuchungen zur deutschen Literatur des Mittelalters 49. Munich: C.H. Beck.
Rohloff, Ernst, ed. 1972. *Die Quellenhandschriften zum Musiktraktat des Johannes de Grocheio. Im Facsimile herausgegeben nebst Übertragung des Textes und Übersetzung ins Deutsche, dazu Bericht, Literaturschau, Tabellen und Indices*. Leipzig: VEB Deutscher Verlag für Musik.
Roloff, Hans-Gert. 1993. "Die Struktur der Erfurter Moralität." In *Von wyssheit würt der mensch geert ... Festschrift für Manfred Lemmer zum 65. Geburtstag*, ed. Ingrid Kühne and Gotthard Lerchner, pp. 391-409. Frankfurt; Bern: Lang. See also Lipphardt-Roloff.
The Roman Missal. 1917. *The Liturgy for Layfolk*. London: Burns and Oates.
Ro[ob], H. 1977. "Das 'Zehnjungfrauenspiel. Über mittelalterliche Schauspieltradition in Thüringen." *Thüringer Tageblatt* 100 (28 April 1977) 8.
Rose, Valentin. 1903. *Verzeichnis der lateinischen Handschriften 2, 2: Die Handschriften der Königlichen Bibliothek zu Berlin 13, 2*. Berlin.
Rothe, Johannes. See Liliencron, ed. 1859.
Rueff, Hans, ed. 1925. *Das rheinische Osterspiel der Berliner Handschrift MS Germ. fol. 1219 mit Untersuchungen zur Textgeschichte des deutschen Osterspiels*. Abhandlungen der Gesellschaft der Wissenschaften zu Göttingen, philologisch-historische Klasse. NF 18.1. Berlin: Weidmann. Repr. 1970. Nendeln: Kraus.
Salmon, Pierre, ed. 1944, 1953. *Le Lectionnaire de Luxeuil* [LLux]. (*Paris, MS. lat. 9427*). 2 vols. Collectanea Biblica Latina 7, 9. Vatican City: Libreria Vaticana.
[1] (CBL 7) (1944): *Édition et étude comparative*.
[2] (CBL 9) (1953): *Étude paléographique et liturgique, suivie d'un choix de planches*.
Sampetrinum. See Holder-Egger, ed. 1899.
Schacht, Edgar, ed. 1925. *Sünte Marie. De Wolfenbütteler Marienklag un Osterspill. Aus alten Bücherschränken*, ed. Wilhelm Stapel. Hamburg: Hanseatische Verlagsanstalt.
Scharnagl, August. 1961. "Offertorium." In *MGG* 9: 1901-1907.

Schipke, Renate, and Franzjosef Pensel, eds. 1986. *Das Brandenburger Osterspiel.*
Fragmente eines neuentdeckten mittelalterlichen geistlichen Osterspiels aus dem
Domarchiv in Brandenburg/Havel. Beiträge aus der Deutschen Staatsbibliothek
4. Berlin: DSB.

Schlager, Karlheinz, ed. 1985. *Antiphonale Pataviense (Wien 1519)* [APat]. Faksimile. Das Erbe deutscher Musik 88, Abteilung Mittelalter 25. Kassel: Bärenreiter.

Schmidtke, Dietrich, ed. 1983. *Das Füssener Osterspiel und die Füssener Marien-*
klage. Universitätsbibliothek Augsburg (ehemals: Harburg), Cod. II, 1,4°,62.
In Abbildung heraugegeben. With an introduction by Ursula Hennig. Litterae
69. Göppingen: Kümmerle.

——, Ursula Hennig, and Walther Lipphardt, eds. 1976. "Füssener Osterspiel und
Füssener Marienklage." *Beiträge* 98: 231-288, 395-423.

Schneider, Karin, ed. 1958. "Das Eisenacher Zehnjungfrauenspiel." *Lebendiges*
Mittelalter. Festgabe für Wolfgang Stammler, pp. 163-203. Fribourg/Switzer-
land: Universitätsverlag.

——, ed. 1964. *Das Eisenacher Zehnjungfrauenspiel.* Texte des späten Mittelalters
und der frühen Neuzeit 17. Berlin: Erich Schmidt.

Schönemann, Otto, ed. 1855. *Der Sündenfall und Marienklage [und Osterspiel].*
Zwei niederdeutsche Schauspiele aus Handschriften der Wolfenbüttler Bibliothek.
Hanover: Carl Rümpler.

Schottmann, Brigitta, ed. 1975. *Das Redentiner Osterspiel. Mittelniederdeutsch und*
neuhochdeutsch. Universal-Bibliothek 9744-9747. Stuttgart: Reclam jun.

S[chröder], E[dward]. 1938. "Das Eisenacher Passionsspiel von 1227." *ZfdA* 75:
120.

Schuler, Ernst August. 1940. "Die Musik der Osterfeiern, Osterspiele und Passio-
nen des Mittelalters." Dissertation. Basel. 2 vols. Vol. 2: "Die Melodien"
[Available at the University Library and Musikwissenschaftliches Institut of
Basel and the Institut für deutsche Sprache und Literatur of the University of
Cologne.]

——. 1951. *Die Musik der Osterfeiern, Osterspiele und Passionen des Mittelalters.*
[Die Texte]. Kassel, Basel: Bärenreiter. [Vol. 1 of the Dissertation].

Schulte, Adalbert. 1916. *Die Hymnen des Breviers nebst den Sequenzen des Missale.*
Wissenschaftliche Handbibliothek 1: Theologische Lehrbücher 17. Paderborn:
Ferdinand Schöningh.

Schüttpelz, Otto. 1930. *Der Wettlauf der Apostel und die Erscheinungen des Pere-*
grinusspiels im geistlichen Spiel des Mittelalters. Germanistische Abhandlungen
63. Breslau: N. & H. Marcus.

Schützeichel, Rudolf, ed. 1978. *Das mittelrheinische Passionsspiel der St. Galler*
Handschrift 919. Mit Beiträgen von Rolf Bergmann, Irmgard Frank, Hugo
Stopp und einem vollständigen Faksimile. Tübingen: Max Niemeyer.

Schwob, Anton, ed. 1994. *Editionsberichte zur mittelalterlichen deutschen Literatur.*
Beiträge der Bamberger Tagung "Methoden und Probleme der Edition mittel-

alterlicher deutscher Texte." 26.-29. Juli 1991. Litterae 117. Göppingen: Kümmerle.

Seay, Albert, transl. 1973. *Johannes de Grocheo, Concerning Music (De musica).* 2nd ed. Translations 1. Colorado Springs: [Colorado College Music Press].

Seelmann, Wilhelm, ed. 1926. "Das Berliner Bruchstück einer Rubinscene" [BeThO]. *ZfdA* 63: 257-267.

Senne, Linda P. 1976. "The Dramatic Figure in *Das Spiel von den zehn Jungfrauen." The Germanic Review* 51: 161-171.

Seuse, Heinrich. *See* Bihlmeyer, ed. 1907.

Sievers, Heinrich, ed. 1936. *Die lateinischen liturgischen Osterspiele der Stiftskirche St. Blasien zu Braunschweig. Eine musikwissenschaftliche Untersuchung der liturgischen dramatischen Osterfeiern in Niedersachsen mit besonderer Berücksichtigung des lateinischen liturgischen Osterspieles Braunschweig IV.* Veröffentlichungen der Niedersächsischen Musikgesellschaft 2. Wolfenbüttel, Berlin: Georg Kallmeyer.

Silagi, Gabriel, ed. 1985. *Liturgische Tropen. Referate zweier Colloquien des "Corpus Troporum" in München (1983) und Canterbury (1984).* Münchener Beiträge zur Mediävistik und Renaissance-Forschung 36. Munich: Arbeo-Gesellschaft.

Siller, Max, ed. 1994. *Osterspiele. Texte und Musik. Akten des 2. Symposiums der Sterzinger Osterspiele (12.-16. April 1992).* Schlern-Schriften 293. Innsbruck: Wagner.

Simon, Eckehard. 1984. "Drama, German." In *DMA* 4: 266-272.

——, ed. 1991. *The Theatre of Medieval Europe.* New Research in Early Drama. Cambridge Studies in Medieval Literature [8]. Cambridge: Cambridge University Press.

Simpson, Adrienne. *See* Buzga–Simpson.

Smedick, Lois K. 1984. "Cursus." In *DMA* 4: 66-67.

Smith, Lucy Toulmin, ed. 1885. *York Plays. The Plays Performed by the Crafts or Mysteries of York on the Day of Corpus Christi in the 14th, 15th and 16th centuries.* Oxford 1885. Repr. 1963. New York: Russell & Russell.

Smits van Waesberghe, Joseph, ed. 1951. *Aribonis de Musica.* Corpus Scriptorum de Musica 2. Rome: American Institute of Musicology.

——, ed. 1953. "A Dutch Easterplay." *Musica Disciplina* 7: 13-37.

Smoldon, William L. 1980. *The Music of the Medieval Church Dramas.* London, New York, Melbourne: Oxford University Press.

Southern, Richard W. 1970. *Western Society and the Church in the Middle Ages.* Pelican History of the Church 2. Repr. 1979. [Harmondsworth]: Penguin.

Stäblein, Bruno. 1949-1951a. "Antiphon(e)." In *MGG* 1: 523-545.

——. 1949-1951b. "Antiphonar." In *MGG* 1: 545-549.

——. 1954a. "Deutschland. B. Mittelalter. I.-V." In *MGG* 3: 272-286.

——. 1954b. "Evangelium. A. Katholisch." In *MGG* 3: 1618-1629.

——. 1957. "Invitatorium." In *MGG* 6: 1389-1393.

——. 1960a ."Lamentatio." In *MGG* 8 : 133-142.

——. 1960b. "Lektionston." In *MGG* 8: 595-596.

——. 1962. "Psalm. B: Lateinischer Psalmengesang im Mittelalter." In *MGG* 10: 1676-1690.

——. 1966. "Tropus." In *MGG* 13: 797-826.

——. 1975. *Schriftbild der einstimmigen Musik.* Musikgeschichte in Bildern III: Musik des Mittelalters und der Renaissance 4. Leipzig: VEB.

Stamm, Gerhard. *See* Heinzer–Stamm.

Stapert, Calvin R. 1974-1976. *Saturday Lady Mass. Two-part Settings of Chants for the Ordinary of the Mass. Transcriptions from the Eleventh Fascicle of MS "W₁"* [*MS Helmst. 628*]. Early Music Series 17 (1974), 18-19 (1976). Oxford University Press.

Stapper, Richard. 1916. "Zur Geschichte des Fronleichnams- und Dreifaltigkeitsfestes." *Der Katholik* 96: 321-330.

——. 1916. *Die Feier des Kirchenjahres an der Kathedrale von Münster im hohen Mittelalter* [OMünst]. *Ein Beitrag zur Heortologie und Liturgiegeschichte.* Zeitschrift für vaterländische Geschichte und Altertumskunde 75. Münster: Regensbergsche Buchhandlung.

Staub, Kurt Hans, and Thomas Sänger. 1991. *Deutsche und niederländische Handschriften mit Ausnahme der Gebetbuchhandschriften.* Die Handschriften der Hessischen Landes- und Hochschulbibliothek Darmstadt 6. Wiesbaden: Harrassowitz.

Steinbach, Rolf. 1970. *Die deutschen Oster- und Passionsspiele des Mittelalters. Versuch einer Darstellung und Wesensbestimmung nebst einer Bibliographie zum deutschen geistlichen Spiel des Mittelalters.* Kölner Germanistische Studien 4. Cologne, Vienna: Böhlau.

Steiner, Ruth. 1980a. "Canticle 3. Roman." In *New Grove* 3: 724-725.

——. 1980b. "Invitatory." In *New Grove* 9: 286-289.

——. 1980c. "Trope." In *New Grove* 19: 172-187.

See also Baroffio-Steiner, Björkvall-Steiner.

Stemmler, Theo. 1970. *Liturgische Feiern und geistliche Spiele. Studien zu Erscheinungsformen des Dramatischen im Mittelalter.* Buchreihe der Anglia. Zeitschrift für englische Philologie 15. Tübingen: Niemeyer.

Stephan, Friedrich. 1847a. "Verzeichnis alter mühlhäusischer Handschriften." *Neue Stofflieferungen für die deutsche Geschichte, besonders auch für die der Sprache, des Rechts und der Literatur* 2: 109-148. Mühlhausen: Verlag von Fr. Heinrichshofen.

——, ed. 1847b. "Zwei vollständige kirchliche Schauspiele des Mittelalters in deutscher Sprache." *Neue Stofflieferungen für die deutsche Geschichte, besonders auch für die der Sprache, des Rechts und der Literatur* 2: 149-184, 195-196. Mühlhausen: Verlag von Fr. Heinrichshofen.

Stephan, Rudolf. 1957. *Musik.* Das Fischer Lexikon 5. Frankfurt: Fischer Bücherei.

——. 1995. "Deutschland I: Einleitung; II: Musikgeschichte bis zum Hochmittelalter." In ²*MGG* 2: 1173-1177.

Stevens, John. 1986. *Words and Music in the Middle Ages. Song, Narrative, Dance, and Drama, 1050-1350.* Cambridge Studies in Music. Cambridge: Cambridge University Press.

Stricker, Stefanie. *See* Bergmann–Stricker.

Stroupe, John. *See* Davidson–Stroupe.

Stummer, Friedrich. 1954. "Vom Satzrhythmus in der Bibel und in der Liturgie der lateinischen Christenheit." *Archiv für Liturgiewissenschaft* 3.2: 233-283.

Suntrup, Rudolf. 1978. *Die Bedeutung der liturgischen Gebärden und Bewegungen in lateinischen und deutschen Auslegungen des 9. bis 13. Jahrhunderts.* Münstersche Mittelalter-Schriften 37. Munich: Wilhelm Fink.

Suppan, Wolfgang. 1969. "Zur Musik der Erlauer Spiele." *Studia Musicologica Academiae Scientiarum Hungaricae* 11: 409-421.

——, ed. 1990. *Texte und Melodien der 'Erlauer Spiele.'* Musikethnologische Sammelbände 11. Tutzing: Hans Schneider.

Suso, Henri. *See* Bihlmeyer, ed. 1907.

Svejkovsky, Frantisek. 1966. *Z Dejin Ceského dramatu.* Latinské a latinskoceské Hry trí Marií. ["From the History of the Czech Drama. Latin and Latin-Czech Plays of the Three Marys"]. Acta Universitatis Carolinae Philologica. Monographia 12. Prague: Universita Karlova.

Tack, Franz. 1960. *Gregorian Chant.* Transl. by Everett Helm. Anthology of Music 3. Cologne: Arno Volk Verlag.

Tailby, John E. 1994. "Schwierigkeiten der Dramenedition." In Schwob, ed., 251-254.

See also Meredith–Tailby.

Taylor, Jerome, and Alan H. Nelson, eds. 1972. *Medieval English Drama. Essays Critical and Contextual.* Patterns of Literary Criticism 11. Chicago and London: University of Chicago Press.

Thalhofer, Valentin, and Ludwig Eisenhofer. 1912. *Handbuch der katholischen Liturgik.* 2nd ed., revised and enlarged by Ludwig Eisenhofer. 2 vols. Herders Theologische Bibliothek. Freiburg i. Br.: Herder.

Thiel, Erich Joseph. 1967. "Die liturgischen Bücher des Mittelalters. Ein kleines Lexikon zur Handschriftenkunde." *Börsenblatt für den deutschen Buchhandel* 83, pp. 2379-2395. Frankfurter Ausgabe (17. Okt. 1967).

Thomas Aquinas (ed. Parma 1864). "Officium de Festo Corporis Christi ad mandatum Urbani Papae IV. dictum festum instituentis." In *Sancti Thomae Aquinatis doctoris angelici Ordinis Praedicatorum Opera Omnia* 15: 233-238 ("Opusculum V"). Repr. 1948-1950. New York: Masurgia.

——, (ed. Turin 1954). *S. Thomae Aquinatis doctoris angelici Opuscula Theologica.* 2 vols. Turin: Marietti.

    1: *De re dogmatica et morali,* ed. Raymund A. Verardo, O.P.

    2: *De re spirituali,* ed. Raymund M. Spiazzi, O.P.

Thomas, Lucien-Paul, ed. 1951. *Le 'Sponsus.' Mystère des Vierges sages et des Vierges folles. Suivi des trois poèmes Limousins et farcis du même manuscrit.*

Étude critique, textes, musique, notes et glossaire. Travaux de la Faculté de Philosophie et Lettres 12, Université libre de Bruxelles. Paris: Presses Universitaires de France.

Thoran, Barbara. 1976. *Studien zu den österlichen Spielen des deutschen Mittelalters. Ein Beitrag zur Klärung ihrer Abhängigkeit voneinander.* 2nd rev. ed. Göppinger Arbeiten zur Germanistik 199. Göppingen: Kümmerle.

——. 1994. "Fragen zu Herkunft und Nachwirkung des Innsbrucker Thüringischen Osterspiels." In Siller, ed., 187-202.

Thurnher, Eugen, and Walter Neuhauser, eds. 1975. *Die Neustifter-Innsbrucker Spielhandschrift von 1391: Cod. 960 der Universitätsbibliothek Innsbruck. In Abbildung herausgegeben.* Litterae 40. Göppingen: Kümmerle.

Touber, Anthonius H., ed. 1985. *Das Donaueschinger Passionsspiel. Nach der Handschrift, mit Einleitung und Kommentar.* Universal-Bibliothek 8046. Stuttgart: Philipp Reclam jun.

——. 1992. "Schreiberfehler in mittelalterlichen Spielhandschriften am Beispiel des 'Donaueschinger Passionsspiels.'" *Editio* 6: 123-130.

——. 1994. "Das Osterspiel im Donaueschinger Passionsspiel. Text und Musik." In Siller, ed., 203-209.

See also Mehler-Touber.

Traub, Andreas. 1988. "Zur Musik der Trierer Marienklage und des Trierer Osterspiels." *Beiträge* 110: 78-100.

——. 1994a. "Der Debs-Codex als musikalische Quelle." In Mehler–Touber, eds., 339-347.

——. 1994b. "Überlegungen zur Edition von Melodien in geistlichen Spielen, an Beispielen aus dem Sterzinger Spielarchiv." In Schwob, ed., 255-259.

——. 1994c. "Zwischen Aufgezeichnetem und Nichtaufgezeichnetem. Probleme bei der Edition der Melodien der Sterzinger Spiele." In Siller, ed., 211-218.

See also Lipphardt-Roloff, eds.

Trauden, Dieter. 1994. "Die Osterspiele der Sterzinger Handschrift VII." In Siller, ed., 219-232.

Treutwein, Christoph. 1987. *Das Alsfelder Passionsspiel. Untersuchungen zu Überlieferung und Sprache. Edition der Alsfelder Dirigierrolle.* Germanistische Bibliothek, NF 4. Reihe: Texte. Heidelberg: Carl Winter.

Ukena, Elke, ed. 1975. *Die deutschen Mirakelspiele des Spätmittelalters. Studien und Texte.* 2 vols. Europäische Hochschulschriften, ser. 1: Deutsche Literatur und Germanistik 115, 1 [*Studien*] and 2 [*Texte*]. Bern, Frankfurt am Main: Herbert Lang.

Unterkircher, Franz, and Otto Demus. 1974. See *Das Antiphonar von St. Peter,* vol. [2], *Kommentarband.*

Väterlein, Christian, ed. 1982. *Graduale Pataviense (Wien 1511)* [GPat]. *Faksimile.* Das Erbe deutscher Musik 87, Abteilung Mittelalter 24. Kassel, Basel, London: Bärenreiter.

Vecchi, Giuseppe, ed. 1954. *Uffici Drammatici Padovani*. Testi Drammatici Medio-evali Latini e Volgari. Testi Latini 2. [Biblioteca dell' *Archivum Romanicum*. Serie 1, 41]. Florence: Leo S. Olschki.

Verfasserlexikon. See *Die deutsche Literatur des Mittelalters*.

Vince, Ronald W., ed. 1989. *A Companion to the Medieval Theatre*. Westport, Connecticut: Greenwood Press.

Vogel, Cyrille. 1975. *Introduction aux sources de l'histoire du culte chrétien au moyen âge*. Biblioteca degli 'Studi Medievali' 1. 2nd ed. Spoleto: Centro Italiano di Studi sull'Alto Medioevo.

——. 1986. *Medieval Liturgy: An Introduction to the Sources*. Rev. and transl. by William G. Storey and Niels Krogh Rasmussen. Washington: Pastoral Press.

——, and Reinhard Elze, eds. 1963-1972. *Le Pontifical Romano-Germanique du dixième siècle* [PRG]. 3 vols. Studi e Testi 226, 227, 269. Vatican City: Bibli-oteca Apostolica Vaticana.

1-2 (ST 226-227) (1963): *Le texte*.

3 (ST 269) (1972): *Introduction générale et Tables*.

Vogt, Ernst. 1913. *Regesten der Erzbischöfe von Mainz von 1289 bis 1396* 1: *[1289-1328]*. Leipzig. Repr. 1970. Berlin: De Gruyter.

Völker, Paul-Gerhard. 1968. "Schwierigkeiten bei der Edition geistlicher Spiele des Mittelalters." In *Kolloquium über Probleme altgermanistischer Editionen. Marbach am Neckar, 26. und 27. April 1966. Referate und Diskussionsbeiträge*, ed. by Hugo Kuhn, Karl Stackmann, Dieter Wuttke. Deutsche Forschungsgemein-schaft, Forschungsberichte 13. Wiesbaden: Franz Steiner Verlag.

Wackernagel, Philipp. 1867. *Das deutsche Kirchenlied von der ältesten Zeit bis zu Anfang des xvii Jahrhunderts. Mit Berücksichtigung der deutschen kirchlichen Liederdichtung im weiteren Sinne und der lateinischen von Hilarius bis Georg Fabricius und Wolfgang Ammonius*. Vol. 2. Leipzig: Teubner. Repr. 1964. Hil-desheim: Olms.

Wackernell, Josef E., ed. 1897. *Altdeutsche Passionsspiele aus Tirol. Mit Abhand-lungen über ihre Entwicklung, Composition, Quellen, Aufführungen und litterar-historische Stellung*. Quellen und Forschungen zur Geschichte, Litteratur und Sprache Österreichs und seiner Kronländer 1. Graz: 'Styria'. Repr. 1972. Wiesbaden.

Wagner, Peter. 1908. "Zur mittelalterlichen Offiziumskomposition" *KmJb* 21: 13-32.

——. 1911-1921. *Einführung in die Gregorianischen Melodien. Ein Handbuch der Choralwissenschaft/Sangformen*. 3 vols. Leipzig: Breitkopf & Härtel. Repr. 1962. Hildesheim: Olms.

1 (1911): *Ursprung und Entwicklung der liturgischen Gesangsformen bis zum Ausgange des Mittelalters*. 3rd ed.

2 (1912): *Neumenkunde. Paläographie des liturgischen Gesanges*. 2nd ed.

3 (1921): *Gregorianische Formenlehre. Eine choralische Stilkunde*.

———. 1926. "Germanisches und Romanisches im frühmittelalterlichen Kirchengesang." *Bericht über den 1. Musikwissenschaftlichen Kongress der deutschen Musikgesellschaft in Leipzig vom 4. bis 8. Juni 1925*, pp. 21-34. Leipzig: Breitkopf & Härtel

———, ed. 1930, 1932. *Das Graduale der St. Thomaskirche zu Leipzig (XIV. Jh.) als Zeuge deutscher Choralüberlieferung* [GLpz]. 2 vols. Publikationen älterer Musik 5. Leipzig: Breitkopf & Härtel. Repr. 1967. Hildesheim: Olms. 1 (1930): *Von Advent bis Christi Himmelfahrt. Mit einer Einführung in das Gesangbuch.* 2 (1932): *Von Christi Himmelfahrt bis Advent; Sanctorale und Ordinarium Missae. Mit einer Untersuchung über den germanischen Dialekt des gregorianischen Gesangs.*

Wainwright, Elizabeth. 1974. *Studien zum deutschen Prozessionsspiel. Die Tradition der Fronleichnamsspiele in Künzelsau und Freiburg und ihre textliche Entwicklung.* Münchener Beiträge zur Mediävistik und Renaissance-Forschung 16. Munich: Arbeo-Gesellschaft.

Wallace, Robin. 1984. "The Role of Music in Liturgical Drama: a Revaluation." *Music and Letters* 65: 219-228.

Walz, Angelus, ed. 1951. *Beati Iordani de Saxonia Epistulae.* Monumenta Ordinis Fratrum Praedicatorum Historica 23. Rome: Institutum Historicum Fratrum Praedicatorum.

Weizsäcker, W. 1961. "Prag." In *Religion in Geschichte und Gegenwart* 5: 499-502.

Wenck, Karl. 1900. "Friedrich des Freidigen Erkrankung und Tod (1321 und 1323)." In *Festschrift zum 75-jährigen Jubiläum des kgl. sächsischen Altertumsvereins.* Beiheft zum Archiv für sächsische Geschichte und Altertumskunde 21: 69-82.

———. 1909. "Die Stellung des Erzstiftes Mainz im Gange der deutschen Geschichte." *Zeitschrift des Vereins für hessische Geschichte und Landeskunde* 43: 278-318.

Weniger, Ludwig. 1894. "Die Dominikaner in Eisenach." In *Sammlung gemeinverständlicher wissenschaftlicher Vorträge.* Neue Folge 9, 199, 1-44.

Werner, Wilfried. 1963. *Studien zu den Passions- und Osterspielen des deutschen Mittelalters in ihrem Übergang vom Latein zur Volkssprache.* Philologische Studien und Quellen 18. Berlin: Erich Schmidt.

———. 1966. Review of Karin Schneider, ed. *Das Eisenacher Zehnjungfrauenspiel* (1964). *ZfdPh* 85: 117-118.

West, Larry E. 1997. *The Alsfeld Passion Play. Translated with an Introduction.* Studies in German Language and Literature 17. Lewiston, Queenston, Lampeter: Edwin Mellen.

Westermann Grosser Atlas zur Weltgeschichte. 1972. 8th edition. Ed. Hans-Erich Stier et al. Braunschweig: Westermann.

Wickham, Glynne. 1974. *The Medieval Theatre.* 1st ed. London: Weidenfeld and Nicholson. 3rd ed. Cambridge, New York: Cambridge University Press. 1987. Repr. 1988.

Wiedemann, Konrad. 1994. *Manuscripta theologica. Die Handschriften in folio.* Die Handschriften der Gesamthochschul-Bibliothek Kassel, Landesbibliothek und Murhardsche Bibliothek der Stadt Kassel 1.1. Wiesbaden: Harrassowitz.

Wimmer, Ruprecht. 1974. *Deutsch und Latein im Osterspiel. Untersuchungen zu den volkssprachlichen Entsprechungstexten der lateinischen Strophenlieder zur deutschen Literatur des Mittelalters.* Münchener Texte und Untersuchungen 48. Munich: Beck.

Winkler, Heinrich Alexander. 1928. "Das Eisenacher Zehnjungfrauenspiel als Fiktionsdrama." *Pflüger. Thüringer Heimatblätter* 5: 385-392.

Wittkowsky, Hartmut, ed. 1975. *Das Redentiner Osterspiel.* Stuttgart: Urachhaus.

Wolf, Herbert. 1973. "Die deutsche Literatur im Mittelalter." In Patze-Schlesinger, eds., 188-249.

Wolf, Johannes. 1913. *Handbuch der Notationskunde 1: Tonschriften des Altertums und des Mittelalters. Choral- und Mensuralnotation.* Kleine Handbücher der Musikgeschichte nach Gattungen 8. Leipzig: Breitkopf und Härtel. Repr. 1963. Hildesheim: Olms.

Wolf, Norbert Richard. 1995. "Sterzinger Passionsspiele." In ²*VL* 9: 316-320.

Woolf, Rosemary. 1972. *The English Mystery Plays.* Berkeley, Los Angeles: University of California Press.

Würdtwein, Stephan Alexander, ed. 1782. *Commentatio historico-liturgica de Stationibus Ecclesiae Moguntinae ex antiquitatibus ecclesiasticis eruta et addito Ecclesiarum Trevirensis et Coloniensis ritu Ilustrata.* Mainz: Haered. Haeffner.

Wutz, Franz, ed. 1926. *Die Psalmen des Breviers. Textkritisch untersucht.* Regensburg: Kösel & Pustet.

Wyss, Heinz, ed. 1967. *Das Luzerner Osterspiel. Gestützt auf die Textabschrift von M. Blakemore Evans.* 3 vols. Schriften herausgegeben unter dem Patronat der Schweizerischen Geisteswissenschaftlichen Gesellschaft 7. Bern: Francke.

1: *Text des ersten Tages.*

2: *Text des zweiten Tages.*

3: *Textteile 1597, 1616. Anmerkungen, Quellen, Glossar.*

Young, Karl. 1910. "Observations on the Origin of Medieval Passion Play." *Publications of the Modern Language Association of America* 25: 309-333.

——, ed. 1933. *The Drama of the Medieval Church.* 2 vols. Oxford: Clarendon Press. Repr. 1967. Oxford.

1: *The Liturgy of the Church of Rome. Plays Associated with the Resurrection and the Passion.*

2: *Plays Associated with the Nativity. Plays upon Other Subjects from the Bible and from Legends.*

Zaminer, Frieder. 2000. "Einleitung." In Huglo et al., pp. 1-10.

Zawilla, Ronald. 1985. "The 'Historiae Corporis Christi' Attributed to Thomas Aquinas: A Theological Study of the Authenticity of Their Biblical Sources." PhD dissertation. University of Toronto.

Zierfuß, Kurt. 1931. *Die Beziehungen der Mainzer Erzbischöfe zu Thüringen. Von Bonifaz bis 1305.* Neustadt a. d. Orla: Wagnersche Buchdruckerei.

Zimmermann, Ernst Wilhelm. 1909. *Das Alsfelder Passionsspiel und die Wetterauer Spielgruppe.* Darmstadt: Wintersche Buchdruckerei. Also in *Archiv für hessische Geschichte und Altertumskunde*, NF 6: 1-206.

Zoepfl, Friedrich. 1955. *Das Bistum Augsburg und seine Bischöfe im Mittelalter.* Munich: Schnell & Steiner; Augsburg: Winfried-Werk.

——. 1957. "Augsburg, Bistum." In *Religion in Geschichte und Gegenwart* 1: 732-733.

General Index

Page numbers prefixed by 'F' refer to the Catalogue on microfiche. Medieval plays other than the *Ludus de decem virginibus* (Lddv) are indexed by their codes (cf. sigla in List of Dramatic Sources, pp. xxvii-xxxvi) only if they have been extensively discussed. Incipits of Latin chants and some prayers are indexed separately.

Index of Latin Incipits

The index includes the beginnings of chants and of a few prayers and readings. Attributions are given in small caps in parentheses. Chants of the Lddv are marked with the given number in square brackets [ ]. The symbol ♪ refers to the melody of the restored chant in Chapter 4; the abbreviation *app.* to the place of the pertinent apparatus in Chapter 3. Other musical transcriptions can be found in the various Figures indicated, or in Table 6.